COLT IN THE CAVE

Mandy moved forward into the pitch black. As the silence deepened, she suddenly became aware of a presence. Something strong and powerful was surrounding her and filled the dark void ahead. Was someone else in the tunnel with them?

She stared hard into the darkness beyond, but could see nothing. She looked over her shoulder and the beam from her headlamp lit up only James's face. Mandy shone the lamp all around her, but it illuminated only the emptiness in the tunnel. Yet, somehow, she couldn't shake off the feeling that they were not alone. A shiver trickled down her spine.

'There's someone here with us,' she whispered to James.

Animal Ark series

LUCY DANIELS

Colt
— *in the* —
Cave

Illustrations by Ann Baum

**Hodder
Children's
Books**

a division of Hodder Headline Limited

Special thanks to Andrea Abbott
Thanks also to C. J. Hall, B.Vet.Med., M.R.C.V.S., for reviewing
the veterinary information contained in this book.

Animal Ark is a trademark of Working Partners Ltd
Text copyright © 2000 Working Partners Ltd
Created by Working Partners Ltd, London W6 0QT
Original series created by Ben M. Baglio
Illustrations copyright © 2000 Ann Baum

First published in Great Britain in 2000
by Hodder Children's Books

The right of Lucy Daniels to be identified as the author of this work
has been asserted by her in accordance with the Copyright, Designs
and Patents Act 1988.

10 9 8 7 6 5 4 3 2 1

A Catalogue record for this book is available from the British Library

ISBN 0 340 78811 9

Typeset by Avon Dataset Ltd, Bidford-on-Avon, Warks

Printed and bound in Great Britain by
Clays Ltd, St Ives plc

Hodder Children's Books
a division of Hodder Headline Limited
338 Euston Road
London NW1 3BH

One

'We're here!' Mandy Hope exclaimed to her best friend James Hunter, as the coach turned off the main road and trundled along a narrow, rutted lane.

A buzz of excitement erupted among Mandy's and James's classmates, who craned their necks trying to catch a first glimpse of the coalmine ahead. Mandy stood up, hoping to spot the mine before James did, but all she could see in the surrounding meadows were horses and cattle grazing peacefully in the soft, autumn sunshine. Two black Shetland ponies lifted their heads and stared inquisitively at the coach as it bumped along the lane.

'Aren't they gorgeous!' Mandy sighed.

James nodded. 'I suppose if they'd been alive when the mine was working, they wouldn't be enjoying the sunshine – they'd have been down the mine instead.'

'I guess so,' said Mandy, frowning solemnly.

'Hey, look!' cried James. He stood up to get a better view of the road in front. 'I think I can see the mine.' He hurriedly began to take his camera out of its case.

Mandy followed James's gaze. An ugly black mound had appeared a few hundred metres ahead. It looked just like the pictures that Mandy had seen in books on coal mining.

The coach passed through an arched gate with a wrought metal sign that read 'Amberton Colliery Museum'.

'This is going to be great!' declared James, taking a photograph of the sprawling mine buildings as the coach came to a stop in the gravelled parking area. 'I can't wait to go underground!'

Mandy smiled. Ever since they'd learned that

their two classes were visiting the mine, James had spoken of little else.

'Did you know,' said James, 'that about a century ago people our age used to have to work in the mine!' He grimaced. 'I wonder what that was like?' He stepped into the aisle of the bus, joining the throng of classmates eager to start the tour.

'Didn't they go to school?' Mandy couldn't imagine having to work for a living yet. She squeezed into the aisle behind James.

'I don't think so,' he answered. 'Mrs Black said that mining was a family tradition in those days. I would've looked up something about it on the Internet last night, but Dad's still having trouble getting the computer connected,' he added glumly.

For months, James had been asking his dad if they could get on to the Internet. Finally, only a few days before, he had phoned Mandy in great excitement to tell her that Mr Hunter had at last given in. However, something was wrong with the equipment and, meanwhile, James was having to wait patiently for the problem to be sorted out.

Everyone clambered out of the bus, then crowded around as Miss Potter, Mandy's class teacher, issued some last-minute instructions. 'Before we start the tour,' she announced, 'I want to remind you about your projects. Remember, you're each to choose a specific aspect of coal mining. Take as many notes as you can on anything you learn about your chosen subject. If you haven't thought of a topic yet, don't worry. I'm sure something will interest you very quickly.'

Mandy had chosen her topic long ago. When Miss Potter first mentioned the project, Mandy knew immediately what she was going to research – pit-ponies – the small but strong horses that had once worked down the mines. Mandy loved all animals and was always eager to learn as much as she could about them. When she grew up, she was going to be a vet, just like her parents, Adam and Emily Hope. Their veterinary practice was called Animal Ark and was attached to their home in the Yorkshire village of Welford.

Mandy had already discovered quite a lot of information about pit-ponies in some of her many animal books. She now knew that the ponies used in the pits were mainly Shetlands or Welsh Mountain ponies. The poor creatures had to pull trolleys heavily laden with coal from the coalface to the lift shaft, which was often quite a distance. But she was hoping to learn much more about the tough little horses at the colliery museum.

The two teachers led the group to a red-brick building. Next to it was a tall steel structure with what looked like a big wheel at the top.

'That must be the winding gear,' Miss Potter told them. 'It operates the lift that goes underground.'

'I hope it's strong,' murmured someone at the back of the crowd. Some of the classmates giggled at the comment while others nodded in agreement.

A young woman dressed in a smart black suit came out of the brick building to greet them. 'Hello, everyone,' she said with a friendly smile. 'You must be the party from Walton Moor School. I'm Lisa Edwards and I'll be looking after you above ground. Before we start the tour, I'll just fill you in on the procedure. First, though, have all your parents signed the indemnity forms?'

Miss Potter took out a thick wad of papers from her briefcase. 'Here they are,' she said, handing the forms to Lisa.

Mandy had read through the form with her parents the night before. It stated that the museum could not be held responsible for any accidents or injuries occurring on their property.

'Just a formality,' her dad had said, as he signed on the dotted line. 'I'm sure they'll look after you all.'

'Thanks,' said Lisa, taking the forms. 'Now, because there are quite a lot of you, we'll divide you into several teams. Some of you may not want to go down the shaft, so you can form one group, which I will take around. Those who *do* want to go underground will make up two parties, each headed by a teacher.'

The big group quickly split up and Mandy and James found themselves in Miss Potter's team.

Lisa then explained that the mine was very old but it had closed down only fifteen years ago. 'That means you'll see a lot of antique tools as well as more modern equipment. The heavy machinery and computer systems once used are in the exhibition hall down that corridor,' she said, pointing to her left.

'Are you going to do your project on the computer system?' Mandy whispered to James.

'No. I'm a bit frustrated with computers at the moment,' James said with a grin. Then he added more seriously, 'I think I'm going to look at the tunnel system instead.'

Lisa continued. 'Some of you might be interested in visiting the farrier's yard next to the exhibition hall – you can learn a lot about the ponies which used to work here.'

Mandy nudged James. 'That's the bit I'm looking forward to.'

'Now, let's decide who's doing the underground tour first,' said Lisa.

Mrs Black tossed a coin. 'Heads!' she announced.

'Oh good!' said James. 'That's us!'

Lisa then explained what would happen when it was time for the underground tour. 'The trip down the shaft starts in fifteen minutes. A bell will warn you to make your way to the lift in a few minutes' time. In the meantime, feel free to have a look round.'

Mandy looked at her watch. 'Let's go to the pony exhibit,' she suggested to James.

'OK,' said James. 'But keep an ear open for the bell. We don't want to miss the lift.'

They hurried through the big hall and out into a courtyard where some enormous machines were on display. James paused as they came to a massive piece of equipment. 'It's a continuous mining machine,' he read out from a plaque. 'It says here that this was one of the machines that replaced ponies in the mines.'

Mandy was pleased to hear this, but it also made her think of something else. 'When you see how huge this machine is, it makes you realise just how hard the ponies had to work,' she said sombrely.

At the far end of the courtyard was a pair of strong wooden doors signposted 'Farrier's Yard'. The two friends pushed open the doors and entered the deserted cobblestoned yard.

Instantly, Mandy felt as if she'd been transported back to another time. The place was steeped in history. Everywhere there were signs of the ponies that had once passed through on their way to their underground lives. Harnesses hung from hooks on the rough brick walls and special head-protection devices were piled on shelves at one end of the yard. Several coal-blackened carts were parked in a row. Mandy tried to picture the ponies that once pulled the heavily-laden carts through the underground passages.

Against one of the walls was a forge. Mandy closed her eyes and imagined a huge fire roaring in the furnace and a blacksmith pounding lumps of red-hot iron into horseshoes. For a moment, she even thought she could hear the ring of the hammer on iron. The loud metallic ringing persisted. Mandy realised suddenly that it was not in her imagination. She opened her eyes to see James banging two bits of rusty iron together.

'What's that all about?' she laughed.

'Sorry. But you were miles away,' he grinned. 'And I thought you'd like to meet the blacksmith.' He gestured towards the forge.

A very old man had come in and was busying

himself at the furnace. Mandy and James went over and saw that he was stoking up a fire. He greeted them as they approached.

'Hello,' he said in a rasping voice. 'Etherington's the name.'

Mandy and James greeted him in turn. 'Do you still shoe horses here?' asked Mandy, surprised to see that the forge was still in use.

'No,' said Mr Etherington. 'I just show visitors how it was back when the mine was working. In those days, I used to be at full tilt pushing out shoes for the ponies – the uneven, rocky ground in the tunnels was very hard on their feet. Nowadays, I just make a few shoes a day and we sell them in the gift shop.'

The blacksmith rolled up his sleeves as the coals caught fire and Mandy could see that, despite his age, the old man had bulging arm muscles. 'It must have been very hard work,' she said.

'Aye, it was tiring all right, but it was honest work,' said Mr Etherington, sliding a long leather apron over his head.

'What about the ponies?' asked Mandy anxiously. 'What kind of lives did they have?'

Mr Etherington poked the fire for a moment then turned round. 'To be honest,' he said, 'they had a really hard time of it. Most of them lived underground their whole lives and many worked very long shifts.'

'Oh, how awful!' exclaimed Mandy, making a few notes on the clipboard she'd brought with her.

'Do you mean that they never came up to the surface?' asked James, shocked. Like Mandy, he loved animals and was always interested in their welfare.

'Well, about once a year or so, they were brought up for a holiday,' Mr Etherington explained. 'But I sometimes wondered if that wasn't worse than leaving them underground.'

'Why?' asked Mandy, biting the end of her pen.

'A lot of them were terrified by the bright light of day when they came up. And then, just when they'd got used to being in the open and were relaxing in the green fields, they had to go back down the pit,' the blacksmith told her.

'That's so cruel!' exclaimed Mandy.

'Perhaps life wasn't too bad for them

underground?' suggested James. 'After all, the miners must have liked having ponies as workmates. Were they well treated?' he asked the old man.

'That all depended on their handlers,' Mr Etherington replied. 'Some of them really loved their ponies, but a few could be really cruel. You could see when a pony was well looked after. He'd do anything for his master.'

'What happened to the ponies when the mine closed down?' asked Mandy.

'Most of them went to live at sanctuaries run by horse protection societies,' answered Mr Etherington. 'In fact, there's a refuge close by. Sunfield Pony Sanctuary, it's called.'

Mandy was amazed. She'd read that the pit-ponies had been phased out many years ago. It hadn't occurred to her that any were still alive.

Mr Etherington continued. 'There are some happy pit-ponies living out in the fresh air at Sunfield, but they're all in their golden years now.' He shook a load of coal from a scuttle on to the fire, then pointed up a short flight of stairs. 'If you want to find out more about our ponies, there's a whole display dedicated to them in the gallery,' he said.

Mandy and James ran up the stairs and had just started reading about the first pony when a harsh buzzing sounded over the Tannoy system.

'The bell! We'd better hurry,' said James urgently. He shot down the stairs and hurtled towards the entrance.

'Wait for me!' cried Mandy.

As they ran past the forge, Mr Etherington called to them. 'Before you go, here's something for you.' He held out two miniature horseshoes.

'They're lovely,' said Mandy, taking them from the blacksmith. 'Thank you, Mr Etherington.'

'They're for good luck,' he said solemnly. 'You never know when you might need it.'

'Well, I feel lucky already,' smiled Mandy, as she and James hurried towards the lift shaft.

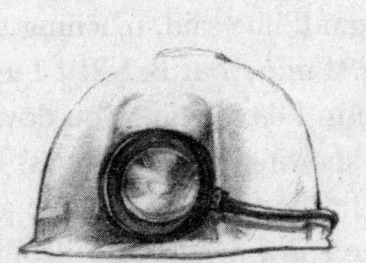

Two

The colliery lift was nothing like the lifts Mandy was used to. It was a big box made out of thick planks that were bolted together on a strong-looking steel frame.

'It looks like a cage,' Mandy said to James, as they waited with their classmates to enter the lift.

'And that's just what we call it, lass,' said a burly man who was threading his way through the excited group. He was wearing black overalls and tough working-boots. On his head was a white safety helmet with a lamp attached to the front.

'Morning, all,' he said, reaching the front of the throng. 'I'm Arthur Bradley. I used to work the coal-beds. I'll be taking you down the shaft today and showing you the ropes. Is everyone here?'

Miss Potter did a quick headcount. 'Yes, all present,' she told him.

'Right then,' said Arthur. 'Before you get into the cage, you'll need to get lamped up.' He pointed to his helmet. 'I'm going to give you all one of these, then I'll show you how to adjust the lamp.'

Christie, who was in James's class, put up her hand. 'Is it *very* dark down there?' she asked nervously.

Arthur smiled. 'Let's just say that it's not like a sunny day at Scarborough. There *are* lights in the tunnels but they're not very bright. Anyway, it's a good idea to have your own – just in case there's a power failure.'

Mandy grimaced at James. 'I don't think I'd like that,' she murmured.

One by one, they all filed past Arthur, who handed them their helmets before they entered the cage. Everyone was in high spirits, chatting eagerly about what they could expect to see when they reached the bottom of the shaft. Mandy donned her helmet and switched on the lamp. She ran her hands over the planks next to her. They were smooth and blackened by years of use. The steel floor was dusty and rang out like a drum as the dozens of feet clattered over it.

At last everyone was kitted out with a helmet and Arthur climbed into the cage, pulling the gate shut behind him. The noisy chatter stopped abruptly. There was a trembling motion as Arthur operated the controls, then suddenly they felt themselves plunging rapidly into the pitch-black darkness. Mandy's stomach seemed to lurch up into her mouth. The feeling reminded her of some of the really awesome rides in amusement parks – only this was the real thing, not just a game.

Then, quite unexpectedly because no one could see around them, there was a loud thud and a sudden jolt as the cage hit the firmness of the floor at the end of the drop.

'Phew,' said James, as Arthur unlocked the

gate and the group began to filter out of the lift. 'That was quite a drop!

Mandy laughed at James's amazed face. 'I wonder how far down we are?' she asked.

'Almost one-and-a-quarter miles,' said Arthur, overhearing her question.

'Wow! That's almost as far as Welford is from Walton,' said James, as he and Mandy took their first steps along the colliery tunnel.

In contrast to the cool air on the way down, it was very warm at the bottom of the shaft. Mandy unzipped her anorak, wishing she'd left it in the cloakroom at the top. She breathed in deeply. The air was thick and carried with it a stale smell of coal. She peered down the tunnel ahead of her. Lamps were attached to the walls every few metres, giving off a dim yellow light. As her eyes became used to the shadowy gloom, she could see that the tunnel was about three metres high and two metres wide. On the ground, a narrow set of rails ran off into the darkness beyond.

'We're in the largest passageway – it's known as the main heading,' Arthur announced and his voice sounded flat in the close and stuffy atmosphere. 'This tunnel leads to the main coalfaces but there are also a few narrow side passages leading off it. Some are emergency escape routes and others are tunnels that were worked by the colliers. We'll keep to the main heading, though – the smaller tunnels aren't lit up.'

Arthur started off down the main heading, the light from his headlamp bouncing against the rough side walls of the tunnel. 'Keep together, everyone,' he said. 'Please don't stray away from the group.'

'I don't think anyone will want to do that,' said James.

'No.' Mandy chuckled. 'It would be a bit too spooky on your own.' She picked her way over the uneven floor. An invisible pothole made her stumble and, as she got her balance, she thought about what Mr Etherington had said about the ground being rough on the ponies' feet.

'On the floor, you can see a pair of rails,' Arthur pointed out. 'Before the mine was mechanised, ponies used to drag tubs of coal from the seam where it was mined along the rails to the bottom of a shaft. There, the coal was tipped into a cage to be hoisted to the surface. The pony would then drag the empty tub back to the seam where his handler would fasten another full tub to the harness, before driving the pony back to the cage.'

'How long did the ponies have to work?' asked Mandy.

'Well, a shift was usually eight hours but sometimes ponies worked double shifts,' Arthur explained.

'That's terrible,' cried Mandy. She was furious at the thought of the ponies being taken advantage of. 'There should have been a law against it!'

'There *was* a law,' Arthur said. 'Double shifts were illegal, but a few mine bosses just disregarded the laws when it came to ponies. You see, the ponies were cheap labour. One did the work of three men. But instead of being grateful and making sure the ponies were well rested after a hard shift, a few bosses sometimes tried to get even more work out of the poor devils.'

'It's a pity they couldn't go on strike – like the

miners did sometimes,' said James.

There were a few bursts of laughter at James's suggestion.

'Actually,' Arthur said, 'in a way, some of the ponies tried to do just that. They could be really stubborn at times, even refusing to budge. But mostly, they were very willing workers.'

Hearing this, Mandy felt even more indignant. After all, if the ponies were so willing, their handlers should have treasured them, not taken advantage of them.

The group came to a fork in the tunnel and Arthur led them to the right. After a short distance, the ground suddenly seemed to fall away beneath them and they soon found themselves going down a steep slope. The roof was lower than before and the walls were so close that everyone had to walk in single file. The wall lamps were much further apart, making the lighting dimmer. Mandy could only just see Arthur a few metres ahead of her in the gloom.

'This is the oldest part of the main heading,' Arthur said, as the group stumbled along.

'That's for sure,' joked James. 'The air in here

must be as old as the tunnel.'

'Mmm,' agreed Mandy. 'It's really stuffy.' She looked over her shoulder. The flickering headlamps behind her cast an eerie glow. She could hardly recognise some of her friends. In the dim and shadowy half-light, their faces looked really strange. *Almost like gargoyles!* Mandy thought to herself. On the walls, their shadows loomed large, vanished, then reappeared as the lamp beams bobbed up and down. Suddenly, someone bumped into one of the wall lamps and it smashed to the ground. There was a dull thud, and then a few cries of alarm.

'What is it?' called Mandy, straining her eyes to try to see what was going on.

'It's Christie,' called one of Mandy's classmates, Susan Collins. 'I think she's fainted. Where's Miss Potter?'

There was much consternation as Miss Potter wove her way from the rear of the group to where Christie lay unconscious on the rough ground. Arthur came back to see what had happened.

'What happened?' asked Miss Potter

anxiously, kneeling down beside the girl.

'I don't know,' said Susan. 'She got a bit nervous when we started going down the hill. And then she just collapsed.'

'It's most likely just a touch of claustrophobia,' suggested Arthur reassuringly. 'It happens down here quite often.'

'Christie,' said Miss Potter soothingly. 'Christie. Can you hear me?'

Everyone clustered around Miss Potter and Christie and there was much jostling as they all tried to get a glimpse of their unconscious friend.

'Could you all move back a bit and give me some room?' said Miss Potter, sounding rather agitated. 'Otherwise, I'll get claustrophobia too.'

Mandy and James took a few paces back into the darkness.

'Let's go a bit deeper,' James whispered to Mandy. 'Nobody's paying any attention to us.'

'OK,' said Mandy. 'But let's not go too far, in case we get lost.'

The two friends moved off quietly down the murky passage. The hubbub behind them gradually receded until it was just a faint hum.

'We shouldn't get out of earshot. Come on, let's go back,' said Mandy after a while, her voice echoing in the narrow space around them.

'Wait,' said James. 'Look here.' He shone his headlamp against the wall. The small beam of light flashed across the glistening black rock face then suddenly faded into nothingness.

As Mandy stared at the vanishing ray of light, she became aware of a shape in the wall. 'It looks like a hole in the rock,' she said.

'I think it's one of those side tunnels that Arthur was telling us about,' said James. 'Let's investigate. Maybe I'll find out something useful for my project.'

Mandy looked back up the main tunnel. The headlamps belonging to the rest of the group shone like small beacons. Mandy could still make out Miss Potter's voice asking Christie if she felt better.

'All right,' said Mandy. 'But we'd better hurry. It sounds like Christie's come round.'

'Let's just have a quick look to see what it's like,' said James.

The two friends stepped cautiously through the hole, which was surrounded by a rough timber framework. They found themselves in a very narrow, unlit tunnel. The sides brushed against Mandy's arms as she inched her way along.

'Imagine spending your life working in a place like this!' said James. Before Mandy could comment, his words echoed back at them both, '... *like this! ... like this! ... like this!*'

'Wow!' said James, sounding a little unnerved. '*Wow! Wow! Wow!*'

Mandy giggled quietly and moved forward into the pitch black, her muffled chuckles bouncing back at her until they faded away, leaving a heavy silence in the air. As the silence deepened, Mandy suddenly became aware of a presence. Something strong and powerful was surrounding her and filled the dark void ahead. Was someone else in the tunnel with them?

She stared hard into the darkness beyond, but could see nothing. She looked over her shoulder and the beam from her headlamp lit up only James's face. Mandy shone the lamp all around her, but it illuminated only the emptiness in the tunnel. Yet, somehow, she couldn't shake off the feeling that they were not alone. A shiver trickled down her spine.

'There's someone here with us,' she whispered to James. '*With us, with us, with us,*' hissed Mandy's words.

'I can't see anyone,' whispered James cautiously.

'Shh, let's listen,' replied Mandy.

They stood dead still. Mandy concentrated hard, listening for the sound of a footfall or the rustle of clothing against the walls. But not even the faintest sound disturbed the stillness.

'There's nothing here,' said James after a few seconds. 'It must be your imagination.'

Mandy shook her head. 'I'm not sure,' she said. 'There's something eerie about this place.' She listened again. Then, shrugging her shoulders, she said, 'I guess you're right. After all, it is pretty creepy in here.'

'Well, we've seen what a side tunnel is like, now,' said James. 'We'd better get back to the others.'

Mandy eased herself round and, just as she began to follow James towards the main heading, she became aware of a faint sound. Slowly, she realised that it was the sound of distant hooves. She stopped and looked back down the inky tunnel. The clopping sound came nearer. She held her breath and listened keenly again. The noise was definitely heading their way! Then, suddenly, it stopped, leaving a silence so heavy that Mandy could hear the regular thudding of her own heartbeat and the rhythmic sound of James's breathing as he moved quietly towards the tunnel entrance.

But what had made that strange sound and why had it stopped so suddenly?

The warm, clammy air had folded itself round Mandy like a blanket. She tried to take a deep breath but the air seemed to stick in her throat. Her headlamp flickered and went out. For a second, a wave of panic washed over her. Then, without warning, her headlamp came back on, revealing a sight that made her heart miss a beat. Staring at her out of the eerie blackness was a pair of eyes. Like lasers they pierced the darkness and shone right into Mandy's own eyes. She couldn't move. The bright stare had transfixed her and seemed to penetrate deep into her very soul.

Mandy gasped and, just as suddenly as the eyes had appeared, they vanished, leaving the darkness unbroken once more. She blinked. Movement returned to her legs. She took a few paces backwards, then turned and scrambled towards the hole in the wall. James had already climbed through and was waiting for her in the main tunnel.

'*Did you see?*' she gasped, as she clambered through the hole.

'What?' asked James, looking puzzled.

'Those eyes – shining in the dark. You *must*

have seen them,' Mandy insisted.

James scratched his head, then pushed back his fringe. 'I didn't see anything,' he said.

'Well that's probably because you were heading back up the tunnel,' said Mandy. 'You *must* have heard the hooves, though. Didn't you?'

'Hooves? What are you talking about, Mandy?' asked her friend, his forehead creased in confusion. 'Come on. We'd better get back.' James shook his head and set off towards the rest of the group.

'I'm talking about the clip-clopping sound I heard back there,' Mandy replied, running to keep up with him.

'Eyes shining out of the dark and horses' hooves! Are you sure you're OK?' asked James, stopping for a moment to let Mandy catch up with him.

'I'm fine!' stressed Mandy. She took hold of James's sleeve. 'Look, I know what I saw and heard. They were real. There was something in that tunnel with us.'

'Maybe you did see something,' said James quietly. 'But you said yourself that it was creepy

back there. Perhaps you were claustrophobic –
like Christie – and that made you see and hear
things that weren't there.'

Mandy thought for a moment. James's
suggestion made sense. Maybe he was right.
After all, *he* hadn't heard or seen anything
unusual. And it *was* very stuffy in the side
tunnel. Perhaps there hadn't been enough
oxygen in there and her mind had played tricks
on her. *I think I'll read up about claustrophobia
when I get home,* she thought to herself.

They reached the others just as Miss Potter
was helping Christie to her feet. No one had
noticed Mandy and James's absence, because
they had all been too concerned about
Christie. She leaned on Miss Potter's arm as
they made their way towards the lift shaft.
Mandy lengthened her stride until she'd caught
up with Christie.

'Are you feeling better?' she asked her.

Christie turned and looked at Mandy. Even
in the dim light, Mandy could see that she was
very pale.

'I guess so,' said Christie quietly.

Seeing Christie looking so pale and shaken,

Mandy knew instantly that her own experience in the tunnel had not been the same as Christie's. Unlike her classmate, she was not trembling and weak. She did feel a little disturbed, but there was also something thrilling about her strange encounter in the tunnel. She looked back over her shoulder. The dull yellow light looked different somehow. It seemed to have taken on a mysterious shimmer and, deeper along the tunnel where there should have been absolute blackness, there was a soft white glow. But who would believe her? Even James was sceptical.

The group reached the lift shaft and Mandy looked back one more time. She knew in her heart that they weren't leaving behind an empty maze. Somewhere in the depths of the mine, was a mysterious presence. And she was quite convinced that what she'd seen and heard was a pony.

Three

An icy draught forced its way down the shaft as the lift climbed slowly to the surface.

'It's even colder and windier in here than when we went down,' Mandy said to James.

'Maybe that's because we've got used to the heat in the tunnel,' James suggested.

The lift lurched to a stop and Arthur pulled open the gate with a clatter. The group emerged, blinking, into the daylight to find that a swirling wind had pushed away the sunny brightness of the morning.

Mandy shivered and zipped up her anorak.

'It looks very stormy,' she shivered.

Overhead, towering black clouds gathered threateningly. It was quite a surprise to find conditions so different from earlier. It reminded Mandy of how odd she felt when she went to the cinema in daylight and came out afterwards into the darkness of evening.

The two friends leaned into the scudding wind and hurried to the shelter of the exhibition hall, where they wandered around looking at the various exhibits. James was fascinated by a display of computers that had controlled the coal-cleaning process, but Mandy found it hard to concentrate on the various items on display. She couldn't forget her strange experience in the tunnel.

They came to a set of photographs that showed the history of the mine.

'Look at those funny old lorries,' said James. He pointed to a faded picture of several old-fashioned bulky vehicles piled high with coal and laughed.

'They're almost as funny as the clothes everyone is wearing.' Mandy chuckled. Then she pointed to another picture. It showed an injured pony receiving veterinary treatment. The caption beneath the photograph explained how some ponies were injured underground – often because of rock falls or because the tunnels were so narrow that the ponies' flanks were badly grazed. Mandy could see huge gashes on the injured pony's side. They looked very painful.

'Do you think the ponies were allowed to rest while their wounds were healing?' Mandy wondered.

'Perhaps we can ask the blacksmith,' said James.

But there wasn't time to return to the yard. The second group had returned from the depths of the mine and the teachers were eager to get going before the storm broke.

Heavy drops of rain began to fall as the coach set off. There were ominous rumblings from the leaden sky and before long they were driving through a torrential downpour. The storm seemed to have put everyone in a solemn mood and hardly anyone spoke during the journey home.

Mandy found herself deep in thought. Now

that she'd seen for herself how harsh the conditions were underground, she couldn't get the pit-ponies out of her mind. Nor could she forget what she was sure that she'd seen in the side tunnel.

James nudged her with his elbow. 'Still thinking about those shining eyes?' He grinned.

Mandy sighed then smiled. 'Yes, but you must have been right. Perhaps I *was* imagining things. After all, *you* didn't see or hear anything unusual.'

James took off his glasses and cleaned a few specks of coal dust off them. 'Perhaps what you saw was just the reflection of your headlamp against the rocks or on a metal hook or something in the wall.'

'And the sound of hooves?' asked Mandy.

'I don't know. Echoes of everyone's footsteps? Remember the echoes in that small tunnel? *Tunnel, tunnel, tunnel,*' said James, playfully.

Mandy laughed. Trust James to come up with a practical solution! 'OK. You win. There must be a sensible explanation to it all,' she agreed. Then, changing the subject, she added, 'Are you definitely going to choose tunnelling for your project?'

'I think so,' James told her. 'I'm going to find out how tunnels are made and also about the different kinds of tunnels.'

'I didn't see much useful information at the museum,' Mandy said thoughtfully.

'Me neither,' said James. 'I wish we'd had more time. I'm sure there's loads of useful stuff on the Internet though. Dad said he might be able to sort out the computer problem today. With any luck, I'll be able to search the World Wide Web tonight!'

'I wish we could get connected at Animal Ark,' said Mandy, a little enviously. 'But Dad says the only web we have time for is on a duck's foot!'

'I tell you what, if Dad does fix the problem, why don't you come round after school tomorrow and we'll do a search together,' suggested James. 'That way, you can decide exactly what you want to download.'

'That would be perfect,' said Mandy.

Later, Mandy told her parents all about the trip.

It was teatime and they were sitting round the big pine table in the kitchen.

'It must be quite eerie in the tunnels,' Emily Hope said. 'The ponies that worked down there would have to be very calm.'

'Mmm, not a place for a nervous pony,' agreed Adam Hope, pouring himself another cup of tea. 'But, even for easy-going horses, I can't imagine that a life in a coalmine would have been much fun.'

'Some of them got quite badly injured scraping their sides on the walls of the narrow tunnels,' said Mandy, remembering the photograph they'd seen of the pony being looked after by a vet. 'But at least there aren't any ponies working underground any more.'

'Would you believe that some of them are still alive?' said Emily Hope, as she began to clear the table.

'That's what the blacksmith told me,' Mandy said, smiling. 'And he said that there's a refuge near the mine called Sunfield Pony Sanctuary. I'd love to go there and meet the ponies.'

Mr Hope got up and started to wash the dishes. 'That would be really interesting,' he said. 'Perhaps we can visit Sunfield. I'll try and find out about opening times.'

'Thanks, Dad. You're the best!' said Mandy, giving him a warm hug. She dried the dishes, then noticed a bowl of leftovers on the table. 'I'll just give this to the birds,' she said and went outside to sprinkle the food on the lawn.

The storm raged wildly. Mandy battled through the roaring gale, barely able to stand upright. It was so dark and misty, she could hardly see her hands in front of her. She wished that she wasn't alone. She pictured the cosy, warm kitchen at home with the fire glowing comfortingly in the grate. She knew that her mum would be anxious about her being out in this weather and that there would be a big mug of hot chocolate waiting for her when she returned.

She leaned into the wind and tried to hurry but the cruel and icy blast just pushed her back. She was making no headway at all. Beads of sweat broke out on her forehead and a tingle of fear ran through her. She turned and tried to retrace her footsteps, but the gale pushed her

back from that direction too.

She tried to go forward again but the wall of wind was solid. She could not break through it. All around her, the storm boiled and seethed, enclosing her in its whirling anger. She knew she was trapped.

Suddenly, amid the howling of the wind and the vicious crack of the thunderclaps, came a new sound. It started faintly. Mandy closed her eyes and tried to block out the roar of the storm and concentrate on this new sound. Perhaps it was someone coming to rescue her. Gradually the sound grew clearer, taking shape above the clamour all around. It was the sound of a pony, whinnying. Urgent, persistent whinnying that bore into Mandy's hearing, like a machine drilling into her head.

She opened her eyes with a start. She was sweating and gasping for breath. The storm had vanished but a drilling sound still rang loudly in her ears. She looked around. She was in her own bed and the noise was coming from the alarm clock on her bedside table. She leaned over and switched off the alarm, then sighed and rested her head in her hands. What a frightening dream! And so real! The animal had sounded so distressed.

She pushed off her duvet then went over to the window and drew back the curtains. The sun was just beginning to climb above the eastern horizon, lighting up a sky that was blue and clear. There was no sign of yesterday's storm. It must have blown itself out during the night. Even though Mandy's dad had picked her up after the trip, she'd got thoroughly drenched just running from the bus to the Animal Ark Land-rover. No wonder she'd had that nightmare!

She washed, then pulled on her school uniform. As she sat brushing her short blonde hair, her eyes came to rest on the miniature horseshoe Mr Etherington had given her at the mine the day before. She'd hung it over the mirror until she could decide on a more permanent place for it.

She reached for the horseshoe. The little iron arc fitted snugly in the palm of her hand. As far as she could tell, it was an exact replica of the real thing. She ran a finger over the smooth surface and round the edges of the holes that, in a real shoe, were for the nails that would attach the shoe to the horse's hoof.

As her finger traced the outline of the horseshoe, Mandy became aware of a raised pattern around the curve of the arc. She looked closely and saw that there was a word carved into the metal. The letters were so small that she couldn't make out what the word was. She pulled a magnifying glass out of a drawer and peered through it: DEFENDER.

Defender? What could that mean? Perhaps it was a business name that the museum used.

As she sat looking at the tiny shoe, her thoughts ran to the pit-ponies. Then she remembered that she was going home with James after school to search the Internet for more information about them. He had rung last night to say that his dad had sorted out the technical problem at last. She checked the time. It was getting late. She replaced the horseshoe, then grabbed her schoolbag and ran downstairs for breakfast.

'Guess what our password is?' James was beaming with delight, as he got ready to connect to the Internet later that afternoon.

'Football?' suggested Mandy who had drawn a chair up alongside James at the desk.

'No,' James said, laughing. 'Guess again.'

The door to the study was pushed open and James's black Labrador, Blackie, came in, with his tail wagging frantically and a feather in his mouth.

'And here's a clue,' said James, swivelling round in his chair.

'Blackie?' Mandy chuckled. 'I should have guessed first time!'

James typed BLACKIE into the space for the password. A series of strange, electronic sounds came from the modem as it dialled the number to connect the computer to the Internet. Blackie frowned and spat out the feather, then cocked his head first to one side then to the other, trying to make out the strange new noise. He growled softly, then, jumping up and putting his front paws on James's lap, started to bark at the modem.

James laughed and pushed him down. 'You'd better get used to it, boy. 'You're going to be hearing it a lot. OK, Mandy, we're on line now. Let's do a search for pit-ponies.'

There were dozens of pages giving information on pit-ponies and other animals that were used in the mines. Mandy and James learned that canaries in cages were used to warn miners of poisonous gas, like methane, underground. If the canaries died in the tunnels, it usually meant that there was a build-up of methane which could cause an explosion. This was a clear signal to the miners to head for the surface straight away.

'Oh, how awful for the canaries,' said Mandy. 'They never stood a chance of escaping. It's so sad that they had to be sacrificed like that.'

'I suppose they rely on modern technology in mines to warn the miners of danger now,' said James, scrolling down a page. 'Hey, look at this. It says here that at the beginning of the twentieth century there were nearly a hundred thousand ponies working underground.'

'What!' exclaimed Mandy, then she read further down the page. 'And here it says that their average lifespan was only seven years. *Seven years!* That's so young. I read that Shetlands can live to be over thirty years old. That just proves how hard pit-ponies' lives must have been underground.'

'At least we know that a lot of them went on to live normal lives in sanctuaries,' said James.

The two friends scanned a few more sites and printed out some details Mandy thought would be useful, then James searched for information on tunnelling. After a while, he disconnected from the Internet. 'I'd better not spend too much time on it,' he said. 'Dad made me promise not to ring up a huge phone bill.'

The door opened and Mrs Hunter came into the study. 'Your dad's on the phone, Mandy. He says he's being trying to get through for the last twenty minutes, but the phone's been engaged the whole time!' She smiled at James. 'I'll have to make sure I make all my calls while you're at school in future!'

'Sorry, Mum,' said James sheepishly.

'That's all right, love,' said his mother. 'I think this Internet thing is fabulous – just as long as you use it for your schoolwork. Anyway, Mandy, your dad says he's got a surprise for you.'

Mandy followed Mrs Hunter to the hall. 'Hi,' she said, picking up the receiver. She listened for a moment, then cried, 'Thanks! I'll tell James right now.'

She hung up and ran back to the study. 'Dad's been in touch with the Sunfield Pony Sanctuary,' she told James. 'They said we can visit any time we like, so Dad's arranged for us to go there this Saturday. Do you want to come too?'

'You bet!' said James, eagerly.

Mandy gathered together the print-outs of the

pages James had downloaded for her. From one of the pages, a bay Shetland pony wearing a heavy harness and dragging a full load of coal stared out mournfully at Mandy. Three miners stood next to the pony, petting him on his neck. 'Poor thing,' she sighed. 'I hope your life wasn't too bad. And at least there are *some* pit ponies leading happy lives now. I can hardly wait to meet them on Saturday!'

Four

Sunfield Pony Sanctuary stood amid green, rolling hills a few miles beyond Amberton Colliery.

'I'll open it,' said Mandy, as Mr Hope pulled up in front of the big wooden gate at the entrance to the sanctuary.

She hopped out and swung open the heavy gate then, once her dad had driven through, checked that the latch was firmly down before climbing back into the Land-rover. They juddered over a cattle grid and followed a meandering driveway to the office. All around them were lush paddocks where ponies, horses and even a few donkeys grazed contentedly.

'They're not *all* pit-ponies, are they?' asked James.

'I shouldn't think so,' Mr Hope replied. He stopped the Land-rover in a parking area next to the office. 'A sanctuary like this might rescue horses from all sorts of situations.'

'Some of them might even be abandoned racehorses or polo ponies, I suppose,' suggested Mandy.

'Probably,' her father said.

They crunched across the gravel towards the office. Mandy breathed in deeply, savouring the rich, earthy scent of horses.

Mr Hope pushed open the office door. Inside, a short, weathered-looking man was speaking on the telephone. He seemed to be in a state of panic and didn't even notice the visitors. A girl about Mandy's age, wearing jodhpurs and riding-boots, was standing next to the man. She had her back to the door and didn't see Mandy, James and Mr Hope come in either.

'Well, do you know when he *will* be back?'

the man was saying to someone at the other end of the telephone. '*This evening!* That'll be too late. You're certain that you can't get hold of him?' The man listened for a moment, then put the phone down. 'I don't believe it!' he exclaimed gruffly to the young girl. 'The vet's away at an equine conference in Bradford and his partner has been called to an emergency on a stud farm fifty miles away.' He opened a book and began flicking anxiously through the pages.

Mandy recognised the book as from the shelves at Animal Ark. It was called *A Veterinary Guide to Horse Care*.

'You're sure it looks like colic, Ceri?' said the man.

The girl nodded. 'He's not eating, but he must be in a lot of pain because he keeps kicking at his belly with his hind legs. He'd just started to roll about on the ground when I left him to come and tell you.'

'Sounds like colic, all right! We can't waste any time,' said the man. He looked up from the book and for the first time noticed Mandy, James and Mr Hope. 'Sorry folks, we've got a bit of an emergency here. You're going to have to come back later.'

'I don't want to intrude . . .' began Mr Hope politely, 'but I think I can help you.'

The man looked at Adam Hope keenly. 'Do you know of another vet?' he asked eagerly.

'Actually, I *am* a vet,' answered Mr Hope. 'And from what Ceri says, I'm sure your horse does have colic. You're quite right, there's no time to waste. The horse needs emergency treatment or I'm afraid you could lose him.' He turned to Mandy. 'Fetch my bag, will you, love?'

Mandy dashed out of the office. It was a good thing her dad took his bag everywhere with him. She heaved it out of the back of the Land-rover. The bag contained instruments and medication that could be used in most types of emergencies. She returned to the office just as the others were coming out of the door.

'He's in the paddock down by the river,' Ceri told Mr Hope and they all set off in that direction. 'His racing name is Woodward's Challenge, but we call him Woody.'

Even from a few hundred metres away, Mandy could make out which horse was in trouble.

Near the far side of the paddock, a big chestnut stallion had thrown himself to the ground and was rolling and struggling in pain. 'Oh, how terrible!' she exclaimed. 'Hurry, Dad.'

'It does look as if Woody's in a bad way,' agreed Mr Hope as they climbed through the railings. 'I just hope there are no complications. Colic is much simpler to deal with if the pain is mostly due to wind in his stomach.'

Mandy crossed her fingers. She knew that complicated cases of colic needed immediate surgery and that, even then, some horses didn't survive.

'Don't worry, Mandy,' said James reassuringly as they rushed across the stubby, cropped grass. 'You know that your dad's a brilliant vet. He'll get Woody right, if anyone can.'

The horse was back on his feet and standing quietly by the time they reached him.

'He's between bouts of pain right now,' said Adam Hope, opening his bag and taking out a stethoscope and thermometer. 'That gives me a moment to examine him. Will someone hold the bridle, please?'

Mandy and James each took hold of a cheek

piece, on either side of the horse's head, while Ceri soothingly stroked his neck.

Mr Hope listened to the stallion's heart and checked his temperature. 'Hmm, his heart rate and temperature are a bit high,' he said. He looked at the horse's eyes and inside his mouth, muttering, 'A bit on the pale side', then carefully examined his belly and flanks. 'Pretty swollen,' he murmured. 'It's definitely a case of acute indigestion. I'll give him some injections to relieve the pain, then look at him more closely.'

He prepared three syringes and one by one injected them into the horse, all the while speaking softly to him. 'There now, boy,' he said, gently rubbing the skin where he'd pushed in the needles. 'That should ease things for you.' He put the syringes into a disposal ba, then looked round. 'Right, let's give him some space while the painkillers work.'

Mandy and James pulled themselves up on the railings and sat watching the powerful chestnut horse. 'He's a beauty,' said Mandy to Ceri who was leaning against the railings next to her.

'Yes, he's an ex-racehorse but he was being badly treated so we rescued him. He came in only yesterday,' Ceri told her.

'Ah, that might explain the colic,' said Adam Hope. 'Woody could have been a bit stressed when he arrived – even hungry – and might have bolted his food and then been too tired to digest it properly. Just as well you picked up the signs, Ceri. Things might have been a lot worse if you hadn't.'

Mr Hope went back to the horse and began to examine him thoroughly. After a few minutes, he called to Mandy. 'Get me a long stomach tube from the bag, please, love. I need to get rid of some of this wind.'

Mandy pulled out a plastic tube and handed it to her dad, then watched as he gently inserted it into the horse's nose and gradually fed it down into his stomach. After a while, the horse seemed to relax and Mr Hope listened once more to his heart rate. 'That's better,' he said. 'Nearly back to normal.' He unhooked the stethoscope and turned to the man. 'He's out of immediate danger and there don't seem to be any problems. It's a classic case of colic. But he'll need to be on medication and a special diet for a few days. Make sure he's rested and kept warm.'

The man shook Mr Hope's hand warmly. 'Thanks so much. I don't know what we'd have done if you hadn't turned up when you did.'

Mr Hope smiled. 'I'm glad to have been able to help.'

'Er, would you mind posting the bill to me?' the man asked, sounding embarrassed. 'You see, we're a bit low on funds at the moment. I'm hoping for a few donations to come in within the next couple of weeks.'

'I wouldn't dream of charging you,' said Adam Hope.

The man looked relieved. 'That's very kind of you.'

'And I think you're very kind to rescue pit-ponies,' put in Mandy cheerfully.

'Well, it's very nice of you to say so,' said the man and then he clicked his fingers. 'Now I know who you are. You're the people who phoned me from Welford the other day, aren't you? And you want to see some pit-ponies!' He scratched his balding head then said, 'Hope? Wasn't that the name?'

Mr Hope smiled and nodded. 'Adam Hope. And this is my daughter, Mandy, and her friend, James Hunter. Mandy needs to find out about the ponies for her school project.'

'And I'm Paul Newbury. Ceri is my granddaughter,' He smiled fondly at her. 'She's my right-hand girl. Comes almost every weekend to help me out. I'd be lost without her.'

Ceri grinned shyly. 'That's not true. You know more about horses than I ever will.' She looked at Mandy and James. 'Grandad used to be one of the country's top jockeys, you know.'

'Of course!' said Mr Hope. 'I thought I recognised that name. But didn't you retire early?'

'Aye,' said Mr Newbury. 'I saw what was happening to many horses in the name of recreation and industry. Racehorses abandoned when they stopped winning big money for their owners; polo ponies whipped brutally by some harsh trainers; old mares left without food when they could no longer breed – I could go on and on.' He shook his head sadly then took a deep breath. 'I didn't want to be part of it. So I pulled out and looked for a way of helping those that were given a raw deal. That's how I ended up here at Sunfield.'

'A worthy change of career,' Adam Hope said sincerely. He turned back to the horse who was standing calmly, swishing his tail slowly from side to side. Mr Hope patted him firmly on the shoulder and said, 'Right, then, let's get you into a stall so that you can rest quietly and get over the shock.'

Mandy and James helped Ceri to lead the stallion to the stable block nearest the office. Adam Hope and Paul Newbury walked behind them, discussing the treatment the horse would need over the next few days. 'If he shows any signs of an infection, you'll need to contact a vet immediately,' said Mr Hope.

Soon the horse was comfortably settled and Mr Newbury suggested that they went back to the office for a cup of tea. 'And one of Ceri's home-baked flapjacks,' he added. 'There's nothing to beat them this side of the Pennines.'

'That sounds good,' said Adam Hope, rubbing his hands together. 'Joining us?' he asked Mandy and James. 'Or are you champing at the bit to see the ponies?'

Mandy laughed. 'What do you think, Dad?'

James was also keen to see the ponies first, so Ceri offered to take them both round the sanctuary.

'Will you take us to meet the pit-ponies first?' Mandy asked Ceri.

As they made their way towards a paddock on the far side of the sanctuary, Ceri told them what she knew about the pit-ponies. 'Most of them have been here for ages,' she said. 'I think the last ones came to Sunfield about twenty-five years ago. But they're still as fit as fiddles, thanks to my grandad. He spends money on his ponies before he spends anything on himself!'

There were about a dozen ponies in the large paddock. Most of them were sturdy little Shetlands but there were also a few beautiful Welsh Mountain ponies. Seeing them arrive, two Shetlands – one brown and the other black – came trotting purposefully over to the railings. They pushed their heads over the bottom railing and began nuzzling at Mandy and James's outstretched hands.

'I know what you want,' Mandy said, laughing. She reached into her coat pocket for some sugar-lumps she'd brought with her and held them out to the ponies on her flattened palm.

While the ponies crunched up the sugar-lumps, Ceri told Mandy and James about the pair. 'This is Margot,' she said, patting the brown pony's neck, 'and this is Duke.' She ran her fingers through his thick, shaggy mane, which flopped forward on the black pony's forehead. 'Grandad says they've been inseparable since the day they came here from Amberton.'

Almost as if he'd understood what Ceri had said, Duke nibbled Margot's neck affectionately.

'They must be quite old,' observed Mandy. She had noticed that Duke's teeth were very long.

'Yes, they're both about thirty-eight. They came here when they were about eleven or twelve,' Ceri told her. 'They're a bit like an old married couple,' she laughed. 'Grandad even calls them Darby and Joan!'

Margot snorted a few times, then began nudging James's jacket pocket, looking for more treats.

'All right, all right!' exclaimed James. 'Give me a chance.' He pulled out two apples, which the ponies gobbled up at once.

'I'll take you to meet some others,' said Ceri, climbing through the railings.

Mandy and James followed her and, with Duke and Margot trotting closely by their sides, went with Ceri to the centre of the paddock where three other ponies were eating hay from a trough.

As they reached the ponies, a chilly breeze suddenly sprang up, finding its way down Mandy's neck. She pulled up the collar of her coat, but the iciness clung to the back of her neck as if it had been trapped inside her coat. She looked up at the sky. A big, grey cloud had appeared from nowhere and was hovering menacingly overhead, blocking out the weak sunshine and casting a deep, gloomy shadow over the paddock. *I wonder if we're in for another storm?* thought Mandy.

'Have you got any more sugar-lumps?'

asked James, breaking into her thoughts. 'I've run out.'

All five of the ponies had encircled him and were mobbing him for treats.

'You look like the Pied Piper,' said Mandy with a laugh. She passed a handful of sugar-lumps to James and was about to ask Ceri about the three other ponies when she felt a gentle nudge in the small of her back. She spun round and almost fell over a handsome strawberry roan Shetland. 'Hello,' she said in surprise. 'You crept up on me very quietly!'

The pony looked up at Mandy and fixed her with an intense stare. She'd brought an apple and offered it to the little horse. But he showed no interest in it at all and carried on staring at her. Mandy found she couldn't escape his gaze. She was compelled to return it. It was almost as if he'd mesmerised her.

Then something stirred deep within her memory. She struggled in her mind to grasp what it was. And all at once, it came to her. The pony was very familiar. Mandy had met him before. But where – and when?

Spellbound, she leaned forward to caress his neck and tried to work out where she could have seen him.

At that moment a strong ray of sunshine broke through the dark cloud above. Like a spotlight, it shone directly on to the pony, making him glow radiantly.

'Wow,' exclaimed Mandy. 'Your coat really shines in the sun!'

Overhearing Mandy's comment, Ceri turned round. 'Oh, I see Flame has introduced himself to you,' she laughed. It was as if her words had switched off the sunbeam, for it disappeared in an instant.

'You can say that again!' said Mandy, still puzzled by the pony's intense interest in her. 'He's very forward!'

Ceri's interruption had also broken the mysterious, invisible cord that had linked Mandy and Flame. The pony bucked his head and whinnied softly, then ambled over to the trough to feed.

'Flame's one of Grandad's favourites,' said Ceri. 'He's been here since he was five, but he wasn't always this bold. Grandad says that when he first came out of the mine, he was really traumatised.'

'Perhaps he wasn't used to the daylight and wide open spaces,' said James. The ponies were still snuffling around his pockets, even though he'd turned them inside out to show that he had no more treats.

'Yes, he was frightened of everything – the light, the trees, the wind, other people – he wouldn't even eat at first and bolted whenever anyone came near him. But Grandad soon got him right. He's got a magic touch with horses.'

'He looks like a very sensitive pony,' commented Mandy, unable to take her eyes off Flame.

'I think he is,' said Ceri. 'And he's very clever. Much cleverer than most of the other horses here.'

'Why do you say that?' asked James, pushing his pockets back into his trousers. The ponies had given up trying to find more food on him and were standing quietly at his side.

'I don't know – it's just that he seems to know things that we don't know,' Ceri answered. 'Like when a storm's coming. Even if it's a bright, sunny day, he'll start getting all edgy and then we know that the weather's going to change. Grandad calls Flame his storm warning.'

'A bit like the weather forecasters on TV!' quipped James.

'Except that they always seem to be wrong.' Mandy laughed.

Mr Hope was waving to them from the office so they started back across the paddock. Before she ducked through the railings, Mandy turned and looked back at the ponies. Flame was standing alone, watching her. And once more he was bathed in light. Another ray of sun had broken through the cloud and was pouring itself down on the little colt.

Mandy felt strangely unsettled. Something mysterious had taken place in that paddock but she couldn't put her finger on it. It was as if she knew him, but how could they possibly have met before? And it was as if he knew her too. There was definitely a bond between them. But what?

Five

Mandy knew, even in her sleep, that she was in the grip of another nightmare. But there was nothing she could do to get out of it. She couldn't even will herself to wake up.

Frightening images and sounds entered her sleeping mind, flinging her on to a roller-coaster of terror. '*Somebody wake me up!*' she screamed as the fear closed in on her like an evil spirit. Then, with a cry for help fading on her lips, she suddenly found herself awake.

Mandy sat up in bed. It was still dark and dead quiet. A creaking sound from somewhere in the house startled her. She held her breath, then realised with relief that it was just one of the usual creaky noises in the old cottage.

She switched on her bedside lamp and looked at the time. It was three o'clock – hours to go before dawn. But the dream had left her wide-awake. She didn't think she'd be able to go back to sleep again.

Mandy leaned back and closed her eyes. The frightening images that had disturbed her sleep were still fresh in her memory. She ran through

the dream again in her mind. She could still see and hear the chestnut Shetland pony that had featured so clearly. At first, the pony had been anxious as he walked through an underground tunnel. Then he became more and more distressed, rearing and bucking with fear. He tried to turn, but the space around him became smaller and smaller until he couldn't move. He whinnied in terror and tried to kick out with his front legs, but to no avail.

Mandy had looked on helplessly. Then, when she couldn't bear his desperation any longer, she'd shouted out and woken herself up.

While the dream replayed itself in her mind, she found herself also remembering her nightmare after the trip to the mine. The sound of the frantic whinnying in that dream had stayed with her for days. Were the two dreams about the same pony? And if so, who was he? Was there something she was supposed to learn from the nightmares? Or was she making something out of nothing?

She remembered what her grandad had told her once when she'd woken up from a bad dream. He'd said that dreams were just the brain's way of sweeping out all the bits and pieces that were cluttering it up. 'A kind of spring-cleaning,' he'd explained. Perhaps her nightmares were because of all the sad things she'd learned about pit-ponies?

Mandy switched off the lamp, then lay down and pulled her duvet cosily around her. She decided to shut out the terrifying images and sounds of the nightmares by concentrating on the happy ponies she'd seen at Sunfield. She thought of Flame. Straightaway, a vision of the handsome pony glowing in the sunshine came to her. She smiled as she remembered the intelligent way he'd looked at her. Then she drifted off to sleep again.

'You look exhausted,' said Emily Hope when Mandy joined her parents for breakfast in the morning. 'Didn't you sleep well?'

'Not really,' said Mandy. 'I had another bad dream.' She helped herself to a glass of orange juice, then flicked through the magazine section of the Sunday newspaper.

'Just as well it's Sunday,' said Adam Hope, buttering a slice of toast. 'I don't think you'd cope too well with school today. Pass me the marmalade please, love.'

Mandy handed him the jar. 'I'll be OK, Dad. I don't feel too bad. It's just that the dream was a bit hair-raising.'

She described what had happened.

'It sounds to me as if you're dwelling on the pit-ponies just a bit too much,' said Mrs Hope, lifting a poached egg out of a pan of boiling water and putting it on Mandy's plate. 'Perhaps you should get out and have a bit of fun today. Think about something else for a change.'

'I can't really do that,' explained Mandy. She slid a piece of toast under the egg. 'I have to work on my project today. It's got to be in on Wednesday and I've still got masses to do.'

'Can't you do it tomorrow? You'll be at home, won't you?' asked Mrs Hope. 'Isn't it a teacher-training day?'

'Yes, but I still have to sort through all the information I've got and decide exactly how I'm going to do the project. Tomorrow, I'll start putting it all together,' said Mandy. She cut into the egg and the yolk oozed into the toast. 'This is delicious. Thanks, Mum,' she said.

'I've got an idea,' said Mr Hope. 'Why don't you spend the morning working? Then after lunch we'll all go for a ramble along the river.'

'That sounds good,' said Emily Hope. 'We'll take a picnic with us.' She pulled her long red hair into a ponytail, then rolled up her sleeves to wash the dishes. 'I'll even bake a cake!'

'Wonders will never cease!' teased Mr Hope. 'We'd better jump at the offer, Mandy. Who knows when Mum will repeat it!'

'OK,' grinned Mandy. She swallowed her last mouthful of egg, then pushed her chair back. 'I'm just going to check on the animals.'

Mandy liked to get involved in the running of Animal Ark as much as she could. She often helped out when the surgery was busy. Then, there were also her regular duties such as feeding the animals that were recovering from illnesses or operations, and cleaning out their cages. Hardly a day went by when she didn't help out with the animals – no matter how busy she was.

There were four animals in the residential unit that day – two cats that had been in a fight, a boxer puppy who had come in the previous evening with a broken leg, and a goat that had eaten some rat poison.

Mandy fed them all, gave them fresh water and made sure they were clean and comfortable. Then she petted each one in turn, saying, 'I'll be back later.'

The puppy whined when he saw Mandy walking away.

'Don't cry, Punch,' she said, returning to him and pushing her hand through the bars of the cage. 'You'll be going home very soon.' She massaged his neck gently until he relaxed, then stood up to sneak away. The puppy immediately started to whine again.

'Oh, Punch, I've *got* to go,' Mandy said. She almost couldn't bear the look on his squashed-up little face. How was she going to get away without him noticing? Punch whimpered and pawed at the gate. Mandy sighed. If only he'd stop looking so pitiful!

And then, something very strange happened. The puppy's eyes seemed to become the eyes she'd seen in the tunnel and it was as if his whining turned into the desperate neighing she'd heard in her dreams.

Mandy took a step back in astonishment and blinked. In that split second, the eyes returned to normal and the whining no longer sounded like neighing.

'That was odd,' Mandy said aloud.

Punch wagged his stubby little tail and then, to Mandy's surprise, settled down and closed his eyes. She tiptoed out of the unit, trying to make sense of the peculiar incident. It must have been her imagination again – especially after such vivid dreams.

She climbed the twisty staircase to her bedroom. Her mum was probably right. She should try to stop thinking about pit-ponies for a while. Then she groaned, remembering all the work she still had to do on her project.

For the next few hours Mandy sat at her desk, sorting through the information she'd gathered so far. She wasn't sure whether to focus on the Amberton ponies or if her project should cover pit-ponies in general. She found herself wishing that Miss Potter hadn't told them to do a project. Perhaps a short presentation about what they'd done at the museum would have been easier – and quicker!

It was hard going and Mandy struggled to concentrate. The nightmare had affected her more deeply than she'd thought. Images of the distressed pony from her dream kept forcing themselves to the front of her mind and she felt a restless anxiety in the pit of her stomach.

Finally, she slammed down her pen. 'It's no good!' she exclaimed in frustration. 'I'm getting nowhere!'

She put her work away and went downstairs to the kitchen where she helped her mum to pack the picnic.

It was a crisp, clear afternoon and the river sparkled in the sunlight as it tumbled and swirled over the rocks lying hidden beneath its surface. A family of mallards swam upstream, battling against the strong current.

'Aren't they funny?' laughed Mandy. 'You'd think they'd swim *with* the current!'

'Perhaps they *need* to go up the river,' suggested Adam Hope.

'They could always walk along the bank,' suggested his wife.

'I don't think so!' cried Mandy as a large and

very wet black dog came hurtling along the bank towards them. 'No, Blackie. Stay there!' she shouted.

But Blackie ignored Mandy's plea. He bounded up to her, then stopped abruptly at her feet and shook himself vigorously, showering her with water.

'You bad boy!' Mandy scolded, laughing in spite of herself. The dog looked up and wagged his tail happily.

'Do you know, I think he's laughing at me,' Mandy said to her parents. 'How can you be cross with a dog that does that?' She looked around. 'I wonder where James is?'

Hearing the name of his master, Blackie turned and charged off, almost bumping into James who was coming round a bend a few metres downstream.

'Sorry,' said James.

Mandy smiled. James knew his dog very well! He didn't even have to guess why his friend was soaking wet. 'It's OK,' she laughed. 'The water didn't get through my anorak. And, anyway, it's quite nice to get such a warm greeting.'

'More like a cold one, if you ask me!' Mr Hope laughed. Then he turned to James. 'You're just in time. We're about to eat.'

They found a suitable spot on the pebbly riverbank for their picnic and tucked into the sandwiches, cake and fruit that Mandy and Mrs Hope had packed.

'How's your project going?' James asked Mandy, helping himself to a slice of Mrs Hope's sponge cake. 'I've nearly finished mine. I just need to do some drawings of the tunnel system at Amberton.'

'Lucky you!' Mandy grumbled. 'I've hardly started.' She told him about her nightmare. 'It's all I can think about. I haven't even really decided what to do my project on.'

'But I thought you were going to look at pit-ponies?' said James, sounding surprised.

'Yes, but I don't know whether I should concentrate on the ponies that worked at Amberton – especially now that we've met a few of them . . .'

'Why not?' asked James. 'Sounds like a good idea.'

'Mmm, but I don't think I've got quite enough

information on them,' said Mandy, giving a small wedge of cheese to Blackie. The black Labrador was exhausted after splashing about in the river and now lay quietly beside her.

'Didn't you see any information about the ponies at the museum?' asked Mrs Hope. She opened the Thermos flask and poured out steaming cups of tea.

'Yes – a whole gallery of photographs,' Mandy told her. 'But we didn't have time to go through it all. I wish we could go back there.'

Mr Hope stretched over and took a cup of tea. 'Thanks, love,' he said. He took a few mouthfuls, then put the cup on a rock and said, 'I think you *should* go back.'

Mandy looked at him quizzically. 'When?'

'What about tomorrow?' replied her father. 'You're not going to school and we have a very quiet morning scheduled. There are only a few animals coming in for check-ups and vaccinations. As soon as we've seen to them, and as long as there are no emergencies, we can leave for Amberton and be back well in time for evening surgery.' He turned to Mrs Hope, 'Does that sound like a good idea?'

'I think it's an *excellent* idea,' said Mrs Hope, enthusiastically. 'I'd love to go on the underground tour and see what it's like in the tunnels.'

Mr Hope looked taken aback. 'You want to go underground!' he exclaimed.

His wife nodded. 'Yes, I do,' she said seriously.

'Hang on,' said Mr Hope, standing up and putting his hands on his hips. 'Aren't you the same person who once refused to go into the Chamber of Horrors at the funfair?'

'Yes, but that was different,' protested Mrs Hope.

'It's different, all right,' agreed James. 'The mine is much scarier than the Chamber of Horrors!'

'Does that mean you won't be joining us?' teased Mr Hope.

James laughed. 'I'm not the one who sees and hears things in dark tunnels!' He glanced at Mandy and she wrinkled her nose at him.

'Perhaps it'll be your turn to imagine things this time,' she joked. She picked up a stick and threw it up the bank. Blackie jumped up and tore off to retrieve the stick.

'Imagine *what* things?' asked Mrs Hope.

'Oh nothing.' Mandy tried to sound casual. Her experience down the mine seemed unbelievable in broad daylight. 'It's just a bit spooky down there, that's all.'

Mr Hope winked at his wife. 'Still game to go?'

'But of course,' she said firmly.

'Right, so that's decided,' said Mr Hope, helping his wife to her feet. 'We'll set off for Amberton at about ten in the morning.'

Blackie came thundering back down the bank, the stick firmly grasped between his teeth. The sound of his paws on the firm ground jolted Mandy's memory. She had a sudden flashback to the eerie clopping sound that she'd heard in the tunnel. And in her mind, she saw once more the blazing eyes that had taken her breath away. A shudder ran through her whole body.

Surprised that she still felt a bit spooked, Mandy decided that it was time to pull herself together. Taking the stick from Blackie, she threw it along the bank. James's lively dog hurtled after the stick and Mandy trudged after him.

Six

'It was *so* real! I was that sure if I reached out, I'd be able to touch him,' Mandy told James on their way to the Amberton Colliery the next morning.

'What did he look like?' asked James, wiping the condensation off the window on his side of the Land-rover.

'The same as in the last dream – a chestnut Shetland – but this time, he was so close to me, I could feel his hot breath on my neck,' said Mandy.

James looked at her in disbelief. '*Feel* his breath! But you were *dreaming*, Mandy!'

'I know. But honestly, James, it felt like it was real,' Mandy explained. She knew that if she shut her eyes now, she'd get a very clear picture of the pony. It was as if he was carved for ever in her mind.

'So what happened in *this* nightmare?' asked James.

Mandy sighed and looked out of her window. The fields and valleys rushed by in a grey, misty blur. Every now and then, she could see horses sheltering under trees from the driving rain and icy wind. Some of them looked really miserable – almost as miserable as the pony in her latest nightmare.

'What happened?' repeated James, looking concerned.

'It was almost the same as the last two dreams,' said Mandy, still staring out of her window. She didn't want to talk about the dream any more, it just churned her up inside. But even though it was the same dream, with the same pony, it *had* been different. This time, instead of watching him from a distance, Mandy had been right next to him. This time she had not only seen, but had also *felt* his desperation.

It was as if they shared a feeling of terror while the space folded in around them.

She closed her eyes and the blackness behind her eyelids was instantly filled with the features of the terrified Shetland – the flared nostrils, eyes wide with fear, the foam round his mouth. In the dream, she'd wanted to turn and run but something had stopped her. She couldn't leave the pony. She knew that they had to face the terror together.

'How did it end?' asked James.

Mandy shook herself. 'Um, I'm not sure. I don't think it did end. I think it just sort of faded away. Or maybe I woke up before the end. I don't know,' she sighed.

'I wonder if bad dreams *ever* have endings?' pondered Mrs Hope, looking over her shoulder at Mandy and James. 'I've never had one that ended definitely – I'm always trying to get away from something terrible, but I'm frozen to the spot!'

Suddenly, Mr Hope braked sharply. 'Oops, nearly missed the turning in all this mist,' he said. He swung the Land-rover down a lane to the right.

There were only two other cars and a workman's van in the carpark outside the museum building. Both cars had bumper stickers, which read *'Amberton Colliery Museum – we go the extra mile'*.

'Must be staff cars,' said Adam Hope, as they walked across to the main building.

Inside the museum, they found Lisa sitting behind the information desk, wearing a thick duffle coat. She smiled warmly at them. 'Hi, there. I was wondering if anyone would venture as far as the colliery with this dreadful weather.' She looked closely at Mandy and James. 'Don't I recognise you two? Didn't you come with the school party last week?'

Mandy nodded, and then explained why they'd returned.

'Well, it looks like you have the whole place to yourselves today. You can spend as much time as you like researching your project. Please ask if there's anything I can help you with,' said Lisa. 'And, of course, Mr Etherington can tell you just about anything you want to know about the ponies.'

Mr Hope pulled his wallet out of his pocket

to pay for the entrance fees. 'Will you give an underground tour for such a small group?'

'Certainly,' Lisa reassured him. 'Arthur – the guide – can take you down whenever you like.' She handed him the indemnity forms, then said, 'I must apologise about the cold in here. We had a power cut earlier this morning. It lasted only ten minutes, but it's affected the heating system. Our electricians are looking into it, so we hope it'll be fixed soon.'

Mandy wrapped her arms closely round herself. No wonder she was shivering so much!

'What caused the power failure?' asked James.

Lisa shrugged her shoulders. 'We don't know. It could have been the weather – there was a raging gale at the time – but apparently Amberton village didn't get cut off and they're on the same grid as us. The electricians have checked all of our systems here but haven't been able to find the fault yet. So, who knows! It's just one of those mysteries.'

James looked at Mandy and winked.

Mandy pulled a face. But she couldn't help remembering how her headlamp had also gone out briefly, and for no real reason, when she and James were in the side tunnel the other day . . .

She tried to ignore a growing feeling of unease. But there was nothing she could put her finger on. Was it just the gloomy weather? Or was she worried that she might have the same creepy experience as last time she'd been down the mine? And then there was the incident with Christie. Maybe she was afraid she'd also faint. After all, it *was* very dark and stuffy underground.

Arthur was sitting in an easy chair reading the *Amberton Village Gazette* in the office next to the lift shaft. Wafts of hot air blew out from a small fan heater making the climate inside the office very different from the chilly conditions elsewhere. As on their previous visit, Arthur handed each of them a safety helmet before they stepped into the big lift.

Mandy braced herself for the mile-and-a-quarter plunge into the dark abyss. Even though she knew what to expect, she couldn't brush aside a small tingling feeling in the pit of her stomach as Arthur dragged the gate shut with a loud clang.

The old miner pushed up a big lever on one of the walls of the lift. There was the familiar jerking movement they'd experienced on their first trip, then the metal cage plummeted down the cold, murky shaft to the hostile depths of the earth below.

'Well, that was quite breathtaking,' Emily Hope remarked once the lift had hit hard ground. 'I hadn't imagined it would be so dark or that we'd drop so quickly.'

The main heading seemed gloomier than before. Mandy reasoned that it was because there were fewer headlamps in the tunnel today – only five this time as opposed to the thirty or so on the school tour.

Arthur led them down the passage, repeating the talk he'd given the school group a few days earlier. 'Amberton is a typical deep shaft mine. This means that the access passages run straight down from the surface to the coal seam.'

'So there's more than one way into the mine?' asked Mr Hope.

'Aye. The way we've just come is how all the miners used to get into and out of the mine. And then there's the coal-removal passage which is about fifty yards further along,' Arthur explained.

'Does this mine have sloping passages?' asked James, who was just behind Arthur.

Arthur sounded a little surprised by James's question. 'Indeed we *do* have a passage dug on a slant. It's further away, where there used to be a coal seam under a hill. A slanting passage is the best way to reach coal in that position. Been reading up about tunnelling, lad?'

James told him about his project. 'I looked up the Amberton Museum web site on the Internet last night. There's a page all about the different types of tunnels in the mine. There's even a map, which shows all the smaller side tunnels and the emergency passages. I've got a print-out with me.'

Arthur seemed impressed but also a little puzzled. 'Well, I know nothing about all this new-fangled computer stuff but I do know about tunnels. And, because you're a small group, what I can do – and your computer can't – is take you down one of the emergency tunnels. That way you can experience for real what it was like for miners years ago.'

'That should be interesting,' said Mr Hope.

James nudged Mandy and she grinned, then lifted a finger to her lips. They'd better not let on that they'd already been along one of the smaller passages – on their own!

They had reached the section where the main heading forked. As before, Arthur led them down the passageway to the right. After a few minutes he stopped. 'The emergency passage is through here.' He shone his headlamp against the wall, revealing a small timber-framed hole that had been cut out of the rock.

Mandy put a hand to her mouth and stifled a gasp. It was the same hole that she and James had clambered through on the day of the school trip. The hole that led to the echoing passage – the passage that, if she was honest with herself, she was still sure hid a secret. But was she brave enough to find out what it was? Part of her wanted to turn and head back to the lift and return to the normal world above. But another part was determined to face whatever the passage might be hiding.

'It looks a bit like an entrance to a cave,' remarked Mr Hope from the back of the line.

He'd brought a torch with him and was aiming the beam at the hole, which suddenly looked very small indeed. 'It's going to be a bit of a tight squeeze for me,' he said.

'Perhaps we shouldn't go in,' said Mandy, giving in for a moment to a feeling of apprehension about the passageway.

'I'm sure if I hold my breath, I'll fit through,' her father answered, chuckling.

'But it looks very narrow in there, Dad,' argued Mandy.

'That's all right. We're not going all the way, are we, Arthur?' asked Mr Hope.

'No – just far enough for you to get a sense of what it was like to work in such conditions,' said Arthur. 'Mandy's right – it does get very cramped after a while. Of course, we *can* go right through if you want to see where it ends up.'

'No thanks,' muttered Emily Hope. 'Just a sense of it will be quite enough for me!'

One by one they crawled through the gap into the unlit and airless space beyond. Even though she'd felt anxious a few moments before, Mandy's heart now raced with excitement.

Could there really be something extraordinary in that tunnel? And would she see it again?

'Ouch!' cried Mr Hope, struggling through the hole. '*Ouch! Ouch! Ouch!*' echoed his voice.

James laughed. 'I think the echo's the best bit about the tunnel, don't you Mandy?' His laughter bounced around them as they filed along the passage.

'So far,' agreed Mandy and she grinned as her own voice came tumbling back at her.

'Can you switch on your headlamp, lass?' asked Arthur after a while, glancing over his shoulder.

Mandy was confused. She hadn't switched it off. She flicked the switch but nothing happened. 'The bulb must have gone,' she said.

'It can't have,' said Arthur. 'I put new bulbs in all of these helmets only yesterday.'

Again, Mandy fiddled with the switch, but nothing happened. Then she looked behind her and noticed that her mum's lamp had also gone out. She felt a sense of foreboding. Something definitely wasn't right.

'Let's go back,' she said, trying to sound calm. She had hardly finished speaking when they were suddenly plunged into total darkness. The rest of the headlamps had been extinguished in one swoop like candles blown out by a strong gust of wind.

Mrs Hope gasped.

'Don't worry,' came Arthur's soothing voice. 'I've got my torch.'

There was a rustling sound followed by a clicking noise, then an exclamation of 'Blast!' and Mandy realised that the torch had also failed. She tried to take a breath, but the stale and clammy air stuck in her throat.

'Keep calm, everyone,' Arthur said from the front of the group. 'We'll just turn and make our way back to the entrance. We're not far from the main heading – you'll even see the light ahead of us.'

In spite of Arthur's reassuring tone, Mandy was convinced that something strange was happening. First the power in the museum had gone off for no reason and now this . . .

The darkness pressed in on her like a sinister force and her mouth felt dry. What explanation could there be for five lamps and a torch all going out at the same time?

They began to manoeuvre themselves around in the narrow space. Mandy's fingers scraped against the jagged wall.

'Are you OK?' whispered James, after accidentally bumping into her.

'Uh-huh,' she said, taking a step forward. 'I just scraped my . . .' She stopped abruptly. There was a new sound in the tunnel. A sound that rose distinctly above the noise of their awkward movements.

'What's wrong?' asked James, bumping into her again.

'Shh,' she whispered. She waited, her senses made acute by the silent darkness. And then she heard it again. A faint, lonely whinnying that came from deep within the tunnel.

'Anything the matter?' Arthur's low voice rumbled in the gloom behind them as he found his way blocked by James.

'I don't know,' Mandy waited and listened again. The forlorn sound rose up to her from the hidden depths of the earth.

'Listen,' she said to the others. 'Can you hear that?' The neighing had grown louder and more urgent.

'Yes,' breathed James in astonishment. 'It sounds like a horse . . .'

'What *are* you two going on about?' Mrs Hope had stopped just ahead of Mandy. She reached back into the dark and caught hold of Mandy's sleeve.

Adam Hope had also stopped to find out what was happening. Mandy could just make out his form against the faint light filtering through the entrance to the passage. He took a few steps back until he was part of the group. They all listened for the sound that Mandy had heard. 'What am I missing?' he asked.

'Some wild imaginings!' Emily Hope chuckled. 'I can't hear anything odd, Mandy.'

'But *I* heard it,' insisted James.

'Listen – there it is again!' Mandy was surprised that only she and James could hear the urgent whinnying. It seemed to fill the tunnel around them.

'Perhaps you can hear the wind whistling down the shaft and along the passages,' Arthur suggested. 'Come on – let's get out of here.'

Mandy was no longer in a hurry to leave the narrow passage. She glanced over her shoulder into the blackness then saw something that made her go cold. 'Wait!' she cried. 'Look there – back down the tunnel!'

Out of the pitch-black darkness flickered a tiny bright light. Mandy strained her eyes, trying to make out what it was. It grew brighter and bigger. It was coming towards them! Then Mandy saw that there were two lights. She felt the hair on the back of her neck stand up. They weren't lights at all. They were eyes. The very same ones she'd seen here before!

James, who had also turned to look behind him, whistled softly. 'Eyes!' he breathed in amazement. 'So you *were* right the other day, Mandy. It wasn't just a reflection – or your imagination . . .'

Mrs Hope touched Mandy's sleeve. 'I think that's quite enough of this little joke now,' she said firmly. 'We're the only ones down here and if you think you can scare me with talk of strange noises and odd sights—'

A sudden loud and heavy thud further up the passage towards the entrance stopped Mrs Hope and made everyone jump. Mandy looked round. The faint light that had shone through the entrance to the passage had gone out. It was darker than ever. *Not another power cut*, thought Mandy.

'What was that?' Mr Hope sounded concerned.

'I don't know,' came Arthur's voice. 'Can you see anything ahead of you?'

'Nothing,' replied Mr Hope. 'But I'll feel my way and see what I can find.' Mandy heard him shuffling towards the tunnel entrance. When he spoke again a few moments later, his voice was brittle. 'I can feel a big rock in front of me. I don't think I can get past it!'

Mandy's heart skipped a beat. What *was* going on down here?

'Does that mean we're blocked in?' Mrs Hope asked slowly.

'Just a sec,' said Arthur. 'I'll see if I can get there to have a look myself. Sorry, lass,' he apologised as he squeezed past Mandy, causing her to be pushed up against the rough wall.

'Do you think your mum's right? Are we blocked in?' James asked Mandy in a low voice.

'Not really – remember, this *is* an emergency exit,' Mandy reminded him, trying not to sound worried. If only they had some lights . . .

She peered past James into the dark space beyond, trying to make sense of everything that was happening to them. There was no longer any sign of the mysterious eyes. She frowned. Even the darkness seemed to be getting thicker

just ahead of them. Mandy wondered if it was a wall. She blinked hard.

Then, out of the solid darkness, a shape began to emerge. It was the unmistakable shape of a small colt! 'It's a pony,' she whispered huskily, forgetting for a moment the crisis at the entrance to the passage.

'Crikey!' exclaimed James. 'It is! How did *he* get here?'

A shimmering phosphorescence radiated from the colt that stood proudly before them. And in the glow, Mandy could see that it was a Shetland pony. A chestnut Shetland pony.

Seven

'Who *are* you? What are you doing down here?'
Mandy mouthed the questions but no sound
came from her lips. The vision of the pony had
stunned her. Yet it was no hallucination. James
could see him too.

'Where did he come from?' James repeated.

At the same time, Arthur called out that a
large rock was indeed blocking the way to the
entrance. 'We might have disturbed the support
frame when we climbed through,' he explained,
'which could have dislodged the rock and made
it fall. I can't think what else might have caused

it. I mean there's been no shaking or rumbling down here so we're probably not in any danger. Lucky we'd stopped for a bit though – otherwise someone might have got hurt or even . . .' He didn't continue.

'So that means we'll have to get out at the other end?' asked Adam Hope.

'Aye,' said Arthur. 'But it'll be fine – just a bit tight in places. I'll go ahead again.'

A heaving noise sounded in the roof above them. Instantly, Arthur yelled out, 'I don't like the sound of that! Don't wait for me up ahead – just get started, and move as fast as you can!'

'Hurry, Mandy!' Mrs Hope prodded her in the back and Mandy started to move as quickly as she could in the cramped space. The sound of everyone's boots pounding on the rough ground echoed around her and, every now and then, she found herself bumping into James who was just ahead of her. She could hear her mother's breathing several metres behind her and she realised that she and James were moving a lot faster than the adults. She pushed a strand of hair out of her face. It was damp with perspiration. Was that just because of the heat down here or was it from fear?

The alarming noise stopped but Arthur urged them to get to the other end fast. 'Just in case the disturbance was bigger than I thought,' he shouted from the back. Then he added reassuringly, 'The tunnel's not very long – we should be out of here in a few minutes.'

Ahead, Mandy could still see the outline of the colt who was standing quietly watching them. When she and James had almost reached him he turned sideways and flexed his neck, then opened his mouth in a silent whinny.

'He's trying to tell us something,' Mandy said breathlessly to James.

'I hope it's that we're not in danger,' answered James, and Mandy could hear the tension in his voice.

The pony snorted. He struck the ground a few times with his hooves, then spun round and stared straight at Mandy. She gasped. His bright eyes seemed to draw her like a magnet. It was as if she was a prisoner of his gaze. And it was a gaze she'd felt before. For a brief moment, she was back at the Sunfield Pony Sanctuary.

Like Flame! she said to herself. *His stare is exactly like Flame's!*

Bewildered by the strange coincidence, Mandy almost lost her balance as she scrambled over the uneven ground. She pushed her hands against the walls on either side to steady herself and, in that moment, the pony reared then vanished.

'Hey!' exclaimed James. 'Where did he go?'

But before Mandy could speak, the tunnel was suddenly lit up by a soft yellow light.

'Oh!' gasped everyone in surprise. Their headlamps were working again!

'Well I never . . .' muttered Arthur from the back.

The beams from their lamps broke the darkness around them and, once Mandy's eyes became adjusted to the light, she could see that the tunnel was much smaller than at the start.

Everyone stopped and looked at one another as if to take stock of their situation. Apart from the sound of their rapid breathing, there was complete silence.

'This is so weird!' James said, shaking his

head, then pushing his tousled fringe off his forehead.

'Uh-huh. It's almost uncanny,' murmured Emily Hope.

'I must say, I've never known anything like it,' Arthur said.

'Well, I don't think we'll come up with any answers down here,' said Mr Hope. 'And I think that the sooner we get out of this place, the better.'

The group pressed on again with James still in the lead. The tunnel was now so narrow that Mandy had to keep her elbows tucked closely by her sides to stop them being scraped by the walls. She looked up and her headlamp shone against the roof which was now only just above her. She'd have to duck her head if it got any lower.

She glanced back over her shoulder and saw that her parents and Arthur were almost bent double. Adam Hope, being the largest of the three, filled the space around him.

'If it gets much tighter, I won't be able to go on,' he grunted.

But the tunnel did get tighter and the roof

lower. Mandy looked back again and saw with alarm that her father was almost on his stomach. What if it got too narrow for him?

'Mandy! Look!' James blurted out, breaking into Mandy's concerned thoughts.

In front of them, standing silhouetted against a dimly lit background, was the colt. He whinnied softly, then struck the ground with his hooves over and over again.

'What do you want?' breathed Mandy.

But the pony gave away no clues about himself. He shook his head vigorously then silently disappeared once more. And in the place where he'd been standing, Mandy saw an illuminated arched hole. It was the end of the emergency tunnel.

'We've made it!' exclaimed James triumphantly.

Mandy tapped him on the shoulder. 'Well done, leader,' she laughed. She felt the tension lifting from her as she clambered after him through the small gap into the airier space of the bigger tunnel beyond. It was great to be able to stand up straight again and not to feel hemmed in on all sides. She looked around to

see if there was any sign of the colt. But there was no trace of him.

'Phew!' That's better.' Adam Hope emerged through the gap behind Mrs Hope, and stretched and dusted himself off. 'Now what?'

'We're in the passage that forks off to the left of the main heading,' Arthur explained, climbing through the hole. 'If we work our way back we'll reach the lift. Would you like to rest first?'

'Good idea,' said Adam Hope. 'I feel as if I've been on some kind of commando course!' He leaned against the wall, breathing deeply.

Mandy didn't want to rest. She wanted to know what had happened to the colt. He had to be somewhere close by. She could see that James was also puzzled by his disappearance. He paced up and down, fidgeting with his glasses, and occasionally kicking idly at the rocky ground. Then he stopped and knelt down, angling his head as if trying to look at something with his headlamp.

'What is it?' asked Mandy, going over to him.

'Hoofprint, I think,' he answered.

Mandy examined the ground. There was a faint horseshoe-shaped impression in the surface where James was pointing. Then she noticed another one close by. She shone her beam along the ground and saw a line of hoofprints going up the tunnel. Were they the prints of the mysterious colt?

'Let's see where they go,' said James, standing up but bending his head so that his lamp lit up the trail.

The two set off up the passage.

'Where are you going?' called Mrs Hope.

'We're just going a little way towards the shaft,' explained Mandy.

'After some phantom horse, I suppose!' Adam Hope said, laughing. 'Don't get too far in front of us.'

Mandy sighed with frustration. Why hadn't the adults been able to see or hear the pony?

The two friends followed the prints for several metres until, near a bend in the passage, the trail stopped abruptly.

'Oh well, that's the end of that,' said Mandy. 'Maybe they're not hoof-marks at all – they just *look* like them.'

'I suppose it was a bit of a wild-horse chase.' James grinned.

Mandy laughed and looked up. Her smile faded instantly for, standing in front of her – so close that, she could have reached out and touched his forehead – was the chestnut pony. Next to her, James sucked in his breath then stretched his hand towards the little Shetland.

The pony bucked his head and snorted loudly, then whirled round and cantered up the passage. Mandy's headlamp lit up his face for a split second before he charged off. But in that brief moment she caught sight of his expression. It was the same as the look of terror of the pony in her dreams!

'He *is* trying to tell us something,' Mandy insisted. 'I *know* he is.'

'Maybe he wants us to follow him,' said James, scrambling off after the colt.

The pony had rounded the bend and was out of sight but Mandy could hear his hooves clattering over the hard ground. 'I think you're right,' she said.

She couldn't understand why, but she had begun to feel a strong sense of urgency. She set off behind James, calling back over her shoulder, 'Mum, Dad, Arthur – you've got to come now. We have to get to the lift quickly!'

She could hear that the pony was now galloping so she quickened her own pace.

'Wait, Mandy,' Emily Hope shouted from behind. 'Not so fast!'

'Hurry!' Mandy cried out, ignoring her mum's plea.

Mandy and James reached the point where the two tunnels merged into the main heading.

'We're nearly back at the shaft,' James reminded Mandy.

Out of the corner of her eye, Mandy saw James suddenly stumble and trip and go sprawling along the ground. His glasses flew off, landing in front of Mandy. She grabbed them and handed them back to him as he pulled himself up to his feet.

'Now perhaps you'll slow down!' said Mrs Hope firmly as she and Mr Hope and Arthur caught up with them.

'Aye,' agreed Arthur. 'I've never known anyone run so fast in a tunnel. Not since . . .'

A distant noise interrupted him. From deep in the earth came an ominous rumbling.

'Quickly!' shouted Arthur. 'Make for the shaft!'

'What's happening?' cried Mrs Hope just as the earth began to tremble and shake beneath them.

'Earth tremor!' yelled Arthur. 'Run!'

The rumbling noise intensified and was accompanied by loud thuds, while in the tunnel the lamps on the walls began to flicker. Ahead of them, the pony whinnied frantically.

Mandy dashed along the tunnel, her heart pounding in her chest. In front of her she could see the pony again. He had stopped and seemed to be waiting for them to catch up. They were only a few metres away from him when Mandy realised that he was standing in front of the cage. He kicked at the gate and it slid open, then he took a few paces to the side.

'He's opened the lift for us!' exclaimed James.

'In you go, little pony,' urged Mandy, running the last few metres to the lift.

The earth shook violently beneath her. She glanced over her shoulder and saw that the others were hot on her heels. Mrs Hope staggered and fell against Mr Hope, who caught hold of her arm and steadied her.

There was another lurch just as Mandy reached the lift threshold and, in that moment, the pony melted away into the darkness.

Mandy blinked then stared hard at the spot where he'd been standing. Perhaps he'd moved into a shadow. But there wasn't even a hint of his presence. It was as if he'd never been there in the first place.

The others leaped into the cage behind Mandy and James, and Arthur pulled the gate shut. 'I hope the hoist is working,' he mumbled apprehensively.

They watched anxiously as the miner took hold of the controls. There was a judder and a creak but the lift stayed on the ground.

'Come on! Move!' growled Arthur, pushing up the lever again.

Mandy crossed her fingers and willed the lift to move. But even as she stood waiting nervously for the machinery to begin hauling them away from danger, a strange calm descended on her. And, with the calm, came a dazzling vision of the colt. Instead of the wild expression on his face, he now wore a look of complete joy. Then he closed his eyes and a split second later, the vision faded.

Mr Hope had put his arm round Mandy's shoulders. In a soothing tone he said, 'Don't worry, Mandy. We'll get out of here.'

Calmly, she looked up at her father. 'I'm not worried. I *know* we're going to be OK.' Then she smiled at James. 'We had a good leader.'

'Oh, yes. Thanks, James, for running on ahead,' said Mr Hope.

James shrugged his shoulders. 'It wasn't me . . .' he began just as there was another jolt and a shudder and the lift began to move slowly upwards.

They stood in silence while the big steel cage carried them up the icy funnel to safety. But Mandy didn't feel the cold wind that hovered and howled in the shaft. A warm breeze tickled the back of her neck like the breath of a friendly pony.

Eight

At the surface, the gate was swiftly drawn aside and daylight flooded into the lift. It was one of the most welcome sights Mandy had ever seen. She stepped out of the lift into the cold, fresh air to find a group of worried-looking people waiting for them.

Lisa was among the group. 'Are you all OK? Did everyone get out?' she asked frantically. When she realised that no one was missing or hurt, she sighed with relief. 'Phew. Thank goodness you're all right.'

She led them to the restaurant where blankets

and pots of hot tea were waiting for them.

'Really, I'm fine,' James protested as Lisa draped a blanket around him.

Mandy thought that he looked a bit dazed but she knew that he'd never admit it. She grinned as he squirmed and shook off the blanket but gratefully accepted the sweet tea that was poured out for him.

Mandy coughed to clear her throat of coal dust. She took a sip of tea and looked across the table at her parents. Mrs Hope's red hair tumbled about her pale face. She smiled weakly at Mandy. 'That was a close call,' she said.

Mandy nodded. 'But we did have help.'

'Oh yes, the pony!' exclaimed James. 'I wonder what happened to the pony?'

'Pony?' Lisa sounded puzzled.

'The pony down the mine,' Mandy explained.

Lisa frowned, then shot a glance at Arthur who shook his head and shrugged his shoulders.

'I expect you were just a bit confused by all the noise and tremors down there,' said Lisa. 'Shock can cause all sorts of reactions.'

'I'm not shocked,' Mandy insisted, 'and there *was* a pony down there. James and I both saw it.

It was a chestnut Shetland pony. We even followed it along the tunnel.'

Lisa smiled at Mandy and James. 'Well, if you say you saw a pony, then you must have seen one. But the important thing is that you're all safe.' She went on to tell them that it was the first time anything dangerous had happened since the museum had been opened to the public. 'And it was just so sudden – we had no warning at all.'

'But we *did*,' declared Mandy. She turned to James and said meaningfully, 'The pony warned us, didn't he?'

'Uh-huh,' said James. 'When we saw him, we knew that something was wrong.'

Arthur winked at Mr Hope. 'It would have helped if he'd warned *me*,' he said and chuckled. Then he stood up, explaining that he'd have to get a team together to go down and check the extent of the damage. 'First time in many years we've had to organise a search party,' he said gravely.

Mandy wanted to ask him to look for the colt, but she could guess that he wouldn't take her seriously. Instead, she asked when the team would be going down the mine. She felt that the sooner they went, the better their chance of finding the pony.

'We'll set off just as soon as we're sure that there are no more aftershocks,' Arthur said. 'I reckon we'll probably be ready to go before lunch. We'll just carry out a quick structural check today, so we won't be very long. If you want to wait until we resurface, I'll be able to let you know how we get on.'

'I think we can wait a while,' said Adam Hope. 'I don't feel up to driving at the moment and I'd like to hear the full details.'

After Arthur left, Lisa offered to organise lunch. 'How about some home-made soup?' she asked.

'Mmm, sounds good,' said Mr Hope, smiling gratefully.

'Right, I'll sort it out with the chef.' She walked towards the kitchen door, then stopped and turned. 'Oh, by the way, the heating's on again,' Lisa said. 'It just suddenly started working at about the same time you were coming up in the lift. It should start warming up in here any minute now.'

Mandy went across to a window that overlooked the courtyard where the large mining machines were displayed. It was still very wet and misty outside, the rain dripping steadily off the huge pieces of equipment.

James came over to her. 'I wish someone would believe us about the pony,' he said, leaning on the windowsill and looking out into the yard. 'But I guess it does sound a bit crazy.'

'I know,' Mandy agreed. 'If I hadn't seen it with my own eyes, I'd agree with you.'

'Hey, look. Isn't that Mr Etherington?' James pointed towards the bent figure of a man sloshing through the puddles in the courtyard towards the farrier's yard.

'Mmm, it looks like him,' said Mandy. 'Oh no, I nearly forgot!' Seeing the blacksmith made her suddenly remember why they'd come back to the museum in the first place. In all the drama of their underground escape, she'd forgotten about her project! 'Let's go and have a look at the pony gallery while we're waiting for lunch,' she said urgently.

Mr and Mrs Hope chose not to go with Mandy and James. 'I'd rather stay here in the warm and dry,' said Adam Hope, paging through a book on the museum.

The two friends made their way out to the courtyard, then darted through the rain to the farrier's yard.

Mr Etherington had lit a roaring fire and was warming his hands in front of it. 'This is the best place to be when the weather's so bad,' he said with a smile when he saw Mandy and James coming towards him.

The heat radiated powerfully from the furnace, penetrating Mandy's anorak and making her feel uncomfortably hot. It reminded her of how sweltering it had been underground. She took a few steps backwards. 'Do you mind if we look around the gallery again?' she asked.

'Be my guests,' said Mr Etherington. 'But I'm afraid that some of the photos are missing at the moment. The people at the pony sanctuary have borrowed them.'

'Sunfield Pony Sanctuary?' asked Mandy.

'Aye,' answered Mr Etherington. 'They want to make a brochure or something about the place. They promised to return them today.'

'Let's hope they bring them back before we

leave,' said James. He picked up a lump of metal. 'Is this what you use to make horseshoes, Mr Etherington?'

The old farrier nodded. 'It's iron. Would you like to try?'

'Yes, please!' James answered eagerly.

Mr Etherington picked up a strong pair of metal tongs and held the lump of metal in the flames. After a while, the iron began to glow red-hot. Mr Etherington pulled it out of the fire and put it on an anvil before pounding it with a hammer. He then offered James a turn.

James took hold of the heavy hammer. He struck the metal with all his might but made little impression on it.

'I think you'd better put it back in the fire to soften the iron more,' said the blacksmith and offered James the tongs.

While Mr Etherington and James worked the lump of metal, Mandy wandered up the steps to the gallery. There was a blank section on one wall where photos had been removed. A few pictures remained and Mandy studied them and the details about each pony, jotting down

comments in the notebook she'd brought with her.

Even though she filled up several pages with useful facts, she wasn't really thinking about her work. Instead she was looking for something else – some information that would throw light on the mysterious colt they'd seen. Surely there must be some clues to his identity? She was quite sure that he belonged to Amberton Colliery so

she had expected to find at least a picture of
him in the gallery.

But she found nothing. Feeling dissatisfied,
Mandy tramped back down the stairs and
returned to James and Mr Etherington who
were still busily hammering the metal into an
arc.

'Did you find what you were looking for?'
asked the old man.

'Not really,' replied Mandy. She pulled herself
up on to the low wall that separated the forge
from the rest of the yard and watched the
blacksmith and his new apprentice.

'What *are* you looking for?' Mr Etherington
pulled the glowing metal out of the fire and
held it still while James flattened it a bit more
with the hammer. 'Are you after evidence
of the colt you saw underground?' A kindly
expression softened his lined, reddened face.

Mandy looked at him in surprise. Then she
realised that James must have told him about
the pony. 'Do you believe us?' she asked.

Mr Etherington lifted up the tongs and
inspected his and James's handiwork. 'We're
getting there, lad,' he said, then turned to

Mandy. 'Who can say what others see? You know, sometimes, I could swear that I hear ponies neighing and trotting in this very yard.' He looked out from the forge and ran his eyes over the cobblestoned enclosure. 'But someone else will only hear the wind howling down the corridors and the crack of breaking branches in the trees.'

'But he *was* real. We could have touched him. Isn't that right, James?' said Mandy.

James stopped hammering. Perspiration lined his forehead and he was breathing deeply. 'Yes, and we even saw his hoofprints,' he said solemnly.

'Well then – if you both agree he was real, that's all the evidence you need,' said Mr Etherington. He flicked the horseshoe out of the tongs. 'I think that's good enough now,' he told James. 'We'll let it cool down.'

'But I want to know who the pony is and what he's doing down there,' insisted Mandy.

'And if he's all right,' added James.

'There are some things in this life we can never know.' The old man's voice made Mandy think of a wise old owl. He turned his head to one side, listening attentively to something. 'That's the hoist,' he said after a moment. 'The search team's coming back up.'

'Great!' exclaimed James. 'Now we'll find out what's really going on.'

Mr Etherington doused the flames, as they hurried out of the yard and back to the restaurant. Mandy's heart had started to thud painfully. What if the colt hadn't survived?

Minutes later, when Arthur came through the restaurant doors, everyone looked up eagerly. His face was blackened with coal smudges and his overalls were covered with a fine layer of coal dust.

'It was definitely an earthquake,' he said, sitting at the table next to James. 'I checked the seismic equipment in the control room before we went down and it measured three on the Richter scale.'

'Three!' James sounded dismayed. 'We were lucky to get out alive.'

'We were,' agreed Arthur solemnly. 'And contrary to what I first thought, it's not a pretty sight down there. We could only investigate the first hundred metres or so . . .'

'Is the whole tunnel system destroyed?' James said quietly.

'We can't say yet,' Arthur answered. 'But we think that the passages beyond the fork are blocked by tons of rock.'

A new pang of fear gripped Mandy's heart. They'd been in far more danger than she'd imagined.

Arthur continued. 'In all my years of mining, I've only once seen a rock-fall like this – more than thirty years ago. That was caused by an earthquake, too.'

'I remember that quake,' Mr Etherington said quietly. 'A terrible tragedy.'

Everyone seemed dazed by the news. Mr Hope stared blankly at Arthur. He tugged at his beard, deep in thought, then at last he murmured, 'It's probably just sheer luck that we got out in time.'

'Probably,' said Arthur solemnly. He reached into his pocket and drew out a dirty, creased sheet of paper.

'What's that?' asked Mandy.

'It's a map of the mine's tunnel system,' explained Arthur, running a stubby finger across it. 'Going by what we experienced in the tunnel, it's my guess that the rockfall started in this area.' He pointed to the right-hand fork of the main heading. 'Then it spread along the emergency tunnel and up the other main passage as far as the fork.'

'If that *is* how it happened, then we were just ahead of the falling rocks,' said Mrs Hope, grimly. 'If we'd slowed down or stopped any longer to rest, we might not have made it!' She shook her head and sighed.

'Well, we did make it – thanks to Mandy and James surging ahead of us,' said Mr Hope. 'Anyway, the main thing is that we're all sitting here together now.'

'I know,' murmured Mrs Hope. 'But, imagine if Mandy and James hadn't held us back when they thought they heard something in the emergency tunnel? We might have been caught in the first fall . . .'

Mandy shuddered. Then, a new thought suddenly came to her. Almost like a cooling breeze, it swept away the turmoil in her head leaving her with a feeling of deep peace.

Mandy was certain that they'd never been

in any real danger. The colt had made sure of
that.

Nine

Mandy didn't feel like eating. She half-heartedly sipped some of the soup that a waitress had brought them. Then she put down her spoon while her mind churned over the events in the tunnel.

The little colt had been so brave. But what had happened to him? Had he managed to find his way out? She remembered what Arthur had told them about the slope entrance to the mine. She nudged James, who was tucking into a crusty bread roll. The events down the mine obviously hadn't ruined *his* appetite! 'I wonder if the pony used the slope passage to get into the mine?'

James shrugged his shoulders while he swallowed a mouthful of bread. 'Dunno. But I hope so. At least then he'd have stood a chance of getting out again.'

Overhearing them, Arthur leaned back in his chair and smiled. 'Still talking about that pony?'

'I *know* there was pony – a very brave one,' insisted Mandy in frustration. 'And he *must* have got into the mine somehow.'

Arthur shook his head slowly. 'Sorry to disappoint you, lass, but there's no way a pony – or anyone else, for that matter – could go down the slope passage. It's been boarded up for years. Anyway, it doesn't lead into the main heading.' He pointed to the slope tunnel on the map. 'But one thing you've said is absolutely true,' he added unexpectedly.

Mandy shot a surprised glance at James who looked equally astounded by Arthur's comment.

'Ponies *can* be very brave. I've known some to stand quite calmly, refusing to budge because they've sensed that a rock-fall is about to happen,' Arthur explained.

James whistled softly. 'Awesome!' he exclaimed. 'Like a sixth sense?'

'That's what many of us who worked with the ponies believe,' Mr Etherington's grave tone made everyone stop eating and look at him inquiringly.

The blacksmith seemed to be lost in thought. For a moment he sat quietly, staring into the distance, then he took a deep breath and shook himself. 'There are many tales of ponies being very perceptive,' he began. 'There was the pony who stopped of his own accord when a miner's foot got caught under the wheels of a loaded car. The creature couldn't see what had happened but, somehow, he just knew. Otherwise, the miner would have lost his foot.'

'That's incredible,' commented Adam Hope, slowly ladling more soup into his bowl. 'I know that horses are intelligent, but that really takes some beating.'

'And if you want to know about real courage,' continued the blacksmith, 'there's the story of the time about a hundred years ago when a pony suddenly refused to go forward. When his handler pushed past him to investigate, he found a young lad sleeping on the ground some distance ahead – right in the path of the pony. If he'd gone on, the heavy truck he was dragging would have killed the boy.'

Mandy's parents shook their heads in amazement. 'That defies all reason,' said Emily Hope. 'How did he know that the boy was there?'

As Mandy took in the remarkable story, a new idea began to form in her mind. Her project would include a special section that described how the instincts of the pit-ponies had saved lives in the mine. 'The miners must have been really grateful for the ponies' warnings,' she said thoughtfully.

Mr Etherington's response surprised her. 'Sadly not,' he said. 'For instance, in the severe earthquake here about thirty years ago when the tunnels were blocked for weeks—'

At that moment, he was interrupted by the waitress who cleared away the plates.

'Thank you very much,' said Emily Hope, passing a soup bowl to the waitress. Then she looked at her watch. 'Mr Etherington, we've loved hearing these fascinating stories, but we really ought to get going now. We haven't got long before afternoon surgery begins.'

'No problem,' replied the blacksmith. 'I was getting carried away there . . .'

'Come on, everyone,' said Adam Hope. He fetched the heap of anoraks and jackets they'd piled on to a chair in the corner. 'You should have enough information on pit-ponies now to fill a whole book,' he said to Mandy, handing over her anorak.

Mandy nodded. 'Just about. And James knows a whole lot more about tunnels now!' She grinned.

James winced briefly then smiled back at Mandy. 'I've seen enough to know that I don't want to go down another tunnel for a long time,' he said.

At the door to the restaurant, Arthur took his leave of them, saying that he'd be sending a report on the incident to the Commission for Mine Safety. 'They'll want to know every single detail. They might contact you if they need to check anything,' he explained, then he set off down the corridor towards his office.

'Wow,' said James. 'We're going to be in an official report!'

'Well, hello again.' Mandy recognised at once the throaty voice behind them.

They all turned to see Mr Newbury and Ceri from the Sunfield Pony Sanctuary.

'Lisa said you were here,' said Mr Newbury. Then he added grimly, 'She told us about your narrow escape. I just can't believe what happened . . .' He looked at his granddaughter, 'Puts our problem in the shade a bit, doesn't it?'

'What problem?' asked Mr Hope.

'Just a financial one,' said Mr Newbury gloomily. 'We're not breaking even with our accounts. I've cut as many corners as I can, but we're still not making enough money to support the sanctuary. If I can't find some way of staying afloat, we might have to close. But really, in the light of your narrow escape, it doesn't seem terribly important.'

'Of course it's important,' cried Mandy. Anything involving animals was always important!

'What would happen to the ponies if you did

have to close?' asked James.

'Grandad would have to find new homes for them,' explained Ceri sadly.

'That would be terrible!' gasped Mandy. The few hours she'd spent at Sunfield had been enough for her to see how happy and well looked-after all the ponies were. She couldn't imagine that they would ever find better homes. On top of that, they'd all been through so much already. It wouldn't be right for the ponies to have to go through another upheaval.

'It could be our only choice,' said Mr Newbury. His weathered face looked more creased then ever. Mandy could see by his expression that his ponies meant the world to him. Despite what he'd said, he was obviously worried sick about his horses.

'Don't you have any other options?' asked Emily Hope.

'I'm pinning all my hopes on registering Sunfield as a charity,' Mr Newbury replied. He went on to explain how he hoped to raise money by asking supporters to sponsor individual horses. They would be able to visit the sanctuary and adopt a pony. 'And for people who live too far away to visit us, we're producing a brochure showing pictures of all the horses. Then they can choose which pony they'd like to sponsor.'

'What a brilliant idea!' exclaimed Mandy.

'Fab!' agreed James.

'Do you really think so?' asked Mr Newbury hopefully. Then he looked at Mandy. 'And we're including a page or two on the pit-ponies to try and create more interest in them.'

Ceri held up a thick envelope she was carrying. 'We borrowed these photos from the museum. Grandad wants people to be able to see pictures of the ponies working underground. We're even going to include the family histories of our pit-ponies.' She reached into the envelope and pulled out a few sheets of paper, which she showed to the group. On each sheet there was a diagram that showed each pony's family tree.

'This is really interesting,' said James looking at the family tree for Margot, the brown Shetland pony they'd met at the sanctuary. 'How did you get all this information?'

'It was quite easy,' Ceri answered, putting the papers back in the envelopes. 'The museum still has all the breeding and veterinary records of every pony that worked at Amberton. So we just had to search through them to find the records for our ponies at Sunfield.'

'Well, it looks like there are going to be two projects about the Amberton pit-ponies.' Mr Hope chuckled. 'We must get going now. Good luck with the fund-raising,' he said, shaking Mr Newbury's hand warmly. 'Send us a brochure when they're ready, won't you?' he added, before turning to leave.

'Wait, Dad,' said Mandy desperately, as a shiver slowly made its way up her spine. 'Could we look through the photos quickly? Please? I might find out something new for my project.' This could be the last chance she'd have to discover who the mysterious pony was.

Mr Hope looked at his watch. 'We really need to be getting back to Animal Ark – but I suppose a few minutes won't make much difference.'

Mr Etherington took the bulky envelope from Ceri and began to take out the photographs. A few fell to the ground. Picking them up, the blacksmith suggested that it would be easier for

Mandy to study the pictures properly if they were back on the wall alongside their accompanying captions in the gallery.

They followed Mr Etherington out into the courtyard, passing the damp metal hulks of the mining machinery before pushing open the big wooden doors to the farrier's yard. The rain was now no more than a soft drizzle and the sky had grown lighter.

'Looks like the weather's clearing up,' said Paul Newbury.

They climbed the short flight of stairs up to the gallery. Then, with Ceri passing the pictures to him, Mr Etherington began pinning the photographs back in their places.

'I remember this fellow well.' Mr Etherington held up a picture of a white Shetland pony. 'Steel, they called him. A right tough one, he was, and clever too. The rascal used to sneak mints out of my pockets when I shod him. His handler told me that he could even open his flask and drink all the tea from it. I didn't believe him until I saw it with my own eyes!'

While he replaced the photographs on the wall, Mr Etherington told them what he could remember about each of the ponies. Mandy listened carefully, occasionally making notes on a small pad. It was wonderful to hear about the individual personalities of the ponies. It made her feel as if she knew them. They were no longer just a collection of photographs of unknown horses. But still the nagging feeling persisted. Somewhere, there was an important clue that she was sure would resolve all her unanswered questions.

'Last one,' said Ceri putting down the envelope on a shelf next to the wall and handing the photograph to the blacksmith.

Mandy felt disappointed. It looked as if she wasn't going to learn anything new after all.

Mr Etherington took the picture and pinned it in the remaining gap on the wall before stepping aside. Mandy leaned forward to get a good look at the pony. What she saw sent a shiver down her spine. Here, at last, was what she'd been seeking all along!

'I know him,' she gasped, taking a step closer. 'It's the colt we saw in the tunnel!'

James peered over her shoulder. 'It is,' he echoed, his eyes wide with wonder.

A sturdy chestnut Shetland pony stared out at them from the photograph. His handsome face wore a proud, intelligent look. But it was his gaze that sent a wave of shock through Mandy. It was the same intense gaze she had felt in the tunnel. There was no doubt in her mind that this was the pony that had led them to safety.

Ten

'I *knew* we'd eventually find out who he was.'

'*And* that he wasn't just a mirage!' said James pointedly.

'You saw *this* pony?' Ceri asked, exchanging a look of bewilderment with her grandfather.

'Yes,' cried Mandy excitedly. 'I'd know him anywhere. Wouldn't you, James?'

'Uh-huh,' agreed James, still examining the picture. 'You can't mistake the white star on his forehead,' he said practically.

The others clustered round the photograph. After a few tense moments, Mr Hope finally shook his head. 'Even if you two *did* see a pony in the mine – and I still think that's unlikely – it couldn't have been this one. Look at the dates under his picture – he died more than thirty years ago.'

Mandy breathed in sharply. She stepped forward to read the dates. It was true. The colt had been dead for a long time. But she *couldn't* have been mistaken!

Mr Etherington, who had been standing quietly to one side, began to speak. 'It's all starting to make sense now,' he said darkly, and Mandy experienced a shiver of anticipation.

'But nothing's making any sense!' Mr Newbury was so confused that his face was more creased than ever. Mandy had to suppress a giggle at the way his friendly features seemed to disappear among his wrinkles.

Mr Etherington began to explain. 'I knew that pony well. He died a hero and became a legend. Even those who never knew him talk about his courage – even now.' He pointed over the balustrade of the gallery towards the yard below. 'We even have a memorial to him down there.'

The blacksmith led them back down the stairs and across the yard to an area which Mandy and James had previously overlooked. The wet cobblestones glistened under the weak sun that had begun to shine down from the watery sky. Autumn leaves scudded across the ground in the gentle, drying breeze that whispered through the yard.

Mr Etherington gestured to the cart that was mounted on a block of concrete behind a chain-link fence. 'The pony pulled a cart like this through the mine.'

A plinth bearing an engraved plaque stood in front of the fence. Mandy bent down to read the plaque. Her heart leaped as she read the first word. DEFENDER.

'*Defender*,' Mandy read aloud. '*In memory of a colt who went beyond the call of duty to save his master and, in so doing, lost his own life. His courage and loyalty knew no bounds. Those who knew him will never forget him.*'

A lump formed in Mandy's throat. She turned to Mr Etherington. 'You said you knew him. What happened? Why did he die?' she asked, her voice faltering.

Mr Etherington swallowed hard. Mandy could see that the memory of the pony still saddened the old man. 'Just over thirty years ago, there was a serious earthquake in the mine,' he began. Defender was on shift that day. His handler was a chap who never really bonded with the ponies. He looked on them just as working machines. They'd been hauling coal up the tunnel to the coal-removal shaft for about three hours and were on their way back for yet another load when Defender suddenly stopped. The handler urged him on but the colt just stood his ground. He wouldn't budge an inch.'

Mandy pictured the handsome little pony stubbornly refusing to move while the handler pulled and tugged at his harness.

'The handler began to beat him, yelling at the poor creature to "get a move on" but Defender resisted him and stayed put. As he carried on with the beatings the colt suddenly started to whinny frantically.' Mr Etherington spoke softly, almost as if he was ashamed to talk about the brutal treatment of the colt.

Mandy had a flashback to the heart-rending whinnying in her nightmares. In that instant she knew without a doubt that the pony she'd dreamed of was Defender. And he *had* been trying to warn her of the cave-in. But there was no time now to ponder the strangeness of it all. Mr Etherington was continuing with his story.

'The colt then started to move backwards, pushing the cart back up the tunnel,' he told them. 'The handler had to turn and go further up the tunnel otherwise he'd have been injured by the heavy cart. He swore and yelled at Defender, but the pony just kept backing up. Then the cart jack-knifed, blocking the pony's path. Defender couldn't go any further – he was stuck fast.'

Mandy held her breath as she pictured the terrible drama in the tunnel.

James, standing next to her, whispered, 'I don't think I want to know the ending.'

'Before the handler could straighten the cart,' continued Mr Etherington, 'a sinister rumbling sound filled the tunnel. He realised then that they were in trouble. He tried to free Defender and grabbed at the cart, jerking and yanking at it with all his might. But it was too late. The roof of the tunnel suddenly caved in right above the colt. Moments later, Defender was buried under tons of rocks. And where they had stood, the tunnel was completely blocked.'

There was not a sound in the yard as Mr Etherington came to the end of his story. Mandy felt hot tears running down her cheeks. She brushed them aside, but fresh ones took their place. She bit her lip as she murmured quietly to James, 'Defender lived up to his name. He protected his master. If he hadn't backed up, the man would also have been killed.'

James sighed. 'If only he'd understood what Defender was trying to tell him. . . . Then the pony would have survived, too.'

Mandy thought about the way the pony had warned her and James of the danger in the mine. It had been almost impossible to ignore him. How could the miner – who worked so closely with him – not have taken the young pony seriously? She shook her head sadly. The colt had sacrificed himself for the sake of a cruel master. And even though he'd been flogged and spurned, Defender continued to help.

Mandy kicked at the cobblestones in anger. 'He shouldn't have died like that,' she murmured. 'His handler *should* have known!'

'I'm sure if it had been me, I would have taken him seriously,' muttered James.

'But you and Mandy did,' Mr Etherington said sincerely. Mandy knew then that the blacksmith was the one adult who believed the colt had saved them, too.

She looked up as the yard was suddenly bathed in bright sunlight. At the same time,

the curious vision of the closing eyes she'd had in the lift earlier flashed through her mind. The real meaning of that image then dawned on her. Defender was now at peace! She could almost imagine him gazing contentedly. She looked at the cart which was shimmering in the sunshine and whispered, 'Goodbye, Defender. And – thank you.'

Mrs Hope ran a hand through her hair. 'It's an extraordinary story,' she said quietly.

'Amazing,' agreed Adam Hope. He looked at the sombre group around him. 'But I don't think we need to be so downcast. After all, it is a heartening story. And it just confirms how dependent we really are on our four-footed companions.'

Mr Hope's words seemed to cheer everyone up. Mandy glanced at her mum who smiled back at her. 'If a pony can save a life in that way,' said Emily Hope, 'I can almost understand why people believe that horseshoes bring luck.'

'Horseshoes! That reminds me,' said Mandy. She turned to Mr Etherington. 'Do you always put Defender's name on your horseshoes?'

Mr Etherington looked puzzled. 'What do you mean?'

'You know! You carved "Defender" on that miniature shoe you gave me,' explained Mandy.

'No, I didn't,' said the blacksmith. 'I don't engrave anything on my horseshoes.'

Mandy was puzzled. She knew she'd seen – and touched – the name on the horseshoe.

She waited for James to back her up, but he just looked back blankly at her. Obviously his shoe didn't have the colt's name on it.

She decided to drop the subject. Perhaps this time she *had* been mistaken. Still, she could have sworn she'd seen the name through the magnifying glass . . . .

Mr Hope jabbed her playfully in the ribs. 'I think we've had enough mysteries for one day,' he said, grinning. 'And I also think that if we don't make a move now, we're going to be horribly late getting back to Animal Ark.'

'Hey! That tickles, Dad.' Mandy laughed and jumped out of his reach.

They walked across the yard towards the wooden doors. At the forge, Mr Etherington stopped and, with a mock salute, said, 'Well, goodbye.'

Mandy and James hung back while the others went on. James shook the blacksmith's hand and thanked him for showing him how to make a horseshoe.

'I enjoyed it too,' said the old man.

'And thank you for telling us about Defender,' said Mandy.

The blacksmith winked at her, picked up an iron poker and began prodding the fire. A huge orange flame leaped up from the coals, casting a bright glow all around the forge.

The flame darted higher as it consumed the coals that cracked and fizzed beneath it. Mandy felt herself drawn to the fire. She couldn't take her eyes off it. The flame danced higher and gradually changed its shape. Mandy's heart skipped a beat. The flame almost looked like a glowing pony!

She shook her head and blinked and the flame resumed its normal shape. What could this mean? But before the question had even finished forming in her mind, she knew the answer. Flame! The pony at the sanctuary! There was just one last thing that she needed to sort out.

Mandy spun round and dashed towards the gallery.

'Hey!' yelled James. 'What's going on?'

'Come quickly, James,' she yelled back. 'I've just realised something very important.' James charged after her, his boots clattering loudly on the cobblestones.

'Mandy! James!' called Mrs Hope, turning to see what the noise was about. 'Where are you going?'

'Just a minute, Mum,' Mandy shouted, taking the stairs two by two with James hot on her heels. 'I nearly left something behind!' She ran to the shelf where Ceri had left the envelope. Picking it up, Mandy pushed her hand inside and felt for the papers she knew were still in there. The family trees – they held the answer. She pulled them out just as Ceri ran up the stairs and into the gallery.

'I wish you'd tell us what you're doing,' said James, leaning against the wall and panting hard.

'Here,' said Mandy, handing him and Ceri a few of the diagrams. 'Look through those for

Flame's family tree.'

James stared at Mandy with raised eyebrows.

'Don't worry,' she laughed. 'I haven't gone crazy. You'll see.'

They scanned the papers until Ceri waved one in the air. 'Here it is,' she announced. 'Flame's family.'

Mandy took the diagram from Ceri and, her heart pounding in her chest, read out the names. 'Dam – Rosy; Sire . . .' she paused then, in a hushed voice, read, 'Defender.'

At last, everything had fallen into place. She closed her eyes and pictured the little strawberry roan Shetland that had so forcefully claimed her attention at the sanctuary. 'I should have known,' she murmured. 'He's got his father's eyes!'

The sun was pouring out of a cloudless, blue sky as they drove back to Animal Ark. The moors and meadows sparkled in the bright sunlight and the air was fresh and clean, washed by the rain of the past few days. Mandy felt relaxed and happy.

Mr Hope glanced at her in his rear view

mirror. 'Do you know, it's the first time in about a week that you've smiled properly?' he said.

'I know,' grinned Mandy. 'And I don't think I'll be having any more nightmares.'

'What about your unfinished project – isn't that becoming a bit of a nightmare?' teased James.

'Don't remind me,' moaned Mandy. 'I think I'll be staying up all night working on it!'

'Talking about projects on pit-ponies . . .' began Emily Hope. 'I've been thinking.' She twisted round in her seat and looked back at Mandy. 'Why don't we all chip in and sponsor one of the Sunfield ponies?'

'Brilliant idea, Mum!' exclaimed Mandy. 'And I know already which one we should pick.'

'I bet I know who that is,' said James.

Mandy grinned at her friend. 'Well, after everything that's happened, who else could we possibly choose, but Flame?'

Another Hodder Children's book

ANIMALS IN THE ARK
Animal Ark 50

Lucy Daniels

A fire at Betty Hilder's animal sanctuary leaves the animals homeless – until Mandy persuades her parents to open the doors at Animal Ark. Obviously the animals can't stay there for long, and money needs to be raised for repairs – can Mandy and James come up with a plan before the sanctuary has to close for good?

MARE IN THE MEADOW
Animal Ark 51

Lucy Daniels

Mandy and James are finding it difficult to spare enough time to give Camomile – a mare whose owner has gone to America – all the attention and exercise she needs. They are hopeful when they meet Rhian, who lives next to Camomile's field, that she will help them out. However, for her own reasons, Rhian doesn't want to get to know the mare. Can Mandy and James persuade their new friend to care for Camomile before she has to be sold?

ANIMAL ARK *by Lucy Daniels*

All Hodder Children's books are available at your local bookshop, or can be ordered direct from the publisher. Just tick the titles you would like and complete the details below. Prices and availability are subject to change without prior notice.

Please enclose a cheque or postal order made payable to *Bookpoint Ltd*, and send to: Hodder Children's Books, 39 Milton Park, Abingdon, OXON OX14 4TD, UK. Email Address: orders@bookpoint.co.uk

If you would prefer to pay by credit card, our call centre team would be delighted to take your order by telephone. Our direct line *01235 400414* (lines open 9.00 am–6.00 pm Monday to Saturday, 24 hour message answering service). Alternatively you can send a fax on *01235 400454*.

TITLE		FIRST NAME		SURNAME	

ADDRESS	
DAYTIME TEL:		POST CODE	

If you would prefer to pay by credit card, please complete: Please debit my Visa/Access/Diner's Card/American Express (delete as applicable) card no:

Signature ....

Expiry Date: ....

If you would NOT like to receive further information on our products please tick the box. ❐

Just Desserts

'I do!' Odette's eager face was in close up, the condom head-dress bobbing. 'I do!'

The shot cut to Lydia, looking staggering in very little at all, a fantastic Asprey tiara balancing on her smooth blonde chignon as she gasped, 'I do.'

Then it cut back to Jimmy's voice behind a panelled wooden door, booming, 'I love you, Odette Fielding.' Even recorded through wood, it was loud and clear. 'How many times do I have to say it? How many mountains do I have to climb to prove it?'

Again, the shot switched with alarming New Wave speed to film of Jimmy walking on the Downs with Winnie, climbing to the ridge that divided Fermoncieaux from his farm and staring into the distance. His voice-over, less distorted but still forcefully loud, said, 'Food Hall is going to be great – one of the biggest sensations in world dining. People will come here from all over the globe, let alone England. But that's not why I'm here. I'm here for love. For Odette Fielding.'

There was a lot of jeering and he hid his face in Odette's shoulder.

Juno, who was weeping openly, reached for another Kettle Chip and said, 'This is the best bit. I just love this bit.'

'Pause the video a moment!' Ally wailed as she spirited China towards the loo. 'We'll be right back. I think Parsley needs changing, Dunc.'

Cyd indulgently filled up the glasses of her many 'children', squeezing Calum's hand as she passed. He had been totally against the idea of a baby party at first, saying it would be all soiled nappies, wailing and post-natal depression, but Cyd knew it would be the roaring success it was. As she had cheerfully pointed out, she'd always liked babies most while still they were inside the womb, so why not hurry up and have the party before they made an appearance? On a Christmas visit to the UK, Juno's huge bump was being fuelled by crisps and stroked by its indulgent father as it awaited its transatlantic flight back to the place of its conception while it was still safe to fly. Saskia and Stan's baby was just a tiny blob on a scan, which they were proudly displaying to anyone who was interested. Still refusing to wear dungarees, Miss Bee was looking utterly content as her unborn child's fathers – Mungo and Jez – lavished attention upon her. Having been practising almost non-stop in the six months since their wedding, Lydia and Finlay hoped to have good news soon. Jimmy's gorgeous brother Felix was still in shock having just learned that the nursery he was decorating in their Yorkshire farmhouse was going to accommodate twins. And, most thrilling of all, her darling Odette, who'd said she and Jimmy weren't planning a family, had stayed off the champagne all day and was showing a strange delectation for chocolates dipped in condensed milk.

As Jez rewound the video by a few frames and paused it again so that Mungo could admire a still of himself in his suit, Odette munched another chocolate drop and looked around the room. She'd seen the video at least a dozen times, mostly at Mungo's behest. They had a television and video at Siddals now, which he kept in the attic annexe they'd converted for him so he could have some privacy when Jez stayed. Love had softened him a lot, although he still tried to bully the dogs into obedience, especially poor Winnie. Odette bit back a smile as she realised that she now lived in a big house with a beautiful man, a crotchety chef and a small dog.

'Have an iced gem,' Cyd offered, floating past. Because neither she nor Calum could cook, she had simply bought piles of sweet children's party food and every table was spilling over with marshmallows, jammy dodgers, sweets, cake and liquorice bootlaces. It was quite the best buffet Odette had ever sampled.

She snuggled tighter into Jimmy's side and glanced up at the two Picasso sketches framed above Cyd's mantelpiece. In exchange for them, Calum had signed fifty percent of his Food

The moment Ally was back, Euan pressed 'play' and they watched the interview with Jimmy Sylvian that Ronny had taped late one night, alone with a camera and a man who had wanted nothing to do with the docusoap until his friend had blackmailed him into it.

'I know who the stars of this thing are going to be,' his bruised blue eyes looked straight into the lens, 'myself and Odette. But that shouldn't be the case. We're just comestibles to Calum. He eats us up. We both love him and he doesn't give a . . .' *bleep*, the censor cut in, '. . . about us. But that's all right, that's the way he works, the way restaurants work. This place is about food. Good food. Consuming, gorging, enjoying. Some people will come here every week, some only once – they'll save and save and remember it all their lives. It's like love. Some of us pig out on love – the rest have maybe one or two binges in a lifetime.'

'Which are you?' asked the anonymous, off-camera voice of Ronny.

'I'm greedy.' He smiled. 'But the love of my life hardly eats at all. I want her to get fat. I love her fat, she likes me lean. We're like Jack Spratt and his missus – or at least that's what I hope we'll be like.' His booming laughter rang out.

Suddenly the screen was full of busy diners in a restaurant being served by super-professional waiters, one of whom was blond and gorgeous Finlay, looking very pleased with himself and charming everyone. The camera shot narrowed to two diners sharing a plate of *fruits de mer*. It showed the woman opening her mouth to accept an oyster, lapping it up greedily. As she reached to wipe the juice dribbling from her chin, her companion leaned across the table and pulled her into a kiss to do it for her.

The famous RSC voice-over actress who had been hired to narrate *Food Fights* cut in with her warm, rich tones: 'Jimmy and Odette are engaged to be married next year. They might choose Food Hall for the venue, but are planning to open a hotel in the Cambrian Mountains, so some healthy competition could be on the cards. Time will tell . . .'

Hall stake over to her and Jimmy, enabling Jimmy to sell enough shares to buy Felix a house and secure all the Sylvians' futures. The stake was a great deal more than the pictures were worth, but that was immaterial to Calum. She knew that he thought of the pair as her and Jimmy, the two people he had hurt most and who had still forgiven him, and he had promised never to sell or separate them. She didn't like their stark naïveté very much – they weren't so much Blue Period as *Blue Peter* – but at least she didn't have to live with them and she liked to imagine Jocelyn Sylvian would take a very black view of their final resting place. For, sitting between them, was one of Dennis Thirsk's pieces from the exhibition, 'Under Where? Underground', which he had given to Cyd and Calum as a wedding present – a red spangled jock-strap set in Perspex. Odette wondered how Calum felt having Jobe's pants above his head whenever he went to stoke the fire.

He looked happy enough now, one leg slung over a chair arm, his leather hat at a jaunty angle as he laughed with his brother. He didn't even seem to mind Cyd playing the video of all six episodes of *Food Fights*, even though he came across as a prat in the series. The hit show of the autumn ratings had, after all, turned Food Hall into a legend and its staff into stars. One had become a national hero.

Odette turned back to Jimmy, her television star, who – far from being embarrassed as he had been when the series had first appeared – now lapped up the attention and adored it when he was asked for an autograph in Tesco's. He cuddled her closer, despite the heat in Cyd's huge sitting room. He still found the British winters too cold. Last week, Odette had bought him a pair of pyjamas, suggesting that he wore the bottoms, she the top. Taking her by the hand, he'd led her outside and set light to them, vowing that nothing would ever come between them in bed. 'You're all I need to keep warm.' Odette loved him for it, although she wished he'd just let her take them back to M & S with the receipt.

'Come here.' He kissed her. 'Mmm, chocolatey. Delicious. You know we're about to have to sit through our big scene again, don't you?'

'Wettest kiss I've ever had in my life.' And they both dissolved into silent mirth as they remembered.

695

the most expensive fittings available which had taken weeks to be delivered – the ovens alone weighed five tons apiece and each cost as much as a small flat. Calum's closest crony, the famously irascible chef Florian Etoile, had so far cancelled five meetings. He wasn't actually going to cook at the restaurant – just conceive the menus with a junior apprentice or something – but without them Odette had no idea who to hire from *sous-chef* to *plongeurs*.

Calum was the one with the contacts. He had promised her a stack of press, celebrity guests, top critics and a charting band on the opening night. But the opening was now a fortnight away and nothing was happening.

The OD was, as usual, full of builders, and looked more like a demolition site than a future media haunt. Thermos flasks were lined up on the dusty bar which was destined to be decked with champagne coolers and dry martinis; plaster-crusted fleece jackets, paint-splashed jeans and scuffed work boots crowded for space, not D & G shirts, Alexander McQueen bondage trousers and Patrick Cox mules. The only designer fixture was Maurice Lloyd-Brewster who was busy attaching découpage cherubs to tens of lavatory cisterns.

'I'm sure Odette said that we were sticking with white marble minimalism,' Odette's assistant, Saskia Seaton, told him worriedly.

Glancing at her watch, she hoped Odette would get back in time for her to dash off to Chelsea for her wedding dress fitting. When she had let her fiancé Stan persuade her into acting as Odette's assistant on the OD, she'd had no idea that the project would be delayed so much it would threaten to encroach upon their wedding.

Stan and Odette had been to school together and were old friends. They originated from the same world – the hardened, quick-witted back streets where kids grew up faster than they did in the country. Saskia knew she was soft and spoiled by comparison. As they had matured, Stan and Odette had gone in opposite directions – Stan to the oblique, cliquey world of modern art; Odette into commercials production and now the restaurant business. They had both excelled in their chosen fields, crashed through the class divide. There was an angry, ambitious bond between them.

For all their differences, Saskia liked and admired Odette. Like Stan, she talked her mind, had a fiery temper and a no-nonsense attitude. She could be brutal in order to get what she wanted, but also honest and loyal. She would always remember a birthday or to ask after an ache or pain, but she'd equally expect you to work through both if need be, because that was what she did herself.

Saskia wondered if Odette would miss a wedding dress fitting. In all likelihood, she suspected Odette would miss her own wedding if it clashed with an important meeting.

Odette eventually tried to flush Calum out at home, but the converted print works in Old Street appeared deserted. She shoved a rude note scribbled on Filofax paper through his door and stomped back to her Vespa. Setting off with a furious whine, she threaded her way through the traffic towards Islington.

The old fire station was locked up behind its chipboard covers when she arrived. Saskia had left a note inside: *'Had to go. Health and Safety rearranged for end next week. Telephones still not in. Maurice says gold and purple velvet is very post-Millennium. Have a nice weekend, darling.'*

Odette closed her eyes and groaned. Weekends meant nothing to her any more. The only thing she noticed about them was that she couldn't call any business contacts until Monday morning. Apart from that all she did was work, work, work, and wait for the Monday tabloids to see what Calum had been up to and whom he had been up.

2

Lydia Morley was working her way through her address book alphabetically, telling everyone she was getting married. This, she began to realise, was perhaps a mistake, as she told her Acupuncturist, Aqua-aerobic instructor, AA counsellor and Antique specialist before getting around to telling anyone she was actually planning to invite to the wedding. But once Lydia embarked upon a project, she saw it through to the bitter end. So she also told her Beautician, Bagel delivery man and Barclaycard Services before she called the first of her real friends, Elsa Bridgehouse, to pass on the news. The moment the receiver was picked up, Lydia launched into a cheerfully flat rendition of 'Here Comes The Bride', although she forgot the words after 'short, fat and wide', so just settled for humming for a while.

'. . . dum da di dum dum, di diddle de dum di dum! You and lovebeast donkey dong Euan aren't the only couple to be tying the knot next year, hon. Guess what?'

Elsa was clearly silenced by the news, which Lydia took as a good sign. 'Yes, it's true, hon. Fin and I are getting hitched, although I'm not up the spout like you or anything.'

There was a very low, very amused clearing of throat at the other end of the line. 'You're talking to the donkey-donged lovebeast, hen. Elsa's at her ma's this weekend. But congratulations – I always say we Scots get the prettiest lasses.'

Lydia wasn't in the slightest bit embarrassed to find herself talking to Euan. In fact she was delighted to receive approval from Elsa's tall, sexy partner who had the same indecipherable accent as her beloved Finlay, only about twelve notes deeper and three grades of sandpaper coarser. 'Don't you just? Now tell me, Eu, are you going to wear a kilt? Only Fin wants to, but I think his legs are too skinny and the Forrester tartan is simply ghastly.'

After talking to Euan, she toyed with the idea of calling Elsa at her mother's, but decided not to intrude. Elsa and Cyd had only recently been reconciled after a lengthy family feud which dated back to Cyd's second marriage, to the legendary hard-drinking rock drummer Jobe Francis. Elsa, the youngest of five children, had been just two when her mother had run away to live with the tortured genius behind some of Mask's greatest hits. The band was known to be as depraved as the cult sixties porn film from which it had taken its name, and rumours of sadomasochism, orgies and drugs abounded.

By loving Jobe, Cyd effectively lost all chance of raising Elsa and her four brothers. The right-wing press lampooned her as a bad mother and a disgrace to her sex. After a lengthy and well-publicised court battle, the children's father won sole custody and brought them up far away from the glare of the media and the excessive attentions of their bohemian mother, who made sporadic and unsuccessful attempts to win them back. The four sons – three of whom now lived overseas – still refused to speak to her.

Elsa had always been loyal to her father, who remained deeply hurt by Cyd's desertion to this day. He had married again in the seventies, to Elsa's stepmother – a loving, gentle little Japanese woman called Po whom everyone adored and no one really knew. She was nothing like the blonde, smoky-voiced Cyd with her rock-star friends and headline-making charisma. Even though Jobe had been killed in a car accident two years ago, Cyd could still get the press camped around her door at the drop of one of her casual one-liners. She was, it was rumoured, close friends with everyone from Bowie to Prince Charles, and Elsa had grown up both captivated by her mother's fame and resenting her neglectful immaturity.

Only recently had they managed a fragile rapprochement. The news of Elsa's pregnancy had finally brought them together, although the relationship was still awkward and tense at times.

Lydia was more fascinated by Cyd than she cared to admit,

and longed to meet her. She guessed her first chance would be at the wedding. She had a feeling they would have rather a ravishing amount in common. She loved Finlay with all her heart, but sometimes wished that he was something a little more glamorous than a trainee sales administrator. When they'd both junked in their slacker jobs at dreary Immedia, Lydia had had visions of their working together from home – herself in her consulting room, Finlay in the attic writing a novel or something. But Finlay found working in a proper job extremely novel, and delighted in the fact he now had a pension scheme, company shares and five weeks' paid leave a year. Lydia was hoping that the fad would wear off pretty soon after they got married. A bohemian life in the country was a rather tempting idea. London was getting extremely passé. Cyd Francis knew what she was doing living in seclusion in Sussex.

Instead of calling Elsa, Lydia closed her address book and tried Odette's number. It was engaged. She pressed the cancel button on her phone irritably and called her best friend Juno for the fifth time that day: 'We can't pick up your call so leave a message'. Lydia twisted her mouth and tutted. That message was really starting to get on her nerves. Telling people you were getting married was a bit boring, she decided. She tried Odette again. Still engaged. Turning back to 'B' in her address book, Lydia dialled her Buddhist adviser, although she'd given up her brief dabble with the faith years ago because she could never remember the chant.

'And then he say, "No, Madame Feeldeeng, you can't have *boeuf* on ze bone – eet ees too dangerous, madame!" So I says to 'im, "Eef zat ees ze case, tell me which street corner I can score some boeuf on ze bone and I weel go zere tonight." Ha! I pull ees foot, ze broadboy.'

Odette was on the telephone to her mother. She loved her mother's brash, non-stop, rusty-nailed voice with its exotic French-meets-Cockney accent, but conversations with her were always tough. They were coming from different directions and travelling very fast. Claudette Fielding (known to all the family as Clod) was a little Edith Piaf in her Stepney neighbourhood, and proud of her Gallic roots. She'd been born in the suburbs of Paris where her family had snobbily seen themselves as petit-bourgeois, and their only daughter as destined for great things. Instead, Clod had met and married Odette's John Lennon look-alike father, Raymond, while he was working in Paris as a session guitarist. Ray's musical career had been short-lived, and when he ran out of work, he returned to England bringing his hot-tempered, fiery-eyed French wife with him. Finding herself living with her very unbourgeois in-laws, Clod had soon realised that the romantic, sexy musician she'd married was a mere assistant in his father's electrical shop in Bow. She'd remained loyal to him and born him two daughters, but never really got over the culture shock.

As the years wore on and she lost her mother to cancer and her two daughters to adulthood, she had grown so homesick that she begged her widowed father to come and live close by in England. The irascible and deaf Grandpère (Grumpy) now resided in Chigwell and pretended to loathe England, although he had started a successful importing business in the eighties and made a tidy profit from the 'filthy mushrooms', selling overpriced French produce to delicatessens and restaurants.

Clod was a great believer in *la famille*. Odette's elder sister, Monique (Monny), had got married at eighteen, to a man of whom Clod did not wholly approve though she tolerated him because he provided well for her daughter and liked his mother-in-law's cooking. Craig was a bully and a thug with a penchant for Escort XR3is – not always his own. He and Monny had two children, with another on the way. They lived in a nice new estate in Thamesmead with a satellite dish and a bidet. Clod felt her eldest had settled well, if not wisely. Odette was a different matter.

'You are in zat 'orrible depot alone tonight, no?' she asked critically, referring to Odette's lofty modern warehouse flat in Islington. 'Why – are you eel?'

Odette was the first Fielding to stay on at school and take A levels, let alone attend university. At the time she'd been baffled by her parents' reaction. She had expected pride, excitement,

32

joy and congratulations; she'd secretly wanted them to boast and brag. But far from being proud parents, Clod and Ray had been confused by her success. 'What do you want to go there for, girl?' Ray had asked. 'Why not get yourself a nice little job round here?'

Even after she had graduated, the confusion had lingered and grown into suspicion as her life became increasingly detached from theirs. They didn't understand her job. They watched the adverts she produced, remembered the copy-lines and the images, but the process itself was a mystery to them however many times Odette tried to explain it. Ray was appalled at how much she eventually earned, and steadfastly refused to accept anything from her, however tactfully she tried to couch it. If she gave an over-generous birthday present, it would be moved into the understairs cupboard unused; if she put fifty quid in the housekeeping tin when he wasn't looking, she'd find it in her handbag the next time she visited. Clod was less sensitive and now had her hair done weekly, wore lots of gold jewellery and sported a manicure courtesy of Odette, but she would never bring herself to ask for anything, or utter a word of thanks for what was given. Only Monny and particularly Craig seemed eager to encourage as many hand outs as possible, usually using the excuse of 'the kids' to whom Odette already gave endless presents and paid regular deposits into two savings accounts.

'Your sister 'as 'ad anozer scan,' Clod was saying. 'She say they weel know the sex soon, but I ask her not to tell me nussink. Eet is unnatural to know. But I am sure it's a girl thees time.'

'That'll be nice for Monny,' Odette sighed, reaching for her Evian bottle, well aware of where the conversation was heading. 'She said she wanted a sister for Frankie.'

'And Craig, he want a bruzer for Vinnie,' Clod cackled. 'But I want a grandchild from Odie, *oui*? If you leave it any longer, you weel have a funny *bébé* – and who weel look after it then, huh, if eet ees a freak?'

Odette looked at her watch. Five minutes. Fairly average. Her mother inevitably mentioned Odette's ovaries and the possibility of her giving birth to a deformed child within the first ten minutes of a call these days.

33

'I know, Mum, and I want *bébés*. Lots of them. It's just not a good time now. You see, the club's due to open in a couple of weeks and things aren't looking too—'

'Your café is still not open?' Clod tutted critically. 'What has taken so long? Eet is simple to cook for people. I sink you are being coined.'

'I'm not being conned, Mum. It's just—'

'*Maman!*' Clod corrected, lighting her second Benson & Hedges of the conversation and inhaling through tight, disapproving lips. 'We ain't common, Odie.'

'Sorry, *Maman*.' Odette picked at the blue plastic hoop still attached to the neck of her Evian bottle. 'It's just that Calum, my business partner, is being very difficult at the moment.'

'Calum?' Clod's voice skipped a few scales excitedly. 'Ees 'e single? Is 'e rich?'

'He's gay,' Odette lied to shut her mother up.

'Well, zat's better than being miserable, ain't it?' Clod refused to learn any English word associated with what she saw as deviance. To her gay was happy, shag was a type of pipe tobacco and bollocks were young cattle.

After she'd rung off, Odette wandered through to the kitchen to fetch another bottle of mineral water. The lights of East London glittered through the vast industrial window which dropped from wooden ceiling to slate floor like a glass wall, but all she could see in it was her own reflection, unflatteringly lit by the halogen spotlights high above her.

Since her teens, Odette had come to realise that she was less than average-looking, and more than capable of making up the shortfall. After three hours at Nicky Clarke and an afternoon sitting at the NARS counter, she could look good – better than good, she could power into a room and find the air was thin because everyone else had taken a deep breath to admire her. On a Saturday evening, home alone with her hair on end and without a scrap of makeup on her face, she looked in desperate need of an oxygen tent.

Her body was as good as she could get it, but the basics weren't great. Her shoulders sloped, she had a short neck and huge boobs, a tummy that ran to spare-tyre fat as soon as a cream bun came within licking distance, and ankles as thick as two pint glasses. She had to eat practically nothing and exercise every day to stay slim, and even then she needed a bra that looked capable of taking the weight of two toddlers, uplift tights and unsexy super-elastic underwear with special Lycra insets to help her out. She never wore polo necks or flat pumps, avoided horizontal stripes and figure-hugging t-shirts, favoured dark colours and tailored lines, and never, ever wore strapless tops. With the help of the glorious Selena at Harvey Nicks, Odette always presented herself impeccably. She liked having a decision taken out of her hands for once, enjoyed being dressed up like a doll and made to feel special, not plain. But designer couture could not be afforded right now, and so Odette had to make do with her own conservative choices, some of which owned more to the *Dynasty* and *Dallas* years of pencil skirts and stilettos than recent designer collections. She liked the look, and didn't care what others thought – it suited her and it suited her square, gym-shaped body. In the absence of a hand-span waist, shoulderpads could do wonders.

The only feature of which Odette was inordinately and justifiably proud was her rear. She had a high, smooth, rounded bottom as perfect as a piece of Cape fruit. In one of her favourite-ever films, *9½ Weeks*, Mickey Rourke had said that Kim Basinger had a 'heart-shaped ass'. Odette knew hers was just as good. She wore tight trousers and short jackets as often as possible to flaunt it, and turned around to pick things up from the ground far too often in male company. These were her only bimbo-legged moments and she enjoyed them rather more than she should. She thought of it as her rearguard action.

Odette patted it fondly and turned back to the kitchen, wondering what to eat. When she had first viewed the flat, rushing around early one morning before catching a flight to Germany, she had fallen in love with this kitchen. It was huge and technical, more like an industrial working kitchen than a private home. The metal shelves and surfaces gleamed like the teeth of a mill wheel, the tower-block fridge was big enough to house three grown men, the vast ultra-modern range was covered with buttons and dials like an aeroplane cockpit.

Because the flat was open-plan, the kitchen sat in its centre like a vast engine. Only this engine had never really been started up and allowed to roar.

She sometimes wondered whether she was buying into the restaurant business in order to keep her relationship with food on a professional level. Odette could control her eating by thinking of food as a corporate tool, an expensive luxury one used to entertain and win contracts. Restaurants were somewhere one worked, whether as a member of staff or a paying client who was entertaining guests. In the house, food was a far more dangerous commodity and needed treating with caution.

She selected a dry rice cake from the almost bare cupboard above the sink and wandered back through to the vast open living area to settle down with her laptop.

Work wasn't much of a distraction. Odette found her gaze continually drawn to the shelf just above the haunted fish tank on which three wedding invitations were neatly lined up – all different, all seeming to taunt her. First there was the tasteful, traditional one which Saskia's parents, Virginia and Anthony Seaton, had sent to her, requesting a reply to their farmhouse in Berkshire by November the twelfth – one month before the Big Day. It was most wannabe brides' dream invite – thickest cream card embossed with one gold-dusted word 'Marriage' on the front and formal, almost archaic, wording inside.

Beside it was Elsa and Euan's invitation, a glittery cardboard case containing a lurid pink CD on which the couple had laid several tracks including a jungle bass version of the 'Wedding March' remixed with Goldie samples, followed by 'Going to the Chapel' recorded by Elsa and Euan themselves.

In sharp contrast, propped up between two photo frames, was a ready-made Andrew Brunswick invitation, the blank spaces of which had been filled in with neat, round biro writing asking Odette to the wedding of her cousin Melanie to long-time boyfriend Dean in April. Above the register office details was a picture of two fat teddy bears, one in a veil, the other a top hat, both being showered with colourful confetti.

The three invitations couldn't have been more different from one another, yet they all had one thing in common. All of them invited 'Odette and Guest' to come to celebrate the contrasting nuptials. That 'and Guest' bugged her. It really pissed her off in fact. She was suffering 'and Guest' angst.

She flipped her laptop shut and headed towards her treadmill, deviating at the last minute and hopping on to the Stairmaster which offered more distraction and effort.

Even so as she pumped her legs up and down, feeling the sweat start to break and the muscles burn with a familiar sting of pleasure-pain, Odette couldn't stop her mind from stewing.

This flat was her proudest possession. She had worked her ass off to get it, and was now working her ass out to furnish it with the ultimate accessory – a man to match her Milanese furniture, her Swedish appliances, her German gym equipment and Limoges porcelain. But Odette was fussy. She had spent years choosing the best of everything, earning it, loving it, fighting hard to keep it. She knew precisely who she wanted to occupy the spare chair at the table, the other stretch sofa and the space beside her in bed. She had designed her flat around him, to his taste and specifications, awaiting his arrival for long, patient years. She had always known he would come, himself waiting until she was ready, until she had her career up to speed, her body honed to perfection, her beautiful, stylish flat completed.

Now the flat was ready. It anticipated seduction. All she had to do was invite him in. But he kept stalling, avoiding her, going missing. She was worried she'd left it too late.

The two most important things in Odette's life were the things she was frightened of and therefore had avoided at all costs throughout her twenties, only ever using them as tools to sell products: men and food.

When she'd hit her thirties, she'd decided she had to face them both head-on, but now wondered whether she'd gone too far, been too typically headstrong by wanting both together. She was starting a restaurant with the man she was certain she would one day marry. She'd broken her business for entrée, pleasure for dessert rule by ordering the main course. And it was too late to change her mind and send it back. The table was laid: she only wished she could be too.

She had asked Calum around to her flat countless times for

an informal meeting and every time he'd blown her out – rarely calling, occasionally faxing, usually simply not turning up. She wanted him to see her flat. The bottles of Peroni beer had been chilling in the fridge for weeks, the Heinz beans and sausage pizzas he was addicted to lined the otherwise empty freezer. But Calum had yet to see her sanctuary, and Odette felt shut out of his life, constantly pacing around and waiting for him to come home.

3

By Monday afternoon, Odette's mobile was out of charge again, and she was feeling about as energetic herself. She only wished that there was an adaptor which she could use to plug herself into the mains and receive a week's worth of power. She flipped the button guard closed and tapped her teeth against its hard little aerial. She needed to speak to Calum urgently.

She went in search of Saskia, tracking her down in the ghastly toilets where her assistant was trying to wash a splodge of paint from her pale camel trousers amidst Maurice's theatrical faux-baroque columns.

'Is your mobile working? I forgot to charge mine up last night.' Odette stifled a yawn. The truth was she had stayed up all the previous night tearing her hair out over her business proposal as she tried to figure out where to get another fifty thousand pounds.

Saskia shook her head. 'Stan's got it for the day. He's still waiting to hear from that Edinburgh gallery, but he can't stay by the phone at home. Are you trying to track Byron down then?' She giggled as she pointed at the swatches of purple velvet pinned beside splodges of gold and red gloss.

Odette wished she could see the joke. The nickname had delighted her six weeks earlier when Maurice the designer had seemed like a fanciful dreamer whom she could curb and control because she was paying his fee. Now she could no longer pay him, he seemed powerful and menacing and elusive.

'I think he mentioned a house clearance in Warwickshire this morning,' Saskia was saying. 'Something about picking up some old-fashioned bathroom fittings. He doesn't seem too taken with these.' She eyed the cool, pale marble lavatories sitting around in their plastic wrapping like passive bullfrogs wearing pacamacs.

'We'll see about that.' Odette gritted her teeth and stormed out into the foyer to tell the builders to plumb in the loos ASAP.

'No can do,' shrugged Errol, her foreman. 'That's a job for Gary and Nev – the aqueous system and filtration facilitation operatives. They're in Hampstead today, fitting fifteen bidets into a gaff on the Bishop's Avenue. Sorry, love. We can fix the doors on the cubicles, if you like? That Maurice geezer dropped them off last night.' He nodded towards a stack of carved, gold-sprayed screens straight out of a Wild West bordello.

Odette hastily shook her head. 'Better wait until after the plumbing's done, mate. Can you do something about the downstairs bar? It looks like the Blind Beggar after the Krays had popped in for a quick shot or two.'

Odette ended up queuing for the pay phone on Essex Road, half-listening as an Asian girl inside the cubicle chatted into the receiver in Punjabi.

She gazed along the length of Essex Road, where passers-by were shuffling along the dirty grey pavements, scarves tucked up to their ears for warmth, gloves buried in pockets. To either side of them was a multitude of bars and restaurants, bistros and cafés, all trying to survive in this popular little stretch of London thoroughfare. She suddenly wondered whether the OD was going to fail. It was the first time she had fully entertained the thought and to her horror tears started clouding her eyes. She blinked angrily and concentrated on breathing slowly and steadily, but her chest felt shrink-wrapped by her ribs and she gulped shallowly for air.

'You okay, miss? Miss – you okay?'

She blinked and glanced up to see the girl who had been in the phone box gazing at her with concern.

'Yeah, fine thanks, love.' Odette tried for a cheery smile, her voice hoarse and airless. 'Just had a bit of a funny turn. Gotta make a call. Thanks, though.'

She stood in the cubicle, holding on to the receiver and staring into the mid-distance, past the postcards advertising 'New Model in Town', past the emergency instructions, the smeared glass, the yellow-grey pavements, the black cabs, buses and courier bikes threading their way through the road-works. Her gaze rested jealously on the anonymous, shuffling passers-by on the opposite side of the street – other people's lives, the envy of the habitually stressed. A flash of bright colour caught her eye and she saw a young mum in a yellow Puffa jacket picking up her toddler and twirling him around and around at shoulder height. The child's face was laughing with glee, his red and orange woolly hat had pom-poms that swung around jauntily, his clothes were a swirling mixture of reds, greens, blues and purples. Odette loved bright colours, although her feelings for small children were, she had always thought, more ambivalent.

Recently, along with the tell-tale stress symptoms of tight chest and shortness of breath, Odette had started to display worryingly maternal urges, which were hitherto alien to her. She'd found herself looking into prams as she passed them by, smiling at those toddlers and babies in cafés who stared into strangers' eyes with unnerving insouciance. She had started leafing through the children's pages of shopping catalogues, admiring those sweet, small, multicoloured faces.

Odette had always assumed she would one day marry, but had never particularly wanted children. She wouldn't dream of admitting it to her friends, but she had a model life to which she aspired, a dream she had clutched close to her heart since childhood, tucked away in her secret mind-pocket of fairytales, along with being Cinderella at the ball on a happy day or the Little Mermaid wading into the sea on a bad one. In the nineties, lifestyle was the buzzword, and every magazine had an opinion as to which particular combination of work, home and cultural assets provided the Über-vogue to which a generation should aspire. But Odette had known for years; she had a formula all worked out. *Hart to Hart*. She had watched every single episode of the eighties' American series with a slavish, almost obsessive compulsion. She had seen the spin-off films, had memorised the plots, knew the layout of the Harts' million-dollar mansion and could recall every one of the tricks Freeway had performed. Odette wanted to be the Jennifer who one day found her Jonathan. She wanted to live in a big, swanky house with a crotchety old butler and a small, intelligent dog – even though she wasn't very keen on dogs. And, as the Harts had never had children, Odette always assumed that nor would she. Only recently her hormones were fighting her all the way to the silver screen.

The receiver had started wailing at her. Odette replaced it and pressed her face into her hands. If this was having a breakdown then she was deeply disappointed. She'd always imagined it would be a Sue-Ellen Ewing combination of drugs, drink, doomed love affairs, suicide attempts, adulterous husbands and trembling lips. Instead it was feeling out of breath and broody in Islington. Hardly very eighties.

But there was no getting away from the fact that she was on a downhill slide, and if she didn't do something to avert it soon, she'd land deep in debt and probably belly up. A flat, ab-flexed, fake-tanned belly with no babies in it.

Odette called Calum's number, but the soft, familiar voice that greeted her was recorded and she'd heard the words too many times before to listen.

She left her usual message 'Calum, it's Odette. Call me.' It was only when she'd hung up that she realised she had no method of taking the call. Her mobile was dead, she wasn't at home and the lines at the OD weren't connected. If only Calum had a mobile of his own, but he refused to own one on principle. Quite what principle, Odette wasn't sure. She found him almost impossible to fathom. He seemed incredibly ambitious and driven, yet there was something of the idealistic dreamer about him too. She knew something about his background, but most of that came from Lydia who was dating – correction, getting married to – his younger brother, the impossibly charming, feckless Finlay.

The Forrester boys' lives had apparently changed dramatically in the early eighties when their father, an unemployed welder, had become one of the biggest ever Pools winners in history. In an era when Camelot was still a legendary Arthurian town and the highlight of Saturday night was still *Blind Date*, the win had been unprecedented.

The publicity thankfully eluded Calum, a solitary and self-motivated student in his third year at Manchester University, but he saw the way his parents were at first trapped in its headlights and then dazzled by its enduring spotlight. The Forresters numbered among Scotland's richest overnight. Within weeks, they had moved to a vast bungalow in the Borders. Finlay – then a bright but uninterested wastrel – was sent to a very expensive fee-paying school nearby which made him miserable yet won him the place at St Andrew's which Calum had once desperately coveted for himself. From student digs in Manchester, he observed in horror as his parents invested in huge, impractical cars they were too afraid to drive, installed a swimming pool in which they could only dabble their feet (neither of them could swim and it was always too cold to try and learn), bought vast televisions, flashy satellite systems, purchased every kitchen gadget Argos had to offer and felt snubbed by their stuck-up, disapproving neighbours. Money made them unhappy and isolated. Unexpected wealth had turned Finlay into a spoilt drug addict until Lydia helped him get straight.

These excesses appalled Calum. When he lost his full grant in his final year at university, he refused to tell his parents, working in bars and garage forecourts to pay his way, sometimes snatching just one hour's sleep in twenty. If they sent him a fat cheque – which they often did – he tore it up.

In business, Calum was equally stubborn and unpredictable. He was undoubtedly a genius at setting up restaurants and clubs, and mixed in an everchanging world of chefs, critics, stars and artists who willingly associated themselves with his every project. Yet for a man with the Midas touch, he chose to wear boxing gloves too often. The wimp was also a bully, and childish to boot. Odette didn't like him very much; in fact at the moment her feelings bordered on hated. What she found more annoying than anything was that Calum the wimp was so bloody fanciable. He was both the ugliest and the sexiest man she had ever met. And the first man with the potential to become her long-awaited Jonathan.

4

Calum had arranged to meet Jimmy Sylvian in the Nero Club, his old haunt of which he had been co-founder. It was the first time he'd been there for several months, and he realised the moment he walked inside the famous smoked-glass doors that it had been the wrong choice. It was starting to look shabby and passé. Once the cliqueiest joint in town, its joints were beginning to click with age as were those of its clientele – famous, rich, household names as well-branded as Heinz, and dated to be consumed several years ago. On the cracked leather sofa which had once been the launching pad for a third series of the cult sit com *Dog*, two alternative comedians were swapping baby photos: 'Frisbee has just started at Montessori in Henley.' 'Really? Jen and I decided to send Betty-Lou to the local prep in Amersham . . .'

Calum now despised new money, and loathed the self-made few who splashed out on frivolous luxuries like swimming pools, fast cars and personal gymnasiums. He saw his parents in each and every flashy lifestyle accessory, even though they themselves had never possessed the awareness to buy into new trends – they still believed in the *Dynasty*-fed eighties aspiration to home cocktail bars and saunas. Calum loathed that lifestyle even more. He had never visited Odette Fielding's huge luxury warehouse conversion, but could guess at its contents. She undoubtedly subscribed to every single one of his parents' notions of luxury, from gym to bar to foot-spa. He might know where she was coming from, but he just wanted her to go.

He had nothing against her personally. In fact, he rather liked her. In her funny, brash, shy way she reminded him of his mother; in her big-breasted, sexy, angry way she aroused him. Yet in her busy, self-satisfied, ambitious way she irritated the hell out of him.

He'd only invested in her club in the first place to impress Lydia, to try and win her favour by supporting one of her dearest friends. She had entreated him to do it, and now appeared entirely to have forgotten the fact. She had no interest in the OD. And as a result Calum had lost interest too – in more ways than one. He needed his money back. Right now, he needed every penny he could get.

Jimmy was already there, occupying a button-backed leather chair in the corner of the smoky bar. He seemed to spill over it, filling every sagging, scuffed inch. Calum had forgotten how enormous he was. Not that Jimmy was overweight; he was simply inches larger than most men in every conceivable direction – taller, broader-shouldered, with huge hands and feet. His hair was white-blond from the South African sun, and his skin tanned to the same colour as his vast leather walking boots. When he spotted Calum, he showed a flash of white teeth in his dark face, as perfect as a slice of freshly cut Granny Smith gleaming from a caramelised apple pie.

'Calum! Great to see you, you old rogue. Looking well.' Leaping up, he crushed Calum's hand within his own and signalled the waiter to bring him a drink, as though it was he who had the long-term attachment to the place, not the new arrival.

Several of the Nero's regular inhabitants eyed him irritably, preferring their peaceful harbour to have the atmosphere of a library in a gentlemen's club rather than that of the noisy media-mob haunt of yesteryear. Calum made a mental note to get the refurbishment underway as soon as possible.

'Here!' Jimmy carried a vast red velvet armchair over one shoulder like a culled antelope, having charmed it away from a table of columnists.

He was as friendly as an oversized lion cub charging around amongst a family of Siamese cats and trying to befriend them all at once. He didn't seem to realise that his sheer size, along with his booming voice and backslapping bonhomie, terrified people. He'd been away from England too long to appreciate the effect he had; was acclimatised to vast tracts of open land, not distrustful, claustrophobic cities. Yet he was so shy, he always seemed to find it impossibly hard to make eye contact. To those who didn't know him well, this could make him appear arrogant, but Calum knew he was the softest, gentlest of hell-raisers.

'How are yous, Jim?' Calum settled on the red chair, which was spewing stuffing. 'How was the funeral?'

'Which one?' For a moment there was a crackle of anger in Jimmy's voice. He glanced away and dropped down into his creaking leather chair.

Calum refused to rise to this. 'Your father's, of course.'

Jimmy sucked in one cheek and then exhaled, his anger forgotten.

'Pretty ghastly.' He pulled a face and darted his blue eyes in the general direction of his host's ear. 'We had trouble getting Pa into the country at all, which was ironic. He was always bringing vast stashes of drugs through Customs when he was alive – the first time he gets searched is in his coffin. They kicked up a huge fuss about the fact he'd lived overseas for more than a decade. Then when the officious little peaked cap who was making all the noise was looking through his paperwork, Mungo spotted one of Pa's paperbacks on his desk and pointed to it, screaming, "That's the stiff!" or something equally poetic. Funeral was a doddle after that.'

Ralph, the waiter, was still hanging around awkwardly, trying not to intrude but aware he had been called over. Calum caught his eye and raised one eyebrow. Ralph understood straight away and headed to the bar to fetch a bottle of Peroni for his former boss, guessing at a Castle beer for Jimmy.

Calum had met Jimmy Sylvian in South Africa. He'd wanted to see the 'Big Five' – leopard, lion, buffalo, elephant and rhino – on safari, but had found himself with only three days at the end of a working stay there. One of his contacts had suggested a private game reserve called Mpona close to Kruger Park but had warned him that it was likely to be booked out. Undeterred, Calum had hired a jeep and driven there alone, arriving on a hot, dusty, airless afternoon to find two unfriendly guards presiding over a high, locked gate.

They'd told him in no uncertain terms to get lost. They had, in fact, pointed rifles at him. And when a very dusty, rusty Land-Rover had pulled up behind Calum's clean jeep they had put down their weapons, beamed out big smiles and started clacking in an incomprehensible, fantastically complicated-sounding tongue to its tawny occupant, Jimmy.

After listening to his guards, he had blustered a little to Calum about being booked up. But when Calum had apologetically admitted that he wasn't certain how to put the unfamiliar Jeep into reverse, Jimmy had given his big lion-bark laugh and told him to drive inside and bunk up in the main house with himself and his partner, Florrie.

Jimmy always joked about that. He claimed he'd liked Calum from the start and had immediately guessed that they were going to be friends. Calum kept his own counsel.

'You planning to stay on here a while, yeah? Spend time with your wee brees?' He watched Jimmy thoughtfully, as ever astounded by the man's ridiculous, film-star good looks. His brother was a model, and no wonder. Yet Jimmy had no idea of his own beauty and was hugely embarrassed if it was ever pointed out.

Jimmy studied the cuffs of his Oxbow fleece. 'Maybe a few weeks. I have no real plans. I guess I'll have to sort out Pa's will. He left his estate in one hell of a mess. Felix and Mungo seem to think it'll get them out of the tight spot they're both in, but I doubt it.'

'You want your money back?' Calum tried to hide his own panic. 'The Picasso sketches?'

Jimmy shrugged. 'I could certainly use them right now. I didn't realise it at the time, but I think the old man was trying to avoid death duties when he sent me that letter.' He winked and Calum stifled a guilty start. What Jimmy had lent him was totally tied up right now. If it weren't for the OD then maybe he could repay some of the loan, but Odette had stripped him of all his spare cash and it was hardly as though he could get the sketches themselves back.

47

He kept his voice as steady as he could. 'With your help, I can double your investment in twelve months and then you'll get twice the value.'

Jimmy's laugh was generous. 'I thought you'd already trebled it?'

'I'll not deny I've done pretty well recently.' He flashed a quick, rare smile which went unnoticed as Jimmy was staring at the ceiling. 'But I'm planning a new venture right now – one that will make the others look like burger bars.'

'Not another restaurant?' Jimmy carried on laughing. He loved Calum's angry ambition, so different from his own diffidence.

But Calum was shaking his head. 'This is more than just a restaurant, pal. Far, far more. This is food made sex.'

Had Odette been there she would have shuddered happily at this. She would have wanted to kiss Calum all over. That is, until he opened his mouth again.

'London's going out of fashion. It's had its day – all this Brit Power stuff is out of date. The future's in commutable commodity, in escapism – in your neck of the woods in fact.'

'South Africa?' Jimmy raised one eyebrow curiously. 'I'd hardly call a twelve-hour flight commutable.'

'No, no – the countryside. Green stuff, old stately piles, hunting, shooting and fishing while you still can. Golf, tank driving and horses. Rural pursuits. Organic Food. Peace. This isn't a loada hippy shit, Jim, this is the future. London's fucking boring – everyone I know is tired o' the place, especially the people in the food industry. We want more space so tables aren't on top of each other or turned around in an hour; we want fresh local ingredients – homegrown even. We want to live on the premises and get to see daylight occasionally. A good place for kids to grow up – safe, unpolluted, innocent.'

'Sounds ideal,' Jimmy sighed, looking around the smoky bar and through the slatted blinds to the crawling London traffic.

'It is!' Calum banged his hand on the table. 'And I think I've found it, Jim pal. I think I've fucking well found it.' He dropped his voice to avoid being overheard. 'All I need is to sell up and go there. What's more, I'm going to take most of London with me, just see if I dinnae.'

Had Odette been there, she certainly wouldn't have been smiling.

'Good luck to you!' Jimmy laughed.

'I want you as part of it, pal,' Calum told him soberly. 'I want you to stay in England and help me out. This way, you'll get your money back with interest. What do you say?'

Jimmy pulled an uneasy face. 'Right now, Cal, I'd appreciate the money back with no interest. I'm sorry, if it weren't for my brothers I'd never—'

'You didn't give me money, pal,' Calum reminded him sharply. 'What you gave me would be impossible for you to sell right now, and you know it. I bust my arse doing it and almost got bust to boot. What I'm offering you is cash. You don't even have to help out – just wait to collect it.'

Jimmy nodded, defeated.

Aware that he had lost any semblance of gratitude in his desperation, Calum ordered another round of drinks and had another go at persuading Jimmy to work with him on his new baby.

'I'm a fucked-up person – I don't need to tell you that. You've seen me at my worst, pal.' He scowled at the label on his beer bottle with genuine shame. 'I wannae get out before I turn into one of these "remember who I was?" has-beens who knock around here, y'know?' He jerked his head at the Nero's clientele.

'You see, pal,' he explained slowly, 'if you open a great bar or restaurant or club in this town, you've got about six months max before the scum move in and claim it as their own – after that it's no longer got cachet, it's no longer exclusive. Membership lists help, but not much. Things go out of fashion in this city faster than bullets out of guns. Now London's out of fashion too. The scum's taken over the whole capital. There are no such things as exclusivity and class. People are opening the best venues to the *masses*.'

'You're right.' Jimmy leaned back in his chair and closed his eyes, long flights and traumatic reunions catching up with him.

'Great!' Calum had known he'd understand. Jimmy had class, after all. 'So you'll—'

'London *has* fucked you up,' Jimmy finished what he was saying. 'And if it gets you out of this place and gets me my money back, then yes, I might even help you make food into sex.' He pressed his palms into his eye sockets and sighed tiredly.

'Sounds just my sort of dish – you must give me the recipe, darling,' purred an amused voice. Smelling the same Chanel No. 5 his mother wore, Jimmy opened his eyes to see a curtain of white-blonde hair swooping down over Calum. 'Sorry I'm late – I waited for Fin for ages, but he didn't show so I came without him. Hello there.' She turned from kissing Calum to smile at Jimmy, revealing a face so flawlessly beautiful he guessed she drank the blood of virgins at full moon to achieve it. As a child, he'd been illogically convinced this was how his mother stayed beautiful, having watched a Hammer horror movie in which she starred as a Hungarian countess who maintained her looks by dressing as a werewolf and slaying all the village totty. Judging from her skinny body, this girl consumed very low-cal virgin's blood.

'Jimmy, meet Lydia Morley.' Calum carefully didn't add that she was his brother's fiancée. He knew full well that Fin had been delayed at work; he'd set it up by calling through a fake order late that afternoon.

Lydia took one look at Jimmy's exquisite face and licked her lips – the only plump thing about her. Sliding her long, lean body into a chair beside him, she picked at the leather buttons on the arm of his. 'So you're the sexy African game ranger Calum told us about?'

Almost suffocating in the cloud of scent and sickened by the memories it churned up, Jimmy leaned away and smiled as widely as he could. 'Well, I'm not sexy or African, but I'm game.' He tried for joviality, but it came out all wrong.

Lydia let out a growl of a laugh, so erotic that Calum felt all the hairs stand up on his neck. Jimmy – who had more self-control – looked at her politely.

'I'll see if our table's ready,' Calum excused himself smoothly, leaving Lydia to use her big guns as he knew she would. With any luck Fin wouldn't make it at all. He was trying hard to prove himself at work, the rot having yet to set in.

But Lydia's big guns had little effect on Jimmy. He longed to leave the smoky bar and get some fresh air but tiredness was weighting his body into the chair. As Lydia caught him in her spot-beam blue gaze, he yawned widely, showing every filling and a lot of pink tongue.

'You poor thing.' She stroked his arm, eager to check out whether the thick fleece covered anything exciting. Feeling the tautness of the muscles beneath made her smile widely. 'You look like you need a lovely warm bed to curl up in.'

Jimmy looked at her mutely, uncertain whether this was an innocent comment or not.

'Where are you staying in London?'

'Notting Hill, with my brothers.'

'I live just round the corner. We could share a cab back later and I'll tuck you in.' Lydia was deeply annoyed with Fin for boringly working late and needed to cheer herself up.

'I don't think so.' Her perfume was making Jimmy feel so sick that he rubbed his nose with the back of his hand to blot it out. 'Excuse me one minute, will you?' He escaped to the loo.

'Great bloke, huh?' Calum slid back into his seat seconds later.

Lydia shrugged, deeply offended at the brush-off. She had only been playing with him to cheer herself up; she'd had no real intention of being unfaithful to darling Fin.

'I'm so glad you asked me along tonight because there's something I've been *dying* to tell you. I've just heard from a very good source that you have the most *gorgeous* admirer.' Her big blue eyes were inches from his and he could smell the toothpaste on her quickened breath.

'Don't tell me you have a sister?' Calum was flattered, despite himself. He only longed for one admirer right now, but she was strictly off-limits.

'No,' Lydia giggled. 'Now she is *far* too discreet to say anything herself, but Elsa told Ally who told Juno who told me that this person is definitely crazy about you.'

Lydia looked as though she was about to hand him a prize

jewel. She positively shuddered with delighted anticipation. Calum tried not to watch the way her long, lithe body slithered closer, or to groan with pleasure as she breathed in his ear.

'Odette Fielding.' She said the word like a chant.

'You're kidding me, right?' He jerked his head away as though she'd bitten him on the ear.

Lydia looked affronted. 'No, it's true. Elsa told Ally who . . .'

'Told you, I know,' he hissed. Why did women work in intricate Chinese whispers? Gossip was swapped between loo cubicles, over desk partitions and down factory conveyor belts like buckets of water being passed along a line to fight a fire. And it had just that effect on him – a slop of cold water in the face.

'Ally told Juno actually.' Lydia thrust out her lower lip sulkily. 'Odette hasn't actually *said* anything, but we all know, and she's *so* choosy, you should be wildly flattered. Aren't you two in business together?'

'You should know, beautiful.' Calum sighed more meaningfully than he'd intended. 'You set it up.'

'Did I?' Lydia looked thrilled at the idea, although she had no recollection of it. 'Anyway, Odette is an absolute darling – not conventionally pretty, but incredibly fit – and you two would be so perfect tog—' Just then her phone trilled in her bag. 'Hang on a sec, darling.' She rooted around in her latest must-have accessory – the Vuitton Cottage Loaf – which was lime green crocodile leather and shaped like a mushroom.

Calum sighed with relief, ignoring the Nero clientele shooting his table evil looks. Mobiles were strictly forbidden in the club. Normally, he loathed them too, but this one was his saviour. So Odette Fielding had a schoolgirl crush? Any remnant of lust he had once harboured for her big-breasted body instantly vanished. In fact, he felt as angry as he had the day the *Observer* had compared him to Peter Stringfellow. He felt offended, belittled and dirty.

He watched Lydia's beautiful face as she located the phone and flipped it open. It was typically capricious of her to turn the tables on him and try to play Cupid when it was he who'd intended to spark true love that night. If this was some sort of competition, then he was determined to win – and the only loser would be plain, lovesick Odette Fielding. But what he heard next made his heart sink.

'Have you, darling? That's so wonderful! They're bound to promote you. Yes, he's right here, do you want to . . . Oh, okay. No, I'm sure he won't mind. I'll be back in ten mins. See you there. Love you, my city slicker. Mpppppppppwwwwwww.' The kiss must have almost deafened his brother, Calum decided with bitter satisfaction.

'You're not going?'

She nodded, gathering up her bag. 'Fin is over the moon. He fulfilled a big order in triple-quick time so he's bought champagne and caviar to celebrate at home. So sweet. He says he knows you'll understand. We can do this any time.'

No, we fucking can't! Calum wanted to scream as he looked around for Jimmy, but his friend had clearly taken a quick walk around the block to clear his head and loosen his cramped muscles.

'Say 'bye to Johnny from me.' Lydia swooped to kiss him on the cheek again and Calum was enveloped in the sweetest of sensual pleasures as her scented hair slithered across his torso before she quickly disappeared into the night.

Ralph waved Calum over to the bar before Jimmy returned. 'Call for you.'

It was his friend Florian. 'Zere is a problem,' he said, his hushed voice almost drowned by the noise of food preparation behind him. 'Ferdy owe a lot of money to 'is dealer. He threaten to sell story about me to the *News*. I need to get 'im out of my 'air wizout pissing 'im off, y'know?'

Calum nodded, a smile spreading across his face as he remembered Lydia's unwanted revelation. 'I have a similar problem myself,' he soothed. 'Don't worry about it, brother. I think we can kill two birds with one stoned chef. Leave it with me.'

Jimmy wandered back in after ten minutes, looking shaken. 'You're right about this city.' He shuddered, having encountered the rowdy after-work drinkers milling outside the pubs, the homeless shivering in doorways and the angry commuters jostling to get home. 'I've never seen so many people trapped in one small space.' He settled back in the chair and rubbed his face tiredly before something occurred to him. 'Where's your girlfriend gone?'

'She's no' my girlfriend, pal.' Calum hid the regret in his voice.

'Phew – that's a relief!' The big lion's bark filled the room. 'I wasn't going to tell you this but within a minute of meeting me, she pretty much suggested we sleep together.' Jimmy seemed to find this totally staggering.

'Did she?' Calum suddenly perked up, despite the jealousy squeezing his chest like a fist. Perhaps things weren't so bad after all. Not only had he dealt with the Odette business neatly, but Lydia seemed to have made a good start too. All he now had to do was convince his friend he should stay in England.

Jimmy wasn't a big drinker, but he was tired and strained and in need of oblivion that evening. Listening to Calum's plans, he made steady progress through several beers and, with Calum's encouragement, chased them down with good Irish whiskey. Soon his laughter was booming out at top volume as he agreed to help with his friend's plans in return for a big pile of interest on his loan. In celebration, Calum tried to encourage him to sample his favourite tipple, absinthe and Smirnoff Black, nicknamed 'absinthe makes the heart grow fonder' because of its anaesthetic effects, but Jimmy refused.

'Absence doesn't make the heart grow fonder, my friend,' he muttered darkly, already three parts cut and with maudlin thoughts rapidly replacing artificial euphoria. 'I should know. My father's been absent from this world for almost a fortnight and I feel less and less affection for him.'

'Oh, yes?' Calum, who had often wished his own father dead before his dream came true, was only mildly surprised by the bitterness in Jimmy's voice. Jocelyn Sylvian had been famously depraved and despite his legendary hell-raising, no doubt had more skeletons hidden in his cupboard than a kleptomaniac medical student.

But what Jimmy confessed surprised even Calum.

'I started to clear the Barbados house while I was waiting for

54

all the red tape to clear so I could fly Pa back here,' he explained, voice thickened with drink and emotion. 'It kept me busy and I thought it would stop me thinking about the old bastard, but of course it did the opposite. There were so many years buried there, so much loneliness. I found something – things – that appalled me . . . disgusted me . . .'

'Like what?'

'You don't want to know, believe me.' Jimmy's voice cracked.

Calum knew that Jimmy was an emotional man. He'd seen him through a shared tragedy in Africa when Jimmy had bawled like a child. Secretly, Calum envied him that ability to let go, but the Nero was no place to do it and he stiffened as he watched his friend take great shuddering breaths. He was so loud and huge and striking that everyone was watching him. Thankfully Jack Nicholson arrived in the bar just a moment before Jimmy spoke again, causing all eyes to turn to the door.

'Videos,' he muttered as Calum strained to hear over the babble of star-spotting recognition. 'Home videos of my father and . . .' He shook his head. 'Use your imagination. He liked them young. Far too young. And he liked to watch himself afterwards and gloat over his conquests. There were hundreds, all labelled with names and dates, and stacked in alphabetical order – the only organised thing in the house. I burned the lot. Shit, I shouldn't have told you! I'm pissed. Excuse me.' He lurched off to the loo.

Calum showed no emotion but his blood was pumping faster, his breath quickening. So old Pa Sylvian had been a man after his own heart.

Talking to Jimmy had finally made up Calum's mind. He no longer wanted to be in London. He regretted his involvement in the OD, which wouldn't be as easy to dispose of as his other interests, but was canny enough not to lose sleep or money over it. He could pull out now, he knew that, but it would be messy. Better to wait. After what Lydia had told him, he wanted to play a little. If Odette Fielding thought she'd met her match, then just let her prove it. If she couldn't take the heat, she could always get out of the kitchen.

5

Florian Etoile had been working since six in the morning. It was now just after three and the lunch rush was starting to die down at last, but he knew that he stood little chance of seeing daylight. He was dripping with sweat despite the fact the temperature was close to zero outside. In truth, it could have changed to tropical sunshine for all Florian and his staff knew in their little hellhole with its artificial light and failing air conditioning. The outside world didn't intrude here, and for the few panic-stricken hours of each day that exquisite food was being prepared for demanding diners, a holocaust could take place without affecting the consistency of the saffron butter sauce for the john dory.

It was in the kitchens of L'Orbital that Florian produced some of his finest food, his most classic dishes. It was here that he had earned his third Michelin star, beaten only to the accolade of youngest-ever three-star chef by his *bête noir*, Wayne Street. This was the restaurant in which he was most often found, although he seldom cooked the dishes he had devised, unless they were new and experimental. Instead, he stalked around, scrutinising and tasting, yelling and berating, seldom complimenting. Most of the time he seemed to be on the phone, tripping up his staff with the long extension wire which led to its wall cradle as he talked and walked at the same time, his eyes always in pots, on plates, studying fingers and amounts and measures and skills.

This afternoon he was taking a call from his publicity agent, who was yet again trying to persuade him to take part in daytime television. 'How many times I have to tell you, Camilla? No way! *Non, non, non!* From now on I only say yes to *Panorama.*' And with this he pompously hung up, returning his attention to his kitchens.

'*Arrêtes!*' he screamed as a junior *commis* headed towards the cramped pass with a dessert. 'What is zat . . . zat . . .' he peered at the offending dish – or rather the decoration on top of it – as the *commis* quailed backward on to his clog heels '. . . ginger *minge*? Whis is he doing zere? Huh?'

'It's spun caramel, chef,' the *commis* spluttered. 'Garret told me to put it there.'

'No!' Florian exploded. 'I say mint – *meeent*. One sprig. No fuss, no minge. *Comprenez?*' He snatched the delicate little net of spun sugar from its resting place and threw it at the wall. 'Garret!' He stormed towards the relative calm of the far corner where his pastry chef, a talented dreamer, was busy piping cassis cream on to a chocolate parfait, making it resemble a garish seventies pouffe.

'Garret, you fuckeeng imbecile! What you do wiz your namby-pamby, fussy leetle touches, huh? You try to make me look like a fool? I tell you many times to keep it simple, and what you do? You stick fuckeeng Phillip Treacy hats on the food. What you do next, huh? Sparklers and cocktail umbrellas? Feathers?'

Accustomed to Florian's furious attacks, Garret rode it through, looking benign and just suitably contrite enough. Pretty soon, he knew, Florian would find another focus for his wrath. It didn't take long as from the corner of his eye, the fiery chef caught a waiter collecting two plates of chervil ravioli from the pass when Florian knew the table had ordered one ravioli and a duck.

'*Arrêtes!*' It was a war cry the kitchen staff heard at least ten times an hour. All the chefs carried on working without flinching. Only the waiter turned pale and awaited Florian's railing, knowing that he had a fifty-percent chance of being fired.

Half an hour later, Garret was having a fag break in the tiny alleyway that led from the mews behind L'Orbital when he was joined by Florian's second-in-command, Fergus Hannon. The lanky *sous-chef* was grinning from ear to ear as he drew out a Rothman's and grabbed Garret's cigarette to light it from.

'What are you looking so cheerful about, Ferdy man?' Fergus had acquired his nickname because his strong Ulster accent made 'food' sound like 'ferd'.

'Got the afternoon off now, haven't I?' The chef winked as he drew in a lungful of much-needed nicotine and blew it out in a cloud of condensed breath. 'Meeting a man about a job, so I am.'

'Shhh!' Garret knew that Florian, who was paranoid, lurked near the door during his staff's cigarette breaks so he could listen to them bitching.

'It's okay, Flo knows.' Ferdy zipped up the coat he had thrown over his chef's whites and shuddered against the cold. 'He was the one who recommended me.'

'Who to?' Garret tried to hide his jealousy.

'Calum Forrester.'

'Fuck me!' No wonder Ferdy was looking so pleased with himself. Calum owned three of the best restaurants in London. 'Which venue?'

'New one – top secret.' Ferdy tapped his nose, which was turning red in the cold. 'Florian was going to cook there himself, but he says he's too busy. Wants to give me a try out on my own.'

'Lucky bastard!' Garret whistled. He was surprised Florian was letting him go.

'I'm only telling you about this because it might mean my job'll be up for grabs.' Ferdy stood back as the recently fired waiter stormed out clutching a kit bag. 'Don't breathe a word to any of that lot in there.'

'Thanks, mate, I won't.' Garret grinned. He'd cut back on spun caramel baskets for the rest of the week. Florian might be a basket case, but to be his *sous* – however tough a job – was effectively a ticket to join the highest stratum of London chefs. He only had to stick with it for a couple of years. Ferdy seemed to have survived; Garret was sure he could.

* * *

Calum called Odette just as she had double-parked her moped to pop into a corner shop for a scratch card.

'Where are you?' She hugged her mobile ecstatically to her ear by a display of Snickers bars.

'In Therapy, sister,' he said coolly, husky voice almost drowned out by background chatter. 'Are you free? There's someone I want you to meet.'

Odette had been in the OD all day and her natty little wool suit was covered with sawdust, one stocking had snagged at the heel and her make-up was in desperate need of a touch-up. She would have liked to pop back to her flat and freshen up, but she didn't want to let the opportunity slip.

'I'll come right round,' she told him as she spotted that the little shop sold a reasonable – if dusty – selection of Pretty Polly tights.

The background noise had reached fever pitch. 'It's dead here,' Calum told her with unconscious irony. 'Meet me at Bar Barella in half an hour, okay?'

Saskia went directly to Stan's studio after work. His old art school chum Fliss was in situ, spray painting one of the huge, bulbous figurative sculptures for which she now commanded ludicrous fees. She lived in Yorkshire, but her latest commission – for a merchant bank – was too large to be transported south.

The air was thick with paint fumes and an old Culture Club cassette was doing its stuff in the paint-stained deck, squeaking with age as though Boy George had a demented budgie trapped in his hat.

'He's in the pub,' Fliss told Saskia when she finally turned off her rattling paint gun and noticed her standing in the entrance. She pulled an apologetic face. 'I'm afraid he lost out on the gallery slot. They've offered it to Tracey Emin to exhibit her dental records.'

Bracing herself for the worst, Saskia tracked Stan down to his favourite barstool where he sat chasing Hoegartens with schnapps, his favourite combined tipple. Far from being furious, he had drunk himself into convivial euphoria.

'Love of my life!' he hailed her loudly, indicating he was at least three up. 'Come here, bird, and snog your fella. Looking fit. I love you in a suit. Odette well, is she?'

Why did he always ask after Odette before her? Saskia thought tetchily. It almost changed her mind about what she was going to suggest but things at the OD were desperate and at least this would give her the opportunity to keep a closer eye on Stan and his drinking.

'Darling Fin,' Lydia wrote on a piece of damp paper, shaking the pen to make the ink flow, *'I love you so much, but I think I might have made a terrible, terrible mistake . . . I'm not sure I want to be married to a junior executive . . .'*

'Sugar!' he called through the door. 'You want me to come in and rub your back?'

'In a minute, darling,' she called back. 'Pour me a glass of wine first and bring it in, will you?'

'I can't write much because you're about to come in,' she scribbled, although the pen was only writing half the words as the steamy heat seized it up. *'I don't think getting married is a very good idea at all. I think we should stay as we are.'*

She quickly folded the paper into a tiny little triangle, as she always did, and threw it into the bin, as she always did. Part of her hoped that Fin, who was wonderfully domestic, would find it when he was clearing out all the bins and read it. But he never had.

Of course Calum was late. He always was. Odette had already downed two Diet Cokes at a sticky marble table and watched the beautiful and the stoned of Soho come and go, and was tetchy with anticipation. She hated sitting alone, and feared being hit upon by the sort of gor-blimey City prat whose eyes never rose above chest level. But Bar Barella was far too old-school indie to attract those. It remained the domain of out-of-work actors and models, struggling musicians and wannabe writers seeking a little quiet in the stony bowels of Frith Street. All around her the thin and the misunderstood gazed at their chewed nails, battered *Outing* magazines or their track marks. Odette thought it typical of Calum to choose somewhere calculated to make her feel completely out of place.

One character in particular intrigued her: a lanky, longhaired figure with soulful eyes and the longest fingers Odette had ever seen on a man. There was something familiar-looking about him which she couldn't place – he could be in a band, one of those Verve/Gomez/Soundgarden Brit Pop ones she only caught snatches of on Virgin Radio. Or perhaps he was an actor? Bar Barella was a classic hangout for the nearly-there star with attitude. What fascinated Odette was the way he sat at the bar in a world of his own, downing shot after shot of neat vodka.

When Calum finally turned up he was alone, which surprised her. He seldom went anywhere without his posse of cronies. Few people turned around when the scruffy little Glaswegian bounded downstairs, but Odette felt as though he'd entered in a spotlight with a trumpet fanfare as his eyes sought her out and then trapped her in their steely missile lock. He was wearing his usual pork-pie hat, football shirt, scuffed pumps and combats, topped off with a vast leather jacket which skirted his knees, the shoulders of which were almost twice as wide as his. Odette tried to tell herself that he looked appalling, but her heart turned over and over like a plump steak being sealed in a very hot pan.

'So you haven't said hello then?' he dispensed with the pleasantries of greeting her, apologising for being late or for staying out of touch for so long. This was classic Calum.

'Hello to who?' She was confused. There was no one nearby – she had deliberately chosen a quiet corner. His cronies must be here after all, she realised with a leaden thump of regret. It would be impossible to talk to him about the crisis at the OD with all of them jeering, leering and beering nearby.

But Calum slapped his cheek in mock-forgetfulness – a curiously jovial gesture Odette had never seen him use before. 'Of course – you two have never met. Ferdy!' he called to someone at the bar. 'This,' he told Odette in an intimate undertone, 'is the second best chef in England.'

But Odette wasn't following his gaze; she was staring at the tiny blond coil of chest hair sprouting from his football shirt. She'd never known Calum whisper in her ear either. These were pitifully tiny changes in his behaviour and yet she was certain they heralded some strange shift in attitude. She was so acutely aware of his every move these days she could sit an exam on his eyebrow-lifting skills alone.

As Calum settled into the chair beside her and adopted his customary slouch, the lanky, longhaired drunk Odette had been watching at the bar hopped off his stool and walked in a perfectly straight line towards them. Apparently none the worse for all the Stolichnayas Odette had seen him down, his sleepy smile was completely disarming.

'How're you doing?' he asked in a lazy Ulster drawl.

'Fergus Hannon, meet Odette,' Calum looked from one to the other with obvious relish, 'your new boss.'

'Wow!' Ferdy's eyes predictably met her chest and stayed glued there like fluff to Velcro. His smile widened. 'I think I'm going to like this job, so I am.'

Odette bristled, the effect of that doe-eyed smile in no way making up for the shock of this introduction. She turned to Calum furiously. 'What's going on here? You promised me Florian bleedin' Etoile, not some drunk I've never heard of.'

Accustomed to Florian's verbal batterings, Ferdy didn't look remotely offended. 'I don't normally drink during the day,' he lied easily, 'but I was so nervous I thought I'd have a couple to still my nerves now.'

'You had more like a dozen,' snapped Odette, who had been watching him for the past half an hour.

'That's what I meant, so I did – *a couple* of dozen.' His dazzling smile didn't flicker as he winked one big brown eye, then seeing Odette's horrified face added, 'That was a joke by the way. Shall I come and see you at the club on Thursday then? We'll talk through menus, like you suggested, Calum?'

'I'll leave that to Odette to finalise.' He patted her knee.

Again, Odette was thrown. He'd *never* patted her knee before. She wasn't sure whether to be ecstatic or insulted. But she was far too angry to enjoy it.

'I'm sorry but I think Calum's misled you.' She fought to

sound authoritative as she looked up at Ferdy. He was far too tall. She stood up, but it made little difference. She'd have to get up on her chair to look him in the eye. 'We haven't finalised the choice of chef at the OD yet, and I really need to know a bit more about you before I make a—'

She shut up suddenly as she felt a warm hand touch the back of her leg. Calum, still slouching in his chair, was stroking the back of her knee reassuringly. One illogical thought entered Odette's head and refused to go away. She was wearing cheap corner shop Pretty Pollys. She normally wore Wolford's best five-denier stockings. Bugger.

Fighting to get a hold of herself, she turned to Calum – so assured and so arrogant. Leaning back in his chair, head tilted upwards, he smiled his rare, toothy smile. 'Trust me, sister.' The hand slipped from her leg to tip back his pork-pie hat so she could see his eyes clearly. They were glittering with confidence. 'Trust me,' he repeated. 'Ferdy's young, talented and a fucking good cook. Florian trained him and they've worked together for years. You won't find better in London right now.'

Odette couldn't argue when he looked at her like that. She didn't know what it was about him that did this to her, but she felt almost sick with longing.

'Okay.' She dragged her eyes away and looked at Ferdy. 'Come and meet me at the club this week.'

'That's great. Look, I've got to skip.' He glanced at his watch apologetically. 'There's some guys I have to meet now. I – er—' he coughed in embarrassment '—don't suppose I could have some sort of advance on my wages? Just to tide me over while we're at the planning stage. I'll have to hand in my notice at L'Orbital, after all, and you know how mean Florian is. He'll not pay me once he knows I'm leaving.'

Odette opened her mouth to argue, but Calum was already reaching into his pocket. He handed over a wad of fifties. 'There you go, pal. Don't spend it all at once.'

'Jesus, thanks!' Ferdy looked ecstatic. He was planning to do just that in order to stop his dealer rearranging his kneecaps.

Calum had reached for his coat too. 'I'll come with you, pal – I'm away to Office Block right now.'

'Wait!' Odette was desperate to have him to herself for a bit. 'Stay for another drink, Calum babes. There are things we need to talk through.'

'No can do, sister.' He was already backing towards the stairs that led out of the bar. 'I'm already late.' Then he paused for a moment. 'Tell you what, are you going to be home later?'

'Yes,' she sighed in frustration, certain she was going to be fobbed off with the promise of a phone call that would never come.

'In that case, I'll call round tonight,' he promised. 'After all, it's about time I saw that great big flat of yours.' With yet another unprecedented gesture – a cool wink – he bounded upstairs after Ferdy.

Stan was not keen on Saskia's idea that he should step in and supervise the décor of the OD.

'I'm stretched as it is,' he told her, running paint-stained fingers through his lion's mane of hair and shaking it out so that it flopped into his beer. 'I know Odette's an old mate, but I ain't a charity.'

'She'll pay you,' Saskia said confidently. 'And think of the showcase this'll be for your work. This place is going to be all over the papers for weeks; celebrities and the idle rich will spend half their lives there. Your work will be right under their noses. That's better than a fortnight in the White Space Gallery, isn't it?'

'Don't knock it, girl – that was going to be my biggest exhibition yet.' Stan looked into his pint gloomily. 'The Leonard Brothers started there.'

Saskia suddenly saw a way to talk him round. 'They were supposed to be designing the OD, but they had to pull out at the last minute.'

'Why's that then?' Stan's ears pricked up. He had always been insanely jealous of the success of the two brothers from Cobham, Jago and Jed Leonard, who were the darlings of the art world.

'Odette's business partner wasn't too happy with their concept,' Saskia said vaguely, uncertain herself why Byron had replaced the famous duo. 'Too tame or something.'

'Tcha!' Stan sneered with delight. 'Told you they'd sell out in the end – everyone does . . . Damien, Chapmanworld, Gilbert and George. I never compromise, y'see. That's why they're worth a fortune and I'm not.'

'Exactly,' Saskia agreed far too heartily, then felt relieved when he didn't pick up on the irony loaded in her response. She was going to take him for richer or poorer after all, and she admired his talented tenacity, even if she secretly preferred his little sketches of their dog, Yuppie, to his big canvases and installations. 'Now I'm giving you the opportunity to prove that you won't compromise. You've got *carte blanche*. Anything goes.'

'You serious?' Stan looked excited. 'I can do anyfink I like with Odette's gaff?'

'Anything, darling.' Saskia stroked his wild hair.

'Hmm. That don't sound like her.' He eyed his fiancée sceptically. 'Left it a bit late to change her mind, ain't she? Talk about putting the *carte blanche* before the horse. You sure she approved this?'

Saskia nodded, certain that she would. Anyone had to be better than Byronic Maurice after all, and Odette and Stan were life-long mates.

She knew Stan's work could be a little controversial at times, but she was sure he wouldn't risk anything too revolting at the OD. He'd once admitted that Odette was the only woman besides his mother who could really frighten him.

Odette was beside herself with excitement. She took a long, hot bath and scrubbed herself pink, removed every unwanted hair, rubbed herself soft and smooth again with oils and creams. She budded her ears, flossed her teeth, flushed out her navel and checked her muff with her make-up mirror.

Dressed in the softest and sexiest of cashmere trousers and top, she lit the fire and put on slow music – her Love Ballads CDs on a stacker system, programmed to random repeat to see them through the night. She chilled champagne, and beer too because she knew Calum preferred it. She re-made her bed and lit scented candles, agonising over whether 'sensual' and 'relaxing' were a better combination than 'invigorating' and 'exotic'. In the end she lit all four.

It takes six and a half hours for a two-inch scented candle to burn out. Odette knew this because she waited until the last flame – 'invigorating' – guttered and died before she went to bed.

Calum hadn't come. He hadn't even called. She felt desolate. So much for aromatherapy.

6

Morgue was one of the most successful restaurants in London. It was almost impossible to book a table, the prices were ridiculously high, the menu required a multilingual dictionary and a degree in bullshit to decipher and the waiters treated the customers with a disdain similar to that afforded to a Woolworth's shoplifter by a snobby magistrate. And yet everyone wanted to eat there.

The bar was a long metal benchtop, behind which several Morgue staff were dispensing drinks into glasses shaped like test tubes which had to be placed in the racks provided or they fell over – as they regularly did when an unwitting drinker forgot the protocol. Odette ordered a Bacardi and Coke from a disapproving-looking barman dressed in surgical greens with an elasticated paper hat, thin rubber gloves and very shiny white wellington boots.

'Still no sign of your companions?' asked a plastic-aproned waitress in a tone that clearly meant '*Have* you no friends?' She smiled coolly when Odette apologised on their behalf and said, 'In that case, may I suggest you wait at your table?'

She was shown to it upstairs – a marble slab surrounded by uncomfortably stylish metal chairs, set beneath operating theatre lights. At the table beside her, a couple had just been presented with their starters which had the unmistakable trade mark of a body-tag tied to a ceramic toe on the plate's rim. Odette studied the menu, which was presented on a clipboard to look like autopsy notes. Before she could take anything in, a familiar voice made her vision blur.

Calum was sitting at a table tucked around the corner almost out of her line of vision. He was with a whole pack of cronies. Craning forward to see, Odette recognised several, including football's hard man-about-town, Denny Rees, and Morgue's designer Dennis Thirsk, whose 'Bludgeoned Seal in Perspex' had been shortlisted for the Turner Prize. Then she caught her breath as she saw that Alex Hopkinson was with them, his trade mark Dracula hair as glossy as a beetle's wing. Calum had offered her the services of the talented PR maverick weeks ago, promising Alex would be in touch, but she'd heard nothing so far. She was still as raw as a skinned rabbit that Calum had blown her out last night, but this was too good an opportunity to miss. He'd probably be glad to bump into her, she told herself firmly, glad to have an opportunity to explain and to introduce Alex at last.

Downing the last of her test tube of Bacardi, Odette stood up and walked easily around the corner, pride intact. The table was thick with smoke and all male, with the exception of one skinny, shaven-headed girl wearing scruffy combats and a nose stud. They were all laughing and arguing and drinking so hard they didn't even look up when Odette approached. She cleared her throat loudly.

'We said we don't want to eat yet, yeah?' the girl carped angrily, mistaking her for a member of staff. 'Don't you know who I am?'

'No,' Odette said honestly, waiting for Calum to notice her, but the rim of his hat was right over his yellow-tinted glasses and his nose was pressed to Alex Hopkinson's lapel as they talked like two spies.

'What's your name?' the girl snarled, anticipating a dismissal.

'Odette.' She tried not to rise to this – she was interrupting their conversation after all. 'And I don't work here, babes. I just popped over to say hello to Calum.'

'Yeah? Well, I'm Susie Thirsk and this is Dennis, and we don't like networkers so fuck off.' She and Dennis cackled with laughter.

At last Calum glanced up and saw Odette. Far from looking contrite, he appeared cornered and shifty, as if she'd caught him flogging her jewellery.

'What do you want?' he demanded, sounding like a teenager whose mother had come to haul him out of a disco.

Far too hurt to be suspicious, Odette just wanted to yell, 'Where did you get to last night? I waited for hours, I changed my bed, I was ready for you!' Instead she mustered a calm smile, anxious not to rile him. This was typical Calum; he'd explain in his own time. His affection was hard earned, and she was still on the minimum wage. She mustn't let him see how inexperienced and insecure she was.

'I'm eating here with some friends.' She smiled into his eyes to let him know he was forgiven, although it hurt as much as gazing at the sun with a broken contact lens. 'Just came over to say hi, babes. And to introduce myself to Alex.' She turned gratefully to the glossy-haired guru. 'I gather we're going to be doing some business together?'

He looked up with interest, calculator eyes appraising her expensive suit. 'Are you involved with the Food Ha—'

'Odette is opening a club in Islington,' Calum butted in. 'The one I told you about, remember?'

Alex winced as an elbow made contact with his ribs.

'Oh, yeah – yeah, sort of . . .'

Sort of? Odette smarted. *Sort* of? He was supposed to be making it the most public launch in history. The doors were opening in just over a week.

'When can we meet up?' she asked him, trying to curb her irritation.

'Shhh . . . shhh . . . let's not talk business. I'm out with my pals.' Calum waved her question away, suddenly all charm. 'Sit down and have a drink with us, sister – let me introduce you to my clan.'

They absolutely weren't her sort of people. They were loud and selfish and drunken and drugged, they slagged off anyone who wasn't there and only wanted to talk about where they were going next.

'Nero's bollocks these days,' Denny complained. 'No fucking style no more. Full of fucking writers. Why don't we go down the local boozer?'

'Too right!' Susie whooped. 'I haven't been in a pub for years. Is there a members-only one round here?'

Odette shuddered and caught Dennis eyeing her tits. 'They real?' He scratched his three-day beard.

She nodded wearily, accustomed to the attention.

'If you ever decide to get them reduced, give me a call.' He handed her his card. 'I could use what comes out – it'd be quite a challenge setting fatty tissue in plastic. I can call it "Breast Implants". Don't go in for tits much myself.'

'Evidently.' Stung by the 'fatty tissue' comment, Odette glanced at Susie's chest, which was as flat as a Thai fisherman's.

Dennis cackled so much the unlit B & H flew out of his lips. 'You like this place, then?' He looked around proudly. 'I'm opening a sister restaurant in Manchester soon. Going to call it Abattoir. Meat-only menu, waiters in bloodstained aprons, racks of carcasses around the place – although Alex reckons Health and Safety might veto that, says I'll have to put them in Perspex. What d'you think?'

Odette felt sick. Sitting beside her, Calum hadn't taken his mouth from his beer bottle since she'd joined them, and his hat was now crammed even lower over his eyes as he listened to Susie and Denny discussing pubs. He clearly wasn't going to apologise, and she couldn't bring herself to challenge him for an explanation in front of all these people. She'd feel too cheap, too desperate. He'd only promised to call around to talk about the restaurant, after all. It was she who'd envisaged the five-act seduction in front of her fire, the planning their lives together, the joint purchase of a scruffy little dog.

To her relief, she spotted Juno and Jay making their way to her deserted table.

'He's sexy.' Susie followed her gaze. 'Shame he's carrying all that excess weight around.' She narrowed her eyes at Juno who was looking ravishing as she spilled out of a too-tight corset dress. 'Flesh is so ugly.'

Odette gave her a withering look and hastily excused herself from the group. Calum barely seemed to notice her go. But as she turned the corner to her table, he caught up with her, spinning her round as his fingers caught the soft flesh between elbow and armpit.

'That hurts.' She snatched her arm free.

The yellow lenses made his eyes look warmer than usual, softening the white steel to gold. 'You mad at me, sister?'

'Should I be?' she bluffed, determined to be cool. 'It was only a chat about the OD after all, wasn't it?'

The corners of his mouth lifted and Odette could have kicked herself. She shouldn't have left that question there. It was clumsy and he knew it.

'Sure it was.' His eyes switched between hers – left, right, left, right – like a hypnotist's pendulum. 'Just a chat. But I'm sorry I missed out. I got totally tied up and couldn't make it. Another time maybe?' It was his turn to leave a question hanging, loaded with meaning.

Odette had to stay professional to stop her knees giving way. She longed to take a risk, to say 'any time', to start making the moves more obvious. But last night had scalded her in more ways than one, and she couldn't risk losing out to passion again. Her feelings for him frightened her. Her business was at stake here. 'The club opens in just over a week, Calum. You've got to come and inspect it soon.'

'Sure, sure,' he soothed, leaning closer to her and dropping his voice. 'I'm working on something for the opening night. That's why I didnae want Alex blabbing back there. And I know I've no' been around as much as you'd like, but that's just the way I operate. We're different, you and me. That's why the dynamic works, why we're going to be so great together.' To her total amazement he cupped a warm hand to her cheek, his little finger resting in the hollow beneath her ear.

Almost fainting with a sudden head-rush of lust, Odette struggled to keep to the point. 'But the club's now so much bigger than I planned. We've hit a cash-flow crisis. There's not enough—'

He covered her lips with his thumb and shook his head patiently, watching her with curious fascination. 'You're a big girl, Odette,' he murmured, cool eyes not leaving her mouth. 'You're in charge. You dinnae need me around all the time. I like to stand back and observe sometimes. Watch you make the moves. Do as I say and it'll work out just fine, trust me. We'll get what we both want out of this. Together, we can do it.' Still watching her mouth intently, his fingers slipped down her cheek and across her lips with exquisite lightness. Had they not been in a crowded restaurant, she was certain he would have kissed her.

Lips buzzing, Odette smiled, suddenly so ecstatic she half-expected an orchestra to loom out of the Morgue kitchens and play 'When A Man Loves A Woman'. It no longer mattered that the building work was so far behind, that Maurice's designs were atrocious, that they'd hired a vodka-pickled chef and had no marketing. Calum said it would work. She was sitting in bed with her Jonathan, he wearing the pyjama bottoms, she the top. They were a team; they were in his words 'going to be so great together'. If she'd been less obsessed, she would have realised that it wasn't Calum's style to sweet-talk, to pump up or to flatter. But her head was too full of Percy Sledge to notice.

Mouthing, 'I'll call,' Calum melted back into his smoky lair. As he passed Susie Thirsk, she reached up and whispered in his ear, 'Enjoy last night, Tiger? I always love tying you in knots.'

Juno apologised profusely for being late, as she always did.

'It's just I popped in to see Lydia, then I realised I'd left my purse there with my travel card in. When I went to fetch it Finlay had got back from work so we had a chat, then I bumped into my friend Lulu on the—'

'Shut up, baby,' Jay laughed, kissing her nose. 'By the time you've finished we'll be through eating. Odette's cool about it.'

In truth, she would usually have given Juno a hard time about it, but tonight she was grinning from ear-to-ear like a Lottery winner.

'You okay?' Juno gave her a curious look.

'I think I'm in love, babes.' She looked from one to the other with glittering eyes. 'No wonder you guys go in for it. It's bloody fantastic, ain't it? Bugger the cost, let's have champagne.'

'In *love*?' Juno almost fell off her chair. 'You? Who with? You don't even date.'

'And I never age neither.' It was an old Gang joke which pre-dated the usual jibe that Odette was a secret nymphomaniac.

Juno would not be deflected. 'Details, details, details!' she demanded, chanting like the Monty Python 'Spam' sketch.

Looking at her friend's gossip-hungry face, Odette realised that perhaps she'd got carried away with her euphoric announcement. 'It's far too early to talk about it,' she backtracked hastily.

'Crap! You're shagging someone, aren't you?' Juno giggled, tucking into a lump of olive bread.

'No!' Odette was appalled.

'Tongueing then?' Juno asked between mouthfuls, looking hopeful.

'Juno, baby.' Jay cuffed her. 'Give the girl a break. Can't you see she don't wanna talk about it?'

With Juno watching her like an excited great-aunt anticipating a marriage announcement at any second, Odette waited for the champagne to be poured and lifted her glass. 'To the OD, and my favourite maître d'.'

Turning as pink as the champagne, Juno knocked back her entire glass in one guilty swig and coughed. 'I was meaning to talk to you about that actually . . .'

Odette was so high – and so relieved that the subject of her love life had been shelved – that she didn't object when Juno dropped the bombshell that she wouldn't be able to take the job as maître emcee on a permanent basis.

'You see, we're going to try out New York for size.' Juno gripped Jay's hand, looking excited. 'They do great doughnuts there apparently.'

'You're moving to the States?' Odette smiled encouragingly, hiding a tight ball of selfish insecurity deep inside her. Juno was one of her oldest friends, the scatty social secretary who organised parties and held the Gang together. Without her, nothing would ever be the same. Thank heavens Odette would have Calum soon.

Juno nodded, still pink with guilt. 'You're the first person we've told outside my family, and it's supposed to be a secret until the visa's sorted out and stuff. But I wanted you to know as soon as possible because of the club. We're not going till next spring so there's lots of time to get a replacement. I'll help out as much as I can till then. God, I can't wait for the launch party. You must be *so* excited!'

'D Day.' Odette closed her eyes and shuddered in anticipation.

'OD Day,' Juno giggled, catching Jay's eye and mouthing 'Definitely shagging'.

'I saw that.' Odette opened her eyes. 'And I'm not.' Yet, she added silently.

One thing was for certain, she decided. She was going to work like a Trojan in the coming weeks. She was going to make Calum proud of her. There was no way their venture would fail. It was the thing that would bring them together, Jonathan and Jennifer united in a common quest. And she'd already decided that the night of the OD opening would be the first night they would make love.

7

On the morning of the OD launch, the building was still an anonymous old disused fire station, much as it had been for the past four years. The possibility that in just a few hours it could be transformed into a desirable media haunt seemed very remote. There was no sign outside to indicate its change of identity, the boarding had gone but the windows were whited out. The interior was coated with dust and littered with timber, coils of wire, cardboard boxes, invoices, partially unpacked crockery, glassware and cutlery, boxes of flowers, piles of linen. Chairs were stacked up to the side walls and covered with dust sheets, tables were kissing tops as they stood in strange, herd-like collections, huddled nervously in the corners while Maurice supervised a third layer of fast-drying polish on his purple painted, mock-marble floor. Up on a ladder, Stan McGillivray was putting the finishing touches to one of his mock-crucifix wall hangings. He and Maurice were not talking, partly because they loathed one another, mainly because they simply didn't understand each other's accent.

Only the kitchen was an immaculate – and near-professional – hive of activity as five chefs prepared stocks, vegetables and cuts of meat for the night ahead along with a mass of tiny, delicate appetisers which would float around the guests' line of vision on vast trays and then soak their taste buds once tried, in the hope that they would stay on and buy a meal after the party had dispersed. The kitchen hierarchy was firmly in place as Ned, the red-haired and loud-mouthed *sous-chef*, stalked around his *chefs de partie* checking that they were carrying out Ferdy's orders. In turn, those *chefs de partie* supervised their *commis* chefs who were carrying out the more mundane work, some of them for the first time ever.

'Where the hell's Ferdy?' Odette was still staring into the kitchen from the 'tube' – the narrow, metal-skirted corridor that ran from kitchen to dining room.

'In his office, I should think,' Saskia told her.

'Shouldn't he be in the fucking kitchen?' Odette railed. 'Doing stuff?'

'He's in his office doing stuff,' Saskia sighed, hoping the stuff wasn't white and Colombian. 'He'll come out and supervise later. Now I really think we should check the bar. Most of the stock is still in cases and we have to chill a lot of it. The optics aren't up and—'

'I don't want fucking optics!' Odette exploded. 'I told Maurice, I want American-style spouts and measuring cups. Shit! This isn't the fucking Bull and Bush. Where is he – Maurice!' She stormed into the main dining room and walked straight on to the still-tacky varnish, almost gluing herself to the middle of the room on her high stilettos.

By lunchtime the situation had worsened. Stan and Maurice disagreed over a large metal statue of the Madonna welded together out of pieces of an old Mini Cooper.

'It's an ocular abomination!' Maurice wailed.

'It's fine art, mate,' Stan muttered. 'That was exhibited at the ICA for three months.'

'Where? In the car park? Don't tell me, Damien Hirst reversed his Porsche into the cleaner's runaround and it's now worth thousands?'

A stand-up fight ensued. Stan's thick blond mane was soon rock solid as a result of the half tin of fast-drying floor varnish that had been tipped on it, and Maurice was fast developing a bump on his head from being crowned with a steering-wheel halo. Both were refusing to work, so the finishing touches remained unfinished and untouched. Odette's high-heeled footprints had dried and were now permanently stamped on the mock-marble floor, the Mini Mary sculpture was sitting bang in the middle of the entrance foyer and the pictures for the basement bar were all stacked in the cloakroom alongside boxes of wooden coathangers and numbered plastic coat tags.

Ferdy had yet to emerge from his office, although it was noted when unpacking the boxes of spirits that two bottles of Stolichnaya were missing. It didn't take a genius to connect the two.

Odette was closer to a nervous breakdown than ever. There was no sign of Juno, Stan had sloped off to the hairdresser's, and the agency from which Odette had hired twenty extra waiting staff claimed that the instructions had been cancelled. If it weren't for Saskia remaining calm and professional, she knew she'd start throwing furniture around in despair.

She had her first laugh of the day when Stan returned just after five. He'd had all his hair shaved off and looked like a very disgruntled Hare Krishna disciple. Not only that, but he'd brought fifty 'Jesus Lives' ashtrays back with him, all replete with a little transfer picture of Our Saviour, who bore an uncanny resemblance to a young David Cassidy with a badly drawn-on ginger beard.

'Got them from a dodgy church wholesalers I know in Dalston – they supplied a lot of the hanging crosses and stuff,' he told her. 'I thought it'd go with your religious theme, mate. Had a bit of cash left over so I also got this.' He produced a lurid lime green cassock and matching bishop's head-dress. 'They said it was a surplus order for some loony cult in Wales that's just gone bust. I thought I could be your mitre d' if you were pushed.'

'Oh, Stan, I fucking love you, mate.' Odette fought tears as she gave him a hug. 'That's inspired.'

He grinned toothily. 'At least the hat'll cover the suedehead, y'know?'

'That's not suede, that's satin.' Odette reached up and polished his freshly shaven pate until he ducked away, grumbling that she'd rub off all the wax.

'I'm here!' A bright, if slightly guilty, voice announced from the lobby. 'Odette?'

'Juno!' She howled in relief. 'Fantastic. I'd given up on you. Now I have two maître d's. Or rather one mitre, the other emcee. I'm sorted!'

'Huh?' Juno was clambering over several boxes of menus and tablecloths. A small, curvy, blonde explosion of energy in too-tight clothes, she was a welcome sight amidst the dusty confusion. 'You are opening tonight, aren't you?'

'Eight o'clock on the dot.' Odette looked at her watch and flinched as she realised time was running out.

'That's good – I thought I'd got the day wrong.' Juno looked around her doubtfully. 'Only I've asked Jay to rally some of his press pack chums to come and snap celebs.' Jay's contacts in the paparazzi world were usually a nightmare when it came to parties because they drank like prisoners on day release, but tonight Juno was happy to extend the invitation.

'Oh, there'll be lots of celebs,' Odette said confidently, her mood suddenly lifting.

Saskia was less hopeful. Unbeknown to Odette, she had just come off the phone to one of her oldest friends and soon-to-be bridesmaid, Phoebe 'Freddy' Fredericks. These days, Phoebe worked for the diary page of a national newspaper and was about as well connected as the Lanesborough switchboard. Her lover, Felix Sylvian, was a some-time model, some-time socialite who was jokingly referred to by the media as the It Lad because he was invited to all the best parties in London and seemed to exist on a diet of chilled champagne and First Class aeroplane food. His circle of friends made Calum's look very small and low-key. Between them they were guaranteed to pull in some very big names, not to mention invaluable coverage.

'I'm really, really sorry.' Phoebe had sounded deeply embarrassed, dropping her voice because Felix was clearly in the room wailing along to a Squeeze CD. 'But Jimmy is taking us all out to dinner. He wants to announce something, apparently. I can't get out of it – had no idea it clashed with tonight until I checked my diary today.'

Saskia was mad with her, but grudgingly understood. Jimmy had been absent for most of the It Lad's charmed but feckless life, and was someone whom Felix idolised in a manner close to obsession. Every minute that Felix and his younger brother Mungo spent with Jimmy was as precious as a last breath of fresh air.

'What's he like?' she couldn't resist asking.

'Lovely,' Phoebe sighed. 'Really calm and easy-going – and so *shy*. Nothing like the other two,' she giggled. 'Not that I'd ever swap. Listen, we'll try to come by afterwards,' she promised. 'And I've already spread the word around, of course. But you do know you're clashing with the Clinic's anniversary bash, don't you? It's a Florian Etoile gig so everyone and his wife are going. Meg Mathews is organising the party.'

'But that's one of Calum's restaurants!' Saskia was appalled. 'He's shitting on his own doorstep. He's due here at eight, and Odette's banking on him bringing a lot more than a bottle with him.' They were all relying on Calum to rustle up most of London's A-list, just as he'd promised.

'Well, he could go to both, I suppose,' Phoebe murmured, adding thoughtfully, 'Amazing coincidence – Jimmy knows him.'

'Jimmy?' Saskia was astonished.

'They go some way back – not sure how. I'll try and find out more tonight. Hope to see you later, darl. If not, I'll be at the dress fitting on Friday.'

'Can I go and change in the loos?' Juno asked Odette. 'I brought a sexy dress.'

'The plumbers are still in the bogs – use my office,' she said cheerfully, looking around. 'Now who's going to help me drag these tables into place?'

'Er – Odette?' Juno emerged from the office less than a minute later. 'Someone appears to have passed out over a joystick in there. Lara Croft is dead and I think he might be too.'

'Shit – Ferdy!' Odette raced into the freshly carpeted, newly painted room with its state-of-the-art computer and desk that still smelled of wood shavings.

Sure enough, Calum's 'rising star' had fallen flat on his face after what appeared to be a bottle and a half of Stolly and four levels of Tomb Raider III.

'Whatever you do, don't tell Ned,' Odette hissed over her shoulder as she straightened her chef up and slapped his cheeks. He managed to grunt, mutter, 'Should have used the shotgun on the T-Rex,' and then pass out again.

8

The first thing Elsa noticed as she and Euan drove past the OD in search of a parking space at seven-thirty was that the windows were still white-washed, obscuring the frantic activity going on behind, although the odd blurred figure could be seen moving at speed, one of which appeared to be very tall indeed and dressed entirely in lime green.

On their second circuit around the block, still in search of a parking space, Elsa saw that a large towelling cloth was cutting great swathes through the white-wash like a laser through a cataract, revealing bright working lights and a jumble of tables and chairs behind. Judging from the pots of paint, stacks of paper and piles of cloth on each table, the place was set up more for a geriatric day care centre than a big media launch.

By the time they'd found a parking space and reached the huge entrance doors on foot, the white-wash was all but gone and what appeared to be a bishop dressed in day-glo lime green was balancing precariously on a stepladder as he tried to hang a mixture of ecclesiastical bell ropes, beaded curtains and plastic shower curtains over the windows.

'Jesus, what a mess,' Euan muttered under his breath as they squeezed past an upside-down Mini in the entrance hall.

'Thank God you're here!' Odette panted up to them the moment they got through the doors to the restaurant. 'Listen, babes, I really hate to ask you this, 'cos I know you're officially guests and that, but can you help out? Half my staff ain't turned up – the agency got mixed up and thought tonight was cancelled.'

Euan looked as though he was about to tell her where to

get off, but Elsa pinched him hard on the arm. 'Sure, hon – just point us where you need us most.'

Within minutes, music journalist Euan was helping out behind the bar and yabbering into his mobile phone to try and arrange a last-minute cover for The Fix, the trendy band Calum had promised and who predictably hadn't turned up. Elsa found herself attaching beads to shower curtains to cover the remainder of the vast windows and standing next to a pretty but slightly horse-faced blonde in a business suit who was holding on to the bishop's ladder and looking up his cassock. Peeping up the cassock too, Elsa spotted a West Ham tattoo on one buttock.

'Hello, Stan.' She glanced around at the paintings, crucifix wall-hangings and disturbing sculptures. Despite the bright working lights, the room had a staggering atmosphere – church crypt meets minimalist warehouse flat. 'Great work.'

'Fanks, Elsa doll.' He grinned. 'Shame I didn't get time to make decent window shutters. You met the wife?'

'Saskia Seaton,' the blonde introduced herself, tucking Stan's cassock proprietorially into his sock and then shaking hands. 'Actually, we're getting married next month.' She fingered Elsa's solitaire diamond with a leading expression that made Elsa laugh.

'Next March,' she nodded, looking from Saskia to Stan. When Odette had told her that 'some posh bird who's marrying Stan' was going to be her restaurant manager, she'd imagined a wild child trustafarian with a thing about torn fishnet and bad boy artists, not a full-scale Sloane complete with pearls.

'You pregnant or just fat, doll?' Stan asked Elsa as he clambered down off his ladder. Not waiting for an answer, he flapped off to supervise the erection of a vast pulpit behind which the maître d' could stand.

'Stan has two blunt instruments,' Saskia apologised, 'and both of them give me no end of pleasure. I've been training him for weeks to say "I do" without adding a "fucking" in the middle.'

Elsa laughed. Odette always maintained that no one in the world was as rude or direct as Stan, although Elsa personally thought Odette ran a close second.

'Is she going to hold up, d'you think?' Saskia asked worriedly. 'You know her better than me. She's worked so hard this week, she's running on neat adrenalin now.'

Elsa nodded, threading on beads faster and faster as she got the hang of it. 'She'll be fine. She was just the same during our finals and she came away with a first.'

'Thank God you're here!' a voice wailed and Juno panted up to Elsa wearing an extraordinary bright yellow rubber dress that made her look like a curvy patti-pan. 'Odette's in tears in the loo. Ferdy the chef's just woken up and told her that Calum's throwing a party to celebrate the Clinic's first anniversary tonight. He's not even coming here, and what's worse, he's stolen half her guest list to lure there instead. Then Ferdy threw up all over her sexy red dress, so she's only got leggings to wear. She'd just about sobered him up when Ned – that's the *sous-chef* – came marching into the office and punched him on the nose and knocked him out cold again.' She lit a cigarette and then held it as far away from Elsa as possible. 'Sorry – I'm sure baby's facing the other way.'

'Right.' Elsa didn't even have to think. 'Give her your dress.'

'What?' Juno sounded appalled, sucking on her cigarette dementedly. 'Do you know how many sit ups I had to do to wear this tonight?'

'Not enough,' Elsa said with the brutal honesty of a long-standing friend who knew she would be forgiven in the long run. 'And it's not in keeping with the religious theme. Just beg or borrow something wacky to match Stan. Tell Odette to hold herself together for an hour – or at least the dress will do that. Guide all the guests downstairs to the bar and get the kitchen to whisk some of those trays of food down there. You know what people are like at launches, no one will arrive here until nine at the earliest. I'll be back by then.'

'Where are you going?' Juno bleated, desperately in need of back up.

'To fetch Calum Forrester. I want to stage a surprise entrance,' Elsa said cryptically, unflipping her mobile as she walked outside. By the entrance, Stan was supervising two drunken builders who were trying to screw the minimalist OD Club plaque on the wall.

'It's upside down, you cretin!' he moaned, turning to Elsa. 'Off so soon?' he hissed irritably. 'So sorry you can't stay. I won't offer you a party bag.'

'I'm just popping out for a few essentials,' she snapped. 'Can you tell the Scottish geezer behind the bar that his missus thinks it's a Dana situation?'

'A what?' Stan took off his mitre and scratched his shaven pate.

Elsa took a step back in shock. Without the stupid hat he looked terrifyingly like Vinnie Jones.

'Just tell him,' she croaked nervously.

'Yeah, okay. I like Dana.' Stan looked quite benevolent and failed to notice that the workmen had screwed the plaque on sideways.

Elsa pressed an auto-dial button and sighed with relief as Jez Stokes picked up the call on his home phone – a rarity. The famously wiry, pock-faced Slang bassist was now a tax exile and lived in Ireland most of the year. She'd had no idea whether he would try to make it tonight, or even if he knew about it.

'Are you coming to Odette's launch?' she asked.

'Elsa, my love! Just setting out. Why? Need a lift?' The familiar Scouse voice was as chirpy as usual.

'No – a favour.' She cut to the chase faster than a kid playing Driver. 'Bring some friends.'

'I'm picking up Olaf,' Jez laughed. 'Don't get much friendlier than that.'

'No – I mean *friends*. Get your arse down to the Cobden and drag them out. Pull favours, use blackmail, give head. Anything.'

'Shit!' he groaned. 'Are we talking Dana?'

'Worse. Possibly even Nicholas Parsons,' Elsa confessed.

'Christ! Robbie's in town – I'll try and track him down,' Jez promised. 'And the Gals might fancy a night on the town.'

'They'll be at the Clinic.' Elsa remembered the Meg Mathews connection. 'I'm fetching them now.' She sounded a lot more confident than she felt.

'Atta girl,' Jez laughed. 'In that case, I'll try for something really sensational.'

'Who?' Elsa couldn't think of anything much bigger than Oasis.

'Wait and see,' Jez cackled. 'Odette's a lovely girl. She needs a break and I have a few rather remarkable beaux whose strings I can pull if desperate. Let's just say I haven't forgotten the sensation of stubble against thigh in a certain public toilet not far from Beverly Hills . . .'

As she flipped her phone shut, Elsa supposed there were benefits to having a friend in a rock band. He might never be around for birthdays, weddings or funerals but he sure as hell knew how to create a media furore in a hurry.

As she trotted to her car, holding on to the bump which seemed to be hosting a minor aerobics work-out inside, she spotted a threatening-looking gaggle coming from the direction of Angel tube station, emitting a plume of combined cigarette smoke as they passed a noisy pub which seemed to quieten and shrink back from the pavement. There was something familiar about the way they walked, about the *Reservoir Dogs* sense of purpose, the don't-mess-with-me stride, the silent determination, particularly of the short, sinister leader. It couldn't be? Surely Odette wouldn't have invited them? She knew how rowdy and dangerous they were, how likely to start a fight and cause a disruption . . .

'Clod?' Elsa asked cautiously.

The shortest and meanest of the group stalled for a moment and peered warily past the after-work drinkers gathered outside the pub.

'Elsa? Ees that you?' a machine-gun voice demanded in a strange staccato accent, which was part French tobacco and wine, part jellied eels and light ale. 'Eeet is! Stone ze crows, you leetle darleen'. Look, Monny, Craig, Papa. Eeet is Odie's leetle school friend, Elsa.'

Clod Fielding always referred to Elsa as Odette's 'school friend' even though the two had not met until university. Several grunts from Clod's throng acknowledged Elsa's presence.

Oh, God. Perhaps she should call Euan on his mobile and

tell him it was beyond Dana and Nicholas Parsons. It was Lionel Blair.

Clod turned beadily to Elsa. 'Where ees thees café of Odette's, huh? Eet's parky out, no? And I need a seat – my feet are keeling me.' Elsa noticed to her amazement that Clod – queen of the fluffy house slippers – was wearing a pair of very high, strappy heels which looked suspiciously designer. No doubt funded by Odette, she decided. Her mother was a shameless freeloader.

'Oh, it's over there.' She waved in the general direction of the club, making sure her expansive gesture took in most of Islington. Finally escaping to her car, she groaned as she spotted a yellow parking ticket tucked under the wiper.

As Elsa sped away from Islington, a long, lean and very old Aston Martin drew up beside the parking space she'd just vacated and started to reverse in at a rakish angle which scraped paint from its wing as it came into contact with the Volvo parked in front. Its blonde driver didn't notice the impact as the loud rock music pounding from the car's stereo obliterated all external noise.

Cyd Francis sang along to one of Mask's biggest hits – 'Sonic Jet to Heaven' – in her famous, whisky-soaked, rasping voice, tears sliding down her face. She wasn't particularly upset; she always cried when she listened to the song and heard Jobe's tarantella beat throbbing beneath the melody as he thrashed his skins as though drumming himself to death. It was frantic, inspired, suicidal, beautiful. Cyd was so transported she unknowingly shifted the Volvo on to the pavement with her crumpled wing as she forced the Aston into the space and cut the engine – and music – to a deathly hush. London bustled around her, but she barely heard it. Dear old London. So quaint. So familiar. So ugly. She hadn't been back for years. Elsa never invited her to visit. She knew so little of her daughter's life here and so few of her friends that when darling Odette had sent her an invitation to her new restaurant, Cyd knew she had to come.

Odette found it next to impossible to wriggle into Juno's yellow dress.

'It's just too tight, Juno babes.'

'Nonsense – I'm much bigger than you,' Juno tutted, heaving a stretch of custard-coloured fabric along her friend's arm with a rubbery squeak. 'It took me almost half an hour to get in and I used talcum powder. Brace yourself.'

'God, I look ridiculous,' Odette groaned, covering her face. It was a far cry from being dressed by Selena at Harvey Nicks. The prospect of Calum seeing her like this was so humiliating her confidence had all but deserted her. 'Why am I so hopeless? I can't organise anything. I was such a fool to think I could do this. And now I look like a fucking yellow pepper.'

'Crap!' Juno puffed indignantly. 'It's a great dress, and it's going to be a great night. Have another slurp of this.' She thrust a vodka and Coke under Odette's nose. The mix was so heavy on the vodka it was the colour of ginger beer.

When at last Odette struggled into the dress and stroked out the rubber wrinkles, Juno whistled. 'Wow, you look fantastic! Like a page-three girl. Those knicks will have to come off, though.'

Odette felt her last reserves of pride trickle away. Her ideal party frock was at least a third bigger, triple the cost and three times as long. Because Juno's high-heeled gold mules were several sizes too small, she was wearing her own black stilettos, intended to be matched with a demure red wool dress. Twinned with the tightest, yellowest, shiniest and shortest dress she had ever seen, they made her look like an extra in a Lynda La Plante vice thriller. She was dressed for a Tarts and Vicars party, not a club launch.

'Perhaps I need another drink,' she told her friend, as much to stop Juno bouncing around telling her how fabulous she looked as anything else.

'Sure thing, boss,' Juno joked, swaggering to the desk to retrieve the vodka bottle.

'Oh, Christ!' Odette covered her eyes. 'I'm not ready. This place isn't ready.'

'You really have to take those pants off.' Juno cleared her throat awkwardly. 'You've got terrible VPL.' She'd never seen her friend like this and it was deeply unsettling. Odette was always so driven. She never experienced crises of confidence or panic attacks like other mere mortals.

'Yeah,' Odette downed a vodka in one, 'Visible Party Lunacy.'

Elsa double-parked the Saab on Dean Street and shoved her Islington ticket under the wiper again in the hope a warden would think they'd already ticketed it.

The press pack was already assembled outside the Clinic, vying for position as they snapped the comings and goings of London's media darlings. As Elsa crossed the road she spotted Tara Palmer-Tomkinson flashing a lot of slim leg between Merc and door amidst a flurry of white-light explosions. A moment later, attention had been turned to a ridiculously long white stretch limo from which spilled the latest boy band sensation, All4One, all dressed in identical long purple satin coats so that they looked more like a bunch of young archbishops than a pop-pouting posse. Elsa was suddenly struck by the contrast between this and the OD Club, with Stan hanging around outside in his ridiculous cult cassock. This was so professional, so slick, so media. Calum Forrester knew precisely what he was doing, so why the hell was he doing it here and not in Islington?

Suddenly Elsa spotted her way in. Shuffling irritably along the crowded pavement towards her was the *Outing*'s notoriously crotchety food critic, Spike Chambers. A short, fat dyed-blond former punk, Spike was an unlikely food critic. He was as laddish as beer and kebabs, lived for Chelsea FC and Sunday league football and liked nothing better than a huge fry-up at a greasy spoon on a Sunday morning. He made no secret of the fact that he loathed most modern British restaurants and the overpriced, over-fancy food they produced. Yet such were the strength of his opinions and the power of his prose that every restaurant longed for the famous old battered leather jacket to be pegged in their cloakroom while he settled down at a table for one to peruse the menu. His weekly column was a London institution. Odette kept every one of them filed on big binders. Elsa had seen them, neatly stacked on one of her minimalist bookshelves, alongside Jackie Collins, Judith Krantz and Odette's literary idol, Barbara Taylor Bradford.

'Spike!' Elsa grabbed a leather-jacketed arm before the reviewer could get close to the door.

'Elsa.' He recognised his colleague's girlfriend straight away, having harboured something of a follicle crush on her since they first met at a gig Euan was reviewing. He was fascinated by her huge cloud of curly hair, and even now could not resist reaching out and giving it an indulgent stroke, poking his fingers through the corkscrews and then pulling them straight as though toying with a telephone wire. 'Amazing stuff – so s-sensual.'

Elsa didn't mind. Spike was immensely likeable, once you got beyond the aggressive prose. In person, he was gentle with a disarming stutter.

'I didn't imagine you'd be here.' She was surprised. 'I thought you hated foodie parties?'

'S-self congratulatory s-social wanking,' Spike agreed heartily, pulling gently at another corkscrew and shuddering delightedly. 'I only c-came because I s-simply have to talk to C-callum Forrester.'

'You and me both,' Elsa said in surprise. She imagined Spike would find Calum as easy to get hold of as an eager double-glazing salesman.

'The little s-shit is s-so elusive that one has to lower one's s-self to attend his revolting s-soirées.' Spike smiled sadly. 'Are you c-coming in?'

'I'm not invited.' Elsa tossed her hair slowly from one shoulder to the other, watching as Spike's eyes almost glazed over with rapt delight. Shaking her hair out behind her, she added, 'Unless . . .'

'Come in with me!' he almost pleaded, taking her hand in his pudgy one.

The restaurant was heaving with famous faces all trying to stand very close to the two or three lucky press photographers who had been allowed inside the sterile, all-white sanctum. Everything inside Clinic was glacial, from floor to ceiling. The crockery was white, the chairs and tables, the pictures, the flowers, the staff dressed in white suits.

Spike shook his head as a waitress offered them white frosted champagne flutes on a tray. 'I'll have a beer and my c-companion would like something non-alcoholic.'

A roving reporter from the regional television round-up, *London Evening News*, was homing in with a small-screen smile and big ambitions. 'Spike Chambers – hello, Fenella Rush, *LEN*. May I have a quick sound-bite?'

'If you must,' he sighed.

Elsa stepped back and instantly saw Calum. He was standing close by, leaning next to a tall, thin man whom she vaguely recognised. A musician, perhaps, or an actor?

But before she had a chance to step forward and say something, Fenella the ambitious local television reporter butted her out of the way and lunged.

'Calum! I'm just about to have a word with Spike Chambers. I wonder if I could do the two of you together? I understand you're great adversaries so the dynamic would make wonderful television.'

Who did she think she was? Elsa thought sourly. Kirsty Wark? Then Calum said something which made her open her eyes wide.

'Far from being adversaries, we're old pals, aren't we, Spike? In fact we're going into business together, aren't we?'

Elsa looked at Spike in surprise.

'Ah, yes, well . . .' He cleared his throat.

'Hold it!' Fenella ordered, taking them both by surprise. 'We'll get this on tape. Just a sec.' She checked that her microphone was switched on and patted her solid helmet of highlighted hair before starting to talk to camera.

'Well, here I am at *the* restaurant party of the year talking to two of London's most influential foodies, the *Outing*'s legendary reviewer and leather jacket wearer Spike Chambers, and restaurant impresario Calum Forrester. Now I always understood you to be old sparring partners, but I gather that's all changed and you're going into business together? Calum?'

'Indeed, but I'm afraid that's all rather secret at the moment. We're both here tonight to celebrate the success of the Clinic in its first year. From its opening last winter to today, a midweek table for four has become the most sought-after location in the whole country . . .'

And so Calum smoothly spieled on in perfect PR press release fashion, while Spike stood beside him looking red and uncomfortable.

Elsa watched Calum murderously, longing for him to mention the OD. She remembered him as being a scruffy, broken-nosed hooligan who always wore stupid pork-pie hats and football shirts, yet tonight he was dressed in understated black Armani, his short, curly blond hair cleanly slicked off his angular face. The customary thick-rimmed, yellow-tinted specs had been replaced by clear, metal-rimmed ones. He had nothing of his younger brother Finlay's beauty, but suddenly Elsa saw the formidable force that lay behind his cold, level gaze and flawless cool. He looked as though nothing on earth could rattle him. There was a strange sort of sex appeal about him, a jagged elegance which was both frightening and deeply attractive.

And then it struck her why Odette was so untogether, why the OD was in such a mess. She'd done it all for Calum.

Fenella the automaton news hound was doing a perfumed Paxman on Spike now. 'Tell me, Jacket, why have you come here tonight when you've been so openly critical of the restaurant in the past? Didn't your review say of it . . .' she glanced at her notes and read out '. . . "an emotionless leuco-cube in which lobotomised, anorexic staff vacillate between the arctic poles of kitchen and customer, delivering dishes so ostentatiously named that ordering feels like delivering a Shakespeare monologue into a void."?'

'You're paraphrasing,' he muttered, turning even redder. 'I would never write a sentence that long.'

Elsa glanced at her watch and wished Fenella would get a wiggle on. This interview was taking so long she could produce a one-hour special. It wasn't even as though Calum and Spike were particularly hot news when all around them stars of film, fashion and chart were slurping champagne, wolfing up bite-sized Shakespearean monologues and discussing whether to go on to the Nero, Office Block or Brown's. Just from where she was standing, Elsa could see at least two major-league soap stars, an All Saint, Jude and Sadie, three supermodels, the Leonard brothers, several Brit Pack film stars and Denny Rees, the gangland-connected footballer-turned-novelist who had a reputation for being the most dangerous man in London. Fenella might want to show off her knowledge of the restaurant scene but she wouldn't impress the Surrey housewife sitting on her floral Draylon sofa who spotted the Fiennes brothers wandering behind the heads of the interviewees in search of their coats.

'Well, thank you both very much,' Fenella was winding up at last. As she drifted away in search of another target, Elsa saw Spike turn to Calum and hiss something, at which Calum batted him away and muttered, 'Later, later.' Returning to Elsa's side, Spike – now puce in the face – stroked her hair for a few seconds to calm himself down.

'What's wrong?' She noticed that his hands were shaking.

'I always get nervous doing interviews.' He shrugged evasively. 'And I fucking hate C-Calum Forrester.'

'So much for old pals going into business together,' she joked. 'What's all that about?'

For a moment Spike seemed on the verge of confessing something, but he looked away, squinted hard for a moment or two and then nodded to where Calum was disappearing through a very discreet white security door hidden behind a tall white cube sculpture.

'If you want to have a word yourself, then now's your chance,' he told her in a low whisper. 'The code's five nine one two – I've just seen him punch it in. Ten to one young Cal's just gone to spy on us all from his flight deck.'

'His what?' Elsa balked.

Spike adopted his conspiratorial about-to-confess look, stopped himself and then seemingly changed his mind once more, sighing irritably. 'Fuck it. The whole place is rigged up with c-cameras, Elsa – or at least so I'm told. All Cal's bars and restaurants are the s-same – a voyeur's playground. He likes to watch people eat. It's like a kinky fetish. But print that and I'd be s-sued to high heaven. It's all very discreet. Very hidden.'

'The OD hasn't got cameras,' she said mindlessly, looking around the room for lenses. She couldn't see any. It all seemed a bit far-fetched.

'The what?' Spike was nonplussed for a moment and then stabbed his finger in the air in recognition. 'Oh, your friend's club in N1. I thought Calum had pulled out of that. Is it ever going to open? It's a bit of a joke, isn't it?'

'It's opening tonight,' she told him in surprise. 'Didn't you get the press pack?'

'Yeah, sure – Euan's been banging on about it for weeks. But I got a fax through today saying that it had been c-cancelled again.'

'What fax?'

'Came through about three. Bloody short notice – must have got a lot of people's backs up. I assume the licences haven't been granted or s-something?'

'It hasn't been cancelled!' Elsa was furious. 'It's going on right now and half the people who are here were supposed to be going there.'

When she slipped discreetly over to the white door and leaned back against the wall pretending to be a lonely guest scanning the room, she was unpleasantly aware that her heart was thumping like mad. She felt as though she was about to leap Avengers-style through a glass window, gun aloft, to catch a Russian super-spy ordering missiles, not slip into a restaurant office and have a quiet word with the owner. It was ridiculous. However unbelievable Spike's voyeur rumours were, she still glanced all around her in search of cameras and then tapped in the number so swiftly she fell through the door in surprise when it opened.

Calum was certainly on the other side. But he wasn't spying on his guests. He was buried inside one of them: the statuesque soap actress girlfriend of the very famous, very aggressive footballing novelist Denny Rees.

'I want to go to the Clinic party,' Finlay grumbled as Lydia told the cabby to stop outside the OD. 'Everyone'll be there, sugar.'

'We're supporting my friend,' she told him sweetly, fishing in her bag for a tenner.

'What about my brother?' Finlay played with the ashtray, refusing to get out.

'He should be here too,' Lydia said simply. She hadn't really bothered following Odette's progress in setting up the club, all that business talk bored her, but she had a vague recollection that Calum Forrester was involved. It seemed a bit mean to host another party on the same night as the OD opened. Not that Lydia imagined Odette would be too bothered. She was such a brilliant organiser that the world and his trophy wife would be here.

'It looks good.' She stood on the pavement and admired the exterior.

Amazingly, now that all the bell pulls, beads and shower curtains were up in the windows, the effect almost worked. Lights filtered out through different layers of diaphanous fabric, sparkled on the beads and laid claim to an exotic, bohemian interior which only the lucky few could access. It was part bordello, part Indian restaurant, but it was certainly eye-catching.

Inside, the lobby was deserted apart from a couple of bored-looking photographers who lifted their cameras tiredly when the doors swung open. Spotting Lydia they both adjusted their zooms excitedly.

'Don't bother, I'm just beautiful, not famous.'

Recognising her friend's voice, Juno exploded out of the cloakroom where she had been trying to make her outfit a little less ghastly by cutting out a cleavage with nail scissors. 'Lyds!'

'Juno, what are you wearing!'

Juno had a reputation for dressing eccentrically, but this was her most extreme fashion choice yet. She was wearing what appeared to be a tablecloth with a hole cut in the middle for her neck. It was belted with one of the thick bell ropes and she had a strange little cream skullcap pinned on her blonde bob that looked at first glance like a bald patch. Draped around her neck was a long chain with a heavy wooden cross on it.

'You look like a student at a toga party, sugar,' Finlay cackled delightedly.

'I'm an acolyte,' Juno bristled, adjusting her tablecloth. 'Stan wanted me to be Joan of Arc but I almost put my back out carrying that six-foot cross everywhere so he's put it in the men's loos. I have an incense burner – look!' She dived into the cloakroom and fetched a long broom handle from which a gold-sprayed cluster of unlit joss sticks was dangling on a loo chain. 'I refuse to wave it around. It's belittling. I haven't let Odette see it. She'd start crying again.'

'But the place looks fantastic.' Lydia had wandered across to peer into the dining room. 'This is sensational – so gothic. Where is everyone?'

'That's the whole point. Practically no one's turned up, not even the staff – just a few friends, Vernon the bank manager and Odette's nutty family.'

'Clod's here?' Lydia groaned.

Juno nodded. 'On her second bottle of red wine and telling anyone who'll listen that her daughter's a lesbian. Odette won't come out of her office. There are fewer than thirty people here and enough food for three hundred.' Juno stashed the broomstick away again and nodded towards the stairs to her left. 'The only saving grace is Elsa's mother, who's arrived looking fantastically sixties and is singing *a capella* in the bar until Euan's band friends turn up. Everyone's enthralled. Jay's down there taking endless photographs. He thinks he's gone to heaven.'

'Cyd Francis is here?' Lydia gasped rapturously. 'I must meet her!' She dashed downstairs on endless legs, desperate to see the woman in whose image she had modelled herself.

'Get out!' Calum screamed, his ugly angular face twisting into a contorted mask of bone and sinew like a Picasso sketch.

'Hello, Tandi, isn't it?' Elsa clicked the door closed behind her and regarded Calum's companion thoughtfully. *Hello!* must have done a heck of a lot of air-brushing in the recent Denny-and-Tandi-at-home spread, she decided.

As Calum hastily pulled himself out, Elsa noted he was using the tradesman's entrance.

Excellent. Now trying to persuade him that legendary football thug Denny might be pissed off to hear that his wife was being screwed just metres from his champagne-quaffing presence would be pretty easy, although Tandi admittedly had a bit of a reputation for wandering. This delightful development was another matter. Calum had entered the sacred hollow. To an old-fashioned East End boy like Denny that would mean only one thing. Revenge. Serious Crime Squad revenge.

'Calum, I have a little favour to ask.' Elsa smiled sweetly. 'It won't take long, but I think you should use the phone and order some taxis straight away to save time.'

He was so shocked that he distractedly asked 'How many?' to stall for time as he pulled his trousers up.

'Oh – about thirty should do it.'

Elsa drove towards Islington ahead of her convoy, amazed that she'd pulled it off. Calum seemed to have convinced his guests that the Clinic party was just a ruse to lead them to the launch of the decade. He might have made his announcement in a voice that suggested he'd just been to the dentist and had five teeth removed, but he had said it, and most of his guests had believed him, and as far as Elsa was concerned, that's what counted. What was even better, he'd ordered all the cabs on the Clinic's account. The trendiest eatery in London was completely empty for the first time in a year and Odette was about to have a very, very busy bar.

Elsa slotted her mobile into the car kit and called Euan on his. The background noise was unexpected: a single, familiar female voice appeared to be singing 'Stormy Weather'. Elsa assumed it was a tape. The band clearly hadn't turned up yet. Nor, it seemed from the lack of crowd chat, had anyone else. Well, that was about to change.

'Prepare yourself for a surprise,' she laughed, suddenly realising what she'd just achieved. 'I'm about to hold a Clinic at the OD Club.'

'Love of my life!' Euan whooped appreciatively. 'Will you have my babies?'

'Yup.' Elsa smiled into her rear-view mirror as the snake of cab lights turned into the Euston Road behind her.

'Prepare yourself for a couple of surprises too,' he told her over a crackle of interference. 'Jez has just turned up with . . .'

'Who? You're breaking up,' Elsa shouted, waiting for a set of traffic lights to turn green.

Euan repeated the name, adding, 'And your mother's here too.'

Elsa ignored the flurry of horns behind her as the lights changed and the Saab stayed put. The news that a hugely famous rock star who had recently been involved in an international sex scandal – and hadn't given an interview since – was currently drinking Watermelon Crushes at the OD was shocking enough. The fact that her own mother was on stage singing live for the first time in ten years was almost enough to induce labour four months early.

Saskia found Odette in her office watching a docu-soap about journalists on the vast flat screen she'd had installed with the singular purpose of catching her favourite soap *Londoners* four nights a week. Her yellow rubber dress was wrinkling up like an old pepper skin, eyes were puffed to nothing, black hair all over the place. She didn't even seem to notice that Ferdy had his head on her lap and was dribbling contentedly into her crotch.

At least the dress was wipe-down, Saskia realised in relief.

'You've got to come out,' she announced firmly. 'People are asking about you.'

'What people?' Odette laughed bitterly, not taking her eyes from the screen.

'You shouldn't have had the offices sound-proofed.'

'I know.' Odette rubbed her face, dragging the last of her wept-away mascara from her cheeks. 'I can't even bear to think what that cost me. I'm fucking ruined.'

'No – it was worth it.' Saskia smiled slowly, reaching for the remote control to mute the television's sound before opening the door behind her again. A wave of chatter and laughter and music and glasses clinking hit Odette like a warm punch in the ear.

'How many?' she croaked nervously.

'Over two hundred,' Saskia laughed. 'And more are arriving every minute. I can't even start to A-list the names. The press are ganging up outside. There's television and everything.'

Odette opened her mouth and then closed it again. She

looked at Saskia, and then at Ferdy, and then back to the screen where the final credits were rolling.

'Veronica Prior,' she read out the producer's name mindlessly, adding, 'I know her – used to work in commercials, too. She's made good, hasn't she?'

'And so have you!' Saskia wailed in delighted frustration. 'It's a complete storm, Odette, listen.' She opened the door again. 'We're turning them away. They love it here.'

Odette still didn't move. She rubbed her eyes again and reached for her vodka glass, but it was empty. 'And Calum?' she asked shakily.

'Oh, he's here,' Saskia giggled. 'He organised the whole thing. Apparently he made an announcement at the Clinic party, saying that he was getting bored and knew of a really exciting new place to go to which was going to be the hottest spot in London. Then he ordered hundreds of cabs and brought everyone here. He had it planned all along.'

'Really?' Two very tiny blue eyes peeked across at her in disbelief.

'Really,' Saskia laughed. 'You can't move for celebrities in the bar.'

'Calum didn't even tell me,' Odette said in a small voice. 'He obviously knew I couldn't take the pressure.' Tears slid down her face.

Saskia shook her head, walking across the room so that she could perch on the sofa arm beside her boss. She couldn't believe she had been so terrified of Odette once. She had seemed so utterly businesslike then, so efficiently prioritised and impatient, that Saskia had quaked. Now she saw that Odette wasn't superhuman after all. Her drive was a defence mechanism. Inside that hard, force-shield shell there was a soft core that was as vulnerable as the little pink pad on a kitten's paw.

'I can get you out there acting like the ultimate hostess in ten minutes flat. Guaranteed,' Saskia promised. 'I have quite a bit of experience at this sort of thing.'

'Make-up?' Odette peered at her scrubbed face doubtfully.

'No, wobblies,' Saskia confessed. 'It's a long story I won't bore you with, but I went totally barmy for six months. Yet I could fool the world into thinking I was outrageously happy; I could make myself look great, even when I'd cried all night and drunk the best part of a litre of vod. I know the techniques.'

'Do it!' Odette laughed, suddenly euphoric and desperate to see Calum.

'No problem.' Saskia chewed her lip worriedly. She'd dealt with a lot of horrifying things – huge weight gain, spots, self-inflicted cuts, rooty hair. But never had she experienced eyes as puffy as Odette's.

'Whatever you do, don't take the dark glasses off,' Saskia muttered into her ear ten minutes later. 'Fantasise you're Magenta Devine.'

Odette wasn't listening. She was staring. Staring at the famous faces, at the beautiful food on trays, at the bustling press, at the sheer numbers. Hundreds and hundreds. All in her club.

'Everyone wants to get in,' Saskia giggled. 'Some tout called Dream Ticket has even set himself up outside selling invites for fifty quid each.'

Downstairs, the bar was heaving. Odette waved at some friends, but they clearly didn't recognise her in her yellow dress and dark glasses. God knows what Saskia had done to her hair – she hadn't bothered taking it in – but it appeared to be all over the place. What was weird was that while she was staring at them, the rich and the famous were staring back. Really staring. A whisper was spreading around, 'That's the owner,' 'Who?' 'Over there – the pneumatic brunette in the yellow dress.' 'Jesus, she's amazing – who is she?' 'I think her name's Odette something.' 'Is she French?' 'Was she in porn films?' 'Must have been – just look at those tits.'

Odette heard none of this. Cyd Francis's sweet, sultry voice was singing 'Fever' with such erotic resonance that beer bottles were being held over bulging crotches all around the bar. Odette watched in awe. She had only ever met Cyd dressed in country scruffs with a scrubbed face and her hair tied back in a scarf. The woman must have been close to sixty but she looked fantastic, that wild blonde mane tipping over the slatey grey eyes, the upturned nose still dusted with summer freckles, the huge, sensual mouth caressing the words in a breathy, melodic union of voice and lyric. She was such a star. Even the dress – a genuine sixties Biba relic with moth holes at the hem and faded coat-hanger marks on the shoulders – looked like the latest Galliano creation on her.

When Cyd headed to the bar for a whisky break, she was immediately surrounded by press and admirers. Brushing them away, she meandered towards her daughter, extracting a Gauloise from her cigarette case and dangling it between her curling lips. It was lit in an instant by a salivating admirer.

Cyd breathed out several smoke rings and turned to Odette. 'Now you,' she said in her deep, hypnotic voice, 'are the most attractive woman in this room. You must tell me who you are.'

'Mum, it's Odette,' Elsa laughed, mouthing, 'She's pissed,' to Lydia who was looking as though a light fitting had just fallen on her.

Cyd blinked. 'Odette?' she laughed – a delighted Ferrari rev of a noise. 'And no wonder – I should have guessed. This place will be the making of you, my dearheart. You have found a stage on which to dance at last, my little ballerina.'

'I think they want you to sing again, Mum,' Elsa urged as the introduction to 'Goodness Gracious Me' started up with camp aplomb. 'Remember when you sang this with Serge Gainsbourg?'

'Ah, dear sweet Serge,' her eyes creased affectionately. 'He only asked me to record that duet because he wanted to bed me. Little did he know I would turn out to have such talent; I have him to thank for the platinum albums and the sell-out Vegas shows. When Jobe stopped recording, this voice saved us from bankruptcy more than once.' She tried out a few rumbling bass notes.

Elsa's eyes bulged. Her mother's albums had always gone straight into the bargain bin. And her one Vegas show had been supporting Mask, who had split up – yet again – after the first night and cancelled the tour, largely because the rest of the band took issue with Jobe's decision to put his wife on the bill. Admittedly Cyd was now a kitsch cult, but her ego was wearing earplugs.

The bar crowd had started a slow-hand clap in eager antici-pation of another set.

'You're audience awaits. Mum,' Elsa managed to keep a straight face.

'Sure, sure – I'm having such fun.' Cyd squeezed Odette's arm. 'Such a success. Reminds me of Studio 54.'

'She was never there,' Elsa laughed as Cyd exploded back on stage. But Odette had already gone.

When the doctor part of the song was taken up, Elsa gaped at the stage again in surprised recognition. The pop star with the international sex scandal hanging over his head was hamming up the old Peter Sellers song for all he was worth, gazing into the eyes of the sixties icon.

'Where did Odette go?' she asked Lydia, who was watching Cyd in mesmerised awe.

'No idea. Do you really think your mother meant that about Odette being the most attractive woman in the room, or do you think she was just trying to cheer her up?'

'Oh, she meant it,' Elsa nodded. 'And she's right. There's something suicidally sexy about Odie tonight. I've never seen it before. She looks feral.' With a lurching start, she realised there was only one other person in the building who possessed the same dangerous, demonic sex appeal. Calum. But he was very controlled, very sober and very, very angry.

At that moment Juno bounced up, face pink from dancing. 'I feel such a prat. I just told Kate Moss she looks a bit like Kate Moss. Come and dance!'

Odette walked into her packed restaurant and stopped in shock. Waiters were galloping between the tables like gymkhana ponies, taking orders, or proudly bearing the specially designed OD plates laden with tens of replicas of those test dishes which Odette and Ferdy had wept over only a week earlier. Then, they had agonised about whether to balance the rice-wine and milk-poached turbot fillet on three mangetout and an asparagus cartwheel or shiitake mushrooms and an artichoke heart. Now dozens of artichoke hearts were being crammed into appreciative mouths all around her.

A fat drunk clutching a cigar and a Cognac lurched past Odette and then backtracked precariously.

'Gather you set up this place – bloody fantastic.' He held out his hand and pumped hers, leering at her boobs in the obscene rubber dress. 'Admit I wasn't planning to come here tonight. Thought all the cancellation stuff – 'specially today – was the last straw in disorganisation.'

'Cancellation? Today?' Odette queried, but he droned on.

'Damned fine marketing that – make a place appear a shambles then reveal it to be an utter gem. Clever of old Calum. And you, of course, m'dear, although I assume it was his idea. Typical of him – bloody shrewd at reading trends that bugger. Was thrilled to bits when he suggested two hundred people move on from the Clinic. Never known anything like it, and we all needed a change of scene. Place has got a bit stale. This is a different matter. Ingenious. Best of luck to you.' He shambled off.

Then Odette saw Calum, and the dress seemed to shrink to the size of a rubber glove, its fingers pinching between her ribs. He was leaning over a table in the far corner, talking to Alex Hopkinson, Florian Etoile and two men in suits who, she noticed in delight, had not only finished their plates of food but looked as though they'd licked them too.

Calum caught her looking and raised a thin blond eyebrow before walking slowly towards her.

A harassed-looking bishop rushed over to her bearing a clipboard, but Odette's eyes didn't move from Calum's.

Stan, who had heard about the Clinic party from Saskia and doubted her belief that it was all a PR exercise, was desperate to warn Odette.

'Odette, I think you should know . . .' he started, but was pulled aside by a very good-looking, very camp blond boy demanding to know when a table would be ready because the restaurant they'd just come from had double-booked them. Not liking his click-fingers superiority, Stan was about to snap there were plenty of tables going at the Clinic right now, but he couldn't deny Odette a single paying customer, however brattish. And there was something curiously familiar about those high cheekbones and swimming-pool blue eyes.

'About an hour – can I have your name?' he fretted, glancing over his shoulder at Odette who was kissing Calum on the cheek and being led to his power table.

'Sylvian,' the boy drawled in the laziest South Ken accent Stan had ever heard. 'Mungo Sylvian.'

Stan spluttered in recognition. 'Felix's brother?'

'Sure – he's here too. Table for four, as soon as you can. Do I know you?' He studied Stan curiously.

'Yeah.' He glanced over Mungo's shoulder to Felix, Phoebe, and a broader, sandier version of Felix who was looking simply amazed by the whole experience. 'You know me.'

His old friend Phoebe had recognised Stan and doubled up with laughter at the bishop's outfit.

'How coincidental.' Mungo flashed an insincere smile and turned back to his family.

'Stan, darl!' Phoebe hugged him. 'You've found your calling at last.'

'It was fucking shouting,' Stan grinned, embarrassed. 'I deserve a medal for this.'

'And this.' She looked around at the room. 'All your doing, I guess?'

She and Stan had dated briefly a few years earlier. Saskia liked to joke that she and Phoebe had traded Stan and Felix, but the truth was a lot more complicated and painful than a simple partner-swap. He watched as Phoebe's bright green eyes drank everything in. She was a clever girl, if a little sharp-tongued. There weren't many people who could live with Felix Sylvian – or any Sylvian for that matter. The experience had almost killed his darling Sask, and Stan disliked the family intensely, however hard Saskia tried to persuade him she bore no more hard feelings.

'Actually, it was Odette who set this all up,' he said humbly, looking at his artwork. 'I was just painting by numbers.' He stiffened as he realised Felix and his brothers had joined them.

'You haven't met Felix's big brother, Jimmy, have you?' Phoebe indicated the big, sandy bear of a man who was gaping across the room at Odette, now sharing a drink with Calum and his cronies.

'So she's the one who owns this place?' he whistled in admiration, his accent strangely exotic compared to the standard Sylvian drawl. 'Stunning-looking creature.'

'Yeah.' Stan decided to put him off. The last thing Odette wanted right now was to get involved with a Sylvian. 'She's a tough old bird. No time for romance, that one. Total ball-breaker.'

'I'll bear that in mind,' Jimmy murmured as Calum called him over to the table.

Odette barely noticed the tall, blond-haired man who was introduced to her as James someone. It was hard to see much wearing her dark glasses – the restaurant was so dim, and she had already met far too many people to remember names. There was nowhere for him to sit and nothing left to offer him to drink so pretty soon he melted away. Odette was relieved. She wanted Calum all to herself. The suits were all talking about Wayne Street's new restaurant, Wardour, which had folded just months after opening.

'Overinvested,' one said darkly. 'Too iconoclastic, food too fussy, waiters too stroppy.' Odette didn't notice him looking around sceptically. She was suddenly aware of a warm hand on her leg. Calum's. She could feel a taut wire of desire pull through from her groin to her toes in response.

'I need to get some air. Come with me, sister.' At last. It was happening. Her plan had been perfect all along.

Beyond the steam-filled, clanking sweatshop of the kitchen, Odette and Calum walked in silence past the bins and into the small staff car park at the rear of the building. It was so cold outside compared to the saturated humidity of the kitchen that Odette felt goose bumps pop up like barnacles through her rubber dress and her short, excited breaths came out steamily in front of her face.

'Thank you,' she murmured. 'Thank you for making it work.'

'You didn't doubt me, did you?' Calum asked in an amused voice, lifting the dark glasses from her nose and then tilting his head to one side so that her face, until then in shadow, was illuminated by the security lights on the building.

'You *did* doubt me.' He studied her puffy eyes closely.

Odette looked down in shame.

'Never doubt me, Odette,' he breathed into her mouth.

She looked up once more into that shadowed, aquiline face, into those frosty white-grey eyes. She had searched for years for her Jonathan. She'd battled and fought misogyny to be as powerful as the man she one day wanted to share her life with. Tonight she'd almost fallen apart thinking it would never happen, yet here he was, breathing into her lips in a way that was just millimetres away from catching the hook of her tongue with his and drawing it coolly into his mouth. He was her match. He'd proven it tonight by taking everything away from her in order to prove just how much he could give.

Stretching across, she kissed him. By god, she kissed him. Mouth against mouth, tongue sliding against tongue, body pressed hotly against body, rubber, skin, wool, cotton, buttons, belly piercing.

Breaking away for breath, Calum fingered her belly ring appreciatively through the rubber, making Odette suck in her diaphragm tautly to flatten her stomach.

'I had no idea you could be so whorey,' he breathed into her ear and then bit the lobe so hard that Odette had to chew her lip to stop herself from squealing. 'You excite me so much tonight. Suck me off.'

'What?' Odette wasn't sure she'd heard him right.

'Suck me off,' he repeated, thrusting a hard, cool tongue into her ear. 'Right here – with the kitchen door open. I want to feel that big, angry mouth of yours wrapped around my cock.'

Odette looked at his ugly-beautiful face, so expectant. It was the first time she had seen him truly excited. His breath was quick, eyes full of pupil, hands squeaking against her rubber dress, moist with anticipation. She licked her lips nervously. Her throat felt dry and hollow as hell, her belly a squirming pit of fear.

'C'mon, sister.' He started to unzip his flies with one hand, the other reaching up to guide her head downwards. 'Don't go all coy on me. It's not as if you've never done it before, is it? I think it's about time you put that lippiness of yours to good use.'

Odette could see a white bulge of underpants poking from the expensive suit fly. In a moment of near-hysteria she suddenly thought it strange that someone like Calum should have such snow-white smalls. How very Jonathan. Then waves of nausea rushed up her throat as fast as a mudslide.

'Fuck off!' She pushed him away violently. 'Who do you think I am?'

He only took a second to recover his composure, zipping himself with a condescending, disappointed sigh.

'No one,' he said simply, backing away. 'You're no one, Odette. You'll always be just that. No one.' With a shrug of his shoulders he wandered inside.

'This place is fantastic!' Jimmy boomed to Calum above the party din in the bar. 'I can't believe you kept it so quiet.' He laughed as he spotted his little brother Mungo dancing with the prettiest member of All4One whilst shooting flirtatious glances at an oblivious Finlay.

Calum didn't reply. He was incandescent with anger, watching his own little brother dancing with Lydia. Determined to score at least one victory that night, he had yet again introduced her to Jimmy, but he had banged on about Africa for too long. In party mood, Lydia had quickly grown bored and drifted back to Finlay's side.

'Beautiful, isn't she?' he tried again, throwing back a mouthful of beer. He'd started to drink fast and hard now, eager for nirvana.

'Who?' Jimmy's restless eyes were searching the room as though looking for someone.

'Lydia.' Calum pointed at her with his bottle, drawing an imaginary line around her perfect silhouette with its rim, his eyes half-focused.

Jimmy shrugged, hardly glancing at her. 'Your brother's a lucky man.'

'It won't last, pal,' Calum snapped. 'Finlay will never make her happy.' He drained the beer, too pissed off, piss-bored and pissed for subtlety.

Very slowly, Jimmy put his glass on the table and turned to him. His deep bass voice was dead-bolted against anger, but Calum could hear it banging to get out. 'You think you could then?'

'No.' Calum shook his head. 'Not me, pal.' His pale eyes bored into Jimmy's. When his friend just looked baffled, he sank tiredly back in his chair. 'Forget it.'

Realising Calum was drunk, Jimmy's shy gaze darted away and scanned the bar once more. 'Fantastic atmosphere. Bloody clever idea of that friend of yours.'

Calum watched Lydia dancing, entranced by the way her body moved.

'London's gonnae be out of fashion in six months,' he muttered.

'This looks set to be a hit to me,' Jimmy laughed.

'Only because I made it one,' Calum snarled. 'I could just as easily let it bomb.' He narrowed his eyes to combat drunken double vision as he watched Odette's posse of friends whooping it up on the makeshift dance floor, Elsa Bridgehouse in its midst with her gonk hair and big Celtic-fan boyfriend. If there was one thing that was guaranteed to make Calum hate a woman it was sharing her bed with a Parkhead pape. Without her, his plan would have worked and Odette would have failed the test as miserably as he'd expected her to.

His efforts so far had been entry level. He'd given her Maurice instead of the Leonards and Ferdy instead of Florian; he'd phoned the agency to fire all her waiting staff and had put on a rival party. There'd been nothing Odette couldn't have coped with, but she had gullibly swallowed the lot. It was what she hadn't swallowed that pissed him off. Seriously pissed him off. Who did she think she was? She was supposed to be mad about him, for Christ's sake.

'Odette Fielding has no idea how hard she'll have to work to keep this place open,' he said to himself with some satisfaction.

'Are you saying she's bitten off more than she can chew?'

Wincing at the unfortunate wording, Calum watched Lydia and Finlay kissing on the dance floor, mouth drinking mouth. 'That depends whether she comes back for a second helping or not.'

Before Jimmy could ask him what he meant, Calum had dropped his beer bottle on the table with a clatter. 'Fuck it, this party's shite. I'm gaun home.'

11

Odette couldn't sleep. Over and over again, she would sit bolt upright in bed with great shuddering gasps of horror and embarrassment. When lying down, she pressed her scrunched face into her pillows and tucked her knees into her chest, curling her toes in shame. She had never felt quite so humiliated in her entire life. The first time she had very truly lost control was the biggest night of her life. Great timing.

She had vague recollections of getting home. Elsa had driven her. 'But I should stay in the club and help tidy up!' Odette had argued. 'The place is a mess.'

'Saskia's sorting that out,' Elsa had countered, waggling Odette's moped keyring fob to let her in through the electronic gates of the warehouse apartment block. 'Let me come in and make you a coffee.'

Odette had refused, storming into her flat in such a drunken rage she'd blackened her knees as she fell up every one of the stairs in her haste, and then snapped the heel off her shoe as she tripped up the last. She'd immediately tried to call a cab to take her back to the club so that she could supervise the locking up, but kept dialling the number wrong. And then nausea took over and she'd bolted to the bathroom to be repeatedly sick before falling into bed.

Now she forced herself to get up and go to the kitchen to make a cup of tea. She didn't really feel like it, but the simple activity distracted her for a moment or two. The flat was freezing; the heating timer was off and the huge space possessed the sombre chill of a church crypt. Odette pressed the over-ride button, cranked the thermostat on to high and turned on the vast fake log fire which she had often imagined her very own Jonathan Hart seducing her in front of. Lately she had envisaged herself entwined beside it with Calum, their naked bodies illuminated by the flickering yellow glow. It was a very eighties mini-series fantasy, very Odette. She'd even contemplated buying a fur rug to replace the old Moroccan one she'd bought on location years ago.

'No point investing in shag-pile if you don't even know how to shag,' she sighed, sinking into her leather sofa. Within seconds she was up again, pacing around, heart thumping, reliving the awfulness of the night.

She'd let everyone down so badly by falling apart like that. Her memory was distorted by too much vodka and overwhelmed by the thought of what had happened with Calum, but she knew she'd lost it big time. She'd branded the club a failure long before the doors opened, had been of no help to anyone at all and – most punishing of all – had acted like a trampy, teenage tease in front of the man she'd set her heart on. The man who, ultimately, had saved her bacon – or should that be *pancetta*? – by staging one of the best publicity stunts in years.

If only she could be mature and modern about Calum. She needed a twenty-first century attitude to life, a Lydia outlook. He'd only wanted a blow job, after all. It wasn't too much to ask.

But for Odette it was much too much to ask. She couldn't just give and take sexual favours as other people seemed to. She knew that most of her friends had slept around before they settled down. From university days until co-habiting cosiness they had all gone out on the pull together. In the early years Odette had been one of the leaders, organising social outings for the specific purpose of meeting her match. But although she was a consummate flirt with a fairly rampant history of kissing in dark night-club corners, at parties, in cabs, and later in private, she had never woken up beside a stranger as the others had. As her job had increasingly encroached upon her social time, she'd gone out on those pulling nights less and hadn't missed the wet, sloppy kisses from beer-breathed men. She'd started to realise that she would never find her Jonathan dancing with his mates in a crowded night club, or clustered in a group of after-work drinkers in the Slug and Lettuce. She'd have to wait for him.

At twenty-one, Odette had seen the decade ahead as one of career progression. She'd calculated that by the age of thirty she would celebrate that hard-won career by matching up with her life partner, possibly her working partner too. While women around her struggled to achieve the Have It All balance of a fulfilling career, a secure home and satisfying love life, Odette concentrated on just two elements. As her beloved Meatloaf put it, 'Two Out Of Three Ain't Bad'.

Over the past decade, she had developed a front to deflect any sexual one-upmanship from both men and women. A combination of earthy tolerance, flirtation and knowing humour worked in her favour. It was a front that insinuated a wealth of sexual knowledge honed from going around the block so often there was a groove worn into the pavement – whereas in truth she'd barely visited the corner shop sexually, and was still on the doorstep in relationship terms.

Odette's sexual history was deeply unsophisticated. She'd had no long-term relationships to speak of and very few short-term ones. Her longest love affair on record had been three months and she attributed that largely to the fact he lived in Amsterdam so they had only seen one another five weekends at most. She hadn't had sex very often at all, and only then with the lights off, in bed, in the missionary position. From the little experience she had, she knew it hurt, it went on too long, it turned men into sweaty, panting, grunting beasts and it made a mess of your sheets. She imagined long-term, companionable love to be very different.

She'd wanted to cut to the chase by missing out on the thrill of the chase and getting the real deal, the *Hart to Hart* marriage. In her total belief that she would get just that, she'd thought she could gain fast-track promotion and by-pass the wandering years, just as she had at work. But it seemed that these days you had to earn your stripes in action, picking any number of targets before you found the right one. Odette had always felt that she'd know when she met him, and this year she had done just that. Only he had qualified through the ranks and she hadn't even sat her entrance exam.

She'd always imagined that Jonathan would teach her all the wonders of the flesh, would free her inhibitions, and that through his love she would stop hating her own body so much. In her self-obsessed vision it had never really occurred to her that he might find that a bit of an effort and would rather she knew what she was doing from the start. If Calum was the other Hart to hers, then all he'd wanted was a blow job, and to her utter shame Odette had never even given one. She hadn't a clue how.

She crouched close to the fire, examining the dark bruises which had formed on her knees like a tomboy's. Running her fingers lightly over the sore skin, she let her hands slide higher so that she was stroking the inside of her thigh, wondering what it would be like to feel Calum touch her there.

'Need a bikini wax,' she told herself, snatching her hand away.

Tonight she had, in all probability, felt the first stirrings of passion at long last. She had no idea what to do with them, how to control the feeling or tame it. She longed for a rulebook, for advice, for clarity. She felt ashamed of her own ignorance.

'Passion,' Odette said the word out loud, playing with the sibilant double 's'. 'Passssssssssion.'

As ever when she was in a state of confusion or crisis, she took out a piece of paper and wrote herself a list. At the top was, 'Get OD in order', with sub-clauses covering staffing, reordering, cash flow and pricing. Beneath it she wrote another heading 'Thank friends for help', with more sub-clauses listing gifts and notes to be bought and written. Underneath that she wrote reminders to arrange another meeting with Vernon, to call Calum and re-establish the working relationship as soon as possible (it had to be done), and to get Juno's dress dry cleaned (could one dry clean rubber?). Finally at the bottom of the list, she wrote the most important reminder of all: 'Deal with passion'. She wasn't sure how, but now that it was part of her schedule for tomorrow, she was certain it was within her capabilities.

It was past six in the morning and still pitch dark outside.

Odette could hear her neighbour's door bang closed as he headed off to his job in the City, anticipating the markets opening. There was no point going to bed again, but it was too early to go to the club or make any calls.

The flat was now sweltering. Ignoring her lukewarm, untouched tea, Odette went to the fridge and took out a bottle of Evian, downing it in one long, thirsty series of gulps so that water streamed down her chin and on to her towelling dressing gown. Chucking the empty bottle in the steel swing bin and sliding the gown off her shoulders, she wandered over to the Stairmaster and set it on its highest level.

It was only when she was pouring with sweat and the light had started to filter in through the windows that Odette realised she was exercising completely naked in full view of every occupant of the warehouse conversion on the opposite bank of the canal.

'Shit!' She jumped off and grabbed her dressing gown, heading into the bathroom for a cold shower.

She hadn't, it seemed, quite got the passion thing under control yet.

12

Calum read the press cuttings from the combined Clinic/OD party as he travelled to West Sussex in the back of Alex Hopkinson's Mercedes. They were as he expected – lots of shots of Cyd Francis and her superstar duet partner, some mention of the odd venue change, a few jokes about the controversial religious drug-addict theme and the green bishop skinhead in particular. There were a fair few name-checks for him and Florian Etoile (ironic, Calum chuckled to himself, as Flo wasn't even involved although he had attended the party). Odette Fielding, her concept, the food, and the exact nature of the club were barely given a passing mention.

The Etoile connection did give him an idea, though. He used Alex's car-phone to call the irascible chef at work in the Desk kitchens, even though he knew it would piss him off.

'Are you sure you cannae make it doon to check out this location today?'

The suggestion was greeted by a tirade of swear words – mostly French and therefore beyond Calum's understanding.

'Okay, okay – I appreciate you're busy, pal,' he soothed. 'Meet me later for a wee blast, huh?'

'I no feeneesh here until after midnight,' Florian exploded. 'I haff to plan menus for next week. What the fuck d'you theenk I am? Superhuman?'

'Sure you are, pal,' he laughed, undeflected. 'Pop into Office Block on your way home. I'll be there from eleven.'

'I try,' Florian huffed. 'Now pees off. I have to stab my pastry chef.'

Calum gazed out of the window as Alex left the M23 and

drove on to the South Downs. The landscape wrapped itself around him like a plump mistress, revealing unexpected beauty in her soft folds. Calum, who preferred his landscapes urban and his women thin, was pleasantly surprised. Even stripped bare and wearing the mottled, grey skin of winter, Mother Nature was a seductive sight.

In the passenger seat beside Alex, Jimmy Sylvian was fast asleep. Thankfully he'd shut up about how much he'd enjoyed last night's party and how sexy the brunette in the yellow dress had looked. 'Shame I didn't get to talk to her properly. She disappeared so early. Bit slack if you ask me – I thought you said she owned the place?'

Calum found his questions unsettling. Odette had dressed like a total tart the night before, so he supposed it was no wonder his friend was mildly interested. Her body was pretty spectacular in a cheap, big-busted way, even if she did have a face like a welder's bench. He'd not been entirely immune himself, although he wouldn't admit it to a living soul. The woman was a pain in the arse, and he needed to keep Jimmy away until he could deal with her.

'She's a total screwball,' he'd murmured. 'Ingenious but unbalanced. Just look at the concept – that druggy Pope thing wasnae a figment of her imagination, you know.'

'How do you mean?'

'She's off her head, pal,' Calum had said, a hint of pity in his voice. 'A Catholic junkie.'

'Christ! Why the hell did you invest money in the place then?'

'She's got a lot worse since I first hooked up in the project,' Calum sighed, and then realising that he needed to keep Jimmy, a big-hearted sentimentalist, on side, loaded on a little pathos. 'She's very charismatic – very persuasive. I think she could be a genius at setting up businesses, but she's got to straighten up fast. The more money we make, the higher the denomination of note she rolls up to snort her fix. I've even contemplated taking her out of the equation entirely – for her own good as much as the future of the business. I want to nurture her, but it's like you used to say about bad cats in the wild. The

116

secret is not to break their spirit, but to remove them from temptation.'

'You mean the cattle killers?' Jimmy's eyes lit up. He was starting to understand a little of Calum's strange environment at last. 'We relocate them far away from cultivated land, in a securely fenced park.'

Calum nodded with quiet satisfaction. 'Odette Fielding needs to be relocated far away from her lines of supply. I've met a lot of women like her, pal. London's crawling with them. Some never straighten out. I'd hoped she would, but . . .' He let the sentiment hang regretfully in the air.

He was relieved when Jimmy's head started lolling sleepily from seatbelt to headrest.

Jimmy could make him feel very small sometimes. In the Mpona game reserve, Jimmy's knowledge of the area and its wildlife had given him enormous power and his word was law – it could make the difference between life and death. His compassion and wisdom were things Calum had admired and envied. In England he had hoped the reverse would be true, that he would be the wise one leading Jimmy around the complicated world of London clubs, bars and restaurants, but it hadn't thus far been the case. Something about Jimmy's huge, loud, powerful presence still made Calum feel weaselly and common. He fingered through the details for Fermoncieaux Hall. It looked magnificent – three times the size of the entire council block his parents had once lived in. He couldn't wait to get there. Alex had been complaining all week that it was too big and too far from London for their needs, but Calum was confident that he could persuade him otherwise. He was in a state of excitement – an estate of excitement. The housing estate kid from the state school wanted to own a stately home.

'Ouch!' Phoebe shrieked as another pin sank into the soft flesh beneath her armpit.

'Sorry, darling – you have to suffer to be beautiful,' Saskia's dressmaker muttered between clenched teeth in which were gripped another five pins.

If she does that one more time I'll punch her in the gob and she can feel what it's like to suffer, Phoebe thought grumpily, narrowing her eyes at her own reflection.

Peach was definitely not her colour. It made her short, mousy hair look mousier, her green eyes look sludgy and her pale skin look positively anaemic. And all those lace ruffles! It was like being measured up for a suburban loo roll cover.

'It looks lovely,' Stan's sister, Helen, sighed dreamily.

She would say that, Phoebe thought murderously. She bloody chose it.

Helen was short and curvaceous with blonde curly hair, very white teeth and a sunbed tan which was about to be deepened by a fortnight in Eilat just before the wedding. Since being asked to be a bridesmaid she'd been on a strict diet and had attended aerobics three times a week. White lace and peach velvet (ending above the knee to show off the toned, tanned legs) had been her idea. She was also keen on a flower coronet from which 'we could trail more flowers like whassername in Hamlet? Orpheus? I loved Mel Gibson in that.'

Phoebe was tall and skinny, with cropped boyish hair, big green eyes and a hooked nose. She'd suggested long, tight tunic dresses in forest green or dark blue with dramatic fur cuffs – not entirely her taste, but suited to a winter wedding. She'd been hoping later to steer Saskia towards something daring like tall fur Russian hats and fur mufflers instead of bridesmaid head-dresses and posies.

Phoebe was Saskia's oldest friend, who had put up with a lot over the years; Helen was about to be part of Saskia's new family. There had been no contest. Peach it was.

'I wonder what's keeping Saz?' Helen glanced at her watch. 'She was supposed to be here half an hour ago. I've got to go in a minute. I've got a lady in for a perm at five.'

'She's probably had second thoughts and is heading towards Rio,' Phoebe said idly.

'Oh, you don't think so, do you?' Helen's big baby eyes widened in horror.

Too easy, Phoebe sighed to herself. Checking out Helen's gullibility rating had been fun at first, but it was getting boring. It was too far off the scale to be challenging. She had no idea how a distrustful cynic like Stan could share so many genes with her.

'Sorry I'm late!' Saskia burst through the door, pulling her coat off as she walked. 'How do you like them?'

'Lovely!' Helen gushed.

Phoebe just smiled benignly. She was determined not to grumble. It was going to be Saskia's big day.

But Saskia was already falling about laughing. 'Oh, darling Freddy. You look like Clinton.'

'What?'

'In imminent danger of being impeached. Do you loathe it?'

'It's not bad,' Phoebe shrugged and then winced as another pin dug in. 'What kept you?'

'Lunch.' Saskia sank down on a sofa covered with fabric swatches and coronets, squishing the lot. 'We had two sittings per table – ninety covers. I'm exhausted.'

'But that's brilliant, isn't it?'

'Not without a maître d' and an executive chef it's not, nor with just five waiting staff and a sommelier who's so hungover he poured out a two-hundred-pound bottle of wine for a customer who'd ordered mineral water.'

'Oh, dear.' Phoebe pulled a sympathetic face. 'Wasn't Ogredette there?'

'She's not an ogre, she's quite likeable once you get to know her.' Saskia picked up a tiara that was lying beside her and tried it on. 'And she was there, actually, working twice as hard as I was. She's amazing. After last night I thought she'd be lying on a therapist's couch all morning, but she was in first thing, stock-checking, reordering and clearing up what was left of the mess from last night. And she bought me this – look.' She pulled a small leather box from her bag. Inside was a Tiffany cross, the latest must-have accessory. 'I'm going to wear it with my going away outfit.'

'Wow!' Phoebe was impressed. 'How thoughtful.'

Saskia nodded. 'And generous. Especially as practically every penny she has is tied up in the club so it's not as though she's got it to burn. I thought she was loaded, but Stan says she's invested the lot – even remortgaged her flat.'

'But the place will make her a fortune, surely?'

Saskia shrugged. 'Hard to tell. Certainly not for a while yet. Even supposing every day is like today, packed out, it'll be months before we break even. And today was what's called "walk-ins", people who turn up in the hope of getting a table. They only did that because of all the publicity last night. That'll last a week at most. What we really need is regular bookings, from regular regulars. And the place is very big.'

'Surely the cabaret club upstairs will help that?'

'Once it's up and running properly,' Saskia agreed. 'But we've only got one-off bookings and unknowns until Christmas. It doesn't get up to speed until the New Year. The restaurant and bar have to carry the place until then.'

'It's all so complicated.' Phoebe shook her head. 'Jimmy completely lost me when he was talking about it last night.'

'Jimmy? Felix's brother?'

Phoebe nodded. 'Didn't he mention anything last night? I thought he'd be picking your brains, and Odette's, but she pushed off as soon as we arrived. I wish you'd introduce me to her.'

'You'll meet her at the wedding. Pick my brains about what?' Saskia wouldn't be side-tracked.

'About opening a restaurant over here. He's thinking about investing in one apparently – with some old friend of his. He wouldn't say much because it's all top secret.'

'He could let Odette have some cash if he likes.'

'They should meet first.' Phoebe hadn't noticed Jimmy being introduced to Odette at the OD opening party. Nor, come to that, had Odette herself.

'I'll invite him to the wedding!' Saskia announced brightly. 'And I'll get Mummy to sit them on the same table.'

Someone else was house hunting that day, although their needs were a lot more modest than Calum Forrester's. Tucked away in a leafy side-street behind Highbury Corner, Euan and Elsa found a tall, thin town house at the rear of which was a walled Japanese garden of such ethereal splendour that at first Elsa thought she'd been transported to a Zen temple.

'The BBC did it in one of those makeover gardening programmes,' the estate agent enthused. 'It would cost thousands to do yourself. Of course, it would only be a matter of throwing some grass seed down if you wanted to put it back,' he added quickly, just in case they didn't like it.

'What sort of grass seed would you recommend?' Euan asked him earnestly to make him think just that. In fact he adored the deep orange walls, the running water border, the gravel swirls and the orange pagoda in the centre, just as he'd loved the simplicity of the slate floors inside the house, the minimalist kitchen, the high ceilings and huge bathroom. Compared to the crowded clutter of their tiny flat it was paradise.

'It's perfect,' he later muttered quietly to Elsa while they lurked at the far end of the daydream garden, out of hearing of the over-eager estate agent.

She gazed towards the rear of the house which was bathed in afternoon sun, its creeping ivy dancing like a thousand green scales on a friendly dragon. 'We can't afford it.'

'We can if we never go out.'

'We're about to have a baby.'

'Exactly. Cancel all evenings out for the next year.'

'Our evenings out are what earn us money,' Elsa reminded him. 'And live-in nannies are expensive.'

'We'll make a huge profit on the flat.'

'Not if you keep telling the truth about the damp and the neighbours, we won't.' Elsa poked him gently in the belly.

'Okay, I'll start lying. And I'll do something else you've been badgering me to do for the last three months.'

'Start flossing your teeth?' Elsa looked delighted.

'Send my novel off to some agents.'

'Oh, Euan.' She hugged him tightly, forcing him to stoop over the bump. 'I mean, that's lovely – really, really good. But it might not buy us this place.'

'We could ask your mother for a loan.'

'No!' She pulled away.

'Why not?' he sighed. 'It's not as though she hasn't offered a hundred times. Or as though she can't afford it. We'll pay it all back.'

'I won't use her like that.'

'She wants to do it, Elsa.' Euan raised his voice in despair.

'Anything I can help with?' The agent had started to hover within earshot.

'We'll talk about this later,' Elsa hissed at Euan, turning to smile at the agent. 'It's lovely, but we have got a couple more to see today so we can't really give you much of an idea until then. We'll call you later.' She marched past him, leaving Euan to wander forlornly behind with the agent, looking at his girlfriend's small footprints in the neat gravel swirls.

'I want you to be executive chef at the OD,' Calum told Florian later that night over a bottle of Rémy Martin in the Office Block's urban chic bar.

'This is a joke, no? I weel not be associated with a restaurant you deliberately want to close.' Florian shook his head violently.

'Keep your fucking voice down,' Calum hissed, looking around the bar.

Florian's anthracite eyes flashed angrily. 'I'm not your pawn, bruzzer. I don't need you to back me any more. I'm a business-man myself now, remember? I haff restaurants of my own.'

'And that's what I'm offering you now.'

'Huh?'

'Trust me, Flo. If you do this then you will own the OD by Christmas. As soon as Odette Fielding is out of the way.'

There was a message from Cyd on the answerphone when Elsa got home from her FMeral show late that night. 'It doesn't matter how late you get back, please call me.' She sounded close to tears.

Elsa pulled off her thick sweater and the old t-shirt of Euan's she was wearing. She loathed the fact that she had to wear all his clothes at the moment to accommodate her burgeoning waistline. Some women hardly showed at twenty weeks, but she was already enormous. Putting the phone on her lap, Elsa settled back in her favourite chair and doodled on her bump with a felt-tipped pen to cheer herself up.

'Mum, it's me,' she sighed as a familiar, throaty voice picked up her call.

'Elsa, is that you? Thank heaven you're back. I've been arrested.'

Her mind spun for a second and then focused tightly. 'Where are you? How much were you carrying?'

'I'm at home – you called *me*, remember?' Cyd sounded confused. 'And I wasn't carrying anything. I was in the car. I wasn't even speeding.'

'So why were you arrested?' Elsa tried to calm down.

'Well, it was last night. I might have had one or two whiskies at the party to calm my nerves. It's good for the voice. They seem to think I was three times over the limit, which is ridiculous. I was driving perfectly well. I'd even managed to change a tape, light a ciggie and navigate my way around the inner London ring road without taking my eyes from the car in front. Unfortunately the car in front had a flashing blue light in the rear window that said "Pull over".'

'Oh, Mum,' Elsa sighed. 'Have you been charged?'

'Afraid so. It was awful, so embarrassing being frisked alongside several ladies of the night and a burglar. I got Charles out of bed. He wasn't best pleased as he says there's no need for a lawyer of his calibre to be present at these things, but at least he drove me home. If he hadn't, the police would have made me stay in the cells overnight to sober up before they'd let me get back in the car.'

'So they haven't taken away your licence?'

'Not yet, thank God, but I don't think I'll be popping to Waitrose much after the court case.'

'Oh, poor Mum. What are you going to do?'

'I suppose I'll have to get a driver.' Cyd giggled huskily, suddenly sounding quite cheerful. 'Actually I rather like the idea of a strapping young man in a peaked cap glancing at me in the mirror and asking where he can drive madam next? I'd be terribly tempted to keep saying "to heaven and back", wouldn't you? Now cheer me up and tell me how the house-hunting is going?'

Elsa could feel her bladder on alert. She'd have to ring off soon and dash for a wee. Bloody pregnancy. 'Not bad – we saw a nice one today.'

'Oh, what's it like? Do tell. Is it that little studio house in Cheyne Walk I told you to look at? It's so pretty around there, and four hundred is seriously good value for the area.'

'Bit cheaper, bit further north.' Elsa looked up as Euan let himself in through the door carrying such a huge bunch of sunflowers that they obscured his view and he fell over the coffee table.

'What was that?' Cyd asked worriedly.

Euan was picking himself up and mouthing 'Who's that?' as he waggled the bent sunflowers at the phone.

'Just Euan coming in,' Elsa told Cyd. 'He's been to a gig. I think he's pissed.'

Euan indignantly mouthed, 'I'm not!'

'Oh, which one?' Cyd asked excitedly, as ever eager to know about the comings and goings on the music scene. 'Any good?'

'A band called Bent Uncle. They're going to be huge.'

'A band called—'

'I heard that too. Where are they from?'

'Ask him yourself. I'll be back in a minute.' Elsa handed the phone to Euan and, kissing him forgivingly on the cheek, galloped to the loo just in time.

Knowing that Euan and Cyd would gas on for as long as they could, Elsa sat back on the loo seat for a moment and pulled her hair off her face. Last night had exhausted her far more than she cared to admit, and she was still deeply worried about Odette, who seemed to be under the impression that Calum Forrester had orchestrated the clashing Clinic party as a deliberate ruse to promote her club. Elsa wasn't sure why he *had* done it, but Spike seemed to be involved in the whole business, as did the smarmy Alex Hopkinson. Elsa had a terrible feeling that her friend was being stitched up.

And despite the tiredness, despite the late night and hard

work, she relished the mental challenge of finding out what it was all about. Pregnancy had restricted her so much in her work. She wanted to use her head, not focus on her navel, or Euan's bloody novel for that matter. Much as she loved it, in the past two months she'd proof read the thing three times for him, checking each edit. She could almost recite it. She might think he was the next Alex Garland, but she wished he'd learn to spell hallucinogenic with two 'l's.

Elsa heaved herself off the seat. She turned on the taps, lit several candles around the room and wandered back into the sitting room.

Euan was arranging the sunflowers in a bright pink vase. The colour clash was delightful. Elsa admired it for a moment and then something occurred to her.

'You didn't give me a chance to say goodbye to Mum. She's a bit needy at the moment – she's been done for drink driving.'

'She said, poor hen.' Euan seemed to be showing unusually perfectionist care in arranging the flowers at exactly the right angles. 'Tragic for her, miles away from anyone out there.'

'She said she'll get a driver,' Elsa murmured, looking at him curiously. 'You asked her, didn't you?'

'About the charge?' He tweaked a bent petal into shape. 'No, she told me.' Still he didn't look at her.

'You asked her for the money.'

He gave a lop-sided grimace and shrugged. 'It was you that mentioned the house, hen. She just asked me why we hadn't put in an offer and I told her the truth. That it's fifty thousand more than we can afford.'

'Jesus!' Elsa turned away in defeat. 'You fucking bastard. You know how I feel and you just go ahead and—'

'She offered!' he howled. 'What was I supposed to say? "No, thanks, Cyd hen, your daughter's a proud bitch when it comes to money!"'

Elsa flinched at the venom in his voice. She had never known Euan speak to her like this. They seldom argued at all, and when they did he was always the one who tried to be conciliatory and soothing, she the irrational hothead.

'You know I don't want to take her money.' She tried to

keep her voice low and even, but fury tightened her vocal chords like piano wires. 'And you know why. I will not let her buy her way into our life, or into this baby's life, especially not with Jobe's filthy lucre.'

'Ach, Elsa, can you not see she's no' trying to do that?' Euan slapped the heel of his hand against the doorframe in frustration. 'She's just trying to help us out here. It's a loan. We'll pay her back eventually.'

Elsa was in despair. 'What we're talking about here is over fifty thousand pounds. We haven't a hope of paying that back in Mum's lifetime.'

'When I sell the book—'

'Oh, Euan, get real! That's just a dream.'

His eyes stayed level with hers and he made no outward sign of registering the blow, but Elsa knew she had committed the unforgivable sin. She'd hit him where it really hurt. Now the gloves were off.

'It's my dream.' His voice was so low it seemed to be coming from the carpet underlay. 'Just like owning this house is my dream. Only this one can come true.'

'Not using my mother's guilt money it won't!'

'What about her grandchild?' Euan looked at the doodle-covered bump. 'Don't you think Buster wants to start life in a nice hoose? You're not even thinking of our baby – of what it might want, Elsa. You'd rather it started life in a damp flat for the sake of your own pride.'

That did it. Not only were the gloves off, but the knuckle-dusters were on and the flick-knives out.

The row raged on at full tilt for almost an hour. It echoed around the tiny flat until their voices were hoarse and their neighbours had banged on the ceiling with a broom handle. Until they said things that hurt because they were so true they never should have been said. They said things that weren't strictly true but were true right now because they were mad at one another. They rowed until their throats hurt. Elsa threw cushions, books, several bank statements, the folder of house details and the sunflowers – vase and all.

It wasn't until the neighbours started hammering on the door screaming that water was pouring through their roof again that they stopped arguing and looked at one another in horror.

'My bath!' Elsa wailed, dashing into the bathroom while Euan ran to apologise.

'There's only one thing for it,' he said sheepishly as she came back out of the bathroom, having stopped the taps and put out the small fire caused by a candle setting light to the shower curtain.

'I know,' she sighed. 'We'll have to move.'

13

Odette watched Calum across her desk as he took off his pork-pie hat, tousled his blond curls and shrugged nonchalantly, like a teenage hooligan offering a friend some free Es, eager not to look too desperate. 'That's the deal. He's keen. I'm keen. I just wannae know if you're keen?'

Odette was amazed how sweetly this meeting was going. No mention had been made of their kiss on Wednesday night. Calum had walked in with an easy smile and an outstretched hand. He was being incredibly helpful – in fact, if she'd asked him to roll over like a dog he probably would have done it – and he was offering her all the things she had wanted in the first place. At least, he was offering her the most important thing she had wanted for the success of the club. Florian Etoile.

'He was seriously impressed by the launch, but he felt the food could be improved upon. Radically redefined, in fact.'

Odette felt she had to defend her kitchen, and Ned in particular. 'We weren't anticipating so many covers – the kitchen was at full stretch and your so-called genius chef was out cold on the sofa in my office.'

'Ah, yes.' Calum cleared his throat. 'Well, I had no idea Ferdy was going to prove so unreliable. He's one of Flo's most talented protégés, but he obviously couldnae take the pressure.'

'Judging by the reports I've been hearing, Ferdy hasn't been able to take the pressure for months,' Odette said, battling to keep her voice calm and unchallenging. She had no intention of baiting Calum while he was being so co-operative, but she needed to stand her ground.

'Perhaps not, but I for one certainly didnae see it coming, and nor did Florian. And he's very, very angry about it. That is one of the reasons he now wants to endorse the place fully with his name and make the menu his own. Come on, sister, you can see the sense in this, surely?' His usually narrowed eyes were wide and lucent.

'And what does he get out of it?'

Calum tapped a very short, very clean fingernail against his thin lips, eyes still boring into hers. 'Ten percent of the profits.'

'We can't afford that.'

'That's because we're no' making a profit yet, and won't be for some time. He's happy to wait until we do. There'll be no capital outlay, but massive returns based solely on the business his name will drum up. Think of the extra publicity.'

'We need capital very badly.' Odette picked up a sheaf of bills. 'Everyone wants paying at once and we now have enormous running costs to contend with. Unless I'm very clever we'll be at least thirty K out of pocket, and the bank simply won't extend the overdraft that much further. It's already well over six figures.'

'That's no' a problem.' Calum winked, a cool smile touching his lips. 'I can arrange to have the money biked over today.'

'There are electronic transfers for these things,' she sighed, noticing in surprise that that his fingers were creeping across the desk towards hers.

'So will you accept Flo's terms? Ten percent?'

'Restaurant profits only?' Odette looked at her cashflow chart. Vernon would freak out.

Calum nodded. 'The rest of the business is entirely ours to get rich on.' He stared at her levelly, those pale eyes drilling into hers. There was something odd about his manner this morning, it could almost be described as flirtatious, but Odette dismissed the idea. After Wednesday night, the notion was ridiculous. He was just being friendly.

Dressed in his usual uniform of tinted glasses, football shirt, donkey jacket and jeans, Calum looked far less intimidating than he had a couple of nights earlier, if no less fanciable. Dressed in her usual slate-grey designer suit, high court shoes and a full face of makeup, Odette felt far more confident.

'I've got to be certain you're being straight with me. I don't want any more secrets like the launch party stunt.'

'I'm sorry, I thought you'd appreciate the surprise.' There it was again. That flirty look, eyes playing with hers. 'I have big plans for this place. I want to make it legendary.' He leaned across the desk and caught hold of the end of her pen to stop it tapping. A moment later he had slipped a warm hand over hers. Odette refused to look into his eyes, just staring fixedly as his thumbnail toyed with the links on her watchstrap.

Jesus, he *was* flirting. Heart slamming, she snatched her hand away and uncapped the pen. She couldn't let him see how excited he made her – she had to stay businesslike. This was a critical meeting. 'In that case I'd better get on with writing up some sort of contract for Florian. I'll get Bill to sort out all the legalities.'

'You don't have to worry about that. I've got my solicitor working on it,' Calum said quickly. 'He can arrange to get that money to you while he's about it.'

'But Bill's the OD lawyer.'

'It's easier this way. Bill can look over it at a later stage.' He stood up. 'Let's go and have a drink downstairs.'

'The bar's not open yet.' Odette was strictly on mineral water for a fortnight.

'Sister, we own it,' he laughed. 'We can do what we like.'

Saskia was standing behind the reception desk looking through the reservations book as they passed through the lobby.

'Fourteen bookings for lunch – fifty-six covers,' she said. 'Not bad.'

'It should be three times that.' Odette shrugged. 'At least half will be no-shows.'

'Early days,' Calum soothed, flashing Saskia his rare smile. 'I hear you're getting married soon?'

'In a fortnight.' She smiled back, totally won over by Calum now that he'd pulled off such a glorious coup on the opening night. She felt hugely guilty for ever doubting him. The man was a marketing genius.

'And you're having a hen party here, I hope?'

Odette rolled her eyes at the prospect of tens of drunken twenty-something women carrying inflatable penises around the club and ordering a fireman strippergram. It wasn't quite the atmosphere she was trying to create.

Saskia was blushing in embarrassment. 'Actually I'm having next weekend away with some friends.'

'Traitor,' Calum teased her, turning to Odette. 'Are you're going too?'

'Of course not.' Odette hadn't been asked and hadn't expected to be. 'I have to stay and look after this place. Cover for Saskia while we're so short-staffed.'

'Nonsense, I can do that.'

'You?' Odette and Saskia both gaped at him.

'I'll cancel my plans for next weekend. You two have both worked so hard, you need a break.

'I'd love it if you could come, Odette,' Saskia said loyally. 'You haven't had a day off in months – and you'd get to meet some of the other girls who'll be at the wedding.'

God, it was a conspiracy. They clearly both thought she was close to a breakdown and needed time off to prevent a repetition of her lunacy of Wednesday night. 'I'm sure it will be too awkward to include me at the last minute,' she said firmly.

'Nonsense! Phoebe's hired a cottage somewhere – she won't tell me exactly.' Saskia smiled, clearly warming to the idea of including her boss in the fun. 'She said there's bags of space. And I know she's dying to meet you.'

'Well, that's settled.' Calum hooked an arm around both of them. 'Now let's go downstairs and crack open a bottle of champagne to celebrate.'

Odette's head spun all night, and from more than just champagne. She couldn't believe that Calum had forgiven her so effortlessly. His attitude was thoroughly twenty-first century and she was determined to match it by being equally calm and friendly. Inside her belly was churning with excitement and hope. She'd been given a second chance to fast-track into her dream. All she had to do was learn the rules and play the game very, very carefully.

Florian Etoile roared into the tiny staff car park behind the OD Club the following day, flattening Odette's Vespa with the bull bars of his glossy Jeep. A nervous young *commis* who was having a quick fag break in the yard gaped at the huge car with its blacked-out windows and sinister silver radiator grille which seemed to snarl at passers by – even more so now that the bull bars were bent into a metal grimace. He knew precisely who it belonged to and dashed inside to warn the rest of the kitchen staff who were in the middle of the lunch rush.

Wearing a vast sheepskin coat and baseball cap, Florian stalked into the kitchen and immediately started moving around behind the cooks, trying everything he could dip a spoon into. Everyone alternately quaked or toadied as he nosed around, but he ignored them all. Only Ned ignored him in return, continuing to yell and berate his staff and tell the waiters they were fucking imbeciles who deserved to be castrated by their own mothers. Florian raised a bushy black eyebrow at the red-faced, red-haired *sous* before marching into the stores, tutting broodily as he swung open fridge and freezer doors, lifted lids on tubs and checked out the fresh vegetables.

Odette was upstairs in the cabaret box office talking a new manager through the computer system and didn't even realise he was in the building until she returned to her office and found him sitting in her chair, leafing through her financial records.

'Florian, I didn't know you were here,' she apologised, trying not to feel pissed off that he was reading confidential paperwork. He was, after all, part of the management team now. 'Can I show you around? Or would you like some lunch?'

'I won't eet that sheet,' he said matter-of-factly. 'And I know my way around. So I would rather be left to do some work, *oui*?' He nodded towards the door.

'But this is my office,' she told him gently. 'Yours is next door.'

'I prefer thees one.' He looked up at her with huge anthracite eyes which had the longest, darkest lashes in history. His expression was of calm expectancy. 'Mine is too small.'

'But I share this one with Saskia,' Odette explained, pointing out the extra desk.

'Now you share that one with Saskia.' He smiled calmly. 'Arrange to haff zat desk moved, weel you?'

His attitude was so autonomous and his force of will so strong that within two days the staff were answering to him and not Odette. He could overrule her on everything, and not just in the restaurant. He wanted snacks in the bar; he got snacks. He wanted the beers changed; the beers were changed. He thought there should be more singers hired for the cabaret bar; singers were hired. He wanted to order seven hundred pounds' worth of supplies from a Japanese food importer, the order was made without Odette's approval.

She found the situation infuriating and tried to square up to him by arguing in French, but he pretended not to understand, telling her that her accent was too bad.

She felt her control over the club slipping away. It was a growing success, she knew that. Bookings were flooding in, the bar was crammed every night. More coverage of That Party had appeared in the Sunday press, along with a multitude of glossy photographs of the guests, and even a couple of pre-Florian reviews which praised the food, although the service was lampooned as 'shambolic'. She wanted to enjoy the success, but barely felt a part of it.

By the end of the week, she was actually glad that she was going away for the weekend. She knew that she should really hang around and see what other changes Florian was planning – his food orders the previous week had caused another furious row because of the gross over-spend on ingredients Odette had never even heard of. She needed to get away and clear her head in order to think of a way to wrest back some control.

She had been signing alarmingly large cheques all week. The money that Calum had arranged to be biked around was in her own high-interest account, earmarked to pay the builders, but she was holding back until they completed work on the cabaret bar which was passable but not to her specifications. It was her safeguard, the only way that she could feel happy about leaving the place to run itself for a couple of days. Without it, she had the weirdest feeling that the locks might have been changed when she returned.

14

Squashed in the back of Phoebe Fredericks' car between a hat designer called Dinny and a quacky blonde called Bibby who said she worked at Sotheby's, Odette battled with motion sickness. Phoebe drove seriously badly. The battered old fifties Ford Zephyr looked like a heap to Odette, but Phoebe claimed it was her partner's pride and joy: 'Felix doesn't usually let me out in this,' she told them over her shoulder, 'but I said I'd record *Emmerdale* over his *South Park* tapes if I couldn't borrow it this weekend.'

In the passenger seat, Saskia was in a state of high excitement, asking over and over again where they were going.

'I think we can safely say it's west.' Odette looked out at the blue motorway signs.

'I love your accent,' Bibby quacked. 'You sound just like what's-her-name from Harry Enfield? The really funny one?'

'Oh, I know who you mean!' Dinny gushed in a breathy voice. 'Waynetta Slob!' She went off into peals of laughter, clutching Odette's arm. 'Gosh, that sounded *so* rude, didn't it? I mean the actress. God, what's her name?'

'Kathy Burke.' Odette forced a polite smile.

'Is it?' Dinny clearly had never heard the name at all.

'No, I think you're wrong, Odette,' Bibby quacked. 'I think she's called Tracey something.'

Odette suddenly caught two green eyes looking at her in the rear-view mirror. Then Phoebe rolled them upwards and crossed them in mock-horror, only stopping when a frantic horn beep from the car behind warned her that she was on the wrong side of the road. Odette liked Phoebe. When they had first all met up

134

at her Notting Hill mews house and she had tried to get Dinny and Bibby into gear, she'd muttered into Odette's ear, 'Murder, aren't they? I hated them at school. We nicknamed them the Yaks – stands for 'Yah' Air-Kiss Sloanes. I know it's not very clever, but we *were* fourteen at the time.'

There were several car-loads of Saskia's quacking, braying and honking school friends travelling in convoy along the motorway. Odette hadn't caught most of their names when introduced, but had noticed in amazement that almost all of them ended with 'y' – Polly, Kitty, Dippy, Hilly, Bunty, Lotty. She figured that most of them were nicknames. Either that or their parents had wanted a dog not a child.

She had a feeling she was in for a rough ride, and she wasn't thinking about Phoebe's driving. It was more than motion displacement she was suffering from; it was demotion put-in-your-placement. These people clearly thought she was vastly inferior to them, what her mother called 'char class', mistakenly thinking that she herself wasn't branded with the same iron-and-dust cleaning-lady status.

'Oh, how simply divine!' Bibby quacked as they bumped over a very pot-holed drive towards a crumbling manor house, the Zephyr's suspension moaning like a mother in labour.

'It's rally, rally amazing,' Dinny gushed breathily, adding, 'I didn't know there were houses like this in Wales.'

Odette opened her eyes for the first time in several miles. Car sickness had dogged her for hours as they'd twisted their way deeper and deeper into the Cambrian Mountains, great waves of nausea snatching her breath from her mouth and filling it with warm bile. Now she blinked as she peered between Saskia and Phoebe at a broad-shouldered and very run-down manor house filling the windscreen like a drive-in horror movie. Surrounded by overgrown woods, the huge stone building was wearing a vast fur coat of ragged wistaria, its stone portico mostly lying on the ground in heaps of rubble, its gardens a rampant and burgeoning wood of saplings, weeds and thistle.

'Phoebe, it isn't!' Saskia was shrieking. 'It isn't, is it?'

As they drew closer, the house looked even more threatening. A single magpie was sitting high on a spiralling gothic chimney stack, dabbing its tail at them. With a low sun trying to break through black clouds behind casting it into silhouetted relief, the mansion looked so like a setting from a Hammer House of Horror movie that Odette expected Vincent Price to welcome them at the door wearing a velvet smoking jacket and carrying the corpse of legendary scream queen Philomena Rialto.

'It bloody well is!' Phoebe laughed. 'Plas Cwyn.'

'Sweet Jesus!' Saskia shrieked even louder. 'I don't believe it. You are so clever. How on earth did you hire it?'

'I have ways.' Phoebe swung the car into an overgrown gravel sweep at the front of the old stone house. 'Of course the centre's long gone. I think it was a youth hostel until about five years ago. The place has been empty ever since.'

'Share the joke, share the joke!' Dinny gushed.

'It looks a bit damp,' Bibby quacked disapprovingly, peering out at the mildew on the mullioned windows. 'Did you hire it from a reputable agency?'

'Phoebe and I came here when we were kids.' Saskia swung around in her seat. 'It was one of those awful outward bound centres then where teenagers are encouraged to toughen up whilst dangling on the end of a rope in a helmet that's too big for them and a harness that's too small. Our parents banished us here for three weeks while they sunned themselves on an adults-only booze-up in the Caribbean. It was about this time of year, wasn't it?' She looked at Phoebe.

'Yup.' Phoebe cut the engine. 'Just before Christmas. We hated it – it was so cold and wet. It rained solidly and the team leaders were sadists. They made us rock climb and abseil and water-ski and we just got wetter and wetter and colder and colder. And what's more we hated one another then, didn't we?'

'Sure did,' Saskia giggled. 'I punctured a hole in your hot water bottle one night, remember?'

'And I took the batteries out of your torch for the overnight orienteering marathon and replaced them with old ones that gave out in the middle of that forest. We had such a dreadful time!'

'So why come back?' Bibby sniffed, no longer thinking the place 'divine' now that she had started to spot the broken window panes, the missing roof slates, the boarded up doors and what appeared to be a tree growing out of one of the chimneys.

'Ah!' Saskia hugged her friend conspiratorially. 'You'll have to get us very, very drunk before we tell you that. Phoebe, I love you.'

'I love you too, sweet thing.' Phoebe kissed her cheek. 'Better do a register.' She picked up a creased spiral pad from the dashboard and jumped out of the car to check that those who had followed them from London had made it all the way.

Odette got out with the others and looked up at the sky. The clouds were full, black and heavy. The only coat she had got with her was the one she was wearing – a huge, fluffy fake-fur one that kept her warm. She hoped it didn't rain. It was bitterly cold. Her face was already turning numb from the icy, breath-snatching wind.

On jumping out of their respective cars, the Yaks all whipped out their mobile phones to call the au pair or Mummy and check on their various offspring, only to let out great shrieks of horror when they realised there was no reception on any of the networks in such an isolated spot.

It seemed the Yaks wanted to recreate the good old days of school by cramming into 'dorms' en masse to engage in pillow talk and pillow fights. Most of the rooms didn't have any pillows with which to talk and fight, or much else in the way of bedding, so they rushed around and claimed every last blanket for themselves.

Odette couldn't get to grips with the geography of the house at all. There seemed to be so many rooms, staircases and corridors. She kept trying to get from one part to another and finding herself walking in big circles. She felt as though she was playing Tomb Raider, running around in search of a power-up.

Apart from the kitchen and domestic offices downstairs, all

the other rooms looked the same – vast, interconnecting wood-panelled tombs with huge stone arches and open fireplaces. Various Yaks were crouching in front of these, blowing madly at smoking, screwed up pages of the *Daily Telegraph*, which they extinguished with a damp log as soon as they caught fire. These rooms were set around the vast flag-stoned hallway with a double sweep of staircases leading up to a galleried landing, off which the bedrooms were huge, with their own fireplaces suffering the same treatment as the ones downstairs.

'I hope the chimneys have been swept recently,' a goat-faced girl told Odette when she looked into one of the rooms. 'My aunt had a terrible time with dry fungus in her breast last year.'

'How awful,' Odette sympathised, having a terror of lumps in her own breasts. 'Was it very serious?'

'What? Yes – it bloody well caught fire. Place was razed. Seventeenth-century thatch. She's living in a squalid little caravan in the garden while they rebuild the place. Bloody awful for her – oh, sorry, I suppose you go in for caravans? Thoughtless of me. Anyway, all these rooms are taken. There are more upstairs.'

Several tiny staircases led up to another floor, and then another. The higher she went, the colder Odette felt, and each room seemed pokier, colder and damper than the last. At the far end of a corridor, she opened a door and almost jumped out of her skin as a fat rat waddled out, shot her an evil look and then disappeared through a huge hole in the floorboards. Dashing back along the corridor and down the stairs, she bumped into Phoebe.

'Odette, are you okay?' She took in the wild eyes.

'I just saw a fucking great rodent!'

'Yes, I'm afraid there are some mice. Have you chosen a room yet?'

Odette shook her head, 'It wasn't a mouse, it was a rat.'

'Couldn't have been.' Phoebe grinned. 'Rats hate heights. Mice live in the roofs, rats in the cellars. It's a well-known fact. The room next to Saskia's and mine is free if you want to take a look – it's got a fireplace and the bed's huge.'

As Odette followed Phoebe through a thick oak door and

up yet another set of stairs, she knew positively that what she'd seen was a rat. Phoebe was talking rubbish. She knew plenty of high-rise council blocks near her parents' house where the rats ran around the walkways on the sixteenth floor.

The room was, as Phoebe had promised, quite habitable, with a huge old wooden bed which had a dry, if lumpy, mattress.

'It's lovely,' Odette lied, throwing her bag on the bed.

'I'm sorry there's no bedding.' Phoebe looked at the bare mattress. 'But I have got an old Georgette Heyer novel stashed under my bed for kindling, so come through and grab a chapter or two when you've collected some wood. But don't tell another soul it's there. Saskia's got a lighter.'

Odette nodded bleakly.

'Hey!' Phoebe cuffed her arm. 'It's what Saskia wanted. No chocolate willies, no strippers, no night-clubs, no health farm – just all her chums suffering like hell.'

'You mean, this is some sort of joke?' Odette was appalled.

Phoebe shrugged, green eyes dancing with mirth. 'Those girls made our lives murder at school. They were bullies. Okay, so Saskia quite liked them then – in fact, she was one of them really. She hated *me* in those days. But when we came here on the activity holiday, something happened and we made this pact that we'd make the Yaks come here as punishment one day. Saskia's very into revenge. It's her one weak spot.'

15

The evening meal had a gung-ho Girl Guide spirit, except that these Girl Guides could consume a bottle of Merlot each, and smoked back-to-back Silk Cut. With the aid of several Georgette Heyer chapters, Phoebe had lit the huge, five-door Aga only to realise that it took at least a day to heat up. So they were forced to try and cook a meal for twenty on two butane gas stoves and a vast, smoky fire in the butler's pantry. The Yaks all rallied round with amazing alacrity.

'When I was a chalet girl in Verbier an avalanche caused a power cut and we had to cook the guests' chickens on a spit roast,' one said cheerfully. 'It's jolly good fun and rally quite easy.' Within minutes she had two fat chickens turning on a makeshift spit constructed out of loose bricks and wire coat hangers.

'Gavin and I trekked through Peru on horseback last year and the guides cooked everything on these little gas stoves,' another announced. 'I think I can rustle up some mulligatawny soup.'

'Let's bake the potatoes in the fire like we did at Pony Club Camp,' Bibby suggested.

'And toast bread on it!'

'And melt marshmallows.'

'We haven't got any frigging marshmallows,' Odette muttered.

The ancient generator sporadically gave up the ghost and they were plunged into darkness, but one of the Yaks inevitably managed to get it going again. 'Had a beast of a horse-box a few years back. Did a mechanics course to get out of scrapes on the way to hunt meets. Bloody useful.'

The meal, the drinking, the gossip, the anecdotes and the

giggles lasted late into the night. Dressed in several jumpers, coats and hats, they all looked as though they were about to set out on an arctic expedition, but it was the only way to keep warm.

Inevitably, as the hens got drunker, the conversation turned to relationships and marriages, as the girls swapped notes on the hopeless nature of men. 'First time I asked Guy to change Georgia's nappy, he took the pack of Pampers back to Tesco and asked for another lot.' 'Henry used to take me out to 192 every Friday night. Now he orders two 192s and prawn crackers to go from the local chinky.'

'I know!' Dinny gushed. 'Let's all play a game. Let's write down how we met our other halves on a piece of paper and then throw them all into a hat. Saskia reads them out and we all have to guess who wrote which.'

'That won't work,' Bibby quacked. 'Most of us know each other too well.'

'What about how we lost our virginity?' Goat-face suggested excitedly.

Odette felt a flash of hot humiliation. She had lost her virginity to a friend in a teenage pact – they both wanted to try it out, neither seemed to attract the opposite sex; it seemed the logical solution. She'd been a fat and unwanted swot; her thighs had rubbed together until they were raw and stinging, until walking was agony. Stan had been a skinny, soap-dodging drop-out. It had been a painful, embarrassing experience that had almost ruined their friendship. He had gone on to become an oddball but irresistible school lothario and later a reputedly fantastic lover, she had never really progressed much further than that first stifled, hasty coupling on Ma McGillivray's sofa.

She swallowed hard, realising that she was on dangerous territory. She had no idea whether Stan had told Saskia about their virgin voyage together, but had no intention of risking indiscretion if he hadn't.

'Let's not play the virginity game.' Phoebe caught her stricken expression.

'Okay, I know.' Saskia's eyes glittered. 'Most of us will have had at least one sexual experience the others don't know about – a one-night stand, an affair, even just something a bit racy with our partners. We write that down and everyone has to guess.'

A round of 'what fun' and 'do we really dare?' greeted the idea.

Odette felt her face redden even more. 'Isn't that all a bit childish? Why not play In The Manner Of or another parlour game – seeing as that's where we are.'

'We're in a pantry actually,' Goat-face corrected haughtily. 'And you don't have to play if you don't want to.'

'I'll play,' Odette said casually, trying to appear mature and arrogant.

As soon as they got their blank sheets, the girls started scribbling furiously, bickering over who got to use the few pens they had between them first.

Waiting for a pen, Odette fingered her piece of paper, feeling more and more nauseous. She thought back over all her sexual experiences. They were hopelessly gauche. She'd only ever had sex in a bed with the lights off, lying beneath someone she didn't fancy very much but had desperately hoped would be her Jonathan. Although she hadn't told her friends much, they all knew she'd had a limited number of affairs.

'Here you are, darl – I've finished.' Phoebe passed her a pen. 'Keep it legal, Bibby's married to a silk.'

Odette watched her naughty-eyed face as she folded up her piece of paper and threw it into a waxed hat in the centre of the floor, and realised Phoebe had no idea how naive she was sexually. None of them did, not even Saskia. Her real friends weren't here. She could, in fact, make up anything she liked.

She hesitated. It was totally against her nature to tell an out and out lie. She always believed in saying things like they were.

Then it struck her. She just had to carry on from where her life had left off. Outside in the car park with Calum. Only for the purposes of her story, she'd reverse the roles.

'". . . and then, pushing me back against a car, Jonathan dropped to his knees, pulled down my knickers and started to lick between my legs,"' Saskia read out in a soft, purring voice so that her audience was hypnotised. '"We were like wild

142

animals. I didn't care that anyone could have seen us if they'd wandered out of the party, I just wanted him to keep on going while I kept coming. He pushed me on to the bonnet, which was still warm from being driven. As I leaned back in pleasure, I looked upside-down through the windscreen and saw the face of my ex-lover watching me from the driver's seat. It was his car we were fucking against, and what was worse, we were far too turned on to stop."' She fanned her face for a moment. 'I don't know about you girls, but this sure as hell beats central heating. I'm going to have to take off my coat.'

The Yaks were all very red-faced, and for once mute. No quacking or honking or braying echoed through the room. It was completely silent bar the hissing and cracking of logs on the fire.

'Go on,' Bibby said eventually. 'Read the rest.'

'That's it.' Saskia turned the piece of paper over and shrugged.

'Whoever wrote that is a cow!' howled Phoebe. 'Reveal your identity right now and tell us what happened next.'

'No, let's guess,' Goat-face insisted, glancing thoughtfully around the room. 'I think it's Bibby and Jonjo.'

'Tilly, you bag,' Bibby quacked. 'You know Jonjo won't go dow – I mean, you know I didn't write that.'

'I know exactly who it is.' Saskia looked at the familiar handwriting and a slow smile spread across her face. 'And I think I know when it happened, too.'

Odette went pale. Oh, God, she hadn't really thought this through, hadn't worked out the consequences of Saskia not only guessing who had written it, but realising that the story was set at the OD launch. She shouldn't have used a real experience like that. She only hoped Saskia wouldn't realise who 'Jonathan' was.

'It's you, isn't it?' She looked at Odette with glittering eyes.

Odette nodded in what she hoped was a nonchalant manner, adding quickly, 'It happened a long time ago.'

'Sure,' Saskia giggled. 'Like last week!'

'You are kidding!' Phoebe whistled. 'Do tell more? What the hell did your ex do when you saw him sitting there?'

Odette took a gulp of red wine and shrugged. She was aware she'd cast herself unwittingly in the role of storyteller, sitting around the fire like this, her audience as rapt as Girl Guides being told a ghost story. She guessed she owed it to them to be entertaining, but she was no Juno when it came to things like this. She hated public speaking, or telling jokes, and most especially she hated lying.

'Not much he could do,' she said eventually. 'He just sat there until we went inside. Then I guess he went home.'

They all looked disappointed at the anti-climactic ending, but even telling them that made Odette feel as though she'd stood in a dock and told a jury an innocent man was a child abuser.

'And Jonathan?' Phoebe looked up between topping up glasses. 'Is he an ongoing thing or was it a one-off?'

'I'm not sure,' Odette muttered, and then realising this sounded weak, added, 'I haven't made my mind up yet.'

'God, Odette, you do get yourself in some hot water,' Saskia giggled, but thankfully she had delved into the hat again and immediately started reading out a very tame story. '"We once did it on the sofa whilst the Labradors were watching . . ."'

Thinking that she'd got away with it, Odette settled back to listen. She felt little pin-pricks of shame digging in all over her body, razor sharp and accusing. One in particular was stabbing away to punish her, a needle-like pain between thigh and pelvis. She crossed her legs to try and make it go away, but it seemed to double and make her wince.

'What's that burning smell?' Phoebe sniffed. 'Like bacon?'

'Good grief!' Arabella boomed, gaping at Odette's crotch. 'You're so sexy you appear to be smoking down there.'

'Jesus!' Odette looked down to see that a large spark from the fire had burned a huge hole through the leather of her trousers. Before she could take in what was happening, Arabella had doused her crotch with a full glass of red wine.

'Are you hurt?' Phoebe asked worriedly. She nodded at the large hole, through which Odette was flashing a lot of singed g-string.

'It's okay – just a bit scalded,' she checked, face flaming with

144

embarrassment. So this was her punishment for telling such lies. Perhaps her mother was right about hellfire and brimstone after all? 'I'll just go and change.'

When she returned, they were honking away trying to identify the Yak who had rogered her lover in the shrubbery at Glyndebourne.

Odette wasn't sure whether her false confession had earned her any more respect amongst the braying masses. If anything they seemed to be ignoring her even more. She no longer much cared. She was feeling such a fraud right now that she hardly listened to the further tales of sexual high jinks. Her head was full of thoughts of that moment outside in the car park with Calum. More than anything, she wished she'd let it continue. She was not only a fraud, she was also a coward. And the realisation appalled her.

As soon as it got light the following morning, Odette pulled on her trainers and crept through the sleeping house, past the debris of the night before in the butler's pantry and out of the kitchen door to go for a run. It was bitterly cold outside, the grass iced with frost, the trees white skeletons, the puddles glass sheets. She had slept in her tracksuit, which she was still wearing, and immediately realised that it offered her no protection from the howling wind. In her desperation to get out, she hadn't warmed up properly and was stiff and sluggish when she started. Cutting through the overgrown garden, she pounded past a drained, moss-encrusted swimming pool and on to a muddy rear drive. The only way to get warm was to start out as fast as possible, despite the risk of cramps. Chest rattling from gasping in cold air, Odette pounded past what appeared to be part of an assault course — old wooden walls, rope bridges and several slides were hidden in a thickly choked wood. The high trees sheltered her from the wind and she started to feel the blood pumping hotly around her body.

At the end of the long drive, she encountered a gravel path that ran around the lake. The door of an old boathouse was slamming open and shut; the few boats that were dotted around were splintered and peeling, half-full of muddy grey water. The wind was sweeping the lake's surface into long, rippling streaks, which reflected the heavy clouds overhead. Cold sawed into Odette's left cheekbone and jaw as she turned right and started jogging around the lake at a more leisurely pace, trying not to let her heartbeat get too high too quickly. The path was very overgrown in places, thick with mud in others. It took her almost half an hour to make it to the far side of the lake, by which time the first few flakes of snow had started to settle in her hair and on her shoulders.

Soon snow was almost blinding her as it fell more thickly, the wind driving it straight into her eyes. She stumbled over tree roots and pot-holes. Her trainers were black with mud and so sodden that she felt as though she was lifting a bench weight every time she took a stride. Her cream tracksuit was filthy with splatters of mud and green streaks of tree mould, and soaked through with sweat and melting snow.

As she embarked on the second crescent of the lake, she realised that, far from being circular as she'd thought, it had a long tributary lake which led off from it and could only be crossed by boat, or by a broken rope bridge which led off from the jetty. It wasn't particularly long, but Odette didn't much like the look of it. She cautiously made her way on to the jetty, trainer soles slipping on the wet, icy wood. Several planks were missing and the black water swirled between the gaps. She looked across the divide of the lake to the far bank and shivered.

Her thoughts were as black as the swirling water beneath her. But for once they weren't of her sickening, hopeless love for Calum, or of the over-ambitious club that had sucked her dry both financially and emotionally. She was no longer angry with Saskia for bringing her here to share time with Sloane monsters. She wasn't thinking about her cold, dysfunctional family, her loneliness, or her friends whose lives were too busy to include her any more.

Odette was furious with herself. She was so incensed and disappointed and humiliated she could barely focus to place her feet on the icy, snow-coated wood. Tears were blurring her vision. She was livid that she had let herself down. She'd made wrong move after wrong move and no longer knew how to get back. She kept running through life because she had no idea how to retrace her steps. She was desperate to be somewhere else, but she was chained to the same treadmill. Even when she ran in the open, she felt lost and trapped.

She wanted to dare herself to do something stupid. Her control was slipping again. Unaware of the tears running a scorching path along her frozen cheeks, she clenched her fists and screamed. She screamed and screamed until her exhausted lungs could no longer make a sound, yet still she forced a hissing wail from their deepest air pockets. At last, the urge started to fade.

She was chased home by the billowing snow. To her amazement, the house looked as warm and welcoming as buttered toast when she arrived. She was so happy to see it that she raced inside, smiling from ear to ear, endorphins finally chasing away the black hollow of anguish inside her.

The kitchen was full of hungover Yaks in voluminous checked pyjamas and brightly coloured bed socks. They all looked at her in horror.

'Where have you been?' quacked Bibby – almost unrecognisable in a man's dressing gown and woolly hat. 'We all thought you were still in bed. You're soaked through, you poor old thing.'

'Went for a run,' Odette muttered through chattering teeth. 'Must have a shower.'

'There's no hot water,' Arabella boomed cheerfully. 'Takes hours to heat up between baths.'

Teeth chattering even more than ever, Odette squelched up to her cold cell of a room and peeled off the filthy tracksuit. Her leather trousers were ruined so the only choice was to climb into her jeans and the red jumper. At least the wine stain didn't show, but it reeked of Merlot. She wished she was in her London flat, able to walk under the hugely powerful shower and pelt her shoulders with hot, steaming water before wrapping herself in her fluffy dressing gown. Instead, she found a free bathroom with a howling draught, and splashed her face with cold water, brushed her teeth and sprayed half a can of deodorant under her jumper.

Downstairs, Phoebe was already dressed in several thick jumpers, trendy combat trousers and hefty boots, chivvying the pyjama party to hurry up and get dressed.

'We're booked in at the trekking centre for ten-thirty. I want everyone down here by quarter-past.'

'Trekking centre?' Odette asked weakly, checking to see if there was any tea left in the pot. There wasn't. She tried to light one of the gas stoves to heat the kettle.

'They've both run out,' Phoebe said apologetically, handing Odette her own half-drunk mug. 'But the good news is you can toast bread on the Aga if you're prepared to wait ten minutes for it to brown through. Do you ride?'

'Ride what?'

'Horses, you dope,' Phoebe laughed kindly.

'Never in my life.' Odette shivered at the prospect. She'd once ridden a donkey on the seafront at Clacton, but she doubted that counted.

Despite the driving snow, the trekking centre – desperate for the off-season custom – felt it was safe enough to let twenty women out for an hour as long as they were supervised by Dai, the huge-shouldered man-mountain who seemed to take particular pleasure in giving them a leg up.

Odette found herself wearing a huge, battered helmet with a dodgy chin-strap and a large '8' painted on the front, being man-handled on to a grubby white horse that was toast-rack thin with mad blue eyes and no mane.

'This is Kojak,' Dai told her in a thick Welsh accent as he put a hand the size of a wicket keeper's glove under her bottom and eased her into the saddle. 'We call him that on account of his mane, see? Bald as an eagle, this one. Rubs it all off on the trees, doesn't he?'

'Is he quiet?' Odette asked worriedly as Kojak sighed sadly and propped his rear leg up on the rim of his hoof.

'Well, he doesn't say much, no.' Dai bellowed with laughter, heaving up Kojak's girth and then adjusting Odette's stirrup length, which seemed to involve feeling her thighs a lot. 'Just getting your leg in the right position, my lovely. I like your boots.' He admired the by now very muddy Guccis which had cost Odette almost three hundred pounds.

Most of the Yaks were experienced riders and jumped on the muddy, scruffy horses without requiring Dai's lascivious help. They all complained that their mounts were too thin, too old and too docile. They also clucked about the state of the tack and the helmets.

'You should have let us know that we were coming riding, Phoebe,' one whinged. 'I'd have brought my joddies.'

'Is this place approved by the British Horse Society?' Bibby quacked disapprovingly as they all set out of the decrepit yard, led by Dai on a horse the size of a tank, with huge feathered feet and a neck as deeply arched as a stone bridge. He took them over a narrow lane striped with tyre tracks in the snow and into a forest, where the trees protected them from the billowing flakes which had not yet settled enough to weigh the branches down too low for them to pass beneath.

Odette wished she had some mane to hold on to too. The saddle felt hugely uncomfortable and unfamiliar beneath her. Her jeans were too tight for her to get a proper grip and Kojak's stride was so long she found herself tipped from side to side like a Val Doonican fan swaying at a concert. She had no idea how to hold the reins and tried to copy the others, but her thick, fur-cuffed gloves weren't designed for riding. What alarmed her the most was how high up she felt. She'd had no idea that riding a horse made you feel you were sitting astride a very high tree branch. She didn't dare look down.

As they plodded on in single file, Dai shouted instructions from the front. 'Don't let the buggers eat the fern . . . don't get too close to each other or they kick . . . watch the branches here, they're very low.'

The Yaks chuntered indignantly that they knew all about the dangers of fern to the equine digestion, that they were accomplished riders and wanted to go a bit faster. Far behind them, Kojak snatched opportunistically at the brown fronds as he loped along, mad eyes half-closed, bottom lip drooping inches below the top while he chewed.

'You want to trot then, girls?' Dai kicked his carthorse into gear, its vast soup-plate hooves hurling up great divots of mulchy, snowy mud which hit his followers in the face.

'Oh, shit!' Odette groaned as Kojak ambled into a faster lope. Jiggly, jiggly, jiggly. She had nothing except the front of the saddle to grab on to, which meant letting go of the reins. Jiggly, jiggly, jiggly. Her legs tried hard to grip but she was being pitched all over the place, her helmet had started slipping over her eyes and her feet had fallen free of the stirrups so that her legs flailed like stubby Pegasus wings at Kojak's side. He took this as a signal to go faster and, groaning with the effort, loped past a couple of the Yaks' horses.

'Steady on, old girl!' Goat-face boomed from the top of a vast, table-wide clopper who flattened his ears and bit Kojak's rump as he passed.

'Okay, we'll have a canter, shall we?' Dai bellowed from the front of the line, not noticing the one-woman charge taking place at the rear.

'Fuck!' Odette felt Kojak surge beneath her and the jiggly jiggly was replaced by an unbalancing rocking. A ball of snow lodged in the hoof of the horse in front chose this moment to fly out and whack her on the nose, making her eyes stream. She wrapped her arms around Kojak's neck and gripped on tight, oblivious of the furious squawks coming from either side as he pitched through the ferns and overtook his companions. He was clearly as unpopular in the yard as Odette was amongst the hens, because almost every horse they passed swung around to try and bite him, spurring him on yet faster towards the front.

'Steady on, lovely!' Dai laughed as Odette caught up with him, by now totally out of control and completely blinded by her helmet. He leaned over and smoothly grabbed her flapping reins, pulling Kojak to a halt beside him.

'Thanks,' she muttered, finding her stirrups and trying to hold on as Kojak flattened his ears and sank his teeth into Dai's vast mount. Behind her, the Yaks had all pulled up and were giggling furiously.

'Good job this big beast between my legs likes being nibbled, huh?' Dai leered as Kojak tried to take another piece out of his horse's rump.

A moment later, a sharp shrilling caused the huge equine tank to rear up in shock and Dai fell off. Not that anyone noticed. Their own horses were charging off in every direction, depositing riders into fern banks, mud and slush, or shying under tree branches so that the Yaks were pulled off to be left swinging. Amidst all this carnage, only Kojak remained motionless, tipping his ugly head from side to side in mild surprise.

Odette suddenly realised he was as deaf as a post.

The shrilling continued in short, faintly familiar bursts. It took her a while to realise it was her phone ringing in her pocket. They'd somehow ridden high enough for her to get a signal. As horses charged madly all around her, thoroughly wound up by one another's fear, she took out her mobile and flipped open the cover.

'Yeah?'

'Odie, fank God!' It was her sister Monny, sobbing. 'Craig's been arrested. Some bloody bastard's stitched him up for handling stolen goods or summink. They've got him at Thamesmead nick. Won't let him out wivout bail.' She sobbed even louder. 'I need you, Odie. Where are you? What's all that noise?'

Horses were still charging around her. The Yaks had started picking themselves out of the mud and were quackily checking that everyone was all right before racing around trying to catch their mounts who were cavorting through the fern, eating great mouthfuls so that fronds hung from their mouths like spaghetti.

'What's happened?' Phoebe panted up to Odette just as she tucked her phone back into her pocket. She'd had enough of lying.

'It was my phone,' she apologised. 'I have to get back to London. My brother-in-law's been arrested.'

She expected them to be appalled, to shoot one another mock-horrified looks or to ask salaciously what he'd been arrested for. But the Yaks did none of these things. On hearing that Odette's phone was working, they abandoned catching their horses in favour of whipping out their mobiles and hastily dialling home: 'Françoise, it's Mrs Farquar here. How is little Hermione? Did she sleep well last night?' 'Mummy, it's me. How's Jamie? Oh, put him on the phone – Jamie-wamie . . . I wuv you, do you wuv me too? Ah, babykins. How's our son and heir by the way?' 'Rolly darling, there's been no bloody signal. How are the girls? Did you take them for a walk? Has Tab come into season?'

Having gathered himself out of the undergrowth, Dai brushed some fox droppings from his trousers and looked at them all in horror. 'What a bunch of madwomen.' He glanced up at Odette, who was the only person still mounted. His leathery face scrunched up in thought. 'Was that your bloody phone ringing?'

She nodded, still thinking about Craig.

To her surprise, Dai started to laugh. He laughed so much that Odette, for all her family worries, couldn't help but join in. 'Funniest thing I seen in years. A load a posh women arse-up in fern. Bloody marvellous! I take my hat off to you, my lovely.' He removed his flat cap to reveal a shiny bald pate.

More shrieks of laughter were playing harmony to Dai's cackling bass.

Looking around, Odette saw that Saskia was standing just behind her, tears streaming down her cheeks.

'I knew I was right to invite you, Odette darling!' she laughed delightedly. 'You did it! You made my hen weekend work. I'll love you forever for this.'

16

It was dark by the time Odette got back to London. In contrast to the snowy surroundings of Wales, the grimy capital was awash with dirty grey slush.

She met Monny in a brightly lit, Formica-clad café around the corner from Thamesmead police station. Phoebe had dropped her off at Notting Hill tube station so Odette was still carrying her overnight bag and wearing her jeans, which smelled strongly of Kojak and were coated with horsehair. Matched with her red-wine jumper, mud-caked boots and black fluffy coat which had become the same matted, manky texture as the trekking horses' coats in the mud and snow, Odette looked very different from her normal businesslike self. Monny was clearly appalled.

'You could have made an effort,' she grumbled, stubbing out her cigarette. 'How are the police supposed to believe you can guarantee bail looking like that?'

'Who said anything about guaranteeing bail?' Odette sat down opposite her where a cup of milky, lukewarm tea was already waiting by the full ashtray.

Monny hung her head, eyes filling with tears. 'You're the only person I know who can do it, Odie. He could be out tomorrow morning if you do – otherwise it'll be bleedin' ages. The police have charged him but are refusing him bail. His first hearing's tomorrow, but the case won't be up in court for months. If he's waiting on remand, he could be sent anywhere. Think of the kids, Odie. I'm bleedin' pregnant. There've been complications . . .' She covered her face, throat closing with sobs.

'What complications, babes?' Odette covered her sister's hands. 'Is the baby okay?'

Monny reached for a napkin from the metal container on the table, blew her nose and shrugged. 'Obsterwhat-not couldn't tell. I gotta another scan next week to make sure. If I was about to have the bleeder next week then the brief says Craig'd be out in a flash – the courts like expectant fathers. But if you might be carrying a deformed baby and you need your hubby's support – forget it. And you know what *Maman* will say if there's anything wrong with this one.' She dabbed the thin napkin at her wet eyes, sobs starting again.

Odette knew just what Clod would say. She held Monny's hand again, trying not to look at the stubs crowding the ashtray. She'd told her enough times to quit smoking while pregnant but Monny needed support right now, not a lecture.

'Why are they keeping him in police custody?' she asked carefully. 'I thought the charge was just handling?'

'Well, there was a bit of aggravated burglary too.' Monny shrugged dismissively. 'And the police seem to think drugs are involved.'

'Drugs?' Odette almost fainted. 'Handling as in drugs? Not stolen goods?'

'I don't rightly know, Odie – they won't tell me nuffink.' Monny took a shaky breath. 'All I know is they bleedin' stormed in first thing this morning, hammered the bloody door down and terrified the kids. Next thing Craig's trying to pull on some clothes to cover his dignity before they haul him down the nick. After that, they were sniffing all over the place, looking in my cupboard drawers. I was the one who felt like she was being naffing burgled.'

'What did they find?'

'Cash,' Monny sniffed. 'Bags and bags of cash. I don't know how much. I ain't never seen it before. Craig swears he was looking after it for a mate. He's bloody terrified, Odette. And now he's been charged with conspiracy to rob and intent to supply along with a load of other stuff he hasn't bleedin' done, and I don't know what to do.' The sobs were louder than ever.

'Jesus!' Odette put down her teacup. 'Does *Maman* know about this?'

'Don't tell her!' Monny started to cry again. 'Please, Odie. I couldn't bear it.'

Odette shook her head. 'Course not, babes. Won't breathe a word. But I'm not sure if they'll take my surety even if we do get a bail hearing.' She dropped her voice as a greasy-haired waitress scuffed her heels across to their table to empty the ashtray before scuffing away again. 'I ain't as cash-rich as I used to be – in fact, I owe a fortune.'

'But you got that big flashy club?' Her sister's eyes widened as she groped for a packet of B & H in her bag. 'You must be raking it in.'

Odette shook her head. 'It's not as simple as that, Mon. I got huge loans, y'know? I ain't got the readies I used to have. If you told Grumpy about this then maybe . . .'

'I fucking knew it!' Monny threw her unlit cigarette down on the table and stood up. 'You're so fucking selfish, you won't even help out your family now you think you're so big. Afraid all your celebrity friends will find out, are you? You ashamed of us or summink? *Maman* said you were, but I didn't believe her till now.'

Odette suddenly felt a huge wave of compassion for her sister, struggling to cope with a husband who continually let her down. Her loyalty might be foolish, but it was admirable in a way – at least she'd found someone to love. She was right, Odette was selfish.

'What you said isn't true. I'll help you all I can, Mon. I'll stand Craig's bail.'

'Yeah?' Monny sat down suspiciously, red-rimmed eyes blinking.

'Yeah.' Odette nodded, picking the cigarette up from the table and handing it to her sister without thinking. 'I'm just warning you in case they turn me down. How much are we talking?'

'Twenty K, I think.' Monny took the cigarette and lit it, breathing in deeply.

'Twenty thousand?' Odette went pale. 'For burglary?'

'Well, he's got a bit of a record as you know.' Monny shrugged, peering intently at the glowing tip, not looking at Odette. 'And they're trying to frame him for some sort of organised crime wave – petrol station raids, I think – then using the money for drugs deals they say. The Old Bill claim they've got video evidence. Bloody crap! He's been home with me most nights.'

Odette watched her sister's face. With a great effort, Monny looked her straight in the eye and thrust out her heavy chin. 'I swear it's the truth, Odie. He ain't got *nuffink* to do with drugs. Not Craig.'

'I believe you.' Odette nodded. Her sister wouldn't lie to her. Well, she might pretend the kids needed new trainers every six weeks in order to borrow a bit of Bingo money, but she wouldn't tell a lie like this. And although Craig was a bit of a small-time swindler, he simply wasn't capable of ring-leading a gang of petrol-station robbers. He was too cowardly and dim.

'Great.' Monny smiled for the first time. 'Now give your mobile over here and I'll call Craig's brief.'

Odette wanted to go home, shower and get to the club to see what was happening there, but it took forever going through the paperwork with Craig's solicitor. She then waited with Monny for the cab she'd ordered to take her sister to the baby-sitter's.

'I'll call you first thing tomorrow morning,' the solicitor had told Odette. 'With any luck we should get a bail hearing in the afternoon.'

'Do I have to come to that?' She thought about the club.

He shook his head. 'We'll just have to meet up afterwards so that you can sign the paperwork. You will need to go to a police station at some point to prove that you have the funds to cover the surety. They'll want to see a bank statement.'

He made it sound so easy. Monny had told him that her sister was loaded, that she could cover the guarantee no problem. Odette's hands had been clammy since shaking his farewell, knowing that the money in her account was there to pay the builders. It didn't even belong to her. She hoped to God Craig wasn't planning to pop over to Rio to visit Ronnie Biggs.

Odette hadn't enough cash for a second cab, so had to get

the tube home. Feeling stale and smelly, she stripped her clothes off the moment she was through the door and headed for her shower. Quickly changing into a smart black trouser suit and very high, spiked heels, she marched out of the flat and into the car park. No Beamer. No Vespa. No money for a cab. Never mind, she could catch a bus.

It was years since she'd caught one, and she'd forgotten they weren't designed for customers with six-inch heels. As soon as she'd paid her fare, the hydraulic doors slammed closed behind her and the bus moved off with a lurch. Unable to make the safety of a seat in time, Odette grabbed the first thing that came to hand and swung from it. When the elderly rabbi finally reclaimed his beard, his eyes were streaming.

As the bus rattled past the OD, she almost didn't recognise it. Stan's ad hoc shower curtains had gone and in their place were amazing wooden shutters inlaid with sand-blasted glass.

Ringing the stop bell, Odette made her way very carefully to the front of the bus and clambered off before clacking back to her club. Each of the shutters was beautifully crafted, the glass sections alternately shaped as a large O or a D. She had no idea how Calum could have had them designed, made and fitted in a weekend, but she loved him for it. His powers were phenomenal.

Rushing inside, past the highly polished brass plaque which was now fixed on correctly, she trotted into the foyer. Behind the reception desk, two very pretty women with glossy hair and smart red trouser suits were taking calls on tiny hands-free headsets. Odette was in too much of a hurry to introduce herself when they told her Calum was downstairs. That could wait.

The bar was remarkably full for a Sunday. Looking around, she noticed that it was basically the Nero crowd, plus a few trendy locals. It was a good combination, a buzz of lively conversation at each table, splashes of weekend colour replacing the usual greys and browns of the working week. She felt rather bleak in her black suit.

Calum was sitting in a far corner, dressed in his customary leather hat and donkey jacket, surrounded for once by paperwork instead of cronies. Odette liked the way his thin fingers poked from his long cuffs like a boy in an oversized school blazer, the dusting of stubble on his angular jaw hinting of late nights and a rock-star life style. She wasn't so keen on the way her own heart hammered inside her chest. He was concentrating very hard on whatever he was reading, a pen poking from his mouth like a cigarette, an empty espresso cup bearing a rim of dried froth just beside him. He looked up when she approached, grey eyes narrowing slightly.

'Back so soon?' The cool smile flicked on and he started piling the papers on top of one another. 'You shouldn't have bothered coming in.'

'I'm not staying – just thought I'd pop in to check you were okay.' An unfamiliar face took Odette's order for a Coke. 'You got a lot of new staff in, huh?' She turned back to Calum.

He had almost cleared the table of paperwork now. Odette wondered why. Most of it they undoubtedly needed to go through together, but when she pointed this out, Calum waved a dismissive hand. 'I wait till tomorrow. I want to hear about your weekend.'

'Blinding.' Odette raised her chin and smiled. 'And honestly, I'm blown away by all this – the new staff and everything. How d'you get them at such short notice? I thought you and Florian would find yourself helping out behind the bar this weekend, state the place was in when I left.'

Calum's eyes glittered with anger. 'I'd rather close the place down than do that.'

'And the blinds in the windows are fantastic,' Odette raced on, aware that she was approaching this all wrong. She wanted to get her edge back, but she felt like a visitor, not the boss talking to the principle investor. Her stupid heart was still hammering away as she took in Calum's smell – part pub, part shower; a heady mix of the seedy and the soapy.

His eyes were still glinting warily. 'I ordered them weeks ago, but they only arrived on Saturday.'

'You ordered them without telling me?' Odette felt two spots of colour hit her cheeks. 'Calum, I've told you that I can't operate like this. I have to—'

'It was before I learned that you dislike surprises. I thought you'd like them, sister.' As soon as her anger flared, it seemed his melted as a disarming smile spread across his face.

Odette was baffled by the disarming mood-swing. 'Well of course I do. It's just—'

'Then there's no argument,' Calum flashed his crooked white teeth. It was the same way he'd dismissed the launch fiasco. Odette hated the randomness of his approach yet she couldn't deny it worked. And despite his infuriating attitude, she couldn't deny she found him at his sexiest when he was like this.

'Now you stay here a minute,' he stood up, 'and I'll see if Florian can come down and join us. Don't go away, beautiful.'

It was the first time he'd called her 'beautiful', not the usual 'sister'. Odette knew she shouldn't let herself be talked down to like that; they were business partners after all. But hearing him say it made her feel ridiculously excited. He was taking an interest in the club at last, and in her. She had to keep a grip on herself, had to play this safe. Yet she knew that if she were given another chance to rise to his challenge and prove that she was his Jennifer, to have twenty-first century sex, to join forces with her other half, she wouldn't hesitate.

'Odette's here.' Calum wandered into Florian's office.

'*Merde!*' he hissed, stubbing out a Disque Bleu. 'Where is she?'

'Downstairs in the bar. You've got to come and charm her.'

'That stupid bitch? Leave me out of eet.'

'I need your help, son,' Calum insisted. 'You're the one who's had shutters put in from a restaurant that went bust just a week before this place opened.'

'The DoDo was in Manchester. No one 'ere will recognise the fittings, least of all that suburban cow,' Florian huffed. 'They look better than ze mess which was there before.'

'And she doesn't know that most of the staff are only borrowed while the Nero is having its refit. It's only a matter of time before they let something slip.'

'Okay.' Florian picked up his cigarette packet and stood up. 'I come. Ned, he can cope in ze kitchen. We only haff fifty covers tonight.'

'Well, don't tell Odette that.'

'Ees Sunday, what d'you expect?' Florian exploded defiantly. 'I shouldn't even be here. I should be at home wiz my wife.'

'You don't have a fucking wife, Florian!' Calum sighed impatiently. Florian liked to pretend that he had a loyal, model wife and two small children. He often said as much to the press who got confused when they looked up cuttings that stated he was a confirmed bachelor. It was a small reverie in which Florian indulged himself when he was feeling bored or fanciful. He certainly wanted children, but he had never met a woman good enough to mother them. Most modern women wanted equality and that, to his mind, was unnatural. He preferred to take lovers. Florian practised the art of seduction, but being seduced was another matter. It offended his pride

Which was one reason why he didn't want to join Calum with the shrewish, eel-faced Odette with her harsh voice and strong, ugly body. For Calum had hinted that Odette was keen on her new Überchef. More than that, he'd insinuated that should she make overtures, Florian shouldn't deflect them.

17

Odette was making a call on her mobile phone when Calum went back into the bar.

'Elsa babes, I wanted to say thank you . . . no, really? Poor thing. D'you think she'll lose her licence?'

She looked up as Calum and Florian approached.

'I gotta go, babes. What? This week – well, it's a bit tricky. I'll be here every night. Yes, that's right – I'm in the club now. Yeah, good vibe – lots of bods. No, not a chance this week. I'm off Saturday for the wedding as it is. Yeah, come in here if you like. I'll try and break off for a natter. Tata.' She slipped the phone shut as Calum uncorked champagne. 'We celebrating something again?'

'Just our combined talents.' Calum winked at Florian and started splashing froth into glasses.

'And ability to drink the profits.' Odette covered her glass. 'Not for me – I had too much last night.'

'Rubbish.' Calum poured the cool liquid on to her fingers so that it foamed in between. Odette pulled her hand away. Their eyes met for a moment and she felt that spark, that uncontrolled ignition, which she'd been fighting to dampen. The cool, pale grey gaze slid away slowly and Odette deliberately turned to Florian with as big a smile as she could muster, determined not to slip out of control.

'You settling in okay, babes?'

'*Oui.*' Florian shrugged sulkily. He, too, was dusted with stubble, she noticed, although it was not nearly so beautiful on his dark, oily cheeks as on Calum's pale, chiselled ones. He was wearing his huge sheepskin coat over his chef's whites, and the faded baseball cap was crammed on to his unruly black curls.

'Okay, shall we schedule a meeting in for tomorrow?' Odette took out her palmtop and looked at Calum, who was still smiling at her. She cleared her throat and flipped up her schedule. 'You and I can have a progress meeting and go through that paperwork, Calum. Say at nine? Then Florian can join us and we'll go through the restaurant receipts, and have a crisis meeting about the cabaret bar. We have a show tomorrow night. I think it needs some—'

'Cancelled. Not enough interest.'

'Shit! Who authorised that?'

'I did.'

'Comedy gigs sell a lot of tickets on the door.'

'We don't want a load of students hanging around in the foyer here, fresh from the Rat and Parrot, waiting for the doors to open. This isn't some dingy pub with a theatre upstairs, sister.'

No more 'beautiful' for her then. Odette rubbed her face tiredly. 'You had no right to take that decision over my head.'

'I tried your mobile, but it was switched off,' he lied.

'Okay, okay, we'll talk about this tomorrow,' Odette soothed, not wanting the argument to rage on. She was too tired and preferred him when he was smiling at her. 'I'll call Val at home and ask her to come in early.'

'Don't bother – I'll do it,' Calum said smoothly. 'Drink up. Let's not spoil the mood.'

Florian became even more sullen and uncommunicative as they moved on to a second bottle of champagne, especially when Calum suggested eating in the restaurant.

'It's after ten.' Odette yawned, looking at her watch. 'I gotta pick some stuff up from my office and then I'll push off home.'

'Nonsense!' Calum's eyes flashed a warning to Florian.

'Yes, nonsense.' He shot Calum a dirty look in reply before stretching a hand across to grip Odette's shoulder. The gesture was more Darth Vader than Valentino, but he was at least trying at last. 'You haff not tried my food. I feel insult eef you no stay and eat.'

Odette swayed slightly as she stood up. She hadn't noticed how many times Calum had filled her glass, but it must have been several. Suddenly it occurred to her that she hadn't eaten all day.

Several diners looked up in surprise to see the chef they had thought was cooking their sublime meal striding across the restaurant with two other people. His reputation was too terrifying for most of them to do more than whisper behind their hands. Florian shot them all dirty looks. Apart from waiters, the people he loathed most in the world were those who ate his food.

They settled at a table by the screened window. The menu design was the same, but its contents totally unfamiliar. Odette looked it over critically, but found nothing to criticise. Before she could make up her mind which dish was the least calorific, Florian whipped it away from her. 'I choose for you,' he said with Gallic masterfulness. 'And what ees more, I cook it.' He strode off to the kitchens, pausing to check the contents of two plates which a waiter was carrying and immediately send them back with a furious series of tuts.

As soon as he was through the kitchen doors, he raced unseeing past his terrified chefs and slipped out into the back yard for a Disque Bleu. 'Chef! *Viens ici!*'

Ned poked his red-mopped head outside.

'*Trois lotte et puis la venaison* for my table, *vite!*'

'Straight away, Chef.'

'And put a hat on, you feelthy bastard!' Florian angrily puffed his cigarette down to a pip and threw it into the slush before heading to his office to drain the remainder of a bottle of Cognac he had in his desk. No woman was going to try and seduce him, he'd see to that! Coming out, he bumped into Calum heading for the smaller office which Odette and Saskia now occupied.

'She thinks I'm having a piss.' He dashed inside and checked the desk. There was a pile of unopened post from Saturday alongside the bar receipts, the printed report of the box office takings, and Val the manager's resignation letter. Calum took the lot and threw it behind a tall filing cabinet. Then he pulled open a drawer and removed several files, sliding them down the back as well. If it was ever discovered, he would blame the cleaners.

Florian stood in the corridor, the Cognac starting to take effect. 'Why you do that?'

'Tidying up.' Calum knew the chef was probably too stupid – and, judging by his breath, pissed – really to care. 'Go and get that food, will you?' He dashed back out into the restaurant, ordering a bottle of very good Riesling en route. That should loosen them both up. He had a feeling things were about to take an expected turn.

The monkfish was one of the most exquisite things Odette had ever set eyes on. It looked more like an exhibit in a gallery than a meal about to be devoured. A single moist, firm medallion of pearl-pale fish languished on a jewelled cushion of red-pepper caviar, criss-crossed with drizzled necklaces of green, yellow and orange pepper *jus*, so delicately traced that they resembled a child's spirograph drawing. Balanced on the fish was a crown of deep fried herb leaves, as glossy and translucent as a jade brooch and an unmistakable Etoile trademark.

The starter tasted almost better than it looked, the flavours delectable, its texture as mouth-melting as a kiss on a four-poster bed. The sauce was so heavenly it made Odette slide her tongue greedily around her mouth as she tried to chase the last of the complicated, light and addictive taste before it melted like a memory.

Florian watched her indulgently. Odette generally didn't like people to watch her eating, but she supposed it was a professional duty to let him continue, and she'd certainly never seen him looking so friendly. Cooking seemed to have cheered him up. He was starting to smile and his coal-dark eyes seemed glazed with pleasure, almost crossed now that she came to look at them.

'You like?' he asked in a voice thick with pride.

'Amazing!' Odette laughed, genuinely blown away. Ferdy's food had been close to sensational, but this was in another class entirely. She took a swig of Riesling, so sharp and fresh that it felt like a breath of air on a mountain summit.

Florian was so proud of his venison he insisted on feeding it to her himself. Odette found the gesture deeply embarrassing, but she complied. Again, the flavours brought to life taste buds she never knew existed before now, making her shudder with greedy delight. Florian's big, sensual mouth smiled wider as he watched her eat, waiting patiently with a fresh forkful of heavenly food like a nanny spooning puréed fruit into a baby.

'I like the way you eat,' he murmured thoughtfully, fingering the stem of his wine glass which now contained a very good Haut Médoc. 'It is greedy and wilful. You are, I think, a very accomplished lover.'

Odette almost choked on a juniper berry. She swilled back some meaty red wine, not noticing that her glass hadn't been empty all night.

She knew that Florian was flirting with her, and while that gave her none of the sweet red-hot sensations that Calum's earlier attentions had, it felt good to be the focus of so much male attention.

Opposite her, Calum picked at his own food, eyes narrowed thoughtfully as he watched her with a curiously intent expression. Odette was too tight to stop herself wondering dreamily what he was thinking. Watching him out of the corner of her eye, she wanted him to be jealous, prayed that he was watching his chef with furiously concealed envy, but she suspected his quiet concentration belied another emotion entirely. Contempt, perhaps? Was he privately thinking that his chef friend, famous for his myriad lovers, had no chance with the frigid tease who had rejected his own approach just ten days earlier? A lot had happened since then, Odette realised. Something had escaped which she couldn't trap and recage. Something she had no control over. But she felt it for Calum, and not for the sexy brute who was feeding her like a lover.

Calum continued filling their glasses with attentive regularity – moving on from the Médoc to an exquisite '82 Chave Hermitage. Not really paying much attention herself, Odette took regular sips at Florian's insistence.

'Wine and food, they are lovers who cannot be taken separately,' he murmured. 'It is a *ménage à trois*, if you like –

yourself and the other two. You take one lover alone and he mourn in ze mouth for 'is companion.'

The wine was one of the restaurant's best-kept secrets, as deep and rich as Barry White's voice. It was only after she had drunk quite a lot of it that it occurred to Odette that Florian had stepped up his attentions to ridiculous heights. He was now flirting with her almost gluttonously. His huge hand was on her thigh, his mouth never more than a few inches from hers as he teased her to take another bite, then a sip, and then another bite until she'd finished all that was on the plate. Odette never finished a meal. She was shocked.

'I give you a break and then I bring dessert.' Florian winked at her, lounging back in his chair and lighting a Disque Bleu, eyes scanning the room as he detached his attention from her as easily as an avid *Coronation Street* addict during a commercial break.

They were almost the only people left eating. A few other diners were still spinning out their meals, nursing coffees and Cognacs or picking over the remainders of a huge cheeseboard. But it was a Sunday night and most had gone home, leaving a stained tablecloth and a hefty tip.

Odette tripped to the loo on a cloud of giddy delight. She was being treated so well. Calum and Florian were spoiling her rotten. Perhaps this restaurant lark was quite enjoyable after all. In a haze of good wine she had forgotten about the closed cabaret bar and the strange new super-efficient staff. She just felt ludicrously happy and, for the first time in ages, really quite sexy.

'"*Ohhhh, I love to love you, baby,*"' she sang off-key as she danced around the hot air dispenser waiting for her hands to dry. She checked her reflection in the mirror. Not bad. Not bloody bad at all. She was a fine stamp of a woman – not conventionally pretty, but definitely sexy. Sexy enough to have the famous Florian Etoile drooling over her. But sexy enough for Calum to love?

For a moment she closed her eyes and saw herself back at her flat, fire roaring, Calum bringing her a glass of brandy, then standing beside her and gazing into the flames. 'I love you, Odette Fielding.' His smooth, light voice was laced with emotion. 'Be my wife. We can get a butler and a small dog and live in a huge house in the country solving mysteries.'

'Odette Forrester,' she tested it out. It sounded good. 'Hello, I'm Odette Forrester, pleased to meet you . . .' Damn! That was common. What was it you were supposed to say? 'Odette Forrester, how do you do?' No – too formal.

Walking out of the men's loos and through the small foyer that bridged the gender-divide, Calum was astonished to hear a familiar voice saying, 'Odette Forrester – great to make your acquaintance – no, that won't bleedin' do. Hi, I'm Odette Forrester, and this is my husband, Calum. Get down, Freeway.'

Unable to keep the smile from his face, he slipped back into the restaurant.

'What's ze joke?' Florian looked at him curiously.

'I think Odette's ready for her just dessert.' He watched her crossing the room towards him. Her shiny black hair was dishevelled, blue eyes sparkling, lipstick applied slightly randomly to those wide lips so that she looked as though she'd been giving head. He still hadn't forgiven her for the launch night. And now he'd worked out a way of feeling better about it, a way that all three of them could enjoy.

Dessert was an even more sensual experience as Florian spoon-fed Odette a three-chocolate mousse as wickedly moreish as shopping with a new black Amex. By the time they had polished off half a bottle of Muscat, petits fours, Cognacs and espressos, the restaurant had emptied and the *plongeurs* were winding up.

Calum told the waiting and kitchen staff they could go home. 'I'll clear this lot.'

Odette laughed. 'You said you'd rather close the club than do manual work?'

'Well, I am closing the club,' he said smoothly, looking so deep into her eyes that she was certain he had memorised every streak on her irises.

Florian cleared their plates and wandered into the kitchen

to give Ned instructions for the following morning. Left alone with Calum in the huge restaurant, Odette found she couldn't stop smiling. He hooked a big, scuffed trainer over one khaki combat trousered knee and grinned back, assured and confident, well aware that he was totally in control at last. It had been easier than he'd ever dreamed.

'I want to show you something,' he said, standing up and, to Odette's amazement, taking her hand.

Her heart didn't thump this time, it appeared to stop altogether. She took a couple of deep breaths and relocated its beat, fast, faint and hopeful in every pulse point. The sensation of his hand in hers was as reassuring as a safety harness on an exhilarating but terrifying fairground ride. It felt dry, warm and firm, and she could all too easily imagine it exploring her body, stroking her naked flesh, cupping each glorious breast, sliding slowly between her legs . . . Shuddering with delight, Odette swung her head to smile across at him and suddenly felt a horrible sensation ricochet through her body.

'Sorry!' She blushed purple as a voracious burp flew out of her mouth.

But Calum smiled indulgently and stroked her cheek. 'Actually it's kinda sexy, sister – like Mrs Peel farting, or Madonna scratching her crotch. Come on, like I say, I want to show you something.'

Odette felt absolutely stuffed with food, her head ludicrously light in contrast to her heavy body. As she followed him towards the office he was temporarily sharing with Florian, she was aware that she was walking differently, part bloated drunken swagger, part sexy sway. She was Mrs Peel – all leather catsuit and chichi cool. She was Madonna – sauntering on stage in a chain-mail corset, with elastic hips and pneumatic cleavage. She was also a little girl, trotting beside the dominant male. She wasn't used to holding hands, to being led. It felt good. She liked the feeling of the palm of his hand, with its soft pads and bony fingers.

Calum seemed unaware of the electric currents which were shooting out of the end of his fingers, through Odette's body and into her skipping toes. He just towed her rather hastily into his 'office'. Two computers were still whirring at each other sleepily behind their OD screen savers – a clever little present which Odette's friend Duncan had created for her.

Letting go of her hand, Calum settled in front of one and brought the screen back to life, revealing a standard green Windows program manager with a stack of icons tucked to the left. Odette was familiar with most of them, having slaved away on the computer late into many nights over the past few weeks.

A warm hand on her leg made her jump, but Calum was still staring intently at the screen.

'Recognise this?' he breathed.

Odette stared. It was the OD bar in grainy black and white, shot from a high angle. The customers were moving around jerkily, the picture seeming to come in erratic bursts from its feed.

'Is this live?' she asked, enthralled.

He nodded, looking up at her. If Odette had glanced at his face, she'd have seen its animation, its excitement, but she was still staring at the screen, utterly rapt.

'This is for security, right?' she breathed, utterly amazed at the changes Calum was bringing to the club. This was so twenty-first century, so cutting edge. He was amazing.

'It's all stored on Zip disks,' he told her, hand still stroking her leg absent-mindedly. 'The camera's digital. It records twenty-four hours a day. The tape never runs out – it's all stored here on computer. No burglar can get in or out without us seeing his every movement on this little darling.'

The hand was getting higher. Odette's voice was squeakier than she would have liked. 'And the rest of the club?'

'This is just a test camera,' he said smoothly, stroking the inside of her thigh with the ball of his thumb. 'If you approve, we can have the whole place rigged up.'

'How much?' Odette could feel her breath punching out the words, but she couldn't control her voice at all now. His hand was reaching around to the curve of her buttocks, her pride and joy, her rear guard action.

'Expensive but worth it,' he said simply, seemingly unaware of his travelling hand. 'There's been a spate of burglaries in restaurants and bars lately. You have a great arse, by the way.'

'What?' She turned from the screen to him so swiftly that her neck cricked.

'You can home in on suspicious-looking characters.' Calum grinned, stooping over her to the keyboard so that she was forced down towards the monitor again. 'Look.' He tapped a couple of cursor keys and the picture shifted, zooming in on a table of rowdy media types. Despite the grainy quality, Odette could make out the lettering on the girls' babe t-shirts.

'The Leonard brothers were talking about using some of our footage for an art installation if we go ahead and rig the whole place up.' Calum's warm hand was back on her thigh again. 'Think of the publicity that would bring in.'

'We'll take it.' Odette shivered as his hand traced the lower arc of one high, round buttock.

Calum grinned up at her. Then, standing in one smooth, flowing movement, he cupped her face in his hands. It was such a romantic, such a Jonathan, move that Odette almost passed out. This was it. It was really happening.

'Florian finds you very attractive, you know that, don't you?' He cocked his head to one side.

A shell of disappointment punctured Odette's lung. 'Well, I suppose tonight he . . .'

'He wants to fuck you.' Calum's eyes bored into hers.

The other lung was punctured. Here we go again, Odette thought sadly, frustration gnawing at her. Sex as I do not understand it. Modern sex. Twenty-first century London sex. Unromantic, clinical, brutal and selfish. Is he coming on to me here or just playing Cupid? Either way, it leaves me cold.

'Does he?' she managed to croak.

'Oh, yes.' He nodded. 'And I can see why.' A slow smile spread across Calum's angular face.

'I don't mix business with plea—'

'Save me the clichés,' he cut through her nervous reply as easily as a sushi cleaver through a strawberry. 'Just do what you want. Fuck him, Odette. For once in your life, do something irrational. Fuck him.'

'Why?'

'For my sake.' His eyes were alight and burning into hers.

A moment later his mouth landed against her lips and he kissed her – hard, sweet and addictive. The first hit of morphine. Only this wasn't the first. The first you still stood a chance of walking away from, of surviving the need for another high. The second began a deadly obsession, a habit too compelling to deny, a fixation that separated your soul from your rationale and took your mind with it.

It was a kiss like no other Odette had experienced. It wasn't gentle or tentative or romantic. Nor was it sloppy or wet or greedy. It was controlled anger turned passion, ferocity with velvet lips, animal instinct with human skill. It was the most exciting sensation imaginable and she never wanted it to end.

When Calum broke the kiss, Odette was hooked. She was pissed, tired, excited and truly, madly, irreversibly in love for the first time in her life. She would have done anything he asked.

'Why him? Why not you?' she breathed, her mouth close to his, eager to be kissed again.

'You heard what he said about wine and food.' He stroked one long, narrow finger down her cheek. 'It's the same with me and Flo.'

Odette raked her mind for dropped metaphors. She vaguely remembered Florian saying something about a *ménage à trois*. 'Are you suggesting some sort of shreeshome?' she slurred, and then corrected herself furiously. 'Threesome?' She blinked, indignant and frankly terrified.

She wanted to scream, 'Just kiss me again and take me home. Me and you. Light a fire. Put on a romantic track – "The Power of Love" or "Careless Whisper". Make coffee. Never drink it. Make love instead. Wake up holding hands. Shower together. Or breakfast in bed. Not this. Not post-Millennium sex. No!' But she said nothing. She stared at him, too terrified of losing the moment, the intimacy, to break away.

Calum was laughing, that low, growling purr of a laugh he emitted so rarely that it was as kind on the ear as a breath from a loved one who'd been declared dead. His pale, pale eyes didn't leave hers.

'No, not a threesome,' he purred, tucking her hair behind her ears and tracing her chin with his lean finger. 'I try Florian's food – I'm his tester. And he does the same for me. He tries my particular weakness, if you like.'

'Tries your wine?' Odette asked hopefully, her voice trembling like a child's.

'Sometimes.' He dipped his finger to her chest, sliding it beneath the collar of her suit jacket. 'But I like him to try my women, too. He's an expert. He likes you all, whereas my taste is more refined. And he knows precisely what I want. He, shall we say, separates the wheat from the chaff.'

Odette pulled away, her mouth dry. 'I can't do this.' She backed towards the door. 'I can't fucking do this! You're crazy.'

'Do it, Odette.' He made no move towards her. 'You want to. I want you to.'

'You're a bleedin' lunatic.' She shook her head. 'You're fucking crazy.'

'Such a shame.' He turned back to his screen, watching the customers milling around the bar. 'I think we'd be good together. I think you might be the one. I thought,' there was a catch in his voice, 'you'd understand.'

She hesitated. 'Understand what?'

'How to love me.' He spoke in a whisper, barely audible over the noise from the bar downstairs.

'Is that what you want?' Her voice was shaking. 'Me to love you?'

He looked up at her over his shoulder, steely eyes suddenly softening. 'I thought you already did. Now all you have to do is prove how much.'

Odette looked at him for one last moment and then ran from the room, stumbling along the corridor into her own office.

Taking huge shaky breaths, she tried to calm herself down. Her head was racing with wide-screen images. She'd once idly dreamed of this happening, but had never imagined the nightmare of reality. Her life was finally imitating her favourite film. She was Kim Basinger in *9½ Weeks*, facing the ultimate demand from Mickey Rourke. Her friends had laughed at it, had pulled the script apart for its soft-porn titillation, its utter shallowness. Odette had cried when the relationship fell apart at the end. As Kim walked away from Mickey's flat after one demand too many, she'd sobbed her heart out and vowed that, given the same circumstances, she would have stayed.

Calum played with his computer-controlled cameras, bored of watching Florian drinking alone in the kitchens. No wonder Ferdy was washed up and drying out – he'd been taught by an expert, simply hadn't had Florian's capacity to soak it all in.

He flicked around the club. Three women were snorting coke in the women's loos downstairs. Too dull. The bar was full. So what? The restaurant was empty. The foyer was now manned by only one receptionist who appeared to be sharing a cigarette, or joint, with the cloakroom attendant. He tutted irritably and made a note.

He could hear someone moving about in the office next door. Odette. He wished the contractors had found enough time to fix a camera there too, but asking them to fit seven in just five hours had been a tough enough deal to negotiate, even paying triple time for the antisocial overnight work.

He rubbed his mouth as he listened, wondering whether he should follow her. But just as he reached out to turn off the monitor, he heard a step in the corridor and held his breath.

Florian was helping himself to a large swig of Cognac from the kitchen stores when Odette walked in. He'd thought she'd gone home – possibly with Calum. There was something funny going on between them, he suspected, despite Calum's assumed indifference. Florian had suggested as much to the classy blonde PA – what was her name, Saskia? She had seemed very taken with the idea if not, alas, with Florian.

'You want some?' He held up the Cognac bottle. 'I find a glass.'

'Don't bother.' Odette took a long pull straight from the neck, trying not to wince too much. Fire leaping in her throat, she moved towards him.

Florian ran his tongue around his mouth speculatively.

Within seconds he was running it around Odette's. It tasted surprisingly good. Sweet, clean and laced with Cognac and chocolate mousse.

Odette felt as though she was sucking an ashtray in a cross-Channel ferry, complete with dried bubble gum and used ear buds. His hands were on her breasts, greedy and excited, pushing them around as though kneading dough. It hurt. She tried to close her mind to it and think herself into a Jackie Collins character.

'Go down on me,' she demanded, wondering if this was perhaps too much.

It clearly was. Florian surfaced angrily from the kiss. 'You want me to taste you like a sauce? I might not like.'

Odette was thrown for a moment, tempted to make a bolt for it. What would Lucky Santangelo do? she wondered.

'Go down on me or I'll fire you,' she ordered.

'You think I'm some kitchen boy you can boss around?' he stormed, but there was a flash of excitement in his eyes.

Odette liked to gamble, and she reckoned the odds on this one were around thirty-three to one. A good outsider. She felt detached yet pissed enough to risk it.

'That's precisely what you are. You're a nobody as far as I'm concerned, Florian. Now get on with it or walk!'

He got on with it. He really got on with it. He licked, and tasted, and kissed and gorged. He added honey and Cognac, butter and cream. He nibbled and sucked and dabbed and suckled. Her turned her this way and that, any way but on. Finally, he turned her around, stripped and entered her. Just the way Calum liked it. All because she'd told him he would walk if he didn't, which excited him more than he'd ever admit. And the following morning, Odette was the one who couldn't walk very easily at all.

18

Elsa arranged a rare girls' night out to go to the OD on Wednesday evening. She was worried about Odette but didn't want the others to guess the extent of her fears so simply told them that going there instead of their favourite pub made sense as it enabled them to see their friend.

Juno grumbled that it was too expensive. 'I can only afford one glass of wine, whereas we could get several rounds in at the Stag for the same money.'

Lydia wasn't keen either. 'I have an appointment with my wedding co-ordinator.'

'Well, come along afterwards,' Elsa insisted.

Only Ally seemed eager for the outing. She and her husband Duncan had missed out on the launch night because they hadn't been able to get a baby-sitter, and so she embraced the chance to have a look around the club she had heard so much about. 'Wow – it's fantastic!' she whistled as she and Elsa headed through the foyer. 'Odette must have worked so hard to put this together.'

'I'm not sure it's the same place.' Elsa was gazing around in surprise.

They settled in the bar. Ally, who was dressed up in her smartest velvet skirt and polo neck, still felt drab and housewifey amongst the London trendies. When Juno arrived – predictably late and dressed in her old fleece – she grumbled that she'd almost not been allowed in. 'They said I was too scruffy. It's worse than the Atlantic bar. I had to point out that a, I know the owner, and b, I bloody work here too.'

'Do you, though?' Elsa asked. 'I thought you'd told Odette you couldn't be her maître emcee on a permanent basis?'

'I did, but she'll still need me to help out occasionally. Compère when the club upstairs reopens.'

'Reopens?' Elsa queried. 'I didn't know it had shut.'

Juno shrugged, 'From what I hear it has – probably fire regulations or something stupid like that. We'll ask her tonight. Anyone seen her?'

They all shook their heads.

Odette was sitting in her office, her face in her hands. She knew her friends were in the club. She'd had a call through from reception, but she couldn't face them. She'd cry. She knew she would.

She had no idea where all the tears came from. All that water. Years of drinking three bottles of Evian a day, she guessed. They just kept coming and coming, throughout the night. The Stairmaster no longer helped. Crying was her new nocturnal activity, along with watching *9½ Weeks* over and over again. By day, she could just about control them so long as she didn't see a familiar face or hear a familiar voice.

Calum hadn't made an appearance all week. On Monday she'd been glad. She'd steered well clear of the kitchens and Florian, had tried to shut herself in her office and sort out the financial mess the club was in, but most of the paperwork was missing. She knew the launch had been hugely loss-making, that she still owed the contractors thousands, that the bar was running low on stock and couldn't reorder until she'd paid off at least part of the wholesaler's bill.

On Tuesday she had walked into a police station and committed a crime right under their noses, giving them a photocopy of her building society account with a healthy five-figure balance, ensuring Craig's temporary liberty. Now that balance had shrunk to a low four figures. The electronic transfer to the builders had gone through, keeping them sweet for a few more weeks. But other bills were arriving every day, and she was appalled at their size. She had a progress meeting with Vernon the next morning. She had no idea how she was going to face him, particularly as she had none of the necessary receipts, facts and figures to hand.

Now tracking Calum down was a priority, but the bastard seemed to be missing. No one knew where he was. She had wasted most of the day calling every club, bar and restaurant he was connected with, but none of them had seen him all week. She'd even resorted to asking Florian, but he didn't know where the Scot was hanging out. Odette had slunk away in shame, certain that whatever test it was she had performed for Calum last Sunday, it was one she had failed miserably.

Far from being embarrassed as she was, Florian was acting as though nothing had happened between them. She was staggered by his gall, yet was also relieved that his arrogant ability seemingly to forget all about it allowed her to continue working alongside him with some semblance of normality.

And yet things were far from normal. Odette was very far from normal. The crying was nothing compared to the panic attacks, the breathless, claustrophobic horror. She was revolted by herself. Her body disgusted her, and now she showered with eyes tightly closed, unable to bear the sight of her own flesh.

She'd had twenty-first century sex. And she'd hated every minute of it.

The fax came through just as Odette was layering on mascara in an attempt to make her eyes look less puffy. She couldn't make it out at all. A very shaky, hand-written scrawl simply read: *'Fermoncieaux Hall – hard to pronounce, harder to renounce'.*

She studied it in confusion. There was no outgoing number on it, just the time. 21.45.

Christ! Her friends. She'd kept them waiting for ages. Throwing the fax down on her desk, she raced towards the bar.

They were twittering away happily downstairs, already two bottles of wine up and deep in discussion. It didn't take Odette long to find out what about.

'Bridesmaids!' Lydia announced delightedly as soon as she was close enough to hear over the hubbub of the bar. 'I want you all. The others have agreed, so you *have* to do it, too.'

'Bridesmaid? Me?'

'Yes. Now that's decided you can join the battle over what

to wear. Juno thinks pink, Elsa favours red, and Ally is so lovely she says she'll wear anything.'

'Oh – right.' Odette wasn't really taking it in. 'As long as it's not yellow rubber, I guess.' She tried to make a joke but it came out horribly wrong – accusing and bitter.

Juno turned very red and hurriedly gulped her wine.

Elsa was looked at Odette in horror. 'What's the matter with your eyes?'

'Spot of conjunctivitis,' she muttered. 'Listen, babes, I can't stay long. Got a meeting tomorrow morning that's a bit vital, y'know? You all all right for drinks?'

'We've got you a glass.' Ally started splashing wine into it.

'I'm sticking to Coke, thanks.' Odette was looking round to see if she recognised any of Calum's friends in the bar.

'It's so busy, I can't get over it.' Ally followed her gaze around the room. 'You must be so happy. Lydia says the launch party was spectacular.'

It was all unfamiliar faces again. They seemed to change every night. No one was coming back. They were all just trying it out.

'Mmm.' Odette sank into a chair tiredly. 'It was spectacularly expensive. Place is ticking over, I guess.'

'Ticking over?' Juno spluttered. 'It's bloody well time-travelling. There must be at least a hundred people in here, and knowing how much you charge for drinks that's lots of lolly in your till. I'd say Big Ben's hands are moving like helicopter rotors if this is ticking over.'

'Yeah, maybe.' Odette didn't want to go into it. Cashflow wasn't her favourite subject at the moment. She groped around for something to take her mind off it. 'Listen, I know it's a bit of an odd question, but have any of you heard of somewhere called Fermoncieaux Hall?'

'Sure, I have.' Elsa nodded. 'I think it's actually pronounced Firm-on-so. It's near my mother's place in Sussex – huge old stately pile. Quite famous, actually. Isn't it up for sale?'

'Is it?'

'Think so – has been for ages, in fact. I read about it in the papers. It's one of the most important houses to come on the market for years. You should see it – it's practically a stately home, although I think it was a mental asylum once. They're asking millions for it. Why?'

'No reason.' Odette decided the fax must have been misdialled. 'Now tell me about this bridesmaid thing again, Lyds? Aren't we a bit old and ugly to follow you around with flower baskets?'

She stayed for just half an hour. The talk was of nothing but weddings. Odette hadn't even thought about Stan and Saskia's, which was just days away. When Lydia asked her what she was going to wear to it, she hadn't a clue. She'd booked her accommodation weeks ago, at the same time phoning up Peter Jones to order a gift from the list, but recently the event itself had been far from her mind, even during the hen weekend. She'd given Saskia the week off to go to Berkshire and help her parents with the preparations. The result was that her own work load had doubled and her thoughts had been even further from her old friend's wedding to her assistant. She'd even wondered whether they'd miss her very much if she didn't go. Being away from the club last weekend had left her feeling like a part-timer, and without Calum to cover for her, she wasn't sure she could leave it. Then again, when he turned up – if he turned up – she wasn't sure she could stay.

Odette stayed in her office until past three in the morning trying to compile enough information to appease Vernon. Armed with till receipts for the week, a rough list of moneys still owing and a projection of income until the New Year, she felt she might just get away with it, but the figures made pretty depressing reading.

As soon as she was back in her flat, the tears started. She couldn't help them. They seemed so illogical, made her so angry, but she couldn't stop them. She cried until dawn.

Vernon made no comment about her dark glasses. He did, however, say quite a lot about her progress report.

'This won't do, Odette,' he tutted. 'This won't do at all. I simply can't allow an extended overdraft based on this. The information isn't here. There are huge holes – most of these figures are estimated.'

179

'Well, they are projections.'

'No, no, my dear – not those. These. Are you telling me you have no idea how much money you made over the last weekend?'

'The receipts have gone missing.' She cleared her throat and told Vernon her first lie in years. 'A computer virus. Terrible thing. Ate the lot.'

'Dear me. Have you tried antibiotics?' It was a day of firsts as Vernon told a joke. Desperate times changed people, Odette realised.

After a lot of thought, he told her that the matter would have to go to a higher level. 'I'm simply not authorised to pay out sums like these. I had no idea your book-keeping would be in such a mess. Your business plan was superb.' He sighed sadly and made a call through to head office to arrange for Odette to meet a manager there.

'He can see you next Tuesday,' he told her as he rang off. 'And may I suggest you try and find those missing figures before then? If he sees this, he may seriously have to consider withdrawing the funding.'

Hollow with fear after the meeting. Odette hailed a cab without pausing to think that she should be economising.

'Where to, love?'

She was so panic-stricken that for a moment she couldn't even think of the OD's address. She just wanted to go home and binge-eat her way through a hundred chocolate bars, but she knew she had to stop herself. Then, in a moment of demented denial, she closed her eyes and murmured, 'Bond Street.'

To stop herself binge-eating, Odette binged on something else. She gorged and glutted, stuffing bags, filling tissue-lined boxes and eating into the credit limit of her one remaining rainy-day credit card.

It was only when she got home hours later that reality bit. Throwing her platinum Visa in the bin, she stomped over to her bookshelves and started gathering up her sex and shopping novels and hurling them at the walls. In her experience, both activities only led to misery.

19

Odette was at Paddington almost an hour before her train was due to leave. She seemed to be getting her timing all wrong lately, panicking that she was going to be late and consequently turning up frighteningly early.

It was a bitterly cold morning. As the two-carriage train trundled beyond Newbury and into the Berkshire Downs, stopping at tiny stations to pick up or drop off just a few well-wrapped passengers, Odette stared out at the heavy grey sky. Inside, the train was tropical. She read a feature in *She* magazine about stress. It had a handy chart so that you could work out how close to a breakdown you were. Odette realised she was off the scale entirely. She closed her eyes and thought about Calum. Why hadn't he got in touch? She'd done what he wanted. What sort of game was he playing to make her feel this self-loathing?

She was one of the few people who got off at Hexbury, a rural Victorian station which was little more than a platform with wrought-iron railings, a covered footbridge and a small unmanned ticket office. A large, empty car park gave away the fact that it was a commuter stronghold, lonely and deserted at weekends. The three spaces in the taxi rank were unoccupied.

As her fellow passengers headed purposefully along an alley sign-posted to the Market Square, Odette looked around for a taxi phone, or even a poster advertising local firms, but there was nothing. Once again, she was reminded how different life was away from London. She had to call directory enquiries on her mobile and take down a number, then shiver for twenty minutes as she waited for it. At least it killed time.

Sid the cabbie was ecstatic the moment he found out she was going to Saskia and Stan's wedding.

'The Seatons? From Deayton Manor?'

'I think they live in a place called Hidden Farm.' She checked her invitation.

'Oh, I know that,' Sid chuckled. 'Had to move, didn't they? Old Tony Seaton lost a lot of money in the recession. But everyone round here still thinks of them as from the Manor out there. Been there forever, the Seatons. You staying at the Crown, you say?'

He took her to the village pub which stood opposite the little flint church where Saskia and Stan were to marry that afternoon. Sid pointed out a huge, exquisite brick and flint manor house in the distance. 'That's where they used to live. They're now at the farmhouse just beyond the wood to the right. See the roof? Locals call it the Villa on account of that.'

Odette could just make out a modern building with a garish orange-tiled roof behind skeletal winter oaks. Billowing beside it was a huge white marquee, almost twice the size of the house itself.

The list of accommodation that Saskia's mother had sent had mostly been of rather grand country house hotels with golf clubs and health spas attached. Odette had chosen the Crown because it was cheap and close to the action, and she was acutely aware of not having a car. But, accustomed to five-star hotels, she hadn't counted on it looking quite so basic.

The front door was locked and she could hear hoovering as she knocked politely to attract attention. The landlady was a thin, agitated divorcee wearing a flowered cleaning apron and fluffy slippers.

'We're not open.' She tried to close the door on Odette.

'I'm booked in to stay. Sorry I'm a bit early. Can I come in and change? It's for the Seaton wedding over the road. I can't go dressed like this,' Odette said jokily.

'Oh – right.' The landlady took in the trainers, tracksuit bottoms and leather jacket with suspicion. 'The Turner party, is it? Three family rooms, full English breakfast?'

Odette wanted to groan. Renee Turner was Stan's aunt and

had at least four sons who had once been the snotty-nosed, foul-mouthed scourge of their Stepney housing estate before being moved by the council to a huge house in Bromley where they terrorised the locals and grew up to be broken-nosed, foul-mouthed adults. Rowdy, hard-drinking Londoners, they had the social graces of England football supporters at a home match. Only today they were playing away and would undoubtedly be even more badly behaved.

'No – Fielding.'

'Oh, single room, right?' The landlady showed her through a very traditional horse-brass-decked bar and up a set of stairs to a narrow hallway, papered in wipe-down pink flowers and carpeted in thick pink nylon pile covered for some reason in what appeared to be gravel.

'We're fully booked so I've put you in here.' She opened the door to a tiny pink cell. 'The bathroom is along the corridor there. Mind the cat litter tray as you pass. I lock the doors at midnight. Breakfast is at eight sharp. And I'd appreciate it if you didn't smoke in here. It's my mother's room, but she's in hospital at the moment. Hip replacement.'

She left Odette in the cluttered pink room, which smelled of incontinent cat and incontinent old lady. A tiny casement window looked out over the main village street. Odette could see a florist's van pulling up outside the church, its rear doors opening to reveal several vast upright displays of winter lilies. She pressed her cheek to the cool glass and watched two ladies in Puffas carry a display carefully through the lych gate and towards the church entrance.

Even though she'd waited so long for a cab, she still had hours to spare. She'd stupidly imagined that she'd have an en suite bathroom in which she could pamper herself with a long soak and a very lengthy makeup application and hair-setting session. It was so rare she had the luxury of time these days.

She unpacked her case and looked around for somewhere to hang up her dress to drop out the creases. The white plastic wardrobe was jam-packed with shirtwaisters that smelled of mothballs. Every drawer was crammed with incontinence pants and nighties. In the end she draped her underwear over a pair of oxygen cylinders by the bed and hung her dress on a hook on the back of the door from which an ancient padded satin dressing gown was already swinging.

When she went to investigate the bathroom, she found a pink three-piece suite jammed into a cerise-painted broom cupboard, smelling strongly of pine bleach with just the subtlest undertone of incontinence. She locked herself in and started running a bath.

Determined to keep the stress demons at bay, Odette soaked for as long as she could, closing her eyes against the assault of several different pinks clashing in such a confined space.

Just as the water was really getting too cold to bear any longer, she heard a great series of heavy thuds coming from the stairs as several pairs of feet pounded up them, accompanied by much yelling and shouting.

'Shut the fuck up, Kylie-Marie. For the hundredth time, I ain't got it. You left your Furbie at home, you stupid little sod.' 'No, Dean, you can't take your tie off yet – we ain't even been to church.' 'This wallpaper's nice, love. Is it Homebase?'

Odette could hear the landlady's thin voice struggling to be heard over the din.

'Now these are the rooms . . .'

'I don't want a pink one,' boomed a deep male voice.

'They're all pink,' the landlady said tightly. 'The bathroom is along the corridor there. Mind the cat litter tray as you pass. It's occupied at the moment.'

'Your cat's taking a dump?' shrieked an excited young male voice, probably Dean's, Odette fathomed. 'Where? Let me see.'

'No, the bathroom is occupied,' the landlady muttered, clearly disapproving of Odette's lengthy bath. 'Another guest. If you'd like to use it afterwards then please wait for me to clean it. Now will you be wanting lunch?'

Once she'd gone back downstairs, Odette listened as a furious row broke out over who would have which room. She recognised Renee Turner's fierce, fish-market voice, which could carry across a football ground and was, as always, punctuated by her hacking smoker's cough.

'Des, Debbie and the baby can go in the one with the cot, you three great lumps in the one with the singles, and me and Mum'll go in this one with Kylie-Marie and Sheena. We can share the double and they'll have the bunks.'

'I'm not kipping in the same room as Gary. He fucking snores,' another deep voice boomed.

'Yeah, and your feet smell,' retorted yet another.

The argument raged on, and at least one child burst into tears.

Odette closed her eyes and slid under water. When she resurfaced, the argument seemed to have abated and a lot of thumping indicated that furniture was being moved around to suit whatever arrangements they'd settled upon. She climbed out of the now cold bath, and wiped the steam from the tiny mirror in the pink cabinet. Her wrinkled fingers were so grippy that the glass door slid open by mistake and she balked as she caught sight of at least three bottles of Librium before she quickly slid it closed again and examined her scrubbed face. A naked canvas which she was about to transform into a masterpiece.

As soon as things fell quiet, she crept out and made a dash for her bedroom, but she stumbled over something and a damp, gritty sensation hit her heel. Looking down she saw that she'd trodden squarely in the cat litter tray.

Renee Turner's voice hacked through a nearby door. 'Are we going down for lunch then? Mum, put your dress back on. You're not going to bed yet.'

Odette hopped back into the bathroom to rinse her foot, trying not to breathe in the foul stench as she washed the cat poo and grit down the plug-hole and, no longer caring, used half a bottle of the landlady's Badedas to cover the pong. When she raced back out again to try and make a run for her bedroom, she was too late. The Turners were re-emerging from their rooms.

Odette put her head down and scurried towards her own.

A series of wolf-whistles greeted her as Gary, Pete and Liam – Des's three shaven-headed younger brothers – emerged from the room beside Odette's. 'Fucking hell, boys, they've laid on the stripper a day late! Weren't you supposed to be at the stag night, love?'

'It's Frenchie Fielding, innit?' Pete, the youngest of the four, stared at her curiously. 'Don't your dad own the electric shop with all the old radios in the window? Me and Gary sell him gear from time to—'

'Shut up, Pete,' Gary muttered, eyeing Odette's small towel. 'You're Ray Fielding's girl?'

'Fucking is 'n' all,' Liam cackled. 'Fancy you staying here. Thought you'd gone all la-di-da now you're a millionaire. Shouldn't you be at the Hilton, darling?' He put on a fake accent, which was extremely hypocritical given that he had offered to put up his entire family in the five-star Courtyard. The most frightening of the Turner brothers, Liam had more scars, tattoos and gold jewellery than the others combined.

With a very weak attempt at a smile, Odette backed hastily into her room.

'Stuck up bitch,' Liam sneered at the door and then kicked it for good measure.

'Nice tits, though,' Gary raised a scarred eyebrow. 'I remember her now – used to hang round with Stan and his dippy mates. Always was top heavy. Tried to grab a feel once, but she was a right frigid cow.'

'What did you mean about her being a millionaire?' Des asked, ignoring Debs complaining that there was cat litter everywhere. 'I thought you said she was old Diamond Ray's girl? That bloke's a loser if ever I saw one.'

'He might be – she ain't. Worth a packet now, that one,' Liam said in a low voice. 'Her sister told me.'

'Monny Fielding?' Des remembered. 'Bit of a looker in her day. Used to put it about a bit 'n' all. Whatever happened to her? Din you used to go out wiv her, Liam? Years ago.'

'Yeah – what a goer,' he growled with far too much familiarity. 'She and Crooked Craig got wed a few years back. But she don't reckon the bastard married her for her Monny – it was for her sister's money.' He laughed uproariously at his own joke. 'Not a bad body on her, that Odette. Used to be a fat little kid, din' she? Looks bleedin' fit now. I'm tempted to have a crack at her later, even if she is a moody bitch. Big tits and wads of cash. Now that's what I like in a woman.'

'Bet you twenty I get in there first,' Gary cackled. 'I fancy being a kept man – yachts, fast cars, big house in the country.'

'She's quite pretty, isn't she?' Pete said as they pounded downstairs.

'Pull the other one!' Liam laughed. 'She's got a face like a smacked arse, but I ain't fussy if they've got it up front. And back off, you're too young for her.'

'Frenchie don't mix with the likes of you, sunshine.' Gary patted his shoulder. 'Squaddies ain't her line these days. She likes the officers' mess.'

Following behind them, Nan Turner looked around in confusion. 'Have we been evacuated again? Is this Devon?'

Odette set about pampering herself with furious determination. She might not want to impress any of the revolting Turner brothers, but she was going to damn well show them who had a smacked-arse face! She put her hair up in Velcro rollers and started on her war paint with unwavering concentration and attention to detail. Not an eyelash was left uncurled, a millimetre of lip unlined or a nail unbuffed.

After an hour, she looked unrecognisable. The Turners were thumping back upstairs from their lunch to collect hats and cameras. Odette peered out of the small window. Beneath her, Liam Turner's flashy Range Rover Vogue was parked several feet from the kerb, armoured with bull bars and light guards, its front grille covered with halogen spots despite never having been further off road than a dodgy car boot sale on an Essex school playing field. A scaled down Tottenham Hotspur strip swung from a coat hanger in the darkened rear window like a rep's jacket. Liam had once served time for organised hooliganism, an achievement of which he was inordinately proud and which he now referred to as his apprenticeship. He'd long since moved on to far giddier criminal heights, which was why he was always decked in gold and designer clothes.

The florist's van was long gone, and the groom's posse was huddling in the church entrance for warmth, puffing on cigarettes. Stan's two ushers were flanking him supportively.

Odette recognised his best mate from school, Reece 'Skunk' Figgis, who still sported a white streak through his hair in the style of Dave Vanian from the Damned. At Stan's other arm, his old drinking pal and fellow artist Vic Dodds was swigging discreetly from a vodka miniature. Handing the three of them thick piles of service sheets was Stan's best man and elder brother, Gilb, who looked even more nervous than the groom.

A few guests had started to arrive by the time Odette had put on her shopping binge outfit, trying hard not to let guilt at how much it had cost burn into her skin.

The dress was sensationally flattering. Its pale blue velvet matched her eyes, the bias cut made her body seem taller, slimmer and, if possible, even bustier. And the hat was something else. Odette wasn't sure whether it was just a bit too London, too outré for a tiny village church like this.

She peeked out of the window. The crowd was thickening. Cars were parking nose-to-tail in the narrow lane and brightly dressed guests were spilling from doors, plumes of condensation puffing from their mouths as they shrieked at one another in recognition. There were lots of silly hats. Just none of them quite as silly as hers.

Oh, God, the familiar symptoms of a panic attack were starting, combining a claustrophobic desperation to get out with an agoraphobic terror of leaving the room at all. Her heart was thumping madly, her chest tightening so that she could barely breathe. She closed her eyes and tried counting, but it was worsening. She took a few more short breaths. She had to get a grip on herself.

She decided she needed a drink. If she nipped downstairs to the bar she just about had time for a brandy. Grabbing her little designer bag, she raced from the room, crunching cat litter underfoot and leaving her camera behind in her haste. She was shivering with fear now, yet drenched in sweat.

The pub was packed with male wedding guests downing swift pints. Odette ordered her brandy from what she took to be the landlady's daughter, a drippy-looking teenager with a big spot on her chin. The brandy optic was empty.

'I'll get another bottle and bring you one over.' The girl

gaped at Odette's hat. 'Go and sit by the fire – you look frozen. Mum said you was in Gran's room. Chilly in there.'

'Thanks.' As she propped herself on the padded leather mantel seat by the open log fire, she heard a loud voice assessing her from behind.

'Is that one of Tony's family, Dan?' The Welsh accent was more refined than Dai the trekker's – Richard Burton to his Ivor the Tank Engine. He made no attempt to lower his voice for Odette's benefit. 'Lovely-looking bit of totty, isn't she now?'

'Shouldn't think she's a Seaton, Garth, they're all blonde and as flat as ironing boards,' said his companion, discreetly dropping his voice to a whisper as he added, 'Probably one of Tony's mistresses. Always suspected he was a tit man.'

Blinkered by her hat, Odette couldn't make them out but prayed Saskia didn't sit her next to either of them. In her current state, she couldn't be trusted with a fork.

'Where's Jilly, Garth?' a posh female voice asked pointedly.

'She left me – didn't even empty the dishwasher first,' the Welshman said without a trace of self-pity or regret, as though talking about a cleaning lady. 'Shacked up with her aerobics instructor. I've joined a dating agency.' The conversation moved on to his recent dates.

When the drippy barmaid brought over a smeary glass of brandy, she was walking backwards and staring in wonder at the bar. She almost tripped over Odette by the fire, continuing to gaze across the pub with a dreamy sigh as she passed the drink. 'That's Felix Sylvian,' she whispered. 'And they must be his brothers – they're just as good-looking, aren't they? Oh, God, I can't go back there. I've got a poster of Felix wearing just his pants.'

Odette followed her gaze to where three staggeringly good-looking blond men were waiting at the bar. She'd seen Felix before, although she'd never met him. Saskia had reported that he and his two brothers were at the OD opening, but she couldn't remember seeing them there. Felix's beautiful face was as familiar in advertising circles as the Lever trademark. His two brothers were, it was true, almost as dazzling. Felix was in the middle – honey blond, six foot, every girl's dream pin-up.

The younger brother was paler blond – almost white-blond like Lydia – and a few inches shorter. The third brother, the eldest, was huge – broader as well as taller – with tawnier, streaky hair and a very loud laugh. He was calling for service in a voice that almost deafened Odette in the corner of the room. Demanding pig, she thought. The Sylvians had a reputation for arrogance bordering on brutality.

The barmaid and Odette then watched in amazement as the tallest Sylvian vaulted over the bar and started helping himself and his two brothers to three glasses of malt whisky from a top shelf before throwing a tenner in the till. 'Now can I get anyone else a drink while I'm here?' he offered in his booming voice, resting both his palms on the bar and beaming round the room, looking for all the world the perfect landlord, except perhaps for the morning suit.

Within seconds he was pouring pints, giving backchat and charging half as much as the drinks would normally cost.

'Bloody marvellous!' the Welshman, Garth, was clearly taken. 'Now he has to be a Seaton.'

'Oh, no.' His male companion laughed bitterly. 'With an attitude like that, he's a Sylvian. Conceited to the last.'

The landlady trotted down the stairs still wearing her pink cleaning tabard and squawked in horror when she saw a tall stranger leaning on the wrong side of her bar, laughing with a customer. She was just puffing and blowing that this was 'beyond irregular' this was 'downright outrageous', when Skunk popped his two-tone head around the pub's door.

'Everyone!' He cleared his throat awkwardly, still as shy as Odette remembered him being at school. 'We've just had to send the bridal party around the block. Can you, like, come into the church, please? Bring your pints if you like,' he added seriously, looking genuinely surprised when he received a delighted round of laughing guffaws.

20

Odette found herself sitting on the edge of a front pew with Stan's Uncle Derek, just behind the dreaded Turners who were offering around Murray Mints and complaining that they wanted a fag.

By her side, Derek was videoing everything that moved on his camcorder, the automatic whirring of his zoom so loud that it almost drowned out the organ as the vicar arrived at the chancel steps and cleared his throat pointedly.

There was the usual anticipatory hush, followed by the usual rustling of service sheets, craning around of heads, tipping up of chins to look over hats, first few strains of the 'Trumpet Voluntary', a louder rustling and clearing of throats as the congregation stood up. Then the game was on.

Odette knew the ropes of old, but every wedding struck her afresh as she took in a new angle, or felt a new emotion. She saw Stan swing around first, watched his delighted reaction. Then she turned herself and saw Saskia making her way slowly along the aisle on the arm of a very fat, very proud-looking father. And well he might be proud. Saskia looked ravishing in what might less kindly be described as a meringue, more kindly as a fairy-tale fantasy of a dress – all duchesse silk, hand-span waist, corseted bodice and huge, full skirt. Her face, beneath the lightest of veils, was glowing with excited happiness. This was her day. She'd dreamed of this moment.

Odette loved every minute, despite Derek's noisy zoom punctuating the more loving moments – such as the 'I do's, the kiss and Gin Seaton crying all the way through her reading of St Paul's letter in *Corinthians*. The Turners crunched Murray

Mints noisily throughout and muttered about Odette's hat, but it didn't matter. It was a beautiful ceremony – traditional, simple, and every girl's dream wedding. For a brief while Odette was spirited away from the horror of her current situation.

Not that every woman there was having a wedding daydream – one in particular was having a lady-of-the-nightmare. Odette caught Phoebe's eye during Tony Seaton's droning reading of a very oddly chosen Tennyson poem about wanting to feel the arms of one's true love, but putting up with a look-a-like. Phoebe grinned broadly and pointed to her tarty bridesmaid's dress, poking out her tongue and pretending to die.

'"*Bring me your arrows of desire* . . ."' Why did everything make Odette think of Calum?

While self-consciously mumbling the familiar hymn, she turned along with everyone else to see who possessed the gloriously rich brown bass voice belting out 'Jerusalem' at the rear of the church, far out-booming the reedy organ. The eldest Sylvian brother sang so loudly he almost blew the hats off the women in the pew in front.

As the register was being signed, Odette listened to Saskia's friend singing 'Ave Maria', and patiently leant to one side as Derek tried to get a better angle for his zoom by dangling a sweaty armpit over her. The church was lit by a hundred fat candles, which had now started to cast their magic as it darkened outside. Looking around, Odette realised how beautiful the dancing light made everyone look. She spotted the Yaks in their finery for the first time, dotted around the church with their husbands and toddlers, looking very different from the way they had last weekend coated in mud, pyjamas or Puffa jackets – like horses plaited up with ribbons for a show.

To her delight Odette spotted Stan's old friend, Fliss Woolf, dressed in an extraordinary lime green fake-fur dress with matching hat that clashed stunningly with her cloud of red hair. They hadn't seen one another for years, but Fliss recognised her straight away and waved enthusiastically before prodding her companion to point her out. A nice, solid-looking bloke in a rather creased morning suit woke up with a splutter and waved too. On his far side sat the three blond Sylvian brothers, looking as long, languid and luminous as the flame-topped church candles around them

At last the bridal party were smiling their way along the aisle, being snapped from all around. Derek's zoom was going mad as it focused in on Helen's high, pert bottom in its flattering peach skirt which, Odette noticed, was far shorter than Phoebe's with a strangely uneven hem, as though it had been taken up at the last minute – with Sellotape.

Outside it was almost pitch dark and thick flakes of snow provided impromptu confetti. Guests pulled on gloves and coats as they puffed away on eagerly awaited post-ceremony fags and chattered over the din of church bells. The inevitable hanging around outside church was curtailed by the father of the bride. Clapping his hands to attract attention, Tony Seaton announced that it was too dark and snowy for the official photographs to be taken, so he suggested moving straight to the marquee, adding, 'I think you'll find the walk rather fun. Dan Neasham, who owns Deayton Manor, has kindly bought it for the bride and groom as a gift.' He indicated an urbane-looking man whom Odette had overheard talking to the Welshman in the pub earlier.

'Who buys a fucking walk?' she heard a harsh voice ask and turned to see Gary Turner, shivering in his shiny grey interview/funeral/court appearance suit as he puffed on a Lambert & Butler beside her. 'Walking's free, innit?'

He seemed to be aiming the question at her so Odette shrugged non-comittally and tried moving away, but he pursued her with an attempt at a gag. 'Unless you're Christopher Reeve of course.'

She winced. He was losing his twenty quid bet faster than a gambling addict at a slot machine.

Fliss came to her rescue, dashing towards her like a fast-moving cactus armed with a huge, fluffy hug. 'Isn't it freezing? Frigging hell, Odette, I almost didn't recognise you back there. You look frigging amazing.'

'Citizen Smith!' Odette laughed, using Stan's old nickname for his mate, 'Wolfy' Woolf. She wanted to keep on hugging the warm, cosy redhead. In the bitter, snowy wind, it was like hugging a hot water bottle in a fake fur cover. 'Boss frock, babes.'

'Yeah,' Fliss scoffed, 'I look like a topiary bush. People keep telling me. Phoebe's sister, Milly, made it. She's setting out as a fashion designer. The little minx didn't tell me we'd look like two Furbies, though,' she pointed out a thin, punky-looking girl in an identically styled fur dress and hat that was the same lurid, disclosing tablet pink as the bathroom suite in the Crown Inn.

'Meanwhile your boyfriend has hypothermia and needs to wrap himself in the foil covering from the finger buffet,' said a chattering-teeth voice as the solid-looking man in the creased morning suit hooked his arm through Fliss's. 'I'm Dylan. And you're Saskia's "stunning boss".'

'Who said that?' Odette flushed.

'This stunning boss of mine,' Dylan kissed a freckled ear. 'Who never tells a lie. Come on my little fluffy catwillow, and you—' he offered his other arm to Odette, '—you stunning boss person. Let's go and seek warmth.'

'Frigging heck – will you look at that!' Fliss whistled as they made their way to the gate that most of the other guests had already passed through. On the other side was one of the most beautiful sights Odette had ever seen.

Dylan immediately started humming the first bars of 'Stairway to Heaven', only to be nudged silent by Fliss whose eyes had filled with tears and who was muttering, 'Whoever would have guessed it? Dan Neasham has a soul after all. Oh, Dyl – it's so lovely! It's like – it's like – a book or a dream or something.'

His arm slipped around her as they gazed in wonder, blinking snowflakes from their eyes

Lighting their way through the Friesian field was a corridor of tall, flaming garden torches, illuminating a path of heavy-duty matting. Almost half a mile long, it led all the way through the Manor's land to the tiny, modern Hidden Farm in the woods beyond. The path cut a warm red glow through the snow-covered field so that it ran like a streak of hot lava down the valley. It was an amazing sight, and so deeply romantic that Odette at first caught her breath and then gently let Dylan's warm arm slide from hers.

'I've left something in the church – you go on,' she told them, backing away. She knew that this was a romantic walk

Fliss and Dylan should enjoy together; they'd never forget it. The snow and the haunting pealing of the church bells were magical accompaniments. She could walk behind alone and indulge herself in solitary, snowy thoughts of Calum.

'All right there, Frenchie?' Liam Turner swaggered to her side and tapped his shiny grey jacket pocket, which looked identical to his brothers'. Odette found herself idly wondering whether the Turners had bought a job lot of suits from Mr Byright and then balked as she recognised it as Versace. Liam's ill-gotten gains could buy him a wardrobe full of designer suits, she realised. So why did he have them all made up to look like cheap, flashy tat?

'I just popped back to the hotel for a little pick-you-up.' He reached into the tapped pocket and retrieved a Tiffany hip flask. 'Care for a snifter, m'dear?' He adopted his mock-posh accent.

Odette was about to snap that the Crown was a pub not a hotel, and that she wouldn't drink from Liam's hip flask without a straw – or cling-film around the rim at the very least – when she stopped herself short. I'm a snob, she thought in horror. I've turned into a snob. I can't let this happen.

'Sure.' She took the flask and swigged, almost choking as she realised it was filled to the brim with gin.

'Eich!' she shuddered.

'It's for me mum,' he apologised, looking sheepish. 'She don't like fizzy wine. Gives her wind.'

Linking her arm tightly through his for warmth and balance, Odette laughed, deciding he wasn't such a mean thug after all. At least he took care of his dear old ma. Not a lot of these stuck-up toffs would do that given the choice of several fine malts – or even vodka – over gin.

'Oi, don't get ideas,' she ordered as he tried to slide a hand around her bottom. 'I have a very big, very mean boyfriend called Jonathan, understand?'

'First I've heard of it,' he said without thinking.

'Why, who have you been talking to?' Odette asked curiously. They hardly mixed in the same circles any more, although she guessed he might know Craig.

'Oh, no one.' He looked suddenly shifty. 'So why ain't he here then, this Jonafan?' He took a defiant swig of gin.

Odette thought about Calum. She had no idea where he was. Not that he was her boyfriend, she realised sadly – just her Jonathan. 'He's overseas,' she told Liam. Remembering the jibe about the officers' mess, she added, 'He's a PT instructor in the army.'

That shut him up.

The receiving line was looking distinctly fed up and desperate for a drink by the time Odette and Liam arrived at the billowing marquee which was, to Odette's delight, blasting out heat. Marching ahead of her in his desperation to get to the 'fizzy wine', Liam mumbled an awkward, foot-scuffing 'pleasedtameetcha' to each and every person before bolting into the hot-air balloon tent.

Odette tried, at least, to say something they might not have heard a hundred times.

'Virginia – I'm Odette Fielding.' She shook a firm, gardening-callused hand, wondering why her own voice was unrecognisably posh on occasions like this. 'I've heard the *Corinthians* verses a hundred times, but that was the first time I've listened to the words. So lovely.'

Gin, a handsome woman in a very well-tailored – if trad – tweed suit, simply glowed and kissed her cheek. 'Must talk later. Saskia adores you. Happiest job she's ever had.'

Odette doubted it, but was flattered. And Tony was already ogling her boobs, so she knew she had a walkover, simply shaking his hand and murmuring, 'You're far too young to give a daughter away, unless you're putting her up for adoption.' Bad joke, but perfectly aimed. Tony pumped her hand in his, blinked at her cleavage and asked her what her name was again.

Along she moved like a mobile feel-good factor, complimenting, charming and joking. She praised Jean McGillivray's ghastly hat and asked Stan's dad for a tip, gently deflecting his loud assertion that 'I always fought it'd be you my boy would marry, love'. She made Saskia and Stan shiver with joy as she reminded them how much happiness they deserved.

It was only when Odette paused at the end of the line and wondered where to head next that she realised who had followed her in line. Standing right behind her was Felix's sandy-haired brother. 'That was amazing,' he said in his too-loud voice. 'I'm not sure whether to be appalled or to applaud.'

'What d'you mean, babes?' she flashed a disarming smile, still in charm-offensive mode. He was even bigger close-to, towering over her despite her high heels. There were snowflakes in his tawny hair and on his broad shoulders, and streaks of ruddy colour in his high, tanned cheeks. He was really just too polo-player, landed gentry attractive, Odette decided. He probably had a hallmark on his bottom.

He screwed up one dark blue eye and looked at her. He also had snowflakes on his pale lashes, Odette noticed, and he was shivering.

'You were working back there, weren't you?' he nudged his head towards the line which was tiredly welcoming the vicar now. 'You made them all want to buy whatever it is you're selling. What are you selling, Miss Fielding?' The formality of his address was strange, along with his accent – part deep public school drawl, part something Odette couldn't identify – exotic, bullish and horribly sexy.

'Myself, Mr Sylvian,' she stared him straight in the eyes, deciding that he'd exposed the truth about her limited social skills – however rudely – so she should tell it back like it was. 'I sold them what they wanted to see in themselves, and that makes people happy. It's a happy occasion,' she plucked two champagne flutes from a passing waitress, handing him one. 'Be happy.'

And then he said the oddest thing. It would stay in Odette's head for the rest of the night, like a lyric from a song she couldn't place, that deep, hypnotically odd voice – all resonance and unfamiliar accent and accentuated emphasis. 'How can I be happy, Miss Fielding, when you are so sad? You're not selling yourself, you are selling your soul. And, believe me, you can't buy it back. I've tried.'

Taking the glass from her with a strangely apologetic smile, he made his way towards his two younger brothers who were dashing around the tables swapping place names. To Odette's amazement, he took them both by the ear like a draconian father and led them to the table plan so that they could remedy their practical joke. Suddenly she realised who the Sylvians reminded her of. They were simply upper-class versions of the Turner brothers. One clan had floppy blond hair and public-school voices while the other sported crew cuts and East End accents, but little separated their behaviour. She didn't like any of them, and was yet again aware of her utter alienation. She never seemed to belong anywhere, eternally destined to be the single woman in a marriage of two extremes – her snobbery and her class.

She drained her champagne and ran the recent comment around in her heart. Selling her soul indeed! What a load of pretentious garbage. She might not have had an ivory-tower education but she knew a pseud from a dude.

As the wedding party posed for endless photographs in front of a cream tent wall, guests milled about, catching up on gossip, complimenting one another's hats and admiring the table settings and the flowers. Two huge gas-burners were pumping so much hot air into the marquee that it almost took off. Outside, it was now pitch dark and the snow was falling even more heavily. In a small annexe tent with a dance floor, a string quartet was playing Winter from 'the Four Seasons'.

Having chatted to a couple of the friendlier Yaks and met their braying husbands and bawling offspring, Odette wandered across to look at the table plan. She brightened happily as she realised that she was placed on the same one as Fliss and Dylan, sitting between dear old Skunk and one of the Sylvian brothers, James. She just hoped he was the giggly younger one and not the big, bullish formal one who disapproved of all things commercial. She loved a good debate, but she wasn't sure her nerves were capable of holding up today.

A gust of very strong, cheap aftershave caught in a warm air pocket from the gas burners warned her that one of the Turner brothers was approaching.

Before she had a chance to escape, Gary had hooked a huge arm around her shoulders and was scanning the plan for his name.

'Bleedin' hell, I'm right at the back. Won't be able to see a thing. Where are you?' When he spotted her choice position on a front table he tutted under his breath, 'Right, we'll see about that.' And marched off to swap the name-places around, dumping James Sylvian at a rear table while he promoted himself to the front. Odette groaned. She'd been right. The Turners and the Sylvians were interchangeable.

'I appear to be called Gary,' Jimmy laughed as he stood behind his gold-sprayed chair, leaning on it and peering at his place-name.

'Gareth, did you say?' chirped a cut-glass voice from beneath a hat so droopy that nothing but a pair of sharp red lips could be seen. 'Good to meet you. I'm Saskia's sister, Sukey, and this is my – er – partner.' She seemed hugely uncomfortable with the word, 'Guy. Guy, this is Gary . . . I didn't catch your second name?'

'Neither did I,' Jimmy laughed, stooping back over the table. 'Turner.'

'Gareth, old boy. I'm Guy.' A balding William Hague lookalike with a very red race pumped his hand and then stood behind his own chair. 'Who are we waiting for?'

'Fliss Wolfe . . . Dylan Abbott . . .' Sukey walked around the table peering at the cards. 'Oh, I know them – friends of Saskia . . . Milly Fredericks, that's Phoebe's sister . . . Reece Figgis,' she snorted in amusement. 'Anyone know who he is?'

'One of the ushers, I think.' Dylan wandered over to take up position behind his chair. 'Hello there, Jim—'

'Gary.' Jimmy held out his hand with a wink which Sukey didn't notice – her hat stopped her line of vision just above her nose.

'And someone called Odette Fielding is sitting beside you, Gareth,' Sukey was reading out the final card. 'Does anyone know who she is?'

'Saskia's gorgeous boss.' Fliss bounced up to the table with Phoebe's sister, Milly. In their two clashing fake-fur dresses they looked like a pair of fluffy dice.

They were hotly pursued by the real Gary, who was eager to claim the new seat he had allocated himself. On spotting its rightful owner already in situ – and clocking Jimmy Sylvian's gargantuan shoulders – he melted away.

'The club owner? Gosh.' Sukey was thrilled. 'We keep meaning to go there, don't we, Guy? See where Sasky works? She loves it. It's supposed to be *the* place to be seen right now.'

'Yes, well, all a bit glitzy for us old-timers,' he said pompously.

Skunk wandered up to the table, said a couple of shy 'lo's to no one in particular and sat straight down in his seat.

'You should stand,' Sukey told him kindly.

'What?' He looked terrified as he took in the talking standard lamp.

'It's etiquette to stand until all the women are seated.' Sukey's little red mouth twitched a condescending smile in his direction. 'Don't worry about it. You weren't to know. I'm sure this sort of formal bash seems terribly antediluvian to you.'

'Oh – right.' Skunk pulled his napkin out of his collar and stood up. Beside him, Milly tried not to giggle. Sukey was such a cow.

'I like your hair,' she told him. 'Is it natural?'

He shyly shrugged in the general direction of the talking pink fluff. 'Sort of.'

'Where is this Odette woman then?' Sukey tilted up her chin and looked around the room. 'I suppose she's used to keeping people waiting. Really, this is quite rude. Everyone else is sitting down – some are starting to eat. What does she look like?' Sukey was scanning the room, desperate to collect Odette and start the meal.

'Huge tits.' Dylan picked up the bottles of red and white wine ready to pour into glasses.

Fliss nudged him hard so that he splodged red wine all over the floral centrepiece, 'She's wearing pale blue velvet and a fantastic hat.'

'Oh, *her*,' Sukey sniffed, having clearly registered Odette earlier. 'Bit tarty.' Not liking the prospect of her hat being upstaged, she lifted it off her head and patted her tight blonde French pleat. Underneath the lamp shade, her face was pudgier than her younger sister's and losing its prettiness with age, but her blue eyes had the unmistakable Seaton twinkle. Now that they could see, she spotted Odette straight away. 'She's over there – talking to that ghastly jumped up estate agent, Garth Draylon. Hasn't his wife just pushed off? No wonder she's in there – he's loaded.'

Odette was trapped. One of the tanned Welshman's huge, burly arms was gripping a ribbon-festooned marquee post, deliberately flashing a lot of chunky gold Rolex. The other was leaning against the corner of the cake table. Pinned into a very small space between, Odette tried to ignore the fact that Garth's dissipated faded denim eyes hadn't left her cleavage for the entire ten minutes he had spent boasting about his property empire. Normally she'd tell him where to get off, but this was a wedding and she knew she owed it to Saskia's family not to explode at one of their friends, however unctuous.

'Shouldn't we be sitting down?' She looked over his shoulder, noticing that almost everyone else had settled at their tables.

'Drink enough of this, my lovely, and we'll both be lying down.' Garth picked up a discarded bottle of champagne from the cake table and filled up Odette's glass. Seeing an escape route, she started edging her way out. But he once again cut her off, discarding the champagne bottle and laying a sweaty hand on her shoulder. 'I hope you don't mind me saying this, but you have the most fantastic pair of brea—'

'Odette, there you are!' Fliss bounced up just in time. A moment later and Garth Draylon would have had a glass of champagne dripping through his grey thatch of hair and onto his moustache. Odette was livid.

She managed to catch a few deep breaths on her way to her table, and was further calmed when Skunk, who was trying to eat his starter while still standing up, looked terribly relieved to see her. She needed someone to look after right now, to take her mind off things.

'There you are!' Sukey stretched out a hand and shook hers. 'I'm Sukey Seaton, Saskia's sister. This is my – er – partner, Guy. Fliss . . . Dylan . . . Milly . . . sorry, I've forgotten your name?' She peered at Skunk who visibly quailed.

'Oh, I know Skunk.' Odette took her place beside him.

'Skunk?' Sukey looked appalled, flared nostrils visibly narrowing as she imagined where the nickname originated. 'What a strange name. And this,' she beamed at the broadest Sylvian brother whom she thought rather dishy, 'is Gary.'

Odette looked at him curiously, then spotted the replaced name-card and realised that some winding-up was taking place here.

'Pleased to met you, Gary.' She held out her hand. His shake was bone-crunching, the dark blue gaze teasing as it held hers for a brief moment before darting away with arrogant restlessness. For someone who thought she was selling her soul, he seemed to have flogged his at a discount.

Why, she thought curiously, does a man who reproaches his two brothers so strongly for playing practical jokes allow himself to play one just a few minutes later? It struck her as hypocritical.

Sukey commandeered 'Gary' the moment they sat down, demanding to know where he came from, 'Is it my imagination or do you have a hint of a South African accent? Were you born in the colonies by chance?'

He laughed. 'I was born in London and went to school in Yorkshire, but yes – I suppose I may have picked up a faint trace of African dust in my throat over the years.'

As she made polite conversation with Skunk during the starter, Odette couldn't help but hear every booming word James Sylvian spoke beside her, and started to realise that he was one huge contradiction. He adored his two brothers, claimed that spending time with them recently had been the best few weeks of his life, and yet he appeared to have lived overseas most of his life with precious little contact.

Odette was about to turn around and find out more when Skunk leaned across and asked her how her family was.

'Heard your Craig was in a spot of bovver with the law?' He sounded excited at the prospect, having always thought Odette's wheeler-dealer brother-in-law the height of cool.

'Who told you that?' She glanced around the table worriedly, but everyone was deep in conversation.

202

Skunk was trying to get a fork into a fat prawn. 'I bumped into your sister in the Greyhound on Thursday night. She said he's up in front of the magistrates this Monday.'

'That's just the first committal hearing,' Odette dismissed hastily, pushing some rocket around her plate.

'That serious?' Skunk whistled. 'Will he be up at Crown Court then?'

Odette was unpleasantly aware that James Sylvian and Sukey were now listening in, eyes on longer stalks than the white lily centrepiece. She tried to give Skunk an easy smile and muttered something vague about unpaid parking tickets.

Skunk gave up on his fork and picked his prawn up in his fingers, taking a huge bite out of it without shelling it first. 'C' mon, Frenchie – everyone knows you don't go in front of a jury for that.' He was chewing frantically. 'I heard he's been doing over petrol stations.' He spat the prawn out. 'Yeuk! This food's bleedin' horrible.'

'Maybe Craig forgot to pay at a self-service Texaco,' Odette muttered vaguely.

But Skunk shook his head. 'Everyone in the boozer was talking about it – saying it's to do wiv a big drug racket. We're talking major league.' He loved to use language from the lousy Segal movies he watched. 'Liam Turner even reckoned you put up twenty K to get old Crooked Craig out.' He cackled in glee, obviously finding this claim beyond belief.

On her other side, James Sylvian lifted an astounded eyebrow. He'd obviously never been a party to this sort of conversation.

'Yes, well, it's all a mistake.' Odette cleared her throat, aware that everyone at the table was now listening in. 'So you still drink in the Greyhound then?' she asked rather desperately.

Thankfully Milly Fredericks chose that moment to swing around and compliment Skunk on his hair again.

'Is that why you're called Skunk? My ex-boyfriend was nicknamed Goat.'

'New Ager was he?' Skunk was too shy to look her in the eye.

'No – he just hung around on mountain tops and ate a lot of

cardboard. Talking of which, would you like me to shell those prawns for you? They taste much nicer and it's really easy – look.' Smiling at him kindly, she started to take off the hard pink coats with deft strokes.

Odette shelled a couple of her own for something to do, but she wasn't at all hungry. Her stomach was churning again, throat tightening, chest full of sand.

'You and I met once before.' James Sylvian turned to her, abandoning Sukey who was describing at length a holiday she and Guy had taken in Cape Town.

'Oh, yes?' Odette thought him hugely rude. She flashed a wary smile.

He nodded. 'At your club in London. I came to the opening night. Fantastic place.'

Odette tried to keep her smile level, tried not to betray the panic and nausea welling in her throat. This table was turning out to be a minefield. That wasn't an occasion she cared to dwell on any more than her brother-in-law's arrest. She had no recollection of the meeting whatsoever, although she knew from the press reports afterwards that Felix had been amongst the guests Calum had drummed up.

'So you own a restaurant in London, Odette?' Sukey was craning around the big blond beefcake, determined to stay in the conversation.

'I don't really own it as such,' she said carefully, testing her voice for any telltale wobble. It held firm, if roughened to a fishwife's caw by the effort. 'My investors have a big stake.'

'And steak is very expensive,' Jimmy laughed heartily. 'They're eating the profits, *ja*?' The 'yah' was odd – not Sloaney or Hooray, far more guttural and alien. She guessed it was something he'd picked up in South Africa.

'Or cooking the books,' she muttered darkly. 'What did you do in Africa?' She hastily changed the subject, knowing that talking about the club would make her feel even shakier.

He explained he ran a game reserve on the South Africa/ Mozambique border, and yet it seemed he was all set to start farming in the UK, a job that involve breeding large numbers of animals for slaughter.

'I want to breed truly organic meat, particularly good game which is so rare in this country. Ostrich is growing in popularity over here, but I'd like to introduce impala, eland, kudu, spring-bok. Whatever settles readily. Very good meat – not fatty, high in protein.'

Odette was shocked. 'I thought you were trying to con-serve them?'

When he started to talk about the reserve, she realised why his big voice carried so far. There he had been solely responsible for maintaining an area the size of Kent.

'Conservation isn't about tucking an endangered species into straw-bedded pens at night and making sure they are safe,' he sighed, clearly adopting a stance he had used for many years, his voice as patient as a nursery school teacher's only about five times as loud. 'My job is to secure the territorial integrity of the park, not to feel sorry for antelope. I want to farm animals that live natural, feral lives – not steroid-pumped cattle that live according to the cut of meat they provide.'

'But why live over here again? Africa sounds wonderful.'

'It's just an idea I'm toying with.' He shrugged. 'A friend is buying an estate. He wants me to manage the farmland, but I'm not sure his idea will work. I may go back to Africa, although I find the bureaucracy there soul-destroying. For now, I want to be with my family.'

'And who are they, Gary?' Sukey clearly felt Odette had monopolised her side-dish long enough.

'They're here.' He craned around to seek out his brothers at other tables, forgetting for a moment that he was supposed to be a Turner.

Sukey, however, hadn't 'Oh, yes – I saw there were quite a lot of you on the seating plan. Are you relatives of Stan's?'

'Yes, that's right.' He flashed her an uneasy smile as he turned back, catching Odette's speculative eye en route.

'Now do tell me about this game reserve. Guy and I are thinking of going on safari next year, although I have to say all the reports of car-jacking and whatnot are rather off putting, aren't they?'

'You wouldn't be car-jacked in Mpona.' He flashed his easy

smile. 'The most likely thing to try and ambush you would be baboons. Believe me, as long as you obey the park rules, you are far safer driving within metres of lion, leopard and elephant than you are driving through central Johannesburg.'

Odette listened to him talking to Sukey about the reserve. His enthusiasm and knowledge were amazing. He talked of big landscapes in his big voice – of deserts, savannahs, bush, mountains, forests and veldt. He spoke of the game which he battled to preserve from poachers and the ever-encroaching sprawl of man, city and pollution. The way he described the turn of the seasons was so poetic it was mesmerising, and yet he also talked like a businessman describing a product which needed to make a profit to survive. He talked of eco-tourism and education, of government funding mixed with high-powered corruption. His view was as wide, it seemed, as his broad shoulders.

On her other side, Odette noticed that Skunk was being thoroughly chatted up by Milly Fredericks. As their main courses arrived, she tried to coax him into eating noisettes of lamb with apricot and caper jam. 'It's not like jam you spread on bread, I promise. Just try a bite.'

To Odette's utter amazement. James Sylvian handed his plate back to the waitress. 'I'm a vegetarian.' She apologised and went to fetch him the alternative.

Now that was one contradiction too far. Odette burst out laughing.

He looked hugely affronted. 'I haven't eaten meat for fifteen years. I can shoot an injured buffalo bull straight between the eyes without thinking twice, but I do not like the taste of animal flesh. Is that such a problem to you?'

'But you're thinking about farming meat!' She tried her own lamb. It was admittedly overcooked and only lukewarm, but the apricot sauce was delicious.

'Knowing how to rear good stock has nothing to do with eating it.' He turned his knife around in his hand, examining it minutely. 'Does your chef eat every dish that he's prepared?'

'He tastes them all, yes.' Odette didn't want to talk about Florian. She abandoned her fork, no longer tempted by the chewy meat.

'Okay, in that case does a male clothes designer wear his dresses?'

'Some probably do,' she said, thinking about it.

He gave his barking laugh. 'You are a tough woman to convince, Ms Fielding. I like that. Final example, and if you still disagree then I will eat your lamb.' He leaned towards her ear and said in an undertone, 'How can a man go down on a woman when he will never know exactly what she is feeling? Because he learns to do so, he acquires the skill, improves upon it. He doesn't need to feel it himself to know that he is giving her pleasure.'

With some effort, Odette flashed him a polite, unfazed smile and tried not to be too disgusted. If she applied logic, she had to admit he had a point, although if the proof was in the pudding then Florian's sweet dessert skills had been sadly lacking. Her instinct told her to take issue, but again her tightening chest and shaking hands warned her she was too emotionally overwrought to risk it. She'd give away her sexual ignorance, or worse still come across as a loud-mouthed slapper. There was nothing more revolting than strangers arguing with cool logic about sex – it was the ultimate thirty-something courtship debate and it left her cold. Why didn't he just leave her alone? She wanted to offload him on Sukey again, so she boringly asked him to tell her more about the farming venture.

His friend – whom he affectionately called 'Woody' – was, it seemed, planning to set up a very grand country club hotel of sorts, and had just found a vast house with a lot of acreage within a short drive of London.

Odette knew she should listen – this was her line of business after all – but she was feeling so tense that her ears were muffled. It was as though every part of her body was stifled. She couldn't breathe enough air, she was moist with chilly perspiration, her shoulders were weighed down with a lead yoke of tension and she was struggling to keep her eyes open – not from tiredness, but from the overwhelming urge to scrunch them shut and blot out the world, the noisy wedding chatter and James Sylvian's rugged, bullish face.

'He thinks he can lure all the rich Londoners from their

favourite spot-a-celeb haunts and feed them like kings,' James was saying. 'Not just at weekends, but during the working week as well. Woody says it'll be part Manoir aux Qua' Saisons, part Babington House, and yet largely original.'

'Sounds wonderful!' Sukey gushed.

Odette heaved a sigh of relief that Saskia's sister was once again in play, but to her irritation Jimmy carried on talking straight at her.

'The luxurious setting and the quality of the ingredients are all important,' he said, his voice dropping for some reason, becoming more intimate as though he wanted to keep the conversation private. 'That's where I come in. The plan is to grow or raise almost every food product which will be used in the restaurants on our own land – from the meat and vegetables to the herbs, oils, and even at a later stage some of the wine.'

'Sounds a hugely expensive venture,' Guy joined in, now well on his way to polishing off a second bottle of red. 'How's this Woody chap raising capital? Who is he, by the way? Must be worth a pretty penny – restaurants don't come cheap as I'm sure Odette would agree, eh, old girl?'

He looked at her intently, along with Sukey, James Sylvian and – it seemed to Odette – everyone in the marquee. For a moment she held it together and tried for a smile, but then the wobblies took over. It was like a flood barrier crashing, a bridge giving way or a roof caving in. She had just split seconds in which to escape.

'Excuse me.' She wiped her mouth and stood up so quickly that she tipped her plate upside down, crashing its contents into the flower arrangement. Not staying to survey the damage, she fled to the loo.

I must not lose it, I must not lose it, Odette told herself firmly, sitting in the freezing portaloos, her breath shallow and laboured.

This was ridiculous. She was a grown woman. She had no idea what was making her feel so childish, so tearful and frightened. She had to fight it.

Taking a deep, juddering breath, she drew on her stockpiles of chutzpah and walked back to her table with her chin held high.

As she passed Liam Turner's table, he reached out a hand and pinched her bottom. She gallantly ignored it. From the other side of the tent, Garth Draylon blew her a kiss. She flashed a cool little smile. That was more like it. The old Odette was back in the driving seat.

'Won't you miss Africa if you stay on in the UK?' Sukey was saying to James Sylvian as Odette sat down. 'The way you describe it is so magical.'

He nodded, beaming his mega-watt smile straight at Odette. 'I adore the place. A lifetime isn't long enough to understand it, but you fall in love with it in one deep breath of its air.'

Her upturned plate and its mess had been cleared away, Odette noticed, although a large orange stain marked the spot. She carefully covered it with her napkin, wanting to blot out the memory of her near-miss.

'So you might go back?' Sukey was munching on what appeared to be seconds of lamb. Her appetite had returned with gusto, it seemed

'Possibly.' Jimmy looked around for a waiter. 'Let me ask for some more food for you, Odette.'

'No – no, it's all right, babes, I'm not hungry,' she said quickly.

Sukey shot her an irritated look, as though she was deliberately trying to drag the gorgeous Sylvian's attention away. 'And if Guy and I go to Mpona, we'd love you to be there. Get a bit of insider knowledge.'

The big smile suddenly faded. 'I'm never going back to Mpona,' he said curtly. 'I can't go back there. Africa, maybe – it is a big continent after all. I speak Swahili as well as Swazi, so I may get work in Zim.'

'Is Swahili the language with all the fearsome clicking noises?' Sukey giggled, aware that she'd trodden on a raw nerve somewhere along the line.

'That's Xhosa.' Jimmy pulled himself together and, again talking straight to Odette, spoke a few words in an amazing tongue, interspersed with several loud and extraordinary clicks.

'What was that supposed to mean?' she asked flatly, certain it would be something lewd again.

'I said "May I dance with you later?"' He leaned back as the waitress delivered his nut cutlet at long last. Before Odette could open her mouth to respond, he asked her what she thought of the situation in the Balkans. Hardly wedding talk, but strangely she was grateful for the opening into a vein which she could happily tap without drawing her own blood. Politics was something she relished, although it was considered the height of boredom amongst most of her friends.

'Yugoslavia is Europe's Heart of Darkness, its Congo,' said Jimmy, filling up both their glasses.

Soon they were talking about issues which Odette hadn't touched upon since her politics A level twelve years earlier. She was surprised how enjoyable and challenging she found the conversation. James Sylvian was too idealistic and poetic, she decided, and he liked the broad sweeping generalisation, but there was no doubting his compassion, and his ability to see the full picture. What surprised her above all was his liberalism. She had expected him to be a bit of an old-fashioned Tory bigot, a colonialist with a whites-of-their-eyes mentality, but he was quite the reverse.

She had almost forgotten her stifling panic, her earlier terror. There was only one moment where she wobbled. Jimmy was talking nineteen to the dozen with his mouth full of nut cutlet. Suddenly he scooped up a large forkful and thrust it at Odette. 'Try this – it's surprisingly good. Go on, you must eat something.'

'No!' She backed away as though he was holding a branding iron to her face. 'Take it away. Please, just take it away!'

'It's only a nut cutlet,' he shrugged, affecting insouciance to save her embarrassment.

How could she explain that the memory of a man feeding her was a trigger that would send the panic attack into a hellish, corrosive fast-forward? The wretched, revolting image of Florian forcing food into her mouth haunted her. She could no longer see it as separate from what had happened in the OD kitchens afterwards. Food was even more inextricably linked to pain and unhappiness in her mind.

Sukey interrupted their *tête-à-tête*, changing the subject to Christmas, asking what everyone was up to.

Odette hadn't even thought about it. The club was only closed on Christmas Day itself, so she'd be working most of the time – especially as they now had several office parties booked into the cabaret bar, which Calum seemed to be treating as a private function room. She supposed she would stay at the flat and go to her parents' house on Christmas Day as usual.

James got up to find the chilly portaloos and a moment later Phoebe was sitting in his vacated chair. 'How's everyone doing? Isn't the food gorgeous? What do you think of Jimmy, Odette? Isn't he divine?'

'Jimmy?' Sukey spoke first, her voice strangely tight. 'Jimmy?'

'Felix's brother.' Phoebe turned to her and then spotted the rogue place-card. 'What's this doing here? Saskia deliberately put the Turner brothers beside all her old school enemies.'

Realising that she'd been the victim of a practical joke, Sukey dabbed her lips with her napkin, muttered 'excuse me' in a strangled voice and bolted towards the portaloos too.

'Oops, was it something I said?'

Odette shook her head. She didn't understand these people. They were all so horrible to each other.

'Sukey always gets upset at weddings,' Phoebe whispered to her, checking that Guy was busy clicking at a waitress for more wine. 'That pig won't pop the question and she's desperate to do the white dress thing. They've been together years, and now she's the only Seaton sister without a bauble on her ring finger. Must be pretty galling, seeing as her relationship has outlasted all her siblings' stormy marriages.'

Odette suddenly felt terribly sorry for poor, shallow Sukey. No wonder she was so familiar with wedding etiquette having played guest at all her sisters' receptions.

'Not that Stan and Saskia's will be stormy,' Phoebe was saying happily. 'So what d'you think of Jimmy? Amazing, isn't he? Has he told you about the country restaurant plan?'

Odette nodded. The truth was she didn't know what to make of Jimmy at all.

'Must table hop.' Phoebe winked as a tall shadow loomed over her and Jimmy returned, adding in a low whisper, 'Just remember what the film said. Most of us meet our future partners at these things.'

Watching Phoebe skip away with a very obvious thumbs-up at Saskia, Odette realised she had been set up.

21

'You're an Ice Queen!' Jimmy laughed delightedly.

Odette couldn't help it. She suddenly felt stilted and arch, on the defensive and impossibly aggressive. 'I am single by choice. That is, I have love affairs when I need to, on my own terms, and I put a stop to them when the time is right. It's like any investment. The secret is knowing when to withdraw.'

'I've never been able to do that.' Jimmy shook his head sadly. 'Or are we talking about two different things here?' He smiled his big, lion-king smile.

Odette winced. So much for not falling into that modern nightmare, the thirty-something love and sex debate trap.

'Not a very suitable conversation for a wedding,' Sukey sniffed disapprovingly, although she was longing to throw her two pennies' worth in when Odette hotly argued that marriage was a singularly false institution. Darling Gary – Jimmy that is – was a believer in true romantic love and the trollopy tart was as hard as nails. 'I thought all that stuff about Kosovo was bad enough, but this . . .' She looked at Guy for support, but he was chatting to Dylan about golf.

'The rules here changed while you were in Africa, Jimmy,' Odette told him pompously. 'Twenty-first century love is all about exercising choice.'

Whenever she was set up with a man, she reacted in the same way – she lashed out as though whoever it was cramped her style. Her cramp was a defence mechanism, she knew that – old maid's knee-in-the-groin.

'Have you never been in love, Odette?' Jimmy looked at her intently. There was nothing whatsoever flirtatious about his

213

manner. He sounded like Anthony Clare grilling a celebrity on his Radio 4 psychiatrist's couch. 'I mean, truly in love.'

'The one where you save your lover before yourself?' she asked lightly. Really this conversation was getting way too deep for wedding banter.

'If you want to put it like that.' His eyes darted away to stare fixedly at a thumbnail. 'Until death us do part.'

Jimmy Sylvian, it seemed, was someone with whom it was impossible to make small talk.

'Till death us do part,' she repeated, thinking about Calum. Sometimes – quite often in fact – she had wished him dead. Or rather never born. Lately, she'd willed him out of her life – under a bus, off a cliff, in front of a train. Anything but there and yet not there – just around the corner, or in another part of London, having fun, making love, laughing, all without her. Had he ever been hers at all? She doubted it. She was intelligent enough to recognise her own obsession, just powerless to stop it. And she knew that the ultimate fantasy solution would be Calum's death. Because then she could mourn, could allow her obsession to become her life's regret and not her whole life. For that tortuous what-might-have-been would have been curtailed by accident and not her own making. What-might-have-been would last for eternity, never answered, always possible.

She looked at Jimmy sadly. 'Ask me that again when he's dead.'

She was so wrapped up in her own thoughts that she didn't catch the look in his eye. It was total, uneclipsed self-torture.

When he spoke again, his voice had dropped too low for Sukey to overhear. 'Do you really want to find out that way?'

'You can love someone to death, but it doesn't necessarily mean they ever love you back,' she shrugged, desperately trying to appear casual. 'It's too risky, isn't it? Like matching numbers on a scratch card. The odds of it working out are so bad. No wonder most people play safe.' Unable to stop herself, she glanced at Sukey and Guy, the long-term bored who stayed together because there was safety in numbers, but would no doubt scream 'each man for himself' if the marquee burst into flames right now.

Jimmy followed her gaze. 'And you don't think it's worth the risk either?' His voice was barely audible over the wedding chatter now.

Odette thought about Calum, about the risks she'd taken and all she stood to lose. Then she thought about her ridiculous *Hart to Hart* dream. 'From what I've experienced, it's all just marketing hype, devised to get box-office ratings or sell crap records. Undying love doesn't exist in real life.'

To her surprise he didn't argue, just nodded thoughtfully. 'I don't think most of us ever find that sort of love, Odette. We find a compromise that we think we can live with, and then we live too long or die too quick ever to know what could have been.'

'Better to die a few months into a relationship then?' she sighed, not picking up on his insinuation.

'Maybe.' He shrugged. 'I'm not the one to ask.'

Again she was too dim to pick up the signals. 'I think we'd all like to have a dead lover to fall back on. Someone with whom we'll never know what might have happened. That's the ultimate love, isn't it? Bereavement. It's self-pity, and that's self-love, which is ultimately what we're all looking for.'

He nodded, lifting his chin and looking at her with those black-blue bruised eyes of his. 'Yup. You said it, Odette. When my lover died, I thought my soul had been taken too. I guess that smacks of self-pity.'

Odette felt the acid of shame drench her body then suck her skin dry.

'How long had you been together?' she asked, frozen with humiliation.

'Just three months.' he drained his wineglass. 'Very self-pitying, don't you think?'

As soon as the wedding guests had polished off their warm chocolate pudding, top table once again resembled a parliamentary backbench during a midnight debate, as everyone except the best man decamped to dash around the room and catch up with friends. Left to read nervously through his speech notes, Gilb scratched his crew cut in horror as he realised some prankster had substituted a photocopy of a hairy bottom.

In a side-tent with a wooden floor for dancing later, all the tots were being kept distracted by a magic show from a children's entertainer.

The Turner children, who had declared the magician 'crap', were running in and out of a flap at the side of the marquee. Great gusts of chilly air blasted in their wake as they started bringing in snowballs and slinging them at one another, turning the dance floor into a sleety ice rink. Pretty soon a pitched battle had broken out. Trying to calm them down, Phoebe was hit full in the face by a backspin from none other than her boyfriend's brother, Mungo.

At that moment the lads from Disco Frisco arrived, heaving their equipment through the tent flap. Slipping on the snowball slush, one promptly flew across the wet floor and crashed into the magician.

'Talk about disco-ordinated,' Phoebe giggled, looking around for Felix.

Odette stared at the cup handle in front of her, knowing that what she had just done was unforgivable. I will not cry and I will not run away again, she told herself with furious determination.

'I'm sorry,' she whispered. 'I'm so very sorry. You must think I'm such a bitch.'

Beside her, Jimmy was staring just as intently at the flower arrangement in the centre of the table, as surprised as he would have been if a leopard had jumped out from under his bed and lunged for his throat, only to loosen its teeth at the last minute and curl up beside him to sleep.

But at that moment Felix walked up to the table and, noticing the atmosphere, chewed his lip. 'Need your help, Jimmy. Mungo's started a snowball fight and Tony wants all his guests back before the speeches start.'

'Sure,' Jimmy said distractedly, not even glancing at Odette before he got up from the table and followed his brother.

She closed her eyes.

'Speeches are about to kick off, thank God.' Sukey lurched back to her seat after a quick gossip with Gin at top table. 'Where's Jimmy gone? Mummy says Saskia asked her to sit you two together, Odette. Not many single players here today.' She made it sound like a bridge pairing. 'You're lucky you weren't put with Garth Draylon – oops! Sorry. You two were getting on like a house on fire earlier, weren't you?'

Odette gritted her teeth.

Oh, yes, she hated being set up. So much so that she almost always opened her machine-gun mouth and annihilated the person her friends thought she should be with. She always, always shot her mouth off and shot herself in the foot. Only this time she'd left her bloodied, pierced slipper at the ball. And no Prince Charming was going to pick it up and trawl the country for her.

Jimmy didn't come back to the table for the speeches. Instead, his place was filled with the stout, grinning form of Garth Draylon, eager to ingratiate himself with Odette and explore her cleavage with his eyes. When he craned around to look at top table, he deliberately shook his wrist out of its folded cuff and stretched it across the table to show off his Rolex. Then he leaned back so far that he was practically lying in Odette's lap. 'Lovely view – reminds me of the valleys back home.'

When Tony Seaton stood up to offer a very clipped and strangely unenthusiastic speech about his daughter and 'Stanley', Garth looked lustily down Odette's dress and said, 'Old bastard resents every penny. Says Stan is a jumped-up little Picasso-lover. D'you know what he's bought them as a wedding present? A Cotman sketch. Bloody marvellous, huh?'

As Stan stuttered lovingly about how proud today was making him and how much he loved Saskia, Garth's nose stretched closer to Odette's breasts and he breathed, 'Somehow that funny accent sounds much better coming out of your mouth, my lovely. Not the only thing I'd like to see coming from your mouth tonight, eh, me old china?' He disguised his insinuation in a bad Dick Van Dyke impression, but it didn't make any difference. Odette was far too frozen to take it in.

217

Finally, Stan's best man Gilb took his stand and read out the endless e-mails from well-wishers, then offered his own monotone, nervous and long speech wishing the couple well. By now, Garth was almost snorting into Odette's chest, his big hands everywhere. At the final 'Be upstanding!' Odette stood up so fast that she almost broke his nose.

Jimmy Sylvian missed all this, just as he missed the speeches. He was playing a very dark, very active game of snowball with the kids outside. Jimmy hadn't seen snow in fifteen years. He only wished Florence had seen it, but now she never would. In the years since her death, only one woman had ever made him as angry and as stimulated at the same time. And that was the furiously proud, and killingly glamorous Odette Fielding. Jimmy knew two things for certain. She wasn't as forgiving as Florrie and she was heading for a breakdown any minute now. Neither of these things particularly ingratiated her to him, but they interested him more than he cared to admit. She might pretend to be hard and clever and, occasionally, quite a good flirt, but he knew she was going to the lavatory every twenty minutes because she needed to cry – or to get herself a fix, or both. Jimmy remembered only too well what Calum had said about her. He knew not to trust Calum as far as he could throw one of these snowballs, but his old friend's comment made sense. He'd never known anyone as changeable as Odette. It was like watching an actress run through expressions for a commercials director – one minute happy, the next distraught, then fear, then egotism, then cool indifference. Only this wasn't acting. This was the real thing. If it wasn't enhanced by some sort of chemical dependence, then she was very, very complicated indeed. For once, he was inclined to believe Calum. Odette was a junkie. A beautiful, fucked-up woman who was too clever by half, so dimmed it by a quarter of a gram.

She was drinking less than anyone else, talking less and laughing less, but making more sense in that lucid, frightening way that people close to the edge do. Jimmy knew the signs. He'd been like that for months, years even. He'd been in grief, as much for the living as the dead. He had a sneaking suspicion that Odette Fielding was in love. Doomed love. He longed to know with whom.

Odette found to her dismayed astonishment that her dance card was as well marked as a prize-winning essay that night. She just wanted to apologise to Jimmy Sylvian and go back to the pink cell in the pub, but she was finding it impossible to get off the wet, skating-rink dance floor in between the Abba and Queen tracks spun by Frisco Disco. All the Turners seemed to want a spin, along with Garth's eyes excuse-meing her boobs every two minutes, Dylan lurching up for a boogie, Fliss and Phoebe on a mission to collect a spare female for every Spice Girl track: 'You can be Posh – you look like her.' Milly was 'Scary', Helen the bridesmaid 'Baby', Fliss 'Ginger' and Phoebe 'Sporty'. At their knees the flower-carriers and their friends were performing exactly the same roll-call with a different cast. Abandoning her hat at long last, Odette did a duty-shuffle with Charlie McGillivray who laid his chin on her shoulder and sighed lovingly, then a quick mosh-pit head-bang to the Damned's 'New Rose' with Skunk. Several Abba tracks were spent bopping opposite Mungo Sylvian for some reason.

'You look so much like Frida,' he yelled over the din. 'I'm fantasising myself the blonde one.'

'Bjorn?' Odette offered.

'No, Agnetha,' he grinned, mouthing the words to 'Waterloo'.

In truth Odette knew why she kept on dancing. It stopped the bloody tears. It stopped the inevitable. For tonight, she knew, was the night that she was going to fall apart. And the pounding of music in her ears was the only thing that was stopping her.

Then the bloody Disco Frisco youths ruined it. When Saskia and Stan came into the centre of the dance floor together once again after much duty-dancing with new in-laws and old friends, the lads saw their chance to hot things up. The happy couple had incongruously started the night's boogying to the theme from 'Vision On' which Tony Seaton and Jean McGillivray struggled to waltz to, although Virginia Seaton and Charlie had managed a brave attempt at a fox-trot. This time the disc-spinners at Disco Frisco decided that they knew best and stuck on a sloppy. Saskia laughed when she heard it, burying her head in her Stan's chest and swaying opposite him. It was 'their song'. A few lonely piano chords rang through the annexe before Patsy Cline sang in her been-there, done-that voice, 'Crazy – crazy for feeling so lonely . . .'

Odette knew that the touch paper had been lit. What she hadn't anticipated was that it would be so short. Without warning the tears positively gushed from her eyes. She raced to the flapping marquee entrance which led to the snowy, muffled safety of outside. Then, just as she reached the cold pocket of air by the exit, a warm hand caught her arm and she heard a strange clicking noise in her ear.

If it's Garth Draylon, I'm going to hit him, she thought murderously, swinging around. But it was Jimmy Sylvian, huge, broad and tanned, his sandy hair covered with melting snow.

'I said,' he repeated his clicking trick, then translated it, 'you didn't save me that dance. I claim it now.'

'I'm crying,' Odette muttered between clenched teeth. She hated him for making her so ashamed, but she knew the fact was too obvious to deny.

'I know,' he said simply, offering her his hand. 'If you don't dance with me, I won't offer you a tissue. And there's no bog-roll left in the portaloos.'

She tried to curb the tears while she danced – well, shuffled really, her face hidden by Jimmy's huge chest which was an amazingly good shield. Her senses were heightened, almost sonic, as acute embarrassment sent her derision detectors into overdrive in case anyone had rumbled her distress. No one seemed to have noticed. She was as stiff and unyielding as an ironing board in Jimmy's arms and yet she was aware of his stolid security, the compassion of another's touch and her desperation to melt into the hug that seemed just inches away. But that was another lifetime. Right now survival was more important. She had started to reach the ungainly snorting stage. Any second now and snot would start streaming out of her nose all over Jimmy's expensive shirt. She had to concentrate on sniffing at regular intervals. If she succumbed to the urge to thaw into his warmth she'd lose all dignity.

She could now hear conversations going on above the droning music so guessed they were travelling to the outer perimeters of the dance floor, but she didn't dare look up. She could feel his warm hand on hers, another touching the nip of her waist with respectful lightness, his breath occasionally stirring the top of her hair. He trod on her toes once or twice without apology. Close-to he smelled of talcum powder and starch spray from his hired wing shirt. She could see his chest breathing and feel the warmth of him lifting from his collar onto her cheeks. Tears still ran along them, hot and salty, landing on the floor beside their shuffling feet – tiny drops lost in the flood of melted snowballs. Only when the track had ended did she feel the icy cool of the exit cutting into her sides again.

'See – I delivered you back to your self-pity. Now go and cry.' Handing her a handkerchief, he turned on his heel and walked away without another word.

Odette slipped outside and immediately felt the bite of the cold chewing her every bone. Teeth chattering, she crunched through the snow, beyond the portaloos and out into a field, hating herself for feeling the cold, for no longer crying. She wasn't numb – she was shivering from head to toe. And she was no longer sobbing, or thinking of herself. She was thinking of Jimmy Sylvian and whoever it was that he'd lost.

Wandering aimlessly away from the party hub, she had no idea where she was heading. She'd danced too long to bad music and sweated too much, turning her skin into an icy cold straitjacket. Her ears thrummed, deafening her to everything. She fell over a sheep, which was as alarmed as she was to find itself in a field with a white-faced coward. Both bleated off into opposite corners.

Odette could see the marquee in the distance, lit up like a giant cubic monster in a *Dr Who* episode, bright lights flashing from within.

She suddenly froze as she heard breathing behind her. For a ludicrous moment she wondered whether it was Jimmy Sylvian, following to check if she was okay. But it wasn't. It was Garth

Draylon, his eyes glittering in the reflected light of the marquee as he panted up to her.

'Thought I saw a vision back there, but it really is you. I was taking a slash by the hedge here – bit of a queue in the bogs. You doing the same?' He seemed revoltingly excited by the thought.

'No – just wanted a bit of space,' Odette hinted heavily.

'Know the feeling, my lovely.' He rubbed his moustache eagerly, eyes darting around for a suitably romantic spot. Seeing that they were in a pitted, snowy paddock in the pitch dark with only a terrified ewe for company, his options were limited. 'Fancy finding a bit of space in my car? It's a Porsche Carrera – red leather interior. A classic.'

'Sorry, I'm no longer a Carrera girl.' Odette backed away and stumbled towards the gate. Garth was much faster than her, but thankfully his aviator prescription sunglasses weren't so hot in the dark and he fell over a sheep trough.

But the vampires were all out. No sooner had Odette made it to the portaloos than Liam Turner exited one and fell into step with her, his menacing face leering down into hers. 'Been looking for you,' he said, doing up his flies. 'D'you wanna go back to the hotel? We could have a nightcap in front of that lovely big fire.' And then, totally without warning, he tried to put his tongue in her mouth.

Odette pulled furiously away. She made to slap him but her frozen hand was so numb it just flopped against his head like a wet fish.

'Oi, you little bastard, get off the poor girl!' Garth had caught up at last, hobbling from his trough-bruised shins. Pausing to take off his Rolex and stash it safely in his trouser pocket, he swung a punch. Before he could land it, Liam head-butted him with an unpleasant crack of skull against toupee tape.

The fight lurched on, seemingly unnoticed by the dancing masses in the marquee annexe. Odette wondered whether to get help, but she just wanted to escape. All she seemed to do was cause trouble. Her hat and bag were still in the marquee, but she couldn't risk Saskia or Stan seeing her leaving. As she raced away, she didn't notice Mungo Sylvian's blond head pop out of the flap, mutter 'Cripes' and pop back in again as he went in search of his brothers.

When Jimmy Sylvian came outside to settle a fight for the second time that evening, he saw a pale blue figure disappearing behind a snow-capped line of trees and somehow knew that the fight had lost its trophy belt.

Odette elected to take the lane back to the village rather than the hessian path through the fields because the latter had lost its torches to the wind hours ago, and the pathway was covered in a thick layer of snow. There was no street lighting or salting-trucks around here. Just the claustrophobic dark crunch-crunch of her feet against the crisp carpet, regularly followed by her own sharp intake of breath as she slid yards on compacted ice. She was forced to take her heels off, which meant that her feet grew damp, and then frozen and then blissfully numb as they creaked on a thin, stockinged layer over what seemed like miles of covered tarmac. It was so dark that she kept walking off the road and stumbling as the pitted verge tripped her up through the snow. The numbness was soon replaced by a penetrating ache. Her feet throbbed so much that she winced every time she trod, and soon groaned with every step, but she trudged on, figuring she deserved it.

She had assumed the lane led straight into the village. When she came to a dark T-junction, she was bewildered. There was no signpost at all, so she just had to guess, heading left and crunching on. Her feet no longer just ached and stabbed but seemed to howl out with every step, cramps contorting her toes like Chinese bindings.

After what seemed like hours of agony, she rounded a corner and was almost blinded as a security light blasted on. She stepped back, eyes watering. Several dogs were barking furiously inside, but the house was unoccupied and in darkness apart from the ferocious white light glaring from high on its side. Odette realised that she was staring at the Seatons' old home, Deayton Manor. The village was in the opposite direction. She had taken the wrong turn and pursued it for close to half an hour.

She retraced her steps, the tears still refusing to come. A great wave of lethargy seemed to have drained her last reserves of energy and she continually wandered off the road – or was it a drive? She stumbled on to her knees twice and fell over totally once, grazing her cheek on the tarmac-hard bank of a ditch. She hated the countryside. As she tottered along, her progress slowing with every painful step, she decided she would never come back. She would stay in London for the rest of her life. She wouldn't even go to Hampstead Heath if she could help it. The only greenery she wanted to see from now on was the organised kind, the sort that came out of a garden centre in seed trays or packets, ranked and serried, in circular beds on roundabouts or perhaps – if she was feeling brave – sharply cut beds in municipal parks.

She was feeling seriously light-headed now and a good deal warmer. She wondered if the wine was kicking in at long last, not that she remembered drinking much. More than anything she was tired. So tired.

Thank God! The T-junction again. If she listened very carefully, she could just make out a thump of music coming from her right – the wedding reception – which meant she had to carry straight on for the pub. With any luck she'd be in time for a brandy with the landlady. Perhaps she could ask her for a tranquilliser? Or a toot from her mother's oxygen cylinder perhaps? Right now sleep was more tempting.

God, she was feeling woozy. She really had to sit down for a minute. She couldn't feel her feet at all any more – just two aching spasms of pain at the ends of her legs.

The headlights of the Zephyr didn't so much catch Odette as slide past her like a spotlight across a prison wall. Its tyres were slipping around far too much on the icy tarmac to get a grip and its progress was one of inertia – weight downhill – more than torque on surface. The brakes engaged but it slithered on regardless, coming to a rakish halt against the verge just feet from Odette.

Jimmy left the engine running, desperately trying to feed some heat into the cab. He didn't know much about hypother-mia – there wasn't much call in Africa – but he guessed that it was essential to warm the victim up as quickly as possible. And Odette was stone cold when he tried to lift her.

'Calum, is that you?' She blinked up at him. Her hair was frozen, he noticed, and so were her eyelashes – like spiders wearing spangled stilettos.

'No, it's Jimmy.' He tried for a better grip. She was damned heavy.

'Jimmy Greaves?' She giggled happily. 'Wait till I tell Stan. He'll be so jealous.'

Jimmy said nothing, picking her up and putting her in the Zephyr with an effort. Her legs seemed to have undergone some sort of rigor mortis and wouldn't go through the door.

'Leave me alone,' she groaned. 'I deserve to freeze in hell. I'm useless. I'm an Ice Queen who's sold her soul.'

Jimmy continued to ignore her. When he finally cranked her feet into the car, her dress had slipped back to reveal long, slim thighs encased in stockings. The pale skin above was covered with yellowing bruises.

'Twenty-first century love,' Odette told him groggily. 'It fucking well hurts.'

As she warmed up, so she seemed to thaw out – perhaps a bit too fast.

At least she made sense. 'I'm staying at the Crown. In the village,' she muttered, pulling down her dress and rubbing her legs through the icy-cold velvet.

But as the car slithered and slid along the narrow lane, she started to cry. Jimmy had heard nothing quite like it in his life. It reminded him of the sad, echoing moans that came from the savannah at dusk – a lost lion calling for her pride. But Odette's sobs were almost more feral, more hopeless.

When he pulled into the car park of the Crown, Odette was crying like a baby elephant whose mother had been poached. By the time Jimmy had worked out how to cut the engine, she had fallen eerily silent beside him.

'Let me buy you a drink,' he offered awkwardly, the sudden silence embarrassing him. 'I think we could both use a brandy.'

But she shook her head, red eyes fixed on the pub sign. 'You shouldn't drink and drive. Thanks for the lift.'

The Crown's neurotic landlady was calling last orders at the bar when the bedraggled wedding guest shot through her pub and up the back stairs. She barely had time to see who it was, but she certainly recognised Jimmy when he tried to follow.

'No visitors in the guests' rooms after ten o'clock.' She barred his way.

For a small woman, she had a formidable arm-lock. Defeated, he left.

When Jimmy got up to open his hotel door the following morning, hangover piercing his temples, he gave the bell hop short shrift. 'I didn't order any damned flowers.'

'Mr James Sylvian?' The boy read the card nervously and backed away before thrusting the huge bouquet at him.

Jimmy had never received flowers before. He wasn't sure what to make of them, or of the card which simply read: 'Thank you for melting me down'.

22

The Christmas decorations twinkled above slush-streaked Regent Street as Odette made her way to the formal and monolithic headquarters of her bank, carrying a briefcase which she knew contained a very fragile lifeline for the OD.

Her balance sheets weren't very inspiring. She calculated that she owed close to two hundred thousand pounds. Her one hundred thousand-pound loan was secured against her flat, a further sixty thousand had been invested by Calum. Yet that went nowhere near covering all the outstanding debts of the club, and her creditors were baying. Odette knew that time was running out. Unless she made a substantial payment on her overdraft soon, the bank would be all over her. The club simply wasn't taking enough money to offer any security. All incomings were being turned straight around to pay the staff and reorder stock. As it was, Odette herself was taking no money at all and living from a small savings account she had stashed aside in case she ran into trouble at a later stage; she hadn't anticipated she would need it so soon.

The bank's senior business manager was younger than Odette with a humorous tie and a humourless face. His desk was a barricaded fortress of executive toys, telephones and computer monitors. He wasted no time in outlining the critical nature of her situation, using as much sexist innuendo as possible with which to run her down.

'You have three weeks in which to pay off at least one-third of your overdraft. If that doesn't happen then we will be forced to freeze your assets and discuss a mutually beneficial solution. As a lone trader, your current position is very tenuous. You are personally responsible to your creditors, ourselves included. That means no extravagant Christmas presents and no party dresses. You must release capital from somewhere to keep on trading, Ms Fielding.'

'I'm putting my flat on the market,' she told him, playing her trump house of cards, certain that it would buy her more time.

He seemed far from impressed. 'Given that it is so close to Christmas and the market is depressed, I would say that only offers a relatively long-term solution.' He smiled frostily. 'I gathered from Mr Dent that you were going to seek further investment from Mr Forrester?'

'He's away on business,' she lied. 'I'll talk to him as soon as he returns.'

'He's not officially a partner, I gather?'

'He's a sleeping partner.' She winced at the *double entendre*. Nothing could be further from the truth.

'But you have no partnership agreement in writing?'

'I've – er . . .' Odette thought about the missing contract and knew that to explain about it would be hopelessly unprofessional. 'Not exactly. It's a gentleman's agreement.'

'In that case, I hope he's gentleman enough to help out a damsel in distress.' He cleared his throat. 'Given the current position, he may think it prudent to withdraw his funding rather than offer more. You will have to be very persuasive. Use your feminine wiles.' His cold gaze predictably flicked across her chest.

Afterwards, she sat in a crowded café clutching tightly onto a watery cappuccino. All around her, exhausted Christmas shoppers were sagging into chairs surrounded by bulging carrier bags. Christmas carols were tinkling from a radio behind the counter and the menu overhead was surrounded by tattered tinsel. Odette could hear a couple of women at a neighbouring table complaining about how much money they had just spent in BHS.

She found herself smiling. She couldn't help it. Her situation was so serious and yet, since the horrific night of Saskia's wedding, she had experienced an extraordinary sense of direction and purpose. For the last two nights she had slept soundly, waking refreshed and energetic each morning. Her appetite had returned with gusto. She had thought that the prospect of losing her flat would cause her to fall apart and yet it seemed to be having the opposite effect. She had relied upon her little powerhouse for too long, had turned it into an emotionless sanctuary. She wanted to strip away her career girl armour and soften up her act. For years she had thought of her home as her haven, as well as the ultimate lifestyle accessory, but lately it had started to trap and stifle her. Every time she ran home to cry, she sullied another few feet of woodblock flooring with bad memories.

She had wasted no time in approaching estate agents. Two had already come around to value the flat the day before, necessitating yet more time away from the OD. It barely seemed to matter at the moment, since the club was running like clockwork, the super-efficient staff that Calum had hired keeping the place buzzing until the early hours each night. It seemed hugely ironic to Odette that the club was so popular yet her financial situation worsened every day.

The Statutory Demand was already sitting on her desk when she got back to the club. It was from Calum's solicitor explaining that he wanted her to return the sixty-thousand-pound loan in full within twenty one days.

Odette's head reeled. She sat down so hard on her office chair that it flew back across the room and hit the filing cabinet, toppling a cactus which was now sitting on top into her lap.

Her phone was ringing, but she ignored it. Calum couldn't do this, could he? What was he playing at? She stormed next door but the office was empty, reeking of Florian's French tobacco. Odette brushed cactus gravel from her skirt and wavered in the doorway, totally confused. The incoming call had automatically transferred from her line to the one on Calum's desk. Mindlessly, she picked it up.

'Odie, it's me.' Her sister's familiar voice was shaking with nerves. 'Craig's done a runner.'

'A what?' Odette wasn't thinking straight. She scanned the desk for signs that Calum had been in the building, but it was covered with pages of Florian's incomprehensible scribbling. Something about the shaky handwriting struck her as familiar.

'He's left me, Odie – walked out on us.' Monny started to cry.

Odette wrenched her mind into gear, almost hearing it straining like an old clutch at the effort of the switch. 'Are you okay, babes? Are the kids okay?'

'Bearing up,' Monny sniffed. 'I'll murder the bastard when he turns up. We haven't been getting on too well lately, but I never fought he'd do this to the kids. He worships those children, Odie. He . . .' she hiccuped with great gulps of despair, '. . . he ripped up all our wedding photos. Didn't even leave a bleedin' note.'

Odette realised how impossible life was for Monny, shackled to someone as feckless as Craig. Her own financial problems seemed so shallow and self-generated by comparison. 'Did you have some sort of row, babes?'

'Sort of – it's complicated.' Monny sniffed again, sounding strangely sulky and defensive, like a small child.

'Well, maybe he'll come back when he's had a chance to calm down.'

'Oh, no.' She laughed bitterly through her tears. 'I don't fink there's much chance of that.'

'Why not, babes?'

Monny's voice cracked with tears again. 'We was in hospital for the results of the scan. There was a bit of a to-do and Craig just does a bunk, leaving me standing there with . . .' She seemed to stop herself and hastily blew her nose. 'When I get home, all his stuff has gone.'

'The scan . . . was it, okay?' Odette chewed her lip, suddenly wondering if that was the tragic reason Craig had done a bunk.

'Fine. A little girl. They reckon she's perfect.' Monny started to sob. 'I'm so sorry, Odie. They'll make you pay that money, won't they?'

'What?' Odette was still sagging against the desk with relief that the baby was going to be all right.

'He missed his committal hearing today.' The sobs were coming thick and fast now. 'The police have issued a warrant.

They've been all over the house again. It's all so bleedin' frightening. I dunno where he is.'

'He missed the hearing?' Odette suddenly knew precisely why Craig had done a runner.

'Yeah. The brief says he's okay for now, but if he don't show for the . . . hang on . . .' Odette could hear her shuffling through pieces of paper. 'For the Plea and Directions hearing then he's in deep trouble. That's next week. If he ain't there then, we're sunk. They'll ask for the bail money – whassit called, surety? If Craig don't turn up soon, the courts will want you to pay up.'

Odette met Bill, her solicitor, for drinks in the OXO bar.

'I'm sorry I couldn't see you earlier – I was in court all day.' He put his briefcase down and started to peel off a heavy black coat and jaunty red scarf. There was melting snow in his grey hair. Odette hadn't even noticed it was snowing again when she'd walked from the tube. She guessed some shocks immunised you against the weather.

When Bill looked through the Statutory Demand, his eyebrows shot up.

'Good grief, he does want his money back urgently, doesn't he?'

'That money is a long-term investment.' Odette slurped her Coke. 'He can't just ask for it back like this, can he?'

'Technically, yes.' Bill chewed his lip and looked around for a waitress. 'Hang on, I'll just get a drink.'

When he returned with a pint of Caffrey's, he explained to Odette the meaning of the demand. 'Generally speaking, a creditor would go to court to obtain a judgement before issuing you with this, but it has been known for a Statutory Demand to be issued pre-litigation. I would never recommend it, but Calum's solicitor must be a crafty sod.'

'But Calum isn't a creditor!' Odette was appalled. 'He's an investor. That money is an investment. You wrote the agreement yourself.'

'I'll look at the contract in the office tomorrow morning,' Bill promised, 'but from what I recall, the manner in which the money was transferred was hardly typical. You had already deposited it into your personal account before we drew up an agreement. From what I remember it was worded more as a receipt than a contract. It could present problems if we can't get this thing set aside in court.'

'Meaning?'

'Meaning,' he pulled an apologetic face, 'that Calum can, in theory, petition you for bankruptcy.'

'What?'

'That's what this is all about, I'm certain of it.' Bill looked at the document again. 'Calum Forrester is trying to screw you.'

Odette winced. She'd initially hired Bill because she liked his no-nonsense, down-to-earth manner and blunt language, but sometimes it was way off the mark.

'I can assure you he's not trying to do that,' she said lightly.

'And I'm telling you he is. He wants his money back in one hell of a hurry.'

'How was the wedding? I'm dying to know – shh, China, darling. Sorry, the baby's crying. Must dash. Duncan sends his love. Call me as soon as you get this message.'

'Odette, it's Juno. Where are you? I'm having everyone round for some grub on Wednesday next week. Try and get a night off from the club and come along. If you do, can I borrow your fish kettle? You never use it anyway.'

'It's Elsa. Call me, I'm really worried about you. I'll try your mobile.'

'Hey, big tits. It's Jez. I'm in LA, but I get back to London for a couple of days next week. Shall we meet for coffee? I'll come to that lovely club of yours if you want me to.'

'Darling, it's Lyds. God, I'm bored. No one's going out at the moment. Listen, I've had an idea about the bridesmaids' dresses. Give me a shout when you get a sec.'

The answer-machine was full to bursting.

Although guilt clawed at her shoulders, Odette knew that talking to her friends would trigger tears, and that would spell disaster. She didn't return their calls.

Florian claimed to know nothing about the Statutory Demand, but Odette didn't trust him.

'When did you last see Calum?' she demanded.

'Not for a long time.' He shrugged vaguely, having in fact played table football with him in his flat until the early hours that morning. 'I sink he's on 'oliday. 'E say 'e need a break.'

'Oh, I agree,' Odette laughed bitterly. 'More than one break. I can think of lots of breaks I'd like to give Calum, all over his body.'

Florian snorted – whether in anger or agreement she couldn't tell – and offered her a brandy, his big, liquid bull's eyes softening slightly. Odette refused.

He was drinking a lot, she noticed. Later that day she found him almost passed out in his office, hunching over those pages of illegible scribbles which no one but himself understood.

'You okay, babes?'

'*Bien sûr.*' His heavy lids were barely open enough to squint up at her. 'It is you I worry about. He has not broken you yet, huh?'

She studied him thoughtfully. His mop of hair was a matted tangle, he had three days' beard growth, a running nose and his chef's whites were filthy. Odette found him repulsive these days. She couldn't believe she had seduced him to please Calum, had agreed to let him debase her like that.

''E is playing a game, you know?' Florian levered himself up unsteadily and leaned back in his chair, then hooked a big clog up on to the desk to push himself backwards on the castors. 'It's – how you say? – a riddle. You just have to figure it out and you win ze prize.'

'What prize?'

'A sur*prize*!' He laughed throatily at his joke, flashing his very pink tongue and silver fillings. 'I dunno. Maybe he want to make you his wife.'

'By suing me?' Odette's voice was caustic, but despite herself her heart almost stopped.

He shrugged his heavy shoulders and lit a cigarette. 'I think about it a lot today.' He closed his eyes against the smoke. 'What he is doing. He is very clever man. He need a very clever woman to make him happy. But you haff to fight him. You haff to solve the riddle. I like that. Is clever, *non*?'

Odette thought Florian was barking, but she said nothing. Instead she clung to that little sliver of hope so tightly it cut her hands to shreds. She longed to ask him more, but Florian disappeared for the rest of the week.

He was putting very few hours into the club now, and relied increasingly upon Ned, the foul-mouthed *sous-chef*. Although the food was still sensational, it had lost its magic sparkle, its Etoile touch. Several key suppliers now refused to deliver goods until their bills were met. One of the expensive ovens in the kitchen had broken down and until Odette could afford to pay the specialist repairers, the staff had to prepare all the food on the other. Two line chefs had already walked out.

The kitchens terrified her now – their noisy, masculine, industrial heat, their anger and aggression, reminding her of the night she had failed to come up to Calum's sexual standard. She only ventured into them long after the restaurant had closed, in the early hours, when just she and the contract cleaners occupied the building. While they tidied and polished, she tried to clean up her balance sheets and vacuumed up the leftovers she found in the fridges. Food was a solace now, a comforter during the lonely shifts at her desk watching the hours creep by until Bill's inevitable morning call with more bad news.

And it was always bad news. Because the outstanding sum was not in dispute, the court would not set aside the Statutory Demand. If she didn't repay Calum within three weeks then she would almost certainly receive a writ for bankruptcy. Meanwhile, her other creditors were becoming more demanding and some were following Calum's lead by going to court.

'It's the rats and ship relationship,' Bill explained. 'Once the biggest rat deserts, the rest run after him. Doesn't matter that the ship is still buoyant and half a mile from harbour.'

Calum wasn't the only rat to have disappeared. When Odette finally told Bill about her brother-in-law, he was livid.

'Why didn't you contact me over this in the first place? I would have tried to talk you out of it in the strongest possible terms.'

'Craig swore he was set up.'

'I think you're the one being set up, my dear.' Bill was characteristically blunt. 'The courts have got very strict about bail infractions lately. And we would have great difficulty proving that you didn't plan to spend that money straight away.'

'Craig will turn up,' Odette promised. She had her hopes pinned on him being there for his children on Christmas Day, had visions of a Santa Claus with arrows on his red suit carrying a swag bag of gifts.

'That may not make a difference in the court's eyes. Your guarantee is already deemed forfeit.'

'Perhaps I should declare myself bankrupt after all,' she laughed hollowly.

Bill had a lawyer's sense of humour and didn't laugh. 'A court fine cannot be written off in a bankruptcy case. You would still be liable for the full twenty thousand, plus costs. In fact, you could find yourself paying it off for the rest of your life.'

The first judgement appeared on Odette's desk later that week, from her building contractors. Maurice's solicitors were on the phone daily, a fax came through from a wholesaler demanding immediate payment. While the pots and pans in the OD kitchen bubbled with heavenly fare, the money pot was empty. Even Bill politely pointed out that his services could not be hired indefinitely without some form of payment.

With Saskia still away on honeymoon, Odette had no one to fall back on at the club during the day. She worked there late at night and in the early mornings to avoid contact with her creditors. She had never been a coward before in her life, but now she was permanently in hiding – from her friends, from bailiffs, from court clerks and from her staff. She wanted to face them when she had some good news, and she struggled night after night to put a new business plan together to achieve that. But it was like constructing a thousand-piece jigsaw puzzle with no picture. Every time she got to the last segment it didn't fit and she had to start all over again. She remembered Florian's ridiculous suggestion that the easiest way to solve her problems was to answer the riddle Calum had set her. But with figures swimming in front of her eyes and a pile of invoices as high as her chin, she had no time for riddles.

The surety summons from the magistrates arrived on Friday, far earlier than either Bill or Odette had anticipated. Reading through all the legal jargon, Odette realised that she would be expected to appear in front of the magistrates just a week before Christmas to show just cause why she shouldn't forfeit the twenty thousand pounds she had guaranteed against Craig's appearance in court.

'You will have to convince them that you did everything in your power to assure that your brother-in-law attended court,' Bill told her, leaving his bill discreetly on her desk.

Odette knew she was doomed. She hadn't even seen Craig between his arrest and his disappearance. Monny still had no idea where he was, and Odette was astonished that she seemed less and less bothered when she called. 'He'll turn up, Odie. Bad pennies always do. I gotta dash – I've got a friend coming round and I've got to get the kids to Mum and Dad's. If you ain't bought the kids their Christmas presents yet, then Vinnie wants the new Tottenham strip. That'll teach his bastard father to go missing – Craig wouldn't let a son of his be seen dead in it.' Craig was a life-long West Ham fan.

The pressure to sell her flat increased daily. It was on the market with both the estate agents who had come around to value it, and a daily influx of viewing muddied the woodblock flooring while the melting snow played havoc with her designer rush matting in the dining area. Odette had been forced to let her cleaning lady go because she couldn't afford to pay her and found that her evenings were spent scrubbing the floor, vacuuming the rugs and brewing gallons of coffee to make the place smell nice. To her shame, she ate as she worked, polishing off all those piles of luxury items that had been stored uneaten in the cupboards for months awaiting Calum's arrival. So jars of olives and antipasti, Belgian chocolates, tins of Oreos, cans of stuffed vine-leaves and boxes of cinnamon toast cereal were wolfed back to clear space in her already minimalist kitchen.

She was on her hands and knees trying to get a particularly

stubborn stain out of one of her Mexican rugs when the door buzzer shrilled. *Londoners* had just gone into a commercial break. Odette wiped her soapy hands on her jogging bottoms and looked at the video entry-phone. The camera was set at such a high angle that all she generally saw was the very top of someone's head. But this visitor was so tall that she saw him full in the face. Jimmy Sylvian.

Odette dropped her scrubbing brush in alarm and looked around. The flat looked immaculate, but she had just scrubbed the day off in the shower and thrown on a few sports clothes to clean in. She couldn't let him see her like this. What the hell was he doing here, anyway? And then she noticed, as he backed away from the camera and checked out a piece of paper in his hand, that he was clutching the glossy brochure her estate agents had produced for the flat. He pressed the buzzer again.

Odette hadn't checked her answer phone yet, too frightened that one of the eight messages flashing on its read-out was from Bill. Listening to them now and guiltily fast-forwarding through those from her concerned friends, she groaned as she recognised the drawling voice of Adrian, one of the less likeable estate agents.

'Hi, Odette – I know you don't like evening viewings as a rule, but I've got a cash buyer who seems really interested – a Mr Sylvian. He'll be along around eight-fifteen if that's okay. Call me if there's a problem. I've left this message on your mobile too.'

The buzzer droned again. Odette wanted him to go away, but Adrian's words rang in her ears: 'cash buyer'.

She pressed the 'open door' button without speaking into the intercom and watched as Jimmy's ludicrously handsome face smiled into the camera before heading inside and out of shot. Odette threw the scrubbing brush into the bucket, which she dumped in the cupboard under the kitchen sink before dashing to the huge driftwood-framed mirror above the fire. She looked hopelessly barefaced and scruffy. In a fit of vanity, she turned on her Stairmaster and leapt on board, hoping that Jimmy would assume her sloppy workout gear had a purpose. He'd knocked on the door before she could even work up the slightest sweat.

'Good evening, Ms Fielding – I hope I'm not inconveniencing you too much by calling around at this hour?'

That odd formality again. Odette couldn't look him in the face at all, but if she had she would have realised he was afflicted with the same problem. While she glared at his coat buttons (a scruffy old trenchcoat, she noted, with a peeling charity sticker on the collar), he was peering awkwardly over her shoulder.

'For God's sake, call me Odette, babes,' she muttered uncomfortably, shifting her gaze back to the safety of the television screen. She had to appear cool at all costs. 'I think we should be on first name terms after—' she couldn't say it. After what? After my breakdown? My total and utter arse-up humiliation in front of a near-stranger?

He came smoothly to her rescue. 'After last weekend?'

'Yes.' She cleared her throat. 'But I'd rather not talk about that if you don't mind.' She feigned fascination as Liam Sullivan got Derek the dim bookie in a headlock for calling Sandra a slapper. Liam reminded her of Liam Turner, and in more than just name.

'I'm not here to talk about that.' Jimmy smiled shyly, glancing around his immaculate surroundings. 'I'm here to view your flat.'

'In that case, just look around.' Odette waved her arms expansively and headed back to her Stairmaster for refuge. 'I'll be right here if you want me to answer any questions.'

She felt ludicrously defensive. She hoped more than anything that he didn't mention the night of the wedding. She wasn't sure she could cope.

He spent ages poking around. Watching him out of the corner of her eye, Odette noticed him behaving very oddly. He ran his fingers along her granite drainer which was still dusted with icing sugar from an earlier gorge-session with some amaretto biscuits. Then he rubbed his sugary finger against his front teeth like something out of a movie. Raising his eyebrows in what appeared to be pleasant surprise, he proceeded to open her designer flour tin and sniff in it. Odette tried hard to ignore him and concentrate on sweating off some calories.

Londoners reached a crescendo of action and its familiar

plinky-plinky theme music played out long before Jimmy Sylvian had even finished in the kitchen.

'For a woman who owns a restaurant, you don't keep much food in the fridge,' he noted.

'The fridge ain't included in the sale,' Odette pointed out.

'Sorry.' Jimmy swung the door shut and disappeared into the bedroom.

Odette took a brief break from the steps, wiping her sweaty forehead with her sleeve. It was the first time she'd been on it in almost a week, she realised in amazement. And she'd been eating like a pig to cheer herself up. No wonder she was feeling the strain.

Jimmy was still in the bedroom five minutes later. Odette hoped he wasn't sniffing through her knicker drawer.

'Do you want a drink?' she called out. 'Tea? Coffee?'

'Scotch, thanks.' He re-emerged through the huge brick arch and wandered into the dining area. 'This flat is quite astonishing.'

'Yes, I've always loved it.' Odette groped through her drinks cabinet for a classy Scotch. She didn't know much about whisky, but she had a huge number of malts on offer, most of which had been corporate gifts over the years.

'Good grief.' Jimmy was gawking at her 'off-licence' with its mirrored recesses which housed a multitude of strange cocktail mixers and exotic liqueurs along with shelves of beautifully simple lead crystal glasses.

'I had it designed to look like the one from *Dallas*,' she explained proudly.

'From what?' He looked blank.

'The television series.' Odette was staggered that he'd never heard of it.

She'd always wanted a huge secret bar like the one J.R. Ewing had behind the panelling of his office, opening up to reveal an Aladdin's cave of crystal decanters, champagne coolers and swizzle sticks. She had once fantasised herself coming home from work to pull it open and sling a couple of ready-cut slices of lemon into two glasses, along with perfect squares of ice from the bucket, splashes of Bombay Sapphire and a dash of Schweppes for herself and Jonathan. But she'd always returned from work alone and preferred a cup of tea to an apéritif so the ice bucket was empty now she plundered it for something to throw into a dusty glass, and the half-full bottle of soda she opened was flat from age.

She poured Jimmy a very healthy measure of neat Allt-a' Bhainne, hoping that he wouldn't ask her what it was as she hadn't a hope of pronouncing it.

'Unusual.' He took a sip. 'What is it?'

'Teacher's,' she told him smoothly, returning to her Stairmaster.

Jimmy watched her curiously. 'Aren't you joining me?'

'No, I'm laying off the juice for a bit.' She didn't look at him as she clambered back on.

'I'm not driving, you know.' He laughed awkwardly.

Odette winced as she remembered telling him not to drink and drive after he'd nobly saved her from hypothermia.

'Thanks for the flowers, by the way.' He moved into her line of vision.

She felt her face flush even hotter and pounded the pedals so hard that the machine beeped an error warning. She hated people who thanked you for thank you presents. It meant you had to reiterate your initial thanks again, which in this case would be mortifying – 'no, thank *you* for picking me off that verge'.

'Don't mention it, babes,' she said with some feeling.

'But they were beautiful,' he said. 'Flowers are very special. You know they all have individual meanings?'

God, it's Charlie Dimmock in drag, Odette thought irritably, muttering, 'Oh, yeah?'

'You gave me a very complicated arrangement,' he laughed. 'But then I've always preferred Tolstoy to Jeffrey Archer, don't you agree?' At that moment he spotted a row of Jackie Collins novels on her bookshelf.

'There's a gymnasium in the building – with a pool,' Odette told him quickly to get him off the floral tribute. 'I only exercise in here because I prefer it. The building's gym is much better equipped.'

He nodded, and turned back to investigate the bathroom.

Odette stopped stepping and gazed irritably at the door. This was *her* home and he had no right to march around intimidating her like this, guzzling her whisky and making her feel a fool about a night she would far rather forget. She had hoped she would never have to encounter Jimmy Sylvian again and here he was less than a week after her breakdown night – a week which possibly rated as one of her worst in history – nosing around her flat counting sockets. She'd only let him in because she was so desperate to sell it.

When he re-emerged, she decided to pitch in with the hard sell.

'Another?' She whisked his glass away and refilled it with an even healthier dose of the unpronounceable malt. 'Let me show you the gallery – there's another sleeping area up there, plus a shower room and a huge space you could use as a study or a third bedroom.' She started up the stairs, wishing she hadn't climbed so many virtual ones on maximum tension in the past half-hour – her legs were aching so much that she was sure she was walking like Mrs Overall from *Acorn Antiques.* It was only when she'd made it to the top that she realised Jimmy wasn't following. Looking down, she saw that he was still dominating the centre of her vast, open-plan room, as tall and rangy as one of her pieces of gym equipment.

'Don't you want to look?' She leaned over the balcony. 'There's an incredible view of West London from here. You can see Telecom Tower.'

'I hate London.' He took a huge slug from his glass and looked up at her. 'I didn't really come here to view your flat, Odette.'

'What?' She sagged against the balcony rails. He'd been doing a pretty good impression so far. 'You mean, you don't want to buy it?'

'Can't afford to,' he said with an apologetic grin, creasing his eyes against the halogen lights as he looked up at her. 'My father's estate is still in probate – it'll be months before any of us sees an inheritance, and even then the tax man will probably lay claim to most of it. I'm sorry.'

'So why are you here?'

'I wanted to see you again.' He looked away, chewing his lip.

'To see me?' Odette couldn't keep the disappointment from her voice. She was flattered, of course she was. But she needed someone to buy her flat so badly that the realisation that her 'cash buyer' was just Jimmy Sylvian checking on her mental health was galling.

'Well, you've seen me,' she muttered. 'Although you didn't have to go to these lengths. I'm in the club every day. You could have popped in for a drink.'

'I wanted to see you alone – not in that place. It's so busy, so loud.' He cleared his throat awkwardly. 'I wanted to ask you out to dinner.'

Odette rapped her fingers against the polished metal rail, watching her long nails as they tapped out a loud percussion. How dare he lie his way into her home like this? She could guess why he wanted to buy her dinner – some sort of misplaced charity because she'd cried all over him, because she'd sold her soul and made a fool of herself. He wanted to be Samaritan Jim for a night, nanny her back into high spirits once again. Well, she had no intention of playing the victim. Her pride wouldn't let her.

'I'm sorry, I'm far too busy to come out. You should have called and saved yourself a journey.'

'So busy that you're staying in to exercise on a Friday night?' He squinted up at her again.

'It's no business of yours what I consider to be busy.' She stomped down the stairs and marched over to him. 'Now, I don't know what you're playing at conning my estate agents like this, or how you even knew that this is my flat, but I think you'd better—'

'Woody told me.' He didn't move an inch.

'I don't know anyone called Woody.'

'Sorry – Calum Forrester. That was his nickname at the camp. Forest – wood. Pretty simple. I wanted to call him Gumpy, but Florrie wouldn't let me.'

'Calum?' Odette froze. '*Calum?*'

Jimmy nodded. 'I saw him this morning and he said that

you'd put your flat on the market. I told him I might be interested.'

'Where did you see him?' She could hardly speak, her throat was so full of lump.

'Some godforsaken pub, he really does hang around in the foulest of places.' Jimmy studied her curiously.

'So he's in London?' she breathed. 'I thought he was on holiday?'

'God, no.' He barked his prairie-crossing laugh. 'I've never known him work so hard. He's really got his teeth into this project, the Food Hall thing.'

'Food Hall?' She shook her head in confusion.

'Remember the restaurant venture I was telling you about at the wedding? I know I had to be vague with Saskia's sister there, but I thought you realised I was talking about Calum's baby. I mean, I appreciate the whole thing's supposed to be hush-hush, but surely he's told you? You're business partners.'

'First I've bleedin' heard of it!' Odette exploded, marching across to her drinks cabinet and pouring herself a large drink from the first bottle that came to hand. To hell with abstinence, she needed it. Then, before she could take a swig, something struck her. 'That's it, isn't it?' She swung around, spilling the entire drink over the mirrored door. 'That's the riddle I couldn't solve! "*Fermoncieaux Hall – hard to pronounce, harder to renounce*".' She put the glass to her forehead in alarm, peering at Jimmy's distorted image through the wet crystal, unable to see his confused expression. 'He's playing a fucking game with my business, and why? *Why* didn't he tell me? Because I wouldn't fucking go down on him, is that it? The bastard. The total fucking bastard. The *cunt*!'

The word hung in the air like a stench. Swinging back in shame, Odette put her glass down and waited for the tears to come, but nothing happened. The same dull numbness lingered, muffling her thudding heart like wadding around a bell hammer. She glanced into the door mirror, which was dripping with drink, and saw Jimmy's horrified expression reflected in it. Looking at the row of bottles in front of her she noticed she'd poured herself a very large lime cordial before throwing it around. She felt a snort of laughter escape from her nose – a revolting sound, scatological, base, crude. Well, that's what she was. Let Jimmy Sylvian think what he liked. She was a foul-mouthed failure.

She waited for him to leave, expected him to walk out in disgust. But he stayed put, saying nothing. After what seemed like an eternity, he drained his glass of malt and put it down on the coffee table.

'I'm taking you out to dinner. Put your shoes on and get your coat.'

Odette waited for him to add 'you've pulled'. She was staggered by his bossy belief that she would do what he said. She was totally overwrought. The last thing she wanted to do was *eat*. At least not in company, not from a menu and not with big, bullying Jimmy Sylvian. She wanted to rip open the freezer and hit the ice cream, sniff out her chocolate stash, cram her mouth until her jaws ached. Now she thought about food, she was desperate for him to go away so that she could binge. She didn't care what she said just so long as it made him leave.

'Sorry.' She whisked his glass away from her coffee table and rubbed the damp ring with her sweatshirt sleeve. 'I'm on a diet. I never eat between chauvinist males. Tata.'

'What?' He looked staggered.

'I want you to leave, babes.' Odette took the glass into the kitchen.

He stared at her in bewilderment for a moment before heading towards the door.

'Tell me one thing.' He paused on the mat and looked at her over his shoulder. 'Why is my handkerchief sitting on your bedside table?'

Odette had forgotten it was there. She'd laundered it that week and wondered whether to post it on to him or just throw it out. In the end she'd popped it beside her bed to remind her to decide. Okay, so perhaps she'd picked it up once or twice to try and remember more about the hopelessly blurred, acutely embarrassing night of Saskia's wedding. She might have sniffed it once or twice in an attempt to stimulate a regressed memory – dancing with him while she sobbed into his shirt, sitting in

244

his car and bawling like a baby. But that meant nothing. It was just a square of functional linen.

'Who the fuck do you think you are? Othello?' she sneered. 'I needed to blow my nose in the night. If you want it back, just take it. Feel free.'

'I'm sure your need is greater,' he said lightly. 'In fact, I'm surprised you've got any nostrils left. Calum was right about you. You are one fucked up, rich cow, you know that?'

When the door slammed, she threw the glass into the sink in despair, letting it shatter against the cool porcelain, its shards spinning a strange dance towards the plughole.

23

Throughout the following week, Odette struggled to make some sort of sense of the ridiculous mess she was in. On Bill's advice, she went to see the debt counsellor at the Citizens' Advice Bureau. They helped as much as they could, but they were more accustomed to sorting out people with mortgage arrears or small debts on credit cards than someone who owed as much as Odette. It was like trying to get a pedicure for an amputated foot. They strongly recommended that she tried to avoid a bankruptcy petition at all costs, but quite how she was going to do that remained unclear. The club was still not making enough to touch her outstanding debts and all the key players had gone AWOL.

Calum was still lying low. Odette had given up trying to track him down by calling every club, bar and restaurant he was involved with. She'd started pissing off the reception staff. She thought about calling Jimmy Sylvian to ask where she could get hold of Calum, but her pride wouldn't let her. He'd rung the club a couple of times. Odette refused to take his calls, paranoid that Calum was using him to break her down yet further.

In the midst of her confused hell, there came the strangest twist of all. Every day a single white rose arrived on Odette's desk. It was delivered by motorcycle courier, packaged up in a little box which to her mind looked like a small pet coffin, the sort young children use to inter their gerbils and hamsters. She found the delivery deeply sinister, and was certain it was another one of Calum's sick mind games.

★   ★   ★

She was arranging her fifth white rose of the week in her mug when her mobile rang. Hoping it was Calum, Odette leaped to answer the call.

'Odette, it's Ronny Prior here,' said a light, sweet voice which sounded infectiously close to laughter. It was very familiar. It was not, however, Calum's and the disappointment made Odette sit down hard on her chair.

'Yes,' she said brusquely.

'I knew you wouldn't remember, darling, it's been too long. We worked on the Purr cat food commercial together. You were my producer.'

'Yes, blimey! Of course I remember, babes. How are you?'

'Sensational.' She really did have the loveliest voice, so close to laughter, it cheered Odette just listening. 'You?'

'Fine.' She didn't want to dwell on her current state. 'You work in documentaries now, don't you, babes? I caught one a while back. Fabulous.' She couldn't remember when, but recalled it being top-drawer, salacious stuff.

'Oh, good, I'm so glad you liked it. That's actually why I'm calling. Listen, I'm trapped in an edit suite all weekend or I'd offer to buy you a drink and talk about this, but I have a little proposition I want to run by you.'

'Give me a quick outline and I'll give you a quick answer.' Odette felt almost her old self again, talking to an old colleague, having a tiny gleam of power.

'Well, do tell me to stop if you think this is ghastly, but we want to fly-on-the-wall a restaurant being set up – planning, opening, first few weeks. Eating out is the new rock and roll after all, chefs are the new superstars, and I hear that you have very cleverly bought into the market.'

'Go on.' Odette was seriously interested. It had publicity written all over it. This could be her life raft at long last. With a camera crew crawling all over the OD Calum couldn't play any more dirty tricks.

'I'm not sure what stage you're at but I wondered if you'd be interested in letting us film you setting up your restaurant?'

'It's already open, babes,' Odette said flatly. 'Has been for weeks. There was quite a lot of publicity.'

There was a long, embarrassed silence at the other end, followed by a hugely apologetic back-track. 'Utterly idiotic of me, I'm so sorry. I've been away, my darling. In Dubai filming ex-pats at play. I feel such a fool. I must have got my information all wrong.'

'Don't worry about it – these things happen.'

'Listen, I'll treat some friends to dinner there next week. What's it called?'

'The OD.'

'How do you spell that?'

Odette winced. 'O and D.' So much for being the most talked-about new venue in London.

The messages from friends had become less regular and less demanding. They were giving up on her, Odette realised with a sting of anger and a pang of guilt. Conversely, she suddenly found that she badly needed to talk. Realising that her troubles were now too large to keep hidden, she arranged to meet Elsa and Juno.

On Saturday evening Odette headed into the jostling West End, her nerves jangling as loudly as the sleigh bells in the seasonal music belching out of every shop she passed. The moment she arrived in the drop-dead trendy bar called Plastic, she realised it had been a mistake to come. Elsa was full of gossip, and stress, and gruesome pregnancy stories. 'I have piles! Can you believe it?' she announced far too loudly. Several super-cool Soho types sucked in their cheeks and looked withering. 'Juno's performing at the Ha Ha so I said I'd page her to let her know where we end up.'

'Can we move on somewhere . . .' Odette wanted to say "less pretentious", but managed '. . . more relaxed?'

'Sure, you name it.' Elsa gathered her bag. 'I thought you'd like this place. Everyone's talking about it.'

Odette gritted her teeth.

Ten minutes later, Elsa was studying the menu in Pizza Express. 'Why did you want to come here?'

'Because it's cheap.' Odette shrugged.

'Oh, you don't have to worry about me – we're set to make quite a lot on the flat, although we were bloody lucky to get a good offer. The market's appalling at the moment. Euan's calling the new place Zen Den II because it's even more minimalist than your place.'

'Actually I'm selling my place,' Odette managed to croak.

'Never! Have you made so much from the club that you're buying Supanova Heights?'

Odette stared at her excited face, knowing that it was her fault Elsa had got it so wrong. If you cut the communication lines, no news quickly becomes good news.

'Calum's playing some sort of dirty trick.' She closed her eyes and took a deep breath, letting it all spill out – the club's debts, the Statutory Demand, the fraudulent surety.

'But I thought the OD was doing really well?' Elsa was staggered.

'We're working on a loss leader basis.' She was fighting hard not to cry. 'Florian and Calum took over so much of the running last month that I lost control. They've spent out on all sorts – but I signed all the bloody orders because Calum told me it would work.'

'A get lost leader,' Elsa joked feebly, struggling to take in what she was hearing. 'But I don't understand *why* he's—'

Odette covered her eyes with her palms. 'It's my fault, Elsa. I let him down. He wanted me to do something.' Her voice cracked as she fought to keep control. 'He asked me to do something, and I failed.'

'What did he ask you to do?'

A black swamp of shame silenced Odette.

Elsa thought about the opening night and her frantic drive across London to persuade Calum to move his launch site. She remembered only too well the tableau that she had stumbled across: Calum buried deep inside Tandi Rees. She'd never told Odette what she'd seen or what she'd done. As time wore on and the club appeared to be such a success, it had seemed less and less important. Now she cursed herself for being too wrapped up in her own world to foresee the inevitable.

'He asked you to have sex with him, didn't he?'

'Not exactly.' Odette couldn't bear to talk about it, not even to Elsa.

'Go on,' she urged.

'I can't.' Odette shook her head. 'I'm sorry, babes.'

They ate in silence. Elsa knew Odette too well to badger her for more. She had a pretty shrewd idea what Calum had tried to make her do. But that wasn't a good enough reason to set out to bankrupt her. First thing on Monday, she planned to call Spike 'The Jacket' Jeffries to find out more about Calum and their deal. Tonight, however, she was determined to take Odette's mind off things for at least a couple of hours.

'Let's go back to your place and watch *9 ½ Weeks* on the vid,' she suggested, abandoning her knife and fork on her empty plate and picking at Odette's barely touched pizza.

'Are you serious?' Odette looked up incredulously. Elsa had always been one of its most forthright critics.

'I haven't seen it in years.' Elsa paid the bill while Odette was in the loo and hastily paged Juno from her mobile. 'The message is "change . . . of . . . plan . . . (full stop) Meeting . . . at . . . Odette's . . . flat . . . (full stop). Mickey . . . alert."' A bemused-sounding Vodazap receptionist promised to relay her message.

As the final credits rolled, the tears returned at last. Odette was grateful. Their hot, stinging presence gave her curious comfort. She wailed and bawled and let rip. She snorted, and snuffled, and dribbled. Until now, she'd dreaded crying again, had avoided contact with her friends because of it. She had been terrified of repeating the same mad, uncontrolled emotion she'd experienced with Jimmy Sylvian, that corrosive hysteria and self-hatred. But this was better, this was purging and cathartic. This was just a good old sob and she needed it.

To her left, Elsa was armed with a pot of tea and a box of handkerchiefs. To her right, Juno had a bottle of Bacardi and a tub of Pringles ready-poised. Both had kindly not laughed during the film, had agreed that Mickey Rourke was the sexiest thing on earth, and had managed to withhold all bitchy comments about Kim Basinger's eyes being too close together.

Juno had, in fact, found the whole thing very educational. The action was set in Manhattan, where she and Jay were moving the following year. She'd already made a note to check out the food markets in Chinatown as soon as she unpacked.

'You can come and stay with us after this place is sold,' she told Odette.

'What, in the States?' Odette laughed through her tears.

'No, you dope – Belsize Park. We're not leaving until March. You'll be back on your feet long before that.'

'Will I?' Odette blew her nose and looked from one friend to the other, desperate for reassurance.

Elsa nodded confidently. ''Course you will. And the same offer stands for us once we're in the new house – there'll always be a room for you.'

Odette smiled gratefully. She felt like a small child surrounded by adults who were kind and lovely and generous but who didn't understand her.

She looked around her flat, its high walls lit only by the flicker of the television and the fire. It was her most precious possession, her honey-pot, her secret weapon, and yet Calum had never even seen it. 'I haven't lost this place yet.'

'That's the spirit.' Juno gave her a cuff and groped for the video remote. 'You bloody well fight for it, Odie. That bastard can't bankrupt you. You haven't done anything wrong.'

Odette watched the movie credits disappear and Pop Up Video leap on to the screen as the tape rewound. It was featuring Meatloaf singing 'Two Out Of Three Ain't Bad', the corny captions making a mockery of one of her favourite songs.

'I fell in love with him,' she sighed. 'Biggest mistake of my life.'

24

Cyd Francis and Odette Fielding appeared before the magistrates within hours of one another, although they were in different parts of London. At Marylebone High Street, Cyd lost her licence for a year and was given a hefty fine, emerging to find a clutch of photographers and a local television news-team crowding around for a quote. In Bexleyheath, Odette risked losing a great deal more, but no one was there to report on it, not even the *Thamesmead Gazette*. It was just before Christmas, and the magistrates were trying to clear as much of the backlog as possible before the holiday. Odette felt like a mince pie at a drinks party, dumped on a plate with a hundred others and presented to people who had already eaten far too much.

The corridors in the building were decorated with tinsel, and she noticed that the clerk who ushered her through was wearing jaunty earrings shaped like Rudolph. The atmosphere in court, however, was more bleak midwinter than season of goodwill.

Her sister was waiting for her outside, her face hopeful.

'They've given me until the New Year to locate Craig and then I'll have to forfeit the surety,' Odette told her, blowing on her hands as they crossed the frosty car park and headed towards the bus stop.

'Oh, Christ, I'm so bleedin' sorry.' Monny stopped and scrabbled in her bag for a tissue. 'I should never have dragged you into this in the first place.'

'You weren't to know that he'd run off like this.' She patted her sister's shoulder. 'None of us thought he was capable of something like this. Have you no idea where he's gone?'

Monny shook her head and blew her nose loudly. 'I've called

everyone – his friends, family, people he used to work with. No one's seen him. I'm really worried, Odie. Something could have happened to him, couldn't it?'

'He'll be okay. He'll come back for Christmas, you wait and see.' Odette rubbed her knuckles together, wishing that she'd worn some gloves. She had a shrewd feeling that wherever her errant brother-in-law was right now, he was warm and cosy.

'Who's to say I want him back?' Monny lifted her chin defiantly. 'I might have met someone else, mightn't I?'

'Monny, you're six months' pregnant!' Odette laughed.

Monny didn't join in, eyes glittering angrily. 'Yeah, you're right – I'm only dreaming. Who'd want a fat cow with two kids – and up the duff to boot?'

At the club, another rose was sitting on her desk. Beside it was a fax that made Odette sink into her chair and wail so loudly that the noise permeated the soundproofed walls.

In reception, an immaculately suited receptionist sweetly smiled at a lunch client. 'Lobsters,' she explained when he cocked his head to listen. 'They emit air when they're boiled – makes a shriek.'

In her office, Odette threw her rose at the wall. Its scattered petals joined the shredded fax on the carpet.

The trendy record label that had booked the cabaret bar for their Christmas party had cancelled at the last minute. The food had already been delivered. Odette had been forced to beg the suppliers to give her more credit. What was worse, she had been so desperate for the booking that she hadn't even demanded a deposit.

Elsa and Euan were due to drive to Scotland for Christmas the following morning, and Elsa should have been buying presents and washing clothes all day. Instead she met Spike Jeffries for lunch at a cult new restaurant, Kennel.

'S-sorry it has to be here, but I'm working.' He reached across the table to stroke her hair when she arrived.

Elsa wasted no time in broaching the point. 'What's Calum Forrester playing at? Why is he deliberately trying to close the OD?'

Spike carefully read the menu and ordered the most easily pronounced dishes before looking up at her.

'Your friend Odette is in a nasty c-corner, huh?' He ran his finger across the prongs of his fork. 'I had no idea Calum could be quite that ruthless, but he does have a reason. I wanted to pull out, but he's got his backers against the wall and is determined to see this thing through. Knowing Calum, it'll probably make us all millionaires. Odette is just an unwanted trespasser in his real estates.'

'Meaning?'

'Fermoncieaux Hall.'

Elsa's eyes widened. 'You are kidding! Calum wants that place? What for?'

'He's already bought it.' Spike tried the Bordeaux and winced. 'He's planning to create the biggest, most extraordinary restaurant in the country. And he probably will. The idea is s-sensational. Almost everyone who is anyone on the London restaurant scene has some sort of stake.' When he started listing the names, Elsa choked on an olive. It was a roll-call of stars and Michelin stars.

'But I haven't read anything about it in the press,' she spluttered as Spike patted her back until the pip flew out.

'All under wraps.' He sat down again, glancing around anxiously. 'Calum will k-kill me if he finds out I've told you.' From the look on his face, Elsa suspected he wasn't exaggerating.

'So if the idea's so sensational, why do you want out?'

Running a hand through his thatch of dyed blond hair, Spike leaned back in his chair and waited for the starters to be arranged fussily on the table before he spoke, voice hushed to avoid being overheard, eyes appraising the food in front of him.

'It takes a lot of money to buy somewhere like Fermoncieaux.' He turned over a rocket leaf without enthusiasm. 'Calum's businesses are worth millions, his new investors are big players as you know, but he owes much more than he's letting on. A while back he went through a very rough time financially – he'd totally overinvested, which is one of his sillier habits. It looked like he was going to lose everything.'

'Sounds familiar.' Elsa tucked into her parsnip soup with noisy slurps.

Spike watched her indulgently for a moment. 'But then, just as suddenly, he was swimming in funds.' He picked up his plate and tipped it sideways to assess the consistency of the sauce. 'As if from nowhere. At the time it just seemed like typical Forrester luck, one of his many insane gambles paying off as they so often do. So when he first approached me with this idea, I thought it couldn't fail, however despicable the little sh-shit behind it. I still think it's a wonderful idea – in principle – but I want my stake back. You see, C-Calum's holy c-cow is riddled with BSE.'

'How do you mean?' Elsa realised she had almost finished her soup, and Spike had yet to pick up his fork.

It was tough trying to have a hush-hush conversation with a food critic in a restaurant. Waiters were hovering everywhere, desperate to be of service. The maître d' hung around, asking whether everything was to their satisfaction. At last Spike waved them all away, his voice now so low that Elsa was forced to lean across the table, hair dangling in her soup bowl.

'You remember what I did before I took this job?' He examined a scallop intently, dabbing his little finger in the sauce and looking up as he sucked it.

Elsa nodded. She had heard all about The Jacket's past from Euan. Spike was something of a hero-figure to him, and Euan was continually frustrated by his refusal to talk about it. Until two years ago, Spike Jeffries had been a leading reporter on a national newspaper, world-renowned for his unique understanding of London's underbelly, its secret criminals and gangland strongholds. He had worked largely undercover and alone, infiltrating groups for months on end to get a scoop. His exposures of protection rackets, paedophile rings, organised crime and football hooliganism were legendary. He'd won awards and risked his life more than once. That was before he'd developed his stutter, before he'd taken one risk too many, gained a big scar across his throat and lost his nerve. Elsa didn't know much about what had happened, but she knew enough not to ask.

'A couple of years ago, I worked on a story about money laundering – it never came out, I couldn't make the mud stick. Recently I bumped into one of the contacts I'd made during that time, and he offered a very illuminating fact about our friend Calum. It seems he raised the money he needed to save his arse by selling a couple of stolen paintings – God knows how he got hold of them, but he certainly got rid of them in a hurry.'

'Who to?'

Spike shook his head. 'Not sure of the name. But we're talking big, big money – all in used fifties if you get my drift. Some still had the Securicor dye on them.'

'Are you saying he's bought Fermoncieaux with – what? Criminal money?'

'He doesn't have a c-clue what he's dealing with.' Spike looked at her nervously. 'Calum thinks he's the big man, thinks all that patter and attitude insulate him, thinks he gets his kicks out of danger. But I know the way these people operate. You just wait until they need that c-cash back. If they do, I don't want my name anywhere near C-callum Forrester's, and neither will your friend. Do her a favour, Elsa, and let C-callum take her to c-court. That way, she can't get hurt.'

Just as Odette was wondering whether things could get any worse, she found out that she would be losing almost half of her employees to the newly revamped Nero just a week before Christmas. The OD kitchens were down to a skeleton staff, everyone was being forced to double as waiters, and the bar was being manned by three people at most with no one working the tables. Things were looking terminal.

Raiding her almost-drained private reserve, Odette managed to scrape enough together to buy each of the few staff left a bottle of port and a fat Stilton.

Her last rose delivery before Christmas was the darkest, deepest blood red – almost black. She carefully pressed it between the folds of her personnel file and closed the drawer before leaving the club.

Christmas at the Fielding house was a gloomy affair. Odette found herself frozen out by everyone except her father because her presents were far more miserly than usual.

Ray took his younger daughter to the pub after lunch to escape.

'What's up, lil' one?' he asked the moment they were alone with two halves of lager.

'I think I'm going to lose it all, Dad – the club, my flat, everyfink.'

He stared into his glass for a long time before looking up at her through his curly mop of thinning hair. 'Maybe it's for the best.'

'What do you mean by that?'

'It didn't make you very happy, did it?'

'Maybe not.' She sometimes wished he wasn't such an old hippy.

On Boxing Day, there simply weren't enough staff at the club to open it fully. The restaurant had just five bookings and no fresh food had been delivered. Ned was going demented trying to chase the suppliers, who refused to co-operate until they saw some cash.

Odette made the agonising decision to keep the restaurant closed and just open the bar for business, causing Ned to walk out in a huff. With three staff in the kitchen covering snacks and everyone else in the bar, it was just about possible to keep things going for a few days with minimal running costs, but soon the customers would look elsewhere. After that, the entire club would have to be closed. The only delivery that Odette could safely guarantee arriving every day was the single white rose.

The Saturday after Christmas was the first night that the OD could not open at all. Only three members of staff turned up, they were out of bottled beer, the phones had been cut off and the previous night's receipts had shown grand takings of just over a hundred pounds. Odette was relieved that the staff who'd appeared were all temps who would still get paid by the agency even though she hadn't a hope of covering the bill.

She showed a couple around the flat later that afternoon, trying to be even more enthusiastic than the accompanying agent.

'Why are you selling if you like the place so much?' they asked in confusion.

'Moving overseas,' Odette lied, letting in the two men from the Islington Auction house who had come to collect the few pieces of very good sixties furniture she owned.

'Whereabouts?' they asked.

Odette was getting more and more adept at lying these days. 'Africa – I'm going to set up a game park.' She smiled sweetly.

They had looked at her smart business suit and high heels with doubtful speculation, but said nothing.

Later that afternoon, her doorbell rang again. Elsa had said she might call around for a coffee. Odette was on the phone trying to arrange for a house clearance valuer to come around and make an offer on her other possessions, so she just buzzed her straight in. She was still talking on the phone when she opened the door to her flat.

Jimmy Sylvian was standing on the threshold clutching a huge bunch of white roses.

'It seems these can no longer be delivered to you at work, so I thought I'd bring them around personally,' he said, marching straight inside and heading for the kitchen to look for a vase.

Odette stood open-mouthed for a moment before a voice yakking in her ear brought her back to life. 'Yes, Monday's fine. I'll see you then.' She cleared the line and watched as Jimmy plonked the roses into a large ribbon vase that Odette had bought in New York and never used. The two-hundred-dollar price tag was still stuck to the bottom.

'What are you doing?' She watched him from beside her still-open door.

'Flower arranging.' He looked up from bashing rose stems.

'It's supposed to be therapeutic. White roses mean truth. The florist told me. I rather like that. Have you sold the place then?' He noticed the missing furniture.

'Not yet – I've just put some stuff in storage.' More lies. It was seriously weird having a conversation with a near-stranger who had barged his way into her flat like a rampant florist.

'There.' He placed the last rose into the very ordered stack. 'I always knew I had hidden talents.' He crossed the kitchen and put them on the zinc-tiled peninsular unit that divided the area from the huge open reception room. 'Did you have a good Christmas?'

Odette blinked and said nothing. He was smiling at her cheerfully, as though he was an old friend calling around for a chat. She couldn't believe his gall. The last time she'd seen him he'd accused her of being a fucked-up drug addict.

'Have you come for your handkerchief?' she asked eventually.

'What?' He looked blank and then laughed. 'No – quite the reverse. Thanks for reminding me. I brought you these. Late Christmas present.' He reached into his long leather coat and pulled out a neatly wrapped parcel, popping it on the peninsular and tapping the top invitingly.

Odette didn't come forward to take it. She was still completely baffled.

'Has Calum put you up to this?' she asked.

'Calum?' He shook his head slowly, his expression suddenly suspicious. 'No. Why? Have you two had a row? Is that why the club's closed for business?'

'I suppose you could say that.' Odette shrugged, looking at the roses. She didn't entirely believe him. She knew Calum had something to do with this. 'So why are you here?'

'I've been away for Christmas.' He ran his hand through his tawny hair so that it stood up on end. The white sun-streaks had started to fade, Odette noticed, so that it looked sandier and shinier, like polished flagstones. 'I wanted to check you were okay – thought I'd pop in to the club for a drink, but it was closed so I came here.'

'Where did you go away to?' she asked, trying to sound

normal as she watched him pace around her flat like a huge animal seeking soft grass in which to rub his belly.

'Switzerland.' He smiled, heading back into her kitchen to nose into her fridge. 'Still living on a diet of Evian and air, I see?' He laughed, drawing out a bottle of very good white wine and reading the label. 'South African wine is far better, and cheaper – you should buy a good Haute Cabrière, save yourself a fortune.' He started ripping at the foil and then rootled around in her kitchen drawers for a corkscrew. 'Yes, Switzerland. Very snowy. Pity it's melted back here. I bought myself some skis. Amazing sport – never tried it before last week, but my mother's new lover is an instructor so it seemed a shame to miss out on the free lessons . . .'

Odette watched as he opened her wine, still chattering on about his Christmas in the Alps with his mother, Fitz the instructor, Mungo, Felix and Phoebe. The way he talked was amazing – familiar, cheery, joking – as though Odette knew them all intimately and would love hearing all the gossip.

'Mungo is madly in love with Fitz which is unfortunate,' he said, handing her a glass of wine. 'He and Mother had a stand-up row in the end and she stormed off to stay in Roger Moore's chalet to cool off overnight. Quite easy to cool off in Switzerland, actually.' He wandered over to her fire. 'Now listen, tonight I won't take no for an answer so I've come around in plenty of time for you to get ready.'

'I beg your pardon?' Odette spoke at last, although she was still standing by the door holding the phone, ready to run or call the police – whichever need arose first.

'Dinner,' he said, rubbing his hands in front of the fire.

'I'm expecting a friend,' she replied quickly. 'In fact, she'll be here any minute so I think you'd better . . .' She almost dropped the phone in surprise as it rang.

It was Elsa, apologising that she wouldn't be able to make it, as she and Euan were stuck at the new house measuring up. 'I thought we'd be finished hours ago, but the place is so huge. We're going straight to a play afterwards. Another time? How are you?'

'Fine, yes, fine.' Odette wanted to say that far from being

okay she needed Elsa here right now to help evict a mad intruder who was trying to lure her out to dinner to bore her about his skiing holiday. She hung up.

'You don't want to come out to dinner?' Jimmy was squatting in front of the fire staring at the flames.

Odette sighed and scuffed her feet. She wanted to yell: 'Listen, babes, right now I'm facing a bit of a crisis. My business is going through the floor and I'm about to lose my home. I really haven't got time to chat to you over tuna carpaccio, d'you understand?' But her pride wouldn't let her. Instead she just said rather blandly, 'No, I don't want to go out to dinner. Now would you mind leaving? Like I said, I'm expecting company.'

'Finc – you only needed to say.' He stood up and walked past her. 'Call me if you change your mind.' And he was gone.

Later, Odette opened the present he had left on her tiled surface. It was a box of cotton handkerchiefs. On the corner of each, picked out in very delicate embroidered stitches, was the word 'Sorry'.

When Saskia returned to work after a blissful three weeks in the West Indies, she found to her surprise that the OD Club was in darkness. She immediately called Odette's mobile.

'Sorry, babes. There's no easy way to tell you this but I've had to close the place down.'

'What!'

'Come round for a drink and we'll talk about it.'

Odette's flat was almost unrecognisable. The designer furniture, the rugs, the high-tech gym and flashy electronic equipment had all gone.

'I sold my stuff,' Odette explained. 'I put the best gear into auction and one of those specialist firms gave me five thousand for the rest. The designer clobber was worth twice that but you take what you're offered, don't you, babes? Or at least the bank do.'

'What's been happening, darling?' Saskia could barely take it in.

Odette wandered over to a kitchen surface on which the

vast array of bottles from her missing drinks cabinet was now lined up. 'What d'you fancy? I haven't got any ice I'm afraid – no fridge.'

'Anything.' Saskia looked around for something to sit on. The leather sofa had gone, she noticed, as had the huge ponyskin chairs. In the end she settled on one of the steps leading up to the gallery.

'Have you sold this place then?'

'No one wants it.' Odette shook her head, handing over a mug of lethal-looking purple fluid. 'Cassis and vodka.' She smiled weakly.

Saskia listened in horror as Odette explained what had happened.

'I can't believe Calum would do something like this!' she raged. 'I thought he was such a nice chap. What does he stand to gain?'

'The OD,' Odette said simply. 'This way, he can buy it at a knock-down price. If I become bankrupt, he writes off his sixty thousand in court, but then buys the club for far less than it's worth afterwards and so recoups all his losses.' Bill had fathomed it out at last. There was nothing Odette could do about it.

'Is that legal?'

'He seems to be getting away with it so far, babes.' Odette took a swig of her cocktail and winced. 'That's foul.'

'Absolutely despicable, darling.' Saskia was thinking about Calum's behaviour. 'Why would he do this to you? I thought he was rather sweet on you actually.'

'I don't know why he's doing it, Saskia,' Odette sighed. 'He won't even talk to me. It's like he's trying to punish me for something. He must really hate me.' She sat beside Saskia on the steps and closed her eyes. 'I hate letting people down, babes,' she apologised in a whisper. 'I hate letting you down, and I know this is the worst thing I could have done to you. No . . .' she talked down Saskia's loud protests. 'You and Stan have a lot to look forward to and this ain't the greatest of starts. I'm certain the new owners will keep you on, babes. And I'll make it up to you, believe me.'

The conversation moved on to the honeymoon and then

back to the wedding. Odette tried to gloss over her encounter with Jimmy Sylvian, but whether Saskia had heard from another source or just had a sixth sense about her set up, Odette was not allowed to get away with a simple compliment about her tall, oddly formal table companion.

'Don't you think he's fantastically sexy?' Saskia laughed. 'I only met him that day and even though it was my own lovely wedding, I swooned.'

'He's very intense,' Odette countered.

'He's very clever.'

'And difficult.'

'And romantic.'

'And he's Calum's friend.'

'You're kidding?'

Odette shook her head. 'I think Jimmy Sylvian is involved in Calum's campaign against me.'

25

Lydia Morley's Maida Vale flat was packed. Her large sitting room with its two sets of double doors leading out on to a balcony was as hard to cross as a busy trading floor before a stock crash. While Finlay – a delightful if unconventional host – ran around topping up everyone's glasses and chatting up the prettiest of Lydia's friends, she herself was sitting in the kitchen talking to Juno.

'Calum said he'd come but he's not here yet.' She glanced at her watch and played with one of the cucumber slices Juno was using to decorate smoked salmon and sourcream sweet potato mash on miniature blinis.

'There's still almost an hour to go before midnight – he's probably at another party.' Juno gritted her teeth. She couldn't think why Lydia had invited Finlay's rotten brother in the first place, but then she guessed Lydia didn't know what Calum was doing to Odette. Juno had been sworn to secrecy by Elsa.

'Calum has such fantastic friends – he said he'd bring some along,' Lydia sighed, looking over her shoulder as Jez lurched to the loo, already plastered. 'Fin's mates are so much duller. Why he had to invite all those people from work I'll never know. And there's no one new here. I hate seeing the same old faces.'

'Remind me to wear a mask next time.' Juno wiped her hands on a tea towel and took a gulp of champagne, wishing she'd gone to Ally and Duncan's dinner like Elsa and Euan. Jay wasn't very happy here; he found big crowds intimidating. And love Lydia as she did, Juno had no wish to count in the New Year with Calum Forrester. She preferred to stay in the kitchen slapping tapenade on ciabatta.

'I wish Odette had come,' Lydia sighed. 'She's gone very funny lately. I didn't even get a Christmas card, did you?'

'I think she's got a lot on her mind, what with the club closing and everything.'

'Yes, I still don't understand that.' Lydia shook her head. 'It seemed to be so popular.'

Juno had a stock response which Odette had asked her to use if people asked why the club had failed: lack of staff, cash-flow problems, the sheer size of the enterprise. Lydia barely listened.

'Odette should have asked Calum for more help.' She played with the foil on the champagne bottle. 'After all, he's the expert. It was a bit silly of her to try and go it alone. I'm sure he would have helped out more if she'd swallowed her pride and asked. After all, he made the launch such a success.'

Juno narrowed her eyes, desperate to spill the beans but equally aware that to do so would be to break a promise. Thankfully her quandary was interrupted by the buzz of the intercom.

'That might be Calum!' Lydia jumped off the surface and dashed through to the hall.

Juno reluctantly left her haven and went through to the sitting room just as Lydia proudly showed in Calum, who seemed to have brought an entire party along with him. He had at least a dozen friends in tow, some of whom Juno immediately recognised as famous hell-raising celebrities. Lydia was beside herself with excitement, clearly feeling she had achieved something of a coup.

Juno loved big parties, but preferred to know most of the people there – especially if one was going to link arms with them and sing about old acquaintances. She had no desire to mingle with the rich and famous.

She made her way across to Jay who was being monopolised by a very thin redhead whose scrawny neck looked in danger of snapping under the weight of crystals swinging from it. She was asking Jay if he'd ever experienced Tantric sex when Juno bustled up jealously.

'We have Transatlantic sex. Much more fun. Come out on the balcony for a fag, darling.' She grabbed his hand.

Jay, an adamant anti-smoker who as an American always thought fag meant gay man, couldn't wait to get outside. Several guests were tipping ash over the balcony as Juno towed him to a shadowed corner.

'Can we go home soon?'

Jay grinned with relief. 'I thought you'd never ask. Won't Lydia be upset?'

'Not now her special guests have arrived.' Juno sighed, curling her arms around his neck and standing on tiptoes so that she could press her nose to his and cross her eyes lovingly. 'You were right. It's much more fun staying at home together.'

Jay kissed her softly on the mouth. 'I'm always right. But I thought you wanted to spend this New Year with the Gang, seeing as it's the last one you'll have in the UK for a while?'

'Most of my real friends aren't here.' Juno rolled her eyes sadly. 'I guess life has changed – they're all doing their own thing. The Gang banged its last New Year in together ages ago. I just never noticed until tonight.' Tears welled up in her eyes.

As Jay squeezed her close in a tight hug, a tall blond man walked out on to the balcony and peered around him as though looking for someone.

'So you're not pissed with me any more?' Jay asked, still scalded from the row they'd had earlier when he'd suggested staying in.

'No – just a bit pissed.' Juno swung from his neck, high on champagne and love. 'I wish the Gang were around, though. I need to hug them a lot before we go and they're always so busy.'

'So where are they tonight?' he asked her.

'Elsa and Euan are at Ally and Duncan's – I guess we should have gone there. Triona's in the States as you know. Horse and Barfly are at Trafalgar Square trying to kiss poor Italian students. And darling Odette's at home on her own refusing to come out or have visitors. She's gone a bit funny lately. I wish I could cheer her up.'

The tall blond man turned around with interest.

'We could try and get there, I guess . . .' Jay suggested reluctantly.

'Nrrr – I called her today and she told me she needed to sit this one out. Believe me I begged. She wouldn't let us in.'

'So you wanna go straight home?' Jay asked hopefully.

'Actually,' Juno snuggled into his warm chest, 'I was thinking . . . Ally and Duncan live south of the river, Juno.' Jay gave his gruff laugh as he guessed what she was about to suggest.

'It'd take forever to get there.'

'Not if we rush back home and pick up the car.' She looked up pleadingly. 'You've been on Coke all night. You and Odette should really own shares.'

On hearing this, the tall blond shook his beautiful head and walked inside.

'Go on then.' Jay tousled her hair. 'Get your coat. You've twisted my arm, baby.'

Jimmy Sylvian beat them to the door. He hadn't even been introduced to his ravishing blonde hostess, but had no interest in being side-tracked by small talk. She was, after all, the fourth hostess of the evening. Waiting until she'd disappeared to fetch more glasses, he patted Calum on the back as he passed by. 'I'm going to beat a path. I said I'd see in midnight with my brothers.'

'You haven't talked to Lydia yet,' Calum argued, looking urgently around for her.

'Who?' Jimmy glanced at his watch.

'You met at the Nero,' Calum snapped impatiently, 'and then at the OD launch.'

'Oh – Christ, yes.' Jimmy had been to so many parties that night and seen so many half-familiar faces, he was disorientated. 'Your sister-in-law?'

'They're not married yet,' Calum hissed, glancing at his brother who was balancing a magnum of champagne on his forehead like a seal to entertain his guests.

Jimmy swung a big arm over his shoulders and towed him away from his cronies before breathing in a fast, low whisper, 'I don't know what your problem is here, Calum, and I don't want to know. But please stop trying to stir things up by involving me. She's a beautiful girl but I'm not the slightest bit interested, okay? If you ask me, your brother's straightened himself out at last. He's on to a good thing, so don't fuck it up, *ja?*'

Jaw clenched with tension, Calum didn't argue. 'You'll never get a cab this close to midnight. Take my car – my driver can drop you off and come back here.'

'Thanks. Happy New Year.'

Lydia barely noticed Juno and Jay leaving. They had both become so boringly domesticated lately, as had so many of her friends. She was terrified that marriage would have the same effect on her. Not that she could resist boasting about her latest wedding plans to Calum.

'Fin and I have managed to book the whole of the William and Mary Museum for the wedding. Can you believe it? Daddy sorted it out. They're getting a special licence so we can marry there. It's so enormous we can invite simply hundreds of people. You can all come!' She looked around the famous Forrester posse excitedly.

Calum's friends were glorious – high-energy, loud, selfish, and very admiring. She let Finlay get on with keeping the rest of the party topped up and geared up for the twelve bongs while she focused all her energy on making sure that Calum and his cutting edge crew stayed as long as possible, most especially Florian who had just arrived in his sheepskin coat, complaining that there was no decent food. 'Blinis are so twentieth-century!'

Lydia looked at him and gasped excitedly, immediately sensing a soulmate. 'Aren't they just? My friend Juno did the catering. She's the daughter of Judy Glenn, the celebrity cook.'

'Ugh!' Florian shuddered, taking in Lydia's tall, whip-thin boyish body with obvious appreciation. 'She is an 'arridan.'

'Yes, dreadful old trollop,' agreed Lydia, who adored Judy. 'Have a pickled onion. They're very morsel *du jour*. Do you know Gordon Ramsay?'

There was no answer when Jimmy buzzed. He backed away from the warehouse and looked up to where he knew Odette's kitchen window was, but the vast stretch of glass was as black as a coal-face. She had to be in there. He buzzed again. It was a quarter to midnight. Had she gone out to celebrate after all? She could be with her friends south of the river, or with her family, or at a local pub. Anywhere. He'd been a fool to come. He looked into the camera lens which was peering at him like a fish eye.

Upstairs, Odette was watching his handsome, worried face in amazement. What on earth was Jimmy Sylvian doing on her doorstep just before midnight on New Year's Eve? He had an uncanny and frankly deranged knack of finding her home alone at unfortunately social times – Friday night, Saturday night, New Year's Eve. She chewed her thumb-nail before glancing at the screen again. He was still there.

'What do you want?' she asked through the intercom, noticing him jump in surprise as the speaker beside him crackled into life at last.

'I heard you were alone,' he said. 'I thought you might use the company.'

'It's very late.'

'It's New Year's Eve, for Christ's sake.'

'I subscribe to the Chinese calendar.'

For a moment he fell silent and she realised in amazement that he believed her. She looked at his face on her tiny screen and saw him backing away. Suddenly not wanting him to go at all, she pounced on the entry buzzer.

He was clearly shocked when he entered the empty flat, which was lit only by the huge fire.

'Have you been burgled or something?'

'I'm trying for a Zen lifestyle.' Odette shrugged. 'So I did a Shirley Conran and sold all my stuff.'

'What, even your fridge?' He looked at the kitchen which seemed strangely bereft without the multi-storey ice chiller.

'You said yourself, I never used it. I keep my water chilled on the windowsill.' She pointed to a row of Evian bottles on the ledge outside. She'd started to refill them from the tap because she had no cash left but she still preferred drinking from the bottle, like a baby seeking comfort from a teat. The sale of the fridge had, in fact, made her close to a grand which she'd used to meet Maurice's monthly mortgage repayment.

Jimmy was looking at her sadly, unable to understand the weird changes she was making. Drugs had really screwed her up. She badly needed help, but he knew she'd reject any he offered. He looked at his watch. It was five to twelve.

'Don't feel you have to stay for a drink,' Odette said in a brittle voice. 'I can tell you're pressed for time.'

'It's almost midnight.'

She looked surprised. 'I thought it was already the New Year. I've had a glass of Malibu to celebrate.'

Jimmy noticed she wasn't wearing a watch. He looked around, but there was no clock in sight. 'I guess you get to celebrate it twice. Uncork that Malibu again.'

She looked at him incredulously. 'You want to spend New Year with me?'

'Well, I'm not going to make it to Trafalgar Square now.' He shrugged.

Odette grabbed her bottle of Malibu and splashed some into two mugs, then looked at her vast array of liqueurs on the kitchen surface, realising they must look very odd. 'I'm not a drunk or anyfink – I sold my cocktail cabinet.'

'Sure.' He poured the contents of his mug into hers and reached for a bottle of Glenmorangie. 'Think I'd prefer a Teacher's if you don't mind.'

He was standing so close to her that his breath lifted the tiny hairs on the back of her left ear as he spoke. Odette ducked away and walked towards the fire.

'Why are you here? Why d'you keep turning up like this?'

'Because I like you,' he said simply, leaning back against the counter and raising his glass. 'We've got a lot in common. I don't know many people in England any more and those I do know are flat out trying to prove something, trying to get somewhere or achieve a goal. We're not like that. You and I don't know what to do next.'

Odette stared at him across the dimly lit flat. Did he mean that they didn't know what to do next in life, or just right now? This was a bloody odd way to fill a loose end.

'Why did you send me flowers?'

'I thought that's what men are supposed to do.' He smiled shyly. 'I'm not very good at making overtures.'

Odette swayed, a combination of no food for several days and a hasty shot of Malibu making her light-headed. How come she hadn't seen it? Could it really be possible that Jimmy Sylvian was 'making overtures' without an ulterior motive? If he wasn't some sort of emissary of Calum's out to get her, to check her out, to try and road-test her for his friend, then what the hell did he see in her? She was such a mess right now. She wasn't the sleek, clever, beautiful Jennifer awaiting her Jonathan she had been for years; she was a complete wreck.

Then a thought occurred to her. At the wedding where they'd first met, everyone had banged on about how successful she was, how much she was worth. Jimmy must have been deaf not to pick up on it.

He was looking at his watch again. 'Two minutes to go.'

'You need to know something,' she blurted urgently, determined to spit out the truth before the final stroke of midnight turned him into a pumpkin. 'I'm not worth a bean. I'm not rich or anything. I've lost it all – the club is technically owned by the bank now. So is this flat. They take possession next week. The reason I didn't go out tonight is because I can't even afford the bus fare anywhere.'

'You poor darling.' His eyes widened. 'I had no idea. I thought . . .'

'I know what you thought,' she butted in hurriedly. 'And I'm sorry, but I'm not some rich career bitch who can bail you out until your father's money comes through. You're a lovely-looking geezer and of course I've been flattered by your attention, but I can't offer you what you're looking for. I'm broke.'

'You think I'm after your money?' Jimmy slammed down his mug in surprise.

'You are, though, aren't you?' Odette backed away a little further into the dancing shadows. 'Most men are – that or my tits.'

'Christ, Odette!' He stormed towards her, making her shoot back even further. He stopped by the fire, a lion lit by dancing flames. 'You really think I'm that shallow? I'm attracted to you, can't you see that? I think you're wonderful. You're glamorous and clever and ballsy and self-destructive.'

'You think so?' Odette was truly stunned.

He nodded. 'You're the most amazing woman I've met in years. Calum tried to warn me off, but if he knew me better he'd realise that would just make me more intoxicated by you. I know how bad life's got for you, Odette – he's told me about the coke habit and I can see it's consuming you right now.' He looked around the empty flat. 'It's ruined your life and I don't want to let it go on any more. I realise I'm practically a stranger, but I can't let you do this. I'm here because I want to get to know you, to help you, as screwed up as things are. I can't walk away.'

Odette stood in the shadows for what seemed like minutes. An explosion of noise from a nearby flat heralded the New Year, but she barely reacted. Jimmy could only see the gleam of her eyes and the faintest glimmer of her white, white face.

'Calum told you I was some sort of addict?' she said at last, her voice shaking.

'You don't have to deny it,' he sighed. 'I'm not judging you.'

'I don't have to deny it at all. It's not fucking true.' Her voice was as cold as liquid nitrogen. 'Calum Forrester is trying to destroy me. I have no idea why. I fell in love with him. Perhaps that's it. He's trying to punish me for daring to love someone who thinks he's so much better.'

'You're in love with Calum?' Jimmy's heart sank.

Odette nodded. 'That's the reason I'm in this mess. That's my addiction, babes. Calum set me a test, which I failed. Now he's never going to love me. He hates me instead because I'm such a gutless, sexless failure.'

'Calum's trying to help you, Odette,' Jimmy offered cautiously. 'He told me a while back that he can't stand by and just watch you self-destruct, and frankly neither can I. I had no idea you two had any sort of romantic history. I'd never have tried to move in on you if I'd known. Jesus, I really respect the guy – I know he has an odd way of operating, but he has a huge soul. And, believe me, whatever he's doing is for your own good.'

Odette's breath caught in a half-choke, half-sigh. She started to shake her head and then stopped. She made another strange gurgling noise and then covered her mouth and moaned with what sounded like ecstatic relief. When, after a minute's more silence, she still hadn't uttered a word, Jimmy took a cautious step forward.

He walked slowly towards her, realising as he approached that she was shaking all over – an eerie, almost unnatural movement that wasn't from cold or fear. It was like approaching a trembling dog. He had no idea whether she was going to snarl and lunge at his throat or fall gratefully into his arms.

She did neither. She lifted her chin, took a deep breath and raised her mug defiantly. 'Let's get drunk.'

'I thought you said you weren't a drunk?' He eyed her suspiciously.

'I'm not yet.' She breezed past him. 'Nor am I a drug addict. But there's a first time for everything. Right now what I want more than anything is to curl up in front of one of my favourite films. Unfortunately I don't have a television, as you see, and I could really use an epic story. So you're going to tell me about yourself, and how you know Calum. Another Teacher's, babes?'

26

Jimmy couldn't get very close to her; it was as though she had an invisible force-shield around her. He settled for lying back against the wall beside the fire, watching her face by the light of the flames.

She didn't talk much. Just drank, and stared into the fire, and occasionally smiled at him. When she did make conversation it was sporadic and confused, the subjects flying around like questions in a general knowledge quiz. She seemed to be waiting for something, for a story, like a child sitting up in bed.

'What's your favourite film?' she asked, staring at a blank corner where he vaguely remembered there being a vast flat-screen television.

'*Betty Blue*,' he answered without thinking.

'Eighties, I approve.' She nodded. 'Mine's *9 ½ Weeks*.'

'I've never seen that,' he apologised. 'We didn't get to the cinema much in Mpona. We had a video player, but we only watched conservation stuff and old Carry On films.'

'Carry On?' she snorted derisively.

'And *Betty Blue*. And for really special occasions we'd get out *Born Free*.'

She had moved on from Malibu to Grand Marnier. He was trying out a rare Islay malt which was like sucking peat, yet strangely addictive.

'Why won't you go back there?' she asked. 'Is it to do with your girlfriend? The one who died?'

His eyes didn't leave her face for a minute; wide, bruised and vulnerable, they watched the flames dancing over that white, white skin without blinking.

'You don't have to talk about it if you don't want.' She looked away, embarrassed.

'No, I don't mind talking about her,' he said quietly. 'I like talking about her.'

Odette flinched, realising that she had been referring to the death, whereas Jimmy was talking about the life that came before. So much more important. It was the woman he loved he wanted to remember, not the manner of her death. Why were humans so obsessed with death?

And yet when he finally spoke again, that was what he talked about, stabbing Odette to the core with guilt.

'Florence died in a car accident. She crashed the car just a few miles from the reserve. It was instant. Head injury. Painless, they say, although I'll never know. And that's not why I won't go back to Mpona. The reason for that is far more . . .' he searched for the word '. . . far more banal. It's too successful. It doesn't need me any more.'

Odette couldn't help herself. Her curiosity burnt the words out of her mouth as she saw a black cloud shadowing Jimmy's normally sunny disposition. 'But it has a lot of bad memories, surely?'

He shook his head. 'Florrie and I fell in love there, spent the few short months we had together there. There are more good memories than bad, but I won't go back. That part of my life's over.'

'And you want to stay here in England?'

'I'm not certain.' He rubbed his forehead. 'I ran away ten years ago. It's a bit of a family habit, running away. I let my brothers down very badly. Coming back's made me face up to a lot of things about myself. About my father.'

There it was again. That black cloud. Odette leapt upon it, feeding off his sadness. 'Your father? The writer?'

His forehead creased as he looked up at her through sandy lashes, head cocked, sensing her interest. More than that he seemed to sense her obsessive need for bad news, for a sob story to allay her own. 'I don't suppose you read the obituaries when he died – why should you? They made him out to be such a fallen hero, a literary genius who sold his soul to commercialism, who lived for excess. He was lauded as a rebellious, likeable hell-raiser with a taste for fast cars and women. He was all those things, but he was also the worst father imaginable. A total and utter unreconstructed arsehole. He's the reason I ran away from England in the first place.'

'You were running away from him then?' Odette understood that feeling only too well. As a teenager she'd dreamed for years of escaping her mother's clutches, finally succeeding by less drastic measures than a one-way ticket to Johannesburg.

But Jimmy shook his head and laughed. 'He hardly ever came here by then. He lived in Barbados. I didn't run away from him, Odette, I ran away to join him.

'His work was in every middle-class bookcase in literary London when I was a boy. When he started writing thrillers, he was everywhere – his big, handsome bully's face leering at me from every airport, newsagent's, railway billboard, magazine. People read him on trains and buses. Boys smuggled his books into schools. There were constant adaptations on television. But I never saw him. My larger-than-life hero father had told me to be a man and look after my brothers while he had fun making love and money in the sun.'

He looked at her thoughtfully. 'I don't know why I'm telling you this. I don't suppose it'll make you like me very much, but as you're in love with Calum there's not much point in trying to seduce you.' He smiled and looked away. 'Calum once told me that the person he least wanted to be when he was a child was his father. I was the opposite. I wanted to be my father. I hero-worshipped him.'

'You know him well then?' Odette asked, grabbing at the mention of Calum like a hungry kid spotting a lollipop.

Jimmy helped himself to another dose of Islay malt, still thinking about his father. 'Jocelyn was an unmitigated shit – I think that's fairly common knowledge. He treated my mother appallingly, she's never got over it. She's very vain, very neurotic; thinks a woman's success is measured by the wealth and power of whichever man she is an adjunct to. She was very beautiful once – still is in her way. She was a star in her own right when they met.

'When he left, Mother tried to kill herself – I found her chasing down fifty painkillers with a bottle of Pa's best brandy. She's made suicide attempts since – she's quite well known for it – but I think that was the only time she really intended to see it through. She's never forgiven me for stopping her, for changing her Marilyn Monroe fantasy into Casualty reality.'

'You found her?' Odette visualised the seventies beauty lying on a four-poster bed, surrounded by scattered flowers and empty pill bottles, a note written in purple ink beside her on the pillow. It was a beautiful image. She empathised with it more than she dared admit, found the curiosity almost too much too bear.

For a moment Jimmy watched her entranced expression, took in her excitement. 'She'd packed Felix and Mungo off to the cinema with the nanny, but she'd forgotten it was my last day of term and that I'd be catching the train home from boarding school. I found her in my father's study. She'd ripped up all the love letters he'd ever written to her – she's always had a terrific sense of dramatic staging like that, although I'm certain she hadn't anticipated being discovered face-down in a pool of vomit. I didn't know what to do. I started cleaning it up with a J-cloth, can you believe that?'

Her vision dispelled by the unpleasant brutality of truth, Odette suddenly saw a smaller, sandy-haired Jimmy in a big oak-panelled office, hopelessly out of his depth as his mother lay dying before him.

He stared into his glass for a long time. 'I'll never forget calling the ambulance and waiting with her, certain she was going to die. They flushed her out pretty smartly, although it was touch and go for a while and she was very ill for a long time afterwards. She claims that was the day she lost her looks. She went straight from hospital to a private nursing home, where she stayed for months. She wouldn't let anyone visit, not even her children.'

'So who looked after you?' Odette was appalled, imagining three small boys left to starve in a huge, empty house.

'My father.' He raised an eyebrow with deliberate irony. 'It was the first time we'd seen him since he'd left home. He sent for us – he had to, there was no one else to look after three hellishly spoiled, screwed up kids over Christmas. He'd already booted out the secretary he'd run away with and taken up with a much younger woman, a model called Sooty. She was sweet – didn't last, mind you. They never did. That holiday was fun. I remember loving Barbados, the freedom and the warmth after months of freezing dormitories. We were allowed to stay up late, to drink rum, to roam around the parties which seemed to take place every night in the house. I talked to my father for hours – most of the time he was pissed and he didn't always make much sense – but one thing was perfectly clear. He blamed my mother entirely for what had happened and felt no pity for her. He said things that a father should never tell his child – certainly not at that age. He told me that she was frigid, that she had never loved him, that the reason he had looked for love elsewhere was because he found none at home. He even hinted that she was a lesbian. And I believed him. As I said, I hero-worshipped him in those days. I never thought to doubt his word.

'After that holiday, I returned to school and Felix joined me there soon afterwards. Poor Mungo was farmed off to relatives and from what I can gather had a pretty shitty time. He was staying in Scotland with a particularly sadistic uncle when Ma came to collect him, looking her old self. Two days later, they were in the States. She's been there ever since, in and out of favour, in and out of rehab, in and out of divorce courts. Mungo was the only one of us she ever wanted to see. Felix was screwed up about it for years – still is. But I never missed her, never wanted to see her. I hated her.

'I went to Barbados every year. Got a tan, played cricket, met my father's lovers and occasionally wives. Women adored him, but he made them bitterly unhappy.

'At eighteen, I won a place at Oxford to read English – Pa's old college, Magdalen. I decided to take a year out and travel, starting from Barbados and working my way back to the UK. I had a route worked out: South America, New Zealand, Australia, South East Asia, India, West Africa – I wanted to make the Cape of Good Hope by the age of nineteen – then back through East Africa to Europe. America was the only destination I wasn't planning to make. My mother was there and even that huge country didn't seem big enough to avoid her in. I had no money but I was convinced I'd get by. Pa always paid for me to fly out to see him, so I thought I could cash in my return ticket to start off with. But that year he didn't want me to visit. He didn't send the money for the flight.

'It didn't put me off – I just guessed he was finishing a book or a relationship and that having me around would be a complication. He was used to me visiting at Christmas, not in July after all. I worked all summer to pay my way there. When I arrived it was the hurricane season and a great brute called Jennifer was ripping roofs from houses. I was on the last plane allowed to land. When I got to Dad's house, all the shutters were closed – against the storm, I figured. I let myself in and I just knew something terrible had happened.

'He'd passed out on a sofa, blind drunk. The cook and the housekeeper were nowhere and for once there was no sign of a lover – no female clothes in the wardrobe, no smell of perfume. He was on his own with just his shotgun for company.'

Odette could hardly bear to think what it must do to a child to endure not one, but both parents' attempted suicides. 'He was going to kill himself?'

'That's what I thought.' Jimmy looked at the fire. 'But when I hid the gun and sobered him up, I found out that it was there for protection, not self-destruction. He'd got a fourteen-year-old girl pregnant – the daughter of one of his friends. She was ravishing – I'd chatted her up at a party the previous Christmas. When Pa refused to take responsibility, her father had tried to kill him. There was a huge fight and my father shot him.'

'Your father killed someone?' Odette almost dropped her glass in shock.

To her amazement, Jimmy let out a short, bitter laugh. 'The girl's father didn't die – he wasn't even very badly injured, just a few pieces of lead in his shoulder. My father was a terrible shot. There was a court case. Pa claimed it was self-defence and was acquitted. Mercifully, the English press hardly covered it. But he was never quite the same again. The Barbados jet set hated him; the big party-animal had gone too far this time. He paid for the poor girl to fly to America for an abortion in a top New York clinic so that she could finish her education. She was very bright – she's a journalist now, I think. Ironic. That summer, Pa changed. He stopped writing, he drank more, he became a recluse. I stayed with him for two months. He was incredibly penitent – he cried a lot.

'When I asked him to explain why he'd made so many sudden changes in his life all those years ago – leaving his family, moving to the West Indies, starting to write under a different name – he told me it was because he thought I'd make a better role-model for Felix and Mungo than he ever could.

'My father categorically didn't want me to travel. He insisted I should go back to England to look after my brothers. We ended up having a huge row – I'm talking life-threatening here. I think all the pent-up fury and disappointment I felt came pouring out that night. I was fed up of being the responsible one, of picking up the pieces where he'd fucked up. Dad still had a little of the old fight in him and threatened to cut me out of his will. I told him I didn't give a shit, and vowed that I'd never see my brothers again unless he became a father to them. The next day, when he was taking his usual drunken nap, I stole five thousand dollars from his desk and left the house. My passport has a stack of different stamps in it, but the first time I stepped back on English soil was three months ago.'

Odette was again caught up in a fantasy – travelling the world on the back of cattle trucks and dusty buses with just a backpack and a roll of stolen cash. No family, no ties, no debts. She wanted to be there. 'So you kept your word? You didn't see your brothers until this year?'

He shrugged. 'I didn't mean what I said at the time. I still intended to take up my university place. But travelling's a curiously selfish occupation, and my route took a lot longer than I'd thought, especially once the cash ran out. I had to work for weeks, sometimes months, before I could afford my fare to the next place. I put my family to the back of my mind and gradually I found it easier and easier to keep them there. Time sort of lost importance. I saw myself as part-Hemingway, part Clint Eastwood – a hell raiser with no name. The moment my feet hit African soil, I knew I'd found sanctuary at last. The most dangerous continent in the world was my safe haven.

'I stayed in South Africa for ten years. De Klerk legalised the ANC, Mandela was released and was elected president. An incredible decade, a wonderful decade. All the time I was buried in the middle of the bush trying to preserve wildlife and hide from my family.'

'And that's when Calum came out?' Odette was ashamed the moment she had asked the question. It was so obvious. She felt as though she'd broken a spell.

Jimmy was still staring at the fire, his face in profile. As he nodded, the sinews in his neck flexed like the furrowed shank of a cedar. 'That was when Calum came out. Do you want me to tell you about that?'

To her surprise, Odette found that her burning desire to learn more about the man who obsessed her had been eclipsed. She needed to hear Jimmy's story through to the end.

'Later,' she muttered guiltily, staring into the fire too. 'Tell me about your father. Did you two ever make it up?'

Jimmy glanced up in surprise and then looked away, eyes scanning the label of the whisky bottle as though searching for clues. 'I visited him just once, about five years ago. I flew in on Christmas Eve. He was still in the same house. He'd just divorced another young wife, Sparkle – his fifth. She was a complete bimbo . . . I think she'd been a porn actress. She'd spent his money and refused to share his bed. He'd started using escort services for sex. He was pretty seedy by then – a revolting old drunken letch. He was quite ill too. Coronary thrombosis. He'd been in and out of hospital, but he refused to have a by-pass. He hadn't written anything for years, but the royalties from his previous books kept him topped up in rum and his ex-wives spent the rest.

'On our last day together, I asked him which of his sons reminded him most of himself and he said Felix. It broke my heart. He said Mungo was like Mother, and I was something else entirely. He kept repeating that phrase "something else entirely". He made me promise that, when he died, I'd bury him in England. He also made me vow that none of his ex-wives would attend the funeral. He said he loathed the idea of them all comparing facelifts around the graveside.'

'And that was the last time you saw him?'

Jimmy nodded. 'But the strangest thing happened after that. He started to write to me. Long, long letters – sometimes ten pages thick in that terrible handwriting of his. Amazing letters. Sometimes he'd illustrate them with crazy cartoons or write a poem. There were brandy splashes and ring marks over each of them, but he kept them coming. Once a week, every week, for five years I'd drive to the local collection office and know there was an envelope waiting. And the week that no letter came, I knew he was dead.

'I flew to Barbados and arranged for his body to be transported to England. Ridiculous bureaucracy. It took forever. Sorting through his belongings was heartbreaking – and I found some things I'd far rather forget.' His eyes rivalled the fire for heat as they sparked with anger.

Odette opened her mouth to ask what and then closed it again. Reaching for her glass, she knew that the story was drawing to a close.

'There were pages of writing all over the house.' Jimmy's mouth twisted sadly. 'He'd started a hundred novels, but only written a few lines. And then, in his desk, I found a very neat cover page entitled "Autobiography". Beneath it was a letter that he'd started to me the week he died and never posted.'

'Those letters to you were his memoirs?'

'Who knows?' Jimmy reached for his glass. 'Mungo thinks Pa wanted the letters published; Felix disagrees. It's all too soon as far as I'm concerned. He made no mention of it in his will, but that was written years ago. He wasn't worth a huge amount by the time he died and I don't want to see a penny of it although the ex-wives are all contesting like mad. The only one of them who doesn't want a share of the pot is my mother.'

'So you two have reconciled?' Odette liked her endings neatly tied up before the credits rolled. 'You spent Christmas with her, didn't you?'

'We try to get along.' Jimmy smiled at her, realising her need for a Hollywood end and supplying what he could. 'But we don't really know each other yet. Felix makes little secret of the fact he thinks she's a lunatic, but I think deep inside he quite likes her these days. Only Mungo really understands her, and their intimacy is something they both need to keep separate from Felix and me. Poor Mungo is the one who's most damaged. You might think it would be Felix. I had the love of my father, Mungo had the love of our mother, and Felix had nothing. But he has an incredible ability to attract, to be loved. Mungo doesn't have that. There's something bitter about him that people dislike.'

'And you?'

'Florrie loved me.' He emptied the malt bottle into his mug. 'I guess that's more than most people get in their lives.'

For the first time, Odette realised he hadn't once mentioned meeting Florrie and falling in love. He had cut it out of the story completely. Now that the credits were rolling, she wanted to grab the video box and stomp back to Blockbusters, complaining that she'd been given the PG edit not the director's cut. But Jimmy was looking her full in the face for the first time in an hour, his big bruised eyes searching, and she simply couldn't bring herself to ask. Florrie was clearly too sacred for her salacious, all-action, flick-chick needs. Instead she threw back a great mouthful of Grand Marnier and nodded.

'More than most people ever get,' she agreed.

Jimmy's face was curiously guarded. After an hour of fire-gazing narration, he was wearing a cool, pale Greek chorus mask. 'More than you have. Calum doesn't love you. You told me at the wedding your parents don't either.'

For a moment Odette faltered. She didn't remember talking about her parents, but then again she remembered very little about that confused, hellish day. 'I shouldn't have said that.' She shuddered, inching closer to the fire. 'It was a mean thing to say. They do love me in their way.'

'And Calum?'

'Oh, he doesn't love me,' she laughed. 'If he loved me he'd be here right now.'

It was one of those uncanny moments which happen perhaps twice at most in a lifetime.

Her door buzzer rang.

27

When the main entrance door to Odette's building flew open, the last person Calum expected to emerge was Jimmy. He was even more astonished when Jimmy grabbed him by the Armani lapels and pulled him up until their eyeballs were level and Calum was standing reluctantly *en pointe*.

'You hurt her one more time and I'll fucking kill you, do you understand?' Jimmy stormed off into the night.

Calum dusted his jacket down, ran an awkward finger around the inside of his collar and walked inside, catching the door just before it closed.

Odette was standing in her empty flat, swaying slightly. Lit only by the fire and luminescent with confusion, she looked strangely beautiful, almost ghostly.

'Where'd he go, babes?' she asked in a slurred voice, tipping right.

Calum was shaken from his encounter with Jimmy, but nevertheless registered one redeeming element to what appeared to be an unpleasant development. Odette was very drunk. And fully clothed. What's more, Jimmy was no longer around so couldn't care too much about her safety.

'He's made a New Year Resolution to spend more time with his family,' Calum said smoothly, putting the leather case he was carrying down on the peninsular top.

'You look like a door-to-door salesman.' Odette squinted drunkenly at him, taking in the suit and the case. 'Don't tell me you've come to offer me the chance to buy back my soul at a discount rate?'

He chose to ignore the question, noticing the malt bottle and homing in it on only to find it was empty.

Odette was still swaying on the spot, looking fazed. 'There's more in the kitchen there.'

Calum flipped a light-switch which illuminated the base of the kitchen wall units and revealed Odette's little collection of horrors like a glass army ranked for inspection. Apart from some very good malts, it was a cocktail for disaster. He selected a Macallan for himself and a bottle of Peach Schnapps for his hostess.

'I must say, I hadn't expected so many visitors,' she muttered. 'You plan a quiet night in and everyone comes out of the woodwork.'

'I thought it was about time we talked.' He watched as she lurched back towards the fire to warm her hands.

'Talk?' Odette swung around to look at him. '*Talk!* Christ, Calum, you've bloody ruined me, and you want to *talk* about it?'

For days she had wondered what she would do if she had to face him; if she had gone to Lydia's flat tonight. She'd known it would be a big, show-stopping, crowd-pleaser of a scene, enacted amongst the party frocks and champagne flutes. And the more she'd thought it through, the less she had wanted to take part.

But the big showdown had come after all. And Odette had no script and no spotlight, just a hollow belly and a dizzy head. She felt totally disorientated to see Calum here in her flat. The setting was wrong now. It should have been the backdrop for her seduction scene but the furniture had all been struck, the props put in storage awaiting a new location. She was starring in her very own actor's nightmare, the sort every luvvie talks about, where they arrive on stage to find they're naked and the play is in Russian.

'By rights I should be searching for a blunt instrument right now,' she snarled. 'But for one, that's not my style and for two, I don't have many possessions left to use. Can it you see what you've done to me? What the fuck are you playing at? We were business partners!'

'Which is why I've come here to offer a solution.' He cleared his throat and rubbed his hands together. 'I don't like this situation any more than you do.'

'Why did you bloody well make it happen then?' she gasped in amazement.

He cackled contemptuously. 'Because you got under my skin, sister.'

Odette was still feeling very, very drunk indeed. She looked at him closely, took in the hunched shoulders, stubbled chin, hooded eyes and stringy hair. He looked tired and shifty. He'd clearly been partying hard all night – probably all week. And he didn't appear to have seen much in the way of soap and toothpaste while dashing between VIP club rooms. Yet he was still staggeringly charismatic and poised, his presence so powerful that all the halogen lights seemed to swivel on their pivots to look at him like sunflowers at the midday sun.

'How d'you mean, got under your skin?'

'You fell in love with me.' He laughed scornfully, as though pointing out that she'd keyed his Merc. 'People don't fall in love with me unless they are very, very damaged, Odette. Ms Squeaky-clean Fielding, Ms Filofax and business plan – people like you don't deserve to love people like me. You have no idea what the pain of love is, how it tears you apart, how many people you have to hurt to get it.' He picked up a trashy airport novel from a box beside him. '*Hearts of Fire*,' he snorted derisively, that Glasgow accent shredding the title as surely as an MOD document destroyer. 'Is that what you thought we could be, Odette? Hearts of Fire?'

She thought about her fireside seduction scene and closed her eyes. 'I never told you I loved you, Calum,' she said, trying to keep her voice level. 'Not once.'

'Did you not?' He looked only mildly interested, flicking through the book. 'It makes no difference. It's a fact, isn't it?'

'So what if it is? I didn't deserve any of this.'

'Yes, you did!' He threw the book at the wall. 'You came along at the wrong fucking time, can you no see that?'

Odette had no idea what to say. She'd never seen him angry before. He was livid, and it terrified her. As he stepped forward, she jumped back in fear but he was simply picking up another book.

'*A Woman Scorned*,' he sneered. 'How appropriate. Hell hath no fury and all that. Well, where's your fury, Odette?'

'I told you, I'm fresh out of iron bars,' she muttered, feeling calmer. For his explosive fury had suddenly given her the strangest sensation of regaining control over the situation, of wresting back a little power. It was Calum who was on edge for once.

'Besides,' she went on, watching as he selected another book and flipped angrily through its pages, 'there's no point in killing you until you tell me why you've done this. That's what happens in those books. The villain always explains his motives before he drives his car over a cliff.'

'I didn't come here for fucking therapy!' He threw the book down and glared at her, the antithesis of soft, soul-baring Jimmy.

Odette swallowed, braving herself to ask. This might be her last chance. 'So why are you here? To kiss and make up? To seduce me in front of the fire? To tell me you love me too?'

'Whoah, back off, sister!' Calum hastily went into retreat behind the kitchen peninsular, scoffing like a teenage bully in a parody of revulsion. 'Don't get any weird ideas just because you've drunk too much and got the horn. I came here to offer you a deal, that's all. I'll buy you out.' He pulled an envelope from his inside pocket. 'I will cover all your debts if you sign the business over to me.'

Odette ran a shaking hand through her hair. She was too pissed to really take much in, to sustain her cool. Calum was standing in her flat, looking as drop dead gorgeous as he had on the opening night of the OD. Her Jonathan was here. She'd longed for this moment, had prayed that this whole terrible business was some sort of bizarre initiation ceremony to see how much she could take. But now that it seemed it was, she craved normality. She no longer wanted to play by his twisted rules.

'It's too late for that,' she sighed, licking her dry lips. 'The bank owns the club. If you'd been around in the past few weeks, you'd know that.'

'We can save it,' he said softly. 'There's still time. All you have to do is agree to a few simple terms and I'll sort everything out with the bank. You'll be able to keep this place, to get another job in time, to carry on as normal.'

Odette peered at him quizzically. 'So you *did* do all this just because you wanted the club for yourself?'

'Not quite.' He tapped the envelope against his knuckles. 'I want something a little more complicated. In fact, the last thing I need to be saddled with right now is a loss-making enterprise. But I'm willing to bear the risk if you comply.'

'Comply with what?'

'Number one: you relinquish all claim to the OD. I may want you to continue managing the day-to-day running, but I can dispose of it as I wish.'

'And?' Odette sighed in defeat. She could agree to that. She wanted no more to do with the place. It had brought her nothing but misery.

'Two: you never see Jimmy Sylvian again.'

'What?' Odette balked in total amazement. What did Jimmy have to do with this? 'I hardly know him. Besides, what business is it of yours whether I see him?'

'Do you agree or not?'

'I don't know.' Odette thought about it. Jimmy confused her. His attentions were flattering, but they had come at the worst possible moment. She wasn't sure what tonight had meant, why he'd chosen to tell her so much about himself. She guessed in a way she'd demanded it of him, asking for a fireside story in place of a soppy film. He was hopelessly good-looking, but he wasn't her type at all and she doubted his motives. He was clearly a do-gooder, a reformed world-travelling hippy with compassion overload. All that baring your soul stuff was hardly macho. And he was so intense. The last thing she needed right now was an admirer.

'I guess I could live with that.' She shrugged.

Calum looked surprised, a fleeting smile touching those narrow lips. 'Good. Finally, you do everything in your power to stop Lydia marrying my brother.'

Odette thought she was hearing things. 'You *are* joking, right?'

'Absolutely not. That is a very important condition and I expect you to comply with it fully.' He sounded like Vernon outlining loan repayments.

Odette's eyes saucered even wider. 'That's just stupid, Calum. Mad. I'll never bleedin' do that and you know it.'

He shrugged insolently, the kid scuffing his trainers and setting his chin in a sulky lockjaw of sullen determination. 'If you don't agree then the deal's off. This time next week you lose everything.'

Odette found herself laughing. She was starting to believe that Calum was truly mad. 'Why the hell do you want to stop the marriage? Lydia's a sweetheart. She and Fin are really good together. And how the fuck do you think I could possibly break them up? I can hardly lure him away from her, can I?'

'You'll think of something. We'll give him a job at the OD, place him close to you. You're already in Lydia's inner circle. I take it you are agreeing?'

Odette looked at him in astonishment. He really was serious about this thing. What had he got against poor Lydia that he wanted her to leave his brother alone? It was crazy. She knew she could – and would – do nothing to try and break them up. Agreeing to it would be ridiculous. And yet, if she did, there was no reason why she need actually carry it through. Calum would pay off her debts, take over the OD and she could walk away. Unlike his bankruptcy petition against her, he could hardly take her to court for failing to stop a marriage. The same was true of seeing Jimmy Sylvian again.

'Supposing I agree and don't manage to do it?' she said idly, spinning him along a little. 'What then?'

Calum smiled coolly. 'If you fail, I might just feel obliged to sell this little jewel to the highest bidder.' He tapped the envelope again.

'What's in there?'

He had extracted a computer disk from the envelope and was tapping it against his uneven white teeth now. 'I must say, I was most impressed.'

Odette was baffled.

Calum walked over to his leather case and opened it up to reveal a snazzy laptop which whirred into life with a series of high-pitched beeps.

'Listen, I'm really not in a fit state to go through any figures right now.' Odette rubbed her face.

'I think this figure might interest you.' Calum popped the disk into a slot at the side of the machine. 'It certainly interested me. I had no idea you were so fit. Quite a delightful surprise.'

'What are you talking about?' Odette stood up with some effort and trailed towards the computer. As she did so, she saw a grainy picture flash up on the screen. A man was stuffing his face in a kitchen, but what he was eating was something of an acquired taste. A moment later, she registered exactly what it was with a horrified whimper.

'Beautiful, aren't you?' Calum looked at the screen indulgently. 'Flo isn't the most original of lovers, but he has a certain brutish ability. You seemed to appreciate it.'

'What the . . . ? How . . . ?'

'Oh, c'mon, Odette. You knew it was there – look at you giving your all for the camera. I told you what was happening. I even showed you the way the programme worked. You agreed to it.'

'No way!' Odette clutched her hands to her face, utterly appalled by what she could see and yet revoltingly fascinated at the same time.

'You must know that's how I get my kicks?' Calum cocked his head to one side to get a better view as Florian turned Odette around and bent her over a steel surface. 'I wanted you to make love to Florian and that's what you did. It was fun. We all enjoyed it.'

'Oh, Christ.' Odette backed away as she saw Florian plunge into her. Her face wasn't in shot, but she could imagine the pain twisting it. 'You absolute shit, Calum. You total and utter shit.'

'Please don't talk dirty, you know how it excites me,' he laughed, flipping the computer closed and popping out the disk. 'Here – this copy's for you.' He threw it at her. It flew over her shoulder and skidded across the woodblock floor. 'I'd offer to have it transferred to video but I see you don't have a recorder any more. You shouldn't have sold your possessions in such a hurry. Now you'll have to start all over again.' Chortling under his breath, he switched off his computer and started to pack it back into the carrying case.

'I won't agree to it.' Odette dragged her fringe back from her face and took a deep breath to stop the room from spinning. 'Never in a million years. I wouldn't do that to Lydia. She loves Fin. I don't agree to any of your terms. Not one. Sue my arse if you like, I don't care any more. Now get the fuck out of my flat.' That didn't sound suitably dramatic so she added, 'And my life!'

It had happened. The ultimate eighties mini-series moment. Odette was slap-bang in the middle of a high-scale melodrama. Big business, sexual intrigue, blackmail. She was where she'd always longed to be. But instead of coming heroically to her aid, Jonathan was causing the whole thing.

To her amazement, Calum made no move to leave. Odette glared at him. He simply smiled in return.

Then he started to clap, slow deliberate applause, his smile widening like curtains opening until it revealed a big chorus line of teeth.

'Bravo,' he laughed delightedly. 'You got there. Fade to black and cue credits. You may go back to your trailer, Ms Fielding, and read the scripts for next week's shoot – the court scene. And let's hope for a little more originality then, huh?'

'What are you talking about?' she faltered.

'It's what you wanted, Odette,' he murmured. 'A little bit of excitement. A little bit of danger. Life's a game, after all. You don't have to play by the rules. You've got to try and expand that small-business mind of yours. Match it up to that big-business body.'

'What are you suggesting now? That I sleep with the magistrates before next week's hearing?'

'Now there's an idea.' He walked towards her until his eyes were level with hers and just inches away, his breath soft on her face. 'Although I was actually going to suggest you sleep with me.'

Jesus! Odette reeled. She never saw that one coming. This was not pleasant, she realised. This was not romantic. But, God, was it exhilarating. Her heart seemed to be thumping between her legs, deep inside her, accelerated like an engine tuned too high. Her lips and groin tingled with chilli-rubbed heat.

'After everything you've done?' She hastily backed away, putting as much woodblock flooring between them as possible.

'You love me.' He continued his lazy, deliberate walk towards her. 'Don't tell me you don't. And watching yourself on camera has excited you, hasn't it? It sure as hell excited me.'

The fire cast their long shadows across the bare wooden floor, Calum's closing in on Odette's, Odette's backing further away, Calum continuing the slow-motion chase.

His quick breath was on her face for just a brief second before his lips were against hers, hard and urgent. That kiss had almost floored her a few weeks earlier, but tonight she was frozen with such numb self-hatred she felt nothing. As his tongue slipped its way between her lips like a knife into an oyster, her hands clenched into tight fists.

She meant to push him away, no more. She needed to explain how she felt, how his demands frightened her, how much he had hurt her. She wasn't Katherina in *The Taming of the Shrew*. He couldn't subjugate her into love when that love had always been unconditional. All he was doing was poisoning it.

But just as she thrust out her arm to make him stop, he slid down her body to kiss her breasts. The full impact of her fist cracked into his forehead and he reeled backwards. Odette hadn't trained with weights for nothing. She had a right hook to rival Lennox Lewis. The next moment Calum was out cold on the floor. His head had made contact with the woodblock with an unpleasantly mortal thud.

'Got to make amends . . . saved my life . . . Florrie . . . disnae mind . . . got to make him love her . . .'

Odette placed a cold flannel on Calum's forehead as she'd seen done in so many movies.

'Got to make amends . . .' he repeated, his lips hardly moving, eyelids fluttering. 'Not Odette, cannae be Odette . . . must be Lydia.'

She stooped low to listen, but he lapsed into gibberish. 'Picasso . . . letter . . . nae matter . . . congratulations, wee bree . . . big hoose, gaun to live in a big hoose . . .'

Odette chewed her thumbnail and wondered whether she should call an ambulance. He was fading fast. It was one thing facing bankruptcy and fraud charges, quite another murder.

'What the fuck!' That sounded more like the old Calum.

Looking down, she saw that his eyes had opened and he was blinking away the water that was running down from the soggy flannel. He whipped it from his forehead and sat up, squinting in pain. 'What d'you fucking do to me?'

'You bumped your head,' she explained, watching his pupils worriedly.

Leaping up and staggering as the room reeled around him, he clutched hold of his head and lurched towards the door. Pausing to gather up his laptop, he glared at her over his shoulder, eyes slightly crossed. 'You'll fucking pay for this, you frigid bitch, just see if you don't!'

'Happy New Year to you too,' Odette muttered, closing her eyes in despair.

When she threw the computer disk onto the fire, it melted into a putrid, viscous black puddle that poured onto the hearth and made the flat smell for days, putting off all who came to view it.

28

The driving range at Wentworth Golf Club was hardly an ideal spot to corner Calum for a quiet word about Odette, but Jimmy was determined to have this thing out. He hated golf, but it was Calum's new passion – typical of him to take it up in the middle of winter, Jimmy realised with dark amusement. He liked Calum deeply, respected his eccentricity and disregard for social graces. But his treatment of Odette Fielding was beyond erratic, it was downright cruel.

'C'mon, Jimmy, put some effort into it. Swing with your body, pal. Like this.' Calum fired off a shot which he promptly hooked into the trees well short of the hundred-yard mark.

Jimmy, with his natural sportsman's ability, took an almighty swing at the ball and it flew in a straight line for almost three hundred yards.

'Jesus!' Calum adjusted his pork-pie hat as he watched the ball bounce another ten yards. 'How d'you do that?'

'Fantasised it was one of your nuts,' Jimmy snarled. 'You haven't answered my question yet. Are you going to put a stop to this ridiculous court action? It's a crazy way of getting back at your ex-girlfriend. She doesn't deserve it.'

Calum shanked a ball angrily into a nearby bush. 'I've told you, Jimmy, this is strictly business. It has nothing to do with whatever went on between us.' He threw his iron back into the bag and selected a wood. He was irritated by the fact that the only way to keep Jimmy in check was to go along with his friend's assumption that he and Odette had some sort of romantic history. 'You know the score – or rather the amount she scores.'

'I've yet to see any evidence of that.' Jimmy thwacked another ball into orbit.

'The really big users are always the best at covering it up,' Calum assured him, digging a tee into the grass and balancing a ball on top. 'Trust me, this is the only way to get her back on par.' He smiled at the metaphor. 'She'll be out of the rough in no time. By doing this, I save the business, and she can get some rehab. She'll nae be declared bankrupt, pal. The suit is just a legal technique to manoeuvre her into a position where she can sort her life out.'

'And what about the money she owes to the courts for her brother-in-law's bail?' Jimmy asked as Calum wriggled his hips and prepared for his back swing.

He missed the ball entirely, almost spinning himself right round as his wood flew through the air.

'The what?'

'You *do* know she owes twenty thousand pounds on top of the money you're asking for?' Jimmy looked at him furiously.

'Christ, she didnae say a thing!' Calum threw down his club in horror. 'The stupid, proud bitch. Why didn't she tell me?'

'It could have something to do with the fact that you're taking her to court for every penny she has.'

Calum shook his head dismissively, quickly covering his shock. 'I gave her the chance to sell me the OD. She could've stopped the petition in its tracks − it was a good offer. Can't you see how screwed up she is? She's way down the line now, pal, mixing with criminals. She'll know what a big mistake she's made when she finally cleans up her act. As soon as she does, I'll take her back.' His eyes burnt into Jimmy's, warning him off.

Throwing his hired clubs down in disgust, Jimmy walked away. Whatever game Odette and Calum were playing between them baffled him. Somehow it felt more like a divorce than a bankruptcy petition. He didn't understand the pair of them at all.

Despite his swaggering bravado, Calum couldn't reach a phone quickly enough. He made a series of hasty, desperate calls before he finally slammed the thing down in disgust. He was too late. Odette should have come clean about the faked surety. It was the first interesting dishonest thing he had known her do, and she had to bloody well keep quiet about it.

Bankruptcy, when it came, was a surprising relief. For the first time in years, Odette had no responsibilities at all. She had no house, no bank account, no business. She felt absurdly liberated. But it was short-lived.

The worse thing of all was the humiliation of admitting her new status. Becoming an overnight charity case for one's friends was deeply shaming. Yet they seemed to thrive on the task, bonded together as they hadn't for years, dragged their husbands and lovers and significant others along to help a woman they'd barely seen in months. She hardly felt she merited such attention, such loving support.

Juno insisted that Odette move straight into her spare room the moment she had to surrender the flat. Odette found the practicalities of moving a godsend as they took her mind off what she was losing. Instead she buried herself in over-efficient lists – inventories and itineraries, meticulously cross-checked and colour-coded. Jay was clearly impressed, Juno just thought it was a sure sign of madness.

Reluctantly, Odette told her family that she'd lost the flat. They reacted far more calmly that she'd anticipated. Her mother simply told her that she couldn't have her old room back: 'Not wiv ze grandchildren staying in it, Odie. Your sister 'as got a job at the supermarket working nights. Maybe she put in a good word for you there, eh? Maybe you meet good man who look after you.' Odette didn't think they really understood the implications of what had happened to her, the years it would take to recover, the limited options that faced her. She wasn't ready to stack shelves yet, but being left on the shelf was the least of her worries.

Her father waited until Clod was out of the way to offer Odette a sad hug, saying, 'Never mind, you'll get another one soon, little 'un.'

'It ain't that easy, Dad,' she sighed.

'Well, let me know if there's anyfink I can do. Anyfink at all.'

She thought about asking him to keep some of her remaining possessions in his shed, but that was his only haven from Clod, especially now that Monny's part-time shift-work meant leaving the kids with their grandparents overnight.

There was still no sign of Craig. Odette admired the way Monny had coped, getting herself a job despite her hefty bump. She was showing the old-fashioned Fielding grit. Taking inspiration from it, Odette struck upon an idea that would help them both out and save Juno and Jay from their gooseberry lodger.

But when she asked her sister whether she could stay with her in Thamesmead, Monny was totally against the idea. She got quite agitated when Odette pointed out that she could baby-sit at night and job-hunt by day, saving her sister the extra hike to drop the children in Stepney each evening.

'No way, babe.' Monny seemed terrified by the prospect. 'I'm sorry, but it wouldn't work out. Just 'cos you've had a flashy job don't mean you know a fing about children, does it? Besides, Mum loves having the kids over their place.'

Staying with Juno and Jay was fun at first. Juno adored having her around and couldn't wait to crack open a bottle of wine and settle on the sofa to gossip or watch *Londoners*, banishing Jay to his darkroom or the pub while they indulged in 'girl-talk'.

With every conversation came a glut of food – Juno could never have a chat without providing a meal, or a bowl of crisps, a packet of biscuits or a box of chocolates. And there was always a bottle of wine open waiting to top up their glasses.

Odette's comfort eating got worse. For once she matched Juno mouthful for mouthful. Living in her baggy jogging gear, she barely noticed the weight starting to pile on.

No one wanted to employ a bankrupt, even as a freelance. Her old colleagues and contacts sympathised with her, offered kind words and vague promises that they'd 'bear her in mind', but she knew that they saw her as untrustworthy. She had, after all, handled her biggest ever undertaking appallingly badly and had made a lot of people redundant.

The irony was that none of them stayed that way for long.

As predicted, Calum bought back the business from the bank almost the moment Odette signed it over. She was still personally responsible for repaying all the club's creditors as much of the debts as she could through her trustees; Calum simply took over the lease and the building, complete with the state-of-the-art equipment and fixtures for which she was still paying. He then sold it a week later to a huge hotel chain as part of one of the biggest deals in restaurant history, a deal which made Calum Forrester one of the richest men in London. Along with the OD, he sold his interests in Desk, Office Block, Therapy, the Clinic, and the revamped and suddenly popular old lady, the Nero. The papers were full of speculation as to why he had done it. The fact that he was Fermoncieaux's mystery buyer was obviously being kept from them. They did, however, report that he and Florian Etoile had fallen out big time and that the big, bullying chef had punched Calum in the face on the fifteenth green at Gleneagles.

Soon afterwards, Saskia called to tell Odette that she'd been asked back as promotions manager by the OD's new owners. 'I was going to refuse, but Stan insists I take it. He wants to keep an eye on his works of art.'

'Do it,' Odette told her. 'Good luck.' It lifted her spirits to learn that it was to reopen almost immediately, with just a very few alterations. The cabaret bar was to become a members-only bar with a private entertainment room. And the name was to change from OD to the Station. Odette knew it would work. It should have worked before.

Her guilty conscience was easing, but not much. Camping at her friend's house made her feel hugely accountable. She tidied and cleaned like a demon to try and pay her way, but that only put Jay's nose out of joint because he claimed actually to enjoy housework. She tried to keep to her room, but Juno was wont to follow her in for a gossip, irritating Jay even more as he remained in the sitting room, excluded from the girly intimacy. She offered to cook, but that was Juno's territory. However hard Odette tried to keep a low profile, she was aware that she was interrupting the rhythm of co-habitational bliss. Every time Juno and Jay had a row, she thought it was her fault.

Her friends had arranged to share her between them like a school hamster during the summer holiday. Life didn't get any easier once she moved into Ally and Duncan's tiny, tastefully decorated box room, although she was secretly grateful to get away from Juno's high-decibel parrot and the constant mess.

At first Ally and Duncan welcomed her with open arms – a live-in baby-sitting service to look after China. Ally went to great efforts to cook good food, enjoying the excuse to use the best wedding china and to give Delia a rare whirl. Duncan bought a case of good wine from Oddbins, knowing that Odette shared his connoisseur's taste for vintage red, whereas Ally was currently sticking to fizzy water.

Still desperately looking for work, Odette lowered her expectations and applied for jobs as assistant producer, PA, even as a runner. But she was overqualified, and in the popular commercials industry there were hundreds of eager graduates who would expect less money and control, who would happily allow themselves to be exploited in order to work in the media. Ally and Duncan both worked from home, and Odette seemed to be under their feet all the time, disrupting their routine.

Late one night, she overheard an argument which she was certain was about her. They tried to keep their voices low enough not to be heard, but the walls of their flat were as thin as rice paper.

'We can't afford another mouth to feed, poo!' Duncan's usually soft voice was taut with frustration. 'China costs enough to keep. She's not even two, for Christ's sake. We were only just making ends meet before she came along.'

'I thought you'd be happy at the idea? We've always wanted China to have some company. I thought you'd be as excited as I am . . .'

Odette listened to her friend sobbing and was lacerated with guilt as she heard Duncan apologising and soothing her, saying that of course they could cope, they always had, things would pick up soon and they'd all be one happy family. Odette felt like a demanding cuckoo chick squashing tiny, fragile starlings into the corner of their nest as she opened her mouth and expected to be fed.

The following day she told them that she'd found some cheap digs and was moving out.

She had less than ten pounds in her purse when she walked to the nearest phone box to call around and beg a room for the night. It was raining and icy cold drops slithered between her neck and her collar like ghostly fingers. As she looked at the familiar coin slots and square buttons, she remembered standing in the phone box on Essex Road just a few short weeks ago, worriedly wondering if she was having a breakdown. If only she'd known how much worse it could get, she thought bleakly. There was a world of difference between finding yourself at Stress Junction, the career and biological clock crossroads, and losing everything you have in the world.

Someone was waiting outside the box now. Odette had to make a decision.

She tried Jez, although she was almost certain he would be out of the country.

'Yes? Hello? Yes?'

'Oh, Jez, fank God you're in, babes.'

'Odette! My favourite little pauper. You just caught me. I'm on my way to the airport. How's things?'

Ten minutes later, she was on her way to Notting Hill with instructions to pick up a set of keys to his flat which Jez – who was running late as usual – would leave with the porter. When she got there, he'd also left two hundred quid under a glass of champagne, along with a note that read, '*My poor little designer vagabond. It's all yours for a week. Get a job, you layabout. Thinking, worrying, caring and fantasising about you. Jez xxxx.*'

Odette stayed on in his flat while he went on tour in Germany with his band, Slang. It was a lonely time. She signed on with as many temping agencies as would take at her, but her bankrupt status terrified them.

Guiltily, crazily, she started binge-eating. Sitting alone at night, she ate her way through Jez's freezer with its exotic luxuries from Harvey Nichols, its tubs of Häagen-Dazs and its sides of Irish smoked salmon. Then, hugely embarrassed at herself, she spent the money he had bunged her on replacing as much as she could. It seemed incredible to be shopping in

Harrods Food Hall once again, as though nothing had changed in her life and buying a square of *pâté de foie gras* was a treat she barely batted an eyelid at. Instead she gaped at the prices in horror, realising that a moment on the lips was not just a lifetime on the hips, it was also three days' temping work.

'Well, strike a light,' a camp *faux* Cockney voice purred into her ear as she rootled through the freezer cabinet for Jez's favourite sorbet. 'If it isn't the East End vamp from Saskia's wedding.'

She swung around to find herself facing Jimmy's little brother, Mungo. He was wearing a peaked cap and the darkest of sunglasses, and looked like a young Warhol.

'Fancy bumping into you in my favourite corner shop.' He kissed her on both cheeks. 'I just popped in for a banana milkshake and a Snickers bar. Perfect hangover cure. How are you?'

'Oh, fine.' Odette was grateful that she was wearing her smart interview suit after a disastrous meeting with a PR company in Pimlico. 'You okay, babes?'

'Well, hungover naturally,' he drawled. 'But otherwise absolutely bloody awful, my dear. You see, I'm about to be made homeless!' He wailed so theatrically that several tourists in the food hall looked at him curiously.

Odette remembered Jimmy saying that the lease had almost expired on the Notting Hill mews house. It was where she'd first met Phoebe, the day of Saskia's hen weekend. Jez's flat was just around the corner.

'You not found anywhere yet?' she asked.

He shook his head and then winced as it reminded him how hungover he was. 'I'm awaiting my inheritance as we toffs say at the DHSS. Honestly you'd think the old bugger had left nothing but debts, the time it's taking. We're practically destitute.' He dropped his voice and whispered in her ear, 'I might even have to get a *job*.' He shuddered at the thought. 'You're so lucky being self-made darling. None of these boring death-duty worries – and look at all your treats.' He eyed her basket enviously. 'All my favourites. You have such good taste. I say, do you want to buy me a drink? I promise to be terribly witty and entertaining.'

Odette smiled despite herself. Oh, the irony. 'I'm sorry, babes, I'm too busy.'

'Oh, shame.' He pushed out his lower lip. 'I really could use a hair of the dog – a bloody enormous voddie and Red Bull would go down so nicely. Never mind, another time.'

Just before he floated away, Odette asked as casually as she could, 'How's Jimmy?'

'Ohhhhh!' Mungo shrieked with no attempt at subtlety whatsoever. 'I'll tell him you were asking after him. He *will* be pleased! He's fine, a pain in the arse as ever. *Such* a bully. Can you believe he told me I drink too much?'

'Never!' Odette feigned horrified sympathy.

'I know, I know.' He shook his head sadly. 'Pol Pot had nothing on him. What's your name again? I'll pass on your love.'

'Odette.' She tried not to feel too offended that he'd forgotten it. They'd only danced to five Abba songs together after all.

'*A bientôt*, Odette, me old China.' He skipped away through the Harrods crowd.

'Did she say where she was living?' Jimmy demanded.

'I didn't think to ask.' Mungo looked sheepish. 'But she was buying caviar so she can't be doing too badly for herself. Probably shacked up with some bully boy trader by now.'

'You know I've been trying to track her down for weeks!' Jimmy stormed.

'Oh, I really wouldn't bother,' his brother drawled lightly. 'She has terribly thick ankles.'

Jimmy slammed out of the mews. Had Odette looked out of her sixth-floor window, she would have seen his blond head far below. But she was far too busy stuffing her face with luxury mince pies that she'd bought in the Harrods sale.

The moment Elsa and Euan took possession of their new house, they insisted Odette move in with them.

'You have to come and help,' Elsa told her. 'I can't bend down enough to lift anything and I'm not letting Euan anywhere near the paint supplier. You know his fetish for electric blue.'

Odette would have loved to refuse. Moving into a new house should be a time to nest and bond, and her cuckoo status was well established, but Jez returned from tour with his lover, Olaf, that week.

The Zen Den II was as spectacular as Elsa had promised it would be. Unlike her other friends' cramped flats, it had acres of space for Odette to lie low in, and huge amounts of tidying, cleaning, decorating, unpacking and sorting for her to do to earn her keep. Better still, there was a pub just around the corner advertising for bar staff so Odette could keep out of her hosts' way when they wanted a quiet evening together.

She liked working in the Pump House. The landlord, a big beefy Stepney lad himself, fussed over Odette and gave her as many bottles of Bacardi as she could carry in exchange for helping him out with his VAT receipts. Whenever she had an evening off, she inevitably found Juno in situ at the Zen Den II, complete with wine, Pringles and unwanted decorating tips. 'I think Euan's right, Elsa, purple foil would look great on the ceiling.'

Between them, Juno and Elsa started planning Odette's future.

'You can't live as a slacker forever,' Elsa told her kindly. 'You're thirty-two, You have to think about the future some-time.'

'I'm thirty-three,' Odette corrected. 'And I rather like being a slacker.'

Her birthday had come and gone without ceremony. Elsa and Juno were furious with her for not saying anything, and guilty as hell for not remembering. Odette's father had sent her a card with a tenner stuck inside, but it had taken weeks to find her because she'd moved so much lately.

The following day, Juno arrived with a lurid purple plastic bag from The Link. She thrust it at Odette. 'So you can never get away. We can call you and track you down even when you're penniless.'

It was a pay-as-you-go mobile phone. Odette felt the first tears for weeks spring to her eyes.

'You can't buy me this,' she said shakily. 'It's too much. I've already imposed on you all.'

'You used to be a poser, now you're an imposer.' Juno kissed her. 'We love you either way. You're our friend.'

There was another thing that Elsa and Juno were plotting between them: Odette's revenge. They were both determined she should enact grisly retribution upon Calum Forrester and delighted in planning it in minute detail, discussing everything from placing a kipper under his carpet to putting out a contract on him.

'She doesn't even seem to be angry at Calum,' Elsa told Juno one evening when Odette was safely working in the pub and Euan was covering a gig.

'I know,' Juno howled indignantly. 'You've seen how rock bottom she is, how little she thinks of herself. She needs to do something to get a bit of the old Fielding chutzpah back, climb up on that moral soap box of hers and puff up her shoulderpads.'

Elsa could only agree. And she reasoned that Odette didn't need to be anywhere near Calum to give him a little divine retribution. In fact she remembered her mentioning something which had seemed awful at the time, but now . . .

'How about a docu-soap box?' she giggled.

'Tell me more?' Juno wrinkled her nose, smelling napalm.

They both rounded on Odette when she came home from work with the usual bottle of Bacardi and several catering packs of Scampi Fries.

'I know you've got a bit of a craving for them,' she told Elsa as she deposited them on the sofa beside her friend.

'That was last week. Can't lay off the mint sauce this. But thanks – perhaps I'll try to combine the two.' Elsa looked quite taken with the thought. So, rather alarmingly, did Juno.

She winked at Elsa. 'We've been having a planning meeting.'

'Oh, yeah?' Odette yawned, whacked out from her shift, much of which had been spent poring over the Pump House accounts.

Juno and Elsa both spoke together. 'Revenge!'

'Revenge for what?'

'Calum, of course!' Elsa spluttered, barely able to believe her friend's indifference.

'I'm not interested, babes.' Odette tried to look detached. She'd thought about it. Of course she'd thought about it. She wanted the ultimate comeuppance. She wanted Calum to suffer, to feel her pain, to squirm with shame and know what it felt like to lose everything. She wanted his balls. But her self-confidence was at such an all-time low, the idea was laughable. He was now one of the most powerful landowners in Britain. She wouldn't know where to start.

Juno shot Elsa another wink. 'It's what Alexis would do.'

For a moment Odette blanked her, then a slow smile spread across her face. 'Okay, what had you got in mind, babes?'

The next day, Odette called Veronica Prior.

'Hi, babes, it's Odette Fielding. You still looking for a restaurant to follow with a crew?'

'It's still in the pot.'

'Is this going to be a hatchet job?'

Ronny laughed. 'Depends who you want to bury.'

'I'm not grinding an axe here, babes, I'm just oiling wheels.'

'Sure.' Ronny dropped her voice. 'Well, between you and me, my executive producer isn't the biggest fan of eating out. The Nero has refused him membership three years running, and he can never get a table in the Ivy. And, yes, it was his idea to try and run with this project, but so far no takers.'

'You willing to shoot out of London?' Odette knew it was a trump card. No parking hell, no local bureaucracy nightmares when it came to external shots, cheaper crews, lavish expenses.

'Do grizzlies dump in the forest?' laughed Ronny.

Do I dump on Forrester? Odette wavered, knowing that once she'd passed on the tip, she couldn't take it back. What the hell? He could always say no. If he had any sense, he'd do just that. At least this way she'd keep Juno and Elsa happy, and she owed them a hell of a lot of favours right now.

'Whatever you do, *don't* tell them this came from me, but I know exactly who you should contact . . .'

29

Elsa organised her own hen party at her mother's house in Sussex, inviting just a very few close friends. Cyd was delighted to be so involved in the occasion and insisted she would arrange all the food and drink. 'You simply have to bring yourself and your friends, dearheart,' she gurgled, greatly cheered by the prospect of some lively young company. She had already rearranged the crystals in her house to emphasise the feminine aura, and ordered a catering-sized box of St John's Wort teabags from an Internet health food site she was very fond of using. She hoped her daughter's party would prove a much-needed tonic. There had been many parties at her Sussex farmhouse once. She remembered few details, although she certainly recalled the day darling Keith Moon had driven an E-type Jag into the swimming pool.

Cyd was not at her happiest. She had employed a very dishy driver called Eric who, far from driving her to heaven, had driven her to distraction. Because he was so pretty, she'd offered him the use of the cars when he was off-duty. And he had taken full advantage, disappearing in Jobe's beloved vintage sports cars for nights on the town in Brighton, returning them scratched and dirty when he turned up to work the following morning.

When several reminders for parking fines arrived through her door, Cyd had simply paid them. When Eric had accumulated six points on his licence for speeding, she'd overlooked them. But when he had driven the Aston – only just back from the body-shop – into a tree, she'd been forced to let him go. She was now relying on local taxis to ferry her around until she found another driver.

Euan had entrusted his stag weekend to the capable hands of Ally's husband, Duncan, his best man. It was only a few days before the event itself that Euan confessed to Elsa that he and 'the lads' were spending the weekend in Brighton.

'But that's just a few miles from where we'll be!' she complained.

'I shouldn't think we'll meet up. You'll be at your mother's all night.'

'She thinks it might be fun to hire a fleet of cabs and go clubbing together.'

'In your state?' Euan wasn't at all happy with the idea.

'I can still boogie.' Elsa demonstrated the fact. 'We'll only go to some naff old seventies night – nothing hard-core. But I don't want to bump into you lot in a club.'

'No chance of that!' he laughed. 'I wouldn't be seen dead in a seventies club. The lads and I are going to be going wild – paint-balling, tank-driving, assault course, go-karting, rally-cross, heavy boozing, moshing to some serious Brighton Rock. And then – of course – a late-night Indian.'

'So Duncan's organised all this for you, has he?' Elsa smiled. She knew through Ally that Duncan was arranging some sort of cheesy retrospective night. She wasn't sure of the details, but Ally had reported that Duncan was busy making Euan a Womble costume (he'd asked her to stitch the eyes on), and that she'd overheard him on the phone enquiring where one could play Bingo in Brighton. Elsa doubted her groom-to-be was in for the all-action adventure he anticipated.

Odette wasn't really looking forward to another weekend in the countryside, although she kept the fact a secret.

A wild Mancunian club DJ, Miss Bee, collected Elsa and Odette from Highbury in her swanky yellow new-style Beetle to travel to Sussex.

As they pelted out of London, music blasting from the stereo, Odette watched civilisation sliding away and braced herself for another weekend in the wilderness. The Sussex countryside came as a delightful surprise. The little villages with their duck ponds and cricket pitches were so picturesque they were almost naff; the huge gate-houses every few miles hinted at great country houses just out of view behind high-banked verges, woods and thick hedgerows. As they wound their way through the lanes towards Smock Mill Farm, Odette started to relax a little. This wasn't the wilds, this was the Weald – really quite attractive and blissfully close to London.

They reached Fulkington in just under an hour, although a lot of that was down to Bee's driving, which was so fast that the big plastic sunflower in her dashboard vase constantly fell out on to Odette's lap.

The village was a cliché of four-acre green with dew pond, wishing well and a host of little thatched cottages clustered around the edge. Two minutes later and they turned left into a long, no-through road which started to climb dramatically and wind its way uphill, flattening out on a shelf of upland, bending dramatically left, ducking through a wood and emerging at the entrance gates to the farm.

Odette had never visited Cyd's home, although she'd seen photographs. It had been featured in several homes-and-gardens magazines and Sunday supplement style sections and she knew it was beautiful in a rural, twee sort of a way. But nothing had prepared her for quite how pastoral it was, nestling in the lap of the South Downs like a clutch of eggs curled in a soft moss basket. The farmhouse itself was a long, creamy-white building of such total irregularity that it looked like a child's sketch – its roof pitching to and fro, its walls bulging and buckling, its tall red-brick chimneys pointing this way and that. The only point of symmetry which could be drawn anywhere close to it was at ground level where it met its reflection in a vast lake. To the left of the house, an amazing combination of outbuildings ranged around a cobbled courtyard – a red-brick barn with heavy black beams, a creamy-white stable block with a bell tower, a crumbling wooden orangery and a whitewashed dovecote. Beyond them was an orchard straight out of a child's story book where ancient, gnarled fruit trees pointed knobbly, bare winter branches at one another like petrified witches having a slanging match. To the right of the lake was the smock mill that lent the farm its name, a huge whitewashed windmill with a top like a pepper mill that revolved to find the wind. Behind it, a long stretch of lawn led to the thick woods through which Cyd walked daily with her Afghan hound, Bazouki, who was reputedly as blonde and scatty as her mistress with a similar bent for breeding.

'This is choice – magic!' Bee drove the Beetle around the lake, past the outbuildings and to the front of the house. 'Is your mam in, Elsa? No cars around. Oh, hell.' She struck her forehead. 'Sorry, I read about her ban in the papers.'

'The cars are all in the garages,' Elsa pulled her curls back from her face and looked at the house. 'I'll show you later. She's in. Listen.'

Once Bee had cut the engine – and consequently the blast from her own stereo – an audible bass boom could be heard thumping from the house.

'Mask?' Odette asked.

'God, no,' Elsa laughed, jumping out of the car. 'Bent Uncle. Mum knows she's got yoof coming, although personally I prefer Boney M.'

Bee caught Odette's eye across the car roof as Elsa wandered around the side of the house. 'Bit tense, isn't she?'

'They have a difficult relationship, babes,' Odette explained cautiously. 'The mother-daughter distinction's a bit blurred.'

Bee gave a say-no-more wink and collected her bag from the boot. 'Can't wait to meet Cyd. She used to be my idol. I hear she's a total babe in the flesh.'

'She is,' Odette assured her.

'Oh, this is going to be heaven,' Bee growled, racing around the side of the house after Elsa. 'I hope she wants a toy-girl.'

It was difficult to know whether Lydia or Bee was flirting more with Cyd that evening. Lydia was at her most charming because she wanted Cyd to recognise her as an equal, to tell her she was the most ravishing woman in the house, as she had told Odette on the opening night of the OD. Bee was flirting for the far simpler reason that she was in love.

Odette watched Cyd and found herself wondering whether she'd known Jimmy Sylvian's mother, Philomena Rialto. They were both former starlets, former Bond girls, sixties pin-ups with middle-class backgrounds and impeccable thoroughbred looks. Both had married drunken, hell-raising men, more famous then themselves. Both had outlived them, both were survivors. Now Philomena was in Hollywood, constantly kick-starting a career or a marriage; Cyd was in rural Sussex kick-starting her lawn-mower and her smoker's cough. They might be a world apart geographically but Odette decided they were eerily similar in other ways.

She was letting her mind wander because the conversation predictably revolved around weddings. While Elsa's married friends swapped notes about their various nuptials, Elsa, Lydia and Juno listened in with eager ears. Cyd, the grande dame of weddings, having taken part in twice as many as anyone else gathered around her bowed scrubbed-pine kitchen table, looked on benignly, entranced by their enthusiasm.

Odette found that she had some allies. Miss Bee, gorgeously gay and proudly single, was munching on olives and looking bored. Elsa's schoolfriend Anna – a recent heartbreak victim who found herself back on the shelf after five secure years in the supermarket trolley rattling along the aisle towards the cash till of marriage – was listening in with the avid determination of someone who wanted to skewer her ex's love tackle with a wedding hatpin. But the conversation showed no signs of abating.

When they started getting down to the nitty-gritty of seating a famous parent at top table, Odette cleared the plates to the dishwasher in the outer-lobby. The house was a maze of odd-shaped rooms, none of which seemed to have much practical bearing on its neighbour; the kitchen led into a conservatory-cum-swimming-pool, beyond which was a laundry room leading into a library and study. The dining room was attached to a vast games room, from which several doors led variously to a gardening room, a sauna, a room which housed nothing but a four-foot-high rose quartz, a pottery and the vast sitting room. That was so jam-packed with sofas it looked like an enormous and very jolly dentist's waiting room.

The babble of conversation filtered through from several rooms away. Talk of dancing, of drinking some more, of clubbing in Brighton.

Odette finished loading the dishwasher and wandered out into the unfamiliar games room. She looked at the vast snooker table and longed to hide in one of its pockets. She'd been fine when she was just surviving, when she was living out of a suitcase in a friend's house certain that things would pick up. But things weren't picking up. Her life was fractured – not a tiny hair-line fracture which she could just about trust her weight on but a great compound one with the bone jutting out of the skin. Her friends were trying so hard to help, she wanted to weep her gratitude in front of each and every one of them, and yet their assistance was the equivalent of sticking a Band Aid on the wound when she needed major surgery. Her life had flat-lined.

Only one person had ever put her problems into perspective. And that conversation hung in the air like a lively radio debate cut short by a technician leaning on the wrong switch. Odette wanted to talk to Jimmy Sylvian again. She needed his wider view. His broad-shouldered, Atlas grasp on the world, his sad stories and his booming laugh.

Odette hadn't noticed Lydia enter the room. She only realised she wasn't alone when the cue ball rattled into a corner pocket with a light thwack as it hit the several reds already in the sleeve.

Lydia was renowned for getting tight on a single measure of vodka. She was legless on two and needed her stomach pumped after three. Tonight she had sipped her way through several glasses of Cyd's favourite tipple besides her beloved whisky – a locally bottled, acidly strong white wine. In her desire to be just like Cyd, Lydia had gamely tried to match her hostess slurp for sip. She was consequently screw-eyed with concentration as she homed in on a table football and spun each row in turn.

'Odette, my sweet.' She tipped her head charmingly and almost fell backwards with the effort. 'You know Calum Forrester quite well, don't you?'

Odette took the opposite side of the table and dropped the

ball into its midst, a sudden tourniquet of emotion gripping her throat and threatening to strangle her.

'We spent some time together,' she said, ramming a goal home with her rear defender. The ball flew between Lydia's posts uncontested.

'Do you think he's gay?' Lydia asked, waggling a few rows of players around without touching the ball.

'That would be far too simple an option for Calum,' Odette snarled, tapping her second goal in with her front striker.

'What d'you mean?' Lydia gave up on play entirely and gazed across the table at Odette.

And that's when she recognised it. Her reflection. Never had she thought to see it in a face as beautiful as Lydia's.

'You fancy him don't you? You fancy Calum?'

Lydia's exquisite head swung from one side to the other on its narrow pivot as her eyes narrowed in momentary, pissed denial. And then she blurted, 'Odette, I adore him. He's so like Fin. And I love Fin, *love* him, but Calum's sexual, you know? He's so seductive and secretive and powerful and just bloody fanciable – whereas Fin is all over me like a puppy, but won't have sex.'

'You and Finlay don't have sex?' Odette scored an own goal without noticing.

'He has this problem.' Lydia wandered towards the darts board. 'It's only temporary – or so we hope. When he was a user, he lost his use. I mean, he became impotent. I thought it would be really good fun trying to work through it. That's my job now after all, and I do love him so much . . .'

'But?' Odette watched worriedly as Lydia dragged the darts from their bullseye and backed drunkenly away from the board.

'But it's taken longer than we thought. Oh, Odie, it's such torture! I love sex so much, and Fin just won't oblige. We were supposed to wait six months at most – that's what the experts say – but when we decided to get married Fin got fixated on this notion we should wait until our wedding night. I mean, it's a terribly romantic idea, darling, don't get me wrong. I love it. It's just that I am feeling so frustrated! It's not as though I haven't had offers . . .'

'Calum?' Odette fed her the name as Lydia threw a dart

which speared an oil painting of a Friesian cow hanging on the panelled and limed wooden wall.

'He's been making sort of overtures.' Lydia threw another dart which shattered a light bulb overhead. 'I made it clear I wasn't interested so he backed off a bit, but I've been thinking about him non-stop lately.'

'What sort of overtures?' Odette's voice strangled itself into a nasal whine.

'A while back he told me he fantasised about me.' Lydia's third dart made it on to the board, jabbing in beside the three of thirteen.

It all sounded so innocent, Odette realised. So blissfully romantic in a steamily adulterous way. Given what she knew of Calum's sexual preferences, it was close to unbelievable and teetering on the edge of killing her with jealousy. Calum had wanted her to stop Lydia from marrying Finlay. She'd thought Calum believed Lydia wasn't good enough for his brother. But now she knew differently. Calum wanted Lydia for himself. Odette's screwed up, complicated, clever, devious Jonathan was just a red-blooded male stereotype after all. Bastard!

As Lydia moved on from darts to the basketball hoop on the wall, Odette headed for the big punch-bag swinging from the ceiling.

She smashed her fist into the stuffed leather so hard that it juddered on the spot like a jelly. If Calum thought she'd knocked him out deliberately on New Year's Day, just wait until she really tried.

'Finlay's far better than Calum, babes,' she said quietly. 'He's honest and open and lively, and remarkably sane given his history. Calum's the most devious, bloody-minded, sadistic bastard I know. He actually asked me to try and persuade you not to marry Fin, can you believe that?'

Before Lydia could answer, Cyd had fluttered into the room.

'Here you are. The cabs are coming in twenty minutes, so get your false eyelashes on. We're going clubbing. Elsa has agreed on proviso I wear a wig to avoid recognition. Rather annoying as I only had my roots done this morning.'

Lydia was looking absolutely devastated. Odette chewed her lip guiltily. What had she done? She shouldn't have said anything. She hadn't just set the cat among the pigeons, she'd set a whole pride of starving lions into a bird sanctuary.

Then Lydia revealed the true reason for her expression of distress as she said to Cyd, 'You mean you're not a natural blonde?'

'I was.' Cyd winked at her, unabashed by a demand for such honesty. 'But everything fades to grey in the end. You, my darling, have many years of looking as luminescent as you do now. You are quite the most beautiful creature.'

Suddenly glittering with satisfaction and happiness, Lydia dashed off to tart up.

'What a dear little thing,' Cyd murmured as her footsteps retreated, 'but staggeringly vain.'

'She worships you,' Odette told her. 'She wants to be like you so much.'

'She is, more fool her.' Cyd gave the punch-bag an affectionate pat. 'Or rather, she is like I once was. Age has a very healthy side-effect. The arteries may harden, the skin sags, the hair grows white and coarse and the memory goes, but wisdom tends to accumulate.

'Now I need your help tonight, my dearheart. I've arranged a rather special display for my darling daughter which means we simply have to get back here by one in the morning.'

'Oh, I love fireworks!' Odette clapped her hands excitedly, instantly guessing what Cyd meant by 'display'.

'I do too, Odette.' Cyd laughed her infectious, honeybee laugh. 'And I'm sure there'll be plenty of them. Wait one moment!' She danced towards a long sideboard and rootled through a drawer full of board games before pulling out a packet of playing cards. 'I'd use my tarot, but we don't have time for a full reading.' She gave the deck a quick shuffle and fanned them out for Odette. 'An old Romany taught me this. Pick a card.'

Odette thought it was hardly the time for magic tricks, but selected one at random and handed it over, wishing Cyd would let her go upstairs and tart up.

'How wonderful!' Cyd gasped when she turned the card over. 'The two of diamonds. The messenger. You have feet of fire tonight, dearheart. Feet of fire.'

Odette smiled humouringly. The old bird was such a hippy. The only reason her feet would be on fire was because she hadn't worn her high heels in so long they were bound to be agony.

30

It was when they were dancing to 'Tiger Feet' that Cyd leaned across to Odette and asked her whether she had a clean driving licence. Odette wasn't sure she'd heard right at first, so asked her to repeat the question. 'Have you ever been banned?'

'God, no!' Odette looked affronted and then remembered too late that Cyd had just lost her own licence. 'I mean, it's easily done, but I never drink and drive. Not me.'

Cyd nodded and danced off, shaking her long silver glitter wig. She was an amazing mover, Odette noticed. Sexy and uninhibited, she seemed to flutter and writhe to the music like a long muslin curtain blowing in the wind. Elsa was having a whale of a time, despite feeling like a whale in her one and only official maternity dress, a clingy green show-stopper from a specialist shop called Bump 'n' Grind. She hadn't stopped laughing and dancing all evening, chatting to her friends, receiving endless non-alcoholic drinks and whipping her curly mop of hair around as she turned from left to right to catch everyone's eyes. Only Lydia wasn't joining in the fun.

'She's throwing up in the loos,' Juno told Odette as she boogied up with two bottles of beer. 'I think she had too much Lower Hurstfield Riesling earlier.'

'D'you think we should get her back?'

'Oh, she'll be okay,' Juno said distractedly as 'Brown Girl in the Ring' started playing. 'Yes! I requested this hours ago. C'mon, Odie. La la la la *laaa*!' She grabbed Odette's arm and dragged her over to the other hens, who were forming a group around Elsa as she danced to her favourite song.

Lydia was not in fact all right. She was sitting on the loo

pan sobbing into her hands – long, bony fingers unadorned by rings. Somehow, she wasn't exactly sure when, she had lost her engagement ring. She'd only just noticed. It could have slipped off her finger when she was changing in the house earlier, or in Mandy Kingston's car on the way from London, but she had a horrible feeling that she'd lost it more recently. Just a few moments ago, when bending over the lavatory throwing up, she'd been vaguely aware of a soft 'clink' beneath her head. She'd reached out and hit the flush button with her eyes squeezed tightly shut. Now the bowl was empty and so was her ring finger. She almost believed she'd deliberately, subliminally, flushed it down the loo.

There seemed to be some sort of symbolism in it. She ignored the fist pounding on the door and the demand for her to hurry up, just pressed her face tighter into her hands to try and stifle the sobs. Calum had asked Odette to stop her marrying Finlay. The stupid fool! If only he'd known that all he had to do was ask her himself.

It was just after eleven when Elsa gathered all her drunken, happy hens and squeezed them into three taxi cabs for the twenty-minute journey back to Fulkington. They would all have been happy to dance the night away, but Cyd was most insistent they had to get back to the farm. 'I can't take the pace any more, my dearhearts,' she'd apologised. 'And this music brings back too many memories – all those dead friends singing. It's like dancing in Heaven.' From the glint in her eye, Odette suspected she had something more up her sleeve than fireworks.

It was only when they were gathered around the kitchen table once more, lifting foil from the supper leftovers and picking at them as they waited for the tea to draw in the pot, that Odette realised Lydia was missing.

'One of us will have to go back and look for her. I'd better call a cab.'

'Why not call her mobile?' Odette suggested, leaping up to gather the phone from the wall. She dialled the number from memory. 'It's ringing.'

A moment later Anna wandered in from a trip to the bathroom, holding a tiny silver mobile phone which was belting out a tinny rendition of the overture to *William Tell*.

'Whose is this?' she asked, looking around. 'Only it was in the bathroom, along with this ring.' She showed them an exquisite solitaire diamond set on a white-gold band.

'They're Lydia's,' Odette sighed, hanging up and redialling. 'I'll call that cab.'

'What on earth was her phone doing in the bathroom?' Ally asked in amazement.

'Perhaps she had to answer the call of nature,' Juno giggled. All in all, they weren't taking the situation very seriously.

When there was a crunch of tyres on gravel twenty minutes later, Odette shrugged into her coat and picked up Lydia's phone from the kitchen table. 'I'd better take this – she might have the presence of mind to call it. I can't get any reception from mine here, so you'd better ring me on this if you hear from her.'

'I'm coming with you!' Juno jumped up and grabbed her bright yellow Puffa.

Sitting in the back of the cab, she admired Lydia's high-tech little phone while Odette chatted to the cab driver, explaining that they'd need him to wait outside the club and then possibly cruise around Brighton looking for a missing hen.

'Amazing technology.' Juno pressed a few buttons. 'Oh, look, it says she has a message. Shall we listen to it?'

A moment later and she was listening to the message, her eyes bulging in surprise. 'You are never going to *believe* this!' she whistled, selecting 'repeat' from the menu and thrusting the phone to Odette's ear.

She stiffened as she heard a familiar rasping but light Glaswegian accent leaving an urgent message which burnt her ear like caustic soda.

'Lydia, it's Calum. We've got to talk about this thing. I'm not sure using my place is such a good idea. We can't keep it a secret from Finlay much longer. Call me when you get this message.'

Odette pressed the 'cancel' button. As she looked out at the darkened windows of the Regency town houses, an image of beautiful Lydia and Calum together tortured Odette's soul. They were already having an affair, she realised wretchedly.

Odette loved Brighton. It was one of her favourite towns. But she wasn't particularly fond of it tonight as she dived in and out of clubs and bars looking for Lydia. There were a remarkable number of places open considering it was off-season.

'This is typical of her,' Juno grumbled as they tramped around the Lanes. 'I bet she's booked into a hotel and is tucked up in a warm bed by now.'

Odette wished she could be so certain.

'No sign,' Juno panted as she came out of an all-night café five minutes later. Odette had been working her way along the taxi rank asking if any of the drivers had seen a tall, good-looking blonde. 'Only in my dreams,' was the standard answer, or, 'We're all looking for one of those, my love.'

Odette checked Lydia's little phone again and cursed as she realised the battery had run out. It was well past midnight. She was exhausted, and freezing cold, but too worried about Lydia to give up. She had to be somewhere.

'We could try Kipper Tie again,' Juno suggested half-heartedly.

'She wasn't there, babes,' Odette sighed sadly. 'We checked it inside out. We couldn't have missed her. I feel so responsible.'

'It's not your fault we left her behind.' Juno shrugged. 'We were all a bit pissed.'

She chewed her lip, 'I'm going to find a phone box and call the farm. She might have turned up.'

'I've a better idea,' Juno suggested through chattering teeth. 'There was a pay-phone in the all-night café on the front. Let's get a hot chocolate and ring from there.'

The line rang for ages and Odette wondered whether they'd all heartlessly just gone to bed. Eventually Cyd's smoky voice picked up. There was music in the background, a thrashing bass which Odette recognised as the CD that had been playing when she and Elsa had first arrived.

'Odette – we've been trying to call you. She's here!' Cyd laughed, clearly covering the receiver and shouting over her shoulder that Odette was on the phone.

'So she did find her way back?' She sighed with relief, realising that she'd underestimated Lydia's self-preservation instinct.

'Not exactly,' Cyd giggled. 'Euan brought her here.'

'Euan?'

'Yes, he and his friends were trying to get into the club when Lydia wandered out. She was a bit upset, so he brought her back here.' She dropped her voice to a whisper. 'The dearheart is dressed as Uncle Bulgaria for some reason. Now we're having a bit of a party,' she started talking in her normal voice again. 'You have to get back here ASAP, my dearheart, or you'll miss out on all the fun.'

'You've got the stags there?' Odette asked, images of an all-night boozathon shattering her hopes of collapsing into bed.

'Not yet. How did you know?' Cyd sounded astonished, and then seemed to realise she'd made a mistake, laughing heartily. 'No, no – just Euan. His friends all went back to their hotel to wait for him. It's the Royal, do you know it? On the front.'

'I think I walked past it a couple of times.' Odette watched the stringy waiter carrying a large bowl of chips to Juno's table, along with the hot chocolates.

'Actually you couldn't pop in there on your way back here, could you? Tell them that Euan's staying here? And hurry so that you get back in time. Darling Elsa thought I'd arranged for Euan to turn up – she's convinced that's her surprise. She has absolutely no idea what's going to happen at one.'

'The fireworks?' Odette remembered tiredly. She no longer felt any enthusiasm for a bunch of squibs and rockets, especially given Cyd's lack of common sense; she'd probably set light to the house.

Cyd's husky laugh crackled down the line. 'No, darling – this is far better.' She dropped her voice to a whisper. 'I've arranged a little floor-show.'

'What have you got planned?' Odette asked suspiciously. There weren't many entertainers who were willing to perform at a private party at one in the morning.

'Let's just say, I think it'll be *staggering*'

Suddenly Odette had a ridiculous notion. Then again, knowing Cyd, perhaps it wasn't so far-fetched . . .

'You've hired the Stage Stags to come to the farm?' she gasped, not noticing that most of the café was suddenly listening in.

'You've rumbled me,' Cyd whispered proudly. 'Their manager, Bryan is a dear old friend of mine – he used to manage the Rumbling Runes and the Why. His boys are doing a show in Brighton tonight and Bry agreed to arrange for them to come here afterwards as a favour. Isn't it thrilling?'

'Unmissable,' Odette laughed. She thought stripping troupes the height of tack, but guessed it was an extraordinary coup to get the most famous one in the country to perform in your front room.

'Now gallop apace, my dearheart,' Cyd urged, making her mission sound far more romantic than it was. 'Fly with those feet of fire, and get back here soon. Don't forget to pass on the message to those nice friends of Euan. He says they've arranged a stripper – in the singular. So last year.'

The Royal was the grand old dame of Brighton's famous sea-front, the diva in the chorus of Georgian architecture. It had survived fire, terrorist bombs and a film crew shooting a docu-soap. The six-foot-wide chandelier in its entrance hall glittered like a hovering UFO as Odette raced in and then ground to a halt as she surveyed a brass signpost which pointed to at least four bars. Beside it a large board welcomed representatives from the Trekkers' Guild of Great Britain and members of the Elvis Impersonators' Society.

'May I help?' trilled a receptionist in a voice so prim she'd have been sacked from an Ayckbourn farce for overacting suburban dimness.

'I'm trying to locate a party you have staying,' Odette dashed up to her. 'They're supposed to be in a bar. They're all men. They're stags.'

The receptionist's eyelashes fluttered knowingly. 'I'm afraid it's residents only in the bars after twelve-thirty ay em.' She sucked the 'm' out like a lollipop.

'Oh, I don't want a drink. I just promised I'd pass on a message.' Odette rattled her fingernails impatiently on the desk. 'Do you know where they are?'

'I certainly do,' the receptionist trilled, on something of a power-bender. 'But I'm not at libertee to tell you. I'm under the strictest instructions not to allow fans to pester the boys after they've finished their show. They need their private time to rest and recuperate. If you want a signed photograph, then leave your name and address with me and I'll pass it on to their manager.'

Odette blinked at her in bewilderment for a moment and then started to laugh. 'I'm not looking for the Stage Stags! I'm looking for a bunch of geezers on a stag night. Euan Cochran's stag night. Duncan Shand's the bloke in charge. They should be here somewhere.'

The receptionist blinked at her distrustfully. 'One moment.' She clicked a couple of buttons on her computer console. 'Yes, we do have that party staying. Would you like me to ring around the hospitality bars to try and locate them?'

Odette looked at her watch. 'Why don't I just pop through and try and hunt them out? I'm on a tight schedule.'

The receptionist sucked in her cheeks and then glanced up irritably as a group of drunks dressed as *Star Trek* characters lurched through the swing doors. 'Perhaps that's best,' she said distractedly, watching a very pissed Captain Kirk urinate in a potted palm.

Odette followed a couple of Uhuras into the Queen Mother Lounge, a vision of pink flock wallpaper, racing prints and old Guinness Is Good For You posters. It was full of Trekkers. She backed away hastily and followed the brass signs to the Duchess of Kent Suite, a tennis-themed bar draped in nets with old racquets hanging on the purple and green-striped walls. It was packed with men sporting greasy black quiffs, sideburns and rhinestone-dotted flares. Back-tracking, Odette galloped down a staircase to the Prince Edward Inn. Sitting on beige pouffes amid a bizarre collection of old costumes from *It's a Knock Out* were a group of Stage Stags knocking back tequila. But they were the wrong ones. These men were fake-tanned, huge-shouldered, thick-necked iron pumpers. Odette was about to carry on her search when something occurred to her.

'Why aren't you at Smock Mill Farm?' she asked one of the brighter-looking strippers.

He blinked at her, opened his mouth, closed it and blinked again. She waited, half-suspecting he would ask her for a clue.

'Cyd Francis?' she name-dropped humouringly. 'You were hired to perform at her daughter's hen night?'

'Streuth, I forgot!' wailed an Australian as wide and golden-brown as Ayers Rock. 'Bryan asked us to go on to some private gig.' He reached into his pocket and drew out a crumpled piece of paper that was translucent with body oil. 'Some old sixties poof he used to hang out with. Sid . . .'

'Francis.' Odette gritted her teeth. 'She's a woman. Starred in *Exhibition* with Bowie, had a number one with "Oyster Diver", married Jobe Francis?'

'Jobe!' A dyed blonde American surfer with forearms as wide as magnum bottles whooped excitedly. 'I loved Mask, man. I mean, their music was so revolutionary. "Sonic Jet to Heaven" changed my life.'

'Well, right now you need a Sonic Jet to Fulkington,' Odette told him. 'Because you've got to get your asses there and waggle them in front of Jobe's wife in Jobe's house.'

'Oh, Christ, Jobe actually lived there?' The surfer was already on his feet.

'Hang on, sport.' The Australian held up a hand as big as a pan lid and then swung it around to offer Odette a hand-shake that almost welded her fingers together. 'Todd Austin. I manage the troupe in Bryan's absence.'

'His absence?' Odette asked worriedly.

Todd was older than the other Stage Stags by a good few years, although his physique was clearly rigidly preserved. There were deep creases around his seedy, lichen-green eyes and his curly ash-blonde hair was thinning at the sun-burnt temples. Odette knew from his little Hitler swagger that he spelled trouble.

'His boy band, All4One, has just lost its lead singer.' He

flashed her a gap-toothed smile. 'Crisis situation. He left me in charge. Now, I know that he and this Cyd Francis sheila go way back when, but my understanding is we're receiving no payment for this show, am I right?'

There were murmurings of dissent amongst the muscle men, and a couple complained they'd already showered their baby oil off and removed their elastic bands, whatever that meant. Odette supposed they used them to tie their hair back. She had never seen so much glossy, high-lighted long hair being swirled about. It was like being trapped in a room with ten Timotei girls.

She could smell mutiny but could hardly offer to bung them a couple of hundred each as she once would have done, desperate for her friend to enjoy the night. She chewed her lip.

'I'm sure you'll be amply rewarded,' she told Todd confidently.

Those gappy teeth flashed once more and he dipped a tinted green contact lens admiringly towards her cleavage. 'Will I now?' he chuckled letchily, looking her in the eyes once again, his intentions perfectly clear.

Odette was aware she hadn't retouched her lipstick in hours and she'd been on the go longer than the arrow on a Monopoly board, but she registered his interest with relief. He wasn't remotely her type – he reminded her unpleasantly of a young, Aussie Garth Draylon – but now she knew how to play him. She stooped a little lower, revealing a chasm rippling with fool's gold.

'Why don't you and your friends pop up to your rooms to collect your thongs together and meet me in reception in five minutes?' she purred seductively.

Todd had them all swaggering towards the lifts in less time than it took to throw off velcro-sided trousers on a club stage.

Buoyed up by her testosterone-heavy admirer, Odette headed on to the Prince Philip Tavern and finally tracked down her quarry amid more Greek paraphernalia than a Crete souvenir shop. Under the watchful gaze of several portraits of the Duke of Edinburgh, occupying a clutch of tartan chairs, Duncan was sitting with a group of half a dozen men and a policewoman.

Odette raced up to them. 'Duncan, mate!'

'Hi, poo.' He looked up at her blearily. 'Don't tell me another hen has flown her coop? Haven't seen Euan, have you? Only he's been under arrest for over an hour now.'

'What?' Odette looked at the policewoman, who seemed to be wearing an awful lot of make-up for a member of the Sussex Constabulary. And she was certain fishnet stockings weren't standard uniform issue. 'No, he's at Cyd's house, babes. He chaperoned Lydia there. I don't think he's coming back.'

'Spoilsport!' moaned a fat skinhead who was leering at Odette's boobs. His cross-eyed squint shifted to the police-woman 'Does that mean you don't get to take your clothes off?'

'I will if I get paid.' She shrugged, sipping from a bottle of Hooch before balancing it on a tartan chair arm. 'Shall I do it now?' She looked at Duncan with dead eyes, practised fingers starting to unfasten her silver buttons.

'No!' He did them up again as fast as he could, suddenly resembling an embarrassed vicar. 'The stag isn't here. It wouldn't be right.' His jeering companions clearly disagreed and started to chant, 'Strip search! Strip search!' in a tuneless football-crowd voice.

Odette turned her palms up at Duncan in defeated empathy, catching sight of her watch face as she did so. Juno and the Stage Stags would all be in reception now. She really had to get a wiggle on.

She blew Duncan a kiss. 'I have to get back to the farm, babes.' She started backing away. 'Catch you soon.'

'Wait! We're coming too.' Duncan was shrugging into his coat, gesturing the policewoman to follow and knowing that Euan's cronies would trot obediently after her.

'You can't!' Odette yelped, imaging their reaction to the Stage Stags. 'It's a hen night.'

'Euan's there,' he pointed out.

'He doesn't count.' She tried to think why. 'He's dressed as a Womble.'

Duncan gave her a hang-dog look. 'Can we please come back with you?'

'No,' she said firmly.

'We'll stay in the garden,' he promised.

Odette felt an involuntary smile twitch at her mouth. If it had been anyone else but Duncan she'd have stuck to her guns. 'Okay, you can come, but you have to promise to behave.'

'Thanks, poo.' He kissed her cheek.

Odette bit her lip, wondering what she'd just let herself in for.

Juno was thoroughly overexcited to find herself hailing cabs for the Stage Stags and Euan's stags combined, her own beloved Jay amongst them.

As she, Jay and Odette settled into the back of a cab while Duncan clambered into the front, Todd Austin thrust his very broad shoulders through the rear door. 'Room for a little one.' He inserted himself into the car with difficulty, ending up with his nose between Odette's breasts.

'Are we being followed?' the cabby asked, glancing worriedly into his rear-view mirror.

'It's just a few friends,' Juno said vaguely, squeezing Jay's knee.

'A few?' The cabby was staring so fixedly in his mirror that he almost drove into a parked car. 'There must be five taxis behind me.'

'Good.' Juno relaxed. 'At least one of them must know the way.'

'Which turning is it?' Odette asked Juno as they cruised along the lane at Fulkington's western limit for the third time.

'I'm not sure.' She wrinkled her forehead at the dark lanes they were passing. 'I had no idea there were this many farm tracks. Hang on – this one looks familiar.'

'We have already tried it,' their driver told them in his flat Eastern European accent. 'It leads to a place called Dyke's Bottom Farm.'

Todd and Duncan both started snorting with laughter again,

just as they had when six taxis had driven up the narrow two-mile track to be faced by three snarling Rottweilers at a security gate, necessitating some very laborious reversing along the narrow drive.

'Wait!' Odette eyed a track she hadn't noticed before, curling away into the hills between two bent trees. 'I think it's this one. Turn here.'

'Are you sure?' Juno looked at the pot-holed drive ahead with much the same distrust as their driver.

'Certain.' Odette was filled with a flood of confidence. 'This is where we're going.'

As they bounced along the rutted track, she could distinctly hear strains of 'Remember You're a Womble' coming from the convoy of cabs following behind.

Half a mile further on, she was still convinced she was right. A further half-mile and the first niggling feeling of doubt crept in. Surely the Smock Mill drive didn't climb this steeply?

'This road, he fuck my suspension,' their driver complained.

'Mine too,' groaned Todd whose love-tackle was being rammed against the window winder on the door with every pot-hole they crossed.

'Oh, I recognise this,' Juno said confidently.

Odette felt a whoosh of relief until she realised that Juno was talking about Jay's Clangers t-shirt which he'd borrowed out of her wardrobe to comply with Duncan's retro theme.

Another mile and she knew this wasn't the way to Smock Mill Farm, yet the convoy couldn't possibly turn back. There was nowhere for six cars to execute a three-point turn along the endless, high-banked driveway which lost the moon overhead every few seconds as it disappeared into a black tunnel of trees. The cavalcade of bright headlights dipped and twisted through the muddy stretches behind their leader for what seemed like an hour.

Odette's ears had popped and fizzed before they finally reached the summit of their climb and twisted through a wood to a house in a clearing.

It was a pure Grimms' Fairy Tales setting. The lights were

all glowing, the chimney emitting a plume of smoke that curled around the moon in the sky like a question mark. A dog was barking its head off indoors.

'Is this it?' Jay whistled in awe.

Doors banged behind them as the assorted stags started emerging from taxis, complaining bitterly about the bumpy ride.

'Odette, you plank!' Juno began to laugh. 'You've brought us to the wrong place.'

'You mean this isn't Cyd Francis's farm?' Duncan groaned.

'Um . . . not quite.' Odette was hot with humiliation. She hated getting things wrong. She must look like such a fool.

'Someone's coming out of the house.' Todd twisted his huge shoulders around and consequently winded Juno. 'You should ask them for directions, Odette.'

She ignored his hand creeping on to her knee as she looked at the magical advent calendar house. It wasn't Cyd's farm, but she was certain some of Cyd's wacky old karma had brought her here tonight. The old bird had been right after all: Odette's feet of fire had delivered her to fate's doorstep. For walking out of the house, dragging a hand through his thick tawny hair and creasing his eyes against six sets of headlights, was Jimmy Sylvian.

31

Odette crouched down as low as she could in the back of the taxi, finding that her nose was almost inside Todd's shirt. 'Turn around!'

'We must at least apologise for driving on to his land.' Duncan wound down his window.

'Ask him for directions to Smock Mill Farm while you're at it.' Juno peered out of the windscreen as Jimmy approached, shading his eyes against the headlights. 'He looks a bit familiar.'

Odette crouched even closer against Todd's shaven chest as Duncan called out, 'Hi there! Sorry about this. We're a bit lost.'

She could hear the crunch of feet on gravel, and Jimmy's booming voice asking Duncan where he was trying to reach.

Assuming they had arrived at their destination, the stags and the Stage Stags were still spilling out of cabs, lighting cigarettes and complaining they needed a drink. Soon Jimmy was surrounded by huge, beefy men. 'Where's the hen party, mate?' one of them asked him.

'Hen party?' he laughed as he counted at least ten men. 'Well, I've got a couple of chickens and three ducks here.'

'We're trying to get to Smock Mill Farm,' Duncan explained.

'I'm not that familiar with the area,' he apologised. 'I just moved in myself last week – hang on, I've got a map in the house.'

Odette could hear more crunching of gravel, and someone asking Jimmy whether they could use his lavatory. Whether it was a stag or a Stag, she had no idea.

Todd was taking advantage of her skulking pose to fondle

her hair. She straightened up for a moment, almost head-butting him on the chin.

'Are you okay, Odie?' Juno was looking at her warily. 'You seemed to be hiding just then.'

Odette stared at the house, the front door of which was partly open, revealing a warm orange glow.

'Just had a bit of grit in my lens, that's all,' she muttered, looking out at all the men milling around Jimmy's gravel drive. She ducked down as he came back out of the house clutching a Landranger map.

'It's just on the other side of that wood there.' He stooped down to show Duncan the map. 'You'll have to drive back down to the road, hook a left and then take the next turning left – here, see.'

'Thanks, that's terribly kind.' Duncan shook his hand through the window. 'Sorry to have disturbed you. Good job you were still up.'

'I don't sleep much,' Jimmy told him, glancing curiously into the back of the cab.

Todd was stroking Odette's hair again, his broad arm resting heavily on her back and making her flesh crawl. She wanted to shrug it away, but that would attract attention.

She tried to reason with herself. Really, hiding like this was ridiculous. But being discovered amid a bunch of strippers and pissed men singing Womble songs was hardly how she'd imagined meeting Jimmy Sylvian again. True, it dispelled the sad no-friends, stay-at-home image he must have gathered from previous encounters, but it was still too much for Odette's pride to take. She could just imagine Jimmy telling Calum all about it and both of them laughing heartily about her decline into debauchery since becoming a bankrupt.

'We'd better be on our way,' Duncan said cheerfully. 'Now someone had better round this lot up and explain we have to drive back along that bloody track again. I dread to think what the fares are going to cost.'

But Juno had spotted a problem. 'Those idiots have already paid off their cabs!' She peered out of the rear window and noticed that the other taxis had all turned around and disappeared. 'They'll have to walk.'

'It's a couple of miles just to get back to the road, and there's no moon tonight,' Jimmy told her. 'I assume you haven't got any torches?'

Odette's head was so low that her nose was almost pressed into Todd's groin. He stroked the back of her neck excitedly.

'They'll manage.' Jay was desperate to get out of the cramped taxi. 'Shall we shoot?'

Jimmy scratched his head thoughtfully. 'Listen, I've got a big backie – why don't we use that?'

'Hey, now you're talking!' Todd sat up enthusiastically, propelling Odette's head into the back of Duncan's seat. 'I could just use a quick spliff right now. Let's all skin up and then walk to the farm through the fields.' He pulled Odette back into his crotch. 'Some of us might get lost along the way.'

Jimmy's booming laugh almost rocked the car. 'You misunderstand me – a backie is a pick-up truck, not wackie baccy. Why don't I round your friends up into it and show you the way?'

Odette bit her lip worriedly, accidentally biting off Todd's fly button. She spat it out hurriedly as he whispered in her ear, 'Steady, hotstuff, wait till later.'

'That's incredibly kind,' Duncan was saying to Jimmy.

'Don't mention it,' he laughed. 'I guess it's about time I introduced myself to the neighbours. I just wasn't expecting to do it at two in the morning.'

With the assorted Stage Stags and stags packed into the back of a huge crew-cab pick-up which was both very new and very dirty, Jimmy drove ahead to the farm. Following behind, their driver cursed the potholes and the mud, telling them that he'd have to charge extra to cover valeting costs.

'Christ, I'm glad that guy's got a map,' Duncan whistled as they threaded their way through the hilly lanes. 'It's in the middle of nowhere.'

When they reached Smock Mill Farm, Odette lurked in the cab long after the others had spilled out of the back, grateful to be able to breathe again. She could see Cyd rushing out of the front door with her Afghan, Bazouki, to welcome them all. Music was booming from the house, indicating the party was still in full swing.

'I had no idea there were so many of you!' She stood beside the truck from which men were jumping like an army squadron arriving at base camp.

'Euan's a popular bloke,' one of them laughed, suddenly launching into song '"Remember you're a Womble!"' Cyd's Afghan hound chased after him, barking excitedly.

Juno trotted up to Cyd and giggled, 'She thinks she's a stag hound.'

Jimmy Sylvian was hitching up the tailgate of his pick-up, gazing around in total bewilderment. 'I thought this was a hen night?'

'It is, it is!' Cyd clapped her hands together delightedly. 'And it'll be the first one where the strippers have outnumbered the hens two to one.' She took in his huge, rangy body with rapturous delight. 'Are you in charge?'

He looked dumbfounded, but before he could respond Cyd spotted a policewoman in a very tight skirt shivering beside the pick-up. 'Don't tell me the neighbours have complained?'

'Actually, I am the neighbour,' Jimmy pointed out, eager to introduce himself and then scarper. 'I've just moved into Siddals Farm – I'm Jimmy.' He held out his hand to shake, but at that moment Bazouki almost flattened him, all flying blonde hair and wriggling enthusiasm as she smelled his dogs and used her nose like a customs official's radar gun to find out more. 'Well, hello there, beautiful.'

'Oh, you're a dog person – how delicious. I'm Cyd,' she gurgled happily. Admiring his bottom as he stooped to pat Bazouki, she added, 'Do you want to buy an Afghan puppy?'

'This man kindly offered the boys a lift when their taxis dropped them off at the wrong farm,' Juno told her.

'So *that's* why they're so late,' Cyd whispered. 'I was beginning to think they'd forgotten.'

'I think maybe they had.' Juno glanced at Todd who was swaggering up with an oily smile. He deliberately placed himself between Jimmy and Cyd.

'Mrs Francis, Todd Austin. Fantastic house. Bryan asked me to pass on his apologies – Darcus Hunt has decided to go solo and he's been in a crisis meeting with the record company all weekend. Now, where can my boys get changed?'

Slipping from the back of the cab at last, Odette started to creep towards the side of the house. She could see Jimmy heading back to his truck. Thank God he hadn't spotted her! He would never know she had anything to do with this.

'There are so many of you!' Cyd was giggling delightedly as she took in all the muscles, although she did notice now she looked closer that a few of them were a little on the weedy side, and one shaven-haired one appeared to have drunk far more six packs than he'd developed.

'We seem to have a few new members.' Todd cleared his throat, looking around for Odette. 'That feisty little East End sheila brought practically every man from the hotel, plus a girl dressed as a copper to appeal to alternative tastes. What an operator! She should run a troupe.'

Odette ducked hastily under a bush as she realised she was about to get a name-check. She was just a few yards from the safety of the far wall of the farm. Jimmy was throwing his Puffa jacket into the rear of the pick-up's cab. Hurry up, she willed. Start the engine. Go.

'I knew it! Those feet of fire!' Cyd looked around for her too, and suddenly noticed that Jimmy was climbing back into his truck. 'You can't be leaving so soon! Do come in for a drink.'

Crouching in the shadows, Odette groaned. She couldn't possibly avoid being recognised now.

But Jimmy was shaking his head, clearly eager to escape this mad house. 'I can see you're busy. Another time. Great to meet you.'

Yes! Odette wanted to do a high five under the bush. As he started his engine once more with a load roar, she knew she was safe.

When Jimmy swung his truck around, the full-beam head-lights caught a movement in the undergrowth. Accustomed to night-drives in Africa, Jimmy immediately recognised the two bright red points of reflection as an animal's eyes staring at the car in total fear. For just a moment, he was almost certain it was a human being. But the figure darted out of the pool of light faster than a leopard.

Slotting a Meatloaf cassette into the stereo, Jimmy drove away yodelling along to 'Dead Ringer For Love'.

It was a raucous party. The hens had found their second wind and, buoyed up by champagne and second helpings of dinner, were lounging around on the six sofas in the farm's central room, which was essentially three rooms knocked into one, with whole tree trunks acting as joists to hold up the ceilings where the original walls had been. Fires were blazing in the inglenooks at either end, and Bazouki's puppies were piled up in front of one like furry pebbles on a beach. Candles flickered on every surface.

Sharing a stool, Elsa and Euan were hammering out 'Chopsticks' together at the grand piano, which was thankfully being drowned out by Mansun, cranked up to maximum volume on the stereo. Euan had changed out of his Womble outfit and was wearing one of Cyd's sarongs and a t-shirt.

'It's Posh and Becks,' the fat skinhead cackled on seeing his friend in a skirt.

'Jesus, who invited yous here?' Euan groaned. He immediately abandoned Elsa to the piano stool and grabbed his beer, hoping most of his mates hadn't spotted him being a total girl's blouse.

As soon as the combined stags swaggered into the room, the atmosphere changed from one of relaxed bonhomie to highly charged hell-raising and almost childish male-female competitiveness.

Elsa couldn't stop laughing as she spotted the familiar faces – Duncan, Spike, Jay, and the rest of Euan's daft friends and colleagues. What made the situation even funnier was that Cyd seemed to think they were all strippers.

'I've hired the Stage Stags for you, dearheart!' she announced proudly.

Admittedly there were a lot of muscle men hanging around

holding suit-carriers, but Elsa thought they were from Euan's gym. Juno quickly disillusioned her.

'That stripping troupe are going to perform here? In Mum's house?' Elsa shrieked with delight. 'We'll have to blindfold the bump. Some of them are gorgeous, aren't they?'

Euan couldn't decide whether to be furious with his friends for inviting themselves along to his future mother-in-law's house or admire their gall, especially as they'd brought their own stripper with them which he thought only fair considering Odette appeared to have returned with half a dozen for Elsa.

'You've still got that wheeler-dealer instinct, hen.' He gave her a kiss, temporarily crossing the male-female divide that had established itself in the room.

'Times like this you need to call the professionals in.' She winked.

'Yous saying we couldnae strip as well as these guys?' Euan feigned hurt pride as his mates started catcalling about his skirt again. 'Euan thinks he's a girl! Euan thinks he's a girl!'

Odette watched as he minced back to his mates, pretending to be on a catwalk. The atmosphere in the room reminded her of a school playground.

She wondered where the naughtiest girl in the school was. Lydia could be counted on to start a game of kiss chase dare. Glancing around, Odette realised she wasn't in the room.

'Gone to bed,' Ally explained when she asked. 'I think she was in a bit of a state.'

Odette crept upstairs to check on her, tracking her down to a dusty bedroom. She'd fallen asleep on top of the old horse rug which was acting as bedspread, still wearing the red dress she'd gone clubbing in, although she'd kicked off her shoes. Someone had thoughtfully placed a bucket by her pillow. Odette stole a blanket from another bed and draped it over her, stroking the flawless pale forehead.

She guessed that Calum would give anything to be sitting where she was now. Gazing at her innocent sleeping face, so utterly beautiful it almost belied belief, Odette could understand why. It hurt like hell, but she didn't blame Lydia. She had loved

Calum too, after all. She only wished she had it in her power to hate him.

She looked up as a shadow moved along the corridor outside. Poking her head out of the door, she saw Cyd carrying a large cardboard box. Bazouki was standing at her knee looking up in concern. In the box five puppies were fast asleep in a warm huddle.

'I thought I should get them out of the way,' Cyd explained, buckling under the weight.

Taking one end, Odette helped her carry them through to her bedroom.

Then Cyd danced back towards the stairs, leaving Odette open-mouthed as she realised Elsa's mother slept in a waterbed made out of an old Rolls-Royce chassis.

A moment later she heard feet thundering on the stairs. Coming out of Cyd's room, she walked straight into Todd Austin.

'There you are.' He slung his super-smooth, shaven arm around her shoulders, breathing in her ear, 'Why don't I give you a private show up here? Fantastic house – can't believe Mask actually used to rehearse here. It gives me a hard on just thinking about it.'

Odette was too shocked to speak.

Footsteps thundered to her rescue as the Stage Stags filled up even more of the corridor, their suit-carriers hooked over their shoulders.

'Cyd said we should change up here,' said a huge West Indian with corkscrew ringlets falling to his waist. 'Any room except the one with the puppies in it, she said.' He reached for the door handle to Lydia's room.

'There's someone asleep in there.' Odette pointed them in the direction of a free room, trying to disentangle herself from Todd.

'You ever see the film Mask? That's how that band got its name. Seriously raunchy stuff.' He nibbled her earlobe. He had such big gaps between his teeth Odette suspected he was flossing them while he was at it. 'You're coming back to the Royal with me later and we'll re-enact my favourite scene.'

'I don't think so.' She tried to wriggle free. 'I'm here for my friend's hen weekend, remember?'

'Sure — Cyd Francis's daughter. Hasn't got her mother's looks, has she?' Todd winked. 'Still, who cares with all that money she's set to inherit? Bet her fiancé's a happy man.'

Odette was livid. She was fed up with having her ear vacuumed every time he directed a comment at her. She had sussed very early on that he was led by the groin, but now saw that he had another master which was an even stronger aphrodisiac. Todd Austin couldn't have been more transparent if he was peeling long bandages from his body in a seventies television series. She tried out her theory with miraculous results.

'I forgot to mention I'm a bankrupt,' she told him. 'I lost everything in a bad business venture.'

The arm was whipped from her shoulders like a feather boa caught in a passing air-vent.

Downstairs, the hens were all still lounging in the huge flame-lit room listening to Cyd playing the piano. The stags had moved to the games room and were indulging in table football, darts, snooker and rumbustious attempts to hit the punch-bag without wincing as their knuckles sank into the leather and made contact with compacted sawdust. The Prodigy was blaring out from the loudspeakers.

When Odette walked into the hen coop, she detected a hush and knew for certain that she had been the topic of conversation. Cyd didn't hit a bum note as she carried on playing 'Sonic Jet to Heaven' on the piano, but she exchanged an 'ooo-eer' look with her daughter's friends.

'Been entertaining the troops, Odie?' Juno looked up from a super-deep leather sofa where she was drinking champagne straight from the bottle with a long straw and munching on a tube of Smarties between sucks.

Odette rolled her eyes. She wished her friends didn't derive so much pleasure from propagating the myth that she was a man-eater.

Beneath her curls, Elsa was raising her eyebrows at Juno, whose own narrow ones were flipping up and down like shunt levers on a pinball machine.

Odette ignored them and headed for a champagne bottle.

'That stripper – the one dressed as a police woman – is in with the stags,' Juno told her jealously. 'I bet she's down to a g-string by now.' The fact that she was about to witness half a dozen muscle-men stripping down to their altogether seemed to be lost on her.

'Actually she's undercover in the kitchen,' Ally said, returning with a half-full casserole of lasagne and a spoon. 'Radioing back to base. I heard her saying that none of the men wanted her to strip because they were all too embarrassed to watch with their wives and girlfriends in the same house.'

There was a round of 'Ah's as the hens realised what reconstructed, liberal men they were married to.

'Where are these bloody Stage Stags then?' Juno helped herself to some of Ally's lasagne.

'Yes, it's about time they showed us what they're made of,' Elsa agreed.

'Roll on the willies!' Juno waggled her spoon.

Loud, rowdy gusts of laughter blasted through from the games room. One of the loudest of all was recognisably Euan's. A loud jungle cry of 'I've got an idea!' was followed by a flurry of conversation, every word of which was drowned by 'Smack My Bitch Up'. A moment later there was another blast of male laughter, followed by an eerie silence.

The hens had all fallen quiet too as they listened in.

'What d'you suppose they're up to?' Bee asked.

'I think Euan's mob are planning to create a diversion during the Stage Stags' performance,' Juno gasped, her eyes suspicious.

'They *wouldn't* try and ruin the show, would they?' Cyd's rendition of 'Can't Always Get What You Want' suddenly developed a few gothic minor chords. 'How unsporting.' She cocked her head towards the games room, which was ominously devoid of male voices although the Prodigy had, unexpectedly, been replaced by Tom Jones.

There was a tap on the door and Todd's tanned face leered around it. 'Ready, girls?' he smouldered straight at Cyd.

'God – no!' She banged the piano lid shut and looked around. 'Where did I put that cassette you gave me?'

'As I recall,' Todd was still leaning through the door, teeth flashing irresistibly, 'you popped it in your cleavage.'

'Oh, yes!' Cyd beamed at him gratefully as she fished it out. 'Give us two minutes. Oh, dear, where can they perform?'

Odette's super-efficient organisational skills were once again called into operation as she orchestrated the repositioning of furniture, sliding every sofa along one long wall to leave the opposite one free as a stage. Poor Elsa's chaise-longue was pushed into a front row of its own at her mother's insistence. 'I hope I can last this out,' she warned cheerfully. 'Only I need the loo every two minutes these days.' She covered her bump with a cushion in case it saw something it shouldn't.

Cyd slotted the tape into the huge stereo system and blew out the candles closest to her before calling out, 'Ready, boys!'

They were undoubtedly gorgeous specimens of male flesh, if a little too greased with baby oil, too thick-necked and too self-satisfied. Of them all, Todd Austin was the most oiled and the most smug. As they paraded in a long line dressed as firemen, Todd's eyes burned into Cyd's with a theatrical display of unadulterated longing. So did the blond West Coast surfer's, but his helmet slipped over his nose after a few choreographed paces and he could see nothing at all.

As the uniforms came off with very professional swishes of well-worn Velcro, Odette screamed and cheered with the rest of the hens, but she was acutely aware that she was just going through the motions.

She didn't find any of them remotely sexy with their gym-pumped muscles and shaven, oiled skin. If anything, they were slightly revolting. As the salopettes flew off to reveal shiny bulging thighs and shiny bulging jockey shorts, she and Ally both looked away at the same moment and caught one another's eye. A look of 'Isn't this embarrassingly awful?' was exchanged before they both concentrated on the action again.

They might both think the situation beneath them intellectually, but they were still fascinated to see just how far the Stage Stags would go and hoped to get a peek at that oh-so-sacred secret hidden from most women, the male genitalia. Most women only got a chance to see five or six close up in their lifetimes, after all. An opportunity to see eight grouped together for comparison was irresistible. Several cameras were being checked for film, flashes winking at the ready.

When the Stage Stags and the cameras flashed at each other, Odette noticed two things. Their penises looked astonishingly small in proportion to their over-muscled bodies, and the owner of the smallest – Todd – had not taken his eyes from Cyd throughout his hip-jabbing, groin-grinding, hose-poking strip. What's more he and the rest of his troupe had erections.

'Ohmygod!' Juno waved her hands around like Kermit the Frog on a bender 'Will you look at those? It's like a giant toad in the hole. Are those whatjamiflips around their whassitsnames whassitcalled rings?' Something about the nude male body could turn even the most straight-talking of modern women into a nonsensical prude.

'Wedding rings?' Elsa suggested with a snort of laughter.

'No – Arab rings,' Bee said sardonically. 'Helps the poor dears maintain a hard-on. Quite the opposite of a wedding ring some might say.'

Odette almost snorted champagne out of her nose as she finally realised what the elastic bands the men had been referring to earlier were for. Each Stag had one wrapped around his manhood to make it stand semi-erect.

'Oh, Christ,' Ally shrieked as a particularly greasy hose-pipe was waggled towards her, splattering her with baby-oil. 'Here comes the audience participation.'

Odette had expected the men to grab their costumes and swagger from the stage the moment all was revealed, but it seemed the fun had only just begun. Now it was time for them to get their own back.

As soon as they were all in the buff, the Stage Stags bounded over to their embarrassed audience to get them involved in the action. Elsa, as chief hen, was dragged to the fore first although her pregnant state – and her desperate need for the loo – saved her from too much oily horseplay. They simply lifted her up between them so that her friends could take photographs.

Letting Elsa escape to the loo to hide her blushes and apologise to Buster Bump, they picked instead on her old school friend, Liz. Her blushes were most definitely not spared and nor was her white chiffon top which greased up to resemble tracing paper as she was forced to her knees and fondled between huge, genetically modified thighs.

Juno was the next victim as the Stage Stags danced her into a club sandwich and then forced her to pluck a rose from between their thighs with a partially erect dick ticking her chin. She co-operated gamely, posing for photographs with her head peeking out, a rose in her mouth like Carmen.

'That's one Jay won't want to put in the album,' Ally giggled to Odette.

Watching in horror, Odette realised that, for all the role reversal, all their pandering to the girl's titillation, she was witnessing a deeply sexist form of entertainment. These men had no respect at all for Elsa and her hens. They wanted to make them look like fools, and they were getting away with it.

Then she cowered back into her sofa as, hands on hips, walnuts and chipolata to the fore, Todd started to grind his way straight towards her.

'Your turn!' Ally clapped her hands, sympathy eclipsed by relief as she realised he wasn't looking at her.

Odette chewed her lip in consternation as he strutted across the greasy floor, eyes boring into hers, the threat implicit – you lead me on, this is what happens. Revenge time, little pauper. This baby-oil bottle has your name on it. Odette's heart thudded with dread, bile rose in her throat, her knuckles went white as she hung on to her seat, willing him to go away.

She wasn't ready for the strength of his grip, and almost fell over as she was propelled in front of her friends as roughly as a small child being hauled up in front of assembly. A moment later a greasy erection was splatted against her thigh.

'Bend over and I'll show you what you're missing out on,'

Todd hissed in her ear. When she didn't comply, he tried to force her downwards.

Furious and terrified, she kicked him very hard on the shins with her stiletto heel.

'Spoilsport!' howled Juno, delighted that her stint was over with and eager for someone else to share in the shame.

The Stage Stags were clearly thrown, their act suddenly out of synch. As his boys lurched about improvising a few moves like bad dancers at a naturists' disco, Todd's mouldy green eyes bored into Odette's and his grip tightened on her arm. This was war.

Elsa was just returning from the loo when she saw Odette being manhandled towards a table. The difference between the way she had been gently coaxed into posing for pictures and this was terrifying. Elsa caught her breath and looked around for help, but the rest of the hens were still cheering and clapping, desperately grateful that it wasn't them.

Ashamed of her own fear, Odette tried to play along, but the experience was horrific as six foot of rock-solid muscle spun her around and bent her over a side table. There Todd pretended to take her from behind with exaggerated hip thrusts, his arm flying around overhead as though riding a bucking bronco.

It'll soon be over, she told herself. Don't make a scene. Put up with it.

Her skirt was soon sticky with baby oil and her eyes screwed tightly shut as she tried not to think of Florian Etoile and that night in the OD kitchen. Hearing a couple of cameras snapping from the sofas, Odette gripped the sides of the table in white-knuckled panic as she envisaged Calum watching his revolting monitor, saving it all on file to blackmail her with like a greasy, bent little private detective investigating an adultery case.

'That's it, hotstuff,' whooped a voice from behind as the thrusts increased. 'Get into the spirit. I want you to lie down on the floor next, okay? And if you kick me this time, I'll stand on your neck, understand?'

Odette lay like a corpse, tears sliding into her hair, listening to the thud, thud, thud of the bass, the squeak, squeak, squeak of Todd's knees sliding on the oil-slick wooden floor, the shriek,

shriek, shriek of her friends, the whurr, whurr, whurr of the camera winders. Twenty-first century sex, she thought bleakly. Fake or real, it feels just the same.

At last it was over and the Stage Stags were gathering up their costumes from the greasy floor. Just before he left, Todd handed Cyd a piece of paper with his number written on it. 'Call me any time you feel lonely. I give a great back-rub.' He flashed his gap-toothed smile

'Thank you.' Cyd cocked her head and smiled. 'That's very sweet but you're not really in my age group, are you?'

'I prefer older women.' He dropped his voice to a sexy purr.

'And I prefer younger men,' she said sweetly. 'You're getting a bit past it now, aren't you?'

Todd consoled himself by chatting up the female stripper in the taxi, more as an ego-exercise than with any serious intent. She simply wasn't in his wage-bracket.

'Ladies, I present to you ... for one night only ... the Stooge Stags!'

As soon as the Tom Jones track started playing, Elsa and her hens guessed that they were about to witness a once-in-a-lifetime show. Howls of laughter greeted the first few bars of 'You Can Leave Your Hat On'.

Euan and his stags made the cast of *The Full Monty* seem highly desirable as they shambled into the room, wearing the clothes they had arrived in plus a bizarre collection of hats they had raided from Cyd's hall. Sporting deerstalkers, flat caps, straw sun hats, riding helmets and a tinted tennis visor between them, they made a vague attempt at keeping time. Chunky little Spike Jeffries started peeling off The Jacket to great whoops of encouragement; Jay tipped his fleece off one shoulder and smouldered at Juno; Duncan began undoing his tie, eyebrows furled in what he clearly took to be a sexy way but which in fact made him look like Norman Lamont.

Elsa and her hens loved every second of it. This was so much more fun than watching the sleek, oiled and frankly revolting Stage Stags. These were their friends, their lovers and their husbands, making delightful, happy fools of themselves in order to get attention. They cheered enthusiastically as shirts came off and were lobbed towards the sofas.

Odette got a sweaty t-shirt full in the face. When she peeled it off, she noticed the fat skinhead grinning at her. Bloody pervert, she thought darkly. This is sick.

But even she found herself hiding a smile as trousers were lowered to reveal an astonishing range of underwear from designer jockeys to M&S Y-fronts. Spike was wearing boxer shorts with Christmas puddings on them; Euan had a tight lime green thong; Duncan had long-johns which made Ally cover her face in shame.

There was a momentary hiatus as the men realised too late that they had forgotten something. Only Euan continued writhing to the music, swinging his sarong around his head. His fellow dancers were all struggling to pull their trousers the last few inches over their feet.

'Shoes!' he wailed, stopping to put his hands on his hips. 'I said shoes first, you great jessies.'

Shoes were clumsily dragged from heels with toes and at least two of the Stooge Stags fell over as they tried to get their trouser legs over their feet before the track ran out. They were still wearing their ridiculous hats.

'Now can you see why I wear a skirt, lads?' Euan laughed, then raised his flowered sun-hat to his future wife before dashing over to the stereo to rewind the tape.

Elsa was positively weeping with laughter now, as was Juno at the sight of Jay dancing in his pants, his long-eyed face concentrating hard as he tried to remember the moves. Seeing as he was the only one to do so, he might as well have started break-dancing for all the difference it made. Odette couldn't fail to notice that he had a fantastically good body, and by far the whitest underwear. Euan, by contrast, who always appeared so sexily narrow-hipped and broad-shouldered in his huge shaggy astrakhan jackets and flat-front trousers, turned out to have a pigeon chest with pierced nipples and a paunch with a belly piercing at its centre. Duncan had incredibly thin, hairy legs; Spike Jeffries had a tattoo of Tweety Pie on his hip.

The cameras were back out and snapping away like mad, accompanied by wails of frustration as hens ran out of film.

Despite herself, Odette was fascinated by the chest-hair issue. Unlike the Stage Stags who'd had all theirs waxed off, this lot had as broad and varied a range as their assorted taste in pants. But unlike their underwear, which had mostly been bought by wives and girlfriends, they were sporting what nature had handed out; some had a general scattering, some had a cross that went from nipple to nipple and collar bone to groin, others had none at all. The fat skinhead, amazingly, had a rug both back and front as thick and bushy as a chimp's.

Odette realised she was humming along to the song and hastily stopped herself. She knew the track off by heart, but not because she – along with half the thirty-something population – had rushed out to buy *The Full Monty* soundtrack. The song was on another sound-track too, a tape Odette had owned for years and still retained in one of her few remaining boxes of possessions in Elsa and Euan's basement. For this was the song playing when Kim Basinger performed a strip for Mickey Rourke in *9½ Weeks*. Odette had danced alone to it many times in her flat, imagining that Calum was watching. She shuddered at the thought.

The stags were turning around and mooning now, revealing several more tattoos and more than a few hairs and pimples. Jay had far and away the best bottom, Odette noted purely as a scientific observation.

As a final coup de disgrace, the shambling but likeable stripping troupe tried smoothly to drop their pants and cover their manhoods with their hats, just as they'd seen in the film. This didn't quite go to plan, however, as the miscellaneous underwear wasn't the sort you could whip off with the aid of a handy hidden velcro fastening, nor were the hats entirely suited for their task. The guy who had the tinted tennis peak soon discovered it covered nothing at all.

There was no audience participation or seedy simulated sex.

As soon as the stags were down to their essentials, they took a bow and shuffled towards the games room as fast as they could manage with hats held to their crotches. A furious round of applause followed them out. A moment later, Duncan popped his head around the door.

'Er – I don't suppose you could gather up some of our clothes and chuck them in here, could you?'

'What lovely, lovely boys,' Cyd sighed as they waved the stags away in yet more cabs.

'Aren't they?' Juno was standing at her side, blowing Jay kisses. There was a hard frost and her breath plumed in front of her face. 'God, call them back. I feel randy.'

'Your Jay has a wonderful body,' Cyd told her. 'Doesn't he, Odette?'

Odette hugged her arms to her torso. 'Does he?' She turned to go back in the house and help the others clear up. 'I didn't notice.'

Cyd looked at Juno and smiled sadly. 'Poor Odette has had a very, very hard time, hasn't she?'

'Terrible,' Juno agreed. 'Losing her business like that.'

'No, no – I mean with men.' Cyd linked arms with her. 'She's terribly damaged. It's awful to watch – like a frightened animal that's been brutalised at the hands of humans. She's simply terrified of them, isn't she?'

'Well, I wouldn't say that . . .' Juno personally thought Odette was one of the best flirts she knew, just very, very choosy. Admittedly she'd made a bit of an error with Calum, but she seemed to have got over that.

'Oh, I'm sure of it,' Cyd insisted. 'And I have a little idea which might just help her . . . tell me what you think.'

32

The following day, the hens staggered up very late, clutching their heads and their bellies. Only Elsa had already been up for hours, giving up on an uncomfortable night's sleep which had been constantly broken by the baby kicking, backache and the urge to go to the loo. Not having drunk anything the night before, she was far brighter and breezier than her friends, doling out tea, toast, glasses of hangover remedy and Nurofen as each appeared.

'I thought we could hang around here,' she suggested, 'have a swim – I'll show you the smock mill afterwards. We could even record a track using Jobe's mixing equipment. I need something sensational for my bride's speech. There's a steam room in there as well, and a gym.'

There was a round of 'whatever's.' Right now, getting through a cup of tea without throwing up was more of a priority for the hens.

'Aren't you going for a run?' Juno asked Odette, accustomed to her blasting off every morning when she was staying with her and Jay.

'I've given up,' she muttered.

Juno grinned, clearly thinking the exercise veto a good development, a sign that Odette was becoming less obsessive, less fucked up about her body, a neurosis which had plagued her since they had first known one another.

But Odette knew that she ran to stop her mind running away with itself, her memory jogging and her head working out what was really going on. Exercise was her therapy, her Prozac and her chick-flick all rolled into one, and she needed to keep it up to keep sane. Lately she'd swapped tying up her Reebok laces for tired lassitude.

By midday, all but Cyd had gathered around the table. Scrabbling in her bag. Odette handed Lydia her little silver mobile phone. 'We took it with us last night when we came to look for you.'

'Yes, thanks for checking I was with you when you left the club.' Lydia stared around at her friends accusingly. 'If I hadn't bumped into Euan I could still be wandering around Brighton now.'

'Sorry.' Elsa went pink. 'It was my fault.'

Lydia was trying to make her phone work. 'The charge has run out. Drat!' She threw it down on the table, not caring that it landed in the butter dish. 'I was expecting a call.'

Odette narrowed her eyes, but said nothing.

Juno wasn't so discreet. 'You had a message. We listened to it, actually – we thought it might be from you, but it was from Calum,' she announced devilishly.

'Was it?' Lydia looked absolutely thrilled. 'What did he say?'

'He said that Finlay is bound to find out,' Odette said with barely concealed venom, wondering whether Lydia had no shame. 'He said that it wasn't safe to use his place any more.'

Lydia's eyebrows shot up in genuine surprise. 'That's odd. Are you sure he said that?'

'Well, I think he actually said he wasn't sure about using his place,' Juno corrected Odette. 'Something about a secret? Are you having a surprise party?'

'No, no!' Lydia suddenly burst out laughing. 'Darling Calum's just getting cold feet about something. He wants to talk about the wedding.'

Odette could guess why. She was staggered by this bare-faced gall. But then Lydia made an announcement which utterly floored her.

'Calum's agreed that Fin and I can use Fermoncieaux to get married in,' she beamed.

'Fermoncieaux Hall?' Elsa gagged. 'Here?'

Lydia nodded. 'So generous. I'm really excited. Don't tell

Fin, though. He doesn't know yet. It's all a surprise – at least it's supposed to be. I'm not going to let Calum change his mind about this.'

Odette was staring fixedly at the window, blinking hard to stop tears of relief spilling from her eyes. So Lydia and Calum weren't having an affair after all.

'But I thought you were getting married in the William and Mary Museum?' Ally was laughing.

'Oh, I didn't fancy getting hitched in front of all those mouldy old relics.' Lydia wrinkled her nose. 'And London's so out of date. Fermoncieaux's destined to be *the* place.'

'Will it be open in time for the wedding?' Juno asked, still suspicious about the call. She'd been secretly hoping it was something far more scandalous. 'I thought the hall was almost derelict?'

'I've never seen it.' Lydia shrugged. 'It's supposed to be magnificent.'

Odette suddenly wanted to see Fermoncieaux too. For the first time since hearing about Calum's new project, she found that she was burning with curiosity. She wanted to see the setting for his next big soap-opera stunt. She wanted to dress in a black cat-suit and creep there under cover of darkness, like Jennifer Hart casing the joint of an evil billionaire she suspected of murder. So what if Jonathan wasn't around? He always left Jennifer to it to begin with and then came in to save the day towards the end when his macho babe-rescuing skills were required. She had her friends to help her instead.

'Why don't we go there this afternoon?' she suggested, looking excitedly at Elsa. 'You said it was just a short walk away.'

'I don't think that's such a good idea . . .' She glanced at Juno for support. 'They don't like people on their land.'

'Oh, do let's!' Lydia looked thrilled. 'It's Calum's land now,' she pointed out. 'And he's practically my brother-in-law.'

And practically your lover, Odette wanted to add. I'm enjoying this, she realised. In a sick, self-punishing way she was actually deriving pleasure from torturing herself. It was the first time she'd felt driven in weeks.

★ ★ ★

Odette missed out on the swimming. She was wearing yesterday's daily disposable contact lenses and didn't want to risk them dissolving in the chlorine. The indoor pool smelled like a steamy laboratory. She was also acutely aware that she hadn't worked out in weeks and that cellulite was spreading across her thighs like dimples in a dinner gong, and her belly was starting to compete with her breasts to enter a room first. She was vain and competitive, and ashamed that she'd let herself go. Leaving them to splash away their hangovers in the deep end, she agreed to investigate the smock mill with Bee who couldn't swim.

The octagonal wooden windmill was clearly rotting away and reeked of damp.

'Man, I'd die for some of this kit!' Bee wandered around the recording studio on the ground floor, most of which was covered with a thick layer of dirt and mould. 'I mean, it's pretty dated, but it was the best in its time. They don't make mixing decks like this any more. Some of these bits are really cult stuff. They're collectors' pieces.'

'They're collecting cultures all right, babes.' Odette brushed her hand along a row of buttons, collecting a glove of dirt. It looked like a lot of grubby old electrical equipment to her.

The place was filthy and creeping with condensation. Every one of the narrow windows was frosted hard with glaciers of ice. The old mill had been gutted in the late eighties, and filled with state-of-the-art recording equipment along with three huge drum kits, a vast range of amplifiers, a high-rise electronic keyboard and enough leather sofas to seat a football team.

In the centre of the huge, circular room the old mill-stone, pierced by a fat mill-pole, had clearly been used as nothing more than a coffee table, and still played host to several dust-encrusted glasses and mugs, ashtrays brimming with cigarette butts and empty bottles of champagne. Jobe could have been chatting to his fellow musicians just a few minutes earlier were it not for the give-away grime of time.

Odette wondered why she didn't find it creepy. It should feel like a mausoleum but instead it felt curiously friendly and companionable beneath its dirt and clutter, perhaps a little like Jobe himself was before the drink turned him into an anti-social hermit.

'Will you look at this!' Bee called up from a purpose-built cellar.

Odette peered down from the top of the spiral stairs, breathing in so much mildew that her lungs felt like bags of compost. It was full of gym equipment. In its midst, like a huge automaton, was one of the first ever Stairmasters; Odette's feet itched longingly, her cellulite-mottled thighs clenched in anticipation and her breath quickened.

'There's a sauna and Jacuzzi down here!' Bee called from out of sight. 'I'm going to try them out. Come down and join me.'

Odette could hear a zip undoing. She'd met Bee many times and was pretty certain that she wasn't the energetic DJ's type, but suddenly felt very narrow-minded and shy. The prospect of sharing a hot tub with Elsa's lovely gay friend made her blush to her roots. She called down a feeble excuse about her contact lenses, and was grateful to hear a step behind her followed by a scrabble of paws.

'Odette, dearheart.' Cyd was standing there in an odd combination of silk pyjamas, welly boots and thick fleece, Bazouki panting at her heels, mane on end. 'Elsa told me you'd come here. I'm so glad. Isn't it gorgeous?' She looked around the dusty room. 'Jobe would never let me in here. It was his little retreat, far enough away from the house to feel I couldn't spy on him. I haven't been in here for months.'

'Too many memories?' Odette asked cautiously.

Cyd cocked her head as she heard the Jacuzzi spluttering into life below. 'Too few, my dearheart.' She smiled. 'Like I say, this was his terrain. I suppose I should get it cleaned up.' She picked up a bottle of champagne and hugged it to her chest, gazing up the spiral stairs.

'It's a shame to let it fall apart.' Odette looked around.

'Mmm.' Cyd smiled thoughtfully. 'It needs to be loved again. Jobe loved it in here. I used to joke that this place was like the inside of his head: messy, twisted and full of booze.'

Odette thought it a very odd thing to say, but Cyd was talking again as she climbed the narrow spiral stairs on the outer wall to the next level. 'He was here for weeks on end sometimes – I barely saw him although he'd pop into the house for food and a change of clothes sometimes, so drunk he didn't notice I was there. Come and see his den – we used to call it the Addendum, because it was a dumb addition to a huge house with more than enough space.'

On the first floor there was even more mess – old newspapers, magazines, open books, music scores, mugs, glasses, bottles, beer cans, plates, crisp packets and dust skirted the fat central pole which had several air-rifle targets pinned to it, most of them untouched by pellets. Glancing at the newspapers, Odette realised they were four years old. This place truly was trapped in time.

There was a huge television positively weighed down with satellite boxes, a vast stereo, a fridge and microwave. Big hatch windows looked out over the South Downs, a frosted landscape obscured by yet more frozen condensation and mould.

'The bathroom's through here,' Cyd said brightly, suddenly reminding Odette of the estate agents who had shown prospective buyers around her flat, eager to impress.

A curved wall of glass blocks concealed a lime-scaled shower and sink, and a loo positively exploding with mould. Cyd hastily flipped down the pan lid and turned back to Odette with a winning smile. 'Come and see the bedroom – you can climb up to the cap from there. That has a tiny window which looks out over Fermoncieaux.'

Up another flight of precariously narrow, wood-wormed stairs, Odette discovered a cramped space housing a vast unmade bed, its crumpled fake-fur spread still playing host to an ancient copy of *GQ*, a packet of king-size Rizlas, several beer cans and an empty vodka bottle. At the end of the bed a terrifying number of cog wheels were attached to the central mill-pole which disappeared through a hole in the ceiling.

Cyd tapped a tiny square window lovingly. 'Jobe used to piss out of this. He thought he was too far up for me to spot him, but I could see him at it if I was backstroking in the swimming pool – look.'

Odette craned around in the tiny, draughty casement and saw the steamy conservatory that housed the farm's pool, its misted glass ceiling reflecting the heavy yellow sky. If she peered very closely, she could just about make out several brightly coloured bathing suits and pale, fleshy limbs moving beneath.

When she turned back, Cyd was waiting at the bottom of a very decrepit-looking ladder. 'Only one more level. Watch out, it's a bit dangerous up here. You have to mind your footing and it can move around a bit if it's really windy. We should be okay. Sometimes it's like standing in a fairground Waltzer.'

Grabbing the uprights, Cyd placed her wellies on the first rung and scaled it in record time, calling down, 'Come and look at this, dearheart.'

Odette climbed the ladder cautiously, listening as Bazouki whined far below them, eager for her mistress to return but too cowardly to risk the stairs. Odette didn't blame her. She was starting to realise just how high up they were. The wind was positively howling through the windows at this level. The tiny chamber at the top of the windmill was rattling with draughts, dripping with damp, and almost entirely filled with the pole and its huge cogs and levers which had once allowed the cap to revolve so that the mill's sails could catch the wind.

'It's been stuck facing this direction for the best part of fifty years,' Cyd explained, edging around the wheels. 'That's why the sails blew off in the '87 hurricane – we couldn't turn them away from the wind.' She was peering out of a window the size of a sheet of A4, rubbing away the frost with her fleece sleeve. 'This looks over Fermoncieaux. On a clear day like today you can count the deer in the park.'

Odette edged around the wheel too and braced herself. Thankfully what she saw hardly took her breath away, although the wind rattling through the loose glass did. Through a very small, bleary window she could just about make out the shape of a house in the far, far distance. From this far away, it seemed minuscule and was surrounded by power pylons.

'Come and live here.' Cyd suddenly turned to her, eyes alight.

Odette felt her jaw drop so far she was surprised her

chin didn't disappear through the trapdoor and land on Jobe's bed.

'Live here?' she managed to splutter.

Cyd nodded and clasped Odette's hands in hers. 'I need a driver, dearheart, and you need a place to live. It's kismet, don't you see?'

Odette stared out at Fermoncieaux, at Calum's new baby. It might look tiny and insignificant from here but she knew it was going to grow and grow in importance as Food Hall took shape. How could she possibly move in next door? She'd feel like a stalker, a crank who couldn't let go. Yet today, for the first time in weeks, she had felt a buzz of excitement and it was the mention of Fermoncieaux that had sparked it. She wanted to stake the place out, find out what Calum was up to. Where better to keep an eye on him than from her very own watchtower?

33

It was a bitterly cold, sunny afternoon. Perfect walking weather. The ramble to Fermoncieaux was to go ahead. Against her better judgement, Elsa handed out hats and gloves and searched for shoes and wellies of the right sizes for her friends.

'How come your mother's got so many different styles and sizes of everything?' Juno took in the multitude of outdoor clothing in the rear lobby. 'It's like the shop that Mr Benn visited out here – you know, the one with the vanishing shopkeeper, where Mr Benn would walk out of the changing room and find he was in Ancient Egypt or whatever.'

'Mum and Jobe always had a house full of friends in the early days,' Elsa explained. 'I think these just got left behind over the years. Mum never throws anything away, as you might have noticed. Just think – you might be wearing Keith Richards' gloves.'

'Wow.' Juno looked at her hands doubtfully. She didn't think sexy Keith would suit pink fluffy knitted ones with bobbles at the wrist, but then again the sixties were a crazy time.

Elsa peered at a map as she trudged on ahead. 'There's a footpath that runs right beside the hall. Shouldn't take us more than three-quarters of an hour to get there.'

'Are you sure you're up to all this walking, Elsa my love?' Ally asked worriedly. 'I know when I was that far gone with China I couldn't manage to get round Sainsbury's without needing to sit down.'

Elsa laughed. 'As long as you lot don't mind me popping behind a bush every five minutes for a wee, I'll be fine.'

'I hope you've brought plenty of tissues,' said Lydia, who

was walking with a strange, long-legged lope because she had insisted on wearing the only fashionable pair of walking boots she'd been able to track down in the farm, which were two sizes too big for her. Despite two pairs of thick socks, she was still struggling to keep them on.

Juno, trudging along in a pair of bright yellow children's wellies because her feet were so small, fell into step with Odette. 'So.' She looked up at her, voice deliberately low. 'Has Cyd asked you yet?'

'Asked me what?' Odette hedged.

'To be her driver,' Juno whispered. 'She told me all about it last night. I think it's a fantastic idea.'

'I told her I'd think about it.' Odette pulled her borrowed woolly hat down over her ears as they crunched through frosted puddles on a track that ran alongside the National Trust wood, wind howling in from the left. She wondered why Juno was whispering like a librarian.

'What's there to think about?' Juno looked surprised. 'I'd jump at the offer to live here and drive all those fabulous classic cars.'

'It's more complicated than that, and you know it.' Odette checked that Elsa wasn't close enough to overhear, but the others were well ahead. 'Elsa's mum is great fun, but they've only just got it together, haven't they? I mean, this might rock the boat between them. And if I do come here, I might never get a job in commercials again – all the work is in London. I'd be so isolated. I don't even like the countryside.'

'Cyd read the tarot cards,' Juno told her wisely. 'She says they told her to take you in.'

'Oh, yes, the "hire a bankrupt to be your driver" card,' Odette muttered sarcastically.

'You could consider this time out. A bit of R & R until you're feeling your old self again.' Juno was trying to be patient but couldn't resist adding under her breath, 'As opposed to just selfish.'

'What did you say?' Odette waited as Juno clambered over a stile.

'That you're being selfish,' she muttered, landing in a frozen puddle on the other side and cracking through it like a spoon through the top of a *crème brulée*.

'*You'd* be selfish if you'd just lost everything,' Odette snapped.

'No, I wouldn't.' Juno had got her trouser leg caught on some barbed wire and cursed. 'I'd have to find the funny side or die. You've just turned into a sort of – sort of—' she searched for the word, her leg still swinging about in mid-air, yellow boot gleaming in the sun as she fought to detach herself from the wire '—sort of *lurky* thing,' she finished.

'*Lurky* thing?' Odette snorted in derision. It was a pretty childish accusation.

'Yes.' Juno wasn't too happy with her choice of adjective either, but decided to stand by it – albeit on one leg. 'You might have had a hard time lately, but unless you lighten up and start to realise how much effort everyone's making for you, you're not going to have any friends left. If you ask me, Cyd could be your last chance.' Releasing herself from the barbed wire with a loud twang, she marched ahead, leaving Odette on the other side, watching a piece of Juno's torn trousers bobbing in front of her.

'Last chance,' she breathed, watching the wire dance.

She followed the others at some distance, hands deep in her pockets, chin deep in her fleece collar and head deep in her thoughts.

What Cyd Francis was offering her was, as Juno rightly pointed out, amazingly generous. A home and a job, the two things she'd lost. It might not be a lifestyle she'd ever aspired to, but maybe it was time to put aside the lifestyle dream and go in search of a life.

Looking down at her feet, she realised that every blade of grass she was flattening now belonged to Calum. She remembered her father's favourite saying that if wishes were horses, then beggars would ride. The combined horsepower of Jobe's incredible car collection was several thousands. That was an awful lot of wishes, and Odette knew she would waste every single one on Calum if she thought it would win his affection.

The others were waiting for her on a long grassy ride which

was set between an avenue of skeletal winter limes. As Odette approached, Lydia was explaining to a far from enthusiastic Juno that she should join some fitness classes in the States to trim herself down for bridesmaid duty.

'They're much more attuned to the needs of bigger women out there,' Lydia told her, unaware that Juno – already in a state of high pique – was close to explosion.

Ally saw it, however, and gently distracted them both with her sweet-natured laugh. 'I'm not sure you're going to want me to be your bridesmaid, Lyds.'

'Of course I will. Why wouldn't I? I want you all.' She looked around them, then spotted Miss Bee looking surprised and hastily added, 'Except you, darling. Sorry, but I hardly know you.'

'Don't mention it.' Bee grinned.

'Bee might have to step in if you insist on ordering me a size twelve dress,' Juno grumbled.

'Of course you can lose the weight, Joo.' Lydia waved a hand breezily as they crossed a cattle grid into the deer park.

'Thing is, I can't.' Ally was once again ready to defuse the situation.

'You don't need to lose weight, my darling.' Lydia looked at the willowy little blonde. 'You're tiny.'

'I won't be in June,' Ally sighed, deciding it was high time to spill the beans. 'I'm pregnant!'

'You're what?' Elsa shrieked in surprise.

'Didn't you notice I hardly touched a drop last night?' she laughed. 'I wasn't throwing up because I was hungover earlier. I had morning sickness.'

'How long have you known?' Juno was jumping around, her black mood quite forgotten.

'About a month.' Ally grimaced. 'It was a bit of a shock. We were planning to wait at least another year. I'm sorry – it must have been pretty bloody for Odette staying with a couple of hysterics.'

'But you didn't say anything.' Odette looked at her in amazement. 'I had no idea.' Then she remembered the night she'd overheard Ally and Duncan arguing about having another mouth to feed. She'd thought they meant her when they were talking about a new baby.

'This is just wonderful!' Lydia burst in. 'You *must* be my bridesmaids – picture the scene. You will have a new marriage and a babe-in-arms, Elsa; Ally has a loving husband, and will have a babe in her belly and one at her ankles; Juno . . .'

'Looks pregnant,' Juno finished for her, eyes flashing angrily.

'I was going to say is in the first months of true love,' Lydia blew her a kiss, 'and darling Odette will represent the single girl. It'll be a symbolic tableau of marriage, love and motherhood. The different stages of our female peer group.'

Odette gritted her teeth. She supposed she deserved to represent the sad minority, the spinster.

'Perhaps you should have me after all?' Miss Bee joked dryly. 'I can be your token dyke.' She clearly thought Lydia's idea batty.

'Perfect!' Lydia clutched her hands together in the way she'd seen Cyd doing and had decided to adopt. 'That would be *so* chichi, wouldn't it? What are you doing in June?'

As they hurried on, Lydia fell in step with Bee, telling her all about her plans, huge walking boots clomping companionably alongside a pair of silver-glitter Doc Marten's. Ally, Juno and Elsa walked three abreast, arms still linked, chatting about babies. Juno confessed she couldn't wait to get pregnant. 'Jay thinks we should try for conception on the flight to New York. It would be kind of fitting, seeing as we're a transatlantic couple. And Jay has a special attachment to JFK. He was practically born there, after all. He calls it his heir-port.'

Tagging along behind, Odette felt very single, very selfish, and very, very broody.

When Fermoncieaux finally came into sight, revealing itself a window at a time from behind a beech wood to their left, Odette knew exactly what the second Mrs de Winter must have felt like when first clapping eyes on Manderley, or Elizabeth Bennett peeking out of her carriage at Pemberley, or even Marie Antoinette at Versailles. The square dot she'd seen earlier from the cap of the smock mill was, close up, absolutely huge, vast, regal, splendid, stately – and staggeringly beautiful.

Calum hadn't just bought himself any old mansion in the country. He'd bought a fairytale palace.

'You're going to get married here?' Ally breathed, barely able to believe the house's beauty.

Lydia nodded mutely, imagining herself standing on the long sweep of stone steps that led up to the vast front entrance, dressed in white, the most beautiful bride who'd ever emerged from a carriage. It had to be a carriage – black glossy wood and glittering brasswork, pulled by six Palomino horses with white feather plumes. There would be liveried footmen, Dalmatians, her father in a morning suit, her gorgeous tableau of bridesmaids (Juno miraculously lost a lot of weight in her imagination, and Odette developed cheekbones), her doting guests, and of course her groom. Her blond, lovely, dashing groom. Mr Forrester. But which one?

'We'd better push back.' Elsa squinted at the sun which was dropping behind the beech wood.

'Can't we go a little closer?' Lydia breathed, wanting to try out the steps, peer in the windows, feel the atmosphere.

'Another time.' Elsa glanced at her watch. 'I told Euan I'd be back in London by six.' She looked at Bee and Odette. 'D'you mind setting off as soon as we get back to the farm? We might have time to splash back some tea first.'

'Fine.' Bee shrugged.

Odette opened her mouth to say something and then closed it again. She was going to stay. She was going to live here, near Calum's castle. She was going to find out what he was up to.

They panted their way back in the fading light, great puffs of condensation clouding around their faces as they raced to reach the farm before darkness fell. Elsa jogged alongside Odette for a while, holding on to her bump for balance and wincing as her back ached with every step.

'I'm not sure if I'm coming back to London.' Odette jumped as an animal screeched in the woods beside them.

'Say again?' Elsa was looking at her as though she'd just announced she was in training for the regional tripe-eating finals.

'Your mother's offered me a job, babes.' She turned Elsa

around and pressed the heels of her hands into her lumbar muscles to relieve some of the tension, working slowly outwards.

'Don't tell me she wants you to produce a commercial for her funny little pots?' Elsa laughed. 'I can see it now – two women in a kitchen window-testing their Smockies.'

'What?' Odette was baffled. 'No, she wants me to be her driver. She says I can live here for free. It would get me out of your hair.'

On cue, Elsa's huge mane swished from shoulder to shoulder several times and almost blinded Odette as she rubbed her friend's back.

'And you've said yes?' she asked tautly.

'Not yet.' Odette noticed all the good work she'd done on Elsa's back reversing itself as the muscles pinched together once more. 'But I'm tempted. I haven't got much else going for me at the moment, have I?'

'What about me and Euan?'

'Like I say, it'll get me out of your hair.' She stood back as Elsa turned to face her, vast speckled eyes boring into her face. 'You've been so good to me over these past few months, babes, and I'll love you forever for it, but it's time I left you and Euan alone to enjoy your time together.'

'We like having you in the house.' Elsa sounded almost pleading. 'It's so big, and you somehow help fill it up. You need to stay in London for work. You love London.'

'I've relied on you too long. I need to get my own life back, and I think that maybe I can find it down here.' Odette look around at the dark woods. 'I know you and your old ma don't always see eye-to-eye, and me staying here might cause a bit of friction between you two, but I don't want that to happen. She'd doing this for you as much as for me, babes. She's helping us both out here.'

Elsa shook her head. 'You don't know my mother, Odette. Honestly you don't. I know you think this is kind of her, but she's really manipulative. And she's impossible to live with – drives me mad after a couple of days. You'd go crazy trying to cope with her moods.'

'But I won't be living with her, will I?' Odette pointed out. 'I'll be living in the mill.'

Elsa baulked, her eyes wide with horror. 'That death-trap? Christ, she is *such* a cow. She doesn't even want you in the house. She's so anti-social.'

'I'd rather live in the mill.' Odette thought Elsa was being irrational. 'And your mum doesn't strike me as anti-social, babes. She's loved having us here. I fink she's a bit lonely to tell the truth.'

'You don't understand.' Elsa sounded desperate. 'She blows hot and cold. Yes, she's been a party animal this weekend, but that's because she knows we're all going to go home today. Sometimes she won't even let people in the house. She's lived alone too long – Jobe was practically a hermit and it's rubbed off on her. She gets these moods where she just can't be reached, wants to hide from the world. And she can be so selfish . . . so demanding.'

Odette realised that Elsa could be describing herself. She and Cyd had more in common than she'd ever imagine.

'I know you don't believe me when I say she's got another side to her,' Elsa tried one last time. 'No one does, she doesn't show it in public. And I know you think I'm just angry about what happened to my dad and about Jobe and stuff, but I promise you it's not that. If you stay here she'll turn on you, just like she did on them.'

'Babes, I'm not marrying her,' Odette laughed. 'I'm just going to drive her around.'

Elsa closed her eyes in defeat. Then they snapped open again and fixed tightly on her friend's face. 'Odette, swear to me one thing?'

'What's that?'

'You're not staying down here because Calum is so close, are you?'

Odette couldn't swear. She'd lied too much to her friends in recent months. If she was going to turn over a new leaf – a hundred fallen leaves by the looks of the paths around her – she owed it to them to be honest.

'Okay.' Elsa nodded when she didn't answer. 'In that case

you should know something – I found out a few facts about Calum. Most of it you already know, I've told you pretty much everything. But I haven't told you how he raised the money for Food Hall.'

'Give me some credit,' Odette snorted irritably. 'He took me to the cleaner's.'

'No, before that.' Elsa's big speckled eyes glittered in the half-light. 'He cut some sort of deal with a bunch of villains. Half the money invested in that place is probably the result of armed robberies.'

To Elsa's surprise, Odette laughed. 'Now that *is* Calum all over.' She almost sounded impressed. 'You've got to hand it to him, he's always coming up with original ideas.'

Elsa felt her anger flare.

'What about the opening night of the OD?' she stormed without thinking. 'Calum didn't stage that publicity stunt through choice. He did it because I forced him to. I caught him with someone, Odette – someone's wife. I told him I'd spill the beans if he didn't help you out, I'd blackmail him.'

Odette winced as the all-too-familiar acid-splash of jealousy ate through her skin. 'Who was he with?'

'That doesn't matter. The point is, he was deliberately trying to ruin you from the start.'

'And you "blackmailed" him out of it?'

'It was the only way, Odette. Don't you see? The place would have died on its feet without his help?'

'Instead of which it died on its concrete-encased feet with his help when he decided to blackmail me in return,' she flared, defending Calum, knowing the way his mind worked. 'He wanted me to make it work without him, against all the odds. He wanted me to prove something to him. He gave me the money, but after that it was up to me. His advice was shit, his staff were diabolical. I should have trusted my instincts and done my own thing, but I loved him and he knew it. That's why he withdrew, waited for me to get things right, to see the game.'

'Odette, what are you talking about?' Elsa fought to keep up as Odette started jogging faster and faster, liking the feeling of breath quickening in her lungs again, her muscles working, her belly tightening.

'Calum set me a test, Elsa. He was waiting for the result. I could have made it work. Instead of which my friends bustled in like a bunch of mothers and ruined it for me.'

'Ruined it?' Elsa was getting stitches in every muscle trying to keep up. 'Ruined it? We saved your arse. For love. Fucking slow down, will you?'

Odette jogged around her, temples throbbing. 'Can't you see, babes? Calum would have loved me if you'd left me alone. I was playing his game. I knew the rules.'

'Crap!' Elsa howled. 'There were no bloody rules. This isn't some sort of courtship ritual we're talking about here, Odette. What planet are you on? It was a courtshit ritual – Calum's a shit and you ended up in court. He only invested the money because he wanted to impress Lydia. When she didn't notice, he got fucked off and decided to play games. Then he started planning Food Hall and wanted his money back in a hurry.'

'That's so wrong.' Odette was speeding up as she ran demented laps around Elsa. 'You don't know how wrong you are. Calum came to see me on New Year's Eve. He offered me a deal and when I didn't take it, he still wanted to have sex with me. There!' She slid to a victorious halt, not caring that Calum's deal had been all about Lydia. She had to win this argument, she just had to. If she didn't, her pride would finally crack. 'Tell me he doesn't want me now? He knows I'm his equal and he's challenging me to duels rather than giving me jewels. It's twenty-first century love, Elsa. Don't you know anything? You've been out of the singles scene too long, babes. That's the way we do it these days.'

'Odette,' Elsa sighed despairingly. 'Odette, darling. Love isn't about duels. It's not a battle of the sexes. It's occasionally battles, true, and hopefully lots of good sex, but it's also companionship and friendship and trust and respect and shared lives and jokes and possessions and memories. It's so, so much more than you think.'

'I know that.' Odette snatched her hands away defensively. 'I know what love is.'

'I really don't think you do.' Elsa shook her head. 'You say you love Calum, but you don't seem to have shared very much with him.'

'Well, we're about to share a bleedin' post-code.' Odette jogged off, leaving Elsa to stumble her way home in the twilight, not knowing that her friend had only jogged a hundred feet or so ahead of her and was keeping an eye on her at all times, stopping every few yards to check that she was okay before pressing proudly on.

34

Working for Cyd Francis was certainly challenging, but not quite in the way Odette had hoped. She was incredibly eccentric, wanting to be driven to strange destinations at all hours. She was also annoyingly vague and grew belligerent if cross-questioned. Odette was never quite sure what she was up to, or why, and had no idea whether it was for business or pleasure, although she soon found out what 'Smockies' were.

In one of the run-down barns at Smock Mill Farm, there was a minor manufacturing empire. Five local women worked together from ten until three, four days a week, casting, firing and painting rustic little figurines of squirrels, badgers, dormice and other assorted woodland creatures, all of whom wore little smocks.

'They're revolting, aren't they? I started making them in desperation when I couldn't pay off Jobe's death duties, and now the business is worth a hundred thousand a year. Come and see the web-site.'

Cyd, it transpired, was an Internet junkie. There was nothing she didn't know about cyberspace. She might be banned from the roads, but she was the Schumacher of the super-highway and was happy to give driving lessons.

With the aid of a state-of-the-art computer in an office set up in the corner of the barn, she showed Odette how the little Smockies were ordered and dispatched, overseen by an elderly Fulkington housewife called Phyllis. All Cyd's team of workers were well into their fifties and most walked to work from the local village, putting in just a few hours a week.

The Smockies were not the only enterprise Cyd ran from

the farmhouse's rambling outbuildings. In an adjoining barn, two retired school-teachers called Derek and Anne worked whilst listening to Radio Four, creating garments for the exclusive designer labels Dog's Spinner and Haute Cature. These turned out to be knitted jumpers for pets – little bobble hats, capes and scarves for the discerning pet-owner, another Internet hit.

In the old dovecote, a stock-pile of jam, honey, mustard, vinegars and dressings made in the summer months was regularly depleted as various local delicatessens and tea rooms ordered fresh supplies. Upstairs in the attics of the farmhouse, another high-tech computer was linked up to the super-highway, and Cyd used it to give live tarot readings, rune throwings and crystal healings three times a week, along with astrological predictions, all of which could be accessed from anywhere in the world with the aid of a modem and credit card.

Odette saw Cyd as a jewelled spider sitting in the middle of the World Wide Web. She admired her ingenuity beyond words.

'It's one of my biggest earners,' she told Odette happily. 'I'm New Ageing gracefully. With any luck I should have enough to open an animal sanctuary soon. That's always been a dream of mine. The Millers work for very little – they seem to enjoy it, and most of our profit is held in a charitable trust.'

Cyd called her workforce the Millers, although it was years since grain had been grown and milled on the farm. Nowadays the land was rented to a local sheep farmer to rear and graze his stock.

Far from a quiet country retreat, Odette felt as though she was staying on a small industrial estate. And far from being a futuristic haven, the smock mill was, as Elsa had promised, riddled with damp, freezing cold, draughty and full of equipment which didn't work. The only electrical circuit which functioned was the one from which the lights ran, the remainder were dead. The high-tech shower consequently just produced an icy dribble, the television and hi-fi looked great but served as nothing but homes for spiders, the Stairmaster was as useless as a library step, and the fan heaters didn't work.

The only way Odette could get warm was to use the spa

bath in the gloomy basement, watching spiders air-sliding along their webs overhead as she gripped hard on to the edges to stop herself being sucked into the valves and pumped out amidst much frothy air.

'I'll get someone to come around and look at the wiring,' Cyd had promised airily the first morning Odette had appeared, teeth chattering, to drive her to Brighton for a meeting. A week later and no one had appeared.

Cyd was hugely forgetful. When describing Odette's 'here and there' job brief, she had forgotten to mention that she expected her to carry out endless chores. Odette found herself doing the shopping armed with a list and a wad of cash, which was never quite enough to cover the bill. She got thriftier and thriftier, learning to bargain with everyone on her employer's behalf. Everyone got paid somehow, except Odette herself.

Cyd didn't rise before midday at the earliest, and so left a note of instructions on the kitchen table the night before, sometimes with a pile of grubby banknotes, sometimes not. Rather than let Odette have a key to the farmhouse, she insisted on leaving one under a stone by the door so that she could let herself in each morning to collect the list. Odette complained that it was a security risk, but her boss insisted it was 'her way'. Cyd used the phrase more often than Frank Sinatra. Sometimes the key was missing. Once or twice, she found that Cyd had left the list under the stone. Another time, she found just a sachet of puppy worming tablets.

When it came to chauffeuring her around, Odette got to know the area quickly, although Cyd never explained where they were going or why. She would produce a scribble on the back of an envelope or a printed letter-head and hand it over when they set out, or simply make Odette drive around Brighton until she recognised a familiar street and shouted out, 'Yes – down here somewhere. I think it might be left – oh, no, that's my hairdresser's. Onwards, dearheart.'

Cyd was, Odette thought, frankly batty. Yet the longer she stayed at the farm, the more she grew to like her eccentric employer with her sad, smoky laugh, her secrets, and her entrepreneurial streak.

Of all the jobs Cyd wanted Odette to do, there was one which she fell into almost by accident, only realising days later that it was probably the main reason Cyd had asked her to come and stay. She needed someone to talk to.

Cyd insisted that Odette eat with her in the evenings. In contrast to the locked, silent farmhouse of daytime, the door was always wide open in the evenings, music blaring, and Cyd was eager to beckon her inside.

She was a hopeless cook who could just about manage to boil a meal for two in a bag provided she pinned the timer to her jumper, and Odette soon realised how she stayed so thin. She hoped to become equally thin by partaking in these inedible meals, but Cyd ruined this plan by providing an outlet for her biggest weakness. There were always bars and bars of the most luxurious, sensuous, melt-in-the-mouth Swiss chocolate on the table. But whereas Cyd might nibble on a single piece, Odette was unable to resist troughing her way through a family-sized bar, sometimes two, to compensate for the indigestible main course.

'The Millers all rallied round and cooked the food for the hen night,' Cyd explained with a guilty chuckle. 'So darling of them – they just appeared with it under foil trays when I was trying to get to grips with Delia. They know I'm utterly hopeless. Jobe and I had a housekeeper, but I had to let her go when the money ran out and I've never bothered getting another. Can't bear the thought of sharing the house with someone else.'

'I can eat in the mill if you'd rather . . .' Odette wondered if she was just inviting her into the house out of politeness.

'God, no – you don't count, dearheart. You're family.'

'That's really kind of you.' Odette felt herself welling up. She hadn't felt a part of a family for a great many years.

'Entirely selfish, I assure you.' Cyd fed the remains of their supermarket curry to Bazouki, batting away the puppies who would undoubtedly later throw up what they managed to grab. 'Elsa's family are her friends, and you are one of those friends. Having you here helps me get an understanding of her world.'

'I wouldn't say we're her family.' Odette thought about it. 'Maybe in the past when everyone was single, but these days most of the Gang are starting families of their own. Euan and Buster the Bump are Elsa's family now. And you, of course.'

'And my ex-husband, and po-faced Po, and my sons who refuse to talk to me,' Cyd huffed. 'They won't let me help with Elsa's wedding at all. I'm astonished I got an invitation. Not that they're doing much – Euan and Elsa seem to have it covered. Her father's just getting in the way. He still refuses to acknowledge me, you know – after thirty years. I mean, how childish. Stupid man.'

'He had his uses in the past,' Odette soothed her. 'You had Elsa together after all. And your sons.'

'Who won't talk to me either.' Cyd rallied a sad smile. 'But you're right, Odette, you wise young bird. He had his uses.' She gave her dry, smoky giggle. 'What a lovely way of putting it! Gosh, it's good to have you to talk to.'

And she did talk. Over the following few evenings, Odette got to know Cyd Francis far better than almost anyone else in her acquaintance, Elsa included. She wasn't quite sure why the famously reclusive, wayward blonde chose to open up to her, but Odette felt as though she was taking an evening course in love and misunderstanding. She had a feeling that Cyd's confession was deliberate, a way of trying to teach her something. There was no doubt that a lot of long-suppressed emotions had chosen to come out because the cork holding them had finally popped under the pressure. But there was more to it than that.

'I wasn't always so good at being a black sheep,' Cyd confessed one evening over ready-made lasagne, which was still frozen in the middle. 'My parents put an enormous amount of pressure on me to forget about modelling and settle down to the only real job a woman should have – raising a family. I think I only married so young to please them.'

'Are they still alive?'

She shook her head. 'Both long gone. They thought I'd done so well marrying Elsa's father, that I'd bettered myself from my 'umble horigins as my mother would say.' She affected a Benny from *Crossroads* voice.

'But I thought . . .'

'That I was born with a silver canteen in my mouth?' Cyd

laughed. 'Gosh, no – ignore the accent. I picked this up from my first husband who fancied himself as Henry Higgins, despite the fact he was entirely self-made and grew up in Solihull. Never underestimate a man's ability to rule the roost with a rod of irony, Odette. He married me for my looks and then spent the best part of a decade trying to persuade me to stop bleaching my hair and to dress like his mother. Instead, I kept on modelling and made the most wonderful friends – such free spirits, such a world apart from my home life. I was rather successful in my day, you know.'

Odette was touched by her unexpected modesty. Cyd was a legend.

She smiled wistfully, her huge smoky eyes creasing at the corners. 'Jobe found me. You could say he saved me – it became his mission in life. I was still modelling from time to time. I suppose my face was quite well known. Jobe saw it in a magazine and went to great lengths to find out who I was. Even the fact I had five children didn't put him off, which I found fascinating. So unexpected. He was ten years younger than me and very cocky. He absolutely bombarded me with flowers and attention. It was at the height of Mask's success and I was rather blown away and very flattered, but it was a long time before I fell in love with him. It wasn't an impulsive decision, although you'd think so to read the press cuttings.

'Leaving the children crucified me. I thought I'd get them back in just a few short weeks, but then there was that awful court case and I lost them. All that publicity . . .' She blotted her spouting tears and blew her nose noisily into her napkin. 'Stupid to get upset still after all this time. Can you drive me to Oddbins, darling? We've run out of whisky and I really need one.'

It wasn't an uncommon request. Odette never drank during their evening meals in case Cyd ran out of alcohol. She was easily capable of polishing off a bottle of red wine and half a bottle of Bushmills Green Label during a talking session.

'I'm terrified of becoming like Jobe,' she explained as they returned along the winding farm track later. 'I have to be careful, dearheart. That's why I only ever keep one bottle in the house.'

Odette privately thought Cyd drank far too much, but she said nothing. She'd already learned that Cyd's temper could flare up at the slightest provocation, and she wasn't averse to reminding Odette precisely who was boss. She now saw what Elsa had tried to warn her about; Cyd blew hot and cold faster than Nicky Clarke's hair-dryer as she changed from genial to hermetic in seconds. This worried Odette deeply, and sometimes she suspected that Cyd wanted to employ her as a Dictaphone, not a driver. Odette had a feeling that the moment she was no longer needed to listen to Cyd's life story she'd be out on her ear and decided to take evasive action.

That night she feigned a few yawns when she delivered Cyd back to the farm.

'You poor dearheart, I've kept you up talking about myself again,' Cyd apologised worriedly. 'You must go straight to bed.'

'Would you mind if I fill my hot water bottle first?' Odette chewed her lip anxiously, dreading the prospect of her damp, chilly bed.

'Of course – drat! I meant to call an electrician today. You must remind me tomorrow.'

Odette did, but Cyd promptly forgot. She also appeared to have forgotten that she'd promised to pay Odette a salary. A rude letter arrived from the Official Receiver demanding details of her new employment. When Odette passed it on to Cyd, she later found it lining the puppies' basket. She would have liked to call in an electrician herself, but had nothing to pay him with and nothing left to sell, nor was it easy to get access to the phone. The line in the tower was dead. Her pay-as-you-go mobile phone was virtually useless this far away from civilisation – there was no clear signal anywhere in the area, and nor did she have any money to put credits on it. Cyd insisted the farmhouse line was for emergencies only, claiming she needed to keep it free at all times for her Internet connection. She was similarly restrictive about her washing machine, insisting that Odette could use her spa bath for cleaning clothes.

*　　*　　*

373

The following afternoon, while Cyd was walking Bazouki, Odette set about investigating the fuse box in the windmill basement. When she opened the door, three bottles of John Power fell out and almost crowned her. Further investigation revealed several more bottles, one of which had tipped over and drenched the circuits many years earlier, blowing all the fuses. She'd helped out in her father's shop long enough to know what she needed. Finding what little cash she had, she took one of Jobe's cars to nearby Chuckfield where she'd spotted a hardware store.

Armed with fuse wire, she set about tackling the problem, proud of her practicality. She doubted most of her friends could do as well. But she howled with frustration when all her efforts came to nothing and the power remained stubbornly dead. What's more, she seemed to have shorted out the spa bath.

'Odette!' Cyd screamed into the tower. 'Where the *hell* have you been? I said three o'clock. And have you used the Ferrari? It has mud all over it.'

She didn't dare tell Cyd what she'd done. That afternoon she took her to Jobe's grave in Brighton Cemetery, a weekly ritual. Cyd returned to the car in tears. 'Those bloody fans have scribbled all over his stone again. I know they loved him too, but it looks so awful. Stop off at Oddbins, will you?'

Cyd drank more than usual that night, and talked herself out. She told Odette about her marriage to Jobe, about his mood swings, his jealousy, his deep, deep depressions and anti-social withdrawal from the band.

'I ended up between a rock-star and a hard place,' she laughed sadly. She was on her fifth or sixth whisky – Odette had lost count – and her eyes were glittering ominously.

'I loved him, Odette,' she snarled with unexpected anger. 'But I hated him too. He took me away from my children. The arguments we had were explosive, violent, passionate beyond belief – they made the rows in my first marriage look like two Regency fops flicking handkerchiefs in each other's faces. It was passion that kept us together, dearheart. Pure, unadulterated passion. It kept on eating us inside out until the day he died. And I still can't get rid of it.' She looked at the bottle.

'Before he met me, he was a wonderful musician – he might only have been famous for playing the drums, but he wrote a lot of the best Mask melodies. He could play practically any instrument. But once he met me, music seemed to bore him. He tried and tried to regain the drive to compose, but it just wasn't there. It was as though his desire for me wiped away all his talent. He lost interest in it. He surrounded himself with instruments and high-tech equipment in that mill of his, but all he did in there was drink. In the end it killed him.'

Then, in one of her now customary about-turns, Cyd's face suddenly softened, big sooty eyes filling with sympathy. 'Elsa's told me about what Calum Forrester did to you, dearheart. She told me how you felt about him, about your passion. You still feel that, don't you?'

Fighting to control anger and shame, Odette said nothing. How dare Elsa tell her mother about that? How dare Cyd bring it up now, when she was tired and emotional and dazed from what she had just heard, when she was feeling so vulnerable, when she had put him so far out of her mind? For that was the crazy thing. In the past couple of weeks, she had been so busy that she had barely thought about Calum at all. All her time had been taken up adjusting to her new surroundings, her new routine. She was now living next to Fermoncieaux, and yet she could have been a million miles away for all the time she'd had to investigate it.

'You can't let that passion destroy you,' Cyd was saying, reaching for the large rose quartz crystal which sat on the kitchen table like a big, angular blancmange, supposedly spreading peaceful and loving vibes. 'You have to use it constructively, Odette, energise it.'

Oh, God, here we go, she thought wretchedly. When very drunk, Cyd started quoting rubbish from self-help books and hippy-tripping about auras.

'Can't you see why fate has brought you here?' Cyd started to laugh in delight. 'You are here because Calum is here. You must act. You must use your passion before it ruins your life as it did Jobe's, as it wasted mine.'

And then it hit her like a large, hardback autobiography in the face. Odette finally realised what this was all about – the evening reminiscences, the long, painful life story.

'Cyd, you can't live your life again through me,' she said gently.

Cyd didn't deny it. Instead she just smiled her enigmatic smile, laughed her smoky laugh and winked. 'Can't I? Just watch. You've got tomorrow morning off. Use it to case Fermoncieaux. If you don't, you're fired.'

35

'Bleedin' *great!*' Odette looked down to where her feet should be and all she could see was a black pool of mud. When she'd climbed over the gate and jumped off, she hadn't checked what she was going to land on. She was now ankle-deep in oozing cow-muck.

A small herd of heifers watched her curiously from the opposite side of the field, limpid eyes impassive, as she tried to step backwards and left her shoe behind with a squelchy popping noise. A moment later it was submerged in mud.

Holding her breath against the stench, Odette groped around like a television contestant looking for prizes in a gunk tank. Unable to find it, she hopped on to more solid ground, cursing under her breath.

She'd been tramping around since eight o'clock and had yet to find Fermoncieaux Hall. She knew she should have brought a map with her, but the farmhouse had been locked as usual that morning and there was no key under the stone so she had not been able to borrow any boots or a decent coat. Her teeth were chattering like a frenzied football rattle and she was certain her kidneys had frozen right through.

The paths all looked very different from the day Elsa had taken her hens for a walk. They were muddier and darker, the heavy rain-sodden skies offering only a murky light. Odette was cold, fed up and badly in need of a spare shoe.

All she'd succeeded in doing was walking in a big loop through the wood and out on to a high field just a few hundred yards from where she'd set out. She could see the farm roof from here, along with her damp little watchtower. She was so high up she was at the same level as its cap.

Hearing an engine in the distance behind her, Odette slipped behind the field's scraggy hedge and watched the horizon. A moment later a huge crew-cab pick-up truck came into sight, trundling along a droving lane and sending up great splashes of water as it bounced through the puddles. Its wipers were on the go, cutting through the muddy film on the windscreen like a child's fingers scraping chocolate icing from a bowl. The driver couldn't see much, but he was keeping a line as straight as a die and positively belting along. Odette admired his skill behind the wheel – she'd tried off-roading as part of a corporate bonding weekend a few years earlier and had almost killed herself and the creative director. As the truck flew past, she saw that he was talking into a mobile phone and eating a sandwich at the same time. It was Jimmy Sylvian.

Whooping delightedly as a thought struck her, Odette galloped back to the farm, wearing one shoe like Cinderella running from the ball.

Up in the draughty windmill cap, she switched on her phone. No signal. She moved around, leaving great splodgy single footprints on the dusty floor. It took quite some time, but she finally cracked the method. If she stood on the biggest cog and leaned half-out of the tiny window, she could get one precious bar. Checking her credits, she found that she had almost two pounds' worth of talk-time in hand. She immediately called Elsa. There wasn't time to say much, and the line was as broken as a teenage boy's voice, but the call made her feel infinitely better, knowing that her friends were thinking about her and that Elsa was well, if enormous.

'How's Mum treating you?'

Odette was wise enough not to sound off. 'Amazing as ever, babes. She cooks for me every night and keeps me entertained with all sorts of stories about her life. I half-suspect she's only asked me here to edit her autobiography.'

'Now that I would love to read,' Elsa laughed, seemingly satisfied that her mother was behaving herself. There was a muffled pause. 'Sorry, Euan's here, trying to listen in. Hang on – I think he wants a word—'

But the phone ran out of credits before he came on the line.

*　　*　　*

Just as Odette had pretended all was fantastic to Elsa, so Elsa had economised with the truth in return. She wasn't at all sure that getting married in the thirty-sixth week of pregnancy was a good idea. Her doctor had strongly recommended against it five months ago when she'd first mooted the idea, but she'd felt gloriously strong and healthy then, had wanted to be fatly, happily pregnant when she and Euan became one family – partners, lovers and parents together.

Her wedding outfit was proving murder to fit. Her weight had stabilised in the last month and she'd only gained a few pounds since she'd last been measured by her friend, the cult club-gear designer Archie Ché. But her bump had changed shape completely, dropping down a few inches as the baby's head 'engaged', causing her painful pelvic cramps. She wasn't sure she could last the length of a civil ceremony, let alone two. They were to marry in the morning at Battersea Register Office with just their parents and closest friends present, and then go on to the film studio which they'd hired where another ceremony would take place – a moving exchange of vows Elsa and Euan had written themselves. Afterwards a party of astronomical proportions was planned, with live bands including Bent Uncle performing short sets, plus a dance-floor presided over by Miss Bee at her decks.

Euan seemed oblivious of Elsa's turmoil. He had another baby to breathe life into, a child that had been born many months earlier but had yet to attract an 'Isn't he beautiful?' comment. Euan's novel had now been rejected by three publishing houses and five agents and he was feeling very, very bitter about it.

He'd thought that he could sell his book and solve their financial worries in one fell swoop of pen over contract, but it wasn't that easy. Of course it wasn't that easy. He vowed that he would give up when the rejection letters eventually outnumbered the pages of his manuscript. Day after day he trailed jealously around his local Waterstone's, wondering what other authors had that he lacked. He stood over the New Fiction table like an allotment owner at a county show the day after his prize leeks have been cut down by a saboteur: envious, suspicious, incensed.

That morning, he walked into the shop during a signing. Some considerable excitement was being generated as a dashing figure in dark glasses sat behind a desk signing copies of his work for a small but eager queue of middle-aged women.

Watching discreetly from behind a revolving card stand, Euan realised it was Micky Moore, the legendary Rumbling Runes guitarist, signing copies of his latest autobiography *They're Playing my Rune Again*.

One of the booksellers, who had seen Euan around a lot and found him wildly attractive, smiled as he passed. 'This is his third set of memoirs in as many years,' he said under his breath, pretending to neaten up the card display. 'All ghosted. He's known in the industry as Memento Moore.'

An idea started to form in Euan's head. 'Is there much profit in celebrity biographies?'

The bookseller shrugged. 'Depends who and how much dirt they spill.'

'What about Cyd Francis?'

'Oh, I *love* her!' The bookseller shuddered appreciatively. 'So camp. She knew them all, didn't she? Jagger, Moon, Richards, Francis himself, of course. *Imagine* the tales she could tell.'

'Imagine.' Euan smiled widely.

Calum Forrester was rather taken with strolling around his estate with a stick in one hand, sturdy boots on his feet, and his wise game-keeper at his shoulder – or rather his estate manager. Calum was always getting told off for muddling the two jobs up. Although dressed in a scruffy shooting waistcoat, ancient cords, a torn Puffa and checked Tattersall shirt, Jimmy looked more poacher than anything else to Calum, who had an image of everyone in the country wearing immaculate herringbone waistcoats and plus fours. He knew that Jimmy had come over from Africa with no warm clothes so was amazed that everything he had looked so scruffy and well-worn. It could almost be second-hand. He supposed he must have borrowed it from his brothers until he had time to go shopping.

'The hunt have had permission to use this land for centuries, but I think we should put a stop to it,' Jimmy told him in his booming voice.

Calum had been toying with the idea of dressing in hunting pink and trying a day himself, so murmured something vague about not wanting to upset the locals at this early stage.

Jimmy decided not to waste time arguing. He liked nothing better than entertaining Calum over a bottle of good malt in his farm late at night, discussing his plans for the estate, but having him around during the day was proving somewhat time-consuming. He'd been forced to cram all his work into a short morning to make time for this; had only agreed to come out with him at all today because he'd seen the oddest sight in Chuckfield earlier that week, and wanted to confirm it. He was certain that Calum would be able to put him straight on the matter.

'Tell me, is Odette Fielding working at Fermoncieaux?'

Calum looked at him curiously. 'Odette Fielding? No, why should she be?'

'I thought you still maintained contact,' Jimmy said cautiously.

'Why should I?' Calum seemed rattled, instantly on the defensive.

'Her addiction?' Jimmy was exasperated. 'You said you took the club away from her for her own good. You said you were going to see that she straightened herself out.'

'What's that?' Calum pointed urgently at a tree as he tried to remember what on earth he'd told Jimmy about Odette and when. He had deliberately blanked that part of his life from his head.

'Another oak, you oke,' Jimmy sighed, refusing to be distracted. 'You told me it was going to be kill or cure. You must be following her progress now, surely? Keeping a eye on her.'

'Sure, sure.' Calum nodded. 'Hasn't Saskia Seaton told you how she is? I thought you two were very close?'

Calum seemed to recall some sort of ancient family history

going on there and didn't want to put his foot in it. In truth, he had no idea where Odette was. He had put her as far out of his mind as he could over the past few weeks, not liking the way she'd made him feel, not wanting to know where she was or how she was. As far as he was concerned she might as well be dead, excised from his life for complicating it too much, getting in the way, making him feel bad about himself. Only sometimes, in the dead of night when he couldn't sleep, he was unable to keep the memories at bay.

'I don't really know Saskia – only through my brother.' Jimmy shook his head. 'I haven't seen her since the wedding. I think she's involved in another restaurant. Somewhere called the Station?'

Sometimes Calum was grateful that Jimmy was so completely uninterested in the London restaurant scene.

'Yes, yes – I think I heard that too,' he nodded, patting the oak. 'Well, Odette is currently in a rehabilitation clinic near Henley. It's very good. My brother went there. I think they'll straighten her out although it doesn't come cheap.'

'You're paying for it?' Jimmy was astonished.

Calum ducked his head dismissively and admired a cluster of wild primroses. 'We go back a long way.'

'I know – and I'm sorry.' Jimmy laughed his booming laugh out of embarrassment rather than amusement. 'I wouldn't have tried to make a move if I'd known. I'm sorry, Cal. I had no idea you two were involved until you turned up at her flat that New Year's Eve. It was idiotic of me to try.'

'Jimmy, you would have every right.' Calum suddenly looked up at him with glinting, anxious eyes. 'After what happened in Mpona, after I . . .'

'I don't want to talk about that,' Jimmy cut in curtly. 'That has nothing to do with what I'm talking about.'

'But it does,' Calum persisted, realising that he was telling the truth for the first time in weeks. 'It has everything to do with this.'

'What happened there is forgotten – forgiven.' Jimmy's big shoulders turned away so that Calum couldn't see the torture on his face. 'Let's leave it there.'

Calum wanted to protest, but realised that it would just make things worse. The stupid great idiot was far too straight for his own good.

'Anyway, Odette and I were never involved,' he said lightly. 'Not romantically.'

Jimmy turned to look at him, dark eyes burning with unspoken anger.

'I think I saw her a couple of weeks ago. Here, in Sussex.'

'Whereabouts? Brighton?' Calum had a sudden and delightful image of Odette living as a New Age crusty with a dog on a piece of string.

'No – here, in Fermoncieaux, or rather at my farm. She and some others were lost on their way to a hen party, although they seemed to have picked up a lot of cocks on the way. I don't think she recognised me. She seemed rather – er – preoccupied.' He didn't want to dwell on the fact that from what he'd seen, she'd practically been performing fellatio on a hulking brute in the back of a cab. He wasn't even entirely sure it *was* her. When he'd dropped the guests at Cyd's farm, she'd disappeared, and he'd decided not to hang around to find out.

Calum realised that his lie about rehab was about to be blown wide open. He'd have to think fast to keep that one spinning. Jimmy was still yabbering on about the party and the bizarre collection of guests he had ferried there in the early hours. 'Like something out of a Carry On film, only with half-dressed men, not women. A bit bloody scary, quite frankly. You know Cyd Francis?'

'The old sixties raver?' Calum nodded. 'She came to the OD opening. Caused quite a stir.'

'Of course – that makes sense then. She owns the farm just beyond those woods.' Jimmy pointed into the far distance. 'Runs some sort of hippy collective there from what I can gather. The woman who runs the dog rescue told me all about her. Cyd's donations practically keep the place open. Quite a local celebrity.'

'Oh, yes?' Calum feigned boredom.

'It was Cyd's daughter's hen party – Elsa, I think they said her name was. Ring any bells?'

Calum's eyes narrowed. The party-pooping Celtic-lover with the gonk hair was Cyd's daughter? That's why Odette had managed to get such a superstar to the OD party and generate all that publicity. 'She's a friend of Odette's.'

'So it was her I saw.' Jimmy seemed curiously disappointed, which Calum took to be a good sign. Maybe he'd swallowed the clinic line after all. But before he could make a carefully barbed comment, Jimmy spoke again.

'Then, a couple of days ago, I thought I saw Odette driving a very flashy yellow Ferrari Testarossa around Chuckfield village.'

'Must have been mistaken,' Calum tutted, mind racing. For a woman brought up in the back streets of the East End, Odette was better connected than the National Grid. The thought of her living so close made cold sweat slide down his sides like icy fingers. He longed to come clean, but instead he flashed a worried smile. 'Unless of course . . .' His brows creased together.

'What?'

'Well, the clinic haven't called but . . .' Calum chewed his lip.

'You think she might have done a bunk?' Jimmy asked, still not entirely convinced by the rehabilitation story.

'Well, it's possible,' Calum sighed sadly. 'And let's face it her options are limited. She hasn't any cash, and Cyd Francis is well known to have been a druggy rock-star groupie all her life. She could well be harbouring Odette.'

'Perhaps I should pop in later and check?' Jimmy suggested.

'No, no – I need you to talk to these television people about access. And they're very keen to feature you in the series,' Calum said hastily. 'I'll pop in on my way back to London. I have a meeting with the bank first thing in the morning. If Odette's there, I'll find her. Believe me, I know her a lot better than you do. If anyone can talk her into going back into rehab then I can.'

Jimmy shrugged. Calum and Odette had history, after all. He had already vowed to keep his nose out. 'You're the boss.'

'I certainly am.' Calum leaned the crook of his arm on his

stick and regarded his acreage proudly, liking the stance. But there was definitely something missing. 'I might get a dog.'

'Really?' Jimmy was delighted. 'I'll take you to the Canine Defence League later, if you like. They'll be thrilled. They've still got a lot of unwanted Christmas presents needing good homes.'

'I don't want a reject mutt.' Calum looked horrified. 'I want something a bit classy. A pedigree. Something to match this place.'

Waking up with a hangover and a bad temper, Cyd seemed to have forgotten about the previous night's conversation, and didn't enquire after Odette's morning off. Instead, she insisted on being driven to her reflexologist in Worthing, disappearing into a small 1950s house while Odette sat in the Aston listening to *Money Box* on the radio. They were having a debt phone-in.

'Whatever you do, avoid bankruptcy,' the financial expert advised.

Gazing bleakly out of the window at the corner shop, Odette recognised a familiar sticker and perked up. She scrabbled in the glove box and found almost five pounds in loose change. Then, feeling like a kid who has raided her mother's purse, guiltily dashed across the road to buy a top up card for her mobile.

By the time Odette had waited on hold for three minutes, she was down to just a few credits. When Ronny Prior finally took her call, she had to speak fast.

'Ronny, it's Odette.'

'*Darling*, how are you? When can we do lunch?'

'I'm working out of town right now, babes,' Odette panted. 'I just wanted to know if you got the restaurant documentary off the ground?'

'Already in production, darling,' Ronny gurgled. 'And thank you so much for the lead. They took some persuading, but we think we're really on to a winner now they're co-operating. The director is talking Baftas. We've already got some marvellous footage – Calum had the most glorious row with Wayne Street last week, all on camera. And then we filmed him toadying up to Florian Etoile to ask him to come back. He has terrific screen presence. I think we might have found a new star. And what's more, he has absolutely *no* idea how famous this is going to make him.'

The phone let out a warning beep that the credits were low. Looking up, Odette could see Cyd reappearing from the house.

'When will the series go out?' she asked Ronny urgently.

'The networks have already agreed to show the first episode the same week as the restaurant opens. We're going to call it *Food Fights*. Rather good, huh? I owe you a slap up meal for this, darling. Maybe I should book a table at Food Hall while I still can? I gather they're already taking reservations for next year and beyond.'

So it was too late to give Calum prior warning. Odette realised. Her revenge was already being enacted.

'Oh, I didn't know you had a phone,' Cyd said accusingly as she climbed into the car. Her temper had clearly not improved during her visit. 'Perhaps your friends could call you on that rather than bothering me to take messages all the time.'

'It doesn't work at the farm,' Odette explained. 'What messages?' Cyd had never mentioned her friends calling.

But she wasn't listening. She was rattling through the glove box in search of a tape. A moment later Radio Four was replaced by the deafening bass of Mask.

'That's better.' She settled back and Odette had to lip-read to find out where she wanted to go next.

As she waited in the car outside Cyd's crystal healer, ears ringing, she fumed about the messages Cyd hadn't passed on. Talking to Elsa today had made her realise how much she was missing her friends, how little contact she had with the outside world down here. When she'd first arrived, she had imagined herself sitting down to write long letters in the mill. But Cyd demanded so much of her time that she hadn't even sent out change of address cards yet. She craved the ease of e-mail, of the fax, the answer phone, a mobile that worked. She also mourned her television and video. She longed to watch a few episodes of *Hart to Hart* right now to cheer herself up. What was worse, she would probably never even get to see the *Food Fights* documentary when it was aired.

Jimmy didn't want to be made into the star of the Food Hall documentary. He had argued against co-operating with the series, but had been shouted down by Calum and more specifically by Alex Hopkinson, who was convinced the show would make Food Hall a national institution. French Merchant were, he said, a very classy production company.

Jimmy, who didn't even own a television, had little understanding of its hold over the public. He did, however, appreciate the hold the television crew had over his time. As if it wasn't bad enough that Calum seemed intent on becoming the David Bellamy of Sussex, Ronny Prior's little team were taking up even more of his time as they insisted they should be able to access all areas.

'This is going to be a no-holds-barred account of renovating one of England's most beautiful houses,' whined a junior researcher who was trying to persuade Jimmy to let her shadow him for a day. 'Your work is an intrinsic part of that. You must sign the release form – everyone else has.'

'I'm just the estate manager.' He stood his ground. 'There's nothing interesting about me supervising courgette potting in the greenhouse.'

'Oh, but there is.' The image of Jimmy, a steamy glasshouse and a courgette was almost too much for her to bear.

'Let's get this straight.' He loomed over the researcher who swooned adoringly. 'I want nothing to do with this enterprise, *ja*? As far as I'm concerned you stay out of my way and I stay out of yours. If I catch you pointing a camera at me or any of my men when we're trying to work, I will sit on the damned thing.'

'Oh, please do,' the researcher sighed after he'd gone. If his arse was anywhere near as photogenic as the rest of Jimmy, it was bound to boost ratings.

When she called Ronny in London to tell her that Jimmy had yet again refused to sign the release form, her boss was furious.

'We need a bloody hero,' she howled. 'Calum Forrester's

accent is too hard to understand and he swears far too much – it'll be all bleep and subtitles. Jimmy Sylvian has it all: looks, sex appeal, glamour. Damn! I suppose we could have another crack at Florian, although God knows he's as bad as Calum.'

'He's about to go to the Continent to get new recipe ideas,' her researcher said excitedly, hoping to be offered some overseas travel.

'May he choke on a bloody mangetout!' Ronny hung up in a huff and marched next door to consult her co-producer, Matty French, who had just come back from filming in the Balkans. Ronny was the tabloid to Matty's broadsheet, and they had worked well together in their two-year partnership. She badly needed his advice on this one. Despite all her Bafta-bragging hype to Odette earlier, she was deeply worried. Matty confirmed her fears.

'The public will demand a storyline,' he told her. 'I've seen the rushes. There's nothing there – just building regulations and moody chefs.'

'I know,' Ronny groaned. 'But the setting's fantastic, isn't it? And you should see Jimmy Sylvian,' she sighed dreamily. 'If *only* we could persuade him to co-operate.'

'Let's not get carried away.' Matty cleared his throat awkwardly. 'I'm not suggesting we impose some sort of Mills & Boon treatment. All we need is an angle. Perhaps I should come down and take a look? If there's really nothing there, we'd be safer to pull the plug on it. We can't risk losing our reputation on this one.'

Ronny, who was very passionate about the project after gaining such a coup, was loath to let it go. She stared out of the office window at the London traffic grinding sluggishly through the rain. The place had started to depress her after spending so much time in Fermoncieaux's leafy park. She disliked Calum intensely, and was looking forward to cutting him down to size in an edit suite later, but there was no doubting his business genius. He was a clever man to predict the current city-fatigue sweeping the capital. Everyone, it seemed, wanted to get out. Odette Fielding was lucky to be working out of town. If only Ronny knew where.

'There is something – or rather someone.' She scrunched up her face. 'But I'm not sure if we could persuade her to co-operate.'

Matty's eyebrow shot up hopefully.

Tapping her pen against her teeth, Ronny pulled out the press cuttings about Calum Forrester. There were three thick files full. For a man who said he had no interest in self-publicity, he certainly attracted an awful lot of media coverage.

Finding the relevant editorials, she passed them over. Matty read in silence, rubbing his mouth as he did so, forehead creased. 'This is the woman who tipped you off about Food Hall?'

Ronny nodded, watching his excited expression. This series doesn't need a hero, she realised. How hopelessly old-fashioned of her to presume that it did. It needed a heroine – a ballsy, go-getting heroine intent on revenge.

'Can we talk to her?' Matty was clearly thinking the same thing. 'Get her in here for a meeting?'

'There's just one slight problem.' Ronny grimaced, cursing herself. 'I don't know how to get hold of her.'

Matty nodded, looking at the cuttings again. 'She'll turn up.'

'How can you be so sure?'

'Calum Forrester did this to her for a reason.' He tapped the pages in front of him. 'And I don't think it was about money. Some killers can't resist going back to check on their victims – particularly in crimes of passion – and I bet you he's one of them. He'll lead us to her eventually. Even better, he's already signed the consent forms.'

Odette was wearing a boiler suit that she had found in the lobby and was peering ignorantly at a thin drizzle of oil seeping from the bottom of the race-prepared 1930s Bentley when she heard a car crunching over the gravel behind her.

She eased herself out from beneath the Bentley and tipped her head up to look. A familiar-looking black jeep was purring throatily towards the garages, its blackened windows revealing nothing except a dusty reflection of the buildings in front of it.

It was another acid-bright late-winter's day with the sun low in the sky, slicing like Darth Vader's light sabre between the garages. It bounced blindingly from the shiny chrome grille on the car.

Odette wiped her oily hands on her boiler suit and sat up, regarding the number plate with alarm. When the engine was cut with an angry splutter, the radio continued blaring. No one got out.

If Florian wanted to sit in the car listening to the last five minutes of Nicky Campbell then it was up to him, Odette decided angrily. But when Calum stepped from the passenger door, and not Florian from the driver's, she felt as though she'd just swallowed a spanner and it was tightening the bolts of her heart.

She hadn't seen him since the early hours of New Year's Day. He hadn't appeared in court, represented there only by his cool, efficient brief. She'd struggled ever since to think of him as a monster, a craven, money-grabbing demon. But in the flesh he was just as desirable as he'd ever been to her, his serene, chiselled face with its unexpectedly babyish eyes, his heel-scuffing walk and hanging head, his daft hat and scruffy clothes. She loved them all.

Vainly, she whipped off her glasses and tucked them into her boiler-suit pocket before he could spot her. When he did, he crossed the courtyard. She couldn't see him too clearly, but she could almost swear he was smiling at her with what seemed to be genuine delight.

'No way – it *is* you!' He tried not to look too appalled by her oil-rag appearance. 'When Jimmy said you might be staying here, I couldnae believe it.'

The friendly approach was so unexpected that Odette blinked, as though she'd expected him to kick sawdust in her eyes only for it to turn into a mist of Optrex.

She found she couldn't say anything. Just breathing was hard enough.

Calum was still standing in front of her, his yellow-tinted glasses at a curiously nerdy angle. Perhaps he isn't so sexually desirable after all, Odette thought wonderingly, although he only had to scratch under his pork-pie hat for her to feel an involuntary shudder of longing. Bastard.

'I've been trying to get hold of you for ages.' He took a couple of paces forwards.

'What for?' Odette found her voice and snorted as cynically as she could manage, still adopting her sulky mechanic's pose. It suited her mood. 'I haven't got any money, if that's what you're after.'

'No – no. I'm no' after money, sister.' He stepped into the garage so that his face was suddenly in shadow. 'What on earth are you doing here?'

'Working,' she muttered, as if it wasn't obvious. 'What are you?'

'*Net*-working.' He rolled the first syllable with some pleasure.

She nodded thoughtfully, taking the blow on the chin. She might have guessed. He hadn't come to see her after all.

'Cyd is in the third barn on your left as you head towards the orchard,' she told him flatly. 'But if you want her to be some sort of piano-bar turn at Fermoncieaux then I wouldn't hold out much hope.' It was as rude as she could bring herself to be. How could she tell him to get lost when she wanted to wrap her oil-stained arms around his khaki ankles and plead with him to love her?

Calum took the tinted glasses from his nose and polished them with the hem of his shiny football shirt. From this low angle, Odette could see his hollow belly with its scattering of moles, a few light blond hairs and an 'outy' belly button like a child's. She felt her own outsized stomach fold over with fat, greedy lust.

'I'm not here to see Cyd, Odette – I'm here to see you,' he said calmly. 'I wanted to know how you're doing?'

'Well, I think you're pretty well aware of my situation, Calum,' she said tightly, angry at herself for feeling so weak with passion.

'I've been thinking about you for a while now.' He screwed up one pale grey eye as he regarded the dusty rafters of the garage. 'In terms of Fermoncieaux Hall – *Food* Hall,' he corrected himself. 'Whether there's a role you could play.'

Odette was too surprised to react. She simply stared at him in wonder.

'I want to make things up to you,' he said with total conviction. 'To make amends. I should have brought you on board from the start. The OD was a very cleverly conceived idea, but it came unstuck shortly after conception. The way it ended was unfortunate.'

'Unfortunate for me,' she snapped, grateful for a surge of self-protective venom at last. She picked up a monkey wrench and examined it thoughtfully. 'You took me to the cleaner's and came away without a stain on your law suit. You didn't give a tossed salad about me, Calum. Admit it, you did it for your own reasons. I just wonder what exactly they were? Had you figured out you could make a killing by taking on someone so trusting then bleeding them bleedin' dry? Did you just get bored? Or was it because of Lydia?' Her voice dropped an octave.

Calum was sucking in air through his teeth anxiously.

'Let's leave Lydia aside, shall we?' he muttered. 'I'm here to offer you a job.'

'Say again, babes?' Odette dropped the wrench with a loud clatter. She gaped up at him.

'At Fermoncieaux. I feel bad about what's happened between us. I never doubted your talents, but now I realise you should have a more clearly defined role.'

'Oh, yes?' Odette could barely believe his gall, her ears, or her luck. 'Doing what exactly? *Plongeur*? Runner? Overnight cleaner?'

'Press liaison,' he muttered.

Odette knew that she was blinking more than Sue-Ellen in a particularly hammy scene with J.R., but she couldn't stop herself. Her eyelashes batted like demented butterfly wings. 'The man who arranged more bad press coverage for the OD than a rusty steam iron is asking *me* to do his PR?'

'Not PR – Alex is in charge of that.' Calum was undeterred by her sarcasm. 'I have a documentary team filming the development of Food Hall. I need someone who understands commercial television to keep them in check, someone who knows how best to use them.'

'Call Jeremy Beadle.' Odette felt a brief frisson of victory as she squatted back down by the Bentley and groped around underneath, pretending to know what she was doing.

'Think about it at least.' He dipped down to her level and peered at her earnestly from under the rim of his hat. 'C'mon, sister.' He cocked his head, voice purring. 'You're no' cut out to be a mechanic for the rest of your life.'

'I'm not interested, Calum.' Odette picked up the wrench again and he backed off. 'Let's leave it at that, shall we?'

'No, let's not.' He pulled out a devastating smile – the sort to melt ice creams, hearts and resolves. 'At the very least can I buy you dinner?'

Odette was tempted to crown him with her monkey wrench, although she suspected that his pork-pie hat was steel-lined given the number of enemies he must attract.

'You've got to be pulling my leg?'

'No, I'm pulling you,' he said calmly. 'Something I should have done months ago. Seeing as I believe in mixing business with pleasure at all times, I was planning on eating at Le Château de Nocturne on Friday night. Will you join me?'

Odette was about to tell him to shove his Nocturne – one of the classiest restaurants out of London – where the moon don't shine when a smoky voice gurgled, 'Odette! You lucky, lucky thing. I haven't been there since Jobe and I celebrated our tenth wedding anniversary. It's so hard to book. Haven't we met somewhere?'

Calum swung around to see Cyd Francis framed in sunshine, her blonde mane a spun-silk halo of light, huge tragic eyes beaming with warmth and affection.

Regarding her boss grumpily, Odette realised that Cyd was radiating so much look-at-me presence and sad serenity it was like being visited by a vision of the Madonna in an Italian cathedral. At least Calum, who was a Protestant, seemed to be taking more interest in her dog. The dizzy, ravishing blonde at Cyd's heels let out a series of husky barks.

'Nice-looking collie.' He ruffled Bazouki's mane, which was

glossy from her once-a-week detangling session courtesy of the local pooch parlour. Her coat was normally full of burrs, fern and carpet fluff. Straightening up, he looked at Odette once more. 'You know where I mean, then?'

'Darling, you must dress up for *Le Nocturne*.' Cyd pronounced it with theatrical emphasis. 'You can't wear one of your track suits there.'

'I'm not going,' she muttered. 'It's Elsa's wedding the next day.'

'Nonsense.' Cyd's syrupy purr was soft and light, but her eyes bored into Odette's. 'I'm sure your friend will get you back in plenty of time. We *have* met,' she told Calum decisively. 'I know we have. You're not one of Rod's boys, are you?'

He shook his head, totally awe-struck by the devastating blonde. Close to, she was luminous. 'We were briefly introduced at the OD opening, I think. Calum Forrester.' He offered an outstretched hand.

Cyd might have had far too many whiskies to drive on that rare night out in London but she certainly remembered the diminutive, scruffy and inexplicably charismatic blond Scot. And she may have had far too many whiskies over the past few nights to remember to ask Odette much about her love life, but she was well aware Elsa had told her that her friend was hopelessly in love with this man.

She looked at Odette with sad sympathy, hoping that her lessons had not fallen on deaf ears, that they were being heard and understood. Odette was a difficult pupil – talented but undisciplined and withdrawn, a problem child. The homework was left undone, the revision ignored, and yet the exam date was already set.

Cyd decided to take control. 'Odette dearheart, I need you to take me to Chuckfield in five minutes. Could you change out of that greasy boiler suit? I want to take the Lamborghini and the upholstery is a bugger to clean.'

Odette was clearly livid at being spoken to like a skivvy, but she said nothing. Standing up and brushing her oily hands on the seat of her boiler suit, she marched away without a word of farewell to Calum.

'See you Friday,' he said hopefully as she retreated towards the mill, although he was finding it hard to take his eyes from Cyd.

'When is your table booked?' She asked him.

'Nine.'

'Pick Odette up at seven, that way you can have a drink here.'

As Cyd floated away, Calum climbed distractedly into the Jeep, eyes smarting as a plume of Disque Bleu smoke hit him in the face.

'She deedn't see me in 'ere, huh?' Florian peered out of the windscreen anxiously.

'No, Odette didn't notice you, brother.'

'Good.' Florian shuddered, starting up the engine. 'Now we must get back to London. I haff to cook at L'Orbital. At least I haff one restaurant left.' He was still livid with Calum for selling the OD – or the Station as it was now called – from under his nose, although he had forgiven him a little now that Calum had chosen him above Wayne Street to oversee the Food Hall kitchens. There had been talk of the two chefs working together, but Florian thought there was more chance of him starting to like vegetarians than Wayne the cheeky-chappy celebrity chef.

'I don't know why you're so frightened of Odette,' Calum laughed as they sped towards the M23. 'She's just a little girl.'

'You no haff sound on that tape of yours, brozzer.' Florian flared his nostrils. 'She was the most demanding fuck I ever had.'

Calum thought about the footage from the digital camera. He was suddenly looking forward to getting back to London. Tonight he planned to spend some time in his old stomping ground, the Nero, to meet up with a couple of investors who were getting itchy feet and then return home and watch it. He had watched it rather a lot lately, freeze-framing different sections and staring at the screen in fascination, torn between lust, jealousy and bitter remorse.

36

That night, after dishing up a particularly revolting ready-made shepherd's pie that had caramelised to the texture of a running shoe, Cyd told Odette that she thought Calum had a marvellous aura.

'He's a twisted sadist,' Odette protested, giving up on the pie after two forkfuls and munching her way through a Lindt Noisette bar to take the taste away. 'He's the reason I'm here in the first place.'

'All the more reason to accept his dinner invitation.' Cyd was unmoved. 'After all, you love it here. He's done you a favour. Without Calum you and I wouldn't be chums, would we dearheart?'

Odette marvelled at her egotism. She was living in a damp shack, had very little time off, had to act as a therapist every evening, was constantly being nipped by dogs *and* she hadn't been paid. In fact, working for Calum was a tempting prospect by comparison.

'Bearing grudges is very negative energy, dearheart,' Cyd started on one of her hippy-trip lectures. 'Elsa may have tried to talk you into revenge, but it really isn't the answer. Far better to strive to understand. Calum is obviously riddled with guilt.'

'He didn't seem very riddled to me,' she huffed, starting on a box of Suchard soft centres. 'Just bleedin' cheeky. I can't believe he came here out of the blue like that expecting me to be grateful when he offered me a job.'

'He offered you a job?' Cyd looked absolutely horrified. 'Bastard!'

'Which is bleedin' crazy.' Odette couldn't help but laugh,

knowing that the moment Calum realised she was the one who had tipped off Ronny Prior, he'd lose his warm front faster than Ian McCaskill dropping his auto-prompter. 'I think he's lost his edge. I mean, what could be more foolish than asking the person he's bankrupted to be his press secretary?'

'Leaving her out in the cold.' Cyd adopted a wise owl look, deciding to forgive him the job offer as Odette had clearly declined. She was in magnanimous mood. 'Despite everything he's done, all the hurt and misery he's caused, all the changes he's wrought in your life, you still love him. That shows some strength of feeling, some loyalty. No wonder he's showing interest at last.'

Odette shook her head. 'He's obsessed with Lydia.'

'Still?' Cyd scratched her head, remembering the conversation she had overheard at Elsa's hen party. 'Oh, dear. I guessed as much on the night you had your feet of fire.'

'Yeah.' Odette laughed bitterly. 'I was certainly walking on hot coals there.'

'Extraordinary.' Cyd clapped her hands together and pressed her forefinger to her wide sensual lips as she thought about it all. 'I'm going to read your cards again. I wasn't going to do it so soon – I promised myself I'd wait until you'd settled here a little more – but I think maybe we need guidance on this one.'

'Whatever they say, I won't go to dinner with him on Friday night,' Odette grumbled, uncomfortable with anything occult.

She watched Cyd with a sceptical eye as she spread a silk cloth out on the kitchen table, lit a lilac candle and shuffled the cards with intense concentration, pausing only briefly to pour herself a glass of wine and apologise that some of the cards were a bit shredded-looking. 'The puppies got hold of the minor arcana a few weeks ago. They were trying their new teeth out – really I must find them homes soon. Are you sure you wouldn't like one?'

Odette shook her head. The thought had crossed her mind that taking on one of Bazouki's unruly offspring might provide a hot water bottle during cold nights in the mill, but it wasn't enough of an incentive to agree. She really didn't like dogs.

'There.' Cyd spread her cards out in a fanned crescent

and sat back in her chair. 'I think we'll do the lesser known Crowley Converse Cross configuration. Chose twelve, will you?'

Odette pulled the cards out at random, her thoughts still occupied by puppies and warmth rather than Calum.

'Ah!' Cyd turned the first over. 'The tower. That must be Fermoncieaux.'

'Looks more like the windmill to me.' Odette looked at the tall thin building which appeared to be falling apart with flames shooting out of the top and people throwing themselves over the side. 'I'm sure those electrics are going to blow up at any moment.'

'Drat! I meant to call someone in to look at the wiring,' Cyd muttered. 'Why didn't you remind me?'

Odette rolled her eyes. She must have reminded her every day that week.

'Anyway, this tower is much more likely to be Fermoncieaux, given that the reading is about Calum.' Cyd tapped it briskly, preferring her own interpretation. 'And it is crossed with,' she flipped over another card, 'the Hanged Man. Oh, dear.'

Despite her cynicism, Odette felt the hairs on the back of her neck stand up.

As Cyd revealed more cards and tried to make the reading sound positive, Odette looked at their faces and realised it was far from that. The cards were universally dreadful – there was the Devil in her past, the Fool in her future.

'It doesn't mean you are necessarily going to be made a fool of,' Cyd told her brightly, 'it means a fresh start, a new phase or relationship.'

Odette raised one eyebrow disbelievingly as the next card turned out to be a dog-chewed one depicting a large red heart pierced by two swords.

'That's not as bad as it looks.' Cyd coughed awkwardly. 'It's really very good . . . yes . . . very good. You have to embrace the twinned swords of passive power lying in your heart, harness your pain . . .'

Odette stopped listening and decided that it actually meant she definitely shouldn't accept Calum's ridiculous job offer. By assisting the documentary team, she could be knifing him in the back twice.

'Ah, that's better.' Cyd was nearing the end of the reading. 'The High Priestess – the eternal virgin. This is a wise adviser, someone who has their eye on the situation and offers guidance, succour and spiritual nurture. She will make sure that no great ill comes to you. I think that's me, don't you?'

Looking at the card, Odette had another explanation. It was herself – the eternal virgin who couldn't cope with twenty-first century sex. The woman sitting on a high tower, monitoring the activity below. She was dark and sultry with pale, pale eyes. The High Priestess was Odette, not Cyd. She was being given an opportunity to oversee things, to keep the documentary team in check, to temper her own revenge plan. Calum's offer was in fact one of unwitting genius.

'And she is being assisted by . . .' Cyd peered at a very dog-chewed card which was so tattered it was hard to see the picture '. . . the Knight of Disks. A very earthy man who has worked hard for status, someone who holds the purse strings. He can be a little ruthless at times, but he also represents security and power. He might seem to leave you stranded and helpless, but then he rushes in at the last minute to save the day. The classic hero.'

'Jonathan,' Odette breathed, suddenly deciding she could get into tarot. Yes, it made a lot of sense. Was, in fact, extraordinary. If she only had the money, she would have rushed out to buy her own pack first thing tomorrow.

'Who's Jonathan?' Cyd looked confused. 'No, I think this is Calum.'

'I agree.' Odette nodded fervently. Her very own Jonathan Hart, the powerful hero who always rushed in to save passionate, headstrong Jennifer at the last minute. Then later they would share a joke in bed while Max prepared breakfast downstairs, occasionally muttering, 'Get off the couch, Freeway.'

'So this is me,' Cyd pointed to the Priestess, 'and this is Calum,' she tapped the dog-chewed square beside it. 'And the next card represents the bond that unites us in your life.' She flipped over another card. Its corner had been chewed off, but it was unmistakably two naked figures entwined together. The Lovers.

'Ah – the Lovers.' Cyd reluctantly placed it so that it overlapped her and Calum. 'That again is not what it seems at face value. It means friendship and trust, not sex. No, not sex.' She cleared her throat. 'I suspect Calum and I will become confidantes in our quest to make you happy . . .'

Odette wasn't listening to Cyd's desperate attempts to hide the fact that the cards clearly indicated the Priestess and the Knight were going to have a shag. She was rather hoping it meant they were. For she was convinced that she, not Cyd, was the High Priestess. And that meant she and Calum – her Jonathan, her Knight of Disks – were destined to be together.

Cyd was hastily continuing with the reading, flipping over the final three cards – Odette's ultimate destiny – and making positive exclamations, even though they looked pretty dismal from where Odette was sitting. The Hermit, which spoke for itself; the Moon – which apparently represented lunacy; and finally Death.

'So I'm going to become a mad recluse and kill myself?' Odette said in a frozen voice. She'd already achieved two out of the three.

'Not at all.' Cyd was incredibly good at making the worst cards sound like the best. 'This is wonderful. You are obviously very, very spiritual at the moment. You must spend time alone to reflect upon this, to take guidance, and then you will be able to start a whole new exciting phase of your life, emerge from your chrysalis. Death means to be born again.'

'But first you have to die, surely?' She made a silent vow never to go back to the fuse cupboard in the mill. The Grim Reaper and the burning Tower were far too closely juxtaposed on Cyd's kitchen table for her liking.

'Exactly!' Cyd enthused, thinking that Odette had started to understand at last. 'You have to let a part of your life go – whether it be a home, a job, a love.'

Odette had already managed two out of the three. That good old Meatloaf song kept coming back to haunt her.

'So what is it telling me about Friday night?' Odette looked at the Lovers overlapping herself and Calum. Perhaps she would go after all. Yes, she would. She and Calum would become lovers at last. The duel was over, the challenge won. She had endured her time in the wilderness and earned his love. 'It seems to indicate I should agree after all, doesn't it?'

'No, no – quite the opposite,' Cyd said firmly, shaking her head. 'I was wrong trying to make you. I knew the cards would hold the answer.' She looked from them to Odette, charcoal eyes sparkling with fervour. 'They are telling quite a different story. This is so amazing, dearheart. You see, they say that I should go in your place!'

Odette stewed this over in her chilly tower bedroom later, hugging a lukewarm hot water bottle. She was certain that Cyd, for all her so-called spirituality, was just a manipulative old crow who knew an opportunity when she saw one. She used the tarot for her own personal profit when conducting her Internet predictions after all, refusing even to shuffle until she'd authorised the Visa card of the questioner. And this time she'd used the cards to get herself a free meal at her favourite restaurant. Odette was livid. She decided she would go after all. She had just two days to prepare herself for it. With no money and no decent clothes left, she would have to use her initiative. She didn't like to ask Cyd for any wages given the fact they'd just had a blazing row about who was going out to dinner with Calum.

'He asked *me*!'

'You said you didn't want to go.'

'But I do now.'

Odette was unpleasantly aware that they must have sounded like mother and teenage daughter arguing.

'You mustn't, mustn't go,' Cyd had insisted darkly, eyes wide and threatening. 'Look at the cards, darling. You have to stay in and heal yourself. You cannot risk damaging your fragile, broken heart. The cards clearly tell you to be hermetic, to regenerate, to shun the world. It might be a long process. You have to resist the temptation to venture out too soon.'

Odette had narrowed her eyes suspiciously and decided to test the strength of Cyd's conviction. 'So you're suggesting I shouldn't go to Elsa and Euan's wedding either?'

'No, you must go to that!' Cyd bleated, aware that to suggest that would be to deny herself a lift to her own daughter's wedding. 'This reading is only about Friday night.'

'So I'll be healed by Saturday morning then?'

'Yes.' Cyd had waved her arms around airily. 'The cards are very accurate.'

'You should ask them for betting tips then.' Odette narrowed her eyes.

'They told you about your feet of fire, didn't they?' Cyd defended her magical pack hotly.

Odette was fed up. Cyd had done nothing but manipulate and bully her since she'd arrived. She remembered Elsa warning that she never quite knew who was the child and who the mother in their relationship. Odette had hoped for a surrogate mother, for loving support and security, instead of which she'd found herself looking after an unpredictable, stubborn teenager. Yet she deeply regretted the way she had stormed out of the farmhouse; it was ungrateful and dangerous, given the fragility of her current position. Her parting shot had been shamefully cheap.

'If they're that bleedin' accurate, d'you think they can tell me when I stand a chance of getting paid?' she'd snarled before retreating to her smock mill tower, which far from burning like the one depicted on the card, was colder and damper than ever. And her feet of fire were now like two blocks of ice.

37

To Odette's amazement, she received her first pay-packet the following morning – or rather Cyd left twenty pounds under a stone outside the mill's door with a note that read, 'Have got computer man coming this afternoon. Take some time off to get haircut for wedding. Curl Up and Dye in Chuckfield v. good, I hear.'

The money had clearly been delivered the night before as it was crisp with frost and had a dried-up bird dropping on the queen's head. Cyd must have stolen out after their argument. It was clearly supposed to be an apologetic gesture, but Odette thought she deserved a slightly higher remittance for a fortnight's hard work. And the insinuation that her hair needed cutting irritated her.

She hadn't paid much attention to it lately, apart from hoping that her short, slick pre-bankruptcy Vidal Sassoon cut would grow out into something vaguely Anna Ford – understated and sophisticated. It had started out rather well – entering a Natalie Imbruglia phase around her court case and then lengthening to a tousled Chrissy Hynde look around the time of the hen party. Since then, she'd pretty much ignored it apart from making sure she kept it clean and off her face. Regarding herself in the rusting mirror above the basin, she pulled off her headband and yelped in horror. Her hair almost reached to her shoulders in ragged layers. Days of washing it in cold water had left it full of shampoo, which had crystallised at the roots like dandruff.

Later, Odette eyed the price-list in the salon window. She realised that if she skipped the tint and went for a junior stylist, then she'd have enough left over to buy a charity shop dress to wear to both dinner and the wedding, provided she scoured the bargain rails and ripped off a button or two before taking them to the counter and asking for a discount.

She was just flipping dispiritedly through the racks of clothes in the Cancer Relief shop and deciding she should drive to Brighton when the door pinged open.

Looking up she saw Jimmy Sylvian stooping to enter under a low beam – huge, unexpected and smiling broadly at the assistant. Odette ducked hastily behind the rail, pretending to examine the cuffs on a nylon shirt with a pussy cat bow.

'Mr Sylvian,' the elderly assistant clucked. 'Didn't think I'd see you again so soon, but I'm glad you popped in. Lady Fulbrook brought in a couple of her husband's old moleskin shirts. There's plenty of wear in them – I've been keeping them aside for you.'

'Thanks, Marge, that's really sweet of you.' Jimmy was looking around the apparently empty shop. 'I thought I saw a friend come in here?'

Marge winked and nodded towards a rack in the corner, whispering. 'Behind ladies' separates.'

Winking in return, Jimmy wandered over to the rack and gave it an almighty spin.

'Ow!' Odette sprang up, covering her eye which had just made contact with a fast-moving fake Chanel button.

'Thought it was you.' Jimmy grinned. 'Got time for lunch?'

'No.' She wasn't about to blue half her wages on a Ploughman's. 'I'm having my hair cut.'

'Looks fine to me.' He smiled.

Odette gaped at him in disbelief. Was he mad? It looked absolutely revolting.

'Special occasion?' Jimmy started picking up the clothes which had flown from their hangers. 'This is nice, you should try it on.' He held up a glittery batwing top which looked as though it dated back to the days of Abba.

'I was just browsing around for something to do until my hair appointment.' Odette cleared her throat. 'I wouldn't actually buy anything to wear here.'

'Why not?' He looked baffled, threading the sleeves back on to a hanger. 'I get almost all my clothes from charity shops.'

'But you can afford to buy new ones.'

'So what? It's just body-covering, after all. The moment you wash a new shirt, it's effectively second-hand, isn't it? So if it's clean and well made it doesn't matter where you get it. You might as well help out a good cause.'

Bloody environmentalist, Odette thought grimly. Had he no idea of the shame of trawling through charity shops when one had once been on first name terms with the staff of Brown's, had employed the services of a personal shopper at Harvey Nicks, and when one's wardrobe had until recently been full of freshly dry-cleaned Miu Miu and Prada?

'So what's the occasion?' Jimmy persisted, still flipping through the rails.

Odette supposed she might as well be truthful. 'A friend's wedding on Saturday.'

'Hmm.' Jimmy eyed her closely and then shifted the revolving rail around from the size twelve section to the fourteens. Odette felt deeply affronted. He thrust a couple of hangers at her. 'Try these on.'

She baulked. 'I'm not trying anything on.'

'Well, you could just buy them, I suppose.' He regarded his choices worriedly. 'But they might not fit. You're – er – quite an unusual shape after all.'

Odette snatched them from him, determined to prove that she was a perfect size twelve. Marge, whose mouth was puckered with amused delight, waved her into a curtained semi-circular area which faced a very short mirror.

She quickly struggled into the separates Jimmy had selected, praying that they fitted. His choices were as deranged as the bat wing top – there was a short lichen green skirt with a frayed waist, a dung brown top with a long seventies collar, and a very long silver grey velvet jacket with bald cuffs and elbows. She was about to take the revolting ensemble off when Jimmy – who had been sneaking looks over the rail – whipped the curtain back to reveal her to Marge and a worthy local who had chosen that moment to ping in through the door with a stack of crockery.

'Not bad.' Jimmy cocked his head as he held the curtain back. 'What d'you think, Marge?'

'Lovely,' she sighed in that I-was-young-once way pension-ers have. Odette guessed she could have been wearing a sack for all it mattered. Marge would agree with anything Jimmy said, and thought that anyone under fifty looked groovy.

'Very striking,' offered the worthy plate-carrier. 'Not sure about the shirt, though. Looks a bit tight.'

'You're right.' Jimmy beamed her his long-distance smile at such close range she almost dropped her plates in delight. 'I think I spotted just the thing over here.' He marched off to a dusty wire bucket containing, to Odette's horror, a jumble of reinforced, flesh-tint underwear.

The item he carried over to the changing room looked at first sight like a surgical truss. Either that or one of Madonna's stage outfits from her Blonde Ambition tour. Palest pink with a hint of silvery green embroidery, it was an old-fashioned boned corset with huge pointy hollows to house an ample bosom.

'Hilary Dickens brought that in three weeks ago,' Marge giggled as she recognised what it was. 'Her husband bought it her for Christmas. There were some matching knickers – the sort with the string – but Debbie from Curl Up and Dye bought those. She said it was for the dusters drawer but Lord knows what you could dust with them.'

'Very small ornaments?' Jimmy suggested with a straight face as he handed Odette the corset.

'Maybe.' Marge thought about it. 'I have a Spanish flamenco dancer with a very awkward crevice.'

'I'm not wearing this!' Odette blustered. 'It's indecent. And it looks far too big.'

'It almost fell off Debbie,' Marge agreed. 'She did try it on, but the poor duck's as flat as a tombstone. It looked like a loo roll on a holder. You're better suited.' She nodded at Odette's chest.

'Telling me.' Jimmy was admiring it too.

Odette realised that almost all of the buttons on the seventies brown shirt had come undone to reveal a sexy blue bra. It was supposed to be only for best, but the spa bath had chewed up all her others before it blew up. She pulled the shirt together and whisked the curtain shut.

Listening to Marge thanking the plate woman and discussing the forthcoming village pancake-tossing match, Odette examined the corset. It had old-fashioned strings at the back, but the front was a hook and eye arrangement. There was no way she was adding to Jimmy's perverted titillation by trying it on. Then she spotted the label and gasped. It was La Perla, her favourite, exquisitely well made, appallingly expensive. She fingered it with new-found reverence although she was certain it wouldn't fit. Perhaps she could just try it on over her bra, though? She hadn't felt quality workmanship against her skin for such a long time.

Over the top of the curtain, Jimmy's eyes widened in lusty delight as he took in Odette's extraordinary proportions and her jazzy taste in underwear.

The corset felt like absolute bliss, but it was, as she'd thought, completely the wrong size. Her blue lace boobs spilled over the top, her belly splayed out of the bottom, and the middle was far too loose. It made her look revolting – her unfit body oozing out in all the wrong places. She looked at her reflection sadly, squinting because she was far too vain to put her glasses back on. She knew she'd let herself go big time. It would take years on a treadmill to get her old shape back. Even her bottom was letting her down.

A moment later all the air was knocked out of her lungs as something which felt like a frantic Heimlich manoeuvre threatened to snap her bottom two ribs and squeeze her intestines into a funnel shape.

'Breathe in,' Jimmy ordered as he yanked the strings from behind. 'Almost there.'

'Are . . . you . . . trying . . . to . . . kill . . . me?' Odette panted as her lungs were compressed into two tiny air pockets the size of piping bags and her vision closed in darkly.

'Sorry.' Jimmy threaded his fingers under the laces and loosened the top, pulling the waist in to account for the slack.

Able to breathe again, the tunnel of blackness vanishing, Odette looked at the surreal figure facing her in the mirror opposite and blinked a couple of times. Only the fact that the pale blue eyes opposite hers moved simultaneously convinced her she was still regarding her own reflection. She had a tiny waist and a flat stomach. Curved in all the right places, tiny in others, as feminine as Chantilly lace, duchess silk and angora wool. Her muscled, exercised, strenuously maintained body had never looked like this. This was glorious.

Jimmy was looking very pink. Odette supposed that tugging at the laces must have been quite some physical effort. He seemed to be so puffed out that he couldn't speak.

Marge and the plate woman were also glazing at her in silent amazement, along with a strange little character of indeterminate sex, wearing a long greatcoat and a fluffy hat who must have pinged in during her near black-out and was lurking by the paperback books section.

'Try the jacket on with it,' Jimmy managed to mutter in a hoarse voice.

Odette shrugged her way back into the tin foil sandwich board. Yet matched with the corset, it no longer looked so big-shouldered and butch. It looked sensationally sexy, picking up the pale tone of her eyes, adding a warmth to her normally blanched skin. The green skirt – although still far too short in Odette's eyes – contrasted absurdly well with the rest of the outfit.

Something was scratching under her armpit. She reached for it and pulled out a price tag.

'Do you like it?' Jimmy was asking proudly.

Odette winced as she realised that the corset alone was five pounds more than she had. The skirt was only three pounds and the jacket fifteen, but the corset – which she wanted so badly – was beyond her means. She couldn't even afford to buy clothes in charity shops these days. The realisation made her throat constrict with bitter self-loathing.

'I'm not sure it's me . . .' she started to make excuses, far too ashamed to admit she couldn't afford the outfit.

'It's wonderful!' The plate woman slapped her hand down on her stack on the counter and cracked at least three like an amateur karate chopper. 'Your boyfriend is a very clever chap. I'd never have thought old Hilly Dickens' smalls could look so smart. Is that jacket from the Christmas panto, Marge?'

'No, I think it belonged to Tristan from the antiques

shop.' Marge squinted at it over her bifocals. 'It's been here years.'

Odette was feeling more and more cornered, and increasingly desperate to own the La Perla corset which she couldn't afford.

'You should try it without the bra,' warbled the androgynous figure in the great coat, leaving Odette none the wiser as to its sex.

'Don't be such an old pervert, Rolly,' the plate woman snapped.

'Rolanda Sherington.' An emaciated, heavily ringed hand shot out of a huge sleeve and offered itself somewhere between Odette and Jimmy, to whom was uncertain. 'Commonly known as Lady Fulbrook. That my husband's shirt you're wearing?' A cataract-misted green eye regarded Jimmy's tatty Tattersall.

'Might be.' He took her hand and pumped it in his own which was about three times the size.

'Looks far better on you,' the warbling voice chuckled. 'And that,' she nodded an approving furry bearskin in the direction of Odette's corset, 'looks quite delicious. You the young couple that have just moved into Siddals Farm? Heard you were a looker.' She tapped Jimmy's sleeve with a long finger.

'I live there, but . . .'

'Must both come round for a drink sometime,' she barked. 'We're just the other side of Fulkington Lane. The Manor House. Can't miss it. Do you shoot?'

'Only big game,' Odette muttered, ignoring Jimmy's dirty look.

'Oh, good – my husband's big and very game,' she chuckled, tapping her hand on Marge's counter with such force that the broken china rattled tunefully. 'No new Dick Francis's then?'

Marge shook her head apologetically.

'Never mind – I'll just read an old one again. Pop in for that drink,' she called over her shoulder and strode outside, coat tails flapping.

Jimmy turned back to Odette in delighted amusement, but she'd whipped the curtains shut. A moment later she re-emerged, once again dressed in her muddy tracksuit bottoms, sports top and leather jacket.

'I don't think it's really me.' She handed him the pile of clothes. 'Thanks for trying – I'll see what Dorothy Perkins in Brighton has.'

She raced outside before he had a chance to argue and ran around the corner to Curl Up and Dye, which reeked of perming solution and was full of little old ladies having their blue-rinses resprayed with super-strong Elesse.

Debbie the senior stylist – who was indeed built like a tomb-stone with huge teeth to match – positively quivered with excitement at the prospect of a client under the age of sixty.

'Don't say a thing!' She held up her hand with rapturous certainty that she was about to change Odette's life. 'I see short at the sides, long on top. I see root lift, I see burgundy tint, I see lots of product to create an avant-garde shape.'

Odette could see stars and backed out of the door.

Debbie chased her. 'I'll do it for free! You can be a model.'

It was the first time anyone had told her she could be a model – even a hairdresser's one – and she had never anticipated running away so fast. She lurked on the bench in the village car park for a few minutes to give Jimmy time to leave the area and then sloped back to the charity shop.

'Hello, duck.' Marge looked up from the *Daily Mail* quick crossword when she pinged in. 'Looking for that nice young man of yours? I'm afraid he's just left.'

'No – I mean, I'll catch him up later,' Odette lied. 'I was wondering. I know it's a bit cheeky given that you're a charity, but could I buy the corset for twenty quid? It's all I've got.' She pulled the tattered and precious note from her jacket pocket.

Marge tutted fondly. 'Already settled. He bought the lot – and those moleskin shirts. Told me you'd change your mind and be back. Seems he was right.'

Pinging out of the shop again, Odette was so enraged by her hopeless destitution that she spent ten pounds on lottery tickets for Saturday's draw, the remainder on toothpaste and much-needed Tampax.

38

'Oh, God, I have *nothing* to wear!'

Odette wanted to go out with Calum on Friday night, but for the first time in her life she could genuinely plead she had nothing suitable to don to a posh restaurant. What was worse, she had grown fat without noticing. Yes, she knew she'd put on a little weight, developed some curves which looked great in a La Perla corset, less so in leggings and a t-shirt, but she hadn't realised she had grown *fat*. Huge fat, obese fat, zips-that-had-once-glided-along-her-hip-now-inches-from-doing-up fat. In just a few weeks she had ballooned.

Her carefully preserved black interview suit, which had been hanging in its plastic chrysalis for weeks, no longer fitted. The faithful, stand-by, flattering, reliable Jigsaw suit she adored. The only suit she hadn't sold. Her stand-by suits-all-occasions suit. It wasn't just a bit tight, oh, no – Odette could have coped with that; she'd yoyoed enough over the years to live with the shame of a safety pin in place of a button, a discreetly draped pashmina to hide the fact her jacket wouldn't do up.

On Thursday afternoon while Cyd was busy reading tarot cards live on the Internet she'd tried it on and, to her absolute horror, found the skirt wouldn't even go up over her hips and the jacket was two whole inches away from buttoning.

Abandoning the suit, she looked around the mill in despair.

The pale blue velvet Ghost dress which she'd been planning to resurrect for the following day's wedding was hanging from a nail in one of the rafters. She'd hoped that the creases would drop out, but it was still covered with ugly streaks, the pile irreversibly tattered by a combination of sweat and snow on Saskia's wedding day. Odette must have sponged the hem a dozen times, but the dirty brown stains from her bare-footed walk through the lanes would not fade. She couldn't afford to have it dry-cleaned.

She searched through two suitcases of clothes she hadn't bothered to unpack. There was no hanging space in the smock mill and she'd hardly needed a varied wardrobe over the past fortnight. But they held no joy. She'd sold all her good stuff, and all that remained was a seemingly endless supply of cycling shorts, Gap t-shirts, sweatshirts, track suits and, for some reason, tights.

She could hardly ask Cyd if she could borrow something to wear. They'd barely exchanged a word since the row, although on noticing Odette's untouched hair, Cyd had commented tautly that it was the last time she recommended Curl Up and Dye to anyone. She had resorted to issuing orders and then playing such loud music in the car they couldn't talk. The farmhouse door remained locked whether she was in or out, and she tutted for England if Odette didn't jump the moment she was called upon. Earlier that day, Odette had ironically been asked to drive her boss to her favourite salon in Brighton, where 'dear Barry' had massaged her scalp, touched up her roots and given her wild blonde mane about three times its usual volume in readiness for Saturday's wedding.

Odette closed her eyes for a guilty moment, wondering what Elsa would think if she knew that her friend was planning to go on a date with Calum Forrester, the man who had ruined her. But Elsa's thoughts would be far, far away from Odette and her troubles this evening. She was getting married in less than forty-eight hours, after all.

Her pay-as-you-go mobile was down to its last minute of credit, which Odette had been saving for an emergency. Today she decided that wishing Elsa luck constituted an emergency.

She clambered up into the windmill cap – the only place she had discovered where she could get a faint signal – and switched it on, gazing out of the tiny, mildewy window towards Fermoncieaux. Even so far away, she could see the scaffolding and plastic sheeting which made it look like a sixties office block. Tiny white dots clustered at its base were transit vans and workers' cars. If she squinted really hard, she could just about make out minuscule ant-like figures moving about.

As the call rang through, she gazed out at the deer-park and the surrounding farmland, wondering whether Jimmy had filled it with antelopes yet. He seemed more preoccupied with buying underwear from charity shops at the moment.

'Hello,' an unfamiliar male voice answered the phone.

'Mr Bridgehouse?' Odette guessed it was Elsa's father.

'One of them.' He laughed far too jovially to be Elsa's dour father. 'There are four of us here. I'm Nathan. Do you want Pa?'

'No, no – Elsa.' Odette was aware that she didn't have much time left on her phone. 'Could you ask her to hurry?'

'Well, she doesn't move too fast these days, but I'll try. Who shall I say?'

'Odette.'

'Sure thing, Annette.' The phone was put down on a surface with a clunk.

Odette could hear talking in the background – the Zen Den II was obviously the scene of much activity, dominated by male voices arguing about who had asked for how many sugars in their coffee. Then, cutting through them all, Odette heard her friend approaching the phone, grumbling that she didn't know anyone called Annette. 'Honestly, Nathan, I told you I was trying to have a rest. If it's someone trying to flog replacement windows, I'll stand on your Crombie – yes?' She picked up the phone.

'Elsa, babes, it's me.'

'Odie! At last. I've been trying to call all day. Did Mum pass on my message?'

'What message?' Odette winced as the thirty-second warning shrilled in her ear. 'Listen, I haven't much time, but I called to wish you good luck. My bleedin' phone's about to pack up.'

'Thanks, my love,' Elsa laughed. 'Hang on, I can call you back, can't I? Ring off and I'll do it.'

It was such bliss to have a proper chat, even though the signal was so bad that Odette cut her friend off every time she moved her head a fraction of an inch from left to right. Odette still felt as though she was in touch with civilisation for the first time in an age. It sounded chaotic at Elsa's end.

'I had another false alarm yesterday,' she grumbled. 'The contractions were so painful I was convinced Buster was coming out. I feel so huge and tired, but now I'm being spoilt rotten. My whole family's here, plus Ally. Juno's coming round later. I wish you were here too.'

'So do I,' Odette sighed.

'How's everything your end?' Elsa asked. 'I know I'm going to see you on Saturday, but you know what weddings are like – you never get to talk to anyone, especially if you're the bride.'

'You know that from personal experience, babes?' Odette joked, deliberately trying to steer off the subject of life at Smock Mill. She'd managed to skirt the issue before, but things had got so much worse since then.

'You know what I mean,' Elsa puffed indignantly. 'Oh, by the way, I asked Saskia and Stan along to the reception.'

Odette felt a huge pang of guilt as she realised that she'd intended to write to them, along with at least a dozen other friends and former workmates. She was hopeless. Thank heavens she would see so many of them on Saturday. Being a semi-professional wedding guest had its uses.

'I met up with her for lunch last week.' Elsa had been cultivating the friendship for some time. 'She's so lovely, and I knew you'd want to catch up with Stan. You must feel so lonely there in the back of beyond.'

'Oh, I keep busy.' Again she tried to deflect the lead.

'I told you Mum's a slave driver,' Elsa snorted, and then dropped her voice as she realised her brothers might overhear. 'It's such a relief that you two get on so well, to be honest. You will keep a close eye on her, won't you? Look after her?'

Odette didn't have the heart to admit that she and Cyd had fallen out big time.

'I'm sorry I got mad at you for wanting to go and live there,' Elsa continued. 'This week will be really traumatic for Mum, but she seems to love having someone around to spoil. It takes her mind off things. You know she sent me a Nicaraguan birthing charm that Bianca Jagger once gave her? And she said she was treating you to a makeover.'

'Mmm,' Odette answered cautiously, 'she gave me some money for a haircut.'

'Typical Mum,' Elsa giggled, covering the receiver and telling someone to hang on while she was on the phone. 'Listen, I'll have to go – my sister-in-law wants to make a call. I can't wait to see the new haircut. I wasn't going to say anything, but I thought it was looking a bit Marilyn Manson at the hen party.'

Odette climbed down the stepladder from the cap in a glum mood. It was getting dark outside. Through her dirty bedroom window, she could see that the kitchen lights were on in the farmhouse and Cyd was moving about. Odette felt desperately torn. Part of her wanted to scream and shout at her employer for being so difficult, so changeable and childishly selfish. Part of her wanted to run inside and make up.

Then something Elsa had said struck her afresh. Cyd needed taking care of during the wedding. It was a huge ordeal for her. It was probably the first time she would see her sons in over a decade. Odette covered her face in shame. It was no wonder Cyd was so tetchy right now.

'It's Elsa's brothers, isn't it?' Odette said, leaning on the kitchen doorframe two minutes later.

Cyd had been pouring herself a mug of herbal tea. Vile purple liquid spurted all over her Shaker worktops and stone floor as she burst into loud, desperate tears.

'They hate me, dearheart. I so want them to try and understand, to talk to me at least, but they absolutely hate me. I'm so terrified!' She was like a small, frightened child. Odette rushed over to rescue the teapot and steer her to the table to sit down.

It was her longest night yet listening to Cyd's terrible tale of remorse and regret. Tonight was filled with questions she couldn't answer: 'What will they think of me?' 'Will they forgive me?' 'Do you think they still love me?' The old kitchen clock hands were both pointing towards four by the time Odette steered a whisky-fuddled Cyd towards the stairs and retreated back to the mill with her hot-water bottle.

*　　*　　*

Odette collected Cyd's shiatsu masseur, a tiny little Chinese man with rampant BO, from his Brighton flat the following lunchtime and dropped him off at the farmhouse before taking the car on to Waitrose with one of Cyd's indecipherable scribbled lists and two fifty-pound notes. It was only when she had rattled a trolley away from its kissing companions and headed past the fresh flowers that she read what was written on the tattered list:

> One outfit for wedding
> One hat to cover Curl Up and Dye disaster
> One apology.

Odette left the trolley by a display of melons and went back out to the Aston, which was being admired by a pasty trolley-collector in an overall. He looked astounded when the scruffy brunette in the grubby jogging bottoms unlocked the door.

She drove straight to Siddals Farm, fully expecting Jimmy Sylvian to be out. The house certainly looked unoccupied, with drawn curtains and closed windows.

She was just scrabbling around in the walnut glove compartment for a pen to leave a note with the money, asking him if he could drop the corset round at the smock mill when Jimmy burst out of the front door, running so fast he almost fell over the two dogs at his feet. For a moment Odette wondered whether he'd set fire to something inside, but then she realised he was grinning broadly.

'Welcome!' He ground to a halt beside the silver car. 'God, this is wonderful!'

Odette realised he must be talking about the Aston.

'Yes – a sixties DBS.' She wound down the window and eyed his dogs suspiciously. They looked terrifying, snarling and snapping – although their aggression seemed to be directed more at each other than at Odette sitting in her protective steel shell.

'What?' Jimmy was shouting above the racket the dogs were making, although he needn't have bothered. His normal talking voice was so loud he could have been heard over a pack of hounds mid-kill.

'A DBS,' Odette repeated, although she was pretty certain

he'd know that already. In her experience, most men could identify a classic car from its tail lights alone in heavy fog. She flinched as a huge, big-toothed grey face leered in at her through the window, barking furiously.

'Don't mind Nelson.' Jimmy hauled him away by a very new-looking leather collar. 'He's still settling in – only arrived yesterday. He and Winnie were supposed to be companions, but they seem to hate each other. I thought they'd be like Lady and the Tramp – you know the film? But she's the tramp. Come in for a cup of tea – you've caught me at a good time. I've just finished a pile of paperwork.' He was talking incredibly fast, like a kid wanting to tell a favourite relative all their news at once.

Odette looked at her watch. 'I'm on duty,' she said rather pompously. Hanging around to deliver Hui Chan back to Brighton hardly merited a pager and a running engine, but she didn't really want to stay. 'I've just come for those clothes – I've got the money,' She reached for her precious fifty-pound note.

'Well, you'd better come in and collect them then.' Jimmy headed back to the house, the squabbling dogs at his heels. He didn't exactly beg her to change her mind about tea, Odette noticed.

Inside, the farmhouse was wonderfully warm. Still unable to adjust to an English winter after so long in Africa, Jimmy had cranked the central heating up to maximum and kept the curtains closed for greater insulation. Accustomed to the chilly mill, Odette felt her face turn instantly pink.

She made her way through a hall that was littered with walking boots, welly boots, trainers and desert boots all in a huge size – at least a twelve – past a banister end which was so over-hooked with coats that it looked like an overgrown bay tree, and into a kitchen where the two dogs were still snarling and snapping at each other. The big grey one had hooked a thick foreleg over the little curly-haired one's neck and was twisting her around. Odette gasped, realising that it was trying to break her neck. She glanced around for Jimmy, but he'd disappeared.

The little bitch, who looked like one of the famous pair of

china Staffordshire mantel-ends to Odette's untrained eye, let out an agonised squeak and rolled over, while the big, ugly grey bully opened its fearsome mouth and wrapped it around her throat.

'Oh, Jesus!' Odette looked around for something to defend the little mite with. 'Jimmy!' she called out, grabbing a long poker from beside the Rayburn stove.

There was no answer. The little female dog was still not moving, and the big grey monster was standing right over her now, jaws still around her neck, the hair on his spine on end, furious growls emitting from its deep chest.

'Get off her, you big brute.' Odette waggled the poker at him. He took absolutely no notice. His tiny victim let out the faintest of dying whines.

'Pick on someone your own size.' Odette jabbed at him with the poker, prodding him very lightly on the rump and then jumping with fear as he turned to her.

Thankfully he didn't lunge. He simply regarded her with speckled, curious eyes before turning back to wrap his mouth around the damp little white neck that was stretched lifelessly beneath him, the snarling redoubling.

'I said, get off!' Odette howled furiously, prodding harder this time. With an indignant yelp, the grey monster sprang away and scuttled to the far corner of the kitchen, tail between its legs.

'That was so funny!' Jimmy was doubled up in a doorway in the white-panelled wall that led to another set of stairs. In his arms were the charity shop clothes.

'It was not,' Odette huffed. 'If I hadn't been here that – that – bleedin' animal might have killed her.' She pointed at the huge grey greyhound-thing which was cowering in the corner, speckled eyes not leaving her face.

'Nelson is indeed an animal – or rather a lurcher.' Jimmy dropped the clothes on the table and walked over to the grey beast to cup its face in his huge hands. It quivered ecstatically at his touch and the forgiveness it bestowed. 'And he was only teasing Winnie. The trouble is, she can't take it.'

'You're telling me – I couldn't take treatment like that

either!' Odette forgot where she was for a moment, rushing to Winnie's defence.

'She's a tart.' Jimmy shrugged, letting Nelson go and heading to the Rayburn to check the contents of the teapot. 'She leads Nel on and then gets furious when he tries to play rough and tumble. He gets carried away. He can't help himself, poor bugger.'

'He should know when to stop,' Odette muttered indignantly, stooping down to give Winnie a stiff pat.

'He's a dog, Odette.' Jimmy laughed his booming laugh as he fetched milk from the fridge. 'Besides, she can look after herself. She just wants to be the boss, that's all.'

'Too right.' Odette and Winnie exchanged a look of mutual support.

'It's my fault for calling her Winnie.' Jimmy climbed over them with two brimming mugs full of brick red tea and stood at the end of the table. 'They haven't cut much off, have they?'

Odette had no idea what he was talking about.

'Your appointment?' He grinned. 'You left the shop in a tearing hurry on Tuesday saying you were late to have your hair cut.'

Odette straightened up, about to let fly, and then felt a sudden attack of self-doubt whip her anger away. She had a date with Calum tonight. She had to look her best, and even her biggest admirer had noticed she was having a bad hair day. This was bad. Very bad. 'You said it didn't need cutting.'

He shrugged, offering her a mug of tea. 'Perhaps a trim. I'll do it if you like?'

'Lay off!'

She wanted to demand that he hand over the clothes so she could leave, but the sight of a cup of proper tea was making her limp with longing. She grabbed at it greedily and sighed as she slurped the top scalding inch.

'Ah – bliss,' she groaned, unaware that she sounded just like Winnie having her tummy tickled. 'I haven't had a proper cuppa in a fortnight.'

'You're living with Cyd Francis now, ja?' Jimmy sat at the table – a cheap pine self-assembly situation with a scratched top.

'I work for her.' Odette nodded, not really thinking as she gave into the urge to whinge. 'But she only drinks disgusting herbal teas. I crave PG Tips.'

'So buy yourself some,' he laughed.

'I can't aff—' Odette stopped herself. How sad to confess that she couldn't afford to buy teabags. 'I haven't got a kettle,' she said lamely.

'In the farmhouse?'

'I live in the mill,' she muttered, unwilling to go into details.

'So what's your job? Don't tell me you're milling grain?' Jimmy's elbows were leaning on the silvery grey velvet jacket now, preventing her from picking it up.

Odette eyed it worriedly, remembering the ruined pile of her Ghost dress. She hoped he didn't spill any tea.

'I'm her driver,' she said vaguely. 'Or at least that's what she calls me, but I think I'm more of a – what's the phrase – "lady's companion"?'

'Why don't you sit down?' he suggested, leaning back in his chair but leaving one hand on the pile of clothes, fingers distractedly stroking the velvet.

'I'd rather not.' Odette scalded her lips as she slurped yet more tea. She longed to ask him if she could take a few bags with her. 'Like I say, I'm on call. I should be getting back.'

'Quite a career change you've made.' He smiled affably.

'I didn't have much choice.' Her teeth were so tightly clenched that she spoke as though her jaw were wired. 'I was declared bankrupt earlier this year.'

'I heard,' he nodded.

Of course, Calum would have told him, she realised.

Deliberately, she backed further away and crossed her arms, trying to sound cool and professional as she changed the subject. It was the only way her scorched pride could cope. 'So when do the antelopes arrive?'

His mouth twisted into a smile. 'After the red deer cull this spring, I hope. The deer-park is huge – the second largest in the country. It's incredible. The farmland isn't quite so good. I have a lot of work to do.'

'How d'you mean?' She cocked her head, maintaining the executive stance.

He rubbed his thumb against his lip, clearly enjoying the opportunity to talk about the project too much to question her sudden Walden routine. 'When Calum did all his calculations, he didn't take into account the fact that ninety percent of the farms are tenanted. Calum wants them to turn around and start producing organic crops on a huge scale within a few months. The subsidies aren't there, and even if they were, there's simply not enough time. It's impossible. His deadline is this summer when Food Hall opens for business, but it will take years. It doesn't help that we've got some bloody television crew following us all around, trying to catch everything on tape – whenever a camera's running every estate worker, gardener and farm hand starts trimming a hedge nearby and showing their best side in the hope of being spotted.' His booming laugh filled the kitchen.

Then, catching sight of her frozen face, he dipped his head. 'Christ, I'm so sorry – thoughtless of me banging on about the place after what's happened between you and . . .' he trailed off hopelessly.

Odette swilled the last of her tea around in her cup, thinking about her stupid revenge, Calum's crazy job offer, his sudden renewal of interest in her. She wondered how much Jimmy knew about it, what the deal was between them.

'Why did you agree to work with him?' she asked with more bitterness than she'd intended.

'He's my friend.' Jimmy suddenly looked cross, the dark blue eyes blinking. 'He's good inside, Odette. It might not seem like it, but he did what he did for *you*, for your sake. Tough love, isn't that what they call it? You should know that by now, but maybe you don't. Maybe that's why things didn't work out between you two. Perhaps you were in love with a man you didn't really know?'

'I've got to go.' She put down her mug crossly. That was getting *way* too personal. She'd forgotten the way the Jimmy Sylvian liked to pick over the contents of one's soul the way other men liked to dissect a football match. 'I'll take these,

421

thanks.' She dragged the pile of clothes out from beneath his arm.

Holding his hands up, he didn't argue. He obviously realised he'd gone too far, and hastily tried to make amends. 'You'll knock them all out at the wedding wearing those.'

She nodded, gathering the clothes to her chest and suddenly feeling ungrateful. He'd helped her choose them, after all. She nodded at the fifty-pound note on the table. 'That's to cover the cost.'

He handed it back to her. 'Buy yourself a kettle.'

Odette shook her head without thinking, 'It wouldn't work.'

'Buy a good one.' He grinned.

'No, the wiring in the mill . . .' She looked at him, eager to leave and certain that this would be monumentally boring to him. He raised his eyebrows quizzically, seemingly fascinated by her wiring. 'It's not working. Only the lights work.'

'You have no heating?' He shuddered at the thought. 'Or hot water?'

He blew out through his lips, clearly staggered. 'In that case, my bathroom and kitchen are all yours whenever you want them – in fact, have a bath now if you want. I have to make some calls.' He stood up, his huge shoulders as wide as the pan-rack overhead. 'Shall I fetch you a towel?'

Odette gaped at him. What sort of person offers someone they hardly know a bath? That was the sort of thing Lydia once did, picking up sad-looking men in cafés and passing them the soap-on-a-rope half an hour later. She'd called it her down-and-out-of-control phase. Maybe Jimmy was on some sort of shabby-chick kick?

'Like I say, I've got to go,' she told him. 'Cyd'll be mad at me as it is.'

'In that case, come back later. I'm in all evening. You can have some supper here if you like.'

'I can't, I'm going out.' Calum obviously hadn't mentioned it.

'Hot date?' Jimmy grinned.

Odette cocked her head, deciding to see whether his altruism came from a natural, affable generosity or the fact that he still fancied her. This was the acid-bath test. 'Calum's taking me to the Château Nocturne.'

He didn't react at all, simply smiled that broad, big view smile of his. 'In that case you must have a bath. Calum is very punctilious about hygiene.'

'Are you suggesting I smell?' Odette bristled.

'Well you could be fresher.' He winked as he passed, heading up the stairs and calling over his shoulder. 'But remember I've lived in the bush. I've smelled far, far worse. Follow me.'

Not saying a word, Odette stomped straight out to her car. As she reversed the Aston angrily towards the gate, she didn't look up to see Jimmy watching her out of his bathroom window. At his side, a long-eared spaniel had her paws up on the sill, big brown eyes mournful.

39

Calum arrived at the farmhouse bang on seven, the first time in Odette's brief acquaintance with him that he had ever been punctual. Standing high in her tower, she watched him crunch across the gravel in darkness until the sensor on the security box picked him up and flooded him with white light. He was wearing the favourite Armani suit, with a crisp white shirt and very shiny black square-toed boots. Instead of slicking his usually tousled blond mane back as he always had before when not wearing his hat, he appeared to have had it cut. It was a crop that was highly fashionable amongst trendy young media men at the moment – razor cut, long over the ears and collar, slightly effete. It suited slender young androgynous pretty boys who wore Farrah slacks with hollow-cheeked irony and used despatch bags rather than briefcases. But it made Calum look faintly ridiculous.

She backed away from the tower window and returned to the mirror. She could hardly preach about haircuts.

She could hear the puppies yapping their way towards the lake, which must mean that Cyd had opened the door. Odette wondered if the manipulative old minx still intended to try and persuade Calum to take her along too – or even substitute herself for Odette entirely. She wouldn't put it past Cyd. She was enviably vain, egotistical and self-deluded.

Oh, God. Odette closed her eyes in horror. She knew what she was doing. She was trying to make Cyd appear as evil in her mind as possible. She badly needed to hate someone right now. She should hate Calum, but she couldn't. She still loved him. Bitter love, angry love, shameful love, but love nonetheless. And so she chose Cyd. Odette needed someone else to hate in order to stop hating herself so much.

She clutched on to the sides of the hand basin and fought back a wave of panic that crashed through her chest with unexpected force, closing her ribs in on each other like a crocodile clip. She shut her eyes tight and then opened them once more, focusing upon the pale face in the mirror. If there was one thing Odette felt she wasn't, it was self-deluded.

I can't do it, she suddenly realised.

She revolted herself too much to go out. Tomorrow's wedding was going to be enough of an ordeal without having to cope with tonight. She couldn't face people, hated being looked at right now, found her appearance so shaming that she didn't want to inflict the sight of it upon anyone else, least of all Calum. She'd wanted to hide in her tower like a character in a fairytale, watching her beloved, black-hearted prince in his big house going about his business, unaware of her presence. For months on end, she would spin a magic cloak, working through the night until her fingers bled. Then she would wrap it around herself, knowing that the first man who laid eyes on her would fall in love. Odette's cloak was her body which she planned to resculpt, to bring it back to its former glory. Calum had wanted it once and would again.

The trouble was, she couldn't hide in her tower because he'd discovered she was there. And she hadn't had time to spin her cloak yet with a demanding boss like Cyd. She hadn't even started to cast on stitches.

She took the nail scissors from her manicure bag and started to clip a few of the longer strands of her fringe. The light was behind her and the scissors were very blunt, but she immediately sensed an improvement as the thatch looked a little less like a bearded collie's coat. A few snips later and her face started to re-emerge from the shagpile. Fetching a hand-held mirror, Odette twisted around and contorted her arm over her shoulder so that she could cut some off the back. It wasn't easy to see what she was doing and her elbow blotted out what little light she had, but she thought she'd done a reasonable job. It looked quite stylish and a lot neater. Her confidence started to flood back. It was only when she dropped her head upside down, ruffled her roots to get some more volume and straightened up again that she realised what she'd done.

With a loud wail, she looked at the mop on her head which was now poking up at all sorts of strange angles, some tufts just a couple of inches long, others sprouting up like antennae. Flattening it back down, she rushed to the window again. The lights were on in the farm's kitchen and Calum's car was parked outside, a driver silhouetted inside, reading a magazine. Calum never drove himself. The big, silver Mercedes estate was new. He must have been splashing out lately.

Odette wavered between the charity shop combination and the creased blue velvet. The velvet was far more Le Château and, provided the lights were low and she sat down fairly smartly, the dirty hemline and balding pile wouldn't be too obvious. She'd sold the matching jacket to a second-hand designer store in London, and abandoned the handbag at Saskia and Stan's reception, but she still had matching shoes and an old blue pashmina which was just about smart enough to pass muster. At least it meant she could cover her hair Jemima Khan-style until they got there, by which time it would be too late for Calum to retract his offer of dinner.

She was so distracted with nerves that she didn't notice the Ghost dress sliding over her body without getting stuck. It fitted just as well as it had the day of the wedding.

When Odette heard crunching on gravel and Cyd's smoky laugh outside, she felt the familiar clawing in her chest, the bile in her throat, the blackening tunnel vision. What was happening to her? She'd thought the panic attacks had gone, but Calum had brought them rushing back again, the cloying insecurity and fear of her own passion.

There was a sharp knocking on the door downstairs before it creaked open.

'Odette?' Cyd called out. 'Your friend's here. Are you ready?'

She wanted to make up any excuse not to go – a cold, a headache, period pains, wind – anything, however shaming. In an instant, she had kicked off the shoes, pulled off the dress and dragged on her old towelling robe, now a very threadbare shadow of its former fluffy self. She threw a towel around her dreadful hair.

'Coming!' she called out as she heard feet moving around downstairs.

'Wonderful news,' Cyd was rasping ecstatically, 'dear Calum has bought two of Bazouki's puppies, Balalaika and Banjo. Derek's friend is taking Koto, and Phyllis knows someone who might want Cithara, so that only leaves little Sarangi. I've decided you must have her. Where are you?'

'Here.' Odette appeared at the top of the stairs and looked down at them, making sure the light remained behind her.

Cyd and Calum both sucked in their cheeks when they saw her, like two snobbish wine-tasters encountering a particularly rough Liebfraumilch.

'I'm afraid I can't come, Calum babes,' she said quickly, trying to sound light and friendly, but in fact sounding like a Smurf in a spin cycle.

'Why ever not?' He seemed very taken aback.

For a ludicrous moment Odette contemplated telling him – quite truthfully – that she had nothing to wear and couldn't do a thing with her hair.

'I have a stomach bug.' She noticed that Cyd's eyes were starting to sparkle as she realised her tarot reading had been spot on. 'Must have eaten something dodgy. I don't think it's serious, but I have a friend's wedding tomorrow and I need to preserve me energy. Sorry, babes.'

'You could have let me know earlier,' he said with steelily controlled fury. 'It's almost impossible to book a table at Le Château, as you know. How am I supposed to get someone else to come at such short notice, this far from London?' He added the final words to make it clear, Odette thought, that were he in London he would have no difficulty in filling her shoes.

She looked at Cyd, who was smiling broadly up the stairs, graciousness personified. 'I'm sure . . .'

'I need to talk to you about the job,' he snapped, winding himself up yet further.

Concealed by the protective shadows, Odette snarled down

at him, 'I've told you, I'm not interested in working for you. Besides, I have a job here.'

'Are you trying to steal my staff?' Cyd's throaty purr was at its most strip-teasing and appeasing. 'Really, Calum, I thought you were a reformed character. I can see we'll need to talk this through. Over dinner perhaps?'

He was speechless. He merely nodded mutely, and – to her amazement – looked up to Odette for confirmation.

She nodded. 'Take Cyd to dinner. She ate at Le Château over a decade ago. She can tell you how much it's changed.'

'Oh, yes, I remember it as though it was yesterday.' Cyd clapped her hands together. 'I would just *adore* to go back.'

'Well, if you're sure you want to come along . . .' Calum seemed strangely doubtful.

'Give me two minutes to change.' Cyd almost danced out of the mill, leaving Calum standing by one of the mildewed recording decks, looking confused.

Odette stayed in the shadows above him, willing him to leave too, but he remained behind, tapping his fingers on the deck, eyes narrowed. Then, before she could scuttle away and hide, he bounded up the stairs as fast as a cat.

'Nice place you have here, sister.'

As he pretended to look around, Odette backed as far away as possible. She felt blistered just standing in the same room as him. It was a sickening fusion of hatred – both towards him and for herself – and desire. She was so raw emotionally, she felt skinned, and so deeply ashamed of herself physically that her whole body was contracted and hunched, trying to swallow itself up. She felt like Caliban in *The Tempest*, the servant-monster: wretched, hideous, resentful and yet desperate for a master.

He was standing just inches away from her now. Odette hunched and cowered even more. When he reached out and touched her, she flinched in horror.

'Calm down, sister – I'm not going to hurt you.'

He scrunched up one eye, examining her face closely. Then he moved away and started nosing around the room again, peering at the television, the stereo and the curved glass wall which hid the shower, adding almost casually over his shoulder, 'Tell me, Odette, d'you still love me?'

She felt two hot spots of colour in her cheeks. 'I never told you that I loved you, Calum.'

'But you *did* love me,' he said with total self-assurance, peering into the shower area and wrinkling his nose as he spotted all the hair cuttings on the white tiled floor. 'The question is, do you still?'

'Is this another one of your tests?' she said in a hollow voice, unable to believe his cruelty. 'Who d'you want me to shag now, Calum, in order to prove I'm worthy?'

'Frankly, I shouldnae think anyone would want to sleep with you looking the way you do.' He walked up to her and grabbed the towel from her head, leaving her cowering even more. 'You're in a fucking state, Odette. You're plain, you're poor, you're common, and you look like you've just laid down under a strimmer.'

'Get out!' she hissed. 'Just get out of my life. You're not so fucking hot yourself, you weasel-arsed, ugly little twat!'

For a moment she thought he was going to hit her and quailed in terror. Then to her astonishment he suddenly laughed in delight, his eyes creasing in rapture, his uneven teeth flashing as never before.

'Thank you!' he gasped, clutching his sides. 'Thank you for getting the joke at last.'

'What?' she scowled, not understanding, one shaking hand raking through her revolting hair. 'Understanding that you're an ugly little runt?'

'You see it!' He howled with mirth. 'You see me for what I am. Odette, you absolute darling.' He grabbed her face and, before she could take in what was happening, kissed her hard on the mouth. She pulled hastily away, anger and self-loathing far outweighing lust.

'I always thought you were ugly, Calum.' She shook her head, totally baffled. 'It didn't stop me fancying you. I thought we had a lot in common, if you must know.'

'And so we do. You sweet darling, I always knew we had what it took. Now you're truly ready.'

'I'm back!' a smoky voice called up from below.

'Ready for what?' Odette asked Calum urgently, but he was already heading towards the stairs, blowing her a kiss over his shoulder.

'Hope you feel better later, sister. Go to bed and get some sleep.'

'Yes, Odette!' Cyd called up. 'You look after yourself, dearheart. We won't be late. Can you be a darling and clean my shoes for tomorrow? They're out on the kitchen table.'

'You shall not go to the ball, Cinderella,' Odette muttered, watching the red tail lights of the car disappearing.

Every time she thought she'd got Calum sussed, he played another trick on her. What was she 'ready' for? She didn't feel capable of boxing her own shadow right now.

Dragging on an old tracksuit, she wandered listlessly to the farmhouse to clean Cyd's shoes, which were red suede and took half an hour's brushing to remove a thick crust of mud. The dishwasher also needed emptying, the puppies required feeding, and there was a heavy tangle of wet towels in the washing machine.

Now reconciled to her Cinderella role, Odette trailed around clearing everything up, stacking the mess into neat piles and keeping the puppies company. She rather liked having the farmhouse to herself. Its cluttered warmth was comforting. And there was one delicious treat she could not deny herself – sitting down with a large Bacardi and Coke in front of the Friday night hour-long episode of *Londoners*.

Topping herself up during each commercial break, she tried not to think about Calum and Cyd reaching the restaurant. She was glad she hadn't gone. Two minutes with him was enough to destroy her confidence; she simply wasn't strong enough to face him yet. But she would be. Tonight had made her absolutely determined to do something, anything, to dignify her shattered life and show him that he had not beaten her, that he couldn't control her any more.

By the time she was halfway down the bottle and *Londoners* had given way to a new sit com, she had decided that the first thing she needed to do was clean up her act.

Now taking her drink neat, Odette reeled upstairs. The thought of a hot, deep bath was absolutely orgasmic. In the plushest of the guest bathrooms, she balanced her glass on the flipped-down loo-seat and kicked off her shoes.

She turned on the gushing taps – hot water that steamed. Bliss! She tried to ignore one of the puppies whining just outside the door, and wandered over to the radio on the windowsill. Selecting an easy listening channel, she hummed along to Frank Sinatra's 'Fly Me To The Moon.'

The feeling of scalding water on skin was absolutely breath-taking, both in its loveliness and its stinging, electric-shock pain as every hair on her undepilated body trapped a tiny tight bubble of air and twisted back on itself. Odette shuddered and sighed and plunged beneath the surface, letting the air slide from her lungs through her nostrils before she resurfaced, pulling her hair from her face and reaching for the shampoo.

She lathered a Lily Savage plume of white froth on her head, grinding her fingers into her scalp as she tried to rid herself of the dull deposits from twenty cold shampoo rinses. Singing along to 'Loving You', complete with high-pitched shrieks, Odette ignored the occasional puppy accompaniment from the landing and plunged back underwater again. When she resurfaced, hair squeaking satisfactorily, she spotted her blurred reflection in the mirrored tiles above the taps, loving the way it had disappeared into the steam like the Little Mermaid turning to foam in the sea. Now that had been a dignified move on her part. She had shown far more nobility than her beloved prince who had taken another bride.

Odette's loathed reflection was totally obscured now. Calum thought she was ugly. He'd taken her back to the base metal she was and was delighting in watching her rust. Well, she was all out of self-rusting tears. She needed a bigger vat of acid to dip herself in.

She set the hot tap running again and climbed out to fetch her drink, standing with it for a long time. Her hated, red-fleshed body was dripping water everywhere and she thought of a suckling pig on a spit, its skin smoking and dripping fat as it turned on its pivot. Calum was right. She was 'ready'.

She'd never been readier. All she had to do was take the first step.

The bath was now scalding hot and almost overflowing. In normal circumstances, Odette would have leaped back out howling, but instead she continued to lower herself down inch by inch, feeling the pain but refusing to acknowledge it, let alone give in. She felt she deserved every long second of agony.

Up to her waist she almost weakened and jumped, but she only had to think of Calum's words – 'you're plain, you're poor, you're common' – to lower herself further, growing immune to the pain with every welt-inducing inch. At chest level she groaned as her hated, swollen breasts were swallowed by the scalding liquid. At her neck, she felt her breath quicken and her chin lift involuntarily. It was only when she was entirely underwater that she was at peace, that she knew she could breathe deeply and easily for the first time in almost six months.

'Bastard!'

Spitting water everywhere, lungs burning, skin raw, Odette leaped out of the bath like a frenzied salmon. Flopping on to the carpet, she choked out great spurts of bath water all over her bright pink flesh.

She would not let him do this to her. She was a fighter. She shouldn't be giving in to her need for oblivion. She should be getting back into training.

Watched by a row of entranced Afghan puppies lined up in front of the Aga, Odette set a mirror up on the kitchen table and set about her damp hair with a pair of sewing scissors. She was too drunk to care if she made a mess of it – anything had to be better than the hacked thatch. As clippings rained down on the flagstones, she started humming 'Eye of the Tiger'. She was back in the ring and ready to spar.

Half an hour later she had a punky new style. A trained hairdresser might sarcastically suggest she must have been wearing boxing gloves while cutting it, but Odette knew it worked pretty well. Part Patti Smith, part Annie Lennox, it was angry and sexy and wholly her.

Looking at her reflection – clear and steam-free – she took a deep breath and tried out an old trick. 'You are getting better,' she told herself. 'You are going to be okay. You no longer give a fuck about Calum.' Laying the mirror face down on the table and closing her eyes, she knew that was too much to ask.

She was fast asleep on the second floor of her mill when the door deep beneath her creaked open and bare feet padded inside.

It was the first time since Odette had been living at the farm that Cyd had let herself into the smock mill to have a chat. Then again, it was the first time since Odette had been staying there that Cyd had been out for the evening.

It was one in the morning when she reeled into the still, silent bedroom which had once played host to the drunken slumbers of her husband.

'He's so vulnerable, isn't he?' she said sadly, plumping down on Odette's mattress, reeking of whisky.

Sitting bolt upright, startled from a dream about giant rampaging metal elephants which had come to life in the Fermoncieaux deer-park, Odette took a while to stop screaming.

Cyd didn't seem to notice, lighting a cigarette and then keeping her lighter running as she spotted Odette's hair. 'That's an improvement. Honestly, he was so hurt that you refused to come. Dear Calum. Such a lost child. So determined to better his parents, so full of piss and vinegar and hatred. Utterly adorable, don't you think, dearheart?' She curled up at Odette's feet.

Odette didn't have to say anything as Cyd's voice murmured on, smoky and seductive. She settled back against her pillows, wondering if this was part of a dream.

'. . . very contradictory,' Cyd was rasping, her voice sleepy and sad. 'So full of desire, yet so angry. So like Jobe. So like you. He's the same age as Gabriel, you know? My eldest son. I'll see him tomorrow. The first time in so many years. Calum Forrester hated his mother too. So do you. So did I. We should start a club.' She was starting to drift off, head growing heavy on Odette's ankles. 'But I found Jobe to love, and Calum loves someone too. D'you know who he loves, dearheart? It's very sweet. I don't think it's sexual. Just love. Very pure. You'll never guess . . .' Her breathing deepened yet further, her head grew heavier.

'Who?' Odette demanded.

'Jimmy,' Cyd sighed, cuddling up to her feet. 'Jimmy Sylvian. Who do you love, Odette? Perhaps that's your problem. We should find you someone to love. How does the song go? "*Can anybody find me . . .*"' She sang a few bars of Queen and then sighed 'Dear Freddie, such a darling friend. So in need of someone to love.' And she fell asleep, fully clothed, on Odette's rapidly deadening, pins-and-needles-filled feet.

She didn't sleep a wink all night. Calum loved Jimmy. Big, loud, crass Jimmy Sylvian. She was caught in a love triangle. How totally *Dynasty*. How bloody awful.

40

When Odette woke up, Cyd was no longer on her bed and she almost wondered whether she had dreamed her early hours appearance the night before. But there was an unfamiliar cork-heeled shoe beside the bed and a tell-tale smudge of grey kohl on the pale green duvet cover near her feet.

She pulled the duvet around her for warmth and shuffled to the window where a very dark sky, weighed down with rain, was offering a bleak outlook weather-wise. Odette abandoned the duvet by the circular glass wall and gritted her teeth as she prepared herself for the usual chilly shower. As she passed the rusty mirror, she caught sight of her short hair. It was like gazing at a stranger. Matched with her charity shop outfit, her friends wouldn't recognise her.

With her face painted, but still wearing her schleppy old joggers and trainers, she headed towards the farm to make sure Cyd was conscious. The wedding wasn't until eleven, and it was only just after eight, but she knew that her boss could sleep through a nuclear attack on Sussex given a bad hangover.

The farm was, surprisingly, unlocked. When Odette let herself into the kitchen, the puppies raced up to her enthusi-astically, minus their mother. Bazouki's lead was missing from her hook and she realised in surprise that Cyd must have risen at an unprecedented hour – that was if she'd slept at all – and taken her dog out for an early walk. It was going to be a nerve-wracking day for her. No wonder she couldn't sleep.

Waiting for her to come back, Odette put out some breakfast to kill time, and made a big pot of Cyd's favourite green tea. As she threw out the old leaves from the pot, she noticed the red suede shoes she'd cleaned the night before sitting in the bin. Odette fished them out and brushed off the worst of the leaves before setting them on the Aga to dry. She knew Cyd was hopelessly dippy and had been more than a little drunk last night, but throwing out her shoes was a classic.

Three-quarters of an hour later, the tea was cold and there was still no sign of Cyd or Bazouki. The puppies were starting to whimper hungrily. Odette fed them some weaning mix and looked at the clock worriedly. They'd have to leave in just under an hour.

It was starting to rain outside – the first spots of the promised downpour. Odette found a pair of wellies, plus a long riding mac and broad-brimmed Australian hat. Looking as though she was about to round up sheep and not a sixty-year-old siren, Odette collected the kitchen timer from the door of the fridge, set it for a quarter of an hour and shut the puppies safely in the back lobby.

She clambered over the stile at the far end of the garden and ducked beneath overhanging branches into the skeletal umbrella of the woods through which only the occasional raindrop permeated.

'Cyd!' she called, hesitating at a fork in the path. She didn't know the routes that Cyd walked. If she wasn't careful, she'd get totally lost and make them late. For all she knew Cyd could be arriving back at the house from an entirely different direction right now.

Odette's jogging momentum was not what it had once been. She was puffed out within a couple of minutes. Wellies were a lot harder going than trainers and made amazingly scatological noises as she panted through the undergrowth emitting squelchy raspberries with every laboured step. She had chosen a bad path – pitted, muddy and heading in completely the wrong direction – and after less than two minutes following it, found she'd just trotted to the edge of the wood.

Then she heard a distinctly canine snorting coming from the opposite side of a huge holly tree.

'Bazouki?' Odette slithered to a halt. 'Cyd?'

The snorting stopped for a bit and then continued in earnest along with a couple of eager barks.

'Bazouki, old gel! Where are you?' Odette followed the noise round.

The dog was almost entirely submerged in a fox hole, only a pair of muddy hind legs poking out, along with a thin wagging tail.

That was why Cyd was late, Odette realised. Bloody Bazouki must have run off. Thank Heavens she'd come out and found her. Now all she had to do was find Cyd.

'Come here, you little cow!' Odette gave the tail a yank.

A loud, deep howl from within the hole was quickly replaced by a far louder growling out of it as the dog backed up and turned to snarl at her.

It might have been coated in mud, and she might be no dog expert, but she knew immediately that this wasn't Bazouki. She'd recognise those bared teeth anywhere. It was Jimmy's misogynist lurcher, Nelson.

Odette screamed and leaped away, tripping over a tree root and falling heavily against a silver birch.

Nelson lunged.

Amidst lots of screaming and growling – both her own, Odette later realised – she was aware of two things: the foul reek of Chappie and the faint peeping noise of the kitchen timer ringing. Such was the ignoble nature of death.

Had she been watching events from Jimmy's perspective, she would also have seen a wagging stringy tail, a welly still trapped by the heel in a tree root, and a bright red bedsock dangling from the end of one thrashing foot.

Pulling Nelson away from his doggy kisses, Jimmy bit back laughter and reached down to press the 'off' button on the kitchen timer which was attached to Odette's corduroy lapel.

'I think your egg's cooked,' he said cheerfully.

She pulled on her welly and reset her kitchen timer.

'Have you seen Cyd?' she asked urgently.

He nodded. 'About half an hour ago on the other side of the woods. Winnie ran off with her in-bred fringe on a stick. I've been hunting them down ever since.'

'Oh, shit,' Odette muttered, starting down the path again. 'We're going to be bleedin' late for the wedding if I don't find her soon. Cyd's wound up about it enough as it is. Sorry, I can't stay and chat.'

'Hang on, I'll help.' Jimmy bounded after her, eyeing the kitchen timer with amusement. 'Why are you wearing that thing?'

'Got no watch.' Odette was jogging along with the inevitable farting boot accompaniment.

He nodded, admiring her ingenuity.

'I think she might be somewhere near the old pheasant coops.' He kept pace with her frantic jog by little more than walking faster – his long, sandy denim legs sweeping through the undergrowth. 'I thought I heard barking there just a moment ago before I lost Nel to the fox.'

Jimmy led the way into the dark, Hansel and Gretel heart of the wood, an eerily silent place in which a clearing had been fenced with chicken wire, with the occasional rusting oil drum acting as feed bin.

Odette looked around and checked her timer. It read three minutes. 'Well, this was a bleedin' waste of—'

'Shh!' Jimmy covered her mouth with a hand that smelled of Imperial Leather and nodded towards a rickety wooden feeding coop with a tiny crossed window from which a faint plume of smoke was billowing. When he spoke again in a hushed whisper he sounded like David Attenborough talking to camera in the Ugandan jungle, telling viewers that there was a gorilla just feet from where he was standing. 'Unless Winnie and that Afghan monster are sharing ten B & H, I think we've tracked her down.'

On cue a rustling in the undergrowth heralded an explosion of rebellious teenage dog activity as Winnie and her new best friend Bazouki burst from their fern layer to ambush a startled Nelson.

Odette crept towards the wooden coop, hoping that the canine distraction had bought her some cover. It hadn't. The moment she was within whispering distance a Marlboro butt flew out of the tiny window and a sighing bear voice muttered, 'Don't get any closer!'

Odette looked over her shoulder to where Jimmy was

standing. He seemed to have pacified the dogs with amazing speed, and even more astonishingly they were sitting at his feet obediently like a bunch of school kids waiting for a story. He raised his eyebrows inquiringly at her. Odette shrugged hopelessly.

'You have to come, Cyd,' she pleaded through the open door, wrinkling her nose at the smell of gamey droppings. 'Elsa needs you.'

'Rubbish!' Cyd scoffed. 'She has her real family there – I was only ever a hopelessly self-obsessed adjunct. I'm not going. I let you duck out of last night so this time you can do the same for me.'

'It's hardly the same thing!' Odette protested, bridling on her friend's behalf. 'This is your daughter we're talking about.'

'And my sons!' came the muffled reply.

'You have to face them today,' Odette insisted. 'This might be your only chance of seeing them for years. You have to grasp it. They're your children after all.'

'I'm just a child myself,' came a sorry whimper.

That was as much as Odette could take. Something snapped. The alarm pinged once more and she ripped it from her collar and threw it into the undergrowth before replying in a furious shout, 'Don't talk shit, you daft mare! You're a sixty—'

A warm hand gripped her shoulder and a soothing voice whispered, 'Cut it out.'

Odette looked at Jimmy furiously, lowering her voice to a hiss. 'Will you just butt out? I don't think you realise what's going on here. Cyd's daughter is about to get married in two hours' time and *she's* hiding in a glorified hen house pretending to be too young to take responsibility for her own actions.'

'I'm aware of the situation.' Jimmy sounded like a senior police officer taking over in a hostage situation. 'I think you should go back to the house, get changed and leave this to me. It's not the first time I've dealt with this sort of thing.'

'You what?' Odette wondered whether he was having a dig at her and felt a flash of illogical anger.

He was unfazed. 'Go back to the farm, get changed and start the car,' he said firmly, clipping the little plastic timer back on to her lapel. 'In thirty minutes, if I haven't brought Cyd back raring to go, then you have my permission to bring the shotgun out here and force her to London. Great haircut, by the way.'

'How did he persuade you to come?' Odette asked for the fifth or sixth time as she tanked the Aston up the M23's fast lane in an attempt to make up time.

Again Cyd said nothing. She could be a stubborn and secretive pain in the arse sometimes, Odette thought darkly as her employer concentrated on applying a second layer of kohl to her eyes, aided by a shaking compact mirror.

Odette was tempted to swerve into the middle lane, but was too eager to catch up a few miles and minutes. They were running hugely late. Cyd had taken almost an hour to get ready and then had the temerity to complain that her red suede shoes were looking stained.

Parking near the register office was murder. Cyd grumbled as she had to walk half a mile through wet, crowded Saturday-morning Battersea to reach it, being recognised all around with the familiar, 'Wasn't she Jobe Francis's wife?'

Elsa's father and Po were already in situ, hovering by the entrance at the top of a flight of steps as they waited for the previous couple to emerge.

Cyd's reunion with her first husband was liquid-nitrogen frosty.

'Aren't you supposed to be giving our daughter away?' she asked in a brittle voice, a bundle of nerves.

'It's a register office,' he sighed caustically. 'She insists on arriving here with just her friend. Besides, you were the one who gave her away thirty years ago – part of a set, if you recall?'

Odette didn't dare look at Cyd's face.

Little Po was as silent and stylish as ever, her bright pink suit clashing disastrously with Cyd's sexy red wraparound angora.

As they loitered under umbrellas waiting for the action to start, Cyd smoked one cigarette after another and grumbled that Odette should have ordered them both some button-holes. Both Elsa's father and Po had huge white roses pinned to their lapels which they ostentatiously sniffed from time to time.

There was no sign of any of her sons.

'They're helping with the transport,' Elsa's father told Odette, whom he'd met a few times before. 'Ah, here are Mr and Mrs Cochlan.'

'God, what dreadful hair,' Cyd muttered under her breath as the Cochlans emerged from the back of a black cab. It was true that Euan's mother had a particularly odd penchant for dyeing her hair bright orange and having it permed into tight little curls close to her head. She apparently thought that she looked like Shirley MacLaine, but the effect was more Ronald MacDonald.

Then everyone heard a loud, spluttering cacophony from Battersea High Street and turned around to see what was causing it.

A cavalcade of classic Italian mopeds was puttering along the wet road, causing passers-by to gape and fellow motorists to slam on their brakes. Looking at them and realising what was going on, Odette burst out laughing.

Leading the gang were Euan and Duncan, one in a gold Elvis suit, the other a collarless sixties suit, both sharing a pale blue Lambretta with ribbons streaming from its mirrors. Behind them a cream Vespa was being driven by one of Elsa's short, curly-haired brothers and riding pillion behind him was Ally, resplendent in a lime green trouser suit. Behind that two Bridgehouse brothers were threatening to crash as they acted as out-riders to a red, white and blue Mini Cooper, festooned in ribbons. The fourth Bridgehouse brother was driving and, beaming from the passenger seat, waving at everyone in sight, was Elsa.

Odette and Cyd both looked at each other and shrieked with laughter. Even Mr Bridgehouse mustered a weak smile although Po remained po-faced. Euan's carrot-haired mother burst into noisy tears as her son brought the leading moped to a rakish halt at the foot of the steps. 'Doesnae he look grand, Wally?'

'Aye,' he agreed, watching as Euan clambered off the moped. 'Now I can see why the boy said he wasnae gonna wear a kilt.'

Cyd was positively vibrating with nervous excitement as she saw her sons for the first time in years, but it was her future son-in-law who greeted her first.

'Cyd – great to see you!' Euan bounded up the steps and gathered her into a golden hug. 'You look sensational.'

'So do you, dearheart.' She wiped a tear from her eye. 'God, I'm starting already!'

'Probably just the light reflecting offa this thing.' Euan brushed raindrops from his shiny suit shoulders. He looked hopelessly excited and couldn't stop smiling and waving at people. 'It has that effect on people. Hello, stranger.' He hugged Odette. 'So we have to get married to get you to come to London these days, huh?'

She cuffed him on the arm. When he released her, she realised that Cyd had left her side and was making her way towards her children. The Bridgehouse brothers – all short, stout and curly-haired like their father – glared at her with ill-concealed dislike, although Elsa was already waiting in their midst with outstretched arms. 'Mummy!'

'You look so, so beautiful baby.' Cyd was sobbing big time now. 'I'm *so* proud of you.' They embraced one another over Buster the Bump. Cyd reached out to stroke the arm of one of her sons who pointedly pulled it out of reach and hissed something under his breath.

Odette watched worriedly as the brothers hastily moved away to stand by their father with whom various Bridgehouse girlfriends and wives had clustered too, having arrived in a taxi earlier.

Elsa did indeed look beautiful. Her wild curls were piled loosely on her head and secured beneath a tiara which had been shaped from shells. Her dress was designed to flaunt and flatter her incredible shape. It was part BBC Jane Austen adaptation – all empire line and classic simplicity – and part seventies disco mermaid, with scale-like green sequins interspersed with the tiniest of shells on the sleeves and skirt. It was outlandish, very kitsch and absurdly camp.

Just behind Odette, the doors of the register office opened and a photographer slipped out. He looked around forlornly.

'You lot'll have to wait on the pavement – I'm about to shoot another lucky couple.'

'Most humane method,' one of the Bridgehouse brothers laughed. No one else took the slightest notice of the photographer as Ally passed Elsa a bouquet which consisted of just three fat calla lilies – one for each member of the family that was due to be united that day.

Moments later, an elderly couple appeared through the doors of the register office. The bride, a curvaceous black grandma wearing a tiny hat with a veil over her white hair, was astonished to encounter a throng of people apparently in fancy dress. For a moment she looked thunderous, and then she burst out laughing.

'Will you look at this, Murray? We have a wedding party after all!' She caught sight of Wally Cochlan. 'A man in a kilt! Now I know I've gone to heaven.'

Euan bounded up to them and introduced himself, and was soon waving at Elsa to come up the stairs and meet them too. 'This is Mr and Mrs de Souza, hen. They've just eloped.'

'Call me Eunice, me darling.' She clutched Murray's arm proudly. 'This man here is my toyboy. You know he's only seventy-two?' She went off into peals of cackling laughter and wiped her eyes.

A spirit of extraordinary, bursting happiness had hijacked the proceedings. Within minutes, Euan had introduced the de Souzas to his entire family and most of Elsa's.

It turned out they were marrying in secret because they couldn't afford a party for their fifteen children from previous marriages, their countless grandchildren and several great-grandchildren. When Wally Cochlan offered to pose for some photographs alongside them, they were delighted. Moments later, Elsa and Euan were inviting them on to their own reception.

'Well, Eunice and I were going to treat ourselves to a rum in the Castle, but that sounds a better offer,' Murray agreed happily.

And so it was that after a short, formal ceremony, Odette found herself driving a weeping Cyd to the reception, still fretting about her sons. 'Not one of them spoke to me, did you notice? Even their girlfriends blanked me. It was so awful.'

Behind them sat Murray, transfixed by the electric windows and constantly whizzing them up and down, which didn't make it easy to talk.

'Give them time. Wait until after the vows – let them have a couple of drinks at the party and then try again, babes,' Odette soothed her. 'It must have been very hard for them back there with their dad looking on and all. Try to get them alone.'

Cyd sniffed doubtfully.

Odette reached the film studio ahead of the cavalcade which had set out late because Euan found it even harder to fit his six-foot-six frame into the Mini's driver's seat than Elsa found fitting her forty-inch waist into the passenger's. The group was now progressing very slowly through the Saturday lunchtime traffic because of the attention it was attracting. She and Cyd were staggered by the number of people milling about outside the studios awaiting the happy couple, sharing brollies and boxes of soggy confetti.

Two huge catering lorries were emitting gorgeous smells, and waiters dressed as frogs for some strange reason were squelching about with trays of champagne glasses full of an alarmingly bright green drink.

'What is it, dearheart?' Cyd almost fell out of the car as she hastened to get her hands on some alcohol.

'Love Drug,' came a muffled voice from deep within a suit. 'Champagne and Crème de Menthe frappé.'

'Sounds wonderful, I'll have two.' Cyd grabbed the glasses before he squelched off, head tipped back so that he could see out of the mouth of the costume.

Watching in amazement, Odette suddenly spotted a group of familiar faces: Juno and Jay chatting to Lydia and Finlay. They all waved when they saw her.

As she helped Murray and Eunice out of the back of the car, Juno bounded over ahead of the others.

'There must be three hundred people here!' she gasped,

kissing Odette on both cheeks and then hugging Cyd. 'You should see the way they've decorated inside. It's inspired – Man from Atlantis meets the Forest of Arden in Gracelands. I've already spotted Zoe Ball and Fatboy Slim mingling with the clubbers. Who are they?' She watched in astonishment as Eunice and Murray disappeared into the crowd beneath a striped umbrella. 'Relatives?'

'It was a sort of double wedding.' Odette smiled, saying hello to the others who had wandered over.

'You look sensationally trendy,' Lydia told her admiringly, herself a vision in second-skin Vivienne Westwood. 'I love your hair. And how did you know glasses are the latest fashion accessory? How amazing – living in the country has turned you into a fashion victim at last.'

Looking around, Odette noticed to her amazement that most of the unbelievably trendy, clubby guests were sporting little frameless glasses like hers, along with quite a number of long velvet jackets and pneumatic bustiers. The men were all wearing drainpipes, waist-long jackets and ugly tufty cuts, long over the ears like Calum's. It suddenly struck her how out of touch she had become since moving away from London.

'That *precise* shade of green is the new black.' Lydia eyed Odette's skirt with continued surprise. 'Did Cyd buy you this outfit?'

'No.' Odette looked around for her and realised with a lurch of panic that she'd dashed off again, probably in pursuit of a frog with a tray of Love Drug.

She had no time to go in search of her as the first of the wedding convoy was puttering into the car park to whoops and claps of delight from the rain-soaked guests. A moment later the huge doors of the studio slid open with a loud groan and the pale blue Vespa – which Duncan was now sharing with Ally – drove inside, followed by the Bridgehouse brothers who now had their girlfriends as pillion passengers. Finally the Mini rattled into view, towing a great timpani of cans, covered in foaming snow spray like a cream cake, and belting out 'The Self-Preservation Society' from its stereo. The welcoming whoops intensified to a deafening pitch.

'Aren't they going a bit fast?' Lydia gasped as the Mini pelted through the studio doors almost mowing down several guests in the process.

They galloped after the exhaust fumes and crowded through the doors with the rest of the guests just in time to hear a squeal of brakes and catch sight of the Mini executing a perfect hand-brake turn in the centre of the huge studio.

'If anything's going to induce labour then that will.' Juno bit her lip worriedly as Elsa and Euan both squeezed their way out of the car with radiant smiles on their faces to be greeted with yet more wolf-whistling applause. One of Elsa's lilies was bent and some shells had fallen off her tiara but she was apparently unscathed.

'My foot got trapped under the brake pedal,' Euan explained to those close enough to him to hear. 'Bit hairy but we made it okay.'

As the ever-ready Bridgehouse brothers reversed the car back out of the studio, Euan took Elsa's hand and led her up to the stage which had been erected at the far end.

Odette stared around the huge, crowded hangar, partly in search of Cyd and partly in absolute awe of the decorations. Juno's description had been spot on. Somehow Elsa and Euan had managed to get their hands on upwards of fifty small trees, sprayed them gold and positioned them around the walls so that the centre of the room resembled a glade in a wood, covered with gold and silver picnic blankets.

'Now I know what they meant by a wedding picnic,' Odette laughed, peeking between the trees for signs of a red angora dress. As the huge doors slid shut behind the Mini, she realised that the place was lit by tens of revolving glitter balls, plus ultra-violet lights tucked in the branches of the trees and a dozen vast, luminous turquoise fish tanks, devoid of fish but absolutely crammed with clear tinted beads which glittered and twinkled. In each tank floated a Barbie and Ken dressed in wedding attire and little snorkels.

More frogs were walking around with big, careful high steps to avoid falling over their green flippers as they offered around trays of Love Drug.

446

It was tasteless, brash, sexily kitsch and very Elsa. Odette adored it, but it was almost impossible to see beyond a few feet. There were simply hundreds of guests. Cyd could be anywhere amongst them.

'Hi there,' Duncan said politely into a microphone which promptly led to a great shriek of feedback from the loudspeakers banked up to either side of the stage, their foam fronts customised with two huge spray-paintings of the happy couple.

'Ghastly, aren't they?' Juno nodded towards them. 'Makes them look like Cleo Lane and Johnny Dankworth.'

'Who did them?'

'Stan, I think.'

Odette turned to her in surprise. She'd had no idea Elsa had become quite so pally with Stan and Saskia – inviting them to the wedding, asking Stan to decorate her reception venue.

'He didn't mention it.' She didn't know why but the fact made her feel childishly jealous and defensive. Stan is *my* friend, she wanted to say.

Odette felt hopelessly out of touch with everyone's news. Life in London moved so fast that she felt as though she'd been away from it for years not weeks. Her social life had effectively stopped the moment she ran out of money. She knew that she'd barely seen her friends when she was in a full-time job, even less when she was trying to get the OD off the ground. But then she'd had a mobile and e-mail and voice-mail and any number of high-tech, low-maintenance ways of keeping up to speed during brief snatches throughout the day.

'Jay and I are off to the States in a fortnight. I wanted to see as much as possible of you before then but Cyd's phone is always engaged or she can't find you. You'd better come to my party, mind you.' Juno was trying on Odette's glasses. 'These are fab.'

'What party?' Odette squinted at a blurred Sue Pollard lookalike.

'Didn't Cyd pass on my message? I phoned ages ago.' Juno looked appalled. 'It's a week next Friday at my parents' house – the day before we go. Just old friends, nothing on this scale . . . just look at all these people!' she whistled as she looked around her.

'I can't see them too well,' Odette pointed out. Juno reluctantly handed the glasses back. She had already decided they made her look ravishing – like Christy Turlington during her academic phase.

Duncan was having another go at attracting attention on the microphone but the sound level was too low and no one was listening.

'They're so popular,' Juno sighed jealously, her competitive streak to the fore. 'I'd be lucky to fill a pub with all the friends I've invited to my party – well, maybe a small club,' she added vainly.

Odette realised to her horror that she'd have trouble filling a telephone box. She was moving in ever-decreasing social circles these days.

'Must find Jay.' Juno grabbed her arm. 'Come with me and we'll nab a good pitch for the stage show.'

By the time Duncan finally got everyone's attention, most of the guests were several Love Drugs up and starting to catcall. Elsa and Euan were sitting on two thrones on the stage, fashioned like giant shells. They hadn't stopped talking to each other and waving to friends since they'd sat down.

'Everyone!' Duncan tapped the shrieking microphone. 'Your attention, please. Hello! Free charlie if you shut the fuck up! Thank you, that's better. For those of you who don't know me, I'm Duncan the best man. As you know, Elsa and Euan got married this morning in—'

He wasn't allowed to finish as a great booming cheer rang around the hangar, making the gold and silver branches on the trees shake. Standing under one, close to the front, Odette noticed that hanging on fishing wire from each were bride and groom glitter shakers.

When the whooping had died down enough to be heard, Duncan started again.

'They may well already be Mr and Mrs Cochlan in the eyes of the law, but as we all know they are not properly married yet.'

At last Odette caught sight of Cyd. She was talking earnestly to one of her lookalike sons who was trying hard to ignore her and pretending to listen to Duncan's droning announcement. Odette edged closer, but she couldn't hear anything over the shrieking PA.

'They've composed their own vows,' Duncan was saying, 'which they are about to exchange, along with the rings and a big snog. If you'll all hush up then we can listen and giggle. So please give the sound of one hand clapping for the bride and groom!'

Misunderstanding him, the raucous guests embarked on yet another booming five minutes of cheers and applause as Elsa and Euan stood up and faced one another over the microphone.

'I, Euan Colin Walter Cochlan . . .' Euan started in a voice gruff with emotion.

'Colin!' Juno snorted in delight.

'. . . do offer my heart, my life and my spirit to you, Elsa Moonbeam Bridgehouse . . .'

'No *way*!' Juno was almost wetting herself. 'She always said the M stood for Marie.'

'. . . to cherish your karma, find yin for your yang, walk in tandem with your soul and dance in rhythm with your passion, whether it be jungle or drum 'n' bass . . .'

'What are they on about?' Jay looked confused.

Cyd had fallen silent to listen, Odette noticed, glancing across worriedly. Big tears were sliding along the laughter lines in her beautiful, sad face. She looked very vulnerable, very lonely, very fragile.

Then Odette watched in dismay as Cyd rested her hand on her son's shoulder and he shrugged it off angrily. When Cyd tried again – this time to link her arm through his – he turned to hiss something at her before moving away. Odette wasn't sure what he had said, but Cyd looked as though he'd just sprayed her with Mace. She clasped her hand to her mouth and bolted towards one of the side doors.

Odette rushed after her. Meanwhile Euan stood on stage solemnly pledging to worship at Elsa's altar and to garage groove at her twin decks. He vowed to leave space for her intellect and make time for her needs, just so long as they both should live 'with a full mental cognisance and reasonable quality of life'.

Juno turned to Jay and muttered, 'Sometimes I think Elsa and Euan suffer from being just too bloody trendy. What's wrong with love, honour and cherish?'

'What indeed?' Jay's yellow eyes glistened lovingly as Euan added that he would take dual responsibility in parenting, and let Buster the Bump support the football team of his/her choice.

A moment later, Duncan had stepped up to the mike, checking his piece of paper before announcing that they would all now join together 'and sing number 76 on your song sheets'.

The vast studio was suddenly flooded with the backing track to Blur's 'Parklife' and everyone started screaming along at the tops of their voices.

Odette tracked Cyd down by the Aston. She was fishing frantically in her handbag, face awash with tears.

'Here.' Odette handed her a tissue.

'I don't want that.' Cyd batted it away angrily. 'I can't find the bloody keys.'

'That's because I've got them.' Odette realised her employer must have polished off an awful lot of Love Drugs in a short space of time. 'And before you ask, no, I'm not going to give them to you. You're missing your daughter's wedding. So bloody pull yourself together and come inside.'

'Don't you dare talk to me like that!' Cyd was almost incandescent. 'You ungrateful little bitch! After all I've—'

'Oh, spare me the clichés and apply a few to yourself,' Odette sighed, finally breaking the end of her frayed tether. 'Starting with the pull yourself together, put a brave face on it, it can't be as bad as all that, you'll regret this for the rest of your life group.'

Cyd opened her mouth and closed it again, caught between blind fury and sudden, astonished amusement. 'That was almost exactly what your friend Jimmy said to me this morning,' she croaked.

A passing frog gave them an odd look as he headed towards the catering truck to fetch more champagne from the fridges.

'Was it?' Odette was amazed the cliché line had worked so

well for Jimmy. She'd been planning to move swiftly on to a little emotional blackmail.

Taking Odette's tissue and blowing her nose on it, Cyd nodded. She was looking highly offended. 'You know, he told me I reminded him of his mother, Philly Rialto? Bloody cheek. I knew her in the seventies – dreadful tart! And between you and me, *very* unstable. She ran off when he was just a child app—' Seeing the connection through her egotism blinkers at long last, she bit her lip and stifled a half-laugh, half-sob.

Odette could hear 'Parklife' coming to a bawdy conclusion inside the studio.

'Let's go inside.'

Cyd nodded, meekly taking Odette's proffered arm and tucking the tissue into the sleeve of her dress. 'I thought he was such a charming young man at first, but he's quite extraordinarily direct, isn't he?'

'Jimmy?' Odette looked at her. 'I don't know him that well to be honest.'

'He has an amazing grasp.' Cyd nodded. 'Such vision. Quite different from your other friend, dear little Calum, who is so desperately disillusioned, so like Jobe. Are you trying to decide between them, dearheart? It must be terribly hard. Both of them so adorably flawed.'

Odette, who had been smiling at the 'dear little' addition to Calum's name, wiped off the smirk. 'Am I what?'

'I'll read your cards for both as soon as we're home.' She squeezed Odette's arm. 'You know, Jimmy said something else which I thought was extraordinary.' Cyd paused by the door. 'He said that some people – like us – are just too bold with our love, whereas others are simply terrified of it. Isn't that a wonderful observation?' She took the tissue from her sleeve again to dab her eyes with it.

'Us?' Odette queried.

Cyd tutted. 'No! Not *you* and me, darling. Jimmy and me. We weren't talking about *you*.'

Odette registered the rebuke with a blush. Cyd wasn't the only one being self-obsessed around here.

'Although he did mention you actually,' Cyd told her with

some satisfaction. 'He said you fell into the category of people who are terrified of love.'

'Who's he think he is, Freud? I always thought he was a pseud,' Odette snarled defensively as she opened the side-door to the studio.

'Dearheart, can't you see? He's your . . .'

The barrage of noise drowned out the rest of Cyd's words, and Odette had no chance to ask her to repeat them as Elsa's echoing voice on the microphone demanded, 'Mum? Where are you? You're wanted on stage. God, I bet she's in the loo.'

As Cyd bolted to the front, Odette stayed at the back of the studio and mulled over the fact that she was certain she'd just heard Cyd saying, 'He's your Knight of Discs.'

As the exchange of vows onstage dragged on longer than swearing in a new government, Odette found herself standing next to Juno's brother, Sean, who was sporting the same ultra-fashionable haircut as Calum, long over his ears and tufty everywhere else. Since Sean was craggy-faced, in his early forties and widening around the middle, it suited him even less. But he was the ultimate trend-junkie and welcomed Odette with surprising enthusiasm.

'You look luminous!' He kissed her on both cheeks. 'I love the specs. Are they Versace?'

'Vision Express,' Odette muttered, although they were, in fact, Gucci. She suddenly realised why she'd been so set against being trendy all these years. It turned friendly acquaintances into Swap-Shop label droppers.

'Hi there.' Sean's designer-junkie wife Triona – the ultimate must-have accessory – smiled her minxy smile and squeezed Odette's arm, nodding toward the stage. 'Isn't that just so lovely? A family fusion ceremony. So *sweet*.'

Odette suddenly realised what was going on. Elsa and Euan had called their respective families on to the stage – Ronald McDonald, Wally the Kilt, Po-face and Pa-face, the Bridgehouse brothers. And finally they were joined by Cyd – who drew a great many gasps of recognition from those guests unaware that

Elsa's mother was none other than the woman splashed across the *Sun* recently with the headline 'Trials Of Jobe's Missus'. With their families gathered together, the couple, known to most of their friends as The Es, were asking them to exchange vows too.

'Bleedin' hell,' Odette said to no one in particular.

'I wish we'd thought of this.' Triona played with one of Sean's tufty sideburns. 'I'd have loved Howard, Judy and Juno to swear a bond of unity with my family.'

'C'mon, your family's so complicated it would have taken twelve weeks. You have more steps than the Eiffel Tower.'

Odette watched in amazement as Elsa and Euan stood ceremonially with their families – Euan's a trinity of weird dress sense, Elsa's a sextuplet of curls plus two mismatched extras, the tiny, seemingly emotionless Po and the tall, emotional Cyd.

'Why are you crying?' Triona asked her a few minutes later as Cyd, her sons, their father, little Po and the hugely embarrassed Cochlans held hands and swore never to hold grudges, take sides, conduct feuds or lose contact. They promised to honour their grandparental duties jointly and without rancour, favouritism or envy. They were also made to promise never to give Buster sexist toys or bad-taste anoraks for Christmas.

'Look at Po.' Odette wiped her eye. Tears were creeping down the little Japanese woman's cheeks. A moment later and she and Cyd were hugging tightly, Amazon and Lilliput. Then, to Odette's delight, three of the four Bridgehouse sons joined in the hug. A moment later the fourth was kicked into place by none other than Pa Bridgehouse himself.

Soon the party was in full swing. The frogs were starting to get the hang of their costumes and bore their trays of food aloft at such passing speed the guests had to jog alongside to get anything to eat.

The music was deafening and the light so dim it was impossible to hold a casual conversation or to find a friend. Happy just to soak up the atmosphere, Odette alternately lingered by gold trees, sat on silver blankets and boogied by the *trompe-l'œil* speakers. She kept a constant look-out for Cyd whom she occasionally spotted in the distance, chatting animatedly with clubby types, looking radiantly happy.

'Fantastic wedding!' Duncan laughed. 'Mind you, the ceremony went on a bit. I thought Buster the Bump would be in nappies by the time his parents finally tied the knot.'

'Lasted longer than most of Rod Stewart's marriages,' Odette agreed, enjoying the chance to strut her stuff, although she was secretly more of a Sinatra fan.

But the most energetic people in the room by far were Murray and Eunice de Souza. Showing a remarkable turn of foot, they boogied, grooved and got down to the music, dominating the dance floor like Fred and Ginger. Their hip-swinging foxtrot proved such a hit that soon everyone was imitating it. Groups of hardened clubbers, who normally danced alone swigging from water bottles, started waltzing up and down the room in pairs, like pensioners in Blackpool Tower ballroom. Odette watched in astonishment as Jeremy Healy tangoed past arm-in-arm with Boy George.

'It's going to be the latest thing, girl, mark my words,' a familiar voice cackled in her ear. 'They'll all be doing it down the Ministry this time next week.'

Stan and Saskia had turned up for the party at last, looking very funky in matching must-have green outfits, punky waxed hair and rimless specs.

'You having fun?' Saskia yelled over the music.

'Terrific!' she yelled back.

'What?'

'Terrific!'

Saskia gave her the polite haven't-heard-but-pretending-I-have nod of the practised London partygoer and started chasing after a frog bearing a tray of food.

Odette hadn't eaten all afternoon and longed for a big bar of chocolate.

'You're looking great, gel!' Stan yelled.

'Thank you,' she enunciated exaggeratedly to be heard over Miss Bee's soundtrack. 'It's lovely to see you and Saskia here, babes.'

'What?'

'What?'

'What?'

It was hopeless. They both shrugged at each other and danced for a while.

Elsa and Euan were mingling easily. Having spent most of their working lives in clubs and music venues they had highly tuned ears, capable of discerning every word of conversation through the floor-shaking bass. Either that or they could lip-read brilliantly.

The party raged on for hours. Feeling deliciously carefree for the first time in weeks, Odette danced and mingled and continued keeping an eye on Cyd who seemed to be having the time of her life dancing with each one of her sons in turn and even managing a brief spin to the latest Aura Grind sound with Po.

When Elsa gathered her friends together to throw her bouquet, she demanded that all the single women came to the front. Odette tried to hang back but Juno towed her forward, whispering, 'Those blooms are *mine*. I'm relying on you to mark the opposition. If you see anyone trying to catch them before me, kick them.'

And so Odette found herself standing behind Juno who was crouched like a wicket keeper at the front of the scrum. Not watching Elsa, Odette checked from left to right. There were a lot of eager wannabe brides lined up, eyes not leaving their intended target, arms outstretched ready. Juno was much shorter than any of them, and Odette suspected she'd had too many Love Drugs to get her eye in. As Elsa turned her back to the jostling crowd and prepared to swing the flowers overhead, the women surged forwards and Juno disappeared under a sea of bodies.

The three calla lilies sailed gracefully into the air.

'Odette, help me!' came a faint cry from deep within the bulldozing, screaming crowd as women elbowed each other out of the way.

Odette looked around for Juno, desperate to drag her out and place her at the front again. But just as she caught sight of a small, crushed-looking figure in the centre she felt something fly past her face and land squarely in her cleavage.

'They don't count,' Juno complained afterwards when Odette handed her the bouquet. 'You caught them.'

'I didn't catch them, they fell down my top.'

Juno examined a big graze on her elbow. 'Ouch! That's a blood sport. It should be banned.'

Elsa and Euan finally left for their honeymoon – one night at the Ritz – in a huge old gold-sprayed Cadillac, its fins covered in tinsel, its fender trailing a glittering, clattering train of CDs like a sequinned fish-tail. They were whooped away by the late-night partygoers whose fun had only just begun. Most were planning to stick it out at the studio until dawn.

Odette suddenly felt incredibly weary. She wasn't accustomed to the London pace any more. She was also desperate to take off the restrictive corset. When her friends finally started to drift home, she went in search of Cyd and spotted her sharing a cigarette with her eldest son, Gabriel, in a tree-lined corner of the hangar.

Leaving them to it, she crept back to the Aston and fell asleep in the driver's seat.

Cyd tapped on the window at three in the morning.

'There you bloody are. I've been searching for you everywhere.' The moment she was sitting inside, she put a Mask cassette on at top volume and fell asleep.

Odette fought lockjaw yawns all the way to the farm. She was amazed at the way her spirits lifted with every mile. When she finally spotted her frosty old smock mill looming over the woods, she felt surprisingly elated.

Under the stone by Cyd's kitchen door was a note that read, *'Please give your driver next Friday off. Insist I take her to dinner. JS.'*

'How shwweet!' Cyd hiccupped as she tripped over the puppies and headed towards the stairs. 'Knight of Discs, my dearheart – after a night of compact discs. It's sherendipity, don't you shee?'

41

Life started to pick up for Odette after Elsa and Euan's wedding. The very next day she was leafing listlessly through Cyd's Sunday paper when it occurred to her that she hadn't checked her lottery numbers from the tickets she'd bought with her haircut money. She had matched four with one ticket and scooped almost a hundred pounds. It was a good omen that seemed to lead to a spell of luck.

Cyd was hugely distracted thanks to a lunch she was planning to host for two of her four sons on Wednesday. The other two refused to come, but it seemed that Elsa and Euan's bizarre ceremony had started to work its magic. She spent most of Monday planning the menu and then sent Odette out on Tuesday morning to buy the ingredients. Odette was pretty certain that the little Chuckfield Budgens wouldn't run to nori or kombu seaweed and rice vinegar, so she popped to Brighton, also treating herself to a new dress for Juno's leaving party with her Lottery winnings.

As she drove back, the sun kicked through the clouds for the first time in weeks, lighting up the new acid greens in the trees and fields. Odette realised with a lifting heart that spring was finally arriving. The hedgerows were foaming with blossom, the verges dotted with yellow clumps of primroses; gardens were crammed with open daffodils and crocuses trumpeting their clashing colours at one another.

When she returned to the farm, Jimmy Sylvian's pick-up was parked in front of the house, with Nelson standing sentry in the back while Winnie, shut in the cab, growled at him through two inches of open window.

Cyd emerged from the side of the house, a pair of dark glasses sliding down her nose.

'Isn't this sun ravishing?' she greeted Odette. 'I was just telling Jimmy, you and I will be able to go topless in the Porsche soon.'

'What?' Odette, who was heaving shopping bags out of the boot of the Merc, dropped two bottles of champagne which rolled away unbroken.

'We'll be able to take the roof off the car, dearheart.' Cyd stooped to pick the bottles up. 'Didn't they have Mumm? I specifically asked for Mumm Cordon Rouge.'

'Sorry – there's obviously been a run on it,' Odette explained. 'Mother's Day next Sunday. I thought Bolly would be okay?'

'I suppose it'll have to be,' Cyd sniffed. 'Come and have a coffee – I've asked Jimmy in for one. Have you bought any? I realised after I'd offered that I only have herbal tea.'

'What's he doing here?' Odette asked suspiciously.

'He came to see me, of course.' Cyd carried the two champagne bottles inside while Odette staggered behind with four heavy bags in each hand and one hooked in her mouth. 'I was, as you might recall, in a bit of a state when he last saw me. What a darling!'

Odette gritted her teeth so hard that the plastic handles she was carrying between them snapped and the bag plunged to the floor. Cyd, having dumped her bottles on the kitchen table, was dancing back through to Jimmy.

'Yes, it was Odette and I've coaxed her in for you, dearheart!'

I was coming inside anyway, she thought irritably, dumping her heavy bags on the table, too high for the puppies to nose through them. How else would I get all the shopping in? Cyd was very good at making it look as though she had gone to considerable pains to engineer a situation that would have happened anyway.

Jimmy was sitting on one of the sofas, surrounded by puppies.

'Have you been in a fight?' Odette asked curiously, noticing a small red scar across his eyebrow.

'Only with a pile of brambles.' He showed her his hands,

which were lacerated with red stripes. 'We're trying to clear the Fermoncieaux kitchen gardens, but it has to be done by hand because the gates in the walls are too narrow to get digging equipment through, and it's taking forever. There's four acres to clear.'

'Redevelopment still not going well, then?' Odette adopted her trusty businesslike stance, trying to look as though she was only interested from an academic point of view.

'Behind schedule, over budget.' He smiled.

'Odette!' Cyd called through from the kitchen. 'This coffee powder won't dissolve. Must you buy such cheap rubbish?'

'It's ground coffee – it needs a filter,' she sighed, trotting through to help out.

Cyd took her cue to rush straight back and chat up Jimmy again. 'Have you got to know many people since you've lived here? The locals are perfectly sweet, but rather clingy. Before you know it you'll be on twenty committees.'

Odette didn't hear Jimmy's answer as the kettle reached a rattling boil and she poured water over the grains in an ancient cafetière which must have stayed unused in a cupboard since Jobe's death.

When she carried it back through, she saw that Cyd was sitting directly under the huge antlers which hung on the far wall, puppies at her feet. She looked curiously like some sort of ancient Norse queen.

'Calum's taking two of my babies,' she told Jimmy, stroking a slipper-soft head. 'I've been trying to persuade Odette to have the last little jewel, but she absolutely hates dogs. Don't suppose you want one, do you?'

'Actually I'm trying to get rid of one myself.' Jimmy smiled up at Odette who was blushing defensively.

'I don't hate dogs,' she told Cyd, still amazed that Calum had agreed to take two of Bazouki's litter. 'I'm just not very good with them.'

'Nonsense!' Cyd jumped up to pour the coffee, waving Odette away. 'You'd be a perfect owner. You never go out, you need the company and you need the exercise. You and I could take Mum and daughter on walks together.'

'I *do* go out,' Odette snapped. Noticing Jimmy's amused expression, she realised they must come across as two lonely, squabbling women living together, which was what they were. A rich widow and her downtrodden, dog-hating companion.

Jimmy cleared his throat. 'Actually, I just popped by to take a look at the wiring in the windmill. You said last week that there was some sort of fault?'

'Oh, you don't have to worry yourself about that, does he, Odette?' Cyd said breezily, pouring out two mugs of coffee from the dusty cafetière. 'I'm going to get an electrician in. Cream or milk?'

'Neither.' Jimmy was looking at Odette. 'Are you sure? I thought you had no hot water?'

'I don't.' Odette glared at Cyd. 'That would be really kind.'

'I was supposed to be in meetings this afternoon,' he told Cyd, 'but the documentary team are there. They spent all morning getting Calum and Alex to pose on the scaffolding in hard hats with the foreman. But they kept getting the giggles and the thing had to be re-shot a dozen times, so everyone's running late. The place is chaos. I'm steering clear.'

'What documentary team?' She was agog.

Odette felt her face drain of colour and stared fixedly out of the window.

'Someone called Veronica Prior,' Jimmy explained, slurping back more coffee, 'wants to do a fly-on-the-wall series about Food Hall – or "fly-in-the-soup" as they've nicknamed it. Calum says it'll be great publicity. I want nothing to do with it. I've made it clear I won't work while they're around.'

'Oh, yes, I've heard all about this.' Cyd gave Odette a very pointed, eyebrow-raised look which was lost on her as she stared out at the lake, praying that Cyd wouldn't mention the fact that that it was she who had called Ronny Prior in the first place. Thankfully, Cyd's memory was as short-term as an exam crammer these days, and she seemed to have forgotten. 'Calum told me something of it. I know he's got a bit of a reputation, but he's too charming to dislike, isn't he? Quite astonishing charisma. We had a splendid dinner together. You two know each other very well, I believe?'

Jimmy nodded, clearing his throat uncomfortably.

'So *how* do you know him?' Cyd persisted, suddenly sounding like Lady Bracknell quizzing a love-struck suitor. When Jimmy didn't answer she dropped her voice to an intimate rasp. 'Did something happen in Africa to make you two so close? After all, you two have a very special friendship, don't you?'

Odette looked at her in alarm. 'Special friendship' was the sort of phrase her parents' generation gave to gay couples. She opened her mouth to say something distracting and then closed it again when she saw Jimmy's expression. His usually open face was guarded. Only his eyes gave him away – they were almost black with anger.

'He came to stay at Mpona,' he said, the rich, booming voice unusually flat. 'He wanted to see—'

But before he could finish, Cyd broke in by clapping her hands together and looking towards Odette. 'Darling, could you put that shopping away before it all goes off? There's a dearheart.'

Skin itching with frustration, she sloped back into the kitchen. She kept the door to the main room open in an attempt to listen in, hoping that Jimmy's loud voice would carry through, but all she could hear was Cyd complaining of a draught and a moment later the door was closed, reducing all noise to mumbles.

Fed up and livid, she turned on the radio. Cyd had it tuned to a local indie music station which instantly started blaring out a deafening Aura Grind dance track. Odette surfed around until she found the soothing sounds of The Corrs.

She threw two packets of smoked salmon into the fridge followed by a bag of salad leaves, slamming the door shut with such force that a fridge magnet shaped like an afghan hound flew off and landed in her cleavage. She fished it back out but the little black magnet had fallen off and no amount of delving and jumping about located it. Odette scoured the floor and then gave up.

Flinging the rest of the shopping away with careless haste,

she followed Jimmy's muffled boom back into the room, but he shut up the moment she entered.

'Done already?' Cyd looked disconcerted. 'You are so efficient. I was just telling Jimmy what an absolute saviour you've been to have around. Best thing I ever did, offering you that job.'

Odette flashed a weak smile. She wanted to point out that most jobs provided at least some sort of wage but she didn't like to say anything in front of Jimmy. She'd promised herself she'd have a word with Cyd after the two Bridgehouse brothers came for lunch, hoping to catch her on a high.

Jimmy looked relieved to see her, polishing off the last of his coffee and standing up. 'So, let's look at this wiring of yours.'

To Odette's amazement, Cyd barred the way out of the farm.

'You really don't want to bother yourself with the mill, dearheart – it's very high-tech and complicated. It just needs a couple of new fuses.'

'Then there's no point in calling out an electrician, is there?' Jimmy gave her a charming smile. 'I can change a fuse. And you can't refuse.'

Cyd laughed with false jollity at his bad joke. 'Well, let me come and show you around at least.' She darted between him and Odette. The phone started ringing before she could get him out of the room. 'Get that will you, Odette? Say I'm out.'

Before Odette could say 'hello' a furious and familiar voice growled sexily, 'And where the fuck are you?'

'Calum?' She froze, clasping the receiver tightly with her hand.

'Odette?' The tone instantly changed from teasing undertone to snappish shock.

A spilt-second later, Cyd had wrenched the receiver from her hand and was breathing into it with smoky soothing balm, 'Calum, dearheart. I've been trying to get hold of you all day. Slight transport problem . . .' She covered the receiver and turned to Odette. 'You'd better show Jimmy around the mill. But don't let him near the wiring. It's very specialist. I'll be along as soon as I can.'

Jimmy had already wandered outside so Odette followed him, half an ear on Cyd's voice fading away behind her. 'Yes, yes, I know today's important, dearheart, but I do have businesses to run this end . . .'

'I can see this mill from my bedroom window,' Jimmy boomed, cutting off Odette's eavesdropping. 'It's even more impressive close to.' He gazed up at the cap. 'So unusual to have survived intact. It must be an amazing place to live.'

'Amazing's not the word,' she sniffed, showing him inside.

A few minutes in the basement and Jimmy started to recognise the difficulties inherent in living in the damp mill. He was a man who could survive in the middle of the bush with no home comforts or luxuries, but the one thing he loathed was cold. He was appalled to think that Odette had gone so long without heating.

'This place is a death-trap,' he boomed when he looked into the fuse cupboard. 'Jesus, someone's really messed these circuits up. I'll just fetch some stuff from the truck.'

Odette sulkily admired her own handiwork. She hadn't thought it a bad patch-up job, even if all she'd succeeded in doing was blowing up the spa bath while she was trying to wash her delicates in it.

'Do you know what you're doing?' she asked worriedly when Jimmy started clanking and cursing in the box, pulling great spaghetti twists of wire out and testing each with a little digital meter. He'd turned off the power so the only light came from the huge rechargeable torch he had given Odette to hold and a small Maglite he had gripped between his teeth.

'I should do – I rewired all the rondavels in Mpona,' he muttered, tapping the little meter irritably. 'Mind you, I hate this new technology. We had a good old-fashioned AVO out there. Size of a brick and never broke down. This thing is as tinny as a . . .' He suddenly let out an almighty scream and jumped backwards.

Almost passing out in fright, Odette stepped back on the little Maglite, which had rolled across the floor towards her. There was a tinny crunch and its beam went out. Jimmy was crouching on the floor by the fuse cupboard.

'D'you get a shock, babes?' She rushed over to him, dumping her torch on a bench press and putting an arm around his shoulders.

'No – the electricity's off, you dolt!' He winced in agony as he clutched his finger. 'I just got bitten by a crocodile clip.' There were tears of pain in his eyes. For a big man with a rugged history of lion-tracking in the African bush, he was incredibly wimpy about pain.

'It's a bleedin' complicated job,' Odette fretted. 'Are you sure you wouldn't rather forget it? I expect Cyd will call out an electrician eventually.'

'And meanwhile you'll wake up one night to find the place in flames around you.' He sucked his cut finger. 'Well, I'm bleeding and I'm complicated too, so I guess I'm man enough for the job. This circuit's been totally overloaded.' He peered at it closely. 'It was never intended to run as much equipment as there is in here.'

He continued unravelling wires, replacing fuses, tinkering and muttering for the best part of half an hour, sporadically banging his head and cursing. Soon the batteries started fading in the light Odette was holding up. The bright white beam dimmed to an amber glow.

'I think this is about to give out.' She waggled it to make her point just as Jimmy was carefully attaching two wires. Losing the light for a fraction of a second made him drop both and curse under his breath.

'It's almost out of charge,' he told her. 'I've only got this last little bit to do – lean as close as you can to get me the light.'

Odette crouched right over him, acutely aware that her boobs were either side of his broad neck, the back of his hair tickling her cleavage. Jimmy didn't seem to notice as he carried on twisting the wires together with deft, swift turns of his pliers.

'A little closer,' he ordered. 'No – move it down, that's right. And again.'

Odette's boobs started sliding down the length of Jimmy's long, warm back.

The light was little more than the brightness of a single candle now. Apart from its one, dim spot, the room was in darkness. Odette felt her face flame as she realised she was in a dark room wrapped around a strange man who, for all she knew, could have murdered someone in Africa. She'd dwelled on Mpona's secrets too much and felt ridiculously jumpy.

'Twist around to my left a bit – that's it – just a few more seconds and we're done.' It seemed to have taken him ages to do the last bit of wiring as he went about it with meticulous, long-winded precision.

Suddenly, Odette realised something very creepy was happening inside her top. It appeared to be moving, pulled down at the cleavage by some unseen force. Peering at it in the gloom, she could distinctly make out her white lacy bra. She hastily looked at the little pool of light, but both Jimmy's hands were still visible.

Christ! She was being groped by a ghost. Jobe Francis's ghost was looking down her top.

She let out an ear-splitting scream just an inch from Jimmy's ear. He head-butted the fuse box in alarm and swung around. The torch fell to the floor and promptly went out.

'What happened?' Jimmy's voice asked in the darkness, reassuringly close.

Odette was shaking like a leaf, heart stampeding. 'I think I was just – touched – by a ghost.'

To her relief he didn't laugh. She jumped as she felt a hand grope for her shoulder, but it was just Jimmy patting her.

'It's okay, I'd get spooked in a place like this,' he assured her. 'Hang on, I'll find that torch.' But as he stooped down, Odette found her top wanted to go too. A moment later and she was flashing in the darkness. The ghost was back. Jobe was up for a threesome.

'What the . . . ?' Jimmy laughed, realising what was happening.

He found the torch and clicked it on. Just for a brief moment it illuminated Odette's lacy front-loader before Jimmy hastily detached her top from his shirt pocket with a metallic click.

'I think that's what you call magnetic attraction,' he laughed, pulling the wire cutters from his pocket. 'Is your bra made of lodestone or something?'

'Oh, God,' She groped about inside her top and, sure enough, found the little fridge magnet she had dropped down there earlier. So Jobe Francis wasn't a tit man after all. And she'd just flashed her boobs at Jimmy Sylvian for the second time in a week.

'That'll have to do for now,' he said cheerfully, clicking on the trip switch and closing the cupboard.

She blinked as harsh artificial light flooded the room once more.

'I'll come back and have another go next time I'm free,' he said, being deliberately businesslike to spare her blushes. It seemed they were both destined to keep behaving like two suits at a conference. 'Right now I'll test the equipment upstairs and see what looks likely to work. Where's the shower – through here?' He opened the door to the spa bath, which was full of wet clothes.

'Your laundry, I assume?' he said in amusement as he backed out. 'My offer of the use of Siddals' washing machine and bath still stands, you know.'

Twenty minutes later he had poked his little device into every plug and socket available, changed at least twenty fuses and ensured that the shower now pumped out a healthy gush of hot water. On top of that, the kettle boiled and the television worked, although it couldn't pick up a signal as the aerial had long-since blown off the cap.

'I can try and fix the video sometime if you like,' he offered, peering at the front panel, the display of which had rusted with condensation.

'Oh, yes, please!' Odette was ecstatic at the prospect of being able to watch her beloved tapes – Hart to Hart, Dynasty, Dallas, Falcon Crest, The Colbys and of course, 9½ Weeks. Her evenings were soon set to be transformed, it seemed.

Jimmy had plenty of opportunity to assess the damp, the leaking windows and the appalling insulation as he poked around. He also found at least thirty empty bottles hidden in the most unexpected locations.

'Very different from your London flat, isn't it?' he laughed. 'You could do a lot with this place, though. It needs patching up, some new paint, a little love, but given a few weeks' work we could make it great for you.'

'I'm not sure how long I'll be staying,' Odette demurred, not liking the 'we'.

Jimmy shrugged amiably and wandered outside, throwing his tool-pack into the back of the pick-up.

Cyd dashed out of the house. 'Dearheart! Have you been here all this time? I hope Odette hasn't been exploiting you, you poor thing. Would you like a herb tea or a coffee before you set off?'

'Odette made me a wonderful cuppa in the tower, thanks.' Jimmy winked at her, climbing into the car.

'With what?' Cyd asked grumpily.

'A kettle and a tea bag,' Odette muttered as Jimmy started up the engine, 'Thanks so much, babes!' she called.

He gave her a mock salute and swung the car around. Cyd watched, tapping her fingers irritably against her thighs.

'I hope you two haven't changed much in there,' she muttered. 'I like to think of the mill as something of a shrine – so full of memories of Jobe.'

'But you said you wanted me to make it into my own little palace,' Odette reminded her. Cyd was so contradictory at times.

Cyd glared at her. 'Now that you've come off your *very* long tea break I'd quite like you to do some work. Can you bring the Aston round?' She dashed back into the house.

Ten minutes later, Odette was driving towards Fermoncieaux. Cyd wouldn't explain why, simply snapped that it was important.

It was the closest Odette had ever been to the house, and the fact unsettled her far too much for her to want to get out and look around. She ducked down in the car as a group of builders ambled past, but of course she couldn't hope to be ignored as they leered first at the Aston and then at her. Why couldn't Cyd own at least one basic runaround amongst her fleet of rusting marques?

After a few minutes of unwanted attention, they pushed off and Odette tapped her fingers on the wheel impatiently.

She hated herself for it, but she was starting to dislike Cyd quite a lot. It seemed so ungrateful, so petty, and yet a creeping mildew of resentment and disrespect had started crawling all over her, clouding her vision and stiffening her eager jump-to-the-call responses. Cyd took advantage too often, changed her mind too often, was mean and childish and a terrible mother to Elsa.

When she wrenched open the car door, Odette jumped guiltily, certain that she would see the festering resentment in her face. But Cyd was far too distracted to notice.

'I need to go to Brighton – we're shopping,' she ordered.

Odette seethed irritably at the familiar finger-snapping routine.

'I've already been shopping in Brighton today,' she muttered under her breath. 'I could have picked up whatever you need.'

'Well, that dress you bought was frightful – I've never heard of the label. River Phoenix, was it?'

'Island.' She deliberately reversed and swung the car around so fast that Cyd slammed into the door trim.

'Yes, you left it in the kitchen – I had a peek in the bag.' Cyd rubbed her ribs. 'Horrible cut, horrible colour. Just like that hair of yours. It won't do at all now. Not at all. You see, I'm firing you as my driver.'

'You're *what*?' Odette slammed on the brakes so that Cyd – who never wore a safety belt – gut-busted the glove compartment.

She sat back in her seat with a resigned sigh. 'Before you rearrange *all* my internal organs, I'm offering you the job of business manager instead. I want you to take over the Miller empire. As of next Monday, you're in sole charge so you'll need to look the part. There are meetings to be conducted, deals to be won. And you'll need to learn how to read the tarot. There's no time to be lost.'

They were halfway along the Fermoncieaux drive, in full view of the house. Not caring, Odette cut the engine, determined to get the facts straight.

'You want me to take over the Millers?'

'Yes.'

'Why?' Odette asked suspiciously. 'Has this anything to do with Calum? With your meeting just now?'

'We need some music.' Cyd fished through the glove box that had just winded her, searching for a cassette. 'Ah – Republica. Saffron is so spunky, isn't she? And she has *wonderful* hair.'

'Why were you meeting Calum?' Odette persisted.

'To negotiate a fee for . . .' Cyd slotted the tape in and sighed as 'Bloke' blared out of the Aston's quadraphonic speakers.

'A fee for?' Odette wasn't giving up, hard as Cyd was trying to appear dizzy.

'The puppies!' she laughed. 'The puppies, you silly dear. Remember Calum is buying Balalaika and Banjo? I was just transferring the – er – Kennel Club papers and what-not. Very boring. Dog stuff, you wouldn't be interested. Now get a wiggle on or we'll miss the shops.'

Odette refused to budge. 'Will I get paid for this?'

'Well, I suppose – if you want a raise.' Cyd looked affronted. 'But I thought I was being quite generous.'

'Cyd, you're not paying me at all!' Odette howled.

'Of course I am,' she huffed.

'With what? Heat-up meals and money for a haircut?'

'No. I put cash in an envelope once a week and leave it in your dove hole.'

'My *dove* hole?' she baulked. Was this another of Cyd's New Age practices?

'In the cote,' Cyd laughed, as if it was perfectly obvious and Odette was being deeply thick. 'It's very safe and tremendously tax-efficient. That's how I pay all my staff. You don't mean to say . . .'

When Odette got back from Brighton two hours later with her second radical haircut in a week and two new suits which she personally thought Miss Whiplash would blush to wear, Cyd showed her the 'dove hole'.

'But you haven't collected any of your wages, dearheart!'

she laughed when she climbed to the top of the ladder and peered in.

Three soggy envelopes were inside, all stuffed with damp ten-pound notes. In total there was more than three hundred pounds. Odette ran her hand through her jet black hair extensions with their stubby Coca-Cola red fringe and stared at Cyd with damp red eyes. 'I'm so sorry – I thought you weren't paying me.'

'Perhaps I should have explained the system.' Cyd wrinkled her nose thoughtfully. 'Anyway – no time to worry about that. Pocket your packets and stay out of the way tomorrow lunchtime, will you? I know I'm a selfish cow but I need to focus on this one. Perhaps you could fix that quad bike to keep you busy?'

Later that evening, the bliss of having a hot shower was beyond Odette's happiness valve. She gave a great wail of pleasure as she stood under the steaming jet, letting it plaster her strange hair to her head. She had seized no more control over her life – if anything it was racketing along runaway train rails even faster than ever. But it *was* on rails again at least.

Afterwards she wrapped herself in a grubby towel, making a mental note to check out the spa bath for hand-washing capabilities again, or as a last resort beg Jimmy for a cycle or two in his machine. She looked around the big mill-wheel room, assessing its potential. It could be quite sensational if brought up to date and given a lick of paint. She turned on the stereo – working at long last. The tape deck and CD were clinically dead, but the radio still managed a few stations and she surfed through them for her favourite, Heart FM. Robbie Williams was blasting out 'Angel'.

It was a seminal moment for Odette. She shuddered happily. Somehow she felt a few angels had entered her life for the first time in ages.

She was so unaccustomed to happiness that her reactions went into overdrive.

That night, Jimmy Sylvian peered out of his attic window towards the tower and smiled as he saw a shadow dancing from window to window, arms waving, hips swinging. Putting down his can of beer, he bounded downstairs to search through his dresser drawers.

The following morning Odette found an envelope pushed under her door. In it was a keyring which bore the sort of plastic, rectangular picture holder that Clod had once carried with school photographs of Monny and Odette on either side. In this one was a cropped-down shot of a familiar-looking long-eared spaniel with imploring eyes. The accompanying note read: *'Please come and visit the sick. Winnie picked fight. Lost. Confined to barracks. Happy to sponge your back in the bath.'* Attached to the ring was a key to Siddals Farm.

Odette found the fault on the quad bike without the aid of the manual. It had no petrol in it. Having siphoned some from the mower, she decided to try it out, letting out a whoop of exhilaration as it zipped out of the cobbled yard, sending up a cloud of dust and straw. Riding it reminded her of her beloved little moped, only here there were no exhaust fumes and kamikaze couriers. The wind whipped her unfamiliar new hair extensions from her head: the feel of close-to-the-ground, open-to-the-elements speed took her breath away as did the jerking, bone-crunching bumps as she and the fat-wheeled bike flew over ruts and divots.

She finally braked at the ridge of the hill above the farm, looking down to Fermoncieaux. In the foreground, Jimmy's ugly farm lay like a blemish on the green skin of the downs.

Having nothing better to do as she killed time, Odette kicked the quad bike back into action and bounced down through the valley, scattering sheep in her wake. Jimmy's key was in her pocket. She saw no harm in checking out his washing machine to see if it had a decent wool cycle.

The little spaniel was indeed in a sorry state, her face crusted with scabs, one big brown eye half-closed. She was wearing a huge bucket collar that made her look like Elizabeth I in a ruff. Odette was flattered by the way Winnie wriggled all around her in ecstatic welcome when she let herself through the door with the new key, shouting a cautious 'Hello?' several times in case Jimmy was in.

The place was empty and as masculinely minimalist as ever, although there were a few additions since she had last visited. There was a new dishwasher in the kitchen, a couple of fat pot plants still bearing their garden-centre labels on the windowsill, a big, scuffed second-hand sofa in the front sitting room and three huge boxes, unopened and stamped all over with Customs and Excise marks. She assumed they must be Jimmy's possessions from South Africa. The urge to rip into them and rifle through surprised her. She supposed it must be the thrill of the exotic. Instead she sat on the big sofa with poor, scarred Winnie and gave her a few awkward pats.

She used Jimmy's phone to freecall BT and arrange to have the smock mill phone reconnected. It was a separate line to that of the farm and she found to her irritation that the reconnection fee had to be paid by cheque or credit card.

'But I have cash!' she complained. 'Tell me where to bring it and I'll pay you.'

They would not be swayed and she gave up in disgust. Being a bankrupt was tantamount to being a non-person. She'd just have to buy some more credits for her mobile instead, and then risk death by swinging from the mill cap to get a good enough signal to make calls. She knew she should head back to the farm, but decided to make herself a quick cup of tea.

An hour later and she was still there, reading an old *Daily Telegraph* and listening to Heart FM.

She was surprised how relaxing it was just to loll around Jimmy's house soaking in the warmth – and it really was blissfully warm. Although at least three of the mill heaters now worked, the place was still an icehouse by comparison. And she quite fancied a bath, too.

At five, she finally quadded her way back to the farm and found Cyd had gone out, leaving the kitchen covered in sticky rice which was so revoltingly overcooked that even Bazouki's greedy puppies had not tried to pilfer it. Starting to clear it up, Odette suspected that her boss's family reunion lunch had not gone well.

Jimmy was far beyond the woods, taking Nelson for an afternoon walk, watching the sun set and the birds roost and smelling the first heady scents of a British spring for ten years. Through his binoculars he'd spotted a multitude of fledglings in their nests, beaks gaping. Buds were exploding into life all around, lambs were bouncing, daffodils creaking open and hibernating creatures waking up for a yawn and a stretch. Nature was awakening once more. Jimmy was enthralled.

Even his ugly farmhouse had looked quite ruggedly handsome in the red glow of sunset, although it had now lost its best feature. The steam on the bathroom window had started to dry, the ravishing silhouette no longer framed within.

Cyd returned at nightfall, slightly pissed and deliriously happy. 'The sushi I tried to make was a disaster. Gabriel took one look at it and took Casp and me to Wok Wok in Brighton. He's flying back to Singapore tomorrow, but he says he'll keep in touch. Casp has promised to try and talk my other two babies into coming down here this week. Such bliss! I'm going to bed. Terribly early start. Can you walk Bazouki, dearheart? She hasn't been out all day.'

Odette was spending so much time with dogs these days, she was starting to feel like Barbara Woodhouse.

Cyd decreed that Odette could have the rest of the week off while she was in 'management training' for her forthcoming role at the head of the Miller empire.

She decided to spend the time scrubbing out the mill. It was a filthy, thankless task, but it kept her mind occupied and she only occasionally bunked off to visit Winnie and use Jimmy's washing machine.

While Cyd stayed locked in the farmhouse by day, the mill had a regular new visitor.

Lurcher barking, music blaring, engine roaring, Jimmy's pick-up would thunder along the drive each day to drop off a delivery. It started with some fuses. To Odette's surprise, Jimmy refused her offer of a coffee.

'Have to dash. Work at Fermoncieaux's really taken off. The young stock has started arriving at last. We're flat out.'

'Thanks for these.'

'Least I can do when you've been visiting Winnie for me.' He grinned. Odette liked this new matey, practical Jimmy. She far preferred him bringing her fuses to roses.

He made no comment about the Republica hair, even though Odette pointed out that Cyd had insisted upon it as part of her new management role.

She was not enjoying being trained for the job. The late-night confession sessions had been replaced by tortuous mystic profiteering lessons over the kitchen table, fuelled by whisky and Aura Grind. Odette ate a lot of bars of chocolate to get her through. She rapidly learned how to read tarots and runes, how to divine with a pendulum and heal with a crystal.

'I really think I should see the accounts first,' Odette insisted, alarmed that her management role would involve long sessions as a live Internet soothsayer.

'Oh, you don't need to bother yourself with those,' Cyd waved her hand vaguely. 'Now what do you know about astrology? As long as you can remember the twelve signs you'll be fine – just make it up. I do.'

Odette was appalled.

'It's all a total con,' she told Jimmy when he popped around on Friday lunchtime with a huge doughnut of gaffer tape to stop up her draughts. 'Cyd's overseeing my first live on-line session tonight and I still have no idea—'

'I thought we were going out to dinner tonight?' He tried to sound casual, unwittingly gaffer-taping a lot of windowsill and wall. 'Just the local pub – nothing fancy,' he added quickly.

Odette chewed her lip, feeling guilty for forgetting. 'I'm not sure what time I'll finish.'

'Forget it,' he shrugged.

Odette was on the verge of suggesting they go to the pub the next night, but stopped herself, guessing it might give the wrong impression. She liked having him around. He was comforting and big-brotherish. He helped her out and he bossed her about without getting her back up too much. He was the opposite of Calum. And that, she realised with a sad lurch, was why she didn't fancy him one little bit.

42

From Monday, Odette embarked upon her new management role with gusto. But the moment she got her hands on the Smock Mill accounts, she needed a long, strong coffee break. They were in a terrible mess. To her alarm, she could find nothing to indicate Cyd had ever paid tax on her little empire or declared a penny of her substantial income from it.

'Cyd should thank her lucky stars that Customs and Excise aren't chasing her yet,' she told Jimmy that afternoon when he dropped off a fan heater he claimed he didn't need.

'Maybe you should be reading the Riot Act rather than the tarot?'

'I'll try but I don't hold out much hope,' Odette sighed. 'That's beyond my horror-scope. You know she actually hid these accounts from me? I found them buried in the puppies' basket.'

On Monday night, armed with a pile of files, she tried to discuss it with her employer, but Cyd was as grumpily uncooperative as anticipated, saying that she'd had a hard day and couldn't get her head around facts and figures. Instead, she burnt a large asparagus quiche for them to share and sloped off to take a long bath and listen to deafening music. Odette retreated to her tower in despair.

The next morning, Cyd once again disappeared on the quad bike. Odette's assumption that she'd been handed the reins of the Miller empire because Cyd wanted to spend more time with her children seemed increasingly unlikely, unless the Bridgehouse brothers were hiding in the woods. She had a shrewd suspicion where Cyd was going. There were a limited number of places a banned driver could reach across the fields on a quad bike from Smock Mill Farm. It didn't take a genius to figure it out.

On Wednesday, Jimmy brought around several panes of glass cut to size to patch the tower's cracked windows, along with a tub of putty and a huge baguette stuffed with roasted tomatoes and goat's cheese.

'You never seem to have any food in the place,' he complained, breaking the baguette in half and handing her the bigger share.

'I'm not hungry, thanks.' Odette glanced at her watch – a cheap new digital which kept far better time than her old designer one had, and played Pacman to boot. 'Cyd's asked me to take a meeting in Hove in half an hour. I really need to push off.'

'I don't understand that woman.' He chewed on his baguette. 'She has all these little businesses on the go, and yet she's started working with Calum.'

'With Calum?' Even though Odette had guessed already, hearing the news was still a shock.

He nodded. 'At Fermoncieaux. I think Cal wanted someone to keep an eye on this documentary crew, but from what I've seen so far this week, Cyd just sits around gossiping about her past – most if it to camera. The show's still set to be a bigger catering farce than *Fawlty Towers*.'

'Calum's asked *Cyd* to oversee *Food Fights*?' Now Odette was genuinely shocked. She'd imagined Cyd was there in some sort of New Age consultancy capacity – advising on feng shui or crystal alignment.

'How did you know the documentary was going to be called *Food Fights*?' Jimmy looked at her curiously. 'We only found that out this morning. Calum's furious.'

Odette froze, her face draining of colour. 'Lucky guess,' she said feebly.

She expected Jimmy to laugh in disbelief. But he looked impressed, finishing his baguette with one big chomp and apologising that he had to rush off. 'The red deer are starting to fawn. I have to check them every couple of hours.'

Calum visited the farm that evening to collect his two puppies. The others had all been fetched by their new owners over the weekend, even little Sarangi, the runt of the litter, who had found a home with Lady Fulbrook of whom Jimmy had lately become a close pal. He had persuaded her to add an Afghan to her ever-expanding pack. Odette was on-line trying to fathom out the wonders of the tarot when she heard Cyd welcoming him into the kitchen.

She flipped over a chewed card and tried to make out what it was before typing into the computer: 'The Prince of Spades, reversed, is the card which indicates the influence of those around you.'

Her questioner – a twenty-seven-year-old woman who refused to give any other details about herself – typed back: 'What does that mean? What are spades?'

Odette was frantically trying to look it up in the reference book and listen to the conversation going on beneath her. She had already invented an identity for the woman to give herself something to work with: Thelma, a New York legal secretary. Pedantic yet impulsive, impatient, single, and desperate for passion and romance to spice up her life.

'Sorry – swords,' she typed distractedly, abandoning the book and making it up. 'You have an admirer.'

'Describe him,' demanded the little typed line which appeared at the bottom of her screen.

Her cursor winked in wait. Odette sighed. 'He is light-haired and dark-souled. He has passion and drive and might upset your life although he has little idea of the havoc he wreaks. He will probably know you through work.'

'What should I do?' flew back the question.

Odette cocked her head as she heard Calum say something which sounded like, 'Where's Odette?'

'I am turning another card,' she typed, straining to

hear more, but the puppies were yapping too loudly downstairs for her to hear. She leaned over so far that she knocked the pack of cards from the table beside her so they spilled everywhere.

'I'm waiting,' Thelma demanded. Odette could almost hear her rapping her fingers against the keyboard.

'The card is the Five of Cups,' Odette typed, noticing with relief that the little alarm clock in the corner of the screen was flashing to show that Thelma's half hour was up. She had no other callers waiting. 'This means that you will be lovers. You should deny him nothing. Whatever sexual requests he makes of you, however extreme, will ultimately give you pleasure. Good luck. Please call again soon.' She pressed the button which would automatically flash up the site's logo and a pre-written thank-you message from Fortune Farm. She knew she was supposed to offer the enquirer a time extension if she didn't have a call waiting, but she was damned if she was going to tonight.

She polished off the can of Coke on the desk, switched off the computer and headed downstairs to find Calum bonding with his new pets. It was an odd sight – the blond sadist in his street-cred anti-establishment clothes holding a wriggling bundle of trouble under each arm. His eyes widened as he took in Odette's haircut.

'That's an improvement,' he whistled. 'You look almost human.'

Cyd was hovering guiltily by the Aga, scratching Bazouki on the head. Odette couldn't tell whether her guilt stemmed from the fact she was robbing her beloved dog of her last two puppies or whether she was feeling guilty about working for Calum. Odette didn't want to confront them. She preferred to let them play their game and see what happened. She felt a hundred times better than she had the last time Calum had seen her, and was determined that whatever happened she wouldn't let him rob her of her new, fragile self-confidence this time.

'Thanks.' She smiled warily. 'Almost human is just the look I was aiming for.'

He was clearly thrown by her breeziness.

Odette had wanted to hang around and try to find out what was going on with the documentary, but she suddenly found she didn't care. She would far rather head to her tower and eat some chocolate than torture herself by hanging around a man who didn't want her. She was on the mend at last. Elsa would be proud.

Smiling at them both, she said farewell to the puppies and scrammed.

In Maida Vale, Lydia frustratedly tried to get back on-line with Fortune Farm, but the link kept freezing out. She wanted to know more about her Prince of Spades. She was almost certain dear, light-hearted Fin wasn't her dark-souled admirer.

After five minutes without success, she gave up on the link and disconnected her modem. The phone rang immediately. It was Fin.

'This training course is such a bore,' he yawned. 'I've bunked off advanced negotiation skills and now I'm raiding my hotel mini bar. Who have you been talking to all this time?'

'Internet.' She settled in a squashy leather chair. 'It's the future for therapy. I'm thinking of starting up a site.'

'Good idea.' Fin was always so enthusiastic about each and every idea she had, however crazy.

Lydia took the red polish off her toenails with acetate while she listened to Finlay telling her about his Better Communication Skills training course in Bournemouth.

'Any plans for tonight, sugar?' he asked her after he'd stopped gassing.

'Quiet one,' she sighed, moving on to her left foot with deft strokes.

'Don't blame you. Looking forward to Friday? Shall I come back to London to fetch you, or go straight to Juno's parents?'

'Whatever,' she sighed, rather wishing Fin wasn't coming at all. Parties were much more fun without him as a rule. Not that he wasn't delightful company and very entertaining, but he did like to hang around with her whereas she preferred to mingle on her own and flirt a little for old time's sake.

'Well, if you think you can get a lift there from someone in London . . .'

'Mmm.'

'Are you missing me then?' he growled playfully. 'Because I'm sure as hell missing you. This bed is enormous. Are you sure you don't want to hop on a train and help me warm it up?'

'I need an early night, Fin,' she sighed, knowing that bed warming was all he wanted her body for.

'We've had a company memo telling us we're liable for pay-per-view porn movies,' he was grumbling. 'Honestly, this firm's so mean.'

'So tell them to stuff their boring old job, darling.' Lydia selected a bright pink polish with which to repaint her toenails.

'I can't do that, sugar – I get my own business cards next month.' He made it sound like a £50K bonus.

'Humph.' She unscrewed the bottle, trying to balance the phone between her ear and her bent-up knee but it kept slipping.

'That sounds horny.' Fin listened to the rustling as she picked the receiver out of her lap. 'Can we have phone sex?'

Lydia clenched her teeth irritably. Phone sex was very good for Fin's on going treatment, she knew that, but she wanted to hang up and try and get Fortune Farm on-line again.

'Okay, but it'll have to be quick.' She recapped her nail polish. 'I'm taking my bra off and playing with my nipples . . .'

'Hang on! I'm still loitering by my Corby trouser press. Let me at least get on the bed.'

On Thursday evening, Cyd was in a particularly foul mood, storming into the tower to tell Odette to stop nosing through the Smock Mill accounts.

'But they're in total disarray,' she pointed out.

'That is *my* choice,' Cyd fumed illogically. 'Just leave things as they are.'

Refusing to discuss the matter further, she stalked around the tower criticising the changes. 'Where will the birds nest now that the windows all have panes in?'

Odette watched her in silence, guessing that Cyd had something she wanted to get off her chest. She was always hopelessly picky before a big confession.

'What are you doing tomorrow night, dearheart?' she asked suddenly.

'It's Juno's leaving party,' Odette said cautiously, suddenly seeing where this was leading. If Cyd asked her to work instead, she'd flip. 'I told you about it ages ago.'

But to her surprise, Cyd looked incredibly pleased. 'Of course!' She clapped her hands together. 'You must wish her *bon voyage* from me. Where's she going?'

'America,' Odette muttered. She must have told Cyd a hundred times.

'How splendid.' She waved a breezy hand, heading towards the door. 'Don't hurry home – I'll be perfectly all right on my own. You enjoy your party. If you want to borrow a car, you can take the Jeep. I don't like the others doing long distances.' The ancient American Army Jeep was by far the most unreliable car in Jobe's fleet. Cold, slow and backbreaking to drive, it broke down on average once every twenty miles.

43

The day of Juno's party started bright and blustery. By teatime, she had helped her mother cook a wide-ranging feast for twenty friends, had tidied up her father's piles of papers as fast as he could spread them around, and had de-fleaed both the dogs. Despite that, Effy and Blind were scratching so violently that their collar tags jingled along with Howard Glenn's favoured choice of music for the day.

From every loudspeaker that was wired around Church House – and there was at least one in every room – his latest recording of music for a National Geographic Channel natural history programme rang out. 'Icelandic Geysers – Parts i, ii and iii' were not soothing. The first movement sounded like the Soup Dragon emerging from beneath her dustbin lid to find the Clangers jumping up and down on top of it; the second like a demented coffee percolator trapped in an echoing biscuit tin. The third, which was playing as Juno wrote out endless change of address cards, was uncannily reminiscent of hundreds of very windy Turks flatulating together in a steam bath.

Jay had suffered almost two hours of the music while chopping up vegetables for Judy Glenn's Steppes Vodka Broth – a big hit from her latest series aired before Christmas. He was now wearing a personal stereo and listening to Vivaldi. Juno pinched his bum as she passed by to answer the phone, causing a celery stick to fly across the kitchen and hit Effy on the head.

Consequently both dogs were barking their heads off and the Turks were reaching a crescendo of wind when she took the call from Elsa.

'I think Buster's coming!' she panted.

'Who?' Juno didn't hear. 'Do I know him? I suppose we've got enough food but I did just want it to be friends and—'

'The baby, you dolt!' Elsa butted in before screaming loudly. A moment later Euan came on the phone.

'We're no' gonna be able to come tonight, hen.' His voice was high and excited. 'I think this is it. Something from *Alien*'s just happened on the kitchen floor and we're waiting on a cab to take Elsa to hospital. Hang on . . .'

There was more demented screaming in the background.

'She says to have a good time – at least, I think that's what she said. It could be "Get me to the fucking drugs". Listen, I'll call with news, okay, hen?'

'Yes. Good lu—' Juno started, but the line was already dead.

Hanging up, she contemplated her seating plan again. Her family's long, thin refectory table could easily seat twenty, but friends kept cancelling and the numbers were going down so rapidly she'd have to issue her guests with loudhailers and binoculars at this rate. Already missing her London flat and her turtle, U-Boat, she felt morose and unloved.

So she was thrilled when Odette called at the last minute, not to say that she couldn't come, but to ask whether she could bring someone else. Odette *never* brought dates to parties. This was an unexpected treat.

In fact Jimmy Sylvian had invited himself.

As if this wasn't embarrassing enough, he insisted on bringing his dogs with him. Because they were using the motorway, both had to travel inside the pick-up. Nelson occupied the whole of the back seat, pacing around and barking alternately out of the window and then at Winnie, who snarled back from the safety of Odette's lap where she was moulting liberally on to the River Island dress.

Odette gripped tightly on to her safety belt at all times. Jimmy drove like a maniac, constantly veering on to the hard shoulder.

'In South Africa we move across when someone wants to overtake,' he explained. 'I keep forgetting you don't do it here.'

Odette held her breath as they narrowly missed an AA van, but diplomatically said nothing. It was very kind of him to offer to drive her, after all. Not that he'd exactly offered – more insisted. When she couldn't even get the ancient Jeep to start, he'd refused to lend a hand. Instead he'd simply turned up at the tower that evening, holding his passenger door open and telling her she looked lovely.

Odette wasn't sure what her friends would make of him. They'd probably think him unspeakably rude and eccentric. He had sung along to Ladysmith Black Mambazo very loudly throughout the journey, laughing when Nelson howled.

'What a dog, huh?' He'd turned to Odette several times in awe. 'Perfect pitch – listen.' Which was more than could be said for his owner.

Odette thought back to the last time she'd visited the Glenns' huge, crumbling flint church conversion. It had been the previous summer. She'd been so full of hope, so excited about the future. She remembered feeling absurdly sexy, dressed in a little mesh cardigan that kept unbuttoning, her body at its most lean and fit. She'd got drunk and sung along to old Buck's Fizz albums; she'd played croquet in the garden and kissed one of Sean Glenn's rowdy friends, Barfly. She hoped with a chilly lurch of worry that he wasn't going to be there tonight.

'You're very quiet.' Jimmy was changing the tape. 'What are you thinking about?'

Odette, who was thinking worriedly about Barfly and his big, sticky Cornish Pasty tongue, hastily improvised.

'The last time I came to a party here it was a really hot summer's day,' she said after a pause. 'It's a shame you won't see the house in daylight. It's so fantastic. There's an ancient chalk horse on the hill opposite.'

In the dark, the former church was barely visible through the gloomy trees when they approached it, although the multitude of cars parked higgledy-piggledy on the steeply banked gravel drive were. Jimmy pulled the pick-up expertly on to the verge, parking it in the soft mud beneath a blossom-heavy horse chestnut.

The dogs were desperate to come out with them, and Jimmy was reluctant to leave them in the car in the cold.

'Just ask Judy and Howard first, huh?' Odette fretted. 'Their dogs might not be too friendly with others.' Turning up with a man no one knew at a leaving party was one thing: bringing along two squabbling dogs quite another.

'God, yes – bring the blighters in!' Juno's mother insisted the moment she met Jimmy, squeezing him into one of her killer hugs which had been known to crack ribs. 'Effy and Blind would love to have some chums, and Rug likes a challenge.'

The party was already in full swing, with a few old friends milling about the house in search of food and drink, the rest sprawling around the wonderful main sitting room with its squashy, dog-eared furniture, its dramatic glass wall, its hundreds of wonky framed cartoons and roaring open fire. The only light apart from that of the fire and the distant light of the kitchen creeping in through the long dining room was from a hundred fat candles flickering and guttering on bookshelves, on the mantelpiece, on tables and on the floor. The place was one huge danger zone for those in cheap man-made fibres like Odette.

'Odie!' Juno spun her around so that they both almost ignited several times. She was dressed in an amazing, waist-squeezing pair of ultra-trendy grey satin pedal pushers and a 'new black' green velvet bustier. She looked plumper and lovelier than ever. 'We're all comparing pics from Elsa and Euan's wedding. Have you brought yours?'

'No camera, babes.' Odette looked around a host of familiar faces for Elsa's.

'Contractions every two minutes last time I heard,' Juno giggled, squeezing her arm and leading her to a spare cushion. 'Euan keeps phoning with updates. I think he's getting a bit bored. Birth is hours away apparently. He says it's just like hanging around in a club chill-out room – Elsa's all sweaty and screaming for drugs non-stop. Talking of which, I'll get you some of Mum's latest punch – it's called Red Eye. Lethal.'

'Does Cyd know?' Odette asked, but Juno had gone and Jez was bounding across the room.

'Where is he then? Your boyfriend?' he demanded excitedly, folding himself down beside her like a pixie.

'If you mean Jimmy, he's not my boyfriend and he's fetching his—'

'Aghh!' Drinks went flying as Winnie scuttled into the room and dived beneath Odette's leg, followed in hot pursuit by a growling Nelson, with Effy and Blind – the Glenns' two singularly stupid mastiffs – close behind. Rug the West Highland terrier was panting to the rear, hopelessly outpaced by the rest of his gang.

Odette was flattened by noisy barks and bad breath. A moment later, Jimmy, Howard and Juno's brother Sean had all waded in to haul off their respective dogs.

'Sorry about that,' Jimmy boomed once Howard had kindly offered to shut Winnie in an upstairs room with a chew and a few toys. 'My bitch has a victim mentality.'

They all gaped at him.

If nothing else, Odette decided bleakly, Jimmy knew how to make an entrance.

As soon as everyone was once again distracted with photographs of the wedding, she sloped off to find a phone and call Cyd to check she'd be okay getting to London for the birth.

There was no answer. Odette let it ring for several minutes before hanging up in relief, certain that Cyd would have got a taxi to the station and was now heading towards London to be in on the scene rather than wait it out by the phone at home.

As Odette walked back into the main room she heard more guests arriving through the door behind her and glanced around to see Barfly's wide girth shambling through the door to receive Judy's rapturous welcome. Not hanging around to be recognised, she scuttled back to her cushion and cowered behind Jimmy.

He was regaling everyone with outrageous descriptions of Odette's death-trap tower. Juno was in stitches and Jez was in love.

'You lucky, lucky thing!' He positively quivered with desire when he cornered Odette by the stereo. 'He is *beyond* sex. Quite, quite beyond. When Juno said you were having it hard, I had no idea she meant that! This calls for Bobby Billions!' A moment later and Robbie Williams was singing 'Angel'.

It was the ultimate couples moment. Juno nuzzled into Jay,

Ally giggled with Duncan, Jez snogged Olaf, Sean and his new wife Triona eskimo-kissed while his hunky friends hit upon two old schoolfriends of Juno's, the perennially single Tina and Fi. Even Barfly shot a few loving looks around the room. Odette fled to Jimmy's side before Barfly spotted her, noticing worriedly that the jug of Red Eye was empty. 'Are you going to be able to drive later?'

'Everyone's staying,' he whispered in her ear, his breath warm and soft. 'Judy told me earlier. She wants it to be a big surprise. We've got to pretend to leave, wait until Juno and Jay go to bed, and then creep back in here to crash out for a few hours. She'll wake us all in plenty of time to hide. Then, come ten o'clock when they're due to set out, we all appear and wave them off. Fantastic idea, huh? Judy couldn't warn you in advance because you're not on the phone, but I said you'd be cool about it.'

Odette could barely believe his cheek, especially as he had known Juno less than twenty-four hours, was already in cahoots with her mother and seemed happy to include himself amongst her closest friends. But she was experiencing far too much of a sentimentality rush to take issue.

It was the first time it had really hit her that Juno was leaving the country the next day. As she looked around the room at her friends, she saw that many eyes were wet with tears as they all sang along to the ridiculously lovely song. And they were no longer looking at their lovers. They were looking at Juno. Only Barfly was gaping – rather alarmingly – straight at Odette.

She stifled a sob and felt a warm, comforting arm around her. Jimmy gave her a quick collarbone-breaking squeeze. No wonder he and Judy had bonded. They both used their weight advantage to the full when it came to hugging.

Howard Glenn had seen the similarity too. When his wife entered the room and banged a wooden spoon against a pan during 'Let Me Entertain You', announcing that they would no longer wait on Lydia but eat straight away, Howard lingered behind the throng and linked arms between Odette and Jimmy. Juno's father was as tall as Jimmy, but half as wide, his white beard stained pink by the lethal Red Eye, although his berry-bright gaze was as clear and innocent as a bush baby's.

'I felt the twinned auras of new life as soon as you two came in,' he announced, ever the old hippy. 'Rebirth is such a refreshing metamorphosis. Like sex after a long period of abstinence, eh?' He cackled delightedly. 'Not that you two would know much about abstinence, I'm sure. Judy and I have kept an inflatable mattress aside for you both in a quiet corner for later.'

Odette was so red in the face that she inadvertently pulled her chair on to her neighbour's foot as she took her place at the table.

'Oi, you clumsy moo!' He turned on her murderously, intent on a fight. She quailed back against Jimmy who was perched precariously on a camping chair on her other side.

'Hello, darlin'.' Barfly's expression changed from fight to delight in an instant. 'Have we met?' he asked her boobs dreamily.

'You two wouldn't know each other, Fly,' Juno called across the table, winking at Odette. 'This is Odie. She works for a feminist women's collective in Sussex.'

'Bleedin' hell!' Barfly gazed one last, lusty time at her boobs and returned to gazing lovingly at his second four-pack.

Just as they were settling down to a lethally boozy, tasty soup, there was another ring of the old doorbell and a tall, cherubic, beautiful blond man walked in.

'I'm not too late, am I? Traffic was murder.'

'Not at all, Fin.' Juno leaped up to hug him. 'Where's Lydia? We thought she must be coming with you.'

He shook his head. 'I came straight from a course in Bournemouth. She said she'd get a lift.'

'Fly!' Juno shrilled at Odette's erstwhile admirer. 'You forgot to pick up Lydia.'

'Skinny blonde thing? Din' forget, girl.' He shook his head, downing a few more splashes of lager. 'She weren't there. We waited bleedin' ages. Right humped off we were. I was dying for a piss.'

'Where is she then?' Fin's eyes blinked worriedly as Judy thrust a glass of red wine at him.

'She'll turn up,' Juno said confidently. 'It's my leaving do. She wouldn't dare not.'

But Lydia didn't turn up.

The dinner was a raucous, delicious success as everyone devoured Judy's divine food, guzzled wine and made more and more emotional speeches wishing Jay and Juno well in the States. As soon as they had finished eating, the entertainment became even more outlandish as Jez got out his guitar and started strumming out every song with the word 'leave' in the title that they could come up with. Howard passed around percussion instruments from his collection; Juno got out her squeezebox to join in but was crying and laughing too much to play properly; Jay's friend Will played the spoons on his knees and Jimmy delighted them all with his gloriously loud – tuneless – singing voice accompanied by Winnie. And so it was that an unruly band sang 'Leaving on a Jet Plane', 'The Leaving of Liverpool', 'Don't Leave Me This Way' and 'Leaving You is Easy' until the early hours. Judy distributed digestifs and coffee, Howard fetched a tape recorder to capture the impromptu jam session and Odette laughed more than she had in weeks.

When the phone rang at two in the morning it was barely audible over the din of 'New York, New York', but Finlay – whose ears had been listening out for it all night – jumped up and rushed through to the downstairs study to take it.

Five minutes later he was back. He tried to shout to be heard, but the band was now belting out 'I Want To Live In America'. Jimmy's boom alone was deafening. In the end he had to stand on a table to get noticed, waving his arms around madly. The singing, clanking, strumming and rattling gradually died down as the revellers turned to stare at his wild-eyed expression. Only Winnie continued howling in honour of Bernstein.

'That was the North London Teaching Hospital,' he announced in a shaking voice.

'What is it?' Juno gasped worriedly. 'Is it Lydia?'

He shook his head, starting to laugh. 'Elsa's had a girl – eight pounds three ounces. Goes by the name of Florence. Mother and baby doing fine.'

Amid the whooping and caterwauling that greeted his announcement, one distinctive, booming voice was noticeably absent. Odette broke away from hugging Jez and looked around for Jimmy. He was standing in a far corner of the room, isolated from the action, his big, bruised blue eyes full of tears. Odette chewed her lip as she made her way towards him.

Florence. Florrie. His lover's name. She knew he must have heard it many times since her death – a call in the street that made him turn, a name on the radio that made him jump, a single word in a newspaper that stood out as though printed in capital letters. He had learned to cope with that. People did. But the birth of a child was different. This was a new life, when his thoughts had been all of death. This was a totally new association with a name that was in many ways his own treasure, his private property to grieve over.

Jimmy looked at her for a long time, his tortured eyes scouring her face – for what Odette didn't know. Then slowly, very slowly, a smile touched his features. It started to spread, gradually at first, as though cautiously testing the way. Then it flooded across his face and lit up the room. A big, happy, life-loving African sunset of a smile.

Suddenly he opened his arms wide, pulling her into a hug.

'Great name, huh?' he breathed into the top of her head, his voice shaking.

'Great name.' She nodded as he patted her on the back, ruffled her hair and then reached for his glass of Drambuie, deafening the room with his loud voice. 'A toast, my friends! To Florence!' He raised the glass.

'Florence!' they all cheered back.

Juno burst into tears for the fifth time that night. 'I won't get a chance to see her before I go. And you're all going to be off home soon.'

Standing at her daughter's shoulder, Judy gave everyone in the room the benefit of one of her famously naughty winks.

44

Lydia knew she'd been very, very wicked. She breathed in her first waking breath of the day and smelled the unfamiliar sheets, then felt the sensation of rough cotton against her skin, not the Egyptian she was accustomed to. Finally she smelled the brackish, gamey smell of an unfamiliar man and unfamiliar sex and felt it on her skin too. It had been a long time, but the cloying, sticky wetness between her legs and that lingering smell were old allies.

The man himself was not in bed with her. She rolled into his creased pillow indent and felt no residual warmth. She was in his flat, so he was unlikely to have done a runner, but he had certainly got up a lot earlier.

She thought of Juno and scrunched her eyes shut. She was such a terrible friend. Juno didn't expect much, but Lydia guessed that this time she might have stretched her pardon-limit a little too far. And as for Finlay . . .

She covered her eyes with the crook of her arm and smiled. She was just having a service check. He deserved to have her in tip-top condition for the wedding. If she'd left it much longer she might have forgotten how, and there was no doubt that last night had been a very thorough refresher course. It had checked out every working, interconnecting part to delicious satisfaction.

She listened out for sounds of life in the flat but there were none. She guessed he must have left after all. Stifling a yawn, she went to check out the bathroom, noticing first a clock on the wall which told her it was only just past seven. She could get to Heathrow in time to see Juno and Jay off. That gave her almost five hours to think up an excuse for missing last night.

Odette had also woken up with the smell of a strange man in her nostrils, although he was still in residence beside her and her head was resting on his huge, socked feet. Sharing the bed with them both was a small, very contented spaniel.

As Odette lay semi-awake for a few minutes trying to assess the extent of her hangover, she also tried to work out whether it was Winnie or Jimmy whose rattling snore sounded like a bone trapped in a hover mower. After a moment's contemplation, she decided it was both. Joining in was a nasal, whining snore that was more like a strimmer encountering chain-link fencing.

Propping her head up, she squinted around the room and realised that there was someone asleep on an old camp bed beneath the window. Someone else was groaning and clutching their head on several sag bags, and a large shape beneath a duvet on another inflatable mattress was muttering to itself and emitting the strimmer noise.

Odette sagged back against the pillow. She felt as though she was in the crowded Red Cross tent on a battlefield, not waking up at a friend's house.

Judy's mad-cap plan to hide them all overnight had worked. Juno had cried a lot when they'd all said farewell and had insisted on coming outside to wave them all off which had necessitated some swift thinking on Judy's part.

'Drive to the Smithy Inn car park just down the road – I'm sure Jerry and Ann won't mind. I'll give them a call in the morning.'

If a squad car with a breathalyser had been lurking in a gateway to monitor the hundred yards between Church House and the village pub they would have bagged more drunken drivers in ten minutes than they usually did in a month, all driving very, very slowly along the white lines in the middle of the lane.

When the by then very tired and cold party guests had walked back to the house, however, Howard had met them to explain that Juno had yet to go to bed. She couldn't find her passport and was unpacking everything from her cases in desperation.

Tapping his index finger to his lips to keep them quiet, Howard had shown the guests into the old barn which was just as chilly inside as out, and also infested with mice. There they'd all waited for the best part of an hour, fending off the cold with the bottles of *eau de vie* they had discovered in a dusty old sideboard, and keeping themselves entertained by torchlight with a pile of old board games. It was no wonder, Odette reflected, that she hadn't complained about the sleeping arrangements when they'd finally got inside. The *eau de vie* had been stronger than methadone.

Howard had finally rescued them at three in the morning.

The house was more or less divided into two halves. In the old tower, all the party guests were crammed into the little rooms. At the opposite side of the house, a separate staircase led to the minstrel's gallery above the sitting room, where the Glenns had their huge, comfortable bedroom and where Juno and Jay were currently occupying the guest bedroom. This meant there was little chance of Juno catching on to her surprise provided her mother woke in time to breakfast and brief them.

Judy overslept as she always did. Howard, who wore earplugs to muffle his wife's tumultuous snoring, didn't hear the alarm shrieking to itself.

In the next room, however, Juno listened to it beeping non-stop. She'd barely slept a wink all night.

'That alarm's still ringing,' she said to Jay. 'And, you know, I'm sure I heard people moving about in the tower last night. I think Ma and Pa might have been abducted by aliens.'

'Huh?' Jay yawned tiredly. He'd barely slept a wink either, constantly woken by Juno's demented chattering. 'It's probably just Sean and Triona.'

'No, they're in the pulpit,' Juno said, referring to the oak-lined room off the minstrel's gallery which Howard had once used as his study before moving into a special studio in the garden.

'Mice then,' Jay sighed, rolling over with a pillow tucked around his head.

Juno jiggled her legs impatiently and peered at the bedside

clock. 'I can't believe it's just after seven, can you? I know Mum told us to lie in, but I'm going to get a cup of tea. D'you want one?'

When Jay didn't respond, she lifted his pillow and hollered, 'Tea?'

He almost fell off the bed. 'Jesus, woman, if you take this attitude with you to New York then I sure as hell ain't gonna marry you to get you that Green Card.'

'Suit yourself.' She clambered off the bed and headed out on to the gallery. A moment later her round, pink face was an inch from his again, eyes glittering.

'Was that a proposal?'

'I guess so.' He levered himself up on to his elbow and rubbed a nub of sleep from one yellow eye, ever the cool operator. 'I kinda like the idea, don't you?'

Juno's eyes crossed, rolled and then bulged. 'Like? Like! Like yes I like, baby.' Then she cocked her head and pouted. 'You could have asked me properly, though.'

'How d'you mean?'

'You know, one knee, take my hand, "Will you do me the honour . . ." type of thing. Grumpily muttering it in bed isn't very romantic, cherub.'

'You said yes, didn't you?'

'No – I said I liked the idea.' She gave him a mischievous smile. 'So go on. Get down on one knee.'

'I'm naked,' he pointed out.

She pulled off her dressing gown. 'So am I. Have you never heard of an indecent proposal?'

Odette was just starting to realise quite how much her head hurt when Ally clanked in through the door carrying a large butler's tray with five rattling mugs on it, along with a jug of water and a family pack of aspirin.

'Wakey, wakey.' She carefully stepped between the bedding and bodies in the room to carry her much-needed medical supplies to the worst casualty.

A tousled blond head poked out from under the duvet with

eyes welded shut like a new-born kitten's. As soon as Ally placed a mug in one of his hands, Duncan and his tea disappeared undercover again. Ally lifted the duvet halfway down, kissed his belly and dropped two aspirin into his navel.

'Juno's up,' she told Odette who appeared to be the only person awake enough to focus on her. 'She came dancing down the stairs singing "Get Me To The Airport On Time" while I was making tea in the kitchen. I had to dive behind a cheese plant in the conservatory. I was sure she'd spot me, especially when those bloody dogs kept poking their noses up my nightie. We'll have to hide in the barn again soon.' She suddenly noticed Jimmy was snoring at the opposite end of the airbed to Odette. 'Do you two always sleep like that? Bit odd, isn't it?'

Before Odette could answer, she heard a gruff cackle.

'He's been in the Southern Hemisphere a long time, hasn't he?' croaked a voice as cracked as old leather. 'Probably gets confused.' Jez was now sitting up on the camp bed beneath the window (Odette was certain Judy had deliberately put him on it as a joke). He was rubbing his neck and groaning. 'Whose idea was it to share a spliff in the barn last night? My throat's shot and we're performing at a benefit concert tonight.' The wheeze faltered to a whisper. 'There it goes. I've lost my voice.'

'You should worry,' another voice rasped and the sag bag shifted to reveal Finlay looking even more like a fallen angel than ever. 'I've lost my fiancée.'

'And I've lost my clothes.' Ally was clambering around in search of her skirt. Then she looked up at Jez in surprise. 'Where's Olaf?'

He let out a strangled wail and then clamped his hand guiltily over his mouth. 'I think he's still in the barn,' he whispered hoarsely. 'He went up the ladder to look at the top floor and never came back down. He was a bit stoned. Oh God, my poor baby.'

Odette marvelled at Jimmy's ability to sleep on, totally unaware of the gradual, groaning awakening around him. Even Winnie was looking around perkily now, stump thumping. But Jimmy snored contentedly, his rugged face strangely childlike in rest. She remembered him telling her he was an insomniac and she'd assumed that he catnapped fitfully, accustomed to the need to leap up and be ready with a rifle if he heard a lion in the camp. But instead he was one of the soundest sleepers she'd ever encountered. Not that she had watched many men sleep.

It was, she realised, the first time she had woken up in the same bed as a man for almost three years. The fact that there were four other people in the room did little to dampen the shock.

'I've already looked in on the others,' Ally was telling them. 'There are a bunch of very smelly men – mostly Jay's friends – in Sean's old bedroom, all of whom look like they need a defibrillator to wake them up. Juno's schoolfriends are in her old room, which smells like the girls' loos. They've stayed up all night talking, polishing off the last of the wine, smoking themselves silly and are still pissed. God knows how we'll get them all out to the barn unnoticed.'

'Can't we just stay hiding up here, babes?' Odette suggested sensibly.

'Hear, hear,' came a muffled boom from the vicinity of her feet as Jimmy finally opened his eyes to the day.

'We can't!' Ally was squeaking. 'Those are Jay's photographic cases.' She pointed to a pile of metal boxes covered with 'Fragile' stickers by the camp bed.

'I know how they feel,' Jez groaned.

Jimmy was looking around in wonder, big eyes blinking. He yawned a huge, jaw-breaking yawn and stretched like an eagle, his huge arm span almost reaching from one wall to the other.

'That,' he said in amazement, 'was the first time I've slept through a night in years.' He looked at Odette and smiled. 'We must do this more often. You are my lullaby.'

She saw Ally and Duncan exchange glances and felt her face flush. She wished Jimmy wouldn't go in for big, sentimental statements. It was embarrassing. Her friends were bound to get the wrong impression.

Jez snorted affectionately, seeing a chance to tease his old mate. 'That's Odette. She's sent more men to sleep than *The Piano*. Mogadonna Fielding we used to call her.'

Odette was appalled. For years Jez had enjoyed making fun of her by insinuating she was a seductress on the sly. It had always made her laugh before, now it just embarrassed her. Jimmy was bound to think she was a complete trollop.

But he didn't seem bothered. He just cuffed her arm chummily.

'In that case I am Mogadon Juan.' He boomed his big laugh.

Jimmy had an uncanny ability to sleep like a baby and wake up like an SAS hero, Odette noticed. As soon as he was dressed and had cleaned his teeth, he set about smuggling the surprise farewell committee into the barn, a few bodies at a time, in total silence. Most were still half-asleep, half-dressed and half-cut, but he took no flak and was amiably, if determinedly, efficient.

While Juno and Jay made love for the last time on English soil, their friends tip-toed across the dew-damp grass beneath their bedroom window and concealed themselves yet again in the sagging old barn that housed several generations of Glenn memorabilia. In all it took Jimmy less than ten minutes to get everyone in.

There was a faint groan from above.

Jez jumped guiltily. 'That's Olaf. Oh, my poor baby!' He slid off the bench and staggered towards the ladder which led through a hatch to the top level. Before he could climb all the way up, a green face appeared through the hole above his head.

'How could you leave me here, you selfish bastard?' Olaf was close to tears. 'We're finished!'

In years to come, when the friends discussed that day, no one could agree whether Jez would have tried to save the relationship were it not for the fact that Olaf chose that very moment to throw up. On balance, most of them agreed the affair had run its course and that, anyway, Jez could never have resisted the joke.

'Well, I've heard of getting chucked,' he'd croaked as he wiped his sodden shoulders, 'but this is quite ridiculous.'

Juno was running a characteristic hour late when she finally announced she was ready to leave for Heathrow. Since waking, she had burst into tears several times, had stopped for several bowls of Coco Pops, vast mugs of tea and just a few cigarettes even though she'd supposedly quit six months ago. She'd unpacked and repacked her suitcases several times, and insisted on calling Sean's flat to leave a message on the answer-phone for her beloved turtle, U-Boat. More than anything else, she hugged Jay over and over again.

'Such a shame you two can't come.' Juno's lips quivered as she watched her brother and Triona heaving camera boxes into the boot of their father's car. 'Can't you follow in the T-Bird?' She looked lovingly at her brother's ancient Land-Rover Defender.

Triona shrugged. 'We'd just hold you up. You're running late as it is.'

Juno's lip wobbled even more, but she managed to control it and hugged the dogs farewell. 'Hang on.' She released one from a tight squeeze. 'This isn't ours.'

The shaggy grey lurcher was looking quite at home amongst the Glenn pack, but Juno was right. It was a new acquisition.

'Someone must have left it behind last night, pusscat,' Judy said breezily as she carried out Juno's squeezebox and tried to cram it into the boot. 'Ready?'

Juno was looking at the unfamiliar dog, which had incredibly sympathetic hazel eyes, a little like Jay's. Then she remembered who it belonged to. Odette's lovely new lover, Jimmy – the sexy South African. The last of the Gang had found happiness. 'Ready,' she squeaked in a tight, emotional voice.

Judy patted her arm. 'Then I'll just fetch you a farewell *cadeau* while you say your goodbyes to Sean and Triona.' She skipped off.

Juno was crushing Triona in a tight hug when she heard strains of 'Leaving on a Jet Plane'. At first she thought it was the recording of her friends that Howard had made last night, but as it grew louder and more unruly she realised it was live.

When the barn doors flew open, she started to laugh and cry at the same time. She hugged Jay tightly to her side and watched her friends approaching, armed once again with instruments and a few Union Jack flags that Judy had purloined from the local school which had recently received a visit from Prince Charles.

'I'm so glad you're all here,' she sobbed and giggled after they'd crowed out the final chorus. 'Because I – that is, *we* – have an announcement to make. The next time you see us, we'll be married!'

The only man strong enough to catch Judy Glenn when she promptly fainted was Jimmy Sylvian. When she opened her eyes again, she burst out laughing. 'My little pusscat's been on the shelf longer than Mrs Beeton. But, God, it was worth the wait!'

When Odette cried most of the way home, alternately dodging Winnie's sympathetic, licky attempts to mop her face up and burying her wet eyes in the little dog's soft forehead, Jimmy said nothing. He diplomatically left the Ladysmith Black Mambazo tape unplayed and kept his eye on the road, only occasionally reaching across to pat her knee.

'I know you're going to miss her,' he said eventually, as he pulled off the M40 on to the M25.

'It's not just that,' Odette sobbed. 'She's got a different life now. We all have. Love changes everything so bleedin' much, and not just your surname.'

Jimmy thought about this all the way to the M23 turn-off.

'Are you upset because she's getting married?' he asked cautiously.

Odette snorted into Winnie's head. At first, Jimmy thought she was sobbing even more violently, but after a couple of minutes he realised she was laughing.

'It's not that,' she hiccuped. 'It's just that I miss them. All my married friends. They're still there, but I miss them like mad. I don't suppose you'll understand, babes. It's pretty sad of me.'

'I understand.' He gave her a swift smile across the cab. 'You think I haven't been through it? We all have. Friends get married, they go away, their focus shifts.'

'They start shopping in B & Q, then in Mothercare.' Odette blew her nose. 'They lose interest in the things you once shared laughs about, they never come out, they move away, they notice what the bloody interest rate is doing. They're no longer so career-obsessed, they start thinking long, long into the future to when their kids are grown up, whereas people like you and me are still waiting to grow up ourselves. I miss them, babes. I really bleedin' miss them.'

Jimmy shot her a shrewd look. 'But you've changed far more than any of them in these past few months, haven't you?'

She stroked the wet patch on Winnie's domed head. 'Yeah, I went a bit mad.'

'Welcome back.' He laughed loudly and drifted on to the hard shoulder.

Lydia went to the wrong terminal at first. Then she was apprehended by a loony Yank fresh off the San Diego red-eye, demanding to know where Buckingham Palace was. Finally she tracked down the right terminal and flight number.

'Has Juno Glenn checked in yet?' she asked a steward at check-in.

'One moment.' He pursed his lips and tapped in a few keyboard letters before peering at his screen intently. 'No – she's very late. Her seat has already been reallocated.'

Five minutes later, Juno huffed into view, scattering travellers with her fast-moving trolley. Jay was trolleying along beside her so that they resembled two drag racers. Any moment now, Lydia expected two little parachutes to fly out of the back to assist them braking. They could have used the help as they crashed into the check-in desk one after the other.

'Lyds!' Juno panted, already heaving her bags on to the weighing conveyor belt and throwing her tickets at the check-in attendant. 'What are you doing here? Where were you last night?'

'Ate something that disagreed with me,' she apologised. 'French, I think.'

Juno was flabbergasted. 'You *ate* something?'

'Only a tiny mouthful, and it was far too salty.' Lydia wrinkled her nose and kissed them both hello. 'So I thought

I'd come and see you off to make up for it. Where are your ma and pa?'

'Dropped us off outside.' Jay smiled his shy smile. 'We're kinda pushed for time.'

'Flight's in twenty minutes and I want a bottle of gin from Duty Free.' Juno squeezed her friend's hand. 'Are you feeling better now, yes?'

'Still a bit queasy.' Lydia pulled a big-eyed face. 'But I had to drag myself here to give you a farewell present.' She fished a small parcel out of her latest must-have Dior doughnut handbag. 'Here. Don't open it until you're on the plane.'

Juno had a seemingly endless supply of tears. Thankfully Jay, who knew her well and loved her anyway, had an equally endless supply of tissues.

'I'm afraid we're overbooked on your plane. You're very late,' the attendant butted in. He would have charged them extra for their overweight baggage, but Jay was so pretty he'd decided to turn a blind eye. 'I'll have to bump you up to First Class, if that's okay?'

'No, it's not!' Juno huffed. 'I'm a Socialist.'

'That's fine, sir,' Jay cut across her as he gratefully took their boarding cards.

As Juno hugged Lydia goodbye at the barrier, she wiped away her tears and suddenly remembered something. 'Did you know Elsa's had a girl? Florence.'

Before Lydia had a chance to let out an excited shriek, Jay butted in with even more thrilling news.

'And by the way, we're getting married.' He was tugging Juno away as the last call for their plane echoed from the tannoy.

'Ah – yes!' Juno wailed guiltily as she was towed away. 'I'm going to ruin your bridesmaids' tableau, Lyds. Sorry. I wouldn't guarantee Odette'll be your single representative either. I'll call!' She finally disappeared around the corner to passport control, leaving Lydia with a kiss frozen mid-way between lips and hand.

Tucking into a champagne brunch in First Class, Juno was already wearing her cotton slippers, had her eye-mask on top of her head like sunglasses, had tried out her toothbrush, executive floss and face mist, and was just examining her aromatherapy flannel whilst spearing a mushroom when she remembered Lydia's present and fished it out of her bum bag. Inside the wrapping were two small leather jewellery boxes containing matching platinum rings.

'Oh, my God!' she shrieked. 'Lydia must have guessed. This is so typical of her. She always was far, far too generous for her own good.'

'Shame she didn't guess our finger sizes quite so well,' Jay laughed as his ring rattled around on his finger like a tag on a pigeon's leg while Juno's barely made it to the knuckle.

'We can have them altered in New York.' She stifled a little sob. Jay was poised with the tissues, but needn't have worried as Juno – close to a food source – sought solace in her First Class breakfast, her new ring on her little finger.

Jay took it off her as soon as she had finished eating, popping it back in the box.

'What are you doing that for?' she grumbled, now hopelessly attached to her new accessory.

Then she started to smile like a loon as Jay stood up in the aisle and went down on one knee, watched by every astonished passenger in First Class.

'Juno Glenn, will you do me the honour of becoming my wife?'

It was only when they were sitting in the back of a yellow cab, heading towards Manhattan with Jay proudly pointing out the sights of his beloved city, that something occurred to Juno. As usual, she realised the truth hours after anyone else would have done.

'These rings.' She looked at her little finger, her lip wobbling like mad. 'I think they're Lydia and Finlay's wedding rings.'

Odette threw herself out of the pick-up and flew around the side of the farmhouse. She was relieved to find the door to the kitchen locked, and gratefully scrabbled for the key in its hiding place beneath the stone. It was there for once. Inside, she was less elated to find that Bazouki had left several puddles and a poo on the kitchen flagstones, and the answer-machine was full of messages from Euan telling Cyd that her first grandchild was on the way. The final message announced that Florence had been born.

Following her inside a few minutes later, Jimmy found her throwing newspapers over damp patches and squirting Dettox around.

'I don't think Cyd came back here last night,' she fretted. 'Bazouki must have been left alone for hours to make this mess, poor old bird.' She blew the dog a kiss as she passed. Cowering in her bed, Bazouki whimpered guiltily and jumped as she leaned back on her squeaky toy.

Jimmy waited until Odette was taking two inverted plastic bags of dog do outside to the bins before he slipped hastily upstairs.

They were, as he'd predicted, both in bed, Cyd's cloud of shaggy hair fanned over the propped-up pillows behind her like a high ruff. She was wearing tortoiseshell half-moons and reading the latest Joanna Trollope. At her side, her sleeping companion lay curled in a foetal ball, his face buried in pillows, one pale arm draped across her belly revealing a faded Rangers tattoo.

Cyd glanced at Jimmy over her glasses when he stepped into the room. Even without a scrap of make-up on, she looked staggeringly good.

'Congratulations, Grandma,' he announced before she could speak. 'You have a granddaughter. Now Odette is taking the day off so I suggest you get your lover to take you to London to see her.'

Banging the door closed on them, he pounded downstairs.

'Feed the dog and fetch what you need for a day out from the mill,' he ordered, plucking the phone receiver from Odette's hand.

'Why?' She was trying to ring the North London Teaching Hospital to trace Cyd.

'We,' he announced regally, as though offering her a trip to Paris, 'are going to B & Q and Mothercare.'

45

Jimmy and Odette joined the hundreds of other couples on the weekend quest for paint in B & Q, baby clothes in Mothercare, and supper ingredients in Sainsbury's. Jimmy insisted that he was going to cook Odette a real South African dish.

She'd never imagined that something so domestic could be quite so much fun, and found herself laughing non-stop as Jimmy towed her around the shops. He attracted attention wherever he went with his loud voice and non-conformist manners. He wasn't exactly rude, but he clearly felt there was no point in queuing politely and quietly along with all the other Saturday-morning shoppers. He insisted upon the best quality of everything and thought nothing of negotiating on price even in huge chain stores; he demanded good service and was rewardingly grateful if he got it, furious if he didn't. Most of all he was intently focused upon what he was buying, however mundane. His cheerful, mad-cap enthusiasm for something as boring as paint was infectious, although his choice in colours was less appealing.

'I can't live with orange walls,' Odette grumbled as Jimmy shuffled paint samples like a card sharp.

'I'm paying for it, I'm applying it, I get to choose the colour,' he insisted, lingering over a very acidic green.

'I can pay!' Odette argued. 'I've got a little bit of money now.'

'Which you'll need to buy Florence a present,' he said pragmatically, finally selecting two pots of saffron yellow emulsion and one of cornflower blue. 'Now, brushes . . .' He rattled off.

We look like a married couple, Odette realised worriedly

as they examined babygros in Mothercare. Even more so when they trolleyed their way along aisles in the supermarket so that Jimmy could select ingredients for the meal that evening. She knew that he was trying to cheer her up, but he was coming on way too strong.

'This is my day for spoiling you,' he laughed when she tried to make him put back a bottle of Bacardi. 'You will eat my food and drink my wine.'

Oh, God. Odette felt her face go clammy. The *ménage à trois*.

'What did you say?' She caught Jimmy shooting her a curious look over a display of real ale.

'Nothing, babes,' she coughed, wondering in alarm if she'd slipped into old habits and said it out loud. 'Just a type of wine I quite like.'

'Well, tonight you're getting your tongue around a big, beefy South African I've been saving especially,' he boomed, trolleying off with a cheery wink at his fellow shoppers.

Once they had got everything they needed, he drove the pick-up back towards Fulkington but took a sharp right before the village instead of heading on towards Siddals and Smock Mill Farms. He took the corner at such speed that all their shopping spilled out of the bags and Nelson almost fell out of the rear of the pick-up.

'Where are we going?' Odette gripped tightly on to Winnie.

'To visit a friend,' He grinned. 'I've just remembered I promised to pop by today.'

'Will they mind me being here?' she asked, looking up at the austere old house they were approaching along a pitted drive. She no longer felt particularly spoiled, tagging along on one of his social calls like this.

'Mind? I've been under pressure to get you along here for weeks.' Jimmy was waving as a tiny, bird-like woman dressed in an extraordinary assortment of different tweeds came out of the house, surrounded by barking dogs.

'Rolanda!' He jumped out of the pick-up and gathered her into a big hug.

Odette stayed inside the cab as she assessed the dog situation.

There were at least six and Nelson had leaped from the back of the pick-up to greet them, rushing around sniffing bottoms. On Odette's lap, Winnie was yapping jealously.

Suddenly a voice which rivalled Jimmy's for depth and strength boomed 'Sit!' and to Odette's amazement the entire pack, including Nelson, lined up beside the tiny woman like the von Trapps. The only disobedient dissenter was a small, familiar-looking Afghan puppy who was sniffing the pick-up's tyres with interest. It was one of Bazouki's litter, Odette recognised, and then immediately remembered Lady Fulbrook, purveyor of second-hand shirts and flattering comments in the Cancer Relief shop.

She cautiously stepped out of the cab.

'My dear!' Lady F took her hand in her frail little one and almost crushed it flat. 'So good to see you. I keep telling Jimmy to bring you round for a snifter. You're both just in time for tea. Come in and have some freshly baked knob. Jimmy can never resist it.'

She clearly knew him pretty well. He devoured the tea she provided, piling jam on to the crusty bread – or 'knob' – and telling her all about the party. Rolanda also clearly adored Jimmy. She wiped her eyes over and over again as he had her in stitches. Starting to relax, Odette surprised herself by joining in and describing their waking moments that morning in the Red Cross tent of a shared bedroom.

'You two do cheer an old girl up,' Rolanda purred with gravelly delight, looking from Jimmy to Odette. 'Most young people get on my nerves, to be frank – all that terrible language and sheer bad manners. Now you two are quite, quite different. You have old-fashioned hearts in young bodies. That is a very rare quality.

'My husband is a randy teenager in a very, very old body,' she sighed. 'Quite a disappointment, but I suppose it's too late to trade him in now. Hold on to this man.' She gripped Jimmy's arm and peered at Odette. 'There's not another like him the length of the country, I can assure you. Now who's for that snifter? Damned yard-arm has tennis elbow.'

Jimmy politely pointed out that they had to be going before the food in the car went off.

As they roared back along the pitted drive afterwards, he turned to Odette.

'Before you say it, I know.' He grinned sheepishly. 'She is my biggest fan. But I swear I didn't take you there to hear what a wonderful person I am and how lucky you are to have me as a friend.' That last word was said with deliberate emphasis.

'So why did you?' Odette was under the distinct impression he had done just that, and far from thinking they were friends, Rolanda was clearly convinced they were the Posh and Becks of Fulkington.

'Because she's lonely,' he said, glancing in his rear-view mirror at Rolanda, still waving from her grand doorstep. 'Meeting you will have made her whole week. Now that's not a bad thing to say you've done, is it?'

Odette felt so guilty for thinking only about herself that she didn't notice Jimmy was driving her to Siddals Farm and not the mill.

'I need to go back, have a shower and change into something fresh,' she protested, looking down at her crumpled dress. 'I slept in this. I'll come over in plenty of time for supper.'

The farmhouse was still deserted when Odette let herself in again and Bazouki was ridiculously grateful to see her, so she realised that Cyd still hadn't got back from London. She took the bored Afghan out into the garden to let her have a run around, carrying the walkabout phone with her to call the hospital. They told her that Elsa and Florence had already gone home. Odette dialled the Zen Den II but it rang and rang without an answer.

Confused, she let Bazouki stay outside while she let herself into the mill to shower and change. She tried to visualise the place painted yellow and failed.

She'd bought herself some more credits for her mobile, which she fired up. To her amazement, it had seventeen messages on it. Odette spent most of the new credits listening to them. Several were from old work contacts who had called to ask whether she was still available. Even more surprisingly, one was from her mother Odette perked up as she realised that Clod was actually concerned for her welfare, and cared enough to check up on her. She called straight back.

'Odie, you are ver' naughty girl!' Clod was livid. 'So selfeesh. Your Auntie Lil is doing 'er 'ead een, y'know?'

'What have I done?' Odette's heart sank as she realised that Clod couldn't care less how or where she was, just so long as she didn't upset the family.

'You haff not replied to the wedding invitation for Melanie. You go or no? They need to know.'

Odette had forgotten all about her cousin's wedding. It was just a fortnight away.

Clod ranted on for ages, eating up yet more of Odette's precious credits. She wanted to know whether she'd be able to drive the family, whether she'd bought the couple a present yet, whether she was going to bring anyone.

'No,' Odette said firmly.

'But you haff to breeng someone, *ma fille*,' Clod thundered. 'I weel not let you embarrass me by coming alone. I weel ask one of the Turner boys eef you no find someone. Monny says they are going.'

'How does she know?' Odette asked sulkily, horrified by the prospect of being accompanied by one of the loutish Turners.

'She says Liam help her out around the house until Craig comes home. He ees very nice boy. I say to Monny that he make good 'usband for little Odette, but she just laugh at me. I sink she is missing Craig very much, *pauvre petite*.'

Odette was still livid at her mother's gall when she took the quad bike and trundled back to Siddals Farm across the farm-tracks, terrifying several flocks of sheep.

Delicious smells were wafting from the kitchen when she let herself in through the back door, knocking as she entered. Jimmy looked up from the Rayburn in shock.

'I told you to call me when you needed a lift.'

'Brought the quad.' She bent down to scratch Winnie who had trundled up to welcome her, jealously growling at Nelson when he tried to do the same.

Odette had put on a pair of old jeans and a comfort jumper and was startled to see that Jimmy – who'd been wearing his usual scruffy gear all day – had changed into cream trousers and a crisp white shirt. Even stranger were the candles flickering in the centre of the table which was laid for two with the best china and cutlery. Jimmy had always struck her as a plates-on-knees round the bushfire kind of a guy, but this looked set to be a night of starched old-fashioned safari tent-dining minus the manservants.

'You have been busy.' She noticed that he'd even put some freshly cut daffodils in a vase. Two bottles of Meerlust wine were breathing on the table, and the Rayburn was covered with bubbling pots and pans.

'I don't often get the chance to cook for someone else.' He smiled, looking strangely edgy – almost nervous. 'You'll have to indulge me in a little formality. Bacardi and Coke?'

He was a very disorganised cook. He clattered pans and spilled ingredients, chattering about this and that, slurping wine at regular intervals. His nervy, energetic enthusiasm reminded Odette of her nephew when he was allowed loose in Monny's kitchen to ice biscuits or stir a cake mix, ending up coated with icing sugar and giggling infectiously.

'In Mpona I was never allowed to cook because I made such a mess. This is a rare treat. I can't be bothered to do it for myself, so I live off toast and peanut butter. Tonight you are my guinea pig.'

'Are you suggesting this stuff might poison me?' Odette looked at the bubbling pots in alarm.

'No – no, not just a guinea pig for my cooking. Although that counts too, I suppose,' he laughed, glancing shyly at her over his big shoulder. 'I'm talking about the whole package: presentation, style, conversation. You have to pretend that I am trying to impress you – like on a first date – and award me points out of ten.'

'Like a date?' Odette stiffened uncomfortably.

'Yeah, sort of.' He shrugged, grabbing his wineglass for a quick slurp. 'You see, I'm so out of practice, I'm sure I'd make a total fool of myself if I asked someone I thought I had a chance with to dinner – like Rolanda, say.' He winked at her over his shoulder. 'You can tell me where I'm going wrong, point me in the right direction so I know how to act like one of those sophisticated city slickers you know.'

The insinuation was that he was happy to make a fool of himself in front of Odette because she was a mate. The idea made her relax, although she didn't like to point out that she no longer knew any sophisticated city slickers and that she personally thought Jimmy was much more fun as he was.

Soon any embarrassment that Odette may have felt on seeing the flowers and romantic candles melted away along with the wax as she went two glasses up and started telling Jimmy about the conversation with her mother. His take on the situation made her laugh.

'You should insist that Cyd lets you borrow a car, but instead of taking the Bentley or the Aston, take the old Jeep. Tell your mother you can give them a lift after all, and then turn up in that.'

Odette snorted with delight at the image this conjured up. 'I couldn't do that.' She shook her head eventually. 'The kids would love it, but my sister's about to have another baby. She might go into labour at the sight of it.'

'Has your brother-in-law been in contact yet?' He screwed up his eyebrows and looked at her.

Odette crumbled bread between her fingers and shook her head again. 'My mother seems to blame me. The whole family do. She thinks I'm legally required to find Craig, which I suppose I am.'

'Do you think he's gone overseas?'

Odette smiled thoughtfully and shook her head. 'He hates foreigners. Never been further than Essex in his life. More than likely he's still in London somewhere. You don't know Craig's friends. They could hide most of the inhabitants of a Parkhurst wing in East London if they wanted to.'

Jimmy raised his eyebrows. He'd already emptied his bowl and was ready for seconds. Odette had barely touched hers.

'Don't you like it?' His bruised blue eyes were anxious. 'Too much *peri-peri*? I like it hot. Sorry.'

Odette ate some more of the big, spicy bean stew he'd made. It was indeed very hot, and full of strange gritty bits. It tasted good enough, but the texture was weird.

Jimmy watched her closely. 'It's *nsima* with relish. Or at least the closest I could make to it. It's staple food for Africans.'

'Very tasty,' she agreed, forcing back a few more spoonfuls.

'You hate it, don't you?' His face fell.

'No, it's not that.' She stirred the stew around in the bowl, willing it to disappear. 'It's just . . .'

'Very spicy, I know.' He rubbed his chin thoughtfully. 'Three points out of ten. Jimmy falls at the first fence.'

'Well . . .' Odette adored spicy food, but she supposed a lot of women didn't. 'If this were a serious dinner à *deux* then maybe something a bit less unusual.'

He nodded, staring thoughtfully at his bowl. 'So what starter would you suggest for a "serious" dinner à *deux*? Oysters?'

She wrinkled her nose. 'Too slippery and not to everyone's taste. You want something simple and foolproof. Half an avocado maybe.' Her belly let out a greedy groan as she thought about the soft green flesh dripping with vinaigrette.

Jimmy heard her rumbling tummy and thought it was letting out a loud complaint about his stew.

He was dishing out a great pile of little savoury patticakes on two plates now and covering them with startling pink gunk.

'Sour fig sauce,' he explained as he brought the plates to the table. 'It's delicious. Try it.' He cut a patticake corner off with a fork and held it up to her mouth.

Odette could feel waves of bile lapping up her throat as she remembered Florian making her eat from his fork. She jerked her head away.

Shrugging, Jimmy ate the piece himself and started whistling as he carried on serving up, slapping dollops of sour cream on top on the sauce.

Odette closed her eyes. Jimmy wasn't Florian. He was nothing like the big, hedonistic drunkard seeking a quick thrill. Jimmy was a deeply complicated individual, seeking something far more profound. That's why he was being so nice to her.

He was looking after her, just as Cyd had at first, in search of some sort of solace, a balm to rub on the guilt gland, a substitute to lavish love upon. But it never worked. Sooner or later, they all realised they had never loved the surrogate in the first place, only the far superior original. Even her friends had grown bored of caring for the needy and greedy cuckoo they had welcomed into their lives to fill a void. She was the ultimate unwanted pet. Everyone loved a victim, just as long as she made a swift recovery and went away sharpish. There was a very exact time limit and to cross it, to outstay your welcome, was to let yourself in for a whole load more victimisation. Odette had already crossed that deadline with Cyd. She had no intention of doing the same with Jimmy. She wasn't going to give him the chance to reject her as she had everyone else. She was strong enough to cope alone now.

'I've got to go.' She stood up hurriedly, throwing her napkin on the table. 'Sorry, babes. The meal looks great, but I have to be somewhere.'

'Where?' Jimmy stood up too.

'Cyd might be back.' She searched around for an excuse. 'She'll need me there.'

He grabbed her shoulder firmly. 'Sit down!'

Odette gaped at him and then, out of the corner of her eye, noticed that both Nelson and Winnie were sitting quaking by the Rayburn and the garden door respectively.

'I said, I've got to go,' she muttered defiantly, struggling against his grip.

'You can wait just five minutes to listen to me,' he insisted, pushing her back down in her chair. 'You have to listen to me, Odette, because if you don't you're never going to crawl out of this hole you're in.'

'What hole?' she baulked.

'The huge one you dig in the floor with your eyes every time you're cornered, about two minutes before you tunnel away from an awkward situation as fast as you can.'

'I never run away.' She stared him out. 'How dare you bleedin' say that? I always stay and face things.'

'So stay now.' He dropped his voice, sitting down again and covering her hand warmly with his. 'Stay and face this

513

situation. You know what tonight's all about. Tell me where to get off if you like. All you have to do is say the word. Just don't run away.'

Odette looked at him in confusion, wondering if he was on one of his social worker-cum-therapist kicks again. 'I don't know what tonight's all about, Jimmy. You said we were pretending that you're cooking a romantic meal *à deux*?'

He smiled into her eyes. 'For a woman who's too clever by point five, you don't half miss the point when it comes to men. I'm not pretending. I've never pretended to care about you because there would be no need. Can't you see that I'm mad about you, Odette? I adore you and tonight I am – or rather I was, admittedly rather badly – trying to seduce you.'

Odette was so surprised that she said the first thing that came into her head. 'Why?'

He let out a short, exasperated sigh and shook his head sadly. 'You really can't see?'

She pulled her hand away from beneath his and automatically crossed her arms over her chest in a defence mechanism. 'I don't know what you're after,' she said suspiciously, her mind racing, thoughts swimming through wine as they tried to sort themselves out.

He looked up at the ceiling in despair. 'I'm not "after" anything, Odette. All I know is that I like being with you. It's as easy as breathing, being with you, only the air is fresher and the sky is brighter, and then the moment you go away again everything goes dim. I've been crazy about you since the first time I ever laid eyes on you. I've never wanted anyone so badly in my life.'

That blew it. He'd been doing all right up until then – the bit about breathing had been lovely, almost Jonathan-like. It was the wanting bit that made her feel ill. It reminded her of Calum. Of twenty-first century love and all it entailed. The whole thing terrified her, from taking her clothes off and revealing her disgusting body to being useless in bed – out of bed, up against the wall, anywhere – useless and frigid and disappointing and a fake.

She looked up at him, feeling cornered and humiliated.

He was so effortlessly good-looking, he obviously had no idea what it was like to be less than perfect. And whereas Jimmy was as body-conscious as a floating spirit, Odette was vain. Deeply, paranoically, jealously vain. She was aware of every fault, every genetic weakness, every hideous inch of her wretched, inadequate body. She had monitored it closely for years, as eagle-eyed as a City whizz-kid checking share prices. She knew each slight fluctuation, and had for years kept on top of things. She had become the ultimate packager, using a glossy wrapping to conceal the sham product beneath. Until recently she had been proud of her outer image. But she had always known that once the glossy paper was stripped away, the luxury box discarded and the lush tissue peeled back, the gift inside was a disappointment.

In the past four months she'd even stopped bothering with her appearance. She'd let herself go completely, coping by living largely in denial, by pretending it wasn't happening. She had gone beyond vain. It hadn't seemed to matter.

Only now it did. It mattered very much indeed. Because she thought she'd been getting better. She'd started to feel okay, to look ahead to the long, grinding recovery slope. And Jimmy had just blown it for her by standing miles away at the finishing line, screaming, 'Why aren't you here yet?'

Now she suddenly saw an image of herself she couldn't face. It was as though she was standing in a neon-lit room, stark naked, facing a mirror. And she was terrified.

Jimmy had no idea what was going on in her head, she realised. He was just a big, hunk-headed man cracking on to her.

'I thought you were—' she started, and then changed her mind. She'd been about to say that she'd thought he was her friend, but in truth she'd always known he wanted more. He had never made a secret of the fact he fancied her. From the roses delivered to the office to the numerous dinner invitations, he had always been clear about his intentions. She'd just found it so hard to believe she'd ignored it.

'You don't feel the same way about me at all, do you?' He suddenly laughed, reaching for his glass and draining it. 'You don't feel a thing for me.'

She shook her head angrily. 'That's not bleedin' true and you know it. I like you a lot, Jimmy. Jesus, you've been so good to me. I don't deserve kindness like yours. This past fortnight, you've kept me going. But I only want friendship, and I don't think it's fair to ask for any more, is it? You want something I can't give.'

It was his turn to say nothing. He just covered his mouth with his hand and stared at her with troubled eyes.

'I'm sorry, I know that's an ungrateful thing to say.' Odette closed her eyes. 'You're so lovely and good-looking and everything – Christ, most women would give their eye teeth to have you cook them dinner and . . .' She rubbed her mouth angrily. 'It's just, I'm not ready. I mean, I'll never be ready. You picked the wrong woman. I was just a passing stranger when you saw me for the first time. Nothing else. Just a stranger.' Unable to express what she was feeling in words, she shook her head.

Jimmy seemed to read her thoughts. His voice was quiet and reassuring. 'You will get to like you, I promise. I do. I adore you. It's only a matter of time before you do too. And we're no longer strangers.'

'No, we're not,' she agreed hollowly, opening her eyes again. 'But we're not lovers either, and we're not about to be.'

He raked his hand through his untidy hair. 'So where do we go from here? I take it you don't want to see me again?'

Odette reached for her glass and took a long draught, letting the delicious wine swirl around her taste buds. The self-hatred had gone for now, she realised with relief. The pressure was off. He was no longer trying to seduce her. She didn't have to pretend to be anything she wasn't.

'You're wrong to say you can't ask for my friendship.' Jimmy filled the silence with his big voice, trying hard to sound light-hearted. 'Totally wrong. I give it willingly. And, face it, you live in the middle of nowhere. There are only a limited number of conversations you can conduct with sheep, such as "Where does one go for a drink around here?" The answer's always "Baa". It's not as if—'

Odette opened her mouth to shut him up. 'Let's . . .' She spoke before she really thought about it and then racked her brain for what to say next. She did want to see him again, she realised. He was a rare friend, immeasurably kind and cheering. When he wasn't announcing he wanted her, he was huge fun to be around.

'Let's stay friends then.' She winced as she realised that the line was so cheesy it had holes in it and a wax rind. 'Let's just hang around together.'

'What, like monkeys?' He cocked his head.

'Yeah, like monkeys.' Odette liked the image of swinging from tyres and swigging from plastic beakers. It was carefree and childish and a million miles from candle-lit meals for two. 'Or washing maybe.'

Jimmy barked out his klaxon laugh and raised his glass. 'I think I'm going to rather like this hanging out thing.'

'To hanging out!'

He clanked his glass against hers, splashing a liberal amount of Meerlust on the table. 'I want you to hang out with me at Mungo's thirtieth. St George's Day. Pencil it in your diary. He's having a *braai*.'

Odette pulled a guilty face. 'That's the day after Mel's wedding. What's a *braai*?'

'Wait and see.' He winked. 'We'll go to both. I'll be your bloke for the occasion. Don't worry.' He saw her wary expression. 'I can hang out without any strings attached. Just a couple of pegs – see.' He patted his big, long legs. 'I'll be your walker – every single woman should take one to a society function. Think of me as the male equivalent of a designer handbag. A hang-out bag.'

She laughed, although she wasn't altogether sure that taking him to the wedding was a good idea. At least it would get her off the hook with her mother's Turner brother set-up, but it was hardly a society function. It was more likely to be a social punch-up.

'Just one other thing . . .' Jimmy smacked his lips as he started tucking into his now cold sour-fig extravaganza.

'Mmm?' Odette was even warier.

'Could you hang out with Winnie, too? She can't live here much longer. Nelson's having a nervous breakdown. She makes

517

his life hell. If you don't want to take me home with you tonight, at least take my dog.'

Quadding back to the mill, Odette listened to the delirious snorting coming from the cubby box behind her as Winnie, sitting in it with her ears inside out in the wind, inhaled the smell of frightened sheep with ecstatic appreciation. Odette guessed she could cope as foster mother until Jimmy found the dog a permanent home. It was the least she could do to make up for the way she had treated him.

The lights were on in the farm, indicating that Cyd was back. Odette rode the quad around to the garages and parked it rather wonkily, lifting Winnie from her pillion box. She felt a bit pissed. She couldn't face Cyd tonight. She had a lot to sleep on and a lot to think about.

As she wandered sleepily and rather drunkenly towards the mill, she didn't notice the silver car parked in the shadows of the topiarised tree, its driver fast asleep over a Jeffrey Archer.

46

Odette could pinpoint the exact moment that she started to feel the warm glow of genuine affection for Jimmy Sylvian. It was the first few waking moments of Sunday morning when she became aware of a fog-horn snoring beside her in bed, and a shaft of bright sunlight blinding one eye like a reverse pirate's patch. She was sleeping with his dog and benefiting from his glazing skills. He had taken over her life.

She felt herself shiver with embarrassment as she remembered her stupid panic attack the previous night. She'd thought the days of self-hating tears had gone, but they were simply lying low, waiting for the slightest trigger to set them off.

Her heart no longer ached so strongly for Calum, but she was terrified of experiencing the same emotions again. Reaching out to tickle Winnie's long ears, she realised that knocking around with warm, trustworthy Jimmy could be just the sort of therapy she needed. Now that they had cleared the air, there was nothing to do but shoot the breeze. She only wished her other troubles could be so easily resolved.

It was Mothering Sunday. She felt a pang of guilt as she thought about Clod and the uncomfortable conversation they'd had the previous evening.

Cyd was predictably still in bed. The farmhouse was locked, the curtains drawn and there was no key under the bay pot. Odette was dying to hear news about the birth and Florence, but realised it would be hours before Cyd got up.

So she took Winnie for a run. It was the first time Odette had jogged for weeks and she was soon puffed out, but nothing could beat the thrill of feeling blood pumping hard through her veins, sweat sticking her clothes to her skin, air rushing in and out of her lungs. She felt as though she was off some sort of ventilation machine and breathing for herself for the first time in several long weeks. The endorphin high was tremendous.

When Cyd finally emerged, she looked like death.

'Hangover,' she croaked as Odette encountered her teetering towards the mill in her usual silk pyjamas and wellies combination.

'Wetting the baby's head?' Odette was fresh from the shower and eager for news.

'What?' Cyd looked blank for a moment and then waved her arm dismissively. 'Oh, that. I've got some photos for you somewhere, dearheart. Funny little soul. Looks like a piglet, but I suppose all babies do.'

It wasn't quite the ecstatic reaction Odette was expecting. She hazarded a guess that Cyd was not only feeling fragile but was also getting used to the idea of being a grandmother. It would take some adjusting for the reclusive rock-chick icon to adapt to the role.

Winnie was sniffing around Cyd's boots with interest. Having already renewed her friendship with Bazouki, she was eager to ingratiate herself with the other glamorous blonde.

'Who's this?' Cyd reached down to give her a pat.

'It's Jimmy's dog.' Odette chewed her lip guiltily, hoping Cyd wouldn't mind. 'I said I'd look after her.'

'Has he gone away then?'

'Not exactly. This one fights with his other dog, so I agreed to . . . um . . . sort of have her here for a bit.'

'Well, that's typical!' Cyd was instantly livid. 'You didn't want a beautiful pedigree Afghan puppy, but you're happy to take on someone else's reject. Honestly, Odette, I despair of your selfishness sometimes.'

She disappeared without explanation for the entire afternoon and most of the evening. In her absence, Jimmy appeared in the pick-up with the paint and a microwave oven. 'I can't fathom out how to use it so you might as well try,' he said, off-loading both his gifts on Odette before jumping back in the cab. He didn't look her in the eye once.

'Aren't you staying for a cuppa?' She was embarrassed by the sudden awkwardness between them, certain it was entirely her fault and that she needed to make amends.

'Can't hang around. I'll see you tomorrow.' He spun the huge truck around and disappeared in a cloud of fumes, big tyres spitting up gravel.

Odette felt absurdly downcast. She'd thought they were going to 'hang out', and instead he couldn't hang around. Perhaps he had been only after one thing.

Cyd didn't reappear for hours.

Odette found it quite creepy being alone in the mill when the farm lights weren't blazing. She knew it was ridiculous, but she felt safer knowing that Cyd was nearby. Sometime after ten, she heard a car and looked out of the window, but there were no lights and the sound was too far away to be near the courtyard. She'd heard the same ticking engine before, and with crawling skin wondered whether someone was casing the joint.

She listened with bated breath. The engine carried on running in the distance for the best part of ten minutes – too close to be on the village lane, not close enough to see. Aware that security at the farm was practically zero, she started creeping along the drive to get a better look when she bumped into Cyd coming the other way, carrying her high-heeled shoes and tiptoeing along barefoot.

'Christ!' Cyd almost fainted with shock when Odette flashed a torch in her face. 'Are you spying on me? Go to bed, Odette, for God's sake.'

She stalked past, cursing when she tripped over Winnie, and then made a sprint for the farmhouse, slamming the door.

The following week did nothing to improve matters between Cyd and Odette. As Cyd got up unexpectedly early to quad off through the fields and oversee the documentary team at Fermoncieaux, Odette tried to get some sort of order into her companies and to investigate the tax position. Cyd paid all her Millers in cash, using her own unique dovecote PAYE system. The Smock Mill companies themselves were far from the 'charity' Cyd believed them to be, but she was certainly building up a huge investment fund ready for the animal sanctuary she planned to build one day. The money from renting out land went into it too. She lived day-to-day on Jobe's Mask royalties, which still provided a hefty income.

Odette calculated that Cyd owed close to thirty thousand pounds in taxes, but when she tried to broach the subject Cyd grew too angry with her to listen. Now she had another illogical axe to grind.

'The Millers have been complaining. They say you want printed records of all the orders.'

'I'm trying to get some sort of financial record together,' Odette explained. 'The administration is chaotic. There are no VAT receipts whatsoever.'

'Well, we don't like wasting paper. It's very unkind to trees,' Cyd fumed. 'It's all worked very well so far. What the Vatman doesn't know won't hurt us. *Vivat diem*, as the saying goes.'

'Actually it's *carpe diem*.'

Cyd looked thunderous.

'Leave the Millers alone. They know what they're doing. You just have to make predictions on the Internet and keep your beak out of the rest. After all, you hardly managed your own company very well, did you, dearheart?'

Ouch! That hurt. Odette blinked as though squirted in the eye with ink.

'So why put me in charge in the first place?'

Cyd tucked her chin in as though the answer was patently obvious. 'Because there was no one else, dearheart. And I really did want to take this job at Food Hall very, very much. Calum says he'd be lost without my help.'

That hurt almost more. Working with Cyd was just like working with Calum except Cyd was, if anything, a little more disorganised and a lot more critical.

Odette no longer went into the farm to eat with her in the evenings. Instead, she and Jimmy had started using the time to decorate the mill. It took a lot of courage to call him and ask for his help – mostly because she was terrified of falling off the cap when using her faint, crackling mobile phone. But she sensed that he was leaving it up to her to make the next move, and the more she dwelled on his no-strings offer of friendship, the more it pulled at her heartstrings. He was the kindest man she had ever met and what's more seemed genuinely to relish helping her out. Even if it meant she had to endure his homespun therapy, strange cooking and the occasional lapse into mild flirtation, she knew it was a low price to pay for his extraordinary generosity and friendship.

On Tuesday he rolled up at just after six, told her to put the kettle on and set about transforming the mill from dingy tower to dreamy bower. He reappeared at the same time each evening, sometimes arriving in his pick-up, other times walking across the fields, always bringing a huge bowl of *nsima* and relish with him which they reheated in the microwave. He was, he explained, perfecting the recipe, and Odette agreed to taste a little more each evening to pass judgement. As his cooking improved, she started to acquire quite a taste for it. They shared it as they worked, listening to old eighties CDs and singing along to the snatches they remembered, chatting about politics, sometimes arguing about them, often laughing too. He had a very good working knowledge of the microwave given that he'd told her he couldn't fathom it out, Odette noticed.

His hair was always full of paint and Pollyfilla, his hands always covered with plasters, but he never stopped smiling and singing along to Queen or Bruce Springsteen. To her delight, he adored Meatloaf and they screeched 'Dead Ringer For Love' at the tops of their voices as they stripped the old gloss paint from the windows.

He talked a lot about the Fermoncieaux Estate and his plans for the future. He was hopelessly idealistic and had already seen a great many hopes dashed.

'It's almost impossible to persuade the tenant farmers to change their practices and be more ecologically sound. Organic farming makes no financial sense to them and they're very heavily subsidised to work the way they do, whereas most of my ideas are still experimental. The situation hasn't been helped by the fact that their new landlord has just put their rents up by almost a third.'

'Calum?' Odette picked up a note of irritation in his voice.

Jimmy nodded. 'He has to. The house is costing a fortune to convert and he's having a nightmare with English Heritage over the changes, as the place is listed. Everything he does must be reversible. It's cranked the cost up beyond belief. But the farmers are livid.'

Jimmy made light of his conflicts with Calum, but it was clear he was growing increasingly unhappy with the situation. 'He thinks he's the lord of the manor,' he laughed. 'You know he's taken up clay pigeon shooting? And I heard him talking about getting riding lessons the other day.'

'I never saw Calum as the country squire type.' Odette was shocked.

'I think it has a lot to do with his father,' Jimmy confided in her when he started tackling the broken video. 'Calum's always had a chip on his shoulder about the way his old pa won all that money and tried to better himself by buying into a world where he didn't belong. Now Calum's doing exactly the same thing on a bigger scale and just can't see it. It's as though he's sticking two fingers up at his dad's memory and saying, "Look what I've bought. Your winnings could never have afforded you this, but I've earned it."'

'He's not going to keep it if he carries on like this.' Odette was amazed. 'It's a business, not a toy.'

'Try telling him that.' Jimmy rolled his eyes, pulling the back off the video with more force than was strictly necessary. 'This bloody documentary team aren't helping either. His ego keeps getting the better of him. He loves coming across as the wild-boy entrepreneur, hogging the screen as he tells them all his plans, showing off when he fires another builder or bawls out one of the managers. They're lapping it up, which he thinks is great for business. But the moment he's buggered off, they're filming the stuff he's too busy Barbouring around to notice – the state of the building, the staff talking behind his back, the surveyors tutting under their breath, the chaos at Home Farm.'

'I thought Cyd was supposed to be keeping them in check?'

'From what I've seen, she's keeping her eye on something

else entirely,' muttered Jimmy, teeth clenched around the handle of a screwdriver.

Odette wanted to ask him more, but he was thoroughly overexcited as he finally got the video to work. He might be a clumsy decorator but Jimmy was a whizz at all things electrical and immediately insisted that they sit down to watch some of the programmes Odette had talked to him about. She'd kept hold of all her favourite videos, although many of them were too mildewed to play, having wintered in the damp tower.

On Saturday night, they went for the big duo – *Betty Blue* and *9½ Weeks*. Cracking open a bottle of Bacardi, they settled down to their favourite films.

Jimmy chattered excitedly as the *Betty Blue* music started, and then fell silent as Béatrice Dalle and Jean-Hugues Anglade appeared on screen making hot and passionate love. Béatrice's orgasmic squeaks echoed around the mill.

Odette went very pink and tried not to make a single movement while they watched. She was convinced the slightest twitch on her part would make her look like a salivating weirdo. She was torn between acute embarrassment and total fascination.

She'd seen the film when it first came out, and had thought it was okay. But she'd been annoyed by the subtitles because her French was good, but not quite good enough to follow every bit of dialogue, forcing her to check on odd words and continually lose the plot. At the time she remembered thinking Betty was a bit too much of a fruitcake to be believable. But she knew it was Jimmy's favourite, so she kept silent and tried to get into it.

It was Jimmy who lost concentration first. He started chatting about his brother's birthday and how much of a shock it would be for Mungo to reach thirty. Soon he was barely watching. He seemed almost surprised when the titles rolled at the end.

'It's not how I remembered it.' He shook his head. 'She's a pain in the arse, isn't she? Let's watch your film.'

Odette felt she had lived *9½ Weeks*. At the height of her obsession with Calum she had watched it almost every day. She knew every scene, every line, every outfit Kim wore, every beautiful and profound expression that crossed Mickey's face.

She knew the layout of both their apartments, the opening hours of the gallery, the names of all the minor characters. Most of all she knew the way it made her feel.

She waited to feel horny, to feel angry and to cry. Instead, she was amazed to find herself thinking that Mickey Rourke has an irritatingly lisping voice and that Kim Basinger's eyes were almost as small as her own. And as for their relationship . . . well, it was doomed from the start. His control-freak attitude wasn't erotic, it was downright Neolithic.

Odette shuddered in revulsion. Leaving Jimmy watching it, she picked up a paintbrush and started dolloping bright yellow on to the dusty plaster, even though the room was only lit by the flickering screen and a few candles so she could barely see what she was doing.

After a while, she realised that the sound of the TV had been muted and been replaced by one of her favourite CDs, Sade's 'Diamond Life'.

Odette felt sexier applying paint than watching her beloved film. Sweeping her brush in time to the music, she let her mind wander for a moment. She painted her way across a window in surprise. She'd just had a very brief involuntary daydream. An image had floated into her head without her realising it. Something totally unexpected and quite outrageous. She had visualised Jimmy walking up behind her and very softly kissing the back of her neck. She closed her eyes and listened to Sade's soft autumnal voice. How could she have thought that? She couldn't want it to happen, could she?

When she opened her eyes again, Jimmy had turned the bright working lights on. He helped her finish in silence. He didn't even comment about the big yellow stripe across the window, or tease her about it. Just after midnight, he said he was tired and headed home.

Odette didn't know why, but the evening left her feeling disappointed and frustrated.

The next evening, after a long walk across the downs with the fighting dogs, they settled down to watch an old episode of

Dynasty. Jimmy – who preferred *Londoners* – fell asleep for most of it, snoring vociferously. Watching alone, Odette, who had always rather fancied Adam, the malevolent younger son, suddenly started to take more notice of Jeff, Fallon's big, reliable and dishy husband.

Jimmy snorted awake just in time to see Joan Collins crowning the calculating Sable with a marble ashtray.

'That's my girl,' he said approvingly. 'Oh, God, here comes Botha in drag.'

As they watched Crystal out jogging with little designer sweatbands around her narrow wrists and over her big, stiff hair, Odette marvelled at her ability to work out in full makeup, something she had tried and failed to pull off for the best part of a decade.

'Did I see you out running this morning?' Jimmy looked across at her.

Odette nodded. 'I've just started again. I'm bleedin' slow.'

'D'you mind if I join you some mornings?' he asked. 'I have to shift this flab somehow.'

'What flab?' Odette laughed sarcastically, looking at his broad but lean frame. She hated it when thin people said they were putting on weight, especially men. If Jimmy thought he was fat then she was clinically obese. She still couldn't get into her little black interview suit, which was her acid test. The waistband was at least two inches away from closing.

But Jimmy seemed convinced he had a problem. 'I hate exercise,' he admitted. 'But if there was ever an incentive to do some it'd be trying to keep up with you – and falling behind might not be too bad a way to lose,' he added with a wink.

Deeply uncomfortable with the conversation, she scowled irritably and snapped that she preferred to exercise alone.

The next morning, as she was bounding along one of the wood's less muddy paths, Jimmy came crashing out of the undergrowth, almost colliding with her. He was wearing an extraordinary pair of bright yellow footballing shorts, a 'Safari Mpona' t-shirt, black trainers and a woolly hat. He looked ridiculous and very, very sweaty.

'Morning!' he yelled cheerfully. Odette groaned as she

realised that despite what she'd said, he was going to exercise with her and would probably run rings around her while she wobbled around like a fat beetroot.

But to her surprise, he crashed into the undergrowth on the opposite side of the path and disappeared, leaving Nelson brawling with Winnie in a thick clump of fern.

47

On Monday morning Odette had her regular appointment to meet up with the trustee at the Official Receiver's office. He was far from happy with her current conduct.

'I can't look after the Smock Mill business any longer,' she told Cyd afterwards. 'He was mad at me for agreeing to in the first place. I'm sorry. I'm not legally allowed to act as director to any company or charity.'

Cyd didn't look remotely surprised. She just smiled a wicked little smile on hearing the news. 'In that case there's only one thing for it!'

'What?' Odette looked at her worriedly.

'We'll have to job swap. I hear it's all the rage these days.'

Somehow Odette was convinced Cyd and Calum had already cooked up the idea between them.

To Odette's surprise Jimmy was all for it.

'With your experience, you'd be perfect at dealing with the production company, getting the best out of them,' he told her over supper that evening, another one of his African bean feasts. He had yellow paint on one cheek and blue on his chin. With his height and his mop of blond hair, he looked like a face-painted Swedish football supporter egging her on from the goal mouth. 'It's what Calum wanted in the first place, after all.'

'So you know he offered me the job before Cyd?'

He shrugged. 'It's not the first thing Calum's offered you that Cyd took instead, is it?'

Odette looked up sharply, but Jimmy was smiling easily, a

dimple cracking through the yellow paint. 'Yes, I knew you turned down the job. And I didn't say anything then because I understood why you did it and didn't really blame you.'

Thinking about Ronny Prior, Odette winced. Jimmy didn't understand at all.

'What Cyd's suggesting is just plain crazy – like telling me not to do anything about her tax liability. She's crackers.'

'On the contrary.' Jimmy spooned second helpings into her bowl too. 'It's the perfect solution. Face it, you hate looking after Cyd's businesses knowing that they're in a mess, and here you're being given an opportunity to tackle something where you can really make a difference.'

She shook her head, spooning up the strange gritty mixture. It was an acquired taste, but she was getting quite addicted to it. 'Calum hates me, Jimmy. I don't think he was serious when he offered me the job. He was just trying to wind me up.'

'Oh, he was serious all right.' Jimmy nodded knowingly.

'How can you be so sure?'

'Because I was the one who suggested it. And Calum takes me very seriously indeed.'

'You told him to ask me?' Odette stared at him in disbelief. 'After what I told you about him bankrupting me? That I was never the addict he pretended I was, just someone who made the mistake of falling in love with him?'

He winced. 'Well, I didn't know the full story then.'

'And you don't now,' she sighed, putting down her spoon and closing her eyes in shame. 'It was me who put Ronny Prior in touch with Calum in the first place, Jimmy. I told her to do a hatchet job. It was my way of getting revenge.'

To her amazement he gave his big, barking laugh, tipping his head back in delight. 'Now that is a very sweet just dessert. You must tell Calum. He'll love it.'

'Are you crazy?' she spluttered, still completely unable to get to grips with their friendship.

'Deadly serious.' His eyes glittered. 'He'll really respect you for that. And he'll definitely want you around to sort things out when he hears.'

*　　*　　*

The next day, Odette took the E-type and drove to London to visit Elsa. She had been planning to offer to take Cyd as a surprise, but there was no sign of her or Bazouki in the farm house. The key was beneath the bay pot so she let herself in and left a note. She wondered whether Cyd had decided to go to London to visit her first granddaughter too.

Elsa shattered her illusions within five minutes. While Odette cradled a small, snuggling bundle of warm skin, tiny hands, thin, uneven hair and sweet, yeasty scents, Elsa muttered a few oaths about her 'adoring' mother's lack of interest.

'She turned up for all of ten minutes the day we brought Florence home. Euan had pulled all the phones out so we could get some peace and I thought Mum was in a panic because she must have got the message about the birth so late that we'd left hospital. But she just said she was in a hurry, plonked a few service station flowers on my lap, told me Florence was sweet and buggered off.'

'You mean, she wasn't with you for the birth?' Odette tucked a little sock back on a creased foot.

'You must be kidding!' Elsa laughed bitterly. 'You can't defend her to me any more, Odette, she's incorrigible. Hang on . . .' Her head tilted thoughtfully. 'If you didn't drive her up here that day, who did?'

'Maybe she came by train?'

'Maybe.' Elsa looked doubtful, although she was soon pre-occupied pulling ooh-er faces at Florence who was droopy-eyed and sleepy.

'So how are things going?' she asked Odette after she'd tucked her precious new jewel into a minimalist Japanese bamboo cot.

There were so many answers to Elsa's question, most of which would involve a five-hour session. Odette didn't want to inflict any of them on her friend. Elsa was totally preoccupied, understandably baby-obsessed, wanting to talk about nothing but Florence, the birth, Euan's unexpected fatherly streak and the whole amazing new experience she was going through. Odette's problems belonged to a whole different era, just a few weeks earlier but a new lifetime apart, a time when career and love had mattered.

'Fine,' she finally answered blandly. 'Still getting my act together.'

Euan reappeared from diplomatically raking the Zen garden, which was now so painstakingly sculpted into overlapping curves that it resembled an Artex ceiling, and Elsa disappeared upstairs.

'Hello, hen – you're looking great.' He winked, helping himself to one of the chocolates Odette had brought and admiring the babygros from Mothercare and the mobile. 'These are neat.'

'The mobile's from Jimmy,' Odette explained. 'It's African.'

He nodded thoughtfully, gathering up a few more chocolates. 'These are delicious, although I'll never know how you women can claim chocolate is as good as sex. I'm on twelve Galaxy bars a day right now and I'm still horny as hell.'

Elsa returned and handed Odette a suit.

'This got muddled up with my stuff when you moved out,' she explained. 'I've got one just the same somewhere – Jigsaw – my funeral suit.'

Odette looked at it. It was her all-purpose little interview outfit. The one she'd been thinking of wearing to Elsa's wedding until she found out it no longer did up. Only she must have taken Elsa's by mistake when she was packing to leave the Zen Den II. No wonder it didn't fit her. Elsa was five foot three and a size six. Realising that she'd been torturing herself for not fitting into a size six suit, Odette suddenly burst out laughing.

'What's the joke?' Euan was wolfing back chocolates at a rate of knots.

'Chuck me one of those, babes.' She grinned. 'I think I might have rediscovered my chocolate drive.'

She excused herself to the loo before she left, hoping that Elsa and Euan were too busy cooing at Florence to notice that she took her suit with her. It fitted perfectly; she was exactly the same size she had been when she'd first bought it. She sat on the side of the minimalist glass bath, feeling almost dizzy with relief. Her head had been playing tricks with her all along. She was slim. She felt fantastic.

When Odette came out, now on an infectious high, Elsa was breast-feeding Florrie. Acutely embarrassed, Odette stared at the light fitting and asked Euan about his book.

'Still being rejected as often as a spotty teenager at a disco,' he huffed. 'No one recognises genius. I'm thinking of diversifying. I might write a biography.'

Elsa snorted with laughter. 'Euan's asked Mum if he can ghost her memoirs.'

'And what did she say?'

'She said something really odd actually.' Elsa unplugged Florence and pulled up her bra before putting her precious little load over her shoulder and patting her back. 'She said, "But my life has only just begun, dearheart. I am nurturing a lost youth." Whatever that means. Her youth was pretty fast-paced from what I know.'

'She took away a Dictaphone and says she'll send me some tapes if she gets time between "nurturing."' Euan grinned, clearly happy with the result. 'She promised that by this summer she might have something truly scandalous to talk about. She's probably shagging Prince Charles again.'

'Euan!' Elsa chastised jokingly. 'NIFTC, please.'

On cue Florence let out a satisfied burp.

'Come back soon.' Elsa squeezed Odette tightly as she left. 'It's been so fantastic seeing you. Next time, stay a few days.'

Odette felt so cheered by her afternoon with the Es that she decided to prolong the pleasure and catch up with another old friend.

She threw her interview suit on the passenger seat, kissed all three of them goodbye, and – stopping off briefly to say hello to her former employer, the landlord of the Pump House, who gave her a wet kiss and yet another bottle of Bacardi – drove towards Maida Vale.

En route, she thought about her friends, who had been so supportive when she'd lost everything. In many ways it had been the final collective war cry of the hunters who had now stopped using their spears to gather men and defend each other, and had started defending and foraging for their families. There were only two hunters left; herself and the supreme marksman who only had to look at a muscled beast for it to drop down on the spot. Lydia might have engagement rings on her fingers and *Belle Rouge* on her toes, but she still heard Barry White wherever she chose to go. And Odette suspected she'd been visiting a flat in Old Street a lot lately.

She was feeling unbelievably high, so high that it hardly hurt at all to think about Lydia with Calum. She supposed it was a heady combination of new baby, old friend, and feeling slim again. She wanted to have a good old catch-up, to hear whether Lydia still wrote secret wish-letters in the bath and went shoplifting for kicks.

She took an age to answer her buzzer. Odette assumed she was with a client and then remembered Elsa saying that Lydia had more or less given up the sex therapy thing after a nasty incident with a premature ejaculator.

'Yes?' Lydia sounded flustered.

'It's Odie,' she announced, full of love and memories.

'Er – can you come back in ten minutes?'

'No, I bleedin' well can't. I've driven all the way from Sussex.' Odette knew how vain Lydia was. She probably wanted to repair her make-up. 'It's an emergency,' she added to hurry her up.

At last, she gained access to the flat.

Lydia greeted her in a long shapeless dress which wasn't her usual style at all. It looked as though she'd just thrown it on in order to run for the door. Odette could smell coffee and sex. She knew without doubt that Lydia had someone else in the flat, and she was pretty certain who it was.

'Sorry, babes,' she whispered in an undertone at the door, desperately hoping she was wrong. 'I thought Finlay would be at work?'

'Oh, he is, darling.' Lydia seemed out of breath. 'What's the matter? It's so delicious to see you. Come through to the kitchen and I'll pour you a coffee.'

There was a hollow, deep-chested cough from the direction of the bedroom. Odette raised an eyebrow.

'Keeping up with the in-laws, babes?' she muttered acidly, starting to back out again. 'Sorry – shouldn't have bothered you. Might have guessed.'

Lydia gripped her wrist before she could escape and dragged her inside. Hustling her into the kitchen, she leaned back against the door as she closed it and breathed, 'Odette, I am so glad it's you. I need your help. I think I've fallen in love with him, and he's just told me he's bisexual and in love with someone called Ned. They're thinking of buying a house in Wimbledon together!'

'Calum's bisexual?' Odette felt her stomach bounce off the floor, twist itself around like a greengrocer's bag of potatoes and then lodge itself beneath her ribs again, tight and lumpy. So Cyd had been right all along.

'No – not Calum.' Lydia's big blue eyes were red-rimmed. 'Florian. I think I love him, Odie, and it turns out he's a bloody queen of puddings!'

48

Knowing that she was still slim, Odette ate with a ravenous appetite. By the weekend of Melanie's wedding, she was fatter by several generous helpings of Cape Pie, courtesy of Jimmy who felt he had perfected his *nsima* sufficiently to start on a new recipe.

Odette had forgone her cousin's hen night. She'd been invited, but she'd preferred to stay in the smock mill on Friday night and paint *trompe-l'œil* London scenes around her bedroom with Jimmy, who had suggested it might relieve her homesickness.

Jimmy was a terrible artist. His attempt at St Paul's looked like a big breast, and the Millennium Dome was even more of a mammary. After a few hours, the landscape on his side of the room resembled a row of sunbathing page-three models. Odette's side, by comparison, looked like post-nuclear Milton Keynes.

At midnight, listening to Madness, she had stepped back and asked if he'd mind very much if they painted it all out and started again with a South Downs horizon, complete with sheep, Winnie, Bazouki and windmills. He'd boomed out that big, horizon-reaching laugh and said he'd love nothing more, just as long as they didn't try it that night. They settled in front of a feature-length *Londoners* 'missing episode' video from years earlier, when Liam Sullivan's long-lost father reappeared briefly before getting murdered in a mistaken-identity gangland killing. It was gripping stuff. Jimmy, already a big fan of the show, was truly hooked. Odette, having seen it before, nodded off beside him on the big leather sofa.

The last time she had woken up beside Jimmy, she'd had a hangover and his big toe had been prodding her ear. This time, when she surfaced from sleep to hear the comforting stereo sound of Jimmy and Winnie snoring, she realised she loved them both.

Odette sat for a long time in the steely half-light of dawn coming to terms with the fact that she might just have done it again. Odette 'I'll never get my heart broken' Fielding had repeated her worst ever executive decision. She'd tried her hardest to avoid it. This time she'd covered her bases, taken out all the insurance policies, told the parties involved she would not invest and protected herself like a fortress against loss, yet still she had been fleeced. Her safe, low-risk investment had just risen to dangerous levels. She was over-stretched. She was back in debt. She was in love. Reluctantly, against her taste and better judgement, she had fallen in love with two hairy, stubborn, bossy and devoted individuals.

She was in the shower trying to wash the realisation away when Jimmy yelled at her to hurry up. So domestic. So lovely. Odette scrunched her eyes shut and concentrated on the day ahead. It wasn't going to be easy. He couldn't know.

'You are a *fermier*, James?' asked Clod Fielding, wearing a hat which looked as though she'd head-butted a mangy old ostrich.

'Call me Jimmy, *madame*.' He winked at Odette. '*Ja*, I'm a farmer of sorts. These are wonderful sandwiches.' He tucked into another anaemic triangle of Mother's Pride, somewhere in which was a scrape of bloater paste.

'I sink ze food at ze reception weel be bleedin' 'orrible.' Clod twinkled her eyes at him, raising her cup of tea to her lips with her little finger crooked. 'Ray's sister, she ees terrible cook.'

'The reception's in a pub, Mum,' Odette said through gritted teeth. 'They're doing the catering.'

'A pub!' Clod shuddered as though Odette had just told her that the reception would be in the whore-pit of Beelzebub.

The best china was out, there were paper doilies on the plates and the Bruges lace coverlets had been put on the chair arms and backs in Jimmy's honour. Odette noticed that her family was being unusually polite to her as they eyed up the tall, well-spoken stranger she had brought into their midst. Jimmy looked simply amazing in a suit – the first time she had seen him wear one. Odette was grateful that she'd taken so much effort with her own appearance, matching the acid-test Jigsaw suit with a blood red top hat, courtesy of Rolanda Sherington who had sported it to the previous year's Ladies' Day at Ascot.

'You look like a film star, little 'un.' Accustomed to drinking out of a mug, Ray had finished his tea in one gulp and was holding his saucer out like a bomb, terrified of incurring Clod's wrath by placing it on the over-waxed furniture.

Her father was, as ever, wholly downtrodden. Despite Jimmy's presence, the family continued to be very rude to him indeed with Clod barking out orders, Monny simply ignoring everything Ray said and Grumpy being openly hostile. That was, until Jimmy singled Ray out for a chat, asking him about his electrical shop and his early musical career. To everyone's amazement – including Odette's – Jimmy and Ray hit it off big time. Soon they were laughing and joking, and Ray's eyes sparkled in a way they hadn't for years.

After that, he came in for the polite family treatment too, if a little resentfully so, as he was clearly seen as a friend of Jimmy's.

Odette gazed around the seldom-used front room of the house she grew up in. It was neat and tidy and smelled of bleach and beeswax, but she knew that it must seem like a very small, grotty cupboard to Jimmy who had grown up in huge, rambling houses and was now accustomed to the echoing emptiness of Siddals Farm.

Her niece and nephew were charging around threatening legs and furniture. Monny had dressed Vinnie in his smartest outfit – his school trousers and a new Tottenham shirt. As his father was a lifelong West Ham fan, Odette guessed it was her way of revenge but she knew not to mention the C word.

Frankie was wearing a grubby velvet dress. Monny was livid that her little girl hadn't been asked to be a bridesmaid.

'Mel's only gone and asked that fat friend of hers, Kelly,' she was moaning to Odette. 'She's bound to try and get off with one of the Turners. Well, they won't have nuffink to do with her – Liam says she's a right old slapper. Kids make all the difference at weddings. It looks so much nicer in the photos, doncha fink?'

Odette looked at her niece. She had a lurid orange smile from guzzling squash, chocolate marks on her cheeks, a front tooth missing, a forty-five-degree fringe cut by her mother with nail scissors and big plasters on each of her knees.

Jimmy had offered to drive them all to the register office.

'Bleedin' heck, it's enormous, in't it?' Monny laughed with a dirty cackle when she caught sight of Jimmy's pick-up which was parked in the street and occupying at least two car lengths. She heaved herself into the front seat, now so heavily pregnant that even fitting in the truck's ample cab was difficult.

It was a short ceremony for just family and friends. Ray's sister Lil was in tears from beginning to end. She was the only parent there; Mel's father had died three years earlier and Dean's parents, who lived in Australia, couldn't afford to fly to England for the wedding. Odette looked around for Mel's elder brothers and sisters, but none of them had come. The family had fallen out after their father's death, arguing over who got what of the little money that he'd left. It was a feud that had smouldered on for years. Apart from Ray's family, the only guests consisted of several of Dean's mates – most of whom were Turners – and their wives, plus bridesmaid Kelly and Barry the best man who was also the landlord of Mel and Dean's local, the Laughing Gnome. In total, they filled less than a third of the register office room.

Mel, the family tearaway, looked surprisingly demure in a hired empire-line wedding dress, which was too tight under the armpits.

'Lil picked up the wrong frock from the hire shop,' Monny whispered in Odette's ear as, beside her, Vinnie made a loud fart noise by thrusting his hand under the opposite armpit. 'There was a huge row about it, but it was too late to take it back.'

No wonder Lil was crying. Mel's temper was legendary, plus Lil had a severe allergy to fur and feathers and was sitting in very close proximity to Clod's hat.

There were more curling sandwiches at the reception in the Laughing Gnome, along with quarters of Scotch egg, pizza pieces, sausage rolls and enough crisps to make Gary Lineker cry.

This wasn't a champagne reception; the men drank pints of lager top, the women drank Bacardi and Coke or vodka and lemonade. The music came from the jukebox, which had every known record ever released by Meatloaf and not much else.

'We don't have to stay long,' Odette told Jimmy as her nephew rushed past throwing sausage rolls at everyone.

'I'll give your family a lift home,' he told her.

Odette was horrified at the thought. 'They always leave parties last. We could be here until two or three in the morning.'

Jimmy just shrugged easily. They were spending the night in Notting Hill with Phoebe and Felix; Rolanda was looking after Nelson and Winnie. He was under no pressure to leave. He wanted to get to know her family better.

Odette, who wanted the reverse, felt a very great pressure to leave as she looked around the small wedding party. At least the Turner brothers were keeping their distance with Jimmy at her shoulder.

But she had started to pick up on an atmosphere she didn't like one bit. There was a lot of bravura going on at the bar, which wasn't in itself unusual, except that the traditional round of jokes were almost all 'Craig' jokes. She listened to a couple and winced. Liam Turner was leading the jeering:

'What do you call a man with 20K on his head?'

'Crooked Craig!' the Turner posse chanted.

'And what do you call getting head from someone who's just lost 20K?'

'Odette of honour, your honour!'

Odette could see Monny looking more and more wound up. She wasn't the only one. Ignoring Jimmy, who was telling her to take no notice, she marched over to them.

'Cut it out!' she demanded. 'You pathetic little creeps.'

A series of camp 'ohhhhs' followed.

'Yeah, yeah, yeah,' Odette mocked them. 'Listen, I don't

bleedin' care what you say about me. Just leave my brother-in-law out of this. For Christ's sake,' she lowered her voice, 'Monny's about to have a baby. She's going through enough as it is. Just leave it out, all right? It's none of your business.'

'Is that a fact?' Liam gave her a dirty look, his big scarred face threatening.

'Of course it bleedin' is,' Odette snarled. 'You know absolutely nothing about this, so butt out.'

'Head-butt out!' Gary lunged off his barstool in a sham head-butt towards Odette's red fringe that made her flinch. Suddenly she felt Jimmy at her shoulder, big and reliable, springing to her defence.

'You all right here, Odette?' His booming voice made Gary quail back.

All the Turners fell noticeably mute and cowered. Except Liam.

'You don't know anything about this, Frenchie,' he hissed, ignoring Jimmy totally. 'You're the one who should butt out.'

'Yeah, it's only a bit of fun,' Gary piped up.

'Fuck off, Gaz,' Liam roared at his brother, flattening him against the bar with fear. He turned back to Odette, his voice very low, very threatening. His mouth was almost in her ear; she doubted even Jimmy could make out what he was saying clearly. 'You are one – stupid – little – cow.' He spaced the words out with pure, venomous hatred. 'You can't get away with it any more, swanning in here and bossing the likes of us around. What d'you think you look like, eh? A bloody joke with your clown hair and your big bully-boy gigolo.'

Jimmy was remaining infuriatingly silent, not springing to her defence at all. In fact he appeared to be listening in with fascination now.

Liam continued hissing in Odette's ear. 'Don't you dare – ever – tell – me what I can or cannot say. You don't know the half of it.' He pulled his head back, his voice audible to all around once more. 'Your family are only good for two things: fencing and fucking.'

Odette swung her arm back to hit him, but Jimmy caught it.

Then, before he could say anything, Monny – who had waddled laboriously across the room during the confrontation – threw her pineapple juice in Liam's face. 'How dare you say that about my family?' She suddenly burst into tears and fell into Jimmy's arms.

Odette froze in shock. What was going on here? It was shamingly like a scene from *Londoners*. No wonder Jimmy was so enthralled.

As Jimmy led Monny away to comfort her, Liam rubbed his face with his hand, chunky gold jewellery glittering. He looked at Odette's appalled expression and winked. 'The bet's still on, you know, Frenchie,' he hissed. 'Twenty quid. Maybe we'll make that a tenner now, though. You're not so hot any more, are you?'

Odette was tough, but she wasn't that tough. She turned and fled. She tried to calm down in the loos, clutching the basin edge and staring at her white-faced reflection.

'I love your hair,' Mel shuffled into the cramped pub ladies' loo beside her to check her makeup. 'It's really wild, doll. You always looked like a bit of a square when you had that flashy job but now you're broke you're ever so trendy.'

'Cheers.' Odette pretended to find this complimentary as Mel pulled a comb from her tiny white leather duffel bag and started raising hers by a couple of inches.

'You should've come on the hen night, doll. It was only me, Mum and Kelly. Monny didn't feel up to it. We ended up having an Indian and getting a video out. *Titanic*. Right bloody miserable it was. Film wasn't much better.'

'I couldn't get to London last night, babes,' Odette lied guiltily. 'I live quite a long way out now.'

'Yeah, your mum said you'd moved somewhere near Dorking.' There was a ripping sound as Mel reached up to tweak the stiff tips of her hair and the seam of her dress gave way under her armpit.

'Sussex.'

'All the same to me.' She stared at the hole which was revealing a lot of gritty stubble. 'Looks better like that, don't it? Hang on – I'll do the other one.' She did a few duck-flaps of her elbow until there was another loud rip. Then she calmly turned her attention to her hair again.

'Anyway, fanks for coming today,' she said, looking through her fringe at Odette's reflection in the mirror, at which she was still trying to comb the tangles from her hair as fast as Mel was combing them in.

'I wouldn't miss your big day,' Odette said, looking at the painted face and trying to remember the child she'd once taught to read the time. 'Sorry I didn't let you know I was coming until the last minute.'

'Don't mention it – wasn't sure I was coming myself until this morning,' Mel smiled wickedly and winked a black-rimmed eye. Then the smile wobbled. 'You don't fink Dean'll turn out bad like Craig do you?'

'Of course he won't, babes,' Odette said with far more conviction than she felt.

Out in the pub, Dean was already five pints up and laughing raucously as he told his favourite 'Mela-knees-apart' joke to the Turner brothers and Jimmy.

Odette did a double take to see him with them. That was the last time she was going to let him watch her *Londoners* videos. She could hear him asking Liam what sort of fencing he specialised in. Walking away, Odette doubted Liam's answer would be 'electric sheep wire'.

'You next, darlin'?' an emotional voice wavered and she found herself next to her aunt Lil, who was still choked with tears, her nose as red as Campari. 'You and that nice young man of yours planning to get wed soon?'

'He's just a friend, Lil,' Odette said gently. As a child she'd run to her kind-hearted, soft spoken aunt for affection many times, loving the big soapy-smelling arms and the packets of Nice biscuits she always had tucked in her cupboards for special occasions. Lil was the only person to have sent Odette a congratulations card when she graduated.

'I wish Melanie had lived a bit more of her life like you have, darlin',' she sniffed. 'Don't get me wrong – Dean's a nice boy and I know he'll look after her – but she's never done nuffink exciting like you have.'

Odette nodded. She wouldn't wish her past few months on anyone, but she was too fond of Lil to argue and she knew what her aunt was saying. Mel had her life mapped out now: babies, housework and Friday night out with the girls when her mum could baby-sit, all other nights running along the same routine of feeding, bathing and bedding kids before feeding, television watching and bedding Dean. Lottery to look forward to twice a week, dreams and disappointment revolving around seven coloured balls dropping out of an Arthurian knight and his mistress while husband and wife clutched bar-coded tickets.

Odette found the occasion a depressing if predictable one. Growing up in the East End, she had always known that the place wasn't the lovely, gorblimey, we-look-after-our-own world of market stalls, friendly boozers and kind-hearted villains it was made out to be on her beloved *Londoners*. It was a tough place to be a woman, and the remnants of the tightly knit, old-fashioned community which lingered also remained anachronistically misogynist. Women could be powerful within the home; matriarchs were at the heart of what was left of the families who had lived in the area for generations as hers had. But they had no financial power, no independence and little chance of any variety in life. They did as every other generation had – followed the same paths from daughter to wife to mother to grandmother, matriarchs in an archaic cycle.

Odette had thought she had escaped to another world, one which really did look after its own, the gang of friends, the educated experience-sharers who chose to stay together and see one another because they had the same philosophy of life even when those lives took different paths.

When her world had crashed around her ears, Odette had known they would look after her. And yet now she came to think about it, the obligation was not necessarily one born of friendship alone. She had been mixing with the guilty, liberal middle classes too long. They all supported charities, wore the red nose when the day came, ran mini-marathons and had their heads shaved for good causes, gave fivers to tramps, sponsored orphans in Romania and fasted for forty-eight hours. It made them feel better about themselves and it made them feel slimmer;

it also kept them within safe but communicable distance of fashionable causes. Was she now just a cause to cauterise their guilt? A conscience clause? A friend-turned-issue? The East End kid who had made good and needed help to stay with them and not slip back into the primordial soup of the working classes?

The biggest charity worker of the lot was Jimmy Sylvian, and he was the one she had leaned upon so heavily that she had started to tip head over heels in love. Mr Reliable, Mr Guilt Trip. She looked across at him, laughing at the bar with the despicable Turners, and finally understood why he was here. He was trying to understand them. Misguided, compassionate Jimmy thought he could befriend them and cleanse their souls of torment to appease his own guilt. He was no different from any of her so-called friends. He was just following a trend. Mel was right; Odette *was* trendy. She was the ultimate designer accessory, a fashionable cause. She was, in fact, so trendy she was the new black.

Feeling very, very trendy indeed, she decided to hit a few stylish drinks. She started with a large Bacardi and Coke – her favourite. Then she slung back a couple of snifters *du jour* – Malibu and pineapple. Delicious. The voddy and Coke went down well, as did the Pernod and black. While Jimmy continued on his guilt-trip with the Turners, Odette chatted about hair-extensions to Kelly, her speech increasingly slurred as she downed two drop-dead trendy Snowballs. Draining a Bailey's before hitting the dance floor, she boogied raucously with her Aunt Lil to 'Locomotion', her father to 'Jumping Jack Flash', and her nephew to Puff Daddy.

All the time she was vaguely aware of Jimmy's scrutiny from the margins of the Turner mob, bruised blue eyes disappointed. Eventually he dragged her away from slow-dancing to 'Two Out Of Three Ain't Bad' with one of Dean's cousins – she wasn't sure which one but she guessed it was the married one because his wedding ring kept catching on her bra strap when he delved into her top.

'Your family are in the pick-up.' Jimmy smiled stiffly as he towed her out. 'Say your 'bye-byes.'

'Wha—?' Odette was rather too Bacardi-heavy to react

quickly. She was outside before she had a chance to say farewell to her cousin.

'You bastard!' She finally connected her spinning head with her manhandled and propelled body just outside the pub door. 'I was enjoying my dance. "*I want you, I need you, but there ain't no way I'm ever gonna . . ."*'

'You're dru—' Jimmy's accusation was cut short as she leaned back to belt out the 'love you!' line and almost tipped herself over backwards.

'I'm with my own,' Odette announced theatrically, fantasising herself as the infamously feisty gangland landlady Lily Fuller from *Londoners*.

'So how come you've behaved like an extra from *Dynasty* all night?' he asked, amused and concerned at the same time. She was very unsteady on her pegs.

'I'm as bleedin' working-class as they come, mate,' she fumed, convinced that he was picking a fight and accusing her of being a social climber. 'It ain't all fucking roll out the barrel, knees up Mother Brown around here, y'know. It's—'

'Please don't swear,' he winced. 'It's so—'

'Unladylike?' she exploded. 'I bloody know I'm bloody unladylike, you sexist bastard. I ain't gonna hang around wiv someone because he likes my fucking language, all right? You middle-class twat! Or are you an upper-class twit? Makes no difference. You still think you're so fucking superior.

'I know you find us all fucking funny – our sad little weddings, our cheap receptions, our bleedin' fights and our drinking. But we're not some sort of trapped-in-time underclass for you to lord it over. We're real and we're hurting and I fucking hate what I am, what I've become. I hate being—'

'A snob?' Jimmy cut in, his usual deafening boom quietened to a deadly hiss which silenced Odette far quicker than his customary bellowing would have. 'Because that's what you are, Odette. You're a snob and you're bitterly ashamed that you've come back to your family with nothing to show off but me. And they are far more impressed by me than they ever have been by your job, or your club, or your flashy cars, or your flat in the right part of London with its Neff cooker and its eco-friendly air-conditioning.'

'You egotistical wanker!' she howled. 'You have no idea what I've been through. What it feels like to lose everything, to love someone who has no feelings for you whatsoever, to be so alienated from your family that coming back and trying to fit in practically kills you.'

'I do know!' Jimmy yelled. This time the deafening Sylvian boom was at such top volume that dogs started howling miles away. 'I know just what it's like to lose everything – that's why I'm here tonight. I know just what it's like to feel alienated from a family – that's also why I'm here tonight. And I do know what it's like to love someone who doesn't love me. I'm looking at her right now.'

Odette's head was on a three-second satellite delay brought on by too many Bacardis. Just as this was registering, she spotted her father hovering in the shadows.

'Piss off, Dad,' she said irritably, looking at Jimmy in bewildered excitement.

'I'm really sorry, Jimmy, my boy,' Ray gibbered with shame-faced embarrassment. 'But I fink Monny's waters have just broken in your motor.'

49

'A big, bouncing girl. Ten pounds three ounces. Looks just like her mum. Would Dad like to come through and see Mum and bubs first?' The nurse indicated Jimmy.

'I'm sure he would.' Jimmy smiled his easy smile. 'But he's working overseas. Why don't Grandma and Grandpa go and say hello?'

'*Grandmère* and *Grandpère*, if you please.' Clod gave him a flirtatious wink and strutted past.

They finally fell into bed at three in the morning after Jimmy had driven Odette's family home. Phoebe let them into the Notting Hill mews house wearing a long Moroccan shirt, bed-socks and an irritated expression with sleep-creases on one cheek.

'You said no later than one,' she yawned.

'Odette's sister had a baby. We've been in the maternity ward,' Jimmy explained.

'Couldn't she have waited?' Phoebe mumbled and trailed off to bed. There was just a small sofa-bed made up in the bright little study area which led off from the kitchen-diner. The spare room which Jimmy had stayed in when he'd first arrived in the UK was occupied by Fliss and Dylan, the other room by Mungo, the sitting room by two more friends who were bunking over for the weekend.

'I guess this means we're sleeping together again.' Jimmy raised his eyebrows.

Odette felt too tired to argue. All she wanted to do was collapse into bed. She scrubbed her face and cleaned her teeth in a very luxurious green marble bathroom. After changing into an old singlet and jogging bottoms, she returned to find Jimmy sprawled out over most of the mattress wearing nothing but his jockey shorts and socks.

'Don't touch me and don't snore,' she ordered, averting her gaze from his rangy body and sliding under the duvet. In an attempt to keep as far away from him as possible, she balanced on the precipice of the mattress, one foot on the floor like a fifties Hollywood star.

'I'm an insomniac,' he reminded her. 'I probably shan't sleep.'

Odette's last, ungrateful waking thought was that he should offer not to sleep somewhere else. What was the point of not sleeping in bed with her and hogging the mattress?

'In that case, just don't touch me,' she mumbled as she drifted off.

She awoke seven hours later curled up against him, listening to a torrent of snores in one ear, a clatter of pans and a sea-on-shingle wash of conversation in the other. Her cheek was as warm as toast from using Jimmy's smooth back as a pillow, the crook between her belly and her thighs nuzzled snugly against a firm bottom. Craning her head up so she could peer short-sightedly over the peninsular unit, she realised that Felix, Phoebe and their other houseguests were fully dressed and trying to breakfast quietly in an open-plan kitchen just feet away.

Odette carefully unthreaded her arms from the heavy-sleeping snorer and crept out of the sofa-bed. Her jogging bottoms had slipped down to give her a builder's bum. Hoicking them up and locating her glasses, she clutched her pounding head and fought nausea as the smell of frying bacon eddied around her.

'Morning,' shrilled a bright male voice as Mungo regarded her over the kitchen peninsular. He was wearing a Flirty at Thirty t-shirt and holding a bright orange gonk. 'You look like this feels.' When he threw it down on the peninsular it cried 'Oh, no!' in a tinny wail.

'Hello,' she croaked. 'Happy Birthday.'

'Come and have some breakfast, Odette,' Phoebe suggested, pulling newspapers from a chair. 'Sorry I was a bit grumpy last night. Felix has a cold and was snuffling like a dirty phone call, kicking all the sheets off. You must think me so rude not even asking about the birth. What did your sister have?'

'Girl.' Odette gratefully accepted a huge glass of freshly squeezed orange.

'Wow!' Phoebe's mint-green eyes softened. 'Natural or C-section?'

'Natural, I think.' Odette noticed Mungo pulling daft faces at Felix, who was sitting at the table looking ludicrously handsome despite the fact he was wearing a towel on his head and inhaling from a bowl.

'Have they got a name for her yet?'

Odette shook her pounding head.

'Told you she was broody,' Mungo cackled at his brother.

'Bugger off, squit.' Phoebe ruffled his hair and smiled at Odette. 'I bet they're arguing like mad. Let me guess. Your sister probably likes something a bit unusual like Caitlin while your brother-in-law wants to call her after his Great-aunt Enid, am I right?'

'Well . . .' Odette chewed her lip. Oh, the picturesque little middle-class family tableau that conjured up – mother in hospital bed cradling baby, indulgent new father kissing his wife's cheek and tickling the newborn's tiny feet as they excitedly chose a name. Instead this father was on the run from the police and probably choosing himself a new name every other day. Odette didn't know what to say. She was ashamed of the truth, but if she lied Jimmy would think she was even more of a snob.

To her relief, a familiar freckled face emerged from the steamy bathroom.

'Hello, chuck!' Fliss bounded over to Odette, red curls flying. 'Didn't know you'd be here. Oi, Dyldo, look who it is. You can stop sulking now.'

'Thank goodness – another adult.' Looking up from the *Guardian*, Dylan blew her a grateful kiss. 'Hello, Odette darling. These two are Mungo's disreputable friends, Lenny and

Bennett.' He introduced two very pretty boys who coo-eed hello and admired her hair extensions.

Mungo threw his 'Oh, no!' gonk at the fridge. 'Have you got me a present?' he asked Odette.

'Sorry, I didn't think . . .' She was appalled at herself. She'd blued the last of her money on a toast-rack for Mel and Dean.

'That's quite all right, darling.' He cocked his head and pursed his lips. 'Birthday kiss-kiss.'

Embarrassed but reluctant to show it, she leaned across the table and pecked him quickly on the lips.

'Mmm – minty fresh.' Mungo wrinkled his nose and closed his eyes afterwards. 'Just like nanny. You know, I rather like you.' He opened his eyes again and gave her a curious look. 'You remind me of Phoebe, only common. Don't you think, Felix? Odette is like a common Phoebe?'

She opened her mouth to speak, but Dylan beat her to it.

'Take that back, Mungo,' he warned lazily, looking up from the *Guardian*. 'Or I'll get Jimmy to dock your pocket money.'

'Actually, I'm quite flattered, babes.' Odette munched on her piece of toast. 'You're like a posh David Beckham.'

He cooed delightedly, 'Now that *is* lovely.'

A loud spluttering from the sofa-bed hailed Jimmy's emergence from deep sleep. 'Odette?' He sounded panic-stricken for a moment, tufty blond hair poking over the peninsular.

'Here.' She peered over at him, chewing her lip guiltily as she remembered that they had both gone to sleep in high dudgeon. A moment later the 'Oh, no!' gonk flew past her shoulder and hit him square on the forehead. It didn't put him in the greatest of moods.

They took advantage of the sun to hold the party on the roof terrace. Mungo donned a pair of lime-tinted sunglasses and lounged on a sunbed while Fliss and Phoebe dashed back and forth from the kitchen with drinks and food. Odette still felt too hungover to drink, but she was starting to enjoy herself. Mungo was spoiled and brattish and far too old to behave the way he did, but there was no doubt he was terrifically entertaining.

Jimmy, however, seemed to be having less fun. He was on

551

edge and at his most bullish. His grumpy irritation dampened the party mood, along with Felix's streaming cold.

Mungo didn't help matters by being searingly rude about Jimmy's gift of a Mont Blanc pen. He'd obviously expected far more. 'You know I hate writing, big brother. My wrist's too weak.' Felix hadn't fared much better when he'd given his brother a new mobile phone which had a little palm-top computer built into it.

'The games on this are useless,' he moaned. 'So far my best pressy has been Odette's kiss. Anyone would think you two were broke or something.'

Jimmy's eyes flashed angrily. 'You ungrateful little sod!'

'Don't talk to me like that on my birthday,' Mungo whined, feigning distress.

'I don't care if it is your bloody birthday,' Jimmy boomed, doing his draconian father-figure act. 'You *are* an ungrateful little sod. You know damn' well that . . .' He stopped himself, glancing around at Mungo's friends who were all agog, desperate for him to go on. Jimmy took a deep breath and struggled to control his anger. It was obvious he wanted to explode, to rant and rage, to remind Mungo of some terrible unspoken truth. But he was far too well-mannered to do it in front of his brother's guests. Instead he announced that he was going for a walk to calm down.

'Odette?' he snapped, not sounding particularly friendly. 'Do you want to come with me?'

She sprang to her feet, but Mungo grabbed hold of her arm.

'I want Odette to stay here with me,' he said petulantly, knowing it would wind his brother up. 'She's my new best friend.'

Jimmy's big bruised eyes lingered on Odette's face for a second before he slammed his way out of the house.

After a moment of embarrassed hiatus, the conversations started popping and bubbling again. Soon Mungo had Lenny and Bennett in stitches. Fliss put on a Buck's Fizz CD and Mungo dragged Odette into the sun for a boogie.

April was enjoying a mini heatwave. The combination of

short sleeves, sunglasses and cheesy music made Odette feel carefree and high. Jimmy just didn't know how to enjoy himself, she decided. He had been the same at Saskia and Stan's wedding – serious and formal compared to his rollicking, high-jinks brothers. He was better one-to-one. He was, in fact, a bit of a party-pooper. And today Odette was part of a high-flying, high-spirited crowd for the first time in weeks. What's more, she was loving it.

She enjoyed catching up with Phoebe and Fliss again. They were a great duo, and clearly missed one another now they lived so far apart. When Odette carried some empty bottles down to the kitchen, she found Fliss trying to encourage Phoebe to move to Yorkshire.

'Property's dead cheap round our way – you and Felix could pick up a little cottage for a hundred thousand.'

'Thinking of buying a weekend place?' Odette asked.

Phoebe shook her head sadly. 'We all have to move out of here next month. The lease is up. It belonged to Jocelyn. Felix and his friends had more or less trashed it by the time I came to live here, but old Pa Sylvian didn't much care. We can't afford to buy anywhere similar around here so we're thinking of moving away from London.'

'But I thought you worked for a newspaper here?' Odette queried.

'I'm only freelance.' Phoebe shrugged. 'They don't use me that often and it's not a good enough income to raise a mortgage. Felix is in the same position – one year he might earn fifty thousand, the next fifteen. We're pretty dodgy. We were hoping Jocelyn might have left enough for a good deposit, but it turns out there's next to nothing. All those off-shore accounts were bled dry years ago. The only thing he had of value was his house in Barbados, which no one wants to buy, and two Picasso sketches which have disappeared. Probably sold or nicked by an ex.'

No wonder Jimmy was snapping at Mungo for demanding extravagant gifts, Odette realised. Between them, the Sylvian brothers were boracic.

'Jimmy's offered to put us up at his place,' Phoebe told

her with a glittering wink. 'We might even be neighbours soon.'

Saskia and Stan turned up just as Fliss was taking over the kitchen to create Mungo's favourite – drop scones with golden syrup.

Saskia couldn't wait to catch up with Odette. 'We didn't get a chance to chat properly at Elsa's wedding. You must tell me all about what it's like living with Cyd Francis. Are Mick and Keith always dropping by? The house must be lovely. How are you feeling now, darling?' She didn't give Odette the chance to answer.

Standing beside her, Stan gave Odette a cheery wink as Saskia proceeded to gush on about the Station, and how well it was doing. She attributed every success to Odette, who tried hard to get a word in edgeways to deny it, but Saskia barely paused for breath as she went on to impart all the latest gossip. She was looking even more of a fashion victim than she had at Elsa's reception, dressed in a complicated combat bondage dress which meant she walked as though she needed the loo at all times

'I've had a tattoo.' She showed Odette a tiny daisy beside her navel. 'I'm thinking about having it pierced but it's a bit *passé*, isn't it?'

'Odette's got a pierced fluff-hole, aincha, girl?' Stan cackled as he helped himself to a beer from the fridge.

'Oh, God!' Saskia covered her mouth. 'I'm sorry, I never thought . . . I mean – it's so *un*-you.'

'I don't wear a ring in it any more,' Odette told her. 'I had it done a couple of years back. Never liked it much.' Elsa and Euan had in fact given her the piercing token as her birthday present. She'd flatly refused to use it until Jez and Juno got her steamingly drunk one weekend and goaded her into it by teasing her that she was a coward.

'I always knew there was a secret vamp beneath all those ghastly eighties suits!' Saskia seemed thrilled at the news. 'I love the hair, by the way. Totally synthesis.' It was a new phrase Odette had heard everyone at the party use, so assumed it was sweeping through London as a *bon mot* right now.

She didn't like to say that she secretly longed for her shoulderpads and stilettos. She had a feeling that she knew precisely why Saskia had suddenly become so trendy. It had a lot to do with getting married. People reacted to it in different ways. Some couldn't wait to throw off the single-girl shackles of mini-skirts and high heels in exchange for comfortable leggings and slippers. Others, like Saskia, were terrified of becoming one of the anonymous retail-park masses. Her career taking off had coincided with her marriage and she needed to prove that she was young and funky enough to juggle both.

Stan, by comparison, had never needed to prove anything to anyone. He helped himself to a large vodka and waited until his wife had finally dashed off to talk to her old friend Phoebe before he asked Odette how she was.

'Still seeking the definitive barnet, then?' He eyed her extensions.

'These were Cyd's idea. I didn't have a lot of choice.'

'That nutty bird you live wiv? Running around with your fella now, ain't she? Saw them together in Plastic last week. Don't know what you ever saw in him. Bleedin' awful taste in hats.'

'You saw Cyd with Calum?'

'Oops.' He nodded. 'Shouldn't have put my foot in it. Still mad at him, are you?'

'He's offered me a job.'

'I don't believe his naffing cheek!' Stan helped himself to another vodka. 'I had a drink wiv the Leonard brothers this week. They're knackered – he's had them out there in that draughty old house day and night for months. They say the place is nowhere near ready. I wouldn't work for a geezer like Forrester if he paid me in Ferraris.'

Odette flashed a weak smile.

When Jimmy finally came back from his walk, his temper hadn't improved. He helped himself to a Coke and perched glumly on the roof terrace wall, watching his brother dancing drunkenly to Barry Manilow.

'"At the Copa"' Mungo sang as he twirled Odette around in frantic circles. '"Copacabana . . ."'

Odette headed dizzily for the loo soon afterwards. When she came out, Jimmy was waiting for her with both overnight bags. Rolanda's crushed hat was under his arm.

'It's time to leave,' he said, not looking her in the eye. Something in the tone of his voice stopped Odette from protesting. Pushing past him she went to say goodbye to everyone. She adored Felix and Phoebe's messy house and Mungo's high-spirited friends. Being with the Sylvians felt far more like being with family than yesterday had.

'D'you want to pass by the hospital and see your sister?' Jimmy asked as soon as they were in the pick-up.

Odette shook her head. 'Monny wouldn't want to see me there. I remind her too much of why Craig's missing.'

'Rubbish! That had nothing to do with you. And she wanted you there yesterday. You're being paranoid.'

'I know Monny,' she said firmly. 'She won't want me around. Mum and Dad'll look after her. I'd just wind them up.'

'Whatever,' Jimmy said huffily, leaning on his horn as they tried to turn out of the mews on to Notting Hill Gate. Odette gritted her teeth. He'd learned 'whatever' from *Londoners* – it was one of the Sullivans' favourite brush-offs and his wound her up like mad. The world was slobbing out. Even Jimmy Sylvian was sounding like a guest on *The Jerry Springer Show*.

Monny's newborn daughter opened her tiny, creased petal eyes and stared up into the face of her father.

'In't she beautiful?' Monny sobbed ecstatically. 'Just like her dad.'

He placed a callused finger against the pad of her tiny hand, watching as the minuscule fingers clutched at his bitten nails.

'As beautiful as her ma,' he said, voice choked with emotion.

'You'll have to go soon,' Monny told him. 'Mum and Dad'll be along any minute. They can't see you here.'

'I know.' He gazed at the tiny face for a few indulgent moments more. 'I'll come back tomorrow, yeah?'

She nodded, tears spilling all over her nightie at the prospect of losing him.

'You take care of that daughter of mine.' He kissed her on the forehead and left.

Monny wiped the snot and salt water from her face and listened to his trainers squeaking away along the corridor.

'Tottenham fan, is he, your hubby?' The woman in the next bed asked companionably, having spotted the football shirt a moment earlier.

'No, my old man supports West Ham.' Monny wiped her eyes on the sheets and cuddled her baby closer to her chest.

Her neighbour raised an eyebrow but said nothing, returning to the real-life confession section in *Chat*.

Odette sat in diplomatic silence as they drove out of London. Jimmy was tense and irritable, taking his anger out on other road-users as he shouted and tutted and beeped his horn at bad drivers, slow drivers, cautious drivers and fast drivers. No car on the road was immune from his wrath, but he saved his bluest language for the cyclists.

'God, I hate London.' He scowled at an old lady wobbling in front of him on her sit up and beg. 'The people are so awful. Get out of my way, you stupid old troll!'

'I'm from London,' Odette muttered as the woman wobbled on to the pavement and Jimmy scorched past.

'You're not a Londoner any more,' he said. 'You hate it here as much as I do.'

'What makes you fink that?'

'Because I know you better than you know yourself.'

Odette rolled her eyes and gave up. He was impossible to talk to when he was in this mood – bullish, angry, arrogant. For all his supposed eco-friendly, laid-back benevolence, he was the most conceited of all the Sylvian brothers.

His mood seemed to lift a little when they finally got out of London and started belting through Surrey. He put on one of his tapes, more African tribal music which he clicked along to and rapped the wheel in time. He always drove with the heating turned up very high. The warm cab thrummed with rhythmic music, becoming comforting and womb-like.

Odette found herself nodding off, her head sliding slowly downwards before she jerked it back as she woke up, cricking her neck. She reached into the back seat and groped around for a jumper which she tucked between her cheek and the side window. It was coarse wool and smelled of earth and petrol. She closed her eyes and dreamed that she was painting the walls of the mill and that Jimmy was kissing the back of her neck.

When she woke up, he had parked the backie in a gateway. It was pitch dark outside and they were far from the motorway. She could smell cigarette smoke.

She straightened up and let the jumper drop on to her knees as she turned to look at Jimmy, only just able to make out his profile in the dark. The red tip of a cigarette glowed as it dangled between his lips.

'I didn't know you smoked,' she said.

He jumped in surprise and then swung around to look at her.

'You're awake then.' His voice was lower than usual, distanced and thoughtful. 'I quit when I came back here, but I needed one today so I begged a couple from Mungo.'

'Do they wind you up that much? Your brothers?'

He shook his head. 'Mungo's very fucked up – that's why he's a pain in the arse. He needs someone to love him. Felix is great, far more level-headed than me, although Phoebe has a lot to do with that. No, it's not them.'

Odette watched him take a long draw, the cigarette tip glowing so brightly that for a moment she could see Jimmy's dark eyes glittering with a reflected orange glow. She wondered whether his tetchiness had something to do with what Phoebe had told her earlier. She knew it was crass to ask, but she had never believed in being namby-pamby about social mores.

'Is it to do with your father's will?' She wound down her window a fraction. The combination of heat and cigarette smoke was stifling.

'Who told you about that?'

'Phoebe mentioned that the lease is up on the house and they can't afford to buy anywhere else because your father didn't leave much and they're—'

'They shouldn't expect to get something for nothing,' he roared. 'Dad's money was his own to squander.'

'I don't think Phoebe meant—'

'I know, I know – I'm sorry.' He took a long drag on his cigarette. 'I shouldn't shout at you. Phoebe's trying her hardest to sort something out. They're looking at renting, but they've got to carry Mungo – he'll never cope alone. I've told them to come and stay in the farm, but I think it might finish me off.' He laughed hollowly.

'It'd give you a chance to get to know them better,' Odette pointed out.

'Oh, I'd love them to stay – but I couldn't cope with the guilt.'

'You can't keep punishing yourself forever. So you stayed away too long? You're back now.'

'It's not that, Odette.' He wound down his own window and ground the cigarette out between his fingers before throwing out the butt. Then he took a deep breath of night air. The temperature had dropped dramatically; it was close to freezing outside. The ground was still cold from winter and unable to retain any heat from a single sunny day.

Odette shuddered and drew the jumper up to her chest.

'Dad left everything to me.' Jimmy suddenly turned back to face her. 'Everything. He cut Felix and Mungo completely out of his will, the drunken idiot! I couldn't tell them – I thought I'd just divide the assets up between us. But then I realised there *were* no great assets, nothing of any value. The Barbados house will make a little if it ever sells, but most of that will be eaten up by tax. The royalties will keep on coming in, so I guess that will help my brothers, but it's not a living and it doesn't make up for the way he neglected them. I thought there'd be so much more to give them. He had very little of any value in the end.'

Odette tucked her icy fingers beneath her knees to warm them. 'Phoebe said something about two Picasso sketches that had gone missing?'

He nodded. 'When my father was a young man, he met

Picasso and thought he was marvellous. The feeling must have been mutual because he gave my father two sketches. They're very good. Must be worth a great deal of money.'

'But they're missing?'

Jimmy shook his head. 'They're in England.'

'You smuggled them back?' she gasped.

'If only! I could give one to Felix, the other to Mungo if I'd done that . . . although I'd need one hell of a lot of Tippex.'

Odette didn't understand, but was too fascinated to question this. 'So where are they?'

He looked out of the window again, listening as an owl shrieked nearby.

'I traded them,' he sighed.

'What for?'

'Beans.' He laughed bitterly and then stopped himself. 'I traded them with Calum.'

'Oh, no,' Odette groaned. 'Please don't say he's involved?'

'He needed my help,' Jimmy corrected her curtly. 'You don't understand what went on between us, just as I don't know what went on between you and him.' He lit another cigarette. 'He's got a thing about you I can't figure out. You two have a history, I know that, and I appreciate you don't want to share it with me. Maybe I feel the same way.'

Odette chewed her lip, tempted to spill everything but simply too ashamed to know where to start. Her soul-destroying obsession, his twisted voyeurism. That awful, hellish night with Florian. It was too humiliating, too tormenting to recount.

The silence crept into what seemed like minutes. Odette could hear the dashboard clock creaking out the seconds.

'Okay, you want to know why I trust him?' Jimmy suddenly slammed his hand against the steering wheel, his voice animated and decisive. 'Why I know he'd never intentionally do anything to hurt me? He had a breakdown in Africa. Big-time lunacy. He tried to kill himself.'

Odette blinked in amazement. 'Calum had a breakdown?'

Jimmy nodded, talking in a frantic hurry, as though betraying Calum's secret at speed made it less disloyal. 'I swore I'd never tell anyone, but you've got to know. You've got to stop hating him and start helping him. When he came to Mpona, I thought he was an arrogant little shit. He was so conceited and crass and pig-headed; he strutted around as though he owned the place, poked his nose in where it wasn't wanted, got himself into unnecessary danger, pissed the other guests off and got the staff's backs up too. I was going to tell him to sling his hook, but when I went to find him in his hut he'd gone walkabout – beyond the security fencing. The guard had been napping. I was so livid, I grabbed a gun and charged out into the reserve looking for him, fully intending to give the little prick the fright of his life. When I found him, he was crying his eyes out like a child. Talking gibberish. I thought he'd already frightened himself enough so I gave him a talking to and left it at that.'

Odette closed her eyes. She had been there. She remembered standing on the edge of the Plas Cwyn lake and walking on to the death-trap jetty. She had followed in Calum's fatalistic footsteps.

'Back in the camp, I talked to him for a bit,' Jimmy continued. 'He was in a terrible state and didn't make much sense, so I let Florrie take over – she was a great listener. I left them to it and did the rounds, checked on the guests. When I came back he was calmer so I kicked him into his hut and went to get drunk with the crew. We laughed about the weedy Scottish oke who'd tried to feed himself to the cats. Later I went to bed and made love to Florrie.

'She couldn't sleep that night – and I never sleep much except with you.' He ducked his head towards the window, pausing for a moment, his face scrunched up in thought as though linking her name with Florrie's made him acutely guilty. 'We stayed up all night, drinking wine and talking – mostly about Calum. Florrie was fascinated by him, by what she called "his pain". It was she who suggested he wasn't just a frightened tourist who'd walked a little close to the wild side. She was the one who made me go back and check on him. She thought he was "sick with the sadness". I remember her words so well. She made me get dressed and walk to his hut. I grumbled the whole time I was hunting for my shorts, tried to get back into bed, asked her to make me another coffee first.

'Five minutes later and he would have been dead – the time it would have taken me to indulge in one more drink, one more kiss, one more cigarette. He'd rigged up a noose from one of the purlins in the rondavel. His body was so limp and his face so white I thought he was already dead. I cut him down and he opened his eyes and looked at me with the sort of sadness I've never felt in my entire life, and a lot of that's been one very long voyage of regret. It was the same sadness I saw in your eyes the first day we met.'

'You saved his life?' Odette stared at him. She had never imagined this twist to the tale.

'In a way. I don't think he wanted to be saved much.' Jimmy shrugged. 'He's certainly never thanked me for it, but he's been a terrific friend. We've got to know each other pretty well. He flew to Africa after Florrie died, talked me through it. He understands grief – he had to come to terms with a lot of demons when he was forced to choose life.'

'But why did he want to kill himself?' The question was out of her mouth before she could stop it.

Not answering, Jimmy took a drag on his cigarette and scratched his teeth with his thumb.

'Why?' Odette was desperate to know. She was back in her eighties melodramas, back in *Dynasty*, *Dallas* and Wilbur Smith mini-series. Suddenly she had visions of Charles Dance smouldering at Greta Scaacchi in *White Mischief*, Meryl Streep tipping back her head and shielding her eyes from the sun as Robert Redford puttered overhead in a bi-plane in *Out of Africa*. She was staring out at the savannah in her mind, watching Calum's body shimmering in a distant heat-haze as he walked among the big cats, seeking redemption, for what she didn't know. 'Why did he do it?' she repeated.

That night, Jimmy played his first ever mean trick on her. 'First, you tell me what he has that makes someone as gutsy as you so frightened of him?'

Odette stared out of the window into blackness, the romantic savannah replaced by a low-pixel image of herself and Florian lashed together in an angry, painful coupling amid stainless steel and red mist.

When she didn't answer his question, Jimmy twisted out the half-smoked cigarette in his fingers and started the engine. Less than five minutes later, they were bouncing up the Smock Mill Farm drive.

'I won't be around for a couple of weeks,' he told her when he pulled up outside the farm, keeping the engine running. 'I'm going back to Africa.'

'To Mpona?' Odette's voice faltered. She felt instantly tearful, a lump in her throat the size of a fist. She felt frightened too, terrified that she wouldn't cope without him.

He shook his head. His face, lit by the security lights on the farmhouse, was set and emotionless, the bruised blue eyes staring fixedly ahead.

'To Kenya to see some friends maybe.' He sounded evasive. 'I need a break.'

'What about Fermoncieaux? Calum? The sketches?' She was appalled. She couldn't believe he would abandon Calum to his demons and his overstretched money-pit of a house.

'Why d'you think I just told you all that?' he muttered in a flat voice, undercut with anger.

'I thought you wanted my help?'

'Precisely.' He was at his most bullying, his most truculent. 'You sort it out, Odette. Take the job. Keep an eye on him while I'm away. Get off your arse for once and do something. If you love Calum, do it for him. If you love me, do it for me. Either way, the result's the same. Now push off. I have a lot of packing to do.'

50

The light was on in the farmhouse when Odette turned away from the cloud of dust and exhaust fumes Jimmy had left in his wake. She longed to talk to someone, to ask what she had done to deserve all this, apart from once wishing for a soap-opera life. This was too operatic for her liking. She craved a little soft-soaping.

As soon as she opened the kitchen door, Winnie body-slammed her in delight, covered her legs in wet kisses and then raced outside into the night, desperate for a pee. She'd obviously been stuck indoors for hours. But she hadn't been alone.

Cyd was sitting at her kitchen table with Calum. A whisky bottle lay between them, empty and dry.

'Dearheart!' Cyd looked up with a strangely guilty expression when Odette walked in. 'How was the wedding?'

'Good.' She cleared her throat, stooping to say hi to Bazouki who was pushing a thin snout up her skirt in a shy welcome.

'I'd offer you a drink but we appear to be out.' Cyd waved a hand at the bottle and knocked it over, causing it to roll the length of the table to the floor where it smashed on the stone tiles.

'I'm not staying.' Odette was already backing away. 'Just popped in to stay I'm back and to fetch Winnie. Thanks for looking after her.'

'Wait!' Calum leaped up and followed her outside, leaving Cyd swaying over the broken glass, trying to pick it up and keep Bazouki at bay.

Odette had rounded the topiary tree and was marching swiftly towards the mill when he caught her up. He grabbed her arm with pinching fingers and twisted her round to a halt.

'Do you hate me?' he demanded. 'Cyd says you hate me.'

Odette pulled away. Her feelings were far more complicated than that. But tonight had been traumatic enough without this.

She fumbled for her keys at the mill door and then jumped in surprise as Calum shouldered the frame beside her, his pale eyes blinking a little too often.

'Jimmy's told you, hasn't he?'

She found the right key, but held it tightly in her fist rather than slotting it into its aperture, the keyring digging painfully between her fingers. 'Told me what, Calum?'

'What happened in Africa?'

She nodded. 'He wants me to help you.'

'I don't need his fucking help!'

'You needed his pictures.'

'What?' For a moment he genuinely didn't seem to know what she was talking about and then, to her amazement, he laughed. 'Oh, Christ, Odette, is that what you think this is all about? A couple of smuggled Picassos? How fucking typical. Your mind is one sordid little action movie, isn't it?'

She heard popping in her ears as blood started pumping faster and faster around her body. But she was determined to stay cool, to stand Jimmy's ground because he was too good and too kind to fight. 'So why don't you give them back to him? You know he wants his brothers to have them. They need the money. He hasn't got anything else to offer them.'

Calum looked at the rotting doorframe. 'They wouldnae do Jimmy any good – he cannae sell them. Even supposing I could give them back to him, Customs and Excise might have something to say about the fact they've been brought into the UK illegally, don't you think?'

'So Jimmy *did* smuggle them here?' Odette gasped.

But Calum shook his head.

She looked at his hunched shoulders, the foot scuffing at the crumbling steps, the belligerent, thrusting chin. 'It was you, wasn't it?'

'Yeah, I brought them back from Mpona.' He sounded almost proud.

'What were they doing in Africa?' Odette stepped back in

confusion and heard a yelp as Winnie, who had crept back from the garden, fled away again on three legs.

He leaned back against the door and regarded her thoughtfully. 'He hasnae told you that, then? Hasnae explained that his father used them as writing paper and posted them from Barbados? Didn't even use a first-class stamp. It's one way to avoid death duties, I guess, although I don't imagine it does a lot for their value, having obscenities scribbled all over the back of fine art. It was one hell of a letter, by the way. Very interesting. No wonder old Jim wanted to give it away.'

'He wouldn't give away one of his father's letters.' Odette shook her head, remembering Jimmy telling her how important they were to him.

'Florrie persuaded him to,' hissed Calum with surprising anger. 'And dear besotted Jimmy would do anything Florrie asked back then. Besides, this letter wasn't like the others.'

'What did you do with it?'

He screwed up his face and looked at her, trying to appear unfazed, but for the first time Odette registered fear in his eyes.

'Where are the sketches now, Calum?'

He shrugged, looking at the doorframe again, pale eyes tracing every grain. 'I sold them.'

'But you said—'

'I didnae fucking auction them at Christie's, Odette!' He rubbed his mouth. 'Denny put me in touch with someone. I could do nothing with them on the open market – what I needed was hard currency, not two illegally imported Picassos in my safe. I was about to lose everything, for Christ's sake!'

Odette took a sharp breath and he dropped his head guiltily before looking up at her, his forehead so creased with tension it resembled a rhino's back.

'I think Jimmy had some sort of romantic notion that I'd sell them to a little old billionaire with more money than sense.' He laughed hollowly. 'Preferably a foreigner who couldnae understand enough English to read what was written on the back. But the idea of the obsessive collector willing to pay millions to have a priceless work of art stolen for his secret collection is a total sham. Stolen canvases are used as collateral in criminal circles

– they're easily transported, easier to roll up and hide than wads of cash, easier to exchange than gold bullion.

'So I traded them for cash. Fuckloads of cash. This guy Denny put me in touch with – calls himself The Knife – got a couple of nice little sketches to pop in his suitcase and use to buy twenty kilos of Columbia's finest; I saved my businesses. It's not hard to launder money through clubs. You pay a few suppliers in cash, along with the casual staff who are already shit scared of immigration rumbling them. Mostly I just put it through the books as income from the bars and restaurants. I must be one of the first people to pay VAT on drug money. Only now . . .' He rubbed his mouth, white with worry.

'Jimmy wants his money back?'

Calum blinked. 'He's not the only one. I've heard The Knife is complaining that he cannae move them around with that shit written on the back. Who'd 'a' thought a fucking gangland heavy would turn out to think he's Brian Sewell, huh?'

'Christ.' Odette looked up at the sky. 'And you say *I'm* the one with the sordid action movie going on in my head.'

Calum scuffed his foot on the step and almost smiled. 'You know why he hasnae cut me up yet?' His eyes blazed into hers. 'Because of you, sister.'

'Come again?' Odette snorted.

'That fucking production company you arranged to have follow me around is putting him off.' Calum laughed bitterly. 'He hardly wants to find himself starring in a prime-time series, does he? He's not called The Knife because he whittles balsawood, y'know? Denny says the police are desperate to stick something on this guy. They've known what he's up to for years.'

'So why don't you go to them yourself?' She was too shaken to register that he knew she was behind the documentary.

'Get real, Odette!' he snarled.

Winnie, who had been hovering around in the bushes licking her squashed paw, hobbled away again when she heard the fury in his voice.

'And what about Jimmy?' Odette stood up to him. 'What does he stand to get out of this mess?'

'I promised him a return when I got him into this thing, and

I meant it. It was guaranteed to make him enough money to see Felix and Mungo through for years.'

'But now you've overinvested, haven't you?' Odette sighed. 'Your backers are running scared, the project's behind schedule and Jimmy stands to make ten percent of nothing. You reward him for saving your business by blackmailing him.'

'I'm not blackmailing him!' Calum was genuinely insulted. 'I took the sketches as an investment, not a gift. And when he came to England, I wouldnae pay him back because that way I knew he would stay here and not fuck off to Zimbabwe or wherever it was he was threatening to go. His brothers need him. And I need him. Food Hall won't work without him.'

'So you did it for your own selfish reasons after all,' she snorted. 'Well, that figures. He saved your bleedin' life, and you return the favour by dragging him in on some doomed project that's nothing to *do* with business and all to do with you wanting a bigger house than your dad ever bleedin' owned.'

'Is that what Jimmy said?'

'Not in as many words,' Odette admitted. 'But he did tell me that you went crackers when you were at Mpona. It's no wonder he gave you those sketches. It was the only way poor, kind-hearted Jimmy could think of stopping you from topping yourself. After all you were pretty determined, weren't you? You'd already tried twice.'

Calum hissed through his teeth and swung his head away so that she couldn't see his face. 'He swore he'd never tell a soul. We made a pact. The fucking, fucking *liar!*' He tipped back his head and yelled up at the sky.

Odette flinched, listening as the word echoed away. Bazouki was barking her head off in the farmhouse. She waited for Cyd to come sprinting from the house, demanding to know what was going on, but the barking stopped and there was no sound of footsteps. Odette found herself craning to hear them, praying that Cyd would come out. There was something about Calum's hunched shoulders and white knuckles that truly scared her.

'I knew he'd never forgive me,' he was saying. He appeared to be talking to himself. 'He said he did. He said he'd forgiven me . . .'

Odette rubbed her lips with her fingers, not understanding. Jimmy had told her everything, hadn't he? What was there to forgive?

Calum's eyes glittered like fireflies as he turned back to her once more. Odette felt her heart hammering hard in her chest. He looked manic, ghostly, terrifying. She was frightened of what he might do next. She should never have told him that Jimmy had betrayed his confidence. Right now, he looked capable of murder.

But when he spoke, his voice was as steady and deliberate as a top cross-examiner. 'What *exactly* did he say went on in Africa?'

Odette cleared her throat. 'That you went walkabout in the bush, and then when he brought you back, you waited until you thought everyone was asleep and tried to swing from a rafter. That the only reason he found you was because he'd been sitting up talking to Florrie.'

Calum nodded, creasing his eyes in thought. Then to her total amazement he laughed – a short, humourless laugh that sounded like the dry, dusty cough of a prairie dog in a canyon.

'He lied.'

Odette shook her head, 'Jimmy wouldn't lie about something like that. You don't have to feel ashamed, Calum.' Suddenly she felt a wave of sympathy for him. 'God knows, I have no idea what sort of devils you were wrestling with out there, but there's no—'

'Oh, the story he told is true enough,' he cut her short, speaking with slow, measured precision. 'Yes, I went walkabout. Yes, he bawled me out. I wasn't trying to kill myself – I was just being a prat. I got off on the danger, needed to frighten myself to feel alive. I'd been working too hard for too many years. I'd run out of money. My wee brother was off his face on drugs and refused my help – I guess I was stressed out and fucked up. My head was so screwed up I don't know what I was thinking.

'When Jimmy brought me back to the camp, he was fucking livid. Told me I was a worthless piece of shite and stormed off to bed.' He took a step forward and placed his hand on Odette's shoulder, his eyes just inches from hers. She knew for certain that he wasn't lying.

'So you didn't try to—'

'Swing from a rafter? Oh, yeah, I did that all right. And when Jimmy found me, I'm surprised he didn't leave me up there to rot. It's what I deserved.' He slid his hand from her shoulder to the crook of her neck, cocking his head and looking at her with a curious mixture of affection and guilt. 'Try to understand, Odette. *I* was the one who stayed up with Florrie that night. I was the one who got a little drunk with Florrie. I was the one who made love with Florrie.'

'No.' She batted his hand away. 'No way!'

'Oh, yes,' he nodded, his voice flat and matter-of-fact. 'After Jimmy hauled me back from the bush, I was seriously fucked off with him; I was seriously fucked off with life. You see, back then he wasn't the sympathetic listener he is now. He was a short-tempered bastard. His reaction to finding me was to tell me he didn't give a fuck if I killed myself that night, but not to do it outside the camp perimeter because losing tourists to lions was bad for business. He seemed to think I was gonnae kill myself, and suddenly it didn't seem like such a bad idea from where I was standing. It would sure as hell solve all my problems.

'But I wanted to do something first.' He reached up to touch her again, but his hand stopped just short of her face as he winced at the memory. 'I needed to give myself one last treat – a few drinks, some dope maybe, and a premium piece of arse. I felt I'd earned it.'

'You mean—'

'I fucked his girlfriend, Odette.' Calum traced his thumb across her cheek to her lips. 'He was a pig-headed bully and I rewarded him by fucking his beautiful girlfriend just once before I died. It seemed like a fair exchange at the time.'

Odette jerked her head away furiously, her lungs deflated by anger. 'But why did she agree to it?'

'Because she wanted to. The sexual tension had been building up all week; she simply couldn't stand it any longer. So we had a few drinks and did what comes naturally. I didn't exactly explain that I was about to top myself. I thought it was the perfect end to a less than perfect life. Florrie felt no guilt; she knew what we were doing was something neither of us could help. The trouble was, straight afterwards, she starts talking about the future, *our* future. I had to shut her up before she ruined my last night on earth, so I threw her out. I think she must have cottoned on to what I was planning and freaked out enough to wake Jimmy and tell him everything.'

'That's when he found you?'

He nodded. 'The stupid, besotted fool! He should've left me there. Instead he saved my life for the second time in a day. What a hero. Shame Florrie didn't see it that way. She was angry with him for not comforting me when he shouldae done, can you believe that? She told him that he'd driven us into each other's arms because he hadn't seen my pain, and that he'd driven me to try and kill myself too. That's why Jimmy gave me his father's letter. Florrie told him to give me the sketches or she'd leave him.'

'How could she treat him like that?' Odette was appalled. 'I thought that she was—'

'Without Florrie, old Jim would still be a pig-headed bastard like his father was. He'd modelled himself on Jocelyn for years. That night changed him. Changed all of us, forever. She was right to get rid of that letter. It was pure poison. Jimmy became the person he is now because of what she did.'

Odette howled with fury. 'So he got to keep his oh-so-generous unfaithful girlfriend and went on to become a compassion junkie. You, meanwhile, walk away with a second chance at life, enough money to cover your debts and the memory of a one-night stand you'll never forget. The only thing you had to grumble about was a slightly sore throat.' She felt the sarcasm burn her tongue like Tabasco. 'Like you said, fair exchange. Bully for Florrie.'

Calum looked at her for a long time before speaking. 'She's dead, Odette.'

She opened her mouth to say something sarcastic about that being no excuse and then closed it again, ashamed of her own anger with someone who could never defend herself.

'She paid the highest price of all,' Calum muttered. 'And she died before she had time to realise she'd fallen for the wrong man.'

'Are you suggesting . . .'

'She thought she loved me, Odette,' he cut in. 'She died loving me, not Jimmy.'

Odette was so stunned she couldn't speak.

'Florrie was beautiful.' He smiled at the memory. 'Truly beautiful – right the way through. She was perfect for Jimmy, but she was crazy about me. When she died, she left a half-finished love letter in her handbag. The police gave it to Jimmy. But when he opened it, he found it was written to me. Do you know, the great big idiot even forwarded it to me in London? It was sweet. She wanted to come to England. She wasn't very well educated. She spelled Calum with a "K", and love with a "u", but she tried.'

'Did you love her too?' Odette's voice trembled as the red-hot lava of anger and shameful jealousy ran down her throat.

Calum sucked his teeth. 'Not in the way Jimmy did. He forgave her. I could never have done that. I'd have thrown her out on her beautiful black arse.'

Odette struck him hard across the face with her hand. Her keys were still gripped between her fingers and they gashed his skin, grazing a deep line from eye to mouth.

'Thank you.' He touched the red gash. It started to trickle with blood as he smiled broadly. 'Thank you, Odette. I deserved that. I knew you could do it.'

'Do what?' she gasped, horrified at herself.

'Truly hate me. Hate me for Jimmy. God knows, I hate myself. But that's never been enough. He refuses to help me out on this one. After her death, he asked me back to Mpona, and I went because I thought he'd punish me, even the score. Instead he welcomed me with open arms. Told me that Florrie had loved me because I was worthy of love, and that was good enough for him because he'd loved her for the same reason. He said he wouldn't have stood in her way if she'd lived long enough to come to England to find me.

'He seems to think I'm responsible for some sort of epiphany in his life. He's the best friend I could ever have, and the dimmest fucker on earth. He forgave me without my ever apologising. He thinks Florrie lives through me somehow. And I want to repay him – I want to repay him so badly! It's an eye for an eye, isn't it? That's the only way. He was willing to give me

Florrie, so I had to do the same. I had to give him the thing I loved most.'

Watching a drop of blood fall from his chin and splash on the ground below, Odette let out a long, sad sigh of recognition. 'Money.'

'No, Odette.' He shook his head. 'It's you.'

Another drop of blood dripped from his cheek, followed by a third. Splash, splash. Then Odette realised they were tears.

'Are you telling me you love me?' she breathed.

He didn't reply. Just looked at the ground, burning a hole in it with his eyes.

Suddenly she was livid, filled with indignation at his inept, manipulative attempt at absolution. 'You can't just *give* people to each other, Calum. This isn't an arranged marriage we're talking about. You can't set yourself up as some sort of compensatory Dateline for all the men you've cuckolded.'

'I'm not fucking doing that!' He continued glaring at the ground. 'Just for Jimmy. He's special. It was supposed to be easy, but you fucked it all up. You're the reason this has become such a mess. It's your fault, Odette.'

'Well, that's just great!' she howled resentfully. 'How was I to know I was your human sacrifice? Is that why you ruined me – to make me more attractive to Jimmy? More like impoverished little Florrie? Well, it might also have escaped your notice when you set about your Henry Higgins transformation that I was the wrong bleedin' colour and in love with the wrong man. Well done – I suppose two out of three ain't bad.'

'I had it all planned. It was going to be Lydia,' he said quietly. 'I fucking adored her then, and she'll never make Finlay happy – he's too weak for her. I figured Jimmy had what it took to tame that wild spirit of hers, and how could he resist someone that beautiful? But Jimmy was just so bloody keen on you, right from the start. I never thought love at first sight existed till I saw that stupid bastard clap eyes on you at the OD opening. He hardly noticed Lydia. I couldnae believe it. I couldn't understand what he saw in you and not her.'

'Thanks,' Odette said drily. 'You came on to me that night, if you recall.'

He pulled a handkerchief from his pocket and pressed it to his cheek, soaking up the blood. 'I wanted to take you out of circulation. And there was an itch needed scratching so I thought I'd boost my own circulation while I was at it, but you surprised me. You wouldnae play the game. After that, I tried to warn Jimmy off, but he wasn't listening. Pretty soon I saw that I was just making him twice as keen – typical, stubborn Jim, picking on the one person I fucking despised. Christ, you really started pissing me off then, y'know?'

'So sorry.' Odette's voice was dry with sarcasm. 'Next time this sort of thing happens, I'll take a six-month sabbatical in Tibet. That way I might avoid bankruptcy.'

'By then, I knew you fancied me – which was astonishing in itself.' Calum laughed bitterly. 'But I didn't know how strongly you felt. When you fucked Florian for me, that blew me away. I couldnae stop thinking about it.'

Odette closed her eyes, bile rising in her throat. That was her *9½ Weeks* moment, her attempt at modern love.

Calum was shaking his head. 'There you were, willing to do anything for me. There Jimmy was, lumbered with one mother of a crush. There I was, stuck with a club I didn't want and an obsessive woman I didn't want. At least, I didn't think I wanted her. Only I started to think about her more and more. I started to wonder if perhaps all this hatred I was feeling wasn't just denial. When it came down to it, I didn't want Lydia at all. She more or less offered herself to me on a plate, but I'd developed a taste for something totally different by then. I wanted the angry, loud-mouthed cow who'd got under my skin and into my head, who would do anything for me. So that's when I knew this thing might work out after all. It was simple. All I had to do was stop you from loving me. The trouble was, I didn't want to do it.'

Odette stared at him, trying to understand his fucked-up, damaged head, his twisted idea of justice, his maverick morality. No wonder he'd taken things so far, given out such conflicting signals. He had tried to force her to stop loving him, and that was the one thing she'd refused to do.

'It wasn't easy at all, was it?' He laughed sadly. 'I turned your life upside down and you still loved me. Christ, that moved me so much!

You'll never know how that made me feel – my head was so eaten up by you, I was sick with longing. When I came to your flat on New Year's morning, I met Jimmy coming out and thought I'd blown it. I thought maybe if I hadn't turned up then, yous two would have got it together. And I was so fucking jealous it hurt! Then I saw your face and I knew it was still me, not him. You still loved me. That ferocious, crazy love was still burning away inside you, forgiving me all my sins.

'That night, I stood in your flat and thought, "I cannae go through with this." I changed my mind about everything; had it all sorted in my head. I decided that Jimmy should meet Lydia again – I hadn't given them a proper chance to spark it off. I was sure I could wean him off you easily enough, keep you all to myself, tell you the truth about what I'd done. But you still wouldn't play the game, would you? You wouldn't take the deal. You wouldn't even make love to me. And you didn't tell me that you owed all that money. Instead you told me to go to hell.'

'So you decided to give me away to Jimmy after all?' Odette laughed hollowly. 'How charitable. Well, I'm sorry it hasn't worked.'

'But it *has* worked.' He folded his handkerchief and put it in his pocket, his voice matter-of-fact.

'Jimmy and I, we're not . . .' she sought the right word '. . . together.'

To her amazement Calum seemed absurdly pleased, looking up at the Big Dipper in the sky as though literally thanking his lucky stars. 'No matter. That was never the deal. All I need is for him to love you and you to love him. Whether you get it together or not isn't up to me.'

'And what makes you so sure he loves me?'

'Because you're just like fucking Florrie, that's why. Only you're wiser, smarter, uglier, and in my fucking head day and night. I love you, Odette. And now Jimmy loves you as well. Congratulations, Miss Fielding, you get the pair.' The joke rang hollow in his cracked voice.

She thought about Jimmy, alone in his huge farm, packing for Kenya. Big, bullying Jimmy who had saved Calum's life even though he'd slept with Florrie and stolen her heart.

Odette now saw that she must have hurt him beyond most

people's highest pain threshold. How he'd tolerated it was beyond her. He'd let her cry on his shoulder about how much she loved Calum, he'd stood back helplessly while Calum set out to destroy her unconquerable love, he'd coaxed her confidence back a smile at a time. And now he'd asked for something in return. He'd told her to get off her arse and do something to help save Fermoncieaux, whether it was for love of Calum or love of him.

Calum was watching her face very closely now. 'You *do* love him too, don't you? Tell me you love him, Odette.'

She looked back at those pale grey eyes, tortured with hope and jealousy. In all her deepest, most desperate fantasies she had never dreamed that when he finally told her he loved her, he'd blow it totally by asking if she loved his best friend. That was a totally new angle.

'I'll take the job,' she told him. 'I'll come and work at Fermoncieaux. First thing tomorrow, okay?'

Calum let out a short, frustrated sigh of resignation. He wasn't going to hear the words. She wasn't going to release him from his pact just yet. Nodding, he turned on his heel and crunched away through the gravel.

Odette let herself into the mill and contemplated her hollow victory. Calum had loved her, maybe still did. He had admitted it. She should be ecstatic but instead she was furious. He'd almost ruined two lives, hers and Jimmy's. He was trying to play Cupid with a poisoned arrow.

She gave Winnie a guilty hug. Those big adoring eyes could forgive her anything. Clutching her solid little body tightly to her chest, Odette clambered up to the cap and perched on the cogwheel, looking out towards the floodlights around Fermoncieaux. Jimmy was going away, leaving his hopes wrapped up in the scaffolding and dustsheets. She longed to jump on the quad bike and race to the farm to beg him to stay, but she knew it would be a mistake. He would demand to know what hold Calum had over her again and she simply couldn't tell him, especially now that hold had tightened to the point of suffocation.

'Jimmy's going to Africa,' she whispered in Winnie's ear. 'And while he's away, I want you to promise to snore every night to remind me why I'm doing this.'

51

As late spring burst and frothed and fizzed across the South Downs like a firework display, Odette found herself working in a job she could understand and relish at long last. Life was still far from normal – she was living in a windmill and commuting to work across fields of sheep on a quad bike – but her head was level and focused. She now knew that it wasn't work she had hated, it was having nothing but work in her life. Now she had a great deal more. She had friends who needed her, two men who claimed to love her, a beautiful tower-house, and a dog.

Accustomed to six months of self-hatred and pessimism, Odette was revelling in a seemingly unstoppable run of optimism. She refused to get down. She missed Jimmy enormously, but she knew that he would be back. So she threw herself into her work, determined that when he returned, he'd be amazed by what she had achieved.

Despite the continuing cash crisis, Food Hall was rapidly starting to come together. Inside, it looked great. The Leonard brothers had muted their usual iconoclastic and overtly sexual art to create very abstract and highly erotic glass murals around the main dining room, the Salon. The two further restaurants, the Pantry and the Refectory, were more experimental but no less lavish. The other rooms and the private suites upstairs were starting to look equally stunning – modern, challenging, and yet undoubtedly aesthetic. No expense had been spared in acquiring the most visual, most beautiful and most desirable furnishings.

Ronny Prior had been both delighted and extremely surprised to find herself working alongside Odette again. She immediately introduced her to the company's executive producer, Matty French, a nervy, fawn-eyed man in his forties with a diffident manner but ruthless eye for good docu-soap. He'd been brought in to give the show a sharper focus, and Odette remembered only too well that Ronny had said he disliked exclusive restaurants. Food Hall had exclusivity stamped all over it, along with the FH logo that had cost a ridiculous two million pounds to develop.

She knew she had her work cut out to salvage Food Hall's reputation. Ronny already had several hours' footage, none of it very flattering.

'What's the deal between you and Calum?' she asked Odette when she took her to lunch to soften her up. 'I was under the impression he'd filed a bankruptcy suit against you. Successfully.'

'He did.' Odette knew that one of her greatest assets was being up front and honest. 'And I hated his guts for it, but it made good business sense at the time and he's making up for it now.'

'Doesn't that strike you as odd, though?' Ronny poured them both a large glass of wine. She belonged to the minority of old-timers who still believed in two-bottle lunches.

'Very.' Odette nodded, again sticking to the truth. Ronny didn't need to know the details, just the tenor. 'Calum *is* odd. Unconventional, eccentric and brilliant with it. He believes that making friends and colleagues of former enemies creates a powerful work dynamic. I could very easily try and play dirty here, turn the tables on him and tell you a lot of stuff which would make for sensational programming, but I won't do that because you've already seen the worst there is. Food Hall is in a mess. He knows that, which is why he's brought me in at this stage.'

Ronny smiled. She knew this woman wasn't stupid. It hadn't taken her long to accept that there was no way she'd be able to persuade Odette to expose Calum to any further humiliation by starring in the show as Matty had proposed. Her executive producer was clever, but even he couldn't have foreseen this twist. Yes, Odette had turned up, just as he had predicted she would, and yes, Calum had led them straight to her. But neither of them had envisaged that she would arrive on the scene as Calum's press liaison. That was crafty.

'So you're his spin doctor?' Ronny laughed. 'I hope you've told him I'm not making commercials any more? This programme tells it like it is. I'm not going to let you write my script.'

'Wouldn't dream of it, babes.' Odette clinked her glass. 'But I can suggest a few key words, can't I? How about starting with "wedding"?'

'What wedding?' Ronny's eyes lit up.

Odette knew it was a gamble. A part of her still doubted Calum's motives for hosting the event, and Lydia was hardly set to be bride of the month as things stood, but she had very few options right now.

'A week before Food Hall opens to the public, it's being used for a big society wedding. Calum's brother is getting hitched to the daughter of one of our greatest sporting heroes. Calum's using the reception as a dry run for the restaurant, and they get free catering and a fantastic venue in return. Weddings are great for ratings, aren't they?'

'Tell me more.' Ronny got out her note-pad. 'Is she attractive?'

Lydia was ecstatic at the suggestion that her wedding could feature at the heart of a programme about Fermoncieaux. Calum was less impressed when Odette told him that this would be far better publicity if he gave his brother a job at Food Hall too.

'I've told Fin I'll never employ him again,' he howled.

'It'll tie the wedding in with Food Hall. What the show needs is human interest. It needs stars. Lydia and Fin would be perfect. That takes the heat off you – I'm sorry, Cal, but Ronny lent me a tape and you don't do yourself any favours on screen. Lydia and Finlay are *Blue Lagoon* beautiful. The public will love them. But we have to keep the focus on Food Hall. If Finlay is part of the restaurant staff then people will want to come here to see him – see the star in action.'

'What did you have in mind?' Calum snapped. 'Head chef?'

'Head waiter.'

'He won't junk in a well-paid job in London to be a waiter here. And besides, he's not French and has no experience whatsoever.'

'So train him.' Odette pulled out her trump card. 'He's already agreed, so long as he and Lydia get a cottage on the estate.'

'What?' Calum was staggered.

It was true. Lydia was fashionably suffering from City fatigue. She couldn't wait to get out. She'd already bought a book on Sussex and enrolled on a gardening course. Finlay was only too happy to resign from his insurance sales post. The novelty of an office job had worn thin. Odette knew his personality was far better suited to hotel and catering work. Lydia, meanwhile, had just discovered e-commerce.

'She plans to use the cottage as a base for a new on-line rebirthing service,' Odette told Calum, gauging his reaction. But he was reassuringly cynical, raising a horrified eyebrow.

'Won't that frighten the sheep?'

Odette's decision to assemble a damage-limitation cast made no allowances for her own battered self-confidence. The brooding heartbreaker, Florian Etoile, had recently headed off to the Continent on a research tour, eating his way from region to region and leaving both Red Ned and Lydia to lick their wounds. As soon as he came back, Odette planned to get him more involved in the documentary. He had great credibility and, although it hurt to remember, he certainly looked good on screen. Adopting Calum's blackmail tactics, she already had a secret weapon tucked up her sleeve in case he refused. She knew something that could blow his carefully maintained French heart-throb status, and it wasn't the fact he was bisexual. She would never dream of outing Florian, but Brussels sprouting him was another matter. For Odette had recently discovered that Florian was not the pouting Gaul he made himself out to be. It was no wonder he'd never understood her French accent. Florian Etoile was Belgian, a fact he had successfully kept from the adoring English press for years. So far, he had been trying to keep his distance from Ronny's crew much as Jimmy had, but as soon as she dropped a few references to Antwerp, she was certain he'd be simpering over a boiled egg like a butch Delia with five o'clock shadow.

Odette tried not to think about Jimmy too much, but it was hopeless. She thought about him endlessly. She spent her evenings watching the old soap videos they'd picnicked in front of when decorating the mill, remembering comments he'd made and now seeing them with new eyes.

The phone line was finally connected in the mill, and Odette was rather overwhelmed to find that she could talk to her friends whenever she wanted. She listened to Elsa's hysterically funny descriptions of the first weeks of motherhood, Ally's gripes about the final two months of pregnancy, Lydia's excited build-up to her wedding.

'What about Florian?' Odette asked cautiously, after a half-hour description of the four-tier cake.

'No, he's not baking it, darling. Mummy's chums with Jane Asher. She's promised something wonderfully fashionable.'

'No, babes, I mean are you feeling okay about him?' Odette was surprised Lydia hadn't mentioned him earlier. The last time they'd seen one another she'd claimed to be in love with him.

'Oh, he's in France, I think,' she said breezily. 'He should be back in plenty of time to prepare the wedding buffet. We've already planned the menus – of course you know that. You popped around the day we were – er – planning.'

'And that was all the "planning" you did?' Odette realised that Finlay must be in the room with Lydia. Why hadn't she said anything?

'Yes, just the one session,' she laughed, sounding remarkably cheerful. 'I know he creates terribly exotic, adventurous things but on the whole I think I prefer home-cooking. I don't really eat much. One always feels so guilty after a huge pig-out.'

'So you felt guilty?'

'Mmm,' she agreed. 'And I've never liked sweet and sour – I always think it should be one thing or the other, don't you?'

'What about Finlay's problem?'

'You know the secret of making cakes rise is never to leave them in too long – always whip them out two minutes before you think you should, and the hot air will do the rest. Jane Asher says that. It's in her book. I'm going to bake lots of cakes when we're in the country – I won't eat them, natch, just bake. Baking is very *now*.'

So it was back to cakes again. Odette wasn't sure what to make of that particular metaphor. Lydia had totally lost her there. Elsa suggested that it meant she and Finlay had progressed to another stage in the impotence therapy, penetration and then almost immediate withdrawal. Odette personally thought that Lydia simply wanted to bake cakes. Either way, she seemed to have gone off Florian. Odette was relieved. She couldn't see Lydia with a bisexual Belgian with a sheepskin coat fetish. The marriage was still on, and conversations with all her friends inevitably revolved around it.

It was back to old familiar roles, Odette realised, as she talked to them about work once again while they talked about marriage and babies. And yet so much had changed. All the time she was aware that there were two people she longed to talk to, neither of whom was available. Juno had still not got in contact from America with her new number, and Odette had no idea where Jimmy was in Kenya.

Cyd continued to lie low. Odette wanted to talk to her about the situation, but the only blonde in residence at the farmhouse was the bored and increasingly irritated Bazouki. She and Winnie played with the Millers' pack in the canine crèche during the day, but her evenings were solitary as Cyd was never in, and Odette had taken to sneaking her into the mill for a few hours to give her some company. It seemed ironic that the latter-day dog-hater was now baby-sitting two mutts. She even visited Nelson at Fulkington Manor because it was the closest she could get to Jimmy right now.

Rolanda was delighted to see her when she walked up the drive on a sunny Saturday morning.

'I was hoping you'd pop by.' She appeared from her grand front entrance doors wearing an extraordinary caftan. 'Had a postcard from Jimmy this morning – or rather Nelson did.'

'From Kenya?' Odette was desperate for news.

'No, Southend.'

'Southend-*on-Sea*?' Odette almost walked into one of the pillars.

'Yes, old girl.' Rolly laughed at her reaction. 'Felt much the same way myself. 'Straordinary place to choose for your hols – far prefer the Norfolk coast m'self. He says he's bought me a stick of rock. Lovely boy. Want to see it?'

Odette followed her into the vast galleried hall.

'Mind those cases,' Rolly barked as Odette fell over several old-fashioned leather trunks. 'Just throwing out some old rubbish – Lord Fulbrook, to be precise. Now where is that postcard?'

Odette gaped at her. 'You're leaving your husband?'

Rolly was searching through a pile of mail on a side table, 'No, he's leaving me. Doesn't know it yet, of course, but he'll find out as soon as he comes back from his round of golf. Ah! Here it is. Take a squizz at that.'

Odette looked at the picture of a donkey wearing a Kiss Me Quick hat, before turning the card over and reading the last line in amazement.

'Bugger!' Rolly was holding her reading glasses to her face and peering over Odette's shoulder. 'Forgot about that bit.'

At the bottom of the card, which was indeed addressed to Nelson and simply promised to bring back a stick of rock, Jimmy had written, *'Please don't tell Odette I'm here.'*

She still had a key to Siddals Farm and let herself in to look around for clues, her skin crawling with guilt. It was monumentally messy and boiling hot because he'd left the heating turned up high. Odette breathed in deeply, smelled Jimmy, and felt a great wave of affection. It wasn't obsessive love, she was sure of that. Maybe it wasn't love at all. Love was the white-hot, searing pleasure-pain she had felt for Calum. This was warmer and sweeter. Friendship, trust, need. She missed him like hell.

She sat in his kitchen for a long time, just breathing every-thing in, remembering the meals they had shared there over the past few weeks, starting with the all-out disaster when Jimmy had announced he was trying to seduce her with grits and relish.

Sitting down at the scrubbed oak table, Odette rested her cheek against the smooth, warm surface and closed her eyes. 'Come home,' she said aloud. 'Please come home. I can't hold out much longer.' The drug was wearing off. She was going cold turkey from optimism.

In the days that followed, Odette popped down to the farm each evening, spending a little longer there each time. She tried to convince herself that she was just checking it was okay, that no burglars had paid a visit and no pipes sprung a leak. As she began to spend a little longer there than was strictly necessary to 'check', she concentrated on resuscitating his pot plants which were days away from death. Then, as half an hour crept towards an hour or two, she started to tidy his mess, run the vacuum cleaner over the crunchy rugs, dust the surfaces and clean the windows, telling herself that she was making it look lovely for his return. But in reality she was drawing comfort from the house, seeking solace and trying to make up her mind whether this warmth, this sweet affection, was really love, and whether she'd left it too late to tell him.

When she had cleaned every inch of the house until it squeaked like a mouse, she started excusing her visits by taking baths. Her toe-swallowing spa bath terrified her, and she loved the old-fashioned cast-iron one in Jimmy's farm with its huge taps and deep sides. She felt distinctly Flake advert wallowing in it.

Which was where Felix Sylvian found her when he and Phoebe arrived for a recce one sunny evening.

Odette was listening to her favourite cheesy listening local radio station which was having 'an Andy Williams' half-hour. She hadn't heard the Zephyr pull up in the drive. Instead, she was singing. 'The boys watch the girls while the girls watch the boys who watch the girls go by' and loofahing her back.

The first she knew of Felix's presence was when he joined in the chorus.

Odette disappeared underwater in shame, covering up what she could with a loofah.

'I take it that was your spaniel who just tried to eat me?' He laughed when she resurfaced just enough to breathe through her nose, blinking bubbles from her lashes. He didn't seem remotely embarrassed.

Odette nodded, causing the bathwater to ripple around her. Thankfully her liberal application of Jimmy's Captain Bubbly to the running water earlier afforded her some degree of modesty.

'Where's Jimmy?' Felix tapped his fingers impatiently on the basin.

Odette lifted her chin out of the water. 'Either Africa or Southend depending who you believe.'

'Typical.' He headed for the door.

Odette dressed in super-quick time so that her clothes still clung to her wet body when she dashed downstairs. Her face glowed pink both from the heat of the water and the embarrassment of being found wallowing in Jimmy's bath, loitering in Jimmy's house, and letting Jimmy's ex-dog terrorise his unsuspecting brother.

Not that Felix or Phoebe seemed to think there was anything suspicious about her behaviour. They clearly considered it totally natural that she would help herself to the farmhouse's facilities in Jimmy's absence.

'I can't believe he's not back yet,' Felix muttered irritably. 'I've left a heap of messages, but I just assumed he'd been too busy to get back to me.'

'Mungo's in trouble,' Phoebe explained to Odette. 'He was arrested in Regent's Park last week. His solicitor seems to think he'll get away with a fine, but it's really screwed him up and he won't come out of his room. We thought Jimmy might talk him round.'

'Why was he arrested?' Odette asked ignorantly.

Felix raised a cynical eyebrow. 'Use your cottage loaf, darling.'

'Let's just say his line of defence is that he thought the young Italian wanted him to help flush the loo,' Phoebe sighed.

Odette's eyes bulged. Of course she knew that gay men did strange things in parks and public lavatories, she wasn't that innocent. Yet she had never imagined someone as beautiful and flirtatious as Mungo Sylvian would be a part of it.

'Poor little sod,' she said without thinking, and then hastily added, 'Jimmy's been away almost three weeks. He promised he'd be back by now. Everyone at Fermoncieaux's frantic. Hasn't he been in touch with you?'

Felix shook his head. 'I might have guessed this would happen. My brother gives with one hand and hangs on to his plane ticket with the other. I knew he'd run away again sooner or later.'

'You mean, you think he might have gone away for good?' Odette felt her warm face cool so quickly she was amazed it didn't crack and fall apart like a clay mould.

'I'm sure of it,' Felix hissed, his anger hiding deep lacerations of hurt. 'It's not like he hasn't done it before.'

Odette sagged against the Rayburn, oblivious of Winnie's sympathetic tongue lapping at her ankle.

She took them to the pub in Fulkington and listened disconsolately while Felix ran down his brother and fretted about Mungo. 'I guess I'm going to have to sort this mess out. It always comes down to me in the end. Jimmy was just as useless when we were at school. Mr Bloody Popular, the golden-haired head boy who was ashamed of his little dropout brothers.'

'I don't think he saw it like that,' Odette said cautiously.

But Felix was unforgiving. 'It doesn't matter how he fucking saw it,' he raged. 'He clearly doesn't give a shit about his family. Why else did he go away for all those years? Why did he abandon us?'

'Jimmy didn't abandon you, babes, your father did,' she defended. 'Jimmy only stayed away for so long because he thought he was like your dad. He thought you'd be better off without him. He hated himself.'

'And how come you know so fucking much about this, huh?' Felix snapped.

She suddenly felt hugely embarrassed to be intruding upon his family history, spilling Jimmy's secrets out into the open. She'd been living under Cyd's influence too long; she was letting things hang loose when she should hang tough and stay tight-lipped.

Muttering a strangled apology, Odette escaped to the loo. When she came out of the cubicle, Phoebe was waiting for her.

'I'm sorry, babes.' Odette looked at her anxious expression. 'I didn't mean to upset him.'

Phoebe shook her head. 'Felix winds himself up all the time – he's the ultimate rechargeable toy-boy,' she sighed with a reassuring green-eyed wink, wholly accustomed to her lover's tantrums. 'It'll play out soon.'

'Has Mungo really gone off the rails?'

'Hard to tell.' Phoebe gave a half-smile. 'He's such a drama queen, he could snap out of it given a few days and a kitsch video – then again, he could have flipped terminally. I think it's shocked him a lot. I guess he has to face up to the fact that sooner or later he'll turn from pretty boy to dirty old man without achieving anything in his life.'

'Shame, innit? Someone so clever slacking out like that?' Odette sighed. 'Y'know, I was thinking of offering him a job, but I guess he won't want to know now.'

'Doing what?' Phoebe pricked up her ears.

'I'm helping Calum out with Food Hall. He's looking for big personalities as meeters and greeters. One up from waiter, not quite maître d'hôtel, y'know? I thought Mungo would be perfect.'

'He probably would.' Phoebe shrugged. 'But try telling him that right now. He's so glum, he's impossible to talk to. All he does is watch TV all day and eat chocolate. He threw the most godawful tantrum the other day because we're so broke Felix has had to cancel the cable subscription and now he can't watch UK Gold. He screamed, "You could at least have waited until Pam's death scene!" and locked himself in his room for twenty-four hours. Felix and I still haven't a clue what he was on about.'

Odette knew precisely – she could pin down the episode. Afterwards, Victoria Principal had decided to return to *Dallas*, necessitating the legendary 'It was all a dream' shower scene. If only poor, feckless Mungo's past week had all been a dream. She felt a pang of recognition. She knew the symptoms, and had a sneaking suspicion she held the keys to at least a tiny part of the cure.

'Tell you what,' she suggested, 'd'you think he'd like some old *Dynasty* and *Dallas* vids to cheer him up?'

'Early episodes?' Phoebe's eyes sparkled.

'Complete first series.'

'No harm trying. Thanks.'

When Odette introduced Ronny to Lydia, Ronny almost wept with happiness. Lydia was a television natural. Not only was she stunningly beautiful, but she was so eager to be a star that she denied the team nothing. They could come to her dress fittings, film her tantrums when discussing costs with her father, follow her and Finlay around an exquisite thatched estate cottage as they planned how to furnish it, witness their petty arguments and Finlay's desperate attempts to make up. Lydia had just the right mix of beauty, vanity, open-hearted honesty, wit and selfish eccentricity to endear her to millions of viewers.

Finlay was so pleased to see her happy that he let her get on with it. She had been very touchy lately, at times picking huge fights over nothing, at others totally uninterested when he made major decisions like working for Calum at Food Hall. She'd also been spending an inordinate amount of time in the bathroom. Its bin was always packed to bursting with paper matter, which Finlay always emptied at arm's length. He worried that she was having women's troubles and bought a discreet book entitled *A Modern Guy's Guide To Down-under*, which had driven many a bookseller to distraction as it was inevitably placed in the travel section by mistake. Finlay found it unexpectedly erotic. He failed to track down the cause of Lydia's bin-filling disorder, but he decided to try out a couple of the more stimulating suggestions from Chapter 12 'Adventures In The Bush'. Pretty soon Lydia's women's troubles seemed to cure themselves of their own accord, he noticed with relief. The bathroom bin was devoid of anything bar the odd loo roll tube and empty shampoo bottle when it came to emptying. Meanwhile her temper improved dramatically.

*   *   *

Calum was spending less and less time at Fermoncieaux. Odette noticed with concern the way that the chain of command was breaking down. Calum was so autonomous that most of his managers, designers, PR and catering staff deferred decisions in his absence, leaving jobs undone and schedules weeks behind target. Without Jimmy around either, the situation was critical. Yet no one seemed to be stepping in to remedy it. The obvious deputies were Florian, who was still away, and Alex Hopkinson, who was too committed to projects in London to spend more than two days a week on site.

She tackled Calum about it when he made a brief appearance with a bunch of investors. It wasn't an ideal time and she certainly didn't want to say anything in front of the Food Hall backers, but she knew that if she didn't, no one would. She was one of the few who wasn't even slightly afraid of him. Not any longer, at least.

Things were complicated by the fact that Matty French had decided to film that day without Ronny, who was editing another project. He was far tougher to talk around. Odette had tried to persuade him to film the new kitchens being fitted but he was much more interested in Calum, pointing out that he was one of the stars of the show and they had seen far too little of him lately. Odette couldn't agree more.

In the end she was forced to follow him into the lavatory in order to get him alone and out of camera-shot.

'What on earth are you doing?' he demanded as she barged into what was destined to be the gents, but was currently a very basic row of lavatories in cubicles without doors fitted.

Realising that he was not at a point where he could easily be interrupted, Odette turned her back on him and spoke over her shoulder.

'Calum, you're making my job impossible,' she blustered. 'You're never here, the contractors and staff are losing faith – and this bloody television crew can see it. I spent the whole of yesterday keeping them away from a furious row between your architect and the geezer from English Heritage. Two of your top chefs have walked out; the kitchen designer is having a nervous breakdown out there; Alex couldn't give a flyer and Jimmy's buggered off to Africa.'

'The place is doing fine. Everything's on schedule. It doesnae need me.'

'It bleedin' well does! Are you trying to make this into another OD disaster? You're doing exactly the same thing as you did then. Withdrawing when the project needs you most. Only this time you're up to your neck. You've got nothing to fall back on. Remember I've got nothing to lose here – you've already bankrupted me. Who are you trying to hurt this time? The only person that I can see is yourself.'

'I thought you'd appreciate the chance to gloat.'

'I'm not gloating, babes, I'm bleedin' worried. You're gonna run out of wonga soon and this thing is gonna come crashing down around your ears. I've been through it, as you know. It ain't nice.'

'I won't run out of money. I have a new investor.'

'If he's amongst that lot out there I wouldn't be too confident if I were you. They look pretty restless to me.'

'No, it's quite a different source.'

'Who?' Odette swung around just as he was pulling his trousers up. It was an ignoble sort of confrontation on both sides, but she stuck it out, determined to get an answer.

'None of your business.'

'Please don't say it's more money laundering? You're up to your neck as it is. The moment the *Food Fights* crew move on, your unwilling Picasso collector's going to be in here waving his *Guernica* around and you know it.'

Only for a brief second did Calum flinch before re-establishing his sang-froid.

'I can safely say there is no laundering involved. That would be ecologically unfriendly. Beyond that, my lips are sealed. This sleeping partner wants to remain anonymous. You don't need to know.'

Odette had heard enough. She was fed up. She might have guessed this would never work out. There was too much history, so much bad blood on the carpet that a fleet of industrial cleaners would take a month to get the stain out. 'In that case, I quit.'

'No, you don't.' He smiled easily as he walked across the white-tiled floor to wash his hands in the basins beside her. 'Because if you do, I'll quit too.'

'You can't!' she yelped, suddenly suspecting that he was doing this as part of his stupid atonement kick, letting his business go to the dogs because he'd ruined hers. 'You can't bail out now. I tried to make the OD work until the bitter end. And it *would* have worked if you hadn't deliberately screwed it up, you know that.'

'Okay,' Calum laughed, having effortlessly manoeuvred her into position. 'If you think you can do better, then be my guest. I'm putting you in sole charge of the opening.'

Odette reeled in surprise. 'I don't want that,' she gulped. 'I can't cope with that pressure.'

'Get used to it.' He turned on the taps. 'From now on you're launch co-ordinator.' He admired the pelting pressure of the water on his hands – the right burning, the left freezing.

She shook her head violently. 'I'm a bankrupt. I'm not allowed a role like that.'

'I'll deal with the bankruptcy order tomorrow,' he said easily, turning off the taps and looking at her reflection in the mirror. 'Give me three days and you'll be out of the woods and in the Forrester empire.'

Odette stared straight at him, horrified. 'Are you doing this for me or for Jimmy?'

He looked around for a towel and tutted as he realised there were none. Quite calmly, he wiped his hands dry on her jacket. 'I'm doing this for the woman I love. Get the plumbers to turn the hot water down a fraction, will you? It'll scald the diners.'

Monny decided to call her second daughter Vogue because it was her favourite song, the kids' favourite Gladiator and, most importantly, it was the place she had been conceived. That was all the rage now; Spice Girls had named children after their conception cities, Phoenix and Brooklyn. Vogue had been conceived in a Range Rover, with darkened windows and all sorts of exciting electrics which had moved the seats backwards and forwards and up and down. Accustomed to Craig's penchant for cramped XR3is and Cosworths, it had been a penthouse of carnal luxury.

As the build-up to both the wedding and the Fermoncieaux opening grew more hectic, Odette found herself at the centre of both. She was busier than she had ever been in her life, and she was now in front of the cameras as well as behind them. One thing had not occurred to her when angling for Lydia to become the media star she had always wanted to be, and that was the fact that she, too, would inadvertently be drawn into the camera's focused gaze along with the other bridesmaids who made up Lydia's living tableau. The first dress fitting was arranged around shooting schedules.

The tableau was divided about being filmed in that most humiliating of all surroundings, the communal changing room. Miss Bee was glad of the publicity although not so delighted by the slinky dresses. Odette was too busy, but knew she had to try and squeeze it in. Juno was Stateside, still incommunicado, and therefore unavailable for comment. Ally was more concerned that there would be a chair to sit on and a loo nearby. Elsa was appalled at the attention, especially as Ronny was keen to involve Cyd as much as possible.

'Why?' Odette was perplexed. She had spent a lot of time convincing Ronny that Cyd should be featured in the programme as little as possible. 'She's not even coming to the wedding as far as I know.'

'Surely Calum's partner would be invited to his brother's wedding?' Ronny laughed.

Odette's eyes narrowed. 'Which precise partnership are we talking about here?'

'Calum Forrester and Cyd Francis. Now that, my darling Odette, is real human interest. I know he told me he'd throw me out of the building if I so much as hinted at the relationship on camera, but I would be so grateful if you could have another try at persuading him otherwise? Cyd is such big news, and the public love glamorous older women with young men – look at Ralph Fiennes and Francesca Annis.'

'Blast!' Elsa groaned, desperately trying to make a joke of it. 'Mum promised Euan he could have that as an exclusive for *Masked Balls*.'

Seeing Odette join in the laughter, she heaved a sigh of relief. So she knew about it already. And she didn't seem to mind one bit that Cyd was currently shacking up with the Machiavellian maverick midget. Odette was officially over Calum. Elsa wanted to cartwheel, put out the flags and do a high five.

'What's *Masked Balls*?' Ally baulked in amusement.

'Mum's memoirs,' Elsa whispered so that Ronny couldn't hear. 'I was dead against it at first, but she slags off Jobe like mad and is terribly nice about my father and Po. She's been sending Euan tapes to transcribe. He gets terribly wound up listening to them because she keeps dating things by Rangers' wins over Celtic. Calum's a Rangers fan so he must be feeding her the statistics. Euan goes into orbit every time she says, "I remember the party when Jack Nicholson fell through the patio door – it was an Indian summer, just after the dreadful two nil Celtic defeat at home to Rangers".'

'Don't you mind that your mum's seeing Calum?' Ally glanced worriedly at Odette. Unlike Elsa, she could read her like a book – *Mask of Indifference*. Inside the covers was a different story.

Elsa shrugged sadly. 'I gave up trying to tell my mother how to live her life the moment I discovered I'd grown up before she had. I just hope they don't marry. Can you imagine having him as a step-father? At least he likes Afghans.'

Odette was waiting in the kitchen of the farm when Cyd returned that night, walking barefoot and carrying her high heels, having been dropped halfway along the drive. It surprised Odette that she went to such lengths to cover up the affair when she was so headstrong and downright selfish in other matters. She badly wanted to think that Cyd was doing it to protect her feelings, but she suspected the wild-child Petra Pan simply got off on the secrecy element.

'I thought I told you only to come in here when I'm out,' she snapped when she encountered Odette sitting at her kitchen table.

'You *were* out,' Odette said, noticing that Cyd looked unspeakably gorgeous. Her hair was more wildly tousled than ever, her eyes painted with smudgier shadows, her luscious wide lips kissed into a sensual daub of red. She was wearing the slinkiest of charcoal silk dresses, high strappy heels and a silver wrap which slithered from tanned, freckled shoulders.

'And now I'm back.' She threw her house keys on to the table, tossed her wrap over the back of a chair, batted Bazouki away and went in search of the whisky bottle.

'Are you having an affair with Calum?' Odette asked. She already knew the answer, but it was a very *Dynasty* question, and so she wanted to ask it. It hung in the air exquisitely, in close up, with just a little haze of flattering gauze.

Cyd didn't disappoint. Her smoky eyes ignited like hot coals crossed by dancing bare feet. Her nostrils flared, her lips parted and the wild mane was shaken from her shoulders as she squared them to face Odette.

'Yes.' The voice was pure peat – dark, rich and smoking with emotion. 'I love him, dearheart. I'm sorry if that hurts you, but it's a fact. I haven't felt this way since Jobe died – long before maybe. I feel passion. True passion.'

Odette took a deep breath. 'And you're investing in Food Hall?'

Cyd looked rather taken aback that Odette had failed to react with anything approaching sufficient hysteria. Instead she had swiftly changed the subject from Cyd's grand passion to her animal sanctuary fund, which was now pretty well employed in saving another exotic, endangered species – the red-blooded male.

'Just a few shares – nothing much,' she dismissed the question, getting back to the point. 'Oh, dearheart, do you hate me very, very much? I know you love him desperately. I know he loved you too, for a brief time, and that must hurt so much.

You both missed out on a great deal of happiness together, and instead you made one another wretched. But he loves me now, you have to see that. He'd do anything for me and I for him.'

'You told Calum to make me launch co-ordinator, didn't you?'

'I told him to make you happy, dearheart.' Cyd refused to be prosaic.

Odette shook her head sadly. 'Work doesn't make me happy, Cyd. It never really has. It just keeps my mind off things.'

'I knew it! You still want him, don't you?' Cyd covered her face in shame. 'I'm such a ghastly old woman, stealing your love.'

'You didn't steal him, Cyd.' Odette shuddered. 'He was there for the taking. And, boy, does he like taking. He takes people for rides.'

'Has he told you then?'

'Told me what?' Odette felt the acid bite of fear in her bones. Cyd must have lent Calum a fortune.

'That I'm teaching him to ride? He's so sweetly hopeless. No natural feel for horseflesh at all.'

The following morning, Odette stole into the Smockie head-quarters and fired up the computer. She knew that the Miller empire was a hopeless mess, but she'd gleaned enough knowledge during her week or two at its helm to figure out how to check up on the main bank balances and the big animal sanctuary fund. There was nothing in them. Six figures had been reduced to one faster than the Nolans breaking up.

In total contrast, her own financial situation suddenly changed beyond all recognition. The Official Receiver sent her a letter later that week confirming that all outstanding debts had been cleared and that the bankruptcy restraints had been lifted.

52

May was a scorcher. Odette burned easily and slapped on the factor twenty-five each morning as she hopped on the quad bike and headed for Fermoncieaux. The builders had all stripped their shirts from their backs, which seemed fitting as the old building had been stripped of its awning and scaffolding. Bared to the world, it looked spectacular again. Clean, pointed, glossy and angular as a model. Odette started to find it less creepy.

Calum rarely came to the hall now, preferring to stroll around the estate with a shotgun slung over one shoulder, although whether this was to bag game or protect himself from a gangland beating, Odette was uncertain. She had only one opportunity to speak to him alone. One evening, when she let herself into the farmhouse kitchen to collect Winnie, she found him sitting at the table reading, to her amazement, *The Road Less Travelled.* Cyd was on-line upstairs making Fortune Farm predictions, and Odette seized the chance to ask whether he'd told her the truth about her investment.

'Has she any idea that all her precious charity money might be used to pay off the low-life art lovers you're mixed up with?'

'Cyd knows everything about me,' Calum said levelly, his eyes lucid with unexpected honesty. 'Every dark, shitty, twisted thing I've ever done.'

Odette was going to ask him whether she knew about the tape he had made of her and Florian but at that moment Cyd appeared, clapped her hands together delightedly and offered Odette a nasturtium and ginger tea.

Odette was exhausted. She'd taken over a lot of half-finished promotion work and was trying to compensate for

Alex Hopkinson's desertion as he dealt with a political scandal in London. She hosted interviews daily now, showing journalists around, pointing them in the direction of Florian who had returned from his information-gathering trip and was experimenting like mad in the new kitchens. Ronny Prior was happy to focus on him, delighted that she was filming cooking instead of building at last, but it was obvious that she knew Food Hall's future was balanced on a knife edge as sharp as one of Florian's steel blades.

Working night and day to whip up as much positive PR as possible, Odette refused to give in and crack up. She knew this was a job with a definite end. She was the lady who launched. Beyond opening was unimportant to her. It gave her something to focus on, something to distract her from Jimmy's continued absence.

Lydia was going frantic trying to get her bridesmaids all together for another fitting. Odette never had time to get to London; Elsa was always tied up with Florence; Miss Bee was manning the decks at Amnesia in Ibiza; Ally was changing shape all the time as her bump burgeoned; and Juno was still incommunicado. 'I'm working from measurements she gave me months ago,' Lydia wailed. 'I don't even know if she's coming, or if she's still alive.'

'You could try calling Howard and Judy,' Odette suggested.

'They say they haven't heard from her either.'

'Perhaps she's eloped?' Odette suggested with uncanny foresight.

With just over a fortnight to go until the opening day, Food Hall was looking immaculate. It was hard to believe that so much was still behind schedule. Odette was spending twelve hours a day on site, and had commandeered a small office on the top floor from which to drum up as much publicity as possible.

The first five episodes of the documentary were already edited and ready for broadcast, but Matty French refused to allow Odette a preview copy. Looking through the contract that Calum had signed with the company, she was appalled to notice that he had agreed that the series could be aired without content approval. She found it hard to believe he could be so naive. The series was due to start just a week after the restaurant opened to the public. The negative backlash could be appalling if they were depicted badly.

She tried not to think about it too much as she set up more press coverage, involved local newspapers as well as nationals, arranged for a top monthly glossy to run a five-page feature, set up a deal with a top charge-card company for discounted meals and worked tirelessly on other leads and sponsors. It wasn't difficult. The product sold itself. Calum had tapped into a gold-mine. They were already fully booked for the first fortnight, the private suites were booked up for weeks and the phone was ringing itself off the hook.

Finlay proved to be a minor miracle. He learned quickly and had such charm that the other waiters responded to him immediately. He spoke no French and hadn't a clue about service, but his enthusiasm won him friends throughout the building. As they embarked upon endless dry runs, he had his team working like clockwork and, what's more, they were happy.

The kitchen staff were content, too, if intimidated by their grand chef who had returned from the Continent with a host of ideas and a new collection of expletives. Florian would work through the night creating new and original dishes. He hadn't been seen in his London restaurants for weeks, and was devoting himself solely to making Food Hall the greatest gastronomic experience in England. He was equally determined that it would win him back his three Michelin stars.

Odette found it remarkably easy to work with him. He was far easier going than he had been at the OD and responded to her better. Not that she had much time to discuss anything with him. She was rushed off her feet, and doubly distracted by the fact that Lydia was always popping in now that Finlay was on board. She kept appearing in Odette's office with new ideas for the wedding, most of which involved changing the menus.

'You know that's not my area, babes,' Odette told her again and again. 'You'll have to talk to Florian about it.'

'I can't talk to him!' Lydia had yelped. 'Not after – you know. What happened.'

Odette tried not to feel too agitated as she compared Lydia's ling with her own experience. If she could still talk to him, then Lydia should be able to sing a duet.

'I thought you were sorted about that – y'know – cakes?' he hinted. 'Jane Asher?'

'What?' Lydia had clearly forgotten her oblique reference to her night with Florian just being a quick pre-wedding lick of he mixing bowl.

'Well, get Finlay to talk to him then.' Odette didn't have ime to go into it. 'They get on really well.'

'Oh, no!' Lydia was clearly appalled. 'What if Flo says omething?'

'What? About being gay and Belgian?'

'No, about *us*.'

'He's hardly likely to, is he? Not with what you know about aim. You're both going to stay stumm, babes. It was a last fling. You both benefited and Fin didn't lose anything.'

'I think I love Florian, Odette.'

'You thought you loved Calum two months ago.' She was not feeling very patient or understanding.

'Yes, I think I still love him too,' Lydia wailed. 'And my bloody hairdresser did a practice run yesterday and it looked terrific – asymmetric chignon, lots of product, very now. That was, until I tried to take the pins out afterwards. It took an hour and I ended up looking like that road protester – Swampy – all tangled dreadlocks. If I come out of the honeymoon en-suite looking like that, Fin isn't going to fancy me on our wedding night and that's the first time we're going to try to have full-blown sex and . . .' she started to sob '. . . and I'm *hungry*!'

Oh, God, the pre-wedding nerves were at their height. Odette simply didn't have time to deal with it. Telling Lydia to buy a good conditioner, she called Elsa.

'I'll do what I can,' she promised. 'But Florence has croup

and Euan is writing this book non-stop. I'm flat out. We need Juno around. Where the hell is she?'

Mungo's arrival was a moment Odette would never forget, nor would most of the Food Hall staff. He had borrowed his brother's Zephyr which was having its first open-topped outing of the year to soak the glorious sunshine into its leather upholstery. The stereo was blaring out Chef's 'Chocolate Salty Balls' from South Park, the white-blond head was bobbing, the mauve-tinted spectacles balanced on the perfect nose. The entrance was picturesque, camp and perfectly timed. The fact that Mungo had failed his driving test eight times had totally passed him by when he set out for Sussex that morning, just as his chronic short-sightedness had been overlooked because he had yet to find prescription sunglasses in mauve.

'Alexis!' he shrieked as he almost ran Odette and Ronny's cameraman over while they were trying to capture a shot of her and Florian admiring the herb garden.

'Stephen!' Odette laughed as the Zephyr came to a halt with the aid of two potted bays and a wheelbarrow.

'Ugh! Credit me with some style.' He pulled a face, jumping out of the car and flashing a ravishing smile at Florian. 'Fallon maybe, or at a push Crystal. Where do I start? I'm a whizz at banana splits.'

'You haff to haff interview first.' Florian eyed him excitedly.

Mungo, it transpired, wanted to learn to cook. Life in the belly of a restaurant was notoriously macho, an old-fashioned iron foundry of sweat and heroics. Odette thought Mungo better suited to the sharp-suited, charming world of waitering rather than the shouting, screaming melting pot of the kitchens. But a smitten Florian was only too happy to offer him a training post and to Odette's surprise the lifelong slacker was a model pupil, getting up at dawn each day in order to drive from London and learn the ropes with the other young *commis* and kitchen hands.

'I'm on a mission, Posh, darling,' he explained. 'Felix and

Phoebe say I eat them out of house and home, so I figured I should learn to cook. They're not getting rid of me without a fight.' He explained they had just a week left together in Notting Hill.

'Why don't you move down to Siddals Farm? It's just lying empty while Jimmy's away,' Odette suggested. She thought it a ridiculous waste of petrol commuting from London daily. But Mungo shook his head.

'Felix says Jimmy isn't coming back, so what's the point? I'll only get thrown out of there once Calum realises his estate manager has done a bunk for good.'

Mungo didn't notice Odette's stricken expression. He was far more concerned with her hair. 'You must get those awful extensions cut out before we open, you know. You've started to look like Alice Cooper.'

One night when Odette was working late in the Food Hall offices trying to drum up interest in America, she stopped tapping her fingers as she waited for e-mails to download and logged on to the World Wide Web instead. She hadn't surfed since she'd been working as Cyd's cyber-psychic and she was dabbling with the idea of setting up a Food Hall site, although Calum thought it was tacky.

She called up a search engine and looked up Food Hall – just a couple of sites mentioned it, the other three million were about shopping for luxury comestibles. She then looked up Juno Glenn and found her mentioned on several New York Comedy sites. At least that meant her friend was still alive.

She took a hot, guilty breath and looked up Jimmy Sylvian. The matches were all to do with Mpona. It had its own site with photographs of wild savannah, red-soiled tracks being crossed by elephant herds, watering holes pebbled with hippos, idyllic rondavels with thatched roofs and little *braais* outside. There were photographs of the Mpona staff, all smiling black faces, smart green uniforms with baggy safari shorts and shirts with epaulettes. Jimmy was easy to spot in a couple of group photographs, as was the girl beside him with her shock of black corded hair and her high, high cheekbones as perfect as two onyx beads. Odette felt sick with jealousy.

She knew it was a sin to ego-surf but she needed a distraction. She entered her own name into the search engine, certain that nothing would come up. To her surprise there were over four thousand matches. To her horror almost all of them listed XXXX in the title, indicating they were adult. Very adult. This was Internet Porn at its seediest. Voyeur-vision Dong Contest.

She closed her eyes and groaned. The bastard had done it after all. He might have taken back his bankruptcy order, given her a job and told her that he'd once loved her in his twisted way, but that hadn't stopped him from carrying out his threat.

She downloaded one of the sites. It took almost twenty minutes to reveal lots of small photographs of naked women with their pinkest bits blurred out. A message flashed 'Live Sex. Photos. Videos'. Then it offered a choice: 'cum shots, oral, anal, girl-on-girl, black-on-white, huge tits, teenage virgins, surveillance camera'. Wincing, Odette clicked on the last on the list. To her amazement, it didn't ask for a credit-card number, simply giving her another list of choices, which took more long minutes to download.

Half an hour later she had looked at lots of blurred footage of couples having sex against walls, but had come no closer to locating her own in-camera seduction. She decided to give it one last shot and check out the Celebrity Sex section.

She was just scrolling through the names looking for Florian's when there was a step behind her and she almost pulled her mouse out of its socket. She spun around on her swivel chair and saw the closet Belgian himself framed in the doorway, carrying a silver tray loaded with tiny dishes.

'You want to try some recipes I experiment wiz?' he asked, creasing his big beetling eyebrows together. 'No one else is here.'

'Thanks, babes.' Odette hastily tried to get the screen-saver to cut in, but she couldn't remember which combination of buttons did it. Instead of seeing the Food Hall logo, she accidentally started downloading what promised to be a censored out-take of Niall O'Shaughnessy and Minty Drover in *Celt*, the huge nineties hit, proving that their sex scene had not been faked.

'What are you doing?' Florian stooped over her. 'Ah! You like ze sexy computer too? You and Calum, you are so similar. I often wonder why you no make good lovers. You are perfect for each other.'

'*Nous dansons sur un volcan,*' Odette muttered, one of her mother's favourite sayings. 'Calum's stitched us both up, babes. His little video of our kitchen sink drama is on the Internet. I just can't bleedin' get at it.'

'Bastard!' Florian exploded. 'He promise he no do thees. I fuckeeng keel him.'

'And I'll hold your coat, babes,' Odette vowed, watching in fascination as the heart-throb Irish actor Niall O'Shaughnessy did indeed appear to be method acting with the curly-haired English starlet. On close inspection, she had terrible cellulite and he had very bushy pubes. It was far from erotic. No wonder the director had cut it out.

'That ees not us.' Florian was pretty slow on the uptake.

'I know. I can't find us. Loads of sex sites came up when I searched my name – our names,' she added quickly, unwilling to confess to ego-surfing. 'But I can't find the thing.'

''Ere, let me try.' He swivelled her out of the way and crouched over the keyboard, tapping away with expert speed.

'I didn't know you were a cyber junkie?' Odette watched him.

'I am man of many secrets.' He puffed out his cheeks. 'Besides, there ees very many good golf sites.'

He surfed around for a few minutes, repeatedly tapping the Back key, finally relocating at Odette's original search and letting out a blast of laughter.

'You do thees all wrong,' he cackled. 'Eef you want to look for yourself, you haff to put brackets around the name, *comme ça* – see? Now we search. *Voilà.*'

There were just three sites that mentioned her. One was an old *The Outing* review of the OD, another was an alumni page from her old University college, the last was a Food Hall advert that she herself had posted on a bulletin board.

'So why did it come up with all those other matches?' Odette asked.

'Eet just match Odette and Fielding, but not the two togezer. Here – I show you.' He took the brackets out and searched again. The sex sites flashed up. Clicking on one, Florian found a picture of 'Odette' within minutes, but this Odette was a busty redhead from Marseilles who promised to do extraordinary things with exotic fruit if you entered your credit-card details.

Odette snorted with laughter, and then started to giggle. Soon, she and Florian were watching Odette play with a carambola courtesy of Florian's Amex.

'Now we are in ze mood, we try my food.' He switched off the computer and led her down to the kitchens.

Odette faltered in the door, fearing demons, skin-crawling memories of that night at the OD, the lung-bursting panic attack and self-torture she associated with it. But to her amazed relief, she felt none of them. She just felt hungry.

They shared a bottle of the best Margaux from the cellars while Florian cooked half a dozen more dishes, chatting about golf and his plans for the Food Hall restaurants.

He was really quite boring and blokeish when you got to know him, Odette realised. She had never really had the chance in London. He'd seemed so despotic then. He still ordered too extravagantly, made impossible demands of his staff, and only worked when he was in the mood. And he was deeply sexist. He ran down almost every other woman working for Food Hall. He was especially blistering about Ronny Prior.

'She haz a face like a stoat and no breasts. I like pretty faces on men and women.'

'And big breasts?'

'Only on women and poultry.' He winked a sleepy eye at her as he grated truffles.

'Lydia doesn't have big breasts,' Odette said idly.

'I know. I told her to get ze boob job as a wedding present for 'er 'usband. She was not 'appy.' He grinned, flashing all three of his dimples. He seemed perfectly happy to talk openly about it.

'Why did you sleep with her then?'

'She has a pretty face.' He shrugged. 'I like sex with boys and girls, you know that, *chérie*. But I could never love a woman. They cannot play golf like a man, they cannot drink like a man and they cannot cook like a man.'

He splashed some Chianti into his sauce with one hand and turned the olive-stuffed lamb medallions in the pan beside it with the other.

Odette knew there was something she had to ask him while he was in this rare, chummy mood, and she had put it off as long as she could.

'How much do you know about the time Calum almost lost his business?' she asked cautiously.

'I remember.' He was arranging lamb and vegetables on a plate with perfectionist concentration, wiping the rim of the plate again and again with the cloth hanging from his belt. 'Two years ago, *oui*?'

She nodded. 'He suddenly got a lot of money, as if from nowhere.'

He nodded, stepping back to admire his work and then tutting. 'It look too heavy, too dull.' He went in search of herbs, talking over his shoulder. 'Calum, he has many contacts, you know? He like to live a little dangerously sometimes.'

Watching him return with a few leaves of basil, Odette guessed that he knew more than he was letting on. She had to take a risk. 'He's in a lot more danger now. The person who gave him that money wants it back.'

'No, he doesn't.' Florian handed her a fork and beckoned her towards the plate.

'You know The Knife?' Odette speared an entire medallion in shock.

'*Bien sûr*,' he laughed. 'It ees a very good joke. Calum, he fall for it like a baby.'

'What are you talking about?' The medallion flew across the room.

Florian had consumed too much wine for discretion.

'You keep a secret?' He carefully dissected what remained of the lamb with a knife and fork, trying just the tiniest sliver of buttery soft meat and shuddering contentedly. 'Taste him – he is ver' good.'

As she ate, Odette listened in wonder to Florian's explanation of the joke played on Calum by what he called '*les Dens*' – hardman footballer Denny Rees and his mate, artist Dennis Thirsk.

'Calum, he sleep wiz both their wives, you know? That make them ver' angry but he ees a friend so they do not plan to kill him, y'know? Just frighten him a little.'

'Bleedin' forgiving of them, don't you think?' Odette fumed.

Florian shrugged. 'You maybe not understand the bond of a man's friendship. He is like the roots of a tree that grow together, where 'is marriage is just a leaf on a branch.'

Florian was full of Eric Cantona-like philosophies, most of them rubbish, all of them sexist. But Odette was too interested in the story to take issue.

'He help them out many times over the years, you know? They get in many bad situations, *les Dens*, and Calum is always there for them. Only once do they help him. Two years ago when he get in trouble, Calum go to Denny and ask him if he knows anyone who want to buy two Picassos, *oui*?'

It turned out that the 'contact' Denny had provided was none other than his old mate Dennis Thirsk who wanted to buy them for his wife Susie as a present. Rather than reveal himself, Dennis suggested playing a trick on Calum by pretending that the money was coming from a dodgy gangland connection, something that Calum had always been unhealthily obsessed with. And so The Knife was born. They heaped on the talk of danger and arranged a terrifying rendezvous in a bleak disused warehouse near King's Cross.

'Calum, he was shit scared,' Florian laughed. '*Les Dens* hide and watch 'im make the switch. They enjoy winding him up for weeks after. But the sketches, they were useless to Dennis. Someone had written on them – feelthy rubbish. He no give them to Susie – they just live in his studio. He talk about setting them in plastic, but then I sink he forget about them.'

'What about the money?'

Florian was wiping the plate with a big hunk of bread now, mopping up the last traces of the delicious sauce. 'You no understand Dennis. Money mean nussink to him. He once burn a million pounds as performance art, remember? He sink of this as just ze same. He and Denny even dye some of the notes to add authenticity, *oui*? It help Calum out and make them laugh at ze time. But zen recently he find out that Calum has been fucking Susie behind his back again. He also screw Tandi, the wife of Denny. Now she haff fantastic breasts.' He sighed appreciatively.

Odette bit her lip, suddenly realising what was going on. 'And they've decided to get revenge by pretending that "The Knife" wants his money back?'

Florian nodded. 'Calum, he sink he has a price on his head.' He started to laugh delightedly, cuffing Odette on the arm. 'Is funny, no? I sink you and I enjoy the joke too, maybe?'

Picking up her glass of Margaux, Odette started to giggle. Suddenly her epic workload, missing Jimmy and panicking about Lydia's wedding didn't seem to matter. Leaning against each other like two winos on a pavement, she and Florian tangoed up and down the long Food Hall kitchens, singing 'Mack the Knife'.

Suddenly Odette stopped, spinning Florian in an unintentional pirouette at the end of her arm. 'Do you think Dennis still wants the Picasso sketches?' She chewed her lip. 'You see, they really weren't Calum's to sell in the first place. They belonged to – to a friend of his whose father gave them to him not long before he died.'

Florian shrugged. 'I ask him for you.'

Cyd rushed out of the farmhouse to greet Odette on her return. Before she had a chance really to register the fact that it was one in the morning and that Cyd was wearing a hat, she was whisked inside and presented with a large whisky. Both Bazouki and Winnie, curled up by the Aga, looked up and lashed their tails sleepily but couldn't be bothered to rise and greet her.

'Do you like this?' Cyd pointed at her hat, which was a Chinese straw triangle, like a rice-picker's hat, that had been sprayed sludge green and covered with gypsy coins. It was hideous.

'Very fashionable,' Odette said diplomatically.

'That's what the assistant said. I thought I'd funk my image up a little for your friend's wedding.' Cyd was highly wired, flitting about her kitchen distractedly. She had at least three cigarettes on the go in different ashtrays, but she lit another one anyway, almost igniting the rim of the repulsive hat. 'We haven't had a chat for ages, dearheart.'

Odette hid a yawn and realised that this was probably her eviction order. She wasn't surprised. She and Cyd hardly got on any more; she was effectively squatting rent-free in her mill, had painted it bright colours, was using her cars and her quad bike and – most importantly – was her current toy-boy's ex of sorts.

'I've been thinking . . .' Cyd tapped cigarette ash into the sink and looked around for her glass.

Odette hoped that she'd have at least a couple of weeks' grace. She needed to get Lydia's wedding and the Food Hall opening out of the way first.

'. . . I've been rather beastly to you, haven't I? Dear Odette.' Cyd settled at the table in front of her, big smoky eyes creased at the corners in sympathy. 'I thought it would be so lovely having someone else around the house – a surrogate daughter, if you like, especially as my own baby was having a little girl of her own. The trouble is, I'm not very good at having people around. I know the Millers are here, but they tend to keep out of my way.'

'It's all right, Cyd.' Odette took a swig of whisky and coughed as it slid its peaty, abrasive way down her throat. 'I know what you're driving at. I can find somewhere else to stay.'

'No, no, dearheart! You don't understand. That's not what I'm saying at all. Quite the reverse, my angel. You see, I adore my children. At least, I love them passionately, but I don't like them all very much. Elsa is quite lovely, but very judgmental, and she has a life of her own. The boys are making an effort at long last but they're terribly like their father – I suppose they're bound to be. You, dearheart, are quite different. You are eccentric and feisty and yet you've looked after me and looked out for me without my thanking you at all. I've been a very mulish old cow these past few months, I know that, and especially lately when I met Calum and felt so jealous that he thinks so highly of you. Now I know what a fool I've been. Calum is madly in love with me.'

'Is he?' Odette spluttered out another mouthful of whisky.

'Of course. Quite sweetly besotted, as I am with him. He's going to move in here. Isn't it perfect?'

Odette forced a smile. In that case she was definitely moving out as soon as she could arrange digs. Rolanda would probably put her up.

'And I know you might feel a little awkward about that, but I want you to feel you can live as my tenant in the mill as long as you like. It's your home now. You're as much a part of the place as darling Bazouki.'

Odette knew that in Cyd's eyes this was a compliment indeed so she tried not to feel too affronted to be bracketed with the ditzy blonde dog.

'Thanks.' She ran her finger around the rim of her glass. After the wine she'd slurped earlier she felt a bit tight, and stuffed to the gullet with wonderful food.

'So are we friends?' Cyd chewed her lip, still uncertain.

Odette looked at her and found her eyes suddenly full of tears. Cyd had been unbelievably good to her, had saved her from homelessness, given her the equivalent of a skip-full of chocolate, persuaded Calum to put her at the helm of the Food Hall launch and injected the cash needed to save the place.

'Of course we're friends.' She stood up and offered Cyd the hug she had always longed to extend during those late-night therapy sessions. Cyd could be extraordinarily funny about hugging and kissing, but now she fluttered into Odette's arms like a leaf to a pond, bobbing against her ample bosom.

'Good!' Cyd clapped her hands together as she backed away, suddenly embarrassed. 'I'm glad that's all agreed. We'll settle the rent another time. Now what else was I going to tell you? Oh, yes, that dreadful hairy old aristo came around earlier. Polly Sherington.'

'Rolly?' Odette wondered what she could have wanted.

'That's the one. She said you are to go there for dinner tomorrow night. Claims it's urgent.'

'But that's Lydia's hen night,' Odette realised. 'I'm supposed to be going up to Maida Vale.'

'In that case I'd just send her a little card saying you had a prior engagement,' Cyd said airily. 'Awful old harridan. Probably just wants you to take envelopes around for the NSPCC or something.'

Odette was less certain. Rolly Sherington was one of her few links with Jimmy. She was the only person he had sent a postcard to, after all. She might know something.

53

Storms rolled up and down the ridge of the South Downs all the next day, dumping vast quantities of rain on thirsty fields and irritated sheep. The gutters were soon overflowing and the lake in front of Cyd's farmhouse started spilling out on to the gravel and lawn. Odette realised that it was a testament to Jimmy's skills that the smock mill was sealed as tight as an anorak.

She knew she should dress up for Lydia's hen night, but she was desperately pushed for time now that she had to stop off and see Rolly en route. The hairdresser had taken longer than she'd expected to cut out all the tangled extensions and re-style her hair. It looked great. For the first time in six months she'd had a say in what she wanted and it was simple, stylish, linear and highly unfashionable. Stunning.

She threw on a crisp white shirt and her leather trousers. She'd recently patched up the scorch mark with a tiny off-cut from the hem that she was certain only an eagle-eyed saddler would spot, and was too delighted to fit into her old favourites again to care. She felt she owed them another outing.

Cyd had told her to take any car she liked, but the only one that started in the moist, damp conditions was the yellow Ferrari. Odette felt ridiculously conspicuous as she growled her way through the village towards Fulkington Manor.

A crew-cab pick-up truck was parked in front of Rolanda's crumbling portico. It was covered in dirt as though it had driven from Southend to Sussex off-road.

Odette was so ecstatic to see it that she almost drove over

Rolly's pack of eager dogs, Nelson included. For once, she didn't cower in the car until the barking had calmed down but threw herself out and ran to the front door.

Rolly's ancient housekeeper answered after an age and asked who was calling. She made Odette hop around impatiently on the doorstep while she shuffled off to inform her employer. Finally Rolly appeared wearing a shooting waistcoat and carrying a twelve-bore over her shoulder. 'Odette. You're early. We've been taking pot-shots at my in-laws. Such fun.'

Odette followed her through the house and out into the rear gardens where a row of gilt-framed portraits of thick-necked inbred Sherington ancestors were lined up on George II dining chairs. Most of the canvas of each, plus a lot of the chairs which supported them, was smashed, ripped and shredded.

'I must say, your brother-in-law is a frightfully good shot,' Rolly sighed admiringly.

Odette spotted two men uncocking their shotguns and leaning back as the spent cartridges smoked their way out. One was tall, broad-shouldered, sandy-haired, and she knew the instant she saw him again that this was, indeed, the real deal. Love. Full-on and passionate. It wasn't the knees giving way or the heart crashing around that told her, nor was it the smile which sawed through her cheeks, the pulse that thrummed in her groin or the tears of relief that sprang to her eyes. It was the warmth, as though she had been caught in a shaft of hot evening sunlight whilst being smeared in Deep Heat, wrapped in cling-film, surrounded by hairdryers and hugged by the Ready Brek kids. Odette Fielding loved Jimmy Sylvian.

The other man gave her quite a different feeling. The cling-film tightened like gaffer tape mummifying her, the Ready Brek kids stabbed her in the back and the hairdryers turned into loaded pistols. Because Jimmy, the love of her life, the stud of her mini-series, the heart-throb of her soap opera, was shooting the past with none other than Craig. Brother-in-law from Hell. Bankrupter. Daughter neglecter. The Enemy. Odette was livid.

'Where the fuck have you been, Craig?' She stormed up to him. 'You bleedin' rat! You ran out on Monny when she and the kids needed you most. You've got a daughter you've never even

612

net.' She was so angry it didn't matter that he was holding a loaded shotgun, that he was six feet tall and three feet wide with a face like a punch-bag and fists the size of cannon balls.

Craig was terrified. Although he towered over her, the expression on his big, battered face was frightened and cornered and he stumbled over his words as he spoke. 'She ain't mine, Odie.'

'What?'

'Liam Turner's.'

'*What?*'

'She's Liam's. He turned up during the first scan. December it was. Started yelling that the baby was his. I did a runner, couldn't cope. But Monny knew where to find me, and she swore blind the kiddie was mine. She told me to stay in hiding, said she didn't want me banged up till after the nipper was born.'

'*What?*'

'But we've just been round to the house. She's moved Liam Turner in there, changed the locks and everyfink. The bastard is living under my roof.'

'WHAT!'

'Are you deaf or summink?' he asked without irony.

'What do you mean, Monny didn't bring her to see you?' Odette tried for the full sentence, but she was finding it hard to speak. 'Where have you been?'

'In a mate's caravan in Essex,' Craig shuffled his big feet. 'I'm sorry, Odie. I just wanted to stay out long enough to see the little one born. I didn't know what had happened to you. Monny didn't say, but she was really off. Then she stopped coming over. She used to catch the bus at nights – your old mum and dad thought she was working in a supermarket. But she just stopped. My mobile packed up. I couldn't get in touch – I knew the Old Bill would get on to me pretty sharpish if I tried, but it was doing my head in. I just assumed she was getting too big with the pregnancy to travel, y'know? Then Jimmy here turns up and tells me the baby's been born nearly a month.'

'You found him?' Odette swung around to look at Jimmy, feeling her heart swell up proudly. They were the first words she had addressed to him since she'd arrived and she found herself fighting a ridiculous urge to add, 'By the way I've missed you like mad, I've worked my heart inside out for you and I think I love you.' But to her surprise, he didn't appear as deliriously excited to see her as she was him.

'It wasn't easy.' He looked tired and needed a shave. He didn't seem able to look her in the eye. 'If I'd known your sister knew exactly where he was hiding, I could have saved myself a lot of time.'

Odette covered her mouth in horror. 'So Monny knew all along and she didn't say anything?'

'She felt bad that the baby wasn't Craig's,' Jimmy explained 'She was in a terrible state when we saw her. She wouldn't let me into the house unless I made Craig promise to wait in the car.'

'She fought I might try and take the kids.' He cocked his gun and blasted a hole in a topiary pheasant, making them all jump in fright. 'They're my kids. I ain't seen them in six months. Bitch!'

Jimmy gripped the smoking barrels and gently pointed the gun downward. 'It's not entirely Monny's fault, Craig. We know that.' His big voice was at its most soothing.

That was too much for Odette. Love him as she did, she felt the compassion junkie had overdosed this time.

'But Monny let me go bankrupt!' she wailed. 'She lied to me, she used me, she watched me lose my livelihood, my flat – everything! I was dragged into court and treated like a criminal, for God's sake! And for what? I lost everything I had for a low-life thief my sister doesn't even *want* any more. Craig's the one who committed the crime, not me. In fact, I'm calling the police right now.' She scrabbled in her bag for her mobile, but Jimmy took it from her before she could dial the number.

His voice was shaking with anger. 'There are more important things at stake here than your money.'

He looked her full in the face at long last, his huge, bruised eyes surprised, tired and unmistakably disappointed. Odette bit her tongue, realising how selfish she must seem, screaming about money at a time like this. It wasn't really the money, she wanted to yell. She didn't give a stuff about the money. It was the betrayal that hurt. But it was too late to take it back.

'Craig was framed, Odette,' Jimmy sighed wearily, deriving no leasure from the gloriously eighties *Miami Vice* phrase. 'We think Liam planted the drugs and cash in the house – he had plenty of opportunity and he certainly wanted Craig out of the way. Monny denies it, but I've talked to this guy for a lot of the past two days,' he slapped Craig manfully on the back, 'and I believe him when he says he's never been involved in drugs. He's certainly no angel and he's up to his neck in other rackets, but not drugs.'

Craig was gazing at Jimmy with such loyal, Rottweileresque adoration that Odette half-expected him to nudge his head under Jimmy's hand demanding to be stroked.

'So what are you going to do?' She looked at them.

'Kill Liam Turner.' Craig slotted two fresh cartridges into the barrels of his shotgun.

'We'll have to go to the police eventually,' Jimmy sighed, 'but we can't prove anything at the moment – they'd just bang Craig up and go straight to court. He'd be behind bars protesting his innocence while Liam Turner's free to swan around congratulating himself. It could take years to prove his innocence that way, if ever. Liam's well known to the local nick, but there's not a shred of evidence against him on this one.'

Odette realised that Jimmy had picked up phrases like 'bang up' and 'local nick' from Craig. He was like a child playing cops and robbers. She hoped he knew what he was dealing with.

'Does Liam know you're on to him?'

'He will do soon – he wasn't at the house earlier, but the moment he gets back Monny's bound to tell him Craig's on the war path at long last. That's why I brought him here. Rolly's going to look after him tonight. Liam will follow us down here, of course, but he'll look at my house or yours or even Fermoncieaux, he'd never think to check out this place.'

'How d'you know Liam will follow you here?' Odette asked. 'Monny doesn't know where you live, does she?'

'She knows where *you* live,' Jimmy pointed out. 'And she knows we're friends.' He said the word with a curious emphasis that made Odette's heart sink.

'She would have just called the police then, surely? They could be on their way now.'

Craig instinctively shuffled his bulky body behind a potted

box and glanced worriedly towards the drive. Spotting the Ferrari for the first time he couldn't help whistling. 'Nice motor, girl. Nicked, is it? I know a great place does cheap paint jobs.'

'Monny won't call the police, Odette.' Jimmy shot Craig a withering look. 'Think about it – she could have done that weeks ago. Liam has no idea that she's known where Craig's been hiding out all this time, or that she's visited him. If that comes out, Christ alone knows what he'll do to her. She's bloody terrified.' He looked at her and for the first time Odette registered his own fear. He wasn't playing cops and robbers. He knew precisely what he was up against. 'In her eyes, it would be much better to tell Liam that Craig's turned up at the house out of the blue.'

'I still don't see why that means he'll come here.' Odette shook her head. 'Monny doesn't think logically like that. If she saw Craig in London, she'll think he's still in London.'

'That's where we need your help.' Jimmy touched her arm. 'You've got to talk to her. Call her tonight and tell her you've seen Craig with me at Siddals.'

Odette carried on shaking her head. 'She'll just tell Liam that, and he'll be the one who shops Craig to the police. It'll backfire completely.'

Jimmy put a warm arm around her. 'Liam won't shop Craig. He'll come here. He has to. You see, Monny gave me a few of Craig's clothes while I was at the house earlier, and this accidentally got in with them.'

Odette flipped through a small rent book. It was full of long lists of numbers written in smudged biro.

'Liam's list of suppliers and users,' Craig told her proudly, again giving Jimmy his loving Rottweiler look. 'I've seen him with it down the Greyhound. It's in code. Won't mean a thing to you, love.'

'Or the police come to that,' Jimmy added. 'But it means one heck of a lot to Liam. He's buggered without it. So he'll certainly be coming in search of it.'

'Monny gave you this?' She turned it over in wonder.

'Well, I don't think it got into the sock by accident.' Jimmy nodded. 'She knows a lot more than she's letting on, and she's very, very frightened. By handing it over, she's forcing some sort of resolution.'

'If what you're saying's true, then Liam would kill to get this book back.' Odette shivered. 'He'll be gunning for Craig's blood.'

Craig was insulted. 'Not if I get there first he won't.'

Jimmy was obviously not keen to umpire a death match. 'Which is why you have to make that call, Odette. Tell Monny Craig's hiding out at my farm. Then wait until Liam is out of the way and go to talk to her in person. She knows the truth. You've just got to persuade her to tell it to the police.'

'How am I supposed to do that?' Odette gasped. 'She's never respected a word I've said.'

'Liam tried to seduce you at Saskia's wedding – even laid a bet with his brothers,' Jimmy reminded her, his voice strangely matter-of-fact. 'He already knew that Monny was expecting his baby then, yet he still tried to sleep with her sister. She'd find that unforgivable. It might just do the trick.' He was already hustling her towards her car. 'Go straight to London and wait for us to get in contact – here's your mobile back. I'll ring when we're ready at this end, and you can make that call and then go round to your sister's. It might be a few hours yet, so don't panic if you don't hear from me for a while.'

'What do you mean, "ready at this end"?' Odette glanced over her shoulder at Rolly who had taken command of the guns and was waving her off with one slung over each tiny shoulder, looking eager for a shoot-out. 'Are you all going out to buy full body armour?'

'Just taking a few precautions.' Jimmy opened the Ferrari door for her. 'I don't want anyone to get hurt. I think I'll plant Rolly on the roof here with a pair of binoculars – keep her out of harm's way. With any luck Monny will be telling all to the police before Liam's got off the M25.'

'And if she isn't?' Her blood ran cold.

'We'll call the police if things get too heated, don't worry.' He stepped back like a doorman as she climbed in. 'What sort of car does he drive, by the way, so we know what to look out for?'

'Range Rover Vogue – you can't miss it, it's covered in bull bars and has blacked-out windows.'

54

'Odette's a bit distracted, isn't she?' Ally asked worriedly, checking her watch again. Duncan had promised to collect her at eleven, and it was ten to already. She was shattered and longed for the buzz on the intercom.

'Maybe she feels like the rest of us do about this wedding,' Elsa muttered while Lydia was out of earshot, fetching another bottle of champagne from the kitchen. She pressed her still full glass to her chest, trying to ease her aching nipples which told her it was Florence's late-night top-up time. She was desperate to get back to her, although she'd expressed enough milk to keep Euan busy. She only hoped he didn't distractedly put it in his tea as he had the afternoon she was at her tum-tightening aerobics class.

'Well, if anyone's going to say something, it'll be Odie,' Ally whispered as Lydia danced back into the room. 'She's not a coward like the rest of us.'

All thoughts of tackling Lydia about her pre-wedding jitters were in fact far from Odette's head. Not that she was thinking much about her sister, or poor Craig and the mess Liam had stirred up between them. All she could think about was Jimmy. He'd seemed so distant, so controlled and in charge. He was sorting out her family's crisis and yet he had hardly looked her in the eye during their brief reunion. There had been no kiss, no hug, no soft focus running-across-fields as she'd imagined. Looking back, she realised that he had never once tried to kiss her, or touch her beyond friendly pats and arm-squeezes. And tonight she was so frightened for him it twisted her lungs together. He was in real danger. Liam Turner was no pushover. He was dangerous. Jimmy was putting his life on the line for her family and she didn't even know if he wanted to kiss her.

She looked at her watch again. It was hours since she'd set out from Sussex and he still hadn't called. It was dark now and that somehow made the danger far more real. Why wait until after dark? If Liam went charging down to the Fermoncieaux Estate now, they would have far less chance of spotting him. Monny might not even want to see her this late on. The kids would be in bed. If Jimmy didn't call soon, Monny and Liam would be in bed too. Odette stared anxiously at the window and then at her phone, wondering whether Jimmy had the wrong number written down. If he did, then she couldn't call Monny to get Liam out of the way or go around to talk to her, could she? That way they wouldn't be put in danger. If they thought about it all again tomorrow, in the cold light of day, then she was certain a more sensible course of action would present itself. The police might know what Liam's little book meant, it might be enough to have him arrested, to sow the seeds of doubt about Craig's culpability for all those endless charges. All this wait-until-Liam's-on-his-way stuff was way too dangerous and relied too heavily on her ability to persuade her sister to see sense. Odette hadn't been able to do that in thirty-three years; she doubted she could start now.

Then a terrible thought struck her. Liam could *already* be on his way. Could already be there, in fact. Jimmy had pointed out that Monny knew her address and that he lived nearby. It was only a matter of time before Liam tracked them down. Jimmy, Craig and Rolanda could all be lying in a bloodied heap right now, their limp bodies peppered with lead shot. Odette groaned out loud and picked up her mobile, but she didn't know the Fulkington Manor number. It was past eleven. Something had to be wrong. Jimmy should have called by now.

In the Smock Mill Farm kitchen, Cyd was turning her chewed tarot cards with delighted wonder. 'These are really very, very good,' she breathed. 'You see the Star card crossing the World there? It means you can have anything you wish, dearheart.'

Calum rubbed his mouth. 'Almost anything, maybe.'

'But this advises caution.' Cyd winced as she turned over the Hanged Man. 'Someone wants to make a fool of you, possibly worse – it indicates a sacrifice, or recompense for a wrong. You must stay close to those you trust, probably close to an older, wiser figure with a wealth of experience and the aura of a young wood nymph.'

Winnie, Bazouki and Calum's two Afghan puppies started barking several seconds before Calum and Cyd heard the sound of tyres crunching on gravel. A moment later the beams from an incredibly bright set of headlights burst through the kitchen window and slid across the ceiling.

'That's funny, I thought Odette said she was staying over in London tonight.' Cyd looked up.

'Maybe the party was nae good?' Calum knew it was Lydia's hen night. He had offered Finlay a big night out in London, but to his surprise his brother said he'd prefer to go out to the village pub in Fulkington the evening before the wedding.

'I don't recognise the car.' Cyd was at the window and shielding her eyes from the glare of its lights which were still on full-beam although the car had pulled up short of the lake. 'Menacing-looking thing – hang on, someone's getting out. Good God!' She took a step back and squinted hard to confirm what she was seeing. 'I think he's got a gun. He looks just like Jobe's old drug dealer. He's heading for the tower. Yes, it *is* a gun – the barrel looks frightfully short as though it's been . . . oh, lord! Calum, what shall we do? Calum?'

When she turned around, he'd disappeared.

Cyd ducked below the level of the window and crawled to the far wall to kill the lights and lock the kitchen door.

Picking up on her fear, Winnie and Bazouki were barking their heads off now. But the dippy Afghan puppies – more like gangly teenagers these days – were distracted by something under the table, their thin tails wagging as they dived underneath to investigate. Looking across, Cyd saw Calum cowering beneath it.

'Shall I call the police?' she whispered as the dogs fell silent and they heard the crunch-crunch of footsteps on gravel heading towards the tower.

'No!' Calum cowered back yet further. 'It's him, don't you see? It's The Knife. I knew he'd come for his money. The police can't know I'm involved in this.'

'What does he look like?' Scuttling across the room on all fours, Cyd joined him under the table, reaching up to pull down the whisky bottle as she did so. 'Shaven head, lots of tattoos and scars, about six foot five?'

Calum's eyes bulged. 'I never met the guy. We made the exchange in a warehouse.'

'Did he drive a huge car with bull bars and blacked out windows?'

Calum started to shake. 'I didnae see that either. I did the switch on my own – I figure he was watching me with a loaded shotgun nearby, you know?'

They both jumped as they heard a furious hammering on the tower door.

'If he's called The Knife,' Cyd unscrewed the whisky bottle, 'why does he carry a sawn-off shotgun?'

'How the fuck should I know? Maybe he's in disguise?' Calum took the bottle and drained it down to the label. 'I think we should make a run for it before he checks out the house.'

As soon as Ally and Elsa left, Lydia poured out two huge goblets of champagne and cornered Odette in the sitting room.

'Do you all disapprove of this wedding, is that it?' she demanded. 'Don't you think Fin and I make a good couple?'

Trying to get her head around the question when it was full of thoughts of gangland killings in Sussex, Odette stalled for time. 'What makes you say that, babes?'

'None of you seems remotely interested in what I've been telling you tonight – you haven't taken much notice for weeks. And Juno hasn't even been in bloody touch. You've talked about this behind my back, haven't you? You don't think I'm doing the right thing.'

'Finlay's one in a million, babes, the real deal. We all think that. Remember when you told me you fancied Calum and I had a go at you because Fin is so much more?'

'But you loved Calum!' Lydia flared angrily. 'You thought he was "the one". You were just saying that to put me off.'

'But it didn't, did it? You went ahead and tried to find brotherly love despite sisterly advice.'

'He wants me,' Lydia said proudly. 'He said he fantasised about me. God, if I marry Fin I'll never be able to flirt with Calum again – not in the same way. Not with all that sizzling sexual potential. And he adores me!'

'He's with Cyd now,' Odette reminded her gently, looking at her watch again. Quarter past. Come on Jimmy, *call*. Let me know you're okay.

'Yes, he passed me up for an ancient old raver,' Lydia sniffed, looking deeply hurt. She tried to make herself feel better by saying. 'What about Florian? The *menage à trois* between wine, food and sex?'

Odette winced. 'He uses that line as often as he uses a pinch of salt, babes. We both fell for it.'

'You too?' Lydia gasped.

She nodded, checking her phone again. 'Besides, you don't eat food, Lyds, and wine makes you incoherent after two glasses.'

'And I don't have much sex,' she hiccupped, rapidly approaching her limit. 'I'm not sure if Fin is capable. What if we marry and he can't perform?'

'Fins are bound to get better,' Odette joked feebly, wondering whether she should call the police – just the local Sussex plods – and get them to check over Siddals Farm and Fulkington Manor.

'Oh, Odette, when are we going to find you a lovely man?' Lydia lolled back in her chair and sighed at the ceiling. 'A lovely Mr Odette – a nice computer programmer or data analyst or one of those clever jobs, hmm?'

'I think I might have already found him,' Odette confessed, almost adding that he was currently lying low, awaiting the arrival of a dangerous criminal who was quite possibly armed. Either that or dead, heroically slain defending her family's honour before she'd ever had the chance to tell him how she felt. Either way, it was a far cry from the usual 'we met in a wine bar last week and he likes Mel Gibson films too'.

'Still Calum?' Lydia's big eyes were twin goldfish bowls of sympathy.

'No.' Odette shook her head. 'I love—'

'I love Florian!' Lydia howled. 'He's just my type, isn't he? Big, dark, sexy, slightly shy in a defensive, rugged way. Fin is a darling, but he's not *me*. He's not—'

There was a loud blast at the intercom. When Lydia picked it up and started to say 'Hello?' a voice was already panting guiltily '. . . MARRIED!'

'What?' She was nonplussed.

'I'M MARRIED! Let me in, you old cow. I've got Duty Free and jet lag!'

Odette only had a moment to register Juno looking twice her usual size and half her age, beaming from ear to ear and swinging bags of fags and gin, before she was propelled into panic by her mobile ringing. She fell on it anxiously, covering one ear to blot out Juno and Lydia shrieking at each other.

'Some party, huh?' Jimmy sounded controlled but urgent. 'I think Liam's already here – Rolly's just spotted a Range Rover heading like a bat out of hell towards Smock Mill. For fuck's sake get Monny to cough something to the police.' His voice was tight, too, tense and nervy beneath a guise of calm. 'Then, when she does, get them to send a squad car here as soon as they can.'

'Was that Odette?' Juno asked as a dark-haired figure bolted past her at speed. 'Still jogging, I see.'

Lydia barely noticed. 'Come and have some champagne, darling. God, it's so delicious to see you. Everyone thinks I shouldn't be marrying Fin. What's your take? Shall I call it off?'

'Let me see my bridesmaid's dress first and then I'll decide. Oh, dear, Odette's left her mobile behind.'

Florian Etoile was high up in the Food Hall offices, idly playing around with Odette's computer, when he looked out of the window and spotted a bright light bouncing towards Fermoncieaux through what he remembered to be a field. The landscape was lost in the darkness, but a few fast-moving shapes caught briefly in the flickering light resembled terrified sheep. Florian couldn't remember there being a road or drive in that direction. The light was moving too fast to be a torch, too slow for a motorbike.

He took a big swig of Cognac and checked again. Now he could make it out clearly: a quad bike with two passengers. It was illuminated by the fiercely bright halogens of a huge off-roader bouncing along behind. As he watched in amazement, Florian started to suspect that the big 4X4 was chasing the little quad. The only reason it wasn't catching it was because its driver seemed to be taking inordinate care not to muddy his paintwork by driving through any puddles.

'Faster!' Calum yelled, blinking mud from his eyes and gazing in terror over his shoulder. 'He's gaining on us!'

'I'm doing the best I can!' Cyd shrieked, blinded by the wind and rain. 'Has he started shooting yet?'

'Fuck!' Calum ducked as a shower of sparks covered them, but it was just Cyd driving through an electric sheep fence. 'We're nae gonna make Fermoncieaux. Go left . . . *left*!'

He almost fell off the quad as it slid on to a narrow path into the woods, heading towards Siddals Farm.

The Range Rover was too wide to follow the quad, and its driver too frightened of scratching his paintwork to try. Florian watched it in fascination as it made its way very cautiously towards Fermoncieaux's floodlit drive before heading out to the village road.

'*Et voilà.*' He shrugged and lit a Disque Bleu. 'Poachers.'

Squinting through the smoke as he returned his attention to the computer screen, he tapped a few more keys and smiled, registering a familiar and quite spectacular cleavage. Bingo! This was easier than making an omelette when you had a copy of *Design Your Own Web Site*.

'You're listening to Chat Radio, the nation's elation station,' the jingle chanted and then an oozing voice cut in, 'Go ahead, caller, you're live on air.' Another listener came on to the line to ask for advice about her complicated personal life.

'Hello, yes, it's Angie from – er – Dorking here. My husband is a lovely fella and we have two great kids, but a while back I took up with another geezer and I've just had his baby . . .'

Odette wasn't listening to the car radio and had no time or inclination to switch stations. It droned on unheard, poor Angie's problems the least of her concerns.

'Thing is, my new fella's a bit of a one,' she announced shakily, 'and I fink he's involved wiv drug deals. I din' know how serious it was until recently, but now he's after my old man and I dunno what to do for the best . . .'

Thamesmead might be a sleepy suburb by East London standards, but it was wide awake to witness a yellow seventies Testarossa roaring through its midst. Odette was in a blind panic. She barely noticed the pub leavers stepping into the road to admire her motor as she threatened to mow them down by breaking every speed limit and cutting every corner en route to Monny's neat little semi.

'You see, I fink my old man's been framed for summink he never done – he's been on the run for monfs,' Angie's voice wobbled, unheeded by Odette.

She flattened a couple of rose bushes as she hand-braked on to the handkerchief front lawn and cut the engine – and Angie's sorry tale – before leaping out to hammer on the door and punch the musical chime doorbell. Lights were flicking on in upper windows all around Edward Heath Grove and nets twitched, but Odette was oblivious as she flipped open Monny's letterbox and yelled for her to get her arse downstairs.

Inside, Monny was livid, but too upset to think straight. Vogue was yelling her little lungs out upstairs, the kids were thumping around in a confused state and she had just been interrupted midway through an emergency consultation with Chat Radio's late-night agony aunt, something she'd had to stay on hold forty minutes to achieve. The nation held its breath and listened as she opened her door.

Odette saw the phone and prayed her sister had been talking to the police.

'Come in,' Monny snapped, glancing at her neighbours' windows and dragging her sister inside. She clutched the phone to her chest, forgetting that she was still on air.

Odette ignored her niece and nephew hurling themselves at her ankles with relief and grabbed her sister's wrist.

'Do you love Liam?' she demanded.

'Dunno.' Monny shrugged.

'Do you love Craig then?'

'Dunno.' Monny started to cry.

'Do you want your kids to have fathers tomorrow morning?'

''Course I bloody do!' Her sister lifted several chins defiantly.

'Good. You see, I love Jimmy and I want him to be alive tomorrow too. But they're all about to kill each other if you don't tell the police what you know.'

'Go upstairs, kids. I said – Get. Up. *Stairs*.' Monny waited until the footsteps retreated before squaring up to Odette with familiar, sullen determination. 'I don't know nuffink.'

Odette was well aware that Jimmy had wanted her to go softly-softly, but that was before Liam had turned up in Sussex. 'He tried to get off with me at Stan's wedding, Mon. Liam tried to sleep with me. You were five months gone at the time.'

'You're lying!'

'Ask Gary. He and Liam had a bet. They made jokes about marrying for Monny's sister's money.' She suddenly remembered something else she had overheard. 'And Liam said he was trying to get back with his wife.'

That did it. Monny's face crumpled. 'The bastard! He's been seeing her behind my back for m-m-monfs,' she sobbed. 'That's why I gave your fella the b-b-book. I fought Liam and Craig could sort it out between them. If they really love me, they'll fight for me.'

'This isn't *Gladiators*, Monny!' Odette howled. 'Someone is going to get seriously hurt here, and I'll never forgive you if it's Jimmy. Never. Now, what do you know?'

'Enough to bury Liam for a long time.' Monny's chins came up again in a moment of pride before she started bawling. 'But I won't do it. I love him, Odie.'

Odette had heard enough.

'Call emergency services and tell them to get a squad car to the Fermoncieaux estate – no, better make that an armed response team – and to send the local CID round here while they're at it. Then call Dad. He can be here in half an hour. He and Mum'll take the kids, meanwhile you can talk to the police. After that, we're going to Sussex. We can talk on the way.'

Nodding mutely, Monny was about to dial out when she heard a voice squawking, 'Angie – Angie! Who's about to kill who? Talk to us, darling, talk to the nation. You're live on air, and we'll be right back after these quick commercials . . .'

Monny hung up in horror and dialled 999.

'Do you think we'll be safe here?' Cyd whispered, pulling a piece of straw from her mouth.

Calum was too frightened to answer, his ears on elastic.

They were hiding in Jimmy's hayloft, along with several bats, a heap of African masks and a month-old copy of *Farmer's Weekly*.

'Do you think the dogs will be all right?' Cyd fretted. 'Bazouki's bladder gets very weak if she's—'

'Shhh!' Calum covered her mouth with a sweaty hand.

Outside, a door slammed. It was too loud to be an ordinary car.

'Shit!' he hissed under his breath. 'The quad bike.'

They'd left it in the courtyard, splattered with mud.

Both of them almost fell out of the loft in fright as the barn door creaked open and a half-million-watt torch blasted straight in their faces.

'It's okay,' Jimmy boomed. 'He's heading back towards Fermoncieaux. The chap drives like a pensioner. Rolly's keeping an eye on him from the Manor roof and is in constant contact, see?' The torch swung back to reveal one of the ancient walkie-talkies that Rolanda had used for many years whilst stewarding local horse trials. He cranked the torch up to his own face. 'It's me. You can stay up there if you like, pretty safe place to hide, although I warn you I caught a rat the size of a terrier just where you're sitting before I went away. Had to stake the bugger out for days.'

They were down the ladder in a flash.

Calum quickly regained his composure in male company.

'Where the fuck have you been, Jimmy?' He was such a pastiche of Glaswegian anger he only just stopped short of a head-butt.

'Staking something else out,' Jimmy told him. 'And I think it's about to fall into my trap. Care to come and watch?'

On cue, the walkie-talkie crackled into life with a geriatric warble. 'Pedigree to Stray Dog. Pedigree calling Stray Dog, do you copy, over?'

'Seen too many war movies,' Jimmy apologised, lifting the radio to his mouth. 'I copy you, Pedigree, over.'

'Bloody frightful cock-up! Heinz 57 has absconded to the Loony Bin. I repeat, Heinz 57 has ab—'

'What are you talking about, Rolanda?' Jimmy interrupted.

'Craig came on the roof here and saw that thug heading back to Fermoncieaux. I told him to wait, but he buggered orff. Took the shooting brake.'

'Shit!' Jimmy cut her off and looked at Cyd and Calum. 'Get in the car, I might need you.'

'You are *joking*?' Calum cocked his head. 'This psycho's after my blood.'

'Don't talk rubbish,' Jimmy snapped. 'He's trying to kill Odette's brother-in-law. I need you as witnesses in case he does.'

'Isn't that a bit sick?' Cyd giggled, following him outside. This was the most fun she'd had since a crazed stalker had held the whole of Mask hostage in the Chelsea Hotel.

Liam had no map and no way of knowing his way around rural Sussex. One lane looked very like another to him, and they were all universally filthy. He carefully drove his beloved Vogue up the centre of the single-track road, his huge headlights bouncing off low-hanging branches and terrified wildlife.

'Oh, shit, not again!' he groaned as a huge great palace of a house came into view once more, this time approached from the opposite direction. How dare rich bastards have so many drives, and such long ones? He was surprised half the landed gentry didn't un out of petrol before they found a main road. He slammed on he brakes, looking over his shoulder to assess how far he had to everse. At least half a mile. He'd be better off turning in front of he house.

As he set off again, he saw a figure dart inside and blinked n surprise. Then he started to chuckle. Crooked Craig *was* well onnected.

t was only when Monny was talking to their father and apologis-ng for getting him out of bed to ask him to come and babysit that Odette realised she'd left her mobile at Lydia's. She waited until her sister had finished before diving on the phone to call Siddals Farm. There was no answer. She called Smock Mill Farm and had the same response. At Fermoncieaux, the lines rang straight o voice-mail and the security guard was clearly not at his desk.

There was no sign of a CID car, which Odette had fully xpected to appear within minutes, a magnetic flashing light lammed jauntily on its roof.

'Maybe it's a busy night?' suggested Monny who had deliber-tely given the wrong addresses for both herself and Fermoncieaux vhile Odette was distracted looking for her mobile.

After twenty minutes, there was still no sign of it. Panic surfing vile in her throat, Odette waited until her father appeared at the door before throwing herself back into the Ferrari and screaming t Monny to join her.

'Where are we going?' Her sister would have refused to come long were it not for the fantastic car.

'Sussex.' Odette was too panic-stricken to think straight. 'We can get there in forty minutes – this thing does well over a ton nd the roads will be quiet. If the Old Bill isn't going to take us eriously, then we'll just have to sort this thing out ourselves. You till carry a can of Mace in your handbag?'

She had just started to explain what was probably happening t Fermoncieaux and the very great likelihood of their both losing he men they loved when she caught sight of a blue flashing light n her rear-view mirror.

There were some things the Old Bill took very seriously

indeed, such as speeding in a restricted urban area while unde
the influence of alcohol.

Juno was midway through her second bottle of champagne and a
lengthy attempt to persuade Lydia that Finlay was perfect for her
when the mobile phone that Odette had left behind rang shrilly
She picked it up with a big wink.

'Odette?' a voice breathed urgently. 'He says he's going to
shoot me in an hour if he doesn't get his book back. Have you
sorted things your end?'

Juno stared at the phone and then pressed the 'cancel' button
in a panic.

'Who was it?' Lydia was only slightly interested.

'Wrong number.' Juno helped herself to more champagne
'Some mad librarian, I think.'

It had all gone horribly wrong, and it was all Florian's fault – or
rather that of his insatiable libido. How was Jimmy to know that, in
the mood for love, he'd switched off the CCTV and got the hunky
young security guard blind drunk, allowing Liam to slip into
Fermoncieaux unnoticed? Or that Rolly would leave her shotguns
unattended where Craig would find them before hot-wiring the
ancient shooting brake? The man was a criminal and, for all their
two days together, Jimmy knew not to trust him. He'd told Rolly
that enough times. 'He's locked in the cold cupboard, don't let
him out!' had been the last words he'd shouted up to her before
leaving to check on Siddals Farm, where Rolly had reported a
quad-bike sighting. How was he to know she'd pop downstairs
for a snifter and take pity on Craig who was whining that he needed
the loo? He'd thought she was made of sterner stuff.

Looking at Liam Turner, Jimmy wished he himself were made
of sterner stuff. The man was clearly out of his pear tree, and had
more than two shot cartridges. He'd sawn his gun off so close to
the stock that it looked like a sixties hairdryer, and he was waggling
it in the faces of his hostages with more than a light scrunch dry
in mind.

'Where. Is. My. Fucking. Book?'

He had Jimmy, Craig, Florian and the comatose security guard held at gunpoint in the Food Hall kitchens, hands tied, backs against the refrigeration units. Craig and Jimmy were absolutely terrified, and the security guard was beyond caring; only Florian showed any semblance of cool.

'Zis book, he is compulsive reading, *non*? You must give me he title. I cannot get srough *High Fidelity*. The hero, he is sex mad.' He admired Liam's broad shoulders, squinting slightly from too much Cognac. He'd stumbled on the siege by accident, having reeled downstairs for a quick surfing snack. He was too drunk to take it seriously. He rather liked being tied up and was pressed very tightly to the butch guard, which wasn't altogether unpleasant.

'Shut. The. Fuck. Up.' Liam was not in the mood for literary criticism. He jabbed the gun threateningly at Craig. 'Go on, tell me where it is, Crooked. Otherwise you're first.' He pointed the lethal hairdryer straight between Craig's eyes.

Lying on the stainless steel surface behind Liam was one of Rolly Sherington's Purdeys which he'd pulled from Craig's grip when he'd held his sawn-off to the back of his enemy's neck. Craig was small-time and no equal to Liam. He'd dropped the gun as fast as a bad relay sprinter's baton. Beside it lay Jimmy's walkie-talkie, which had long since fallen silent.

Jimmy had already calculated the distances. Even supposing he could leap up and wrestle the sawn-off from Liam, the Purdey was too close for his liking and the walkie-talkie too far away. He had his hands tied behind his back. It was suicidal.

'Like Jim says, Odette's got your book,' Craig was gabbling. 'She won't be here for anuvver hour at least. She's got to drive from London.'

Jimmy closed his eyes. He hoped to hell that Odette had understood his call. He'd managed to stall Liam by pretending she had the book and was on her way, but he wasn't sure the ruse would work much longer. His only hope was Calum and Cyd, who had stayed in the car when he'd jumped out ten minutes earlier only to walk straight into Liam's barrels. They must have escaped into the night, and Jimmy was certain they were calling the police right now.

At the very least, he prayed that Rolly, spying on the cars clustered outside Fermoncieaux from her roof, would start to suspect something.

When the walkie-talkie behind Liam crackled into life, they all jumped out of their skins and Liam almost shot the fridge.

'Pedigree to Stray Dog, Pedigree calling Stray Dog. Have spotted badgers. Repeat, have spotted *badgers*! First sighting in a decade. 'Straordinary creatures. Bloody marvellous. Recommend you return to base to take a squizz if you're finished there, over.'

Jimmy closed his eyes. Now Calum and Cyd were his only hope.

In the Food Hall offices, Calum was hyperventilating with fear as he tried to dial the police with clumsy fingers. 'The lines are down. Must be the wind.'

'Don't be silly, they're buried underground.' Cyd took a look under the desk. 'Someone's plugged a modem in there – look.' She squatted down to pull it out.

'Wait!' Calum hissed, suddenly noticing the screen in front of him for the first time. 'Shit . . . oh, no! Oh, shit. I never meant for this to happen. Cyd, I need your help.'

'What's that, dearheart?' Cyd, who was still under the desk and thoroughly overexcited by danger now, had been contemplating his fly thoughtfully.

'Is there any way you can get this off the web?' Calum demanded, thrashing the computer mouse around like Tom in a very mean mood with Jerry.

Settling beside him, Cyd drew her reading glasses out of her back pocket and had a look. 'Good God, it's Odette. What *is* she doing? I never thought she had it in her.'

'Can you remove it?' Calum groaned, closing his eyes to the delicious sight one last time.

'Sure – at least I think so.' Cyd started tapping a few buttons and then peered up at him over her glasses. 'Don't you think we should call the police first?'

'That can wait,' Calum hissed. 'This is an emergency.'

'As you say, dearheart.' Cyd started working, tucking her chin back into her neck and squinting at the screen. 'But I warn you, even if I remove it, it could already have been copied all around the world – depends how many people have accessed the site. And it'll be on the computer's hard drive. I have no idea how to delete it from that – I only dabble.'

'Just do what you can.' Calum kept his eyes clenched tightly shut. 'I'll deal with the rest.'

'Tick-tock, tick-tock.' Liam was looking at the clock on the tiled kitchen wall. He was not the most original of armed villains, but he was no less threatening. 'Odette's taking her time, in't she? She drive a hearse or summink? Might come in handy.' He curled his lip at Craig who was now pasty-faced and fighting to control his bowels.

'Actually she drives a Ferrari Testarossa,' he bleated.

Liam raised his scarred eyebrow.

Jimmy was looking at the Purdey again. He'd been trying to work loose the tapes on his wrists for the best part of an hour, but Liam was obviously *Blue Peter*-trained and could do things with sticky tape most mere mortals hadn't a hope of achieving. Twisting his head to one side, he saw that the security guard was still out cold and that Florian had nodded off beside him. Something metal was poking out of his back pocket. Shuffling towards him an inch at a time, Jimmy managed to work it free of the chef's Levis and stealthily tuck it behind his own back before Liam noticed.

He closed his eyes in despair when he felt what it was. Some sort of computer disk. He'd hoped it was a paring knife or, at the very least, a bottle opener.

'Always rather fancied Odette,' Liam was saying to no one in particular, waving his hairdryer gun around with theatrical aplomb. He was getting into his role now, his menacing expressions perfect, just the right level of psychotic abandon and a very good line in vicious sneers. 'Fantastic body, that girl. Mind you, face like a—'

A mobile phone was ringing in his jacket. Liam smiled evilly at

Craig and Jimmy before drawing it out. ''Scuse me, lads – hello?'

Taking advantage of the momentary distraction, Jimmy was trying to pull the metal clip from the computer disk when he saw Cyd Francis appear in the kitchen door behind Liam. She caught his eye and put a finger to her lips.

'Mum!' Liam was whining into the phone, his voice instantly losing its threatening edge. 'What did I tell you about calling me at work? Yes, I know it's one in the morning but I . . . So what if it's my access weekend? I'm busy. What do you mean, she's dumping the kids on you? At this time of night? Where's she say she's off to?'

Cyd removed her reading glasses and stole across the room towards the Purdey, as light-footed as a phantom.

Liam was given no time to react as two barrels were poked between his shoulder blades at exactly the same moment as his sawn-off was whipped from under his hand.

'Er – call you back soon, Mum, okay?' Liam spluttered, switching off his phone. It seemed he wasn't so different from Craig after all. The moment he had two barrels in his back, he surrendered.

'Lie face down on the floor!' Cyd ordered, a gun in each hand now, like an ageing Lara Croft. Pressing the heel of her boot into his neck, she reached for a knife and slid it across the floor towards Jimmy.

Before he had even cut the tapes on his wrists, he heard sirens wailing their way towards Fermoncieaux.

'Thank Christ someone's called the police at last,' he laughed, freeing his hands and setting about cutting the others loose.

'Oh, God, I knew I'd forgotten something.' Cyd covered her mouth guiltily.

The walkie-talkie crackled into life once more. 'Pedigree to Stray Dog, Pedigree calling Stray Dog. Badgers are mating. Repeat, badgers are *mating*. Outdoors. In summer. 'Straordinary. Over.'

55

Returning to Sussex just after dawn, Odette found no one at Siddals Farm, Fulkington Manor or Smock Mill Farm. They were all eerily deserted.

She'd left Monny in Stepney with their parents, along with the kids and a huge guilt complex. Odette had hugged her very tightly before leaving, grateful that she'd put things right at last, knowing that doing so had cost her more than just the liberty of her children's fathers. It had been a long night, and Monny had coped all alone. Seeing her sister locked in a cell had obviously been the final straw. For, while Odette was awaiting her formal charge, Monny had finally decided to spill the beans on the man who had torn her family apart. She'd spent all night talking to the police, going over and over what she knew about Craig's arrest, how often Liam had visited the house immediately before the police raid, his comings and goings after that. The police realised she personally was blameless, but had found enough damning evidence both in her statement and in her house to warrant Liam's arrest.

'That's one hell of a shopping trip your sister's been on,' the arresting WPC had joked when she finally got around to processing Odette. 'She's shopped both her husband and her lover tonight. Talk about retail therapy!'

Last night, Odette's soap-opera life had hit a new high when she was caught champagne-drunk in a Ferrari – Cyd would be proud – and inadvertently triggered a chain reaction. As soon as Monny started talking, the Met had radioed through to the Sussex Constabulary. Liam Turner had been arrested, Craig rearrested, and Jimmy had been questioned. If justice had its way, the first would be banged up, the second exonerated and the third seduced by a randy witness for the prosecution.

Odette felt randy – she felt very randy and very loving. She also felt frustrated that the recipient of her randy love was not around, nor was her dog, his dog or her landlady and the quad bike, although poor Bazouki wriggled with delight to see someone at long last.

When Odette and Bazouki took a quick jog to Fermoncieaux they found the reason for the mass desertion. Plumes of smoke were belching out of three upper-storey windows. Fire engines, police cars, ambulance crews and television vultures were all clustered on the carriage sweep in front of the huge old house. A fire fighter on a crane was hosing a great jet of water through a shattered casement, into what Odette recognised to be her own office.

She raced towards the first familiar face she saw, Ronny Prior.

'What's happening?'

'All under control,' Ronny assured her. 'Just an electrical short apparently. Something to do with a computer left running – only the offices are affected. Neither the dining rooms nor the kitchens have been touched. This smoke is just the last gasp. Shame, really. If the place had burned down we'd have made an absolute killing. Sorry, darling.'

'No, I get your point,' Odette was reeling with relief. No one was hurt. Jimmy was safe.

Then she saw him talking to a fireman, his face so blackened by smoke that his bruised blue eyes shone out as bright and startling as the police lights she had seen the night before. The love welling up inside her had nowhere else to go but out. It was too big for her now, too powerful, too fat, too angry and happy and joyful. She had to share it. She sliced through the crowd like a border collie through sheep.

Jimmy was thrown backwards by the force of her hug. For a moment they teetered on the verge of tipping over and then he dug deep into his reserves of strength to right them both and gather her into the longest kiss she had ever experienced. This was perhaps less long than most people, but Odette was a tyro when it came to love and Jimmy was one hell of a kisser. He clearly felt no embarrassment that they were surrounded by press, the emergency services were looking on, or that his face was black with smoke and his mouth tasted of soot. Odette liked the taste, in fact she loved the taste as they kissed on and on. She would never turn her nose up at burnt cooking again.

When he surfaced, his eyes blazing with surprise and love, he cupped her face in his hands.

'Where on earth have you been?' He rubbed her cheeks with his sooty fingers, eyes ablaze with worry. 'The police said something about you getting arrested?'

'I lost my licence and my heart.' She reached up to kiss him again. 'Thank heaven you're safe.'

The sound of breaking glass made them both jump, but it was just the fire fighter on the crane smashing the last of the glass from the broken window so that he could climb inside and assess the damage. The smoke had thinned out now, although great sooty flakes were still floating down like grey snow. No longer needed, the ambulance started to trundle away.

Odette watched it worriedly before putting her hands over Jimmy's and looking into his big, kind eyes. 'You shouldn't have gone in. It was just a faulty computer.'

He drew her to one side, 'I got Calum out. He was going mad in there.'

'Calum started it?' Odette gasped.

'Shhh.' Jimmy looked over his shoulder. 'I don't know. He was trying to put it out when I found him, waggling a fire extinguisher around like a bloody woman with a scent bottle. I'd just brought Cyd back from the police station, and when we found Smock Mill deserted, we came here to see a top-floor window lit up with flames.'

'Cyd was at the police station too?' Odette was puzzled.

'Yes, I'll explain later.' Jimmy hugged her tight, pressing his blackened chin to the top of her head. 'I'm just so glad you're safe.'

'And you.' Odette watched over his shoulder as two policemen walked across to talk to a senior fire fighter. 'Do you really think Calum started the fire deliberately?'

Jimmy stroked her hair, his voice muted. 'He kept muttering about the evidence – destroying the evidence. Something about a tape. Cyd's taken him for a walk to calm him down. With any luck the fire investigation team won't suspect anything. It'll all come off the insurance. That could even be why he did it.' Jimmy shrugged sadly.

Odette knew for a fact it wasn't. She knew what Calum had been burning and he'd almost destroyed his dream while doing it. Calum had been severing his last hold over Odette. She was free now. The pact was fulfilled. He'd delivered his promise. Odette loved Jimmy; Jimmy loved Odette. And yet . . .

'I love you,' she said it. It badly needed saying.

Jimmy didn't even wait a beat. 'I love you too!' His loud, booming voice caused heads to turn.

Ronny Prior's voice was far quieter, murmuring from behind the shrubbery, 'And cut. Get that, boys?'

Her sound recordist took off his cans and nodded sulkily. It wasn't easy hiding a furry boom in a rhododendron. There'd be a lot of interference.

Ronny's cameraman was far happier. The close up on the kiss had been sensational. He'd almost steamed his own lens up, and the angle was just right to catch Odette's huge boobs in glorious profile.

Jimmy drove Odette back to Siddals across the wet fields – not easy to negotiate when he wouldn't let go of her hand or stop looking at her in wonder, his eyes blazing with love. On the way, he excitedly told her about the siege in the kitchen.

'Christ!' Odette was horrified as she imagined Jimmy tied up at gunpoint. 'I had no idea you were in that sort of danger. From what the police told us, it sounded like Liam just gave himself up.'

'He did eventually,' Jimmy laughed, recounting the story of Cyd's dramatic rescue with obvious relish. 'Bloody amazing woman. I've always thought she was a bit of a lightweight rock diva, but she really showed her heavy mettle last night. You should have seen it!'

Odette shook her head in amazed admiration, secretly rather appalled by her foolhardy bravery. Cyd couldn't operate a can-opener, let alone a twelve-bore. 'What was she doing there in the first place?'

'That's the weirdest thing.' He shook his head, squeezing her hand and gazing at her so lovingly he almost drove into a gatepost. On the back seat, Winnie let out a yelp as she slid from one window to the other. Nelson was flat to the floor in the rear, hanging on for grim life. 'Calum seemed to think Liam was after *him*.'

Odette opened her mouth to explain and then closed it again. She couldn't shatter Jimmy's high by mentioning the sketches, and the stupid practical joke *les Dens* had played on Calum, which had inadvertently cost Jimmy his fortune. Not yet. She'd tell him soon. Florian might still be able to strike up some deal with Dennis Thirsk to get them back. Better to tell Jimmy then.

She looked at his big hand holding hers, still sooty and scratched, and callused from months of work around the estate. They were hardworking hands, strong hands, kind hands. She wanted to feel them against her skin. Glancing up at Jimmy again, she shivered with excitement as she saw that he was brimming with anticipation too. Unable to stop himself, he leaned across and kissed her, almost driving the pick-up straight into a ditch this time.

As they bounced on to a drover's lane and climbed the final hilly field before Siddals' little valley, Odette felt a smile spread across her face like a fire catching, only this one hadn't a hope of being extinguished. We're going to go straight to bed, she decided. We're going to make love – delicious, slow, gently old-fashioned love. Jimmy will be a wonderful lover, just as he's a wonderful man. He'll be patient and giving and passionate. And I will learn. With his help, I'll learn fast. I'll be the best pupil ever, full of bright ideas. Boy, I can't wait to start learning.

'I can't wait to have a bath.' Jimmy sighed happily at the

thought. 'I've been wearing those clothes for two days. You'll be wanting one too, I guess?'

Odette tried not to feel too disappointed. Of course, he was right. He must feel sweaty and stale. So did she. Far better to go to bed when squeaky clean and soft-skinned from a long soak. Then she perked up as she realised he probably meant for them to have a bath together – the big claw-footed one at Siddals could easily accommodate two.

'You can go first, and I'll use the water afterwards,' Jimmy suggested, reaching up to stroke her face, unable to stop touching her. 'It's good ecology. And I'm going to cook you a simply enormous breakfast after that.'

Odette smiled, drinking in his lovely face and the big white grin that looked bigger and whiter than ever against the sooty cheeks. Yes, we'll go to bed after breakfast, she decided. Jimmy's right. We need some energy food first. We're head-over-heels, after all, so why not breakfast-then-bed to match?

'And after that?' she asked, reaching out to stroke his thigh.

But Jimmy didn't have time to answer as they belted into the courtyard behind Siddals and almost crashed into the back of a Budget Hire van.

'What the . . . ?' He bounced back off his steering wheel.

Winnie, who had fallen off the back seat during the emergency stop, started barking feverishly and jumped over the gearshift to clamber on to Odette's lap and growl at the van, from which a particularly well-formed male bottom was protruding.

'Someone's obviously making a delivery.' Odette shushed Winnie and undid her belt, wondering who delivered on Sundays. But Jimmy was already out of the pick-up and making loud, excited greeting noises while he bounded up to the van.

Watching from the cab, Odette saw the owner of the bottom turn around and she groaned. For there, holding a pot-plant in one hand and a box of CDs in the other, was Felix. Behind him, Phoebe was trying to grapple with a coffee table. Odette had a feeling they weren't just planning to store their stuff with Jimmy. They were moving in.

As she got out, Mungo came trotting through the kitchen door carrying two Meatloaf albums at arm's length, pincered between his fingers like dead mice. 'I'm sorry, Jimmy, but these have *got* to go.'

Jimmy didn't seem prepared for this turn of events either.

'Now, forgive me if I got this wrong, but I thought you lot were moving into a flat in Little Venice today?'

'We were,' Phoebe dropped the coffee table on the cobbles. 'But Felix conveniently forgot to sign the tenancy agreement and it went to someone else.' She glanced at Mungo who was trying to bat Winnie away with the Meatloaf albums.

'We thought we'd come and crash here instead, if that's okay?' Felix didn't seem too bothered by the loss.

'For how long?' Jimmy picked up the coffee table and slung it over one shoulder.

'Just a few days.' Felix handed the pot-plant and CDs to Odette before clambering back into the van. 'Most of our stuff's coming down tomorrow in a lorry. Don't worry, we can keep it in a barn. And we won't get in your way.' He re-emerged carrying a huge, stuffed crocodile. 'Mungo will be working, and Phoebes and I are going up to Yorkshire to look at cottages next week.'

'Yorkshire?' Jimmy laughed, starting to head towards the house. 'That's a long way from Little Venice.'

'And from here,' Mungo shuddered, giving Odette a sad look as he threw Meatloaf in the bin. 'Oh, look, that big shaggy thing's attacking Handbag.'

Nelson, having staggered weakly from the back of the pick-up, was in an evil mood and keen to pick a fight. Winnie had sensibly hidden beneath the hire van, but the huge stuffed crocodile made a more than adequate stand in and Nelson leaped on it with hackles raised, wrestling it from Felix's grip and flailing it around in his jaws.

'Do you mind them staying?' Jimmy asked Odette worriedly when she followed him inside.

'I don't live here, babes,' she sighed, dumping the pot-plant on the table. Of course I mind! she wanted to wail. What about our bath and breakfast and bed and day of lovemaking? We can't do that now your family is here.

But she knew that Jimmy's relationship with his brothers

remained shaky. She didn't want to make it any worse. Until this week, Felix and Mungo had assumed their big brother had done a permanent bunk. Now he was back, they deserved to see him.

Sitting in the bath ten minutes later and listening to the laughter drifting up from below, Odette told herself to stop being so selfish and impatient. She and Jimmy had a lifetime to share; she shouldn't be in such a hurry to get his clothes off.

She reached a bubbly hand out and dabbed froth on Winnie's nose to cheer herself up. The little spaniel had joined her in the bathroom in a panic, afraid that Nelson would tire of savaging Handbag and pick on her again.

The smell of frying bacon had drifted upstairs and Winnie crept to the door to take an indulgent – if quiet – few sniffs, causing the foam on her nose to fly up in the air.

Clambering out of the bath and pulling the plug, Odette realised that there was no reason why she and Jimmy couldn't go to bed after breakfast anyway. They'd been up all night and needed a 'rest'. The others were bound to understand. They could go to the village for a pub lunch or something, then a long walk and maybe a cream tea. With any luck they'd be gone for hours.

Humming happily as she wrapped a towel around herself, Odette pulled open the door and walked straight into another long kiss.

'Brought you some tea up.' Jimmy handed her a mug with a wink. 'I was going to offer to rub your back, but never mind – you can do mine.' He kissed her back into the bathroom and kicked the door shut with his heel. But just as his hand had started to slide beneath her towel to loosen it, the bath let out a satisfied burp.

'You let the water out!' Jimmy spun around to see the last few inches of Captain Bubbly racing towards the plug hole. 'I said I'd take seconds.'

'Sorry, I forgot.' She hastily put the plug back in and started the taps running, feeling ridiculously like a total failure. 'Won't take a second to fill.'

But he leaned past her to turn them off again. 'There won't be enough water – it's okay. I'll wait till after breakfast.' He dropped a kiss on her clean, wet neck.

With the length of his body against her damp skin and his groin pressing against her bottom, Odette felt a pulse positively pounding away between her legs and started to loosen her grip on the towel, her nipples almost bursting out of their own accord as they hardened excitedly. But the next moment, Jimmy – who didn't seem to have noticed – was pounding downstairs again and calling over his shoulder for her to hurry up so as not to miss out on a fried egg.

Phoebe, Felix and Mungo showed no intention of going for lunch in the village, or a walk, or a cream tea. They all sat with Jimmy and Odette at the kitchen table, and talked, and talked, and talked . . .

Odette liked them all. In fact she adored them, but she yearned to get Jimmy on his own. He caught her eye all the time, his hands never left her fingers or her wrists, her arm, her cheek, her leg. Aware of his family's presence, they were all touches of affection rather than lust, but guaranteed to drive Odette into an orbit of fizzing desire in her current state. He bent to kiss her on the ear, or cheek, or mouth – mostly when he was standing up and walking past, but often while he was just sitting beside her and there was a lull in the ebb and flow of conversation. Not that there were many. Boy, could the Sylvian men talk.

Odette smiled at Phoebe as Jimmy recounted his cross-country chase the night before. Phoebe rolled her eyes to the ceiling and faked a yawn, but was secretly enthralled.

'I was so worried about Odette,' Jimmy said, stroking her cheek as he talked. 'I mean, I'd seen her for all of ten minutes since getting back from Essex, and here we were relying on each other for both our futures.'

Nice one, Jimmy, thought Odette, looking around the table expectantly. Take a hint, folks. All of *ten minutes*, he said. In a whole month. Geddit? We. Want. A. Shag.

'I'll make more tea,' Felix offered, loafing over to the sink to rinse the mugs and looking out of the window. 'Your lurcher's really got it in for Handbag, Jim.'

'That's why Winnie's looking so happy.' Jimmy laughed at the little spaniel, who was belly-up in front of the Rayburn looking quite relaxed now that she realised Nelson was going all ten rounds with the stuffed croc. 'You should stick around.' He looked up at Felix. 'You're obviously good for relations around here.'

Odette gaped at him as he squeezed her hand tightly and gave Winnie another indulgent look. Was he mad?

He didn't get to have his bath in the end. As they moved through to the sitting room and settled on sofas, Jimmy's eyes started to droop.

'Do you want to go to bed?' Odette suggested. 'Have a nap? It's been a long night.' She was ready to carry him upstairs if necessary.

'In a minute,' he yawned. 'Just finish my tea then I'll have a bath maybe. You have to scrub my back for wasting all that water.' He nuzzled her ear and Odette wriggled deliciously. A moment later and his chin was as heavy as a bowling ball on her shoulder. And then she was almost deafened by the unmistakable sound of snoring.

'I'd better wake him and make him go to bed,' she said more eagerly than she intended, carefully taking the tea mug from his hand and giving him a gentle shake.

'Need more force than that if he's anything like Felix,' laughed Phoebe who had Winnie on her lap and was doing aeroplane-wing impressions with her long ears.

Odette upped the shaking, but Jimmy just tipped over on to the sofa arm and started snoring more voraciously.

'Slap his face,' suggested Mungo from the corner of the room where he was working his way though Jimmy's record collection and sorting it into piles.

'You'll never wake him.' Felix stood up and stretched. 'He was just the same as a kid. He doesn't need much sleep, but once he's off, he's off – look.' Taking one of Mungo's record piles, he brought it down on Jimmy's head. Apart from a sleepy grunt, he didn't move.

Jimmy didn't wake all afternoon and was soon joined by Winnie, who clambered on to his snoring chest and pressed her nose against his. Even with a spaniel practically French kissing him, he snored on. Nelson had dragged his catch into an outhouse and buried poor Handbag amongst the straw before coming inside to find his master with another woman. Lying by the door, eyes narrowed, he growled resentfully from time to time. Odette felt like joining him. Instead, she showed Phoebe, Felix and Mungo around the farmhouse, where they chose the bedrooms to either side of Jimmy's. Pretty soon yawns were tugging at Odette's own mouth, reminding her that she hadn't slept in thirty-six hours.

'Why don't you get your head down for a bit?' Phoebe suggested. 'There's no food in the house, so Felix and I are going in search of a takeaway to bring something back for supper. By then Jimmy will have woken up and we can all eat together.'

Nodding, Odette headed towards a spare room.

'Aren't you going in here?' Phoebe laughed, pointing out Jimmy's room. 'Christ, you are tired, aren't you? I'll bring you a drink up just before we're ready to eat.'

Fully clothed and all alone wasn't quite the way Odette had anticipated falling into Jimmy's bed for the first time. As she closed her eyes, she was comforted by the fact that she could still hear him snoring very faintly through the floorboards.

56

When Phoebe brought Odette a drink in bed it wasn't later that evening, but first thing the next morning.

'Jimmy's just left for work,' she whispered, putting the mug on the bedside table. 'Do you know you've still got your clothes on? It's no wonder I couldn't wake you last night.' She perched on the bed.

Odette rubbed her eyes, then winced as she realised she still had her lenses in. Blinking furiously to straighten them out, she looked around the unfamiliar room, which smelled of Jimmy but showed no other sign of his recent occupancy.

'Did you say he's gone to work?' She felt absurdly disappointed that he hadn't even woken her to say good bye, let alone joined her.

'Someone from Home Farm called with a serious endive emergency.' Phoebe giggled. 'He had to drop everything and run. He was making you this tea, so I said I'd bring it up. You know he was crashed out on the sofa the entire night, the poor darling? He says he only really sleeps well when you're around.'

'I have that effect on men,' Odette said weakly, glancing at her watch. It was just after six. 'You're up early.'

'Hangover.' Phoebe rolled her eyes, still whispering. 'We drank rather a lot of Jimmy's wine last night while you two were out cold. Made up for the disgusting takeaway. Do you know how *far* the nearest Chinese is from here? My chow mein had grown cultures by the time we got it back. We stayed up planning life in Yorkshire. Felix is going to write a brilliant screenplay and I'll have lots of babies.'

Odette took a slurp of tea. 'You serious about moving there then?'

Phoebe nodded, green eyes glittering with excitement. 'Felix is all for it now, can't wait to look at cottages. We're going up there tomorrow – staying with Fliss and Dyldo until next week.' Her voice was barely audible now.

'You got a sore throat, babes?'

Phoebe put a finger to her mouth. 'No, the others are asleep and the walls here are paper-thin. Listen . . .'

True enough, Jimmy's old farmhouse seemed to have internal walls built from *papier mâché*. Odette could distinctly hear muttering.

'That's Mungo – he talks in his sleep,' Phoebe smiled fondly. 'And unlike his brothers, he's an incredibly light sleeper. I wanted to have a word with you before he gets up for work. You see, he can't come to Yorkshire with us. And he's been so happy since he worked here, I thought . . .'

'That he could stay here?' Odette looked at her mug, suddenly worrying how she and Jimmy would ever consummate their love with a light-sleeping mutterer in residence next door.

Phoebe nodded. 'He's such fun to live with and he's a great cook. You and Jimmy will love having him around.'

Odette shrugged. 'It's not up to me, babes. You'll have to ask Jimmy.'

'Perhaps you could talk to him?'

Odette suddenly felt a flash of anger on poor Mungo's behalf. 'I don't think he wants to leave you two, babes. A few weeks back, I suggested he should live here and he was dead against it.'

'That was before Jimmy came home. You two could offer him stability.'

Odette wasn't sure she and Jimmy could offer each other much stability yet – they hadn't even made it to second base – but she could hardly say that to Phoebe who was treating her like a sister-in-law already. 'You can't just pass him on like an unwanted pet, Freddy.'

'I know, I know. The thing is,' Phoebe looked deeply

647

embarrassed, glancing at the wall, 'he's already decided to stay here. He said so last night. I think you're stuck with him.'

Jimmy came to collect Odette from work that evening, still wearing the same clothes he'd had on yesterday, and this time he did pong.

'Been up to my arms in rotten vegetables all day,' he apologised, holding open the car door. 'Endive's got blight. Christ knows where from, we're so careful. It's a disaster – all that produce rotting away just a week before opening.'

Odette hadn't had a much better day. Almost all of the promotional material had been lost in the fire, plus files of contacts and ongoing work. But she didn't want to think about it. Just seeing Jimmy made her delirious with happiness – even stubbly, smelly and dirty as he was. And from the look on his face he was equally pleased to see her.

'Christ, I've missed you!' He gave her only the lightest of kisses. 'Mouth like a gumboot,' he explained. 'I'll make up for it later. Got any plans tonight?'

'No.' Odette wriggled in anticipation as she thought about her fresh sheets and naughty ideas. Well, she wasn't so hot on those but she was sure Jimmy could help her out and the flesh was more than willing, ready and able.

'Good,' he said, heading towards Siddals. 'Because Felix and Phoebe want to take us out to the pub for dinner to make up for last night. I can't believe I was stuck down on that sofa with you all alone in my bed, can you?'

Odette's skin itched with frustration throughout dinner, although the food was fantastic and the conversation as funny, varied and non-stop as it always was with the Sylvians. She knew she should be ecstatic that this cliquey, beautiful family had taken to her so easily, but she was so desperate to get Jimmy alone that she started to contemplate faking all sorts of outrageous illnesses to force him to drive her home. She only gave up on the idea when she realised this would make seduction tricky unless she faked an equally swift recovery.

'I can't wait until you meet Mother,' Mungo giggled over pudding. 'She will *so* love you, although I warn you I already know exactly what her first words will be.'

'"Who did those breasts?"' Felix did a glorious impression of his mother's syrupy voice, '"Give me his number right this minute!"'

Odette, who normally dreaded any reference to her breast size, smiled into Jimmy's eyes and chewed her lip excitedly as he winked back and had a very quick ogle. Only Jimmy could ogle with totally and utterly inoffensive charm.

Back at the farm, Phoebe and Felix excused themselves straight to bed to get ready for their early start but Mungo made himself immediately at home in the kitchen, revving up three Irish coffees in between making sporadic attempts to discipline the dogs. 'Do you think it's right to let animals perch on the kitchen chairs, Jimmy? Get down, Winnie.'

Odette looked at him sharply. Who did that remind her of?

'She's sitting up there to feel superior to Nelson,' Jimmy explained. 'Although she needn't worry because he's out in the barn with his crocodile. He's getting obsessed with that thing. I had to drag him away from it to get him in the truck this morning.'

'Well, I don't think it's right.' Mungo tipped Winnie off the chair. 'Things will have to change around here.'

Odette watched Jimmy's reaction, but he just laughed heartily and kissed her on the head. 'Too right! Starting with the sleeping arrangements. I am definitely in my own bed tonight.' A warm hand slipped beneath her hair, causing every single follicle on her body to stand to attention.

Odette felt a hot lava stream of excitement course through her belly and between her legs, then it was instantly extinguished as Mungo announced that in that case he would make their coffee stronger and his decaff.

'Although, Christ knows, I shan't sleep tonight – I'm *so* excited. You know, I didn't think I'd like living in the country, but I actually heard an owl hoot last night. Can you believe that?' He made it sound like the bicentennial mating cry of the last lesser-spotted wombat on earth. 'I hope you two aren't noisy shaggers because I've heard a rumour there are badgers around. I plan to keep an eye out later.'

The thought of Jimmy's little brother lying awake listening to their first ever seduction was like a cold shower to Odette's libido, although it quickly picked up again at the thought of her own crisp sheets in the isolated, thick-walled tower. She drank her coffee so quickly she scalded her mouth raw before suggesting that Jimmy drive her to Smock Mill.

'I don't have my contact stuff here.' She thought she should at least try for an excuse to save their blushes.

To her delight, he was already grabbing his keys from the dresser, along with a heap more clutter he'd emptied from his coat pockets earlier.

'Is this yours, Odette?' He held up a Zip disk questioningly.

She shook her head. 'They all got torched in the fire.'

Shrugging, Jimmy pocketed it and whistled for Winnie. As they got in the pick-up, they could hear Nelson still savaging Handbag in the barn.

'It gives him something to do,' Jimmy laughed, putting a hand on Odette's knee. He drove obscenely fast, but had Odette not been worried for Winnie's safety, she would have urged him to go even faster.

It all started so well. They were halfway out of their clothes before they were even through the door, tripping over discarded coats, over Winnie and over their own feet as they rushed inside, kissing all the time. By the time they were on the first level, they were down to their underwear and so happy to be free to touch anywhere and anything at last that they tried for all at once. Stroking, licking, caressing, kissing and tangling limbs and lips, they stumbled up to the next level and fell on to the bed. Odette could see Jimmy's erection poking through his pants, a glorious muscular redhead sprouting from the most beautiful lond body she had ever seen. And he was staring at her in wonder. 'You are so beautiful. So totally, totally beautiful.'

Afterwards, Odette went through various stages of apportioning blame. Firstly she blamed poor Winnie for following them upstairs and deciding to join in the fun by launching herself on to the bed with abandon before they'd even really got started. Of course, Odette could have blamed herself here for not training Winnie better, or not getting her claws trimmed in weeks, but she preferred to blame the dog. The huge red scratches the encounter left on both Odette's and Jimmy's bodies hardly added to the passion, not did the dog slobber or the hairs she and Jimmy both found in their mouths when they next kissed, trying to laugh the invasion away.

After that, there was the inferior bed linen. How was she to know the so-called King Size fitted sheet she'd bought would be so meanly cut that it sprang from each corner of the mattress after two minutes, trussing her and Jimmy together like two kids in a hammock? It was humiliating, especially as this revealed the dubious stains on Jobe's old mattress.

'It dried out years ago, and Cyd swore they were whisky not pee,' Odette gabbled as she tried to fit the sheet back on again, her bra on one tit and off the other as though she was about to breast-feed. Another passion-killer, although Jimmy laughed delightedly throughout. Again, she could have blamed herself for not fitting the sheet correctly in the first place, and for wearing her ghastly minimiser bra, but she chose not to.

Then came the lights debate. Odette wanted them off, Jimmy wanted them on. Not that they argued, but when Odette killed the switch, Jimmy manoeuvred himself around to kiss her one exposed nipple and kicked it on again with his foot. Odette kissed her way right down his body – nothing she had ever dared try on a man before but quite unexpectedly delicious and a good way of getting in position – and reached out to flip it off once more. Jimmy felt his way to her body in the dark – wonderfully erotic as fingers accidentally brushed all sorts of bits they had yet really to examine – and, spinning her back on to the mattress with such glorious force that she shrieked in delight, he hit the lights with his shoulder. This forty-watt foreplay went on for several minutes until Odette started enjoying herself far too much to care whether the lights were on or off. They stayed on. But, looking back later, she decided that leaving them on had just added to her edge of self-consciousness. For that, she blamed Cyd for not providing a decent low-watt bedside light.

Mostly, Odette blamed the condom situation. Jimmy brought it up far too early and she hadn't even thought about it. She was normally so efficient, but she hadn't bought a pack of three in years and it simply hadn't occurred to her to stock up.

'So have you got one?' he asked, kissing his way down her belly.

Odette wriggled downwards too, terrified that he was about to plunge his head between her legs. She wasn't ready for that. She wasn't sure she could cope. Why, oh, why, hadn't she bought condoms? She could do ordinary quick in-out sex, she was relatively experienced at that, and with Jimmy it was bound to be bliss. It would have made the perfect start. They could move on to more experimental things later on.

'No,' she admitted.

'Okay.' He grinned, looking even more beautiful with his hair flopping over his face as he gazed down at her. 'We'll do without.'

'No!' Odette sounded more starchy than she'd intended. 'I mean, I'm sorry, Jim, but I'm not having unpro—'

He shut her up with a kiss. 'I'm just saying we can do other things.' He started back down her belly again. 'And I've been wanting to do this for so damned long.'

'No!' Odette grabbed his hair to stop him.

'What's wrong, darling?' He stroked her belly. 'Don't you like it?'

'It's not that, it's just—' Oh, Christ, how could she explain she was hopeless at sex? That it frightened her? That she saw herself as dirty and poisoned and anaesthetised down there, however much he loved her? She'd thought it would be different with Jimmy, that she'd be able to be open and honest, but when it came down to it she was still just too bloody proud. And it had all gone so horribly wrong so quickly, before she'd

652

ad a chance to relax and confide; it was already too tainted
o enjoy. She wanted just to start out all over again, to get
he buzzing wings, the fast-moving lava, the melting chocolate
nd foaming soap-suds feeling between-the-legs back again,
ot this awful awkwardness in a brightly lit room on a badly
tting sheet.

And that led to the final fault on Odette's blame list.
mmy's misunderstanding. He jumped to the conclusion that
he didn't want him to go down on her because she was having
er period.

'You should have said, darling.' He'd cuddled her tightly,
issing her neck and stroking her belly. 'I don't mind. Have
ou got cramps? Would you like me to fetch you a hot water
ottle? You don't mind if I stay and cuddle you tonight, do
ou? Now I'm so close to your body, I never want to spend
nother night without at least one leg, one arm and one chest
air touching you.'

Lying awake later, listening to his lovely snoring, Odette
ssembled her blame list. Her body was thrumming with
rustration, aware of every contact with Jimmy's skin – and
here was a lot of that as he slept wrapped around her like
 comforting human duvet – but Odette made lists to stay
alm. Winnie. Cheap linen. Cyd's lighting. Condoms. Man's
nnate ignorance of menstruation. My crappy technique. That
vas her list. No wonder it had all gone so wrong. Tomorrow
vas another day, and she planned to start getting things right
rom the crack of dawn.

t was yet another very good start. Odette peeked under the
luvet as soon as it was light and came face-to-face with Jimmy's
norning glory. Having had plenty of opportunity to assess male
genitalia at Elsa's hen party, she was more than happy to note
hat Jimmy's was a spectacular specimen. Even its imperfections
eemed magnificently well-suited. It leaned a little to the left
only fitting for a guilty liberal) and had a big blue vein running
ip it (well, he was practically blue-blooded after all) and was
erhaps a little more purple on top than she remembered others

being (nothing wrong with having lots up top). No, she loved everything about it. She was almost tempted to get cracking straight away and kiss it (something she had definitely never done before) but she was dying for a wee and she wanted to clean her teeth before she kissed anything – her mouth felt like a bear's pit.

Getting ready for her second assault on seduction took longer than she'd anticipated. She couldn't find her glasses, Winnie needed letting out, the boiler had packed up and needed relighting, and Cyd had thrust a long rambling note under the door – obviously written when pissed – apparently saying that this week's rent was due. Odette looked at it for a long time, trying to remember if they had ever discussed rent. She was happy to pay it, but she needed to know how much.

When she finally got around to cleaning her teeth she'd already been up twenty minutes and was leaping with excitement. She could hear Jimmy still snoring and decided to have a quick wash between her legs, which was already slippery and therefore, Odette suspected, smelly. But further investigation revealed three days' stubble on her legs. Not wanting Jimmy to see her as less than perfect, Odette dedicated herself to the full works, quickly lathering herself under the shower. She was just bending down to Bic her ankles when she felt a hand slither across her back. 'Morning.'

'Aghh! Shit!'

'Oh, Christ! Oh, God, I'm sorry. Jesus, it's like a bloodbath. Get *back*, Winnie. I'll get something to stem the bleeding.' Jimmy reappeared with two tea towels – one to mop up the flood of red water, the other to cover his wilting hard-on.

'It's all right – ankles always bleed like mad,' Odette explained later over a cup of tea, all thoughts of the Second Assault abandoned in the wake of so much blood. 'It's only a nick.'

Jimmy drove her to work in high spirits, despite the disastrous night. 'I'll pick you up later. Shall we eat at Siddals? I'll make Mungo stay in his room and listen to records or whatever it is you're supposed to do.'

'No, my place.' Odette decided she'd have to do something

out Mungo's choice of bedrooms. 'I've got to pay Cyd
r rent.'

'Cyd's asking for rent?'

She nodded, spotting Florian standing sullenly outside the
od Hall entrance smoking a cigarette. 'Oh, great, I hoped
'd be here today. Look, I've got to dash, babes. I love you.
you get a chance, buy some condoms,' she whispered before
owing him a kiss and slamming the door. She laughed as she
w him drive away punching a high five.

Florian was waiting for her.

'I talk to *les Dens* last night, *oui*?' He kissed her hello on
th cheeks. 'Dennis, he say he give you the sketches, but he
ant somesink in return.'

Odette had been dreading this, although she knew to expect
'I don't have any money, Florian. I mean, nothing like I'd
ed to buy—'

'Like I tell you, he is not interested in money.' He ushered
r into the topiary walk beside the house. 'Ronny, she film
e all day so I haff to talk to you quickly, *oui*? Dennis want
mesink for his art. You know he puts sings in plastic?'

'In Perspex? Yes, I – oh, no, not that.' Odette suddenly
membered her one and only conversation with Dennis
hirsk, when he had asked her for the by-product of any
east-reduction she may have.

But when Florian told her what Dennis actually wanted,
e burst out laughing. 'Well, it might be just as hard to get
what I was thinking of, but nowhere near as painful. When
e you seeing him again? I'll see what I can do.'

've got the condoms.' Jimmy grinned, showing Odette the
acket as they belted towards Smock Mill that evening. She
as gratified to see that he'd bought a pack of eighteen, so
ey could have lots and lots of practice at getting it right. She
as certain tonight would be much better.

'Shall we go straight to the tower?' she suggested. 'I can
op in on Cyd – later.' She almost said afterwards, but that
unded far too crass.

This time there was no Winnie to fall over, and the were less impatient, removing their clothes, kissing with leisurely delight, slowly letting hands dive and delve and unbutton.

Which meant they were still just about decent when Cyd burst in through the door.

'There you are, dearheart – and Jimmy too! How lovely I can't believe we've none of us seen each other since the assault on Fermoncieaux, can you?' She made it sound like a noble WWI battle. 'Now you must both come over for a drink straight away, and I won't take no for an answer.' She clapped her hands together.

'No.' Odette thought it was at least worth a go.

'Come on.' Cyd handed Jimmy and Odette their jackets

'Will we need these?' Odette shrugged hers on. 'I thought you said we were having a drink.'

'It's still raining and Calum and I have to show you something first.'

He was waiting in the old stable yard, looking absurd in breeches and long riding boots matched with his standard pork-pie hat and yellow glasses. He had a lot of mud on his backside indicating several falls, but his usually dour face was wreathed in smiles. 'Come and look at these beauties Pure-bred Arabs and fast as Lear Jets.'

Two mad, inbred but undeniably pretty faces bobbed over the stable doors.

Having admired the new acquisitions – named Drum and Cymbal – Odette and Jimmy trailed into the house behind the happy couple. Jimmy squeezed her hand as they walked whispering, 'One quick drink and we'll beat a path. I told you we should have gone to Siddals.'

'I need a word with her anyway,' Odette reminded him realising that as soon as she had done so, she and Jimmy could run back to the tower and get naked. The thought made her want to sing.

Cyd allowed no words to be inserted between hers, edgeways or otherwise, as she poured out vast whiskies and purred in throaty ecstasy about her incredible bravery 'with no though or my own safety, dearhearts'. Having relived the siege, she moved on to her beautiful horses.

'Do you think I should offer Drum and Cymbal to Lydia or the wedding?' she asked Odette. 'She and Finlay would ook so ravishing riding up to Fermoncieaux on them.'

'Slightly less ravishing when they bolt past all their guests nd disappear over the horizon.' Jimmy's laughter boomed out nto the room.

'Oh,' Cyd looked mortally offended.

'I think they've got their transport all sorted, Cyd,' Odette aid kindly, trying not to giggle. 'And the weather looks a it iffy.'

'Yes, yes, maybe you're right – awful to sit through one's wedding smelling of wet horse.' She nodded sympathetically. 'Now, while Calum's dosing us all up, can we discuss the little natter of rent?'

'Oh, yes.' Odette scrabbled in her bag, noticing that Calum was filling Jimmy's glass straight through the fingers he had put across it to say no. Great timing, Cyd. 'I haven't got much cash, I'm afraid, but I thought a hundred pounds would be okay for now.'

'For what?' Cyd snapped. 'A night?'

'No, a week.'

'Dearheart,' Cyd inserted herself between Odette and Jimmy with some difficulty and cocked her head beguilingly, 'you know I would love you to stay on rent-free – or even for some sort of peppercorn rent like you're offering – but as you know I'm downsizing my business interests.' She let out a regretful sigh. 'I've checked it against similar-sized properties and I'm afraid I can't accept less than seven hundred and fifty.'

'A month?' Odette baulked.

'A week.'

'Where are these properties?' Jimmy laughed drily. 'Hampstead?'

'The smock mill is entirely unique. There's not another like it.'

'Unique price, too.' Jimmy rolled his eyes. 'Well, it's immaterial, because Odette's coming to live with me.'

'What?' Cyd gaped at him. So did Calum. So did Odette for that matter.

'From tomorrow, Odette will be living at Siddals.'

Opening her mouth to protest that she might like to have some say in the matter, Odette suddenly closed it again. She loved Siddals. She loved Jimmy. She couldn't wait to live there with him.

'And so this is farewell, my little vixen.' Cyd's eyes were full of tears as she geared up for another theatrical soliloquy. 'I hope you will look back on our time together and realise that I have helped, in some small measure, to get you back on your feet.' She took a deep breath to say more, but Odette saw that Jimmy was close to explosion on her other side and so quickly jumped in.

'Of course I will. You've been helpful beyond measure, Cyd.'

'Oh – yes, well, I suppose I have.' Cyd looked pleased. 'And if there's *anything* I can do to help you on your way now that your broken wing has healed and you can fly—'

'Actually there is one thing.' Odette hoped she didn't sound too precipitate.

'Go on?' Cyd looked miffed, so she clearly did.

'Well, it's rather private . . .' Odette looked over Cyd's shoulder and pulled an apologetic face at Jimmy, who rolled his eyes and then grinned. She knew he was as desperate as she was to get this over with and get back to naughty pursuits in the mill.

Clapping her hands together, Cyd was thrilled. 'Oh, girl talk – I understand. The advice of an older woman is invaluable at times like this. Calum, dearheart, why don't you and Jimmy go to the games room or something?'

'Sure.' Calum raised an eyebrow. 'Actually there's something I've been meaning to talk to you about, Jimmy pal.'

As soon as Odette explained what she needed, Cyd burst into delighted peals of laughter. She laughed so much that she cried. 'My dear, dear Odette, I would never have expected in a million ears to be asked for that – least of all by you. How utterly elightful. You are full of surprises this week.'

Odette wasn't sure what she meant by that but pressed on, ardly able to believe Cyd was taking it so well. 'You mean, ou really don't mind?'

She thought about it for a bit and then shook her head. 'I hink it's rather a lovely testimony to his life – and civic statues re so dull, aren't they? This is so unusual and quite the most ovel way of remembering his talent I've ever heard of – and e really was quite wonderfully gifted in that department before he drink got him. No, I don't mind at all. Thank goodness I ever throw anything out. Let's go in search, shall we? How nany pairs did you say you needed?'

'What d'you suppose they're up to?' Calum asked curiously s he heard Cyd and Odette giggling their way upstairs.

'As long as she's not indoctrinating Odette into some weird antric sex ritual, I'm not bothered.' Jimmy shrugged, squinting p at the fifty-inch flat-screen monitor Calum had rigged up in he games room. 'How do you do this again?'

Calum took his joystick and showed him. 'You should try antric sex, Jim – it's quite good. Just takes time and lots of neditation.'

Jimmy looked at him in amazement, but Calum's eyes were ixed on the screen once more. 'See how good the graphics re? There's nothing else like it in the country. I had to get his sent over from Japan – it's still a prototype.'

Jimmy wasn't particularly interested in computer games and Calum knew it. He'd always failed to understand his friend's utter fascination with a world that doesn't exist, but then again immy guessed a lot of things Calum believed in hadn't really appened.

'So why did you get me here?' He gave up as his racing ar once again crashed and burned. Now benefiting from a guilty conscience courtesy of Cyd, Calum was taking forever o get to the point but he clearly wanted something. 'Spit it ut because Odette and I have much more important things o do.' He couldn't help a big smile crossing his face.

Jimmy was so entranced by the thought that he didn't

see Calum wince and crash his own virtual car into a barrier.

'I want you to sign Ronny Prior's release form.' Calum turned to look at him, the car bursting into a ball of fire on the screen behind him.

Jimmy shook his head. 'You know I won't do that. And besides, I thought that was Odette's jurisdiction now?'

'She sure as hell won't ask you, so I am. Believe me, Jim, it could make all the difference to Food Hall's future. You have to let them use you in the show.'

'I don't want to be immortalised by cathode ray.' Jimmy looked up at the huge screen in front of him. 'It's the cheapest way of selling your soul in the world.'

'She just wants to do a face-to-face interview. It's no fucking *Faustus*. If you agree to do it, I promise I'll get the sketches back for you, whatever it takes.' He shuddered at the prospect. 'I'll even fucking frame them so Odette never need know what's written on the back – nor your wee brees for that matter. We'll forget the deal. You'll still keep your ten percent so you never have to sell the bloody things.'

'All that in exchange for my fifteen minutes of fame?' Jimmy shook his head. 'Why is it I get the feeling I'll be the framed one here?'

Calum scowled at him, unable to believe the ingratitude. Couldn't the man see an olive branch when he was being offered one? The deal was more than generous. All Calum was seeking was a little humility from the man who'd won Odette's heart.

'I'll leave you to think about it while I check on the horses.' Saying this with some satisfaction, he left the room.

Jimmy buried his head in his hands. He could still hear Odette and Cyd laughing upstairs; a moment later the door banged as Calum headed outside. Looking up, Jimmy watched the cars still burning on the huge screen, the graphics as clear as Calum had promised. He felt like it was his own heart going up in flames. He couldn't drag his eyes from the picture now, remembering the twisted wreck he'd seen after Florrie had died, trying to remember what it had looked like when it was still a car, trying not to imagine . . .

He was desperate to get rid of the picture, but nothing on the joysick would respond. In the end, he flipped out the game's disk, noticing as he did so that it was the same type he had in his pocket.

In search of a distraction to take his mind off the image of the car, Jimmy fished the disk out of his jacket and inserted it. It started to play straight away.

He didn't notice the back door slam again, nor did he see the games room door open a fraction before quickly closing again. His eyes were glued to the screen, his ears too full of the sound of rushing blood to hear anything. It was only when he pulled the disk from the slot and furiously snapped it in two that he realised feet were thundering downstairs and Cyd was saying. 'You, my darling Odette, have just sampled the contents of a legend's trousers.'

'What's the matter?' Odette asked as they walked back to the tower together. She was certain that Calum must have said something to upset Jimmy when they were alone together. She was bubbling over with excitement and anticipation again, but he seemed dour and distant.

'Nothing.' He looked at the bag she was carrying, clearly eager for a change of subject. 'What's in there?'

'Pants!' she laughed, pouncing on the chance to cheer him up by fishing out some extraordinary tiger-skin seventies Y-fronts. 'They were Jobe's. They're for a new exhibition Dennis Thirsk is putting together called "Under Where? Underground". He plans to set dead icons' pants in Perspex, can you believe that?'

'Isn't that a bit sick?'

'Totally.' Odette let them into the tower, waiting for Winnie to chase them inside. 'But that's modern art, and it turns out Dennis is one of the biggest Mask fans ever – he followed them everywhere as a kid. So when Florian asked me if I would—'

'Florian?' Jimmy interrupted, sounding extraordinarily terse.

Still feeling incredibly pleased with herself, and wanting to shake him out of his black mood, Odette decided to tell Jimmy about the sketches. She could just imagine his face when she announced that he was going to get them back any day now. 'Oh, Jimmy, there's something I'm just dying to get off my chest and you mustn't be mad at me for keeping it a secret until now. You see, I was with Florian in the Food Hall kitchens the other day and we got a bit pissed and—'

But Jimmy had heard enough. Covering his face with his hands, he said the one thing guaranteed to shut her up fast. 'Jobe died in a car crash, didn't he?'

Suddenly scorched with guilt, Odette nodded. 'Oh, God, I'm sorry, Jimmy. I didn't think.'

'Forget it.' He turned away, deeply ashamed for using it against her.

When she got into bed after cleaning her teeth, Jimmy had his back turned to her and the light switched off. Odette knew he was only pretending to be asleep because he wasn't snoring. She snuggled up to him, dropping light kisses on his back. 'Jimmy? Jimmy, babes?'

When he didn't respond, she wondered whether he was playing some sort of game. It would be just like Jimmy to wait until she'd given up before rolling over like a ship in a storm to tickle her. She reached over the arm that he had clamped to his side and started to stroke his chest, to draw circles around the tiny nipples, to delve lower, daring herself to take his beautiful lop-sided cock in her hand.

It felt sleepily soft and warm. Odette worked it a little, kneading and stroking, teasing and caressing. She wasn't certain what she was doing, but as soon as she felt it starting to respond, to stir and shift, she bit her lip happily. It was so lovely and exciting to feel it change in her hands. She felt powerful and wonderfully erotic.

'Does that feel good?' she asked cautiously.

Jimmy didn't answer, but she could hear his breath quickening.

Gaining in confidence, she increased the pressure a little. She ran her fingers along the big blue vein and around the smooth, taut tip. Because she had avoided anything this intimate before, she wasn't certain where to go, but she stroked everything, opping more kisses on Jimmy's back, getting more and more xcited by what she was doing and the effect it was having.

'We're going to enjoy this so much, babes.' She sank her eth gently into his shoulder as she remembered Beatrice Dalle oing in *Betty Blue*, her hand moving faster and faster. 'It's so eautiful,' she breathed, thinking how much sexier it was than the Stage Stags' – huge and lop-sided and full of enthusiasm, quite the most beautiful thing ever.'

But then it suddenly seemed to grow soft again. Odette antically tried to stop it, but it was slipping out of her grip ke grains of sand.

When Jimmy spoke, his voice was choked with unhappiness. 'lease don't, Odette.'

'What?'

He didn't move, his face still turned away from her. 'Please op it. Just go to sleep.'

Rolling over to face the other wall, Odette let her tears slide n to the pillow and into her ears and hair as she realised she'd iled the test once and for all. Even Jimmy no longer found her esirable. She was absolutely, categorically, the worse lay in the rorld. When she finally heard the rumbling echo of his snore, ie could let herself cry out loud, great mournful sobs echoing rrough the mill until Winnie crept upstairs to lick her face.

The next morning, piggy-eyed, she asked him whether he ill wanted her to move into the farm with him.

'Of course I do, Odette. I love you.' He gave her a tight hug, ut when she stretched up to kiss him, he patted her on the back nd pulled away, pointing out that they had a lot to do. He was in a reird mood – brusque and father-like, yet still strangely affection-te. And then she realised where she had seen it before. It was the vay he treated his brothers when he was annoyed by their excesses, y what he pompously saw as their self-destructive depravity.

Watching him packing her stuff into the pick-up, occasionally ausing to give her shy, sad smiles, she decided she could live vithout sex for now. She'd coped without sex for years – it vas living without love that had almost killed her.

*   *   *

Calum's London flat had been empty for weeks. He'd already had an offer for it from Wayne Street, who loved the place but because it was mortgaged up to the hilt, Calum had been dabbling with the idea of taking inspiration from Cyd and renting it out for a vastly overinflated sum instead. Now he changed his mind.

'How quickly can you get me the cash?' he asked Wayne that morning.

Wayne was wily enough to know a desperate man when he heard one, and he knocked twenty thousand off his offer. To his amazement, Calum agreed without argument just so long as he had the money in his hands the next day.

He could sort it out with the building society later. Right now he needed to speak with Denny Rees. But when Calum finally got him on the phone late that afternoon, Denny had some news that made him slump down in a chair in despair. 'The Knife's sold them, mate, dunno who to. I fought you'd be pleased? It means you're in the clear. Not that I'd put it past him to come looking for you still after you've mucked him about like this,' he added menacingly.

But Calum wasn't relieved that he was in the clear. If the sketches were in the wrong hands, Jimmy stood to lose everything. The moment he appeared all over the nation's television screens on *Food Fights*, it was only a matter of time before whoever had Jocelyn's letter put two and two together and made a fortune at his friend's expense. And Calum had been the one who'd goaded him into the public eye in the first place, forcing him into a position where he stood to be recognised after years of anonymity in Africa.

He raced to Fermoncieaux to find Jimmy, tracking him down knee-deep in organic herbs in the kitchen garden.

'You dinnae have to do the interview,' panted Calum.

'Too late.' Jimmy straightened up, his eyes narrow with anger. 'I did it this morning.' He handed Calum a clutch of sprigs. '"Here's rosemary; that's for remembrance." Remember when we used to be friends?' With that he walked away.

*　　*　　*

Mungo was delighted when Odette moved into his brother's house. He offered to cook them both a big moving-in-together meal, but Jimmy and Odette suddenly started working late into the evenings, often not returning until after midnight. Feeling lonely, Mungo befriended Winnie and even managed to coax Nelson away from Handbag to join them over chocolate drops in the kitchen.

'I have no idea why Jimmy claims that these two fight,' he told Phoebe when she called from Yorkshire to see how he was getting on. 'They seem to get on like a Food Hall on fire – get *off* the couch, Winnie!'

'Don't say couch, Mungo, it's terribly American. Say sofa.'

'You sound just like Felix,' he giggled. 'I'm longing to be a sofa potato, if only Jimmy would get a television. He absolutely exploded last night when I said we'll have to get one for when *Food Fights* is aired. Talk about mean – he's robbing me of my chance to watch myself on primetime and I've got *the* most sensational suit for the wedding.'

The build-up to the weekend's wedding was causing frantic activity at Food Hall and both Jimmy and Odette were flat out, collapsing into bed late at night.

They chatted about their days, laughed and scrapped, rubbed tired tense muscles into sleepy submission and said how much they loved each other, but they still could not make love. They made fumbled, embarrassed attempts, but Jimmy couldn't perform and Odette couldn't relax enough to help him. He blamed tiredness, but she knew it was her fault. After each fruitless try they kept their distance in the darkness, falling asleep back to back like strangers. It was only when they woke up in the morning that they found their bodies had turned around and curled together like two entwined roots.

Downstairs, Winnie and Nelson had no such qualms. They had taken to sleeping together on the sofa, shaggy grey hair nestling companionably against silky skewbald, legs twitching and chests rising and falling as one dreamed of chasing rabbits, the other of slaying crocodiles.

57

Lydia's wedding day was well documented. Not because a famous tennis star's daughter was marrying the son of the biggest Pools winner on record, nor because it was the first function at Food Hall.

The day itself was legendary. It followed the night of the biggest storm on record in England since the fifties. Hurricane winds, monsoon rain, tropical lightning and explosive power cuts looked set to welcome the guests at what was destined to be the most luxurious country-house retreat in England. News bulletins reported millions of pounds' worth of damage nation-wide and warned the public to stay indoors and avoid travelling at all costs.

'It's not a very good omen, is it?' Cyd asked cheerfully on the morning of the big day, as force-ten winds threatened to blow the cap from the smock mill and lift the roofs off the barns.

Finlay, who had spent the night before his wedding at the farm, looked up worriedly as his brother staggered back into the kitchen from the yard, fighting to close the door against the wind. Calum had lost his hat and his hair was plastered to his face, his shoulders black with rain. 'You can hardly walk oot there.'

'I just tried to call Lydia but the phones here are all down,' Finlay gibbered.

'She'll be fine, pal, her family are there to look after her.' Calum took off his yellow glasses to wipe the water from them. 'The horses are going nuts. I tried to give them that herbal stuff like you said, Cyd, but they're too frightened to eat.'

But she had far more urgent worries to dwell on.

'I hope my hat stays on,' she fretted, looking out of the

window as Calum's missing leather pork pie flew past ten feet off the ground.

Odette was making breakfast for ten people at Siddals Farm, tripping over dogs and baby-changing bags en route between Rayburn and toaster as she slithered fried duck eggs on to doorstep slices of toast.

'Get a wiggle on, Juno babes!' she yelled up the stairs, not noticing the contents of the plate she was carrying being licked by Nelson. She turned back to the kitchen. 'Jay, can you get that wife of yours out of bed? That bleedin' documentary crew will be here any minute, and we're supposed to be at Fermoncieaux in less than an hour. Lydia will be going spare. D'you want to take her an egg up?' She offered him the plate.

'I'll pass, thanks.' He gave it, and Nelson, a wide berth.

Jimmy had offered the farmhouse to Odette's friends and fellow bridesmaids. The bridesmaids were due to meet Lydia at Fermoncieaux to change in the private suite of rooms on the first floor which had been intended as Calum's home but remained just empty shells now he lived with Cyd. Thankfully they had been untouched by the fire on the floor above and were still deemed safe.

Jimmy had dashed to Fermoncieaux at first light to assess the damage, calling at regular intervals to let Odette know the worst and to whinge about the documentary team who had braved the weather to get startling shots of tables and chairs flying past at head height. After Ronny's windswept crew had got their fill at Food Hall, they planned to call on Lydia's cottage for some preparation footage and then move on to Siddals Farm to capture the bridesmaids *au naturel*.

Crowded around the kitchen table, Ally and Duncan and Elsa and Euan were cooing over their respective progeny, Miss Bee was doing the *Telegraph* crossword, and Mungo and Jez were flirting outrageously with one another – much as they had been the previous evening. Nobody looked remotely ready to get dressed and rally round to help out at Food Hall despite Odette's goading. Jimmy had insisted that she stay behind to look after them, but she longed to be with him right now; she needed his solidity and his loud voice to snap them all into action.

The phone rang again. Odette tripped over a baby buggy and Winnie as she raced to grab it.

'Jimmy?' she asked eagerly. 'How's it going, babes?'

'It's Lydia,' spluttered a tearful voice. 'I don't think I want to go through with this, Odie. I feel sick and I've plucked my eyebrows all wrong.'

'Calm down, babes,' Odette soothed. 'It's going to be fine. Don't let the weather put you off.'

'What weather? Is it raining?' Lydia asked vaguely. 'I had a Mogadon last night and still feel a bit groggy.'

Odette chewed her lip worriedly. 'Haven't you looked outside yet?'

'No, the curtains are shut although it's a bit noisy. I thought it was farm machinery or something – hang on.' There was a rustling and then a loud shriek of alarm. 'Oh my God! There's a tree across our drive! It's landed on Daddy's Lexus.'

The only way to get to Fermoncieaux was by four-wheel drive across the fields. The lanes were all blocked by fallen trees, which the estate workers, dragged from their beds in the small hours, were now frantically trying to saw up and haul away in order to let the wedding traffic through later that day.

Odette just about had her gang of bridesmaids gathered and was preparing to pile them into Jobe Francis's US Army Jeep when Ronny Prior trundled up in the French Merchant OB van.

'Couldn't get through to Lydia's cottage.' She leaped out of the van. 'Trees in the way – only made it here by the skin of our teeth. Any chance of twenty minutes' footage of you lot getting up and realising there's a hurricane?'

'Most of us have been up since six,' Ally pointed out huffily. 'And we know there's a bloody storm. My daughter didn't stop crying all night and I'm seven months pregnant.'

'Wonderful!' Ronny beamed. 'Can you try to recreate that?'

*　　*　　*

Odette was certain that Lydia and Finlay wouldn't get married. Everything appeared to be conspiring against them. The weather, Lydia's nerves, Calum's brooding disapproval. The latter was the most threatening and unpredictable of all the negative influences. She was certain he had something up his sleeve.

She took the quad bike and headed for Lydia's cottage, zipping along the all-too-familiar sheep drives of the estate – now covered with branches, some so big she had to get off and haul them out of the way. When she reached the brow of the hill that divided the Fulkington valley from Fermoncieaux, she dropped the engine to a ticking rev. The wind was slicing right through her and rain seemed to seep into every crevice of her body like liquid nitrogen, chilling it to the core. She could see the devastation the storm had wrought all around. Trees were felled from the root, fence posts lay like Picastix on field borders, their wires tangled. There were branches everywhere and huge floods were making lakes of fields.

Odette wondered what sort of malicious spell Calum had cast.

The tree in front of Lydia's cottage was being chain-sawed into pieces, but was still blocking the entire entrance. Odette heaved a sigh of relief as she spotted Calum's sinister silver car parked in front of it. He was sitting inside, alone, listening to Robbie Williams. He'd put on his favourite Armani suit for the wedding, with a rose button-hole and a shiny acid yellow Paul Smith shirt that clashed with his hair but was this season's statement buy. Odette slipped in beside him, making him jump.

'Don't drip on my upholstery,' he muttered.

She ignored him. 'D'you think they'll do it, babes?'

He shrugged. 'Even if they don't, it'll be a bloody good party.'

Odette studied him closely. 'You really don't mind what they do?'

He shook his head. 'I figure it's their call. I can't control Fin any longer. He's stopped being fucked up all of a sudden.'

'So you're all alone on that one?' Odette looked at him. 'Carrying on the family tradition.'

Suddenly smiling, Calum said nothing. He just tipped his head back and stared at the roof of the car.

Her favourite song came on. Odette closed her eyes as Robbie blasted out 'Angel' straight into her chest, peppering it with bullets of friendly fire.

'When are you going to stop being fucked up, Calum?' she breathed.

He took what seemed like minutes to respond, although Robbie had only moved on a few lines. 'I've got a way to go yet. You helped me a lot. I'm glad you and Jimmy have worked out.'

'You *didn't* help a lot.' Odette smiled sadly, looking out of the window and remembering her old dream of cutting to the chase and missing out on all the passion in order to get straight to cosy *Hart to Hart* coupledom. Now she'd done that it wasn't a dream come true at all. She loved Jimmy with all her heart, but she felt almost more rejected and sexless than she had when she'd been single for years.

'It has worked out, hasn't it?' Calum looked at her worriedly.

'Sure, babes.' She wasn't about to tell him about her sexual problems, even if he did pride himself on being the poison-arrow Cupid who'd got them together in the first place. 'And you and Cyd?'

He scrunched his face up as he thought about it. 'She's like a truth drug – I can't keep secrets from her. And I haven't made her sleep with Florian, so I guess I'm making progress.' He let out a sardonic laugh. Then he twisted his mouth guiltily as he peered out of the windscreen at the tree removal. 'Jesus, I'm sorry about that, sister. But I guess Cyd's truth drugs worked for you too. Christ, you're brave being up front with Jimmy about it, even giving him that disk, especially with his heritage. I only wish you'd told me what you were planning to do before I started that fire. You could have saved me the bother.'

'What on earth are you talking about?' Odette froze.

'The surveillance footage from the OD.' Calum swung around to look at her.

As the wind buffeted the car from side to side, Odette

ught the urge to throw up. 'You bastard! You told him, dn't you?'

'I didn't fucking give it to him!' Calum stormed indignantly. nd I've never breathed a word about it. I tried to burn it, for hrissake. If Jimmy doesn't have your copy, then . . . Shit! I ought it was still in the computer.' He rubbed his face as the uth dawned. 'Florian has the only other copy. He'd been trying log it on to the net – he thought he could quash these gay imours that are knocking about. Jimmy must have got hold f it somehow, but couldn't look at it because the Food Hall imputers had all been torched. That's why he was using the ie in the farm Tuesday night. I thought he'd put it on to show ie that he didn't give a fuck what I threatened, but the poor astard was seeing it for the very first time. On a screen the size f a fucking cinema's.'

'Oh, Christ.' Odette felt great tears splashing out of her eyes. No wonder he didn't want to . . .' She started to sob. Reaching r the door handle she tried to get out, but she couldn't make it ork. Howling in fury, she tried to kick and punch it open until alum grabbed her hands to stop her. 'Get off me! This is all your loody fault, you fucking pervert. If Jimmy hadn't seen that tape verything would be all right. Instead he can't bear to touch me, in't bring himself to . . .' She couldn't finish, pressing the balls f her hands tightly into her eye sockets.

'Blame Florian, not me.' Calum was clearly worried she was oing to start beating him up. 'It's the only tape he ever wanted keep. You made quite an impression. If you were a guy I think e'd propose. Maybe that's why he gave it to Jimmy.'

Odette slammed her fists on the dashboard. 'The double-rossing shit! I should have known there'd be a bigger price to ay than Jobe's moth-eaten pants. Life's just an ironic joke to him. Ie's probably suggested that Dennis Thirsk Perspex-wraps iso-ted stills of that surveillance tape and calls it "Anal-by-mouth". 'll bet he hasn't even got the sketches. For all I know, The Knife alive and kicking.'

'What?' Calum gripped tightly on to the wheel.

Odette closed her eyes. 'Florian's supposed to be giving me immy's Picasso sketches at the wedding. Dennis had them all along – it was part of some elaborate joke at your expense. Now I'm the one paying the price with Jimmy.' She started to cry again the moment she said his name. 'I thought this way he might start to fancy me again, might . . .' She couldn't go on.

To her horror, Calum started to laugh. 'Dennis the Menace you fucking bastard! I mightae guessed.'

Odette had another go at getting out of the car, this time trying to force the door with a series of body slams.

'Whoah, stop it!' Calum was trying hard to curtail his laughter. 'Don't you see? This makes it all right, sister. You and Jimmy just have to tell the truth at last – and Christ, I never thought *I'* be the one to tell you that. In fact, I'll do better. I'll tell you th truth myself.'

He punched the car into gear as a tree clearer signalled for him to reverse a few feet. 'You probably don't know that after Jocelyn's death, Jimmy found a stack of home videos his father had made of himself screwing different women. It really did Jimmy's head in.' Catching her eye as he swung around to reverse Calum smiled apologetically.

'Oh, Christ.' Odette buried her head in her hands. 'Are you trying to torture me?'

He braked. 'That letter written on the back of the sketche you're so keen to deliver back to Jimmy describes the plot of one of the movies Jocelyn was most proud of. One Jimmy starred in too.'

'No!' Odette yelped, covering her ears.

Calum pulled her hands away. 'But, you see, that video wasn' with the others when Jimmy found them in Barbados. It wa made on a much bigger budget and had a much wider – if very exclusive – distribution. I have a copy; many of my friends have copies – it's quite a collector's item. Unfortunately old Jimmy doesn't get a credit. Nor does anyone else for that matter.'

'What are you talking about?'

'In her long and varied career, Philomena Rialto made a great many movies. The majority bombed, most went straight to TV. but only one was banned from this country. Not that she's ever admitted starring in it, which is odd given that it's attracted more press over the years than almost any film ever made. It's a cult classic – there's even a rumour that Kubrick directed it although that's never been proven. The band Mask was named in its honour. You know what I'm talking about now, Odette?'

She nodded mutely, staring out of the window as the huge tree-trunk was cleaved apart. She felt like the chainsaw was ripping into her own flesh. Everyone knew about that film, although she'd never met anyone who'd actually seen it. She knew there had long been rumours that the female star was Philomena – it was popular folklore, although just as many people claimed it was Bardot or Birkin or Pallenberg. She'd even heard somewhere that Cyd had starred in it and that's why Jobe married her.

'As I'm sure you haven't seen it, I will very briefly describe the plot: a masked woman is taken every conceivable which way by a masked man. Only now, it seems, she also *con*ceived her first child during filming – while the cameras were rolling. Who'd have guessed that the masked man was none other than her own husband, literary giant Jocelyn Sylvian? That's one rumour I'd never heard. Quite a scoop, don't you think? It's all in the letter, in unnecessarily graphic detail. Jimmy's birthright – the ultimate home video described on the back of two Picasso sketches, the most valuable things Jocelyn had left in his possession. The old bastard knew that by doing that he'd made sure Jimmy would never be able to sell them or give them to his brothers.'

'Why are you telling me all this?' Odette wailed. 'Poor, poor Jimmy. Oh, Christ, he must hate me for what I've done.'

'He doesn't hate you. He loves you. That's why he didn't want you to know all this, in just the same way you kept your biggest secret from him. You both think the other won't be able to handle it, and look at you now – are you packing your bags? Has Jimmy thrown you out of Siddals Farm because he's seen the tape? He moved you into his house the very next morning, didn't he?'

'Yes,' Odette said in a small voice. Calum Forrester, relationship counsellor and love guru. Who would have thought it?

'All you've got to do is tell Jimmy the truth – why you fucked Florian, and when. Jimmy can't tell one kitchen from another, for all he knows it was last week.'

673

'But what makes you so sure he'll forgive me?'

'Don't you see, you thick bitch?' Calum cut the engine 'He'd do anything for you. You'd do anything for him. You don't understand what there is to forgive here, and neither does he – he just doesn't think he can give you what you want and it's crucifying him. Now push off and find him. I'll see that Fir and Lydia get to the wedding even if there is no ceremony.'

Jimmy was trying to re-erect a marquee when Odette tracked him down. The wind had dropped dramatically, but rain still lashed his ruddy face and flattened his tawny hair.

'I've lost my erection!' he announced cheerfully as he saw her mulching through the sodden, twig-strewn lawn.

Odette winced.

'Is Lydia okay?' he asked as she drew close, handing his rope to someone else and drawing her to one side.

All this jolly camaraderie was too much for Odette to take.

'I know you saw the video of me and Florian,' she said, wiping wet tendrils of hair back from her forehead. 'And I know what's written on the back of those sketches.'

'Who told you that?'

'It doesn't matter,' she sighed sadly. 'Is that why you can't make love to me?'

His bruised blue eyes looked away, skirting the top of the clipped yew walkways. 'I can't give you what you want, Odette. I know I'm prudish and old-fashioned and, God, I love you to hell and heaven and purgatory and Ruislip and back, but I'm never going to match up to that . . . to what you . . .' He frantically tried to rub the deep, troubled grooves from his forehead. 'This thing, that bloody tape, it's opened up a whole hell pit in my head. You were right all along just wanting me as your friend. I've pushed it too far and totally fucked up, haven't I? And now you know why, I'll understand if you want to move out. I know I'm never going to make you happy.'

'Can we go to bed?' Odette's teeth were chattering.

ydia and her tableau were squabbling as they dressed in the
rivate suite. Garment bags were strewn everywhere along with
roissant crumbs and champagne foil. Only one garment bag was
ill hanging from the picture rail.

'This is so unlike her,' Juno was saying as she munched on
Danish pastry. 'She definitely said she'd be here by ten.'

'Maybe there's some sort of crisis on elsewhere in the house?'
lly suggested.

'Oh, spare me!' Lydia was flapping as she balanced her
ead-dress on her perfectly sculpted white-blonde Princess
Grace chignon which had taken her hairdresser, Robin, almost
n hour to perfect. 'What d'you think, my darlings? Too
airytale?'

Juno choked on her pastry, Ally's mouth hung open, Elsa
lmost dropped Florence and Miss Bee let out a loud wolf
vhistle.

'Aren't you going to put your dress on?' Juno spluttered.

'Don't be silly, Joo,' Lydia giggled. 'This *is* my dress.'

eeling off her wet clothes, Odette tried not to show how much
he was shaking as she draped them over a chair back and then
lipped into bed beside Jimmy. She was still wearing her old
-shirt and knickers, but felt more naked than she ever had
efore. She knew it was she who had instigated this situation and
he so wanted to make it work, yet she felt stupidly frightened
nd doubtful. The timing was crazy. Her friend was about to
et married, she had a stack of things to do, but instead she

was sitting in bed beside the man she loved, both propped u
on the pillows like Jonathan and Jennifer, picking over a crim
they had just solved. Only they'd solved the crime, unravelle
the riddles and saved one another from certain death whilst a
the time keeping the two most vital clues to themselves.

Jimmy was still fully dressed and decidedly damp. Whe
Odette reached across to hug him, he stayed very still, b
bruised eyes watching her worriedly.

'Why didn't you tell me you'd seen the tape, Jimmy?' Sh
stroked his face.

'I wasn't sure you even knew it existed.' He bit his lip.
thought it might freak you out. I thought you might not wa
to . . .' he looked at the ceiling and smiled ruefully '. . . live her
with me if I told you that I knew what you and Florian ha
been . . . that you and Florian . . .' He couldn't bring himse
to say it.

Odette winced. Outside the door, she could hear Winni
and Nelson snuffling away like mad, eager to know what wa
going on.

'And you still wanted me to move in here, even know
ing that?'

Jimmy shifted on the pillows and reached out a gentl
hand to touch her face. 'I know I can't offer you the sam
pleasure, that I'm next to useless to you at the moment, tha
I'm conservative and repressed and impotent . . .' He wince
at the word. 'All I'm asking for is time. I love you so much
I can't bear to lose you. Mungo told me once that you'r
the type of woman who's given up on sex but now I kno
you're not like that. And even if I never manage to . . . if
can't ever . . . maybe we can work something out. Maybe
could learn to cope with you finding what you need wit
someone else.'

'No!' Odette yelped in horror.

'Florian's no good for you, Odette, just as Calum wasn't
They abuse love. He'll hurt you, he'll just use you and—'

'I'm not in love with Florian! I never was.'

'So it's just physical then?' He turned his head away, no
understanding her world. 'Christ, I must be such a let dow

676

fter that – or maybe you're still enjoying what he can offer? wouldn't blame you.'

'There's nothing going on between us.' She held on tightly o his wet jumper. 'You've got to believe me – you saw the um total of our relationship on that awful tape. I had sex vith Florian that night because Calum told me to. He said ae'd love me if I did it and I believed him. I was so obsessed vith him then, I'd do anything. It was last year – just after the OD opened. It seems like another lifetime now.'

'Last year?' Just for a moment she heard an upbeat in nis voice.

'It only happened once.' She pulled her knees to her chest und pressed her face to them as she fought not to remember. I cried all night afterwards.'

'Because it didn't work,' Jimmy said flatly. 'It didn't bring nim any closer to loving you, did it?'

'No, it just made him despise me all the more,' she vhispered, numb with pain. 'It was the dumbest thing I've ver done in my life. And I hated every minute of it. When found out Calum had caught the whole lot on his security :ameras I freaked out, but he said that was all a part of the leal. I'm not very experienced sexually, you see. I thought hat's what people do these days, that's what love is all about, hat the rules changed without me noticing.'

'C'mon, Odette, you don't really expect me to swallow :hat, do you?'

'It's the truth.' She wiped his damp hair from his forehead, out he still wouldn't look at her. 'Before I fell for Calum, I'd only had one or two relationships and I'd never been in love – nowhere close. No one had ever chased me or tried to woo me, so I learned not to expect it, to find solace in films and soaps instead. I grew to believe that in real life it was phoney, that only adulterers buy flowers and that romance was just a commercial gimmick. I found being chatted up quite offensive. So it didn't matter to me when Calum didn't show any apparent interest; I knew we got on well and that there was a spark. I was certain we'd end up together, but I didn't expect him to do a Milk Tray man act and abseil from the roof of my block of flats bearing champagne. I thought inflicting pain was all part of the modern mating ritual, some sort of endurance test.

'Then you came along and changed all that. When you started sending me flowers, I didn't trust your motives, and I was too wrapped up in Calum to notice that the person I'd been looking for all my life was right there under my nose doing the whole old-fashioned romance routine. It was only after I left Calum's world of faces and places that I could see it, and by then I'd lost everything – my dignity, my self-respect, any hope of being able to match up to twenty-first century love, twenty-first century sex. I hated myself too much to let anyone close enough to see how damaged I was.'

'But I just wouldn't give up.' Jimmy turned to look at her at last, his kind face creased with guilt.

She nodded, so brimful of love that tears began to slide down her cheeks. 'Then it started to dawn on me that all the stuff I thought was just in fairytales and soap operas existed in real life after all. It was there, living and breathing and beautiful and called Jimmy Sylvian. You seemed too good to be true, and you just kept on getting better and better until I knew it *was* true – the film wasn't about to end; I wasn't going to turn the page and find it was the last one in the novel. Until this week, I thought you were invincible, that you could repair all the damage in my heart just as you did in my tower. I was so self-obsessed I didn't see that there was a chink in your shining armour, and that the single most damaged thing about me was the one thing you couldn't help me with.

'You see, I didn't know about your father, about the tapes and the film and . . .' she faltered, seeing the pain in his face. 'And I hadn't told you what Calum had made me do because I was so ashamed. It hurt me so much; I thought I'd never be able to have sex again – I mean, I was bad enough at it before, but after that . . .'

'Oh, my poor darling.' He cupped her face in his hands.

'With you, I felt so different.' She closed her eyes, unable to bear the sadness in his. 'I suddenly realised that I wasn't getting a second chance, I was getting my first ever taste of what it was to really love someone, to want to share body and soul with

em. Only now I remember the first thing you ever said to
e. You told me I looked like someone selling her soul. And
u were right. I'd already sold it. It's no wonder you don't
nt my body when the soul's gone missing.'

'You have more soul than Motown.' He started kissing away
r tears. 'I never doubted that. It was the world you lived in
at had lost it. And when I saw that tape, I thought you still
longed there, that you expected so much more excitement
an I could ever give. That's why I screwed up so badly, why
e pressure got to me. And I let you suffer rather than tell
u the truth. I'm the one who blew it.'

'I love you, Jimmy,' she laughed, finding his mouth and
ssing him back. 'Being with you is the most exciting thing
at's ever happened to me. But I want us to be more
an friends, more than a couple of old bookends sleeping
ck-to-back with a great volume of misunderstanding lying
tween us. I can't go through another night or day or even
other minute knowing that this is as far as we're going to get.
don't expect you to dress up as a fireman and do kinky things
ith your hose attachments or organise a five-in-the-bed orgy.
d be horrified. I just want to be with you and I want you just
e way you are.'

Outside the door, Winnie let out a shrill bark demanding to
e let in. Standing up, Jimmy bellowed for her to shut up. Then,
Odette's amazement, he dropped his trousers, whipped off
s jumper, kicked away his socks and jumped out of his pants
the fastest strip show she'd ever seen.

'Well, if I'm not allowed to dress as a fireman,' he laughed,
hen there's no need to put out the fire, is there? And I don't
now about you, but I'm burning up here.'

Odette's eyes widened in delight. 'Where do you want me
start?'

'Well,' Jimmy followed her gaze to where he was stand-
g very proudly to attention, 'seeing as we both blew it
efore, you could start there. I'll blow yours if you blow
ine.'

*   *   *

679

Lydia's mother, Ingrid, was a tall Swede with exquisite bon
structure. She'd had one face lift for every affair her husband ha
conducted and consequently looked like a Siamese cat peerin
through a very tight mouse-hole. She had the same distracte
air as her daughter, and hardly seemed to notice that there wa
a wedding taking place at all, let alone that the bride was he
only child.

Her husband, the dashing and legendary former Wimbledor
Champion, Digby Morley, was happily marching around givin
everybody double handshakes of congratulations for making
through the storm. Numbers were way down on expectation
with fewer than half the guests in the house just minutes befor
the ceremony was due to kick off. And one of the bridesmaid
was missing.

Odette had never felt pleasure like it. So warm, so comfortin;
and yet so strange and unfamiliar. She was being licked deep
inside with hot, soft tongues of sensation. It was bliss. She neve
wanted it to stop.

This time, when the condom question came up, she wa
so happy and relaxed and excited that she couldn't wait to
rip it out of its purple foil and start learning how to put i
on. Between them, she and Jimmy giggled their way through
several attempts.

'Are you sure you bought the right size?' Odette asked a
she abandoned another, which had only unrolled an inch or
to his magnificent hard-on before getting stuck.

'Only come in one size,' he told her, plucking the fifth
from the packet.

'Good job you bought in bulk,' she laughed as, a momen
later, she reached down for number six.

'I'm sorry,' She kissed him after a few more minutes' highly
enjoyable fumbling. 'I'm truly hopeless at this – perhaps you
should have a go?'

'I'm having far too much fun letting you try,' he laughed
lying back against his arm and watching indulgently.

But Odette wasn't getting any better. One by one, she

orked her way through the entire packet until only one as left.

'Okay, I surrender!' Jimmy took it, kissing her indulgently nd sitting up to start gloving up. 'Er . . . Odette . . . I hate to ll you this, but . . .'

'Definitely a defective batch.' She examined the box, deeply isappointed.

'Never mind.' Jimmy started kissing her throat. 'There'll be lenty more chances and we really should get to that wedding.' 'hen he ruined it by admitting what they were both feeling. Oh, Christ, I'm going to explode if I don't take you right ow, right this minute!'

Odette rolled back against the mattress and shuddered in cstasy as he started licking and sucking her nipples. She could eel his weight shifting on top of her, the soft hair of his thighs gainst her smooth ones, the long springy erection moving gainst her pelvic bone. She couldn't control herself now; ie was too slippery and hot and she could feel her muscles umping in frenzied anticipation. It was as though she had wo hearts beating away like mad – one in her chest, the ther between her legs. Unable to stop, she raised her hips p further and further until, like opening a secret door at long, ong last, she released a great depth-charge of pleasure as Jimmy ipped inside.

'I can pull out just before,' he breathed in her ear.

Oh, Christ, it felt good to have him inside her. As she slid er legs up his body to let him in further, Odette knew for ertain that there was no way either of them was going to pull ut of this one for a long, long time.

This is getting critical.' Elsa looked at her watch. 'She's got ive minutes to get here and get changed. What on earth is she laying at?'

Lydia was flapping about in a complete state of headless hicken mania.

'I can't believe Odette could do this! She knows how mportant my tableau is to me. I need my single representative.

I thought Juno had mucked it up by getting married, for God's sake, but this is so much worse.'

'Glad you feel so positive about my nuptials,' Juno sniffed, adjusting her bridesmaid's outfit which was far too tight because she had put on a lot more weight in the States. 'I'm sorry, Lydia, but I am absolutely *not* wearing the glasses.'

'They are vital for the tableau!' she wailed. 'The lenses are just plain glass – you won't fall over.'

The lenses were the only plain thing about the grotesque 1950s bins which looked like something Dame Edna Everage would reject as too ostentatious. Juno's still had wet glue on them, which made her eyes run. Lydia had decorated the frames herself to match each bridesmaid's outfit and Juno was certain she'd only thought up the idea to make her maids look as ugly as possible. They'd clearly been bodged together at the last minute to make up for the fact the tableau's outfits, although strange, were surprisingly flattering.

They had all been schemed carefully according to Lydia's rather eccentric view of the stages of womanhood. The dresses were essentially the same short silk shifts in different colours – only the bouquets and the hairdressing were symbolic and different, as created by Robin who it transpired had worked as a theatre designer before becoming a top stylist. As 'new love', Juno was wearing a bright pink dress, and had pink glittery love-hearts pinned throughout her sculpted beehive. As newly married, Elsa was wearing a yellow dress with a tiara made up of wire and tiny doll's house kitchen equipment scattered with glitter to represent setting up a home. Florence had been dressed in a yellow babygro and matching bonnet embroidered with brides and grooms. As the Earth Mother, Ally had a green dress and her pale blonde hair had been twisted up into a sprouty bun from which several tiny wire mobiles dangled with tiny birds, bees, lambs and kittens, while China who was just walking had a similar little tufty bun with sprouting leaves and flowers. Miss Bee had flatly refused to crew cut her short, punky hair, so Robin had sculpted it into waxed peaks and sprayed the ends bright blue to match her dress and Doc Marten laces, and she was sporting a tiara made up of circles with crosses, the symbol of women. Her glasses were the worst of all as Lydia had tracked down a pair of blue plastic National Health frames in a charity shop and glued a row of Smarties across the top so she now looked like she had a blue Liam Gallagher mono-brow.

'What does this symbolise?' she asked as she tried to reattach the two that had already fallen off.

'I don't know,' Lydia confessed, 'but Finlay doesn't like the blue ones so it seemed a shame to waste them.'

'I feel bloody ridiculous,' Bee moaned. 'This is weirder than your wedding, Elsa.'

'Thanks.' She was peeking out of the door to look down the stairs where the main hall was full of milling guests. There was no sign of Odette, although Elsa saw Finlay running past the bottom of the stairs looking fraught.

'We'll just have to go ahead without her,' she sighed, turning back into the room.

'No!' Lydia screeched. 'I need my single woman. If she doesn't turn up I'm wearing the outfit myself.'

'But you're the bride,' Ally pointed out gently.

'Exactly. I'm still a single woman! And if Odie doesn't turn up, I'm staying that way.'

The guests had all taken their seats in the long banqueting hall, although so many rows were empty that a casual observer might think the wedding was twenty minutes away, not half an hour late. Finlay was pacing about at the head of the central aisle while his brother talked calmly to the registrar.

Outside the wind was howling angrily and the guests gasped as an umbrella flew past the long windows and smashed against one. It didn't break the glass but the clatter made Finlay jump so much that his collar stud gave way.

'Calm down, Fin,' Calum hissed. 'She's always late. You know that.'

'About bloody time!' Ally wailed as Odette floated in, still high on sex and love.

683

'I'll be ready in no time, babes,' she sighed, wandering towards her garment bag while Robin immediately started hopping along beside her and combing her hair, kirby grips clenched between his teeth. 'Can I borrow some tights?'

Ally and Elsa both watched her with open mouths. Juno started to laugh. 'You've had a shag, haven't you?'

Odette poured herself into her purple dress and smiled beatifically at them all. 'I've got a boyfriend.'

'Shhh!' Miss Bee rolled her eyes towards Lydia who was talking to herself dementedly by the window. 'Say that and you'll bugger up her bloody tableau again.'

'Is she okay?' Odette looked at her worriedly, realising that Lydia hadn't even noticed her coming in. 'Where's her dress?'

'That *is* her dress,' Juno giggled.

Jimmy wandered into the banqueting hall, running his finger around the wing collar of his shirt. He disliked wearing formal clothes, and judging by the assembled guests, most of them probably went to bed in evening dress.

When Calum spotted him, he left his jittery brother with the registrar and dashed to the back of the room.

'You any idea what the delay is?' he asked.

'I've a fair idea,' Jimmy said coolly. 'Won't be too long now, I'd say. Can I have a brief word somewhere quiet?'

Raising an eyebrow and glancing at his watch, Calum followed him through a side door to an empty office.

'Lydia? You okay, babes? Robin's done my hair up smashing, don't you think?'

Lydia's big blue eyes were staring with semi-focused and unblinking wonder into the garden where tablecloths, chairs and branches were still flying around being pursued by Food Hall staff.

'Are you ready, babes? 'Cos I think everyone's waiting,' Odette tried again.

Lydia still gazed at the garden in *Cherry Orchard* fashion.

'I'm sorry I was late. I know I pissed you off, but I'm here now and gagging to see you and Fin tie the knot. He's waiting.'

'Oh, darling Fin!' Lydia's lip wobbled.

'Lydia, do you want to call this whole thing off?' Odette asked gently. 'Do you want me to get Finlay to come up here?'

'Yes!' Lydia suddenly looked at her, eyes animated. 'Get Finlay up here. And the registrar. And take off those stupid glasses!'

Odette hardly dared look at Ronny Prior and her film crew as she slipped along a side aisle and signalled for both Finlay and the registrar to follow her through a door in the panelling which led to a servants' staircase.

Only a very few guests noticed her, one of whom was Mungo Sylvian who roared with laughter and turned to Jez. 'Did you see that? Odette has a head-dress made of coloured condoms!'

Finlay's face was almost pure white with worry when Odette hustled them upstairs.

'She wants to call it off, doesn't she?' he whispered.

'Not exactly.' Odette cocked her head as she heard raised male voices from one of the domestic offices on the left, a room that currently stored boxes of glasses. 'Ask her yourself.' She led him out on to the landing and through the door to the private rooms, where Lydia positively fell into his arms and started sobbing. Odette caught her fellow brides-maids' eyes and jerked her head towards the landing to get them outside and give Lydia and Finlay some time alone together.

They all started whispering like snooker commentators.

'Oh, God, this is so awful.' Ally batted a mobile sheep from her eyes.

'It's Odette's fault for being late,' Juno chuntered.

'If Odette hadn't been late Lydia might have changed her mind halfway through the ceremony,' Elsa said pragmatically, bouncing her yellow attendant in her arms and then wrinkling

685

her nose. 'This one needs changing. They'd better hurry up in there or she'll start bawling.'

'Are the couple getting married or not?' the registrar asked impatiently. 'Only I have a wedding at Brighton Pavilion at one.'

Ally pulled an apologetic face. 'I think maybe . . .'

The door flew open and Lydia and Finlay, giggling like children, put their fingers in front of their mouths and dragged their friends inside.

'We want to get married in here,' Lydia whispered. 'With just you lot. I can't face all those people I hardly know, or my parents. Fin agrees, so we're going to do it here. Straight away. Is that okay?' she asked the registrar.

'Well, it's most irregular but I don't see any legal reason why not . . .'

'Great.' Finlay kissed Lydia on the cheek. 'In that case, all I need is Calum with the rings. Where is he?'

'I'll fetch him,' Odette offered quickly.

Racing down the back stairs once more, she paused outside the office.

'My brother is about to get married,' Calum was saying. 'I don't want to get into this now.'

'I want those sketches,' Jimmy boomed in his prairie-crossing voice. 'We had a deal. You said that if I did it, you'd let me have them. Well, I've fucking done it and I hated every bloody second so you'd better bloody come up with the goods. Now!'

Odette felt the floor drop away beneath her and reeled as she fought to stay upright. He had to be talking about her. The deal was to do with her. It was just another of Calum's sick jokes. He'd made Jimmy agree to sleep with her in exchange for his drawings. Jimmy didn't love her at all, his poor performance all that week was simply because he was forcing himself to do something he hated. He'd probably got hold of some Viagra for today. She closed her eyes and let her face crease ready for tears but then reined the emotion back, spurring it into a tight corner before snatching hold of the door handle and marching inside.

They both stared at her guiltily.

'Calum, can you go upstairs to the Long Gallery, babes? Fin wants to see you.'

He blinked and then nodded brusquely, racing past her. Odette looked at Jimmy for a brief moment before turning to follow.

'Odette!' he called her back. She paused at the door, but couldn't turn around.

'You look beautiful,' he told her.

'Jimmy, I have a set of flavoured condoms on my barnet. I only wish we'd used one earlier. I'm sorry you had to sleep with me to get your sketches back. I guess Calum made a joke of us both, after all. Now, if you'll excuse me, I've made a bride happy so I'm going to act the happy bridesmaid.'

She tried to walk upstairs with dignity, but the pair of tights she had borrowed from Elsa was too low in the crotch and made her walk as though she was taking part in the game where you try to grip an orange between your knees.

Jimmy caught her up just as she was about to make her knock-kneed way on to the main landing.

'Is that what you think?' his foghorn voice boomed. 'That I slept with you to get the drawings? Jesus! I love you, Odette Fielding. How many times do I have to say it? How many mountains do I have to climb to prove it? How many episodes of *Dallas* do I have to endure? I love you so much, don't you bloody dare tell me what I'll do for love! You loved me back for about five minutes before changing your mind and doubting me.'

'But . . .' Odette cowered under her condoms. 'You just told Calum you'd hated every minute.'

'I was talking about the interview I gave to that bloody documentary team,' he boomed. 'Which is not entirely true, because I ended up just talking about you and how much I love you, and that's made me happier than anything else in the world.'

Odette felt a lump in her throat the size of an entire wedding cake. 'You did?'

He nodded. 'I did and it does.'

She reached up to kiss him and then stopped as something occurred to her. 'Hang on, did you say Calum made you agree to do it in return for your drawings?'

'Yes, that was the deal. And I want them back so I can blot out that letter of my father's with white bloody emulsion. Stuff what it does to the value.'

'But Calum doesn't even have them. *I* got them back for you.'

'What?'

'They're in the kitchens right now.' She bit her lip. 'I was going to tell you earlier, but you took your clothes off and then I sort of forgot.'

She thought he was going to kiss her inside out when she explained how she'd managed to get hold of them. 'You did that for me? Christ, I love you! Bloody Calum. He hasn't changed, has he? Although he did offer to get them framed which I still plan to take him up on. Oh, God, this means I'm going to appear looking like a prime prat on primetime for nothing.'

Odette chewed her lip. 'I'm sorry. If it's any consolation you're not the only one – look!' She pulled out the pair of revolting red plastic glasses to which Lydia had tied yet more condoms.

He burst out laughing when she put them on. 'I guess that means we're both making spectacles of ourselves.'

'You really don't mind appearing on television, becoming a star? Because maybe I could have a word with—'

'No, it doesn't matter.' He dropped his direct, fiery gaze. 'The fact that I love you is what matters. If I had the chance, I'd appear on every show on every channel across the globe to announce the fact I intend to marry you.'

'You . . . ?' Odette's eyes filled with tears.

He nodded, still staring at the floor like a stubborn child. 'I want to share my life with you. You are the most amazing, sensitive, emotional, stubborn and sexy woman I have ever met. I know you'll never love me as much as I love you but I don't mind. I only need a little of your love.' His voice shook as he reached across and removed her ridiculous glasses. 'Enough to get by.'

'In that case,' Odette's voice was shaking stupidly too, 'I think you're going to get a little more than you bargained for. A lot more.'

As she connected with the full, solid, familiar length of him, she revelled in her newfound, super-randy lust which almost dissolved her from the waist down, and more or less melted the low-slung tights.

'I hate to repeat myself,' Jimmy emerged from a kiss about a millennium long, 'but don't we have a wedding to get to?'

When Odette took his hand and swung through the door to the landing, she heard an agonised yelp on the other side followed by a crash before realising she had just knocked a soundman over.

Ronny Prior's team was filming outside the door to the new 'wedding room'.

With frantic hand-signals to her cameras to keep rolling, Ronny collected the boom from the prostrate soundman and pointed it at Odette and Jimmy.

'Tell me, are the rumours right? Are Lydia and Finlay the head waiter getting married in private up here instead of in front of their guests?'

Jimmy looked dumbfounded for once, so Odette flashed a media-friendly smile. 'You'll have to ask them that.'

'In that case, did we just overhear you agreeing to a proposal of marriage from Jimmy Sylvian, the estate manager?'

It was Odette's turn to be dumbfounded. Jimmy gripped more tightly on to her hand and looked lovingly at her. 'She didn't actually accept.'

'Oh, but I do! I do!' Odette was appalled that he hadn't realised how ecstatic she was to have the chance to share her life with him. 'I love you, babes. I love you, and I accept. I do!'